About

Addison Fox is a lifelo... happy-ever-afters. She l... much as reading it. Addi... apartment full of books, ...laptop that's rarely out of sight and a wily beagle who keeps her running. You can find her at www.addisonfox.com, facebook.com/ addisonfoxauthor or on Twitter (@addisonfox).

USA TODAY and award-winning author **Janie Crouch** has loved to read romance her whole life. She cut her teeth on Mills & Boon Romances as a teen, then moved on to a passion for romantic suspense as an adult. Janie lives with her husband and four children in Germany, in support of her husband's U.S. Department of Defence job. Janie enjoys travelling, long-distance running, movies of all kinds, and coffee. Lots and lots of coffee. For more: www.janiecrouch.com

Cindy Myers became one of the most popular people in eighth grade when she and her best friend wrote a torrid historical romance and passed the manuscript around among friends. Fame was short-lived, alas; the English teacher confiscated the manuscript. Since then, Cindy has written more than fifty published novels. Her historical and contemporary romances and women's fiction have garnered praise from reviewers and readers alike.

Heroes in Hot Pursuit

Heroes in Hot Pursuit:
Line of Duty

ADDISON FOX

JANIE CROUCH

CINDI MYERS

MILLS & BOON

First Published in Great Britain 2021
By Mills & Boon, an imprint of HarperCollins*Publishers,* Ltd
1 London Bridge Street, London, SE1 9GF

www.harpercollins.co.uk

HarperCollins*Publishers*
1st Floor, Watermarque Building,
Ringsend Road, Dublin 4, Ireland

HEROES IN HOT PURSUIT: LINE OF DUTY © 2021 Harlequin Books S.A.

Secret Agent Boyfriend © 2015 Harlequin Books S.A.
Man of Action © 2016 Janie Crouch
Undercover Husband © 2017 Cynthia Myers

Special thanks and acknowledgement to Addison Fox for her contribution to *The Adair Affairs* series.

ISBN: 978-0-263-30247-9

MIX
Paper from
responsible sources
FSC™ C007454

This book is produced from independently certified FSC™ paper to ensure responsible forest management.

For more information visit: www.harpercollins.co.uk/green

Printed and bound in Spain
by CPI, Barcelona

SECRET AGENT
BOYFRIEND

ADDISON FOX

To Family

The ones we're blessed to be born with and the ones we're lucky enough to find along the way.

Chapter 1

Landry Adair flipped and pushed herself off the concrete wall of the pool. The heated water kept her body comfortable while the cool morning air coated the back of her skin as she swam lap after lap.

Forty-four.

The words echoed in her head, a promise that she had only six more laps to reach her daily goal.

Spring was in the air, and each time she took a breath the light scent of alfalfa mixed with a deep, rich citrus that wafted up from the lush valley that formed the backdrop of Adair Acres.

Home.

Even if it had felt more like a prison these past months.

She turned off the pool wall with an extra hard push, images of her father's funeral and the ensuing madness since filling her thoughts. Secrets. Kidnapping. And murder.

Her father might have been a distant man, but she'd never given up hope Reginald Adair might come to be the real father she'd always craved.

The pain she'd worked so diligently to push to the back of her mind reared up and swamped her, choking her throat and pushing her up out of the pool, gasping for breath. Hot tears spilled over her cheeks, made even hotter by the cool spring air that blew over her skin.

When would it stop? The moments of abject pain that came up and simply swallowed her when she thought of her father, his life snuffed out by the will of another.

A hard cough drew her from her thoughts, and she ran wet hands over her cheeks to remove the tears before turning. No one interrupted her morning sessions in the pool, and it was jarring to know someone was there.

And they'd seen her tears.

Whatever embarrassment that might have caused faded as she took in the large male form that stood at the edge of the pool. Long and lean, she caught only a vague sense of dark features as the early-morning sun limned his frame, highlighting an impressive set of shoulders in a rich patina of gold.

Wrapping the haughty demeanor she'd perfected through the years around her own shoulders like a shawl, she climbed up the pool ladder to get a better look at their visitor. Because of the lingering threats of the past few months, no one got onto Adair property without passing several security checkpoints.

If he was here, he was meant to be here.

But who was he?

"Miss Adair?"

He spoke first, his voice rich and deep. She ignored the outreach as she grabbed her towel, curious when a buzz of nerves lit her stomach.

Landry dried her face but let her body drip water on the Spanish tiles that made up the length of the pool terrace. Although she hated scrutiny, she knew well enough how to use her long, lithe body as a weapon, and the water would only highlight her curves.

It might have been a trick as old as time, but it remained a surprisingly effective tool against the male of the species.

"Landry?" Sharper now, but with a hint of something husky and warm in that deep baritone.

"Yes?"

"I'm Derek Winchester. I'd like a moment with you."

"It's awfully early for a moment, don't you think?" She kept her gaze cool but allowed it to roam over his body. Was this the man her brother Carson had spoken to her about?

He certainly fit the bill with that long, rangy form so tall and straight he appeared to stand at attention.

Tight.

Contained.

Controlled.

Reluctantly fascinated, she continued her assessment, cataloging his features as she looked her fill. His skin was a rich bronze, set off by short black hair and deep, piercing eyes nearly as dark as his hair.

He was attractive in a wholly masculine way. There was nothing pretty about him; rather, he exuded a mix of confidence and stoicism that drew the eye.

"It's early for a swim that could fell an Olympian, too. That doesn't make my business any less urgent."

Business?

Although the urge to bait him was strong, she reached for her pool wrap and slipped underneath the thin black material. Showing off her body to gain an advantage was one thing. Sitting there half naked during a business transaction was tantamount to stupid.

And she wasn't stupid.

"Please have a seat." Landry gestured to the long glass-topped table that dominated a section of the patio. "Help yourself to whatever you'd like."

She busied herself with drying her hair and took a few more moments to assess her adversary. He crossed to the long table the kitchen staff set up each morning, filled with coffee service, an assortment of pastries and fresh fruit. When he returned with nothing more than a cup of black coffee, she was curious.

Was he nervous?

In her experience—and she had plenty with the size of her family—men ate breakfast.

She crossed to the buffet to fix her coffee, then her usual plate of fruit. The kitchen's world-famous blueberry muffins beckoned, but she suppressed the urge to take one and added a few extra pieces of melon.

"So, Mr. Winchester. What can be so urgent you needed to interrupt my morning?"

Her brother's earnest request that she play along echoed through her thoughts but she tamped it down. If Derek Winchester was the man they thought, then he should be able to handle anything she threw at him, too.

"I thought it made sense to get started."

Started?

And why did that word sound like a promise?

A shudder of awareness prickled her spine that had nothing to do with the light breeze that coated her skin. She turned away from the buffet and kept her voice light. Unaffected. "Started for what?"

"Effective immediately, I'm your new boyfriend."

* * *

Derek sat back and waited for the fireworks as a series of reactions flashed across Landry Adair's expressive face. For the first time since receiving this asinine mission from his old boss and trusted friend, Kate Adair, he actually had a moment to enjoy himself.

So the resident princess did have a bit of heat underneath that cool demeanor.

The thought surprised him as it took root and he turned the words over in his mind. Why should he care if Landry Adair ran hot or cold? She was a job, nothing more.

Even if he hadn't felt any heat—for anything—in far too long.

Nor had he found himself captivated by the long arch of a woman's neck, where it tapered down to meet her shoulder in a delicious dip just made for his mouth, in an equally long time.

Shaking off the lush images of running his lips over her skin, he shifted his attention to the valley that spread out as far as the eye could see.

Adair Acres.

Or simply "the ranch," as he'd already heard it called more than once.

A shockingly gorgeous stretch of land that spoke of money and promise, hard work and fierce ambition. His gaze drifted over the lush vista, the light scent of citrus wafting from the rolling hills full of grove after grove. Oranges and avocado, grapefruit and lemons.

It was a far cry from the street gangs of LA or the more refined—yet no less devious—minds of Washington, DC.

Which only reinforced the question he'd been asking himself since fielding a phone call from Kate Durant

Adair O'Hara, former vice president and current whirling dervish.

What had she gotten him into?

While he respected the heck out of the former vice president—and he appreciated her belief in his abilities more than he could ever put to words—he still didn't fully see how he could help her.

But no amount of skepticism had put Kate off her plan.

"What are you playing at, Mr. Winchester?"

Landry had stilled at his rash comment, and while he'd expected the hostility, he hadn't expected the cool, assessing look in her vivid blue eyes.

Or the sudden realization that fake or not, no one would ever buy Landry Adair hanging off his arm.

"Your aunt Kate wants me to look out for you."

"And what makes her so sure I need looking after?"

Whatever momentary gain he had with his opening salvo faded as she collected herself, wrapped in an aura of predatory cool.

Damn, but the woman was a looker. Tall—he'd put her around five foot ten to his six one—which gave him the unusual opportunity to practically look her in the eye without craning his neck. Her body was long and lean, lethal in its perfection.

He contrasted that perfect form with memories of Sarah's petite frame. They'd never quite fit, and he'd always felt like a giant standing next to her. He'd never have hurt her, of course, but he could never quite shake the feeling that he lumbered next to her small, pixielike build.

Shaking off memories of his ex-fiancée—memories that belonged in the locked box where he'd shoved them six months ago—he refocused on the here and now.

And the very real fact that he needed to convince

Landry Adair that it was in her best interest not only to cooperate with him, but to work with him, too.

She brushed past him with her plate of food and took a seat at the large patio table. The morning sun beat down on her still-wet hair and he guessed at the shade he'd seen only in photographs. Dark layers, mixed with a refined blond.

The fresh scents of citrus from the groves below enveloped him while something more potent mingled underneath. Lush and erotic with the lightest touch of honeysuckle.

Landry.

Heat still sparked under his skin where she'd brushed his arm, and he lifted his coffee mug for a sip, taking a moment to right himself.

Focus on the job.

It should have been easy, Derek knew. He'd been the job for so long he didn't even remember how to be anything else.

"Surely you're not immune to what's happened here. Your father's killer is still on the loose."

Pain flashed in her eyes, electrifying those blue depths, before she laid down her fork. "You think to come into my home and scare me?"

"I'm here to protect you."

She reached for a pair of sunglasses lying on the middle of the table and twirled the frame as she kept her gaze steady on his. "I'm a big girl, Mr. Winchester. I haven't needed protecting for a long time."

A wholly inappropriate thought sliced through his midsection at her words. She *was* all grown-up, with a woman's curves and a woman's beauty. Although she'd put on a wrap, the swells of her breasts were visible through the dark V-neck, a greater temptation than when she'd worn only her swimsuit.

Steeling himself against the temptation, Derek focused on why he was here. Whatever arguments she attempted to push his way, he'd deflect.

For Kate.

And for the very real chance to earn back a bit of the self-respect he'd lost over the past six months. He needed this job. And he needed some damn sense of purpose again.

"You may want to rethink that, since you've never been up against a nameless killer or a missing-person's case."

"Ah yes, family drama worthy of a nighttime soap." She eyed him over the rim of her coffee mug, more amusement in her gaze than any trace of fear, before leaning forward. "Does my aunt Kate think my mother killed my father, too? That's the prevailing wisdom, you know."

The urge to hold back was strong, but he went with honesty. For her own protection, Landry deserved at least that much. But on a deeper level, he sensed he'd gain far more by appealing to her inherent intelligence than placating her as he suspected too many others did. "She hasn't ruled anything out. And your mother's mad dash to Europe hasn't put suspicious minds to rest."

"She's also an easy target. Kate has never cared for my mother."

"From what little I've gathered, I'd say that's a sport around here."

Derek saw the moment his words registered, her eyes going round in her face before the first genuine smile curved her lips. "Now that's one you don't hear every day."

"I'm not here to placate anyone. And I suspect I'd be rather bad at it if I tried."

Her smile faded, their moment of connection lost. "What else did my aunt say?"

"She believes you're all in danger, you especially. And she believes that danger won't pass until the identity of your brother Jackson is discovered."

Landry settled back in her seat, the aggression fading from her shoulders. "Ah yes, the missing Adair heir. It's all anyone can talk about."

If the past few days had shown him anything, it was that the Adairs knew how to keep to themselves. Yes, they had a legion of staff at their disposal, but they were a family that lived at the highest echelons of society. Babbling about their family business wasn't in their nature. And he suspected that what conversation had gone on was done behind closed doors so even the servants couldn't hear all the details.

"No, it's all you and your family can talk about. And it's the real reason Kate asked me to come."

Her gaze roamed over his face, and he fought the urge to shift in his seat under that direct stare. Before she could say anything, he pressed on. "My expertise is missing-persons cases. It's what I do for the FBI and I'm damn good at it."

Until recently.

That admonition whispered like smoke through his mind, and he ignored it. Ignored that pervasive sense of failure that had dogged his heels like the hounds of hell since his last case went unsolved. Ignored the resulting sense of loss at his failure to protect an innocent young girl.

Landry Adair wasn't Rena.

And he wouldn't fail again.

"So that's the gig? You pose as my new boyfriend so you can nose around here and dig into the past?"

"Pretty much."

Landry slipped on her sunglasses, the shielding of her eyes as clear a message as simply standing up and walking away. "I'll consider it on one condition."

"What's that?"

"We're partners on your little investigation."

"I work better alone."

"Then you can head right back the way you came. Despite what she may think, my aunt doesn't have a say in what goes on in this house. Neither do my brothers. And while I may love all of them to pieces, I'm not going to follow along like some frightened puppy."

"I'm a trained professional."

"And I live here. You'll do far better as my ally than my enemy."

Derek knew he had a stubborn streak a mile wide and twice as deep. He also knew when it made sense to step back and let the target think they had the lead. He'd give Landry Adair her head for a few days. From all the intel he had, it was easy to assume she'd get bored in less time, anyway.

"No one can know what I'm after."

"Of course."

"Not even your mother."

"Then it won't be a change from how we usually get on. I don't tell my mother anything. And as you so succinctly mentioned, she's out of the country right now anyway."

With her eyes shaded, he couldn't see any hint of emotion deep in her expressive gaze, but even sunglasses couldn't hide the subtle tightening of her slim shoulders. "So we're agreed?"

"Agreed."

She extended her hand across the table and Derek hesitated, the implied contract not lost on him. When she only waited, he slid his fingers over hers, her delicate skin soft under his calloused palm.

It didn't make sense, nor was it rational, but in that moment he knew his world had reordered itself. And he knew with even greater certainty that nothing would ever be the same again.

Her hand slipped from his as she stood, her breakfast untouched. "Well, then. You'd better get ready."

"For what?"

"We've got a governor to go meet."

Landry slipped her cell phone into her caramel-colored clutch purse and left her room. She'd already fastened on her suit—Armani, of course—and the subtle jewelry that had become her trademark. Her heels sank into the ranch's plush carpet as she moved from her wing toward the main staircase.

Although she'd been raised with the understanding that not much was expected of her beyond perfect hair, impeccable manners and a few well-chosen charities, she'd determined early on that she wasn't going to let that be an excuse. So she'd channeled the frustration born of low expectations—along with boredom and a damn fine business degree—into making life better for others.

It had been a fulfilling choice until recently.

Until the bottom had dropped out of her world and she'd been forced to wonder about the morals, ethics and basic decency of her loved ones.

And her mother sat at the top of the list.

As Patsy Adair's youngest child—and only daughter—she'd grown up with the knowledge that her mother was different. Cold and brittle, she wore both like a battle shield against the world. And wielded them equally well.

As a result, Landry had gone to the right schools. Had the right friends. Hell, she'd nearly even married the *right* man because it fit what was expected of her.

Wealth brought privileges and expectation in equal measure, and Landry had always understood that. What she couldn't understand was how her mother could live a life so devoid of warmth and kindness.

Or love.

She turned down the last corridor toward the stairs and came to a stop at the top, thoughts of her family and their low expectations vanishing as if they'd never been.

Derek Winchester stood in the great hall, a phone pressed to his ear, and she gave herself a moment to look her fill. The same impression she'd gotten this morning of subtle strength and power was still there, but she let others swirl and form around it. He was tall and whip-cord lean, but the strength in those broad shoulders was more than evident.

His coloring was dark—darker than she'd realized in the sun—and she placed his ancestry as holding some, if not all, Native American. Unbidden, an image of him on horseback filled her mind's eye, roaming the High Plains and protecting his family from harm.

Protecting what was his.

She fought the fanciful notion and continued on down the stairs, already on the descent before he could catch her staring at him. Landry fought the slight hitch in her chest when she cleared the last stair and came to stand next to him.

And she refused to give an inch by relaxing the haughty demeanor that she swirled around herself like a cloak. "Do you have a suit jacket?"

"In the car."

"And a tie?"

"Right next to the jacket."

"Then let's get them and go."

Twenty minutes later they were on their way toward San Diego in her BMW. Unwilling to ruin her hair, she left the top up all while cursing herself for the choice. She should have selected her large SUV instead of the tight confines of the two-seater.

Serious mistake.

Derek's large body filled up those confines and she could swear she felt the heat rising off the edge of his shoulders, branding her with its intensity.

"What event are we going to?"

Landry filled him in on the work of her favorite charity, the project's focus on children an ongoing highlight in her life. Although she'd let several of her other commitments lapse over the last few months since her father's death, she'd refused to cut ties with the bright and able-bodied leaders who worked tirelessly to ensure that the children of Southern California had enough basic necessities to not only survive, but blossom.

Weekend camps, tutoring and days out simply enjoying their youth were a mainstay of the organization, and in the past three years she'd seen the children who took part begin to thrive.

"Sounds like a special group. Why is the governor attending?"

"He promised some additional funding if we met certain testing criteria, and the children in the program exceeded every goal set for them."

"You're proud of them."

"Absolutely." The response was out, warm and

friendly, without a trace of her "haughty demeanor" cloak.

"Everyone needs a champion. Those children are lucky to have you on their side."

Whether it was the close confines or something more, Landry didn't know, but she sensed something underneath his words. Treading carefully despite the curiosity that ran hot in her veins, she nodded and kept her tone neutral. "All children deserve that."

"Even if there are too many who don't get that opportunity. Or a chance to shine."

And there it was.

That subtle suggestion of something indefinable. Of something *more*.

"You speak from experience?"

"My work revolves around missing-persons cases. There aren't nearly as many happy endings as there should be. Or beginnings, for that matter."

The urge to remain distant was strong, but something long dead inside her sparked back to life. "It sounds like a taxing profession."

"At times. But it's also one I'm good at. Your aunt was a part of that." She shifted into another lane, the sign for their exit coming up, and he continued on. "I was on her protection detail, but she saw something in me. She knew I had ambitions beyond security, and when a job opened on the FBI's missing-persons team she gave me a glowing recommendation."

"You must have impressed her. Kate Adair doesn't do 'glowing' lightly."

"She's a special woman."

Landry risked a glance at him as she slowed for her exit ramp. His face was set in hard lines as he stared straight ahead, his gaze set on something only he could see. Once more, the realization that something hovered just under the surface tugged at her.

The hotel came up on her right, and she pulled into the valet station. Two valets rushed to open their doors, the man on her left all smiles as he gave her his hand. "Welcome back, Miss Adair."

"Thank you, Michael."

Landry didn't miss Derek's widened eyes over the top of the car or the assessing gaze that accompanied his perusal. Annoyance speared through her at the speculation she saw there—and the surprise that she'd know the name of a hotel employee.

Whatever he thought—or whatever she believed she'd seen—vanished under a facade that was all business as he rounded the front of the car. With swift movements, he took her hand. "Come on, darling."

Heat traveled up her arm, zinging from her fingers to her wrist to her elbow before beelining straight for her belly. She kept her expression bright and her smile wide, even as she clamped down on her back teeth. "What do you think you're doing?"

His grip tightened, his smile equally fierce as another set of employees opened the hotel's double front doors. "Why, escorting you, of course."

"I hardly think this is necessary."

"Of course it's necessary. People see what they want to see, and we've got something for them to talk about. You're showing off your new love, whom you can't bear to be parted from."

While she'd later admit to herself she had no excuse, in that moment she could no more stop herself than she could have voluntarily stopped breathing. The combative imp that liked to plant itself on her shoulder—the one that regularly whispered she needed to push against con-

vention and what was expected of her—couldn't resist
putting her earlier impressions into words.

"So it's all about distraction, then."

The rich scent of lilies filled the air around them,
dripping from the six-foot vases that filled the lobby of
the hotel, a vivid counterpoint to the foul stench of her
father's murder that had seemingly clung to her—to all
of them—for the past two months.

"Distraction?" Derek's eyebrows rose over the almost-
black depths of his eyes.

"Of course. It helps hide the secrets. Like a sleight of
hand, it focuses attention elsewhere."

"Are you suggesting you're hiding a secret?"

"No. But I think you are."

Landry had to give him credit, he held it together, his
poker face firmly intact. If she hadn't been looking for
it, she wouldn't have even noticed that slight tightening
of his jaw that gave him away.

"Everybody's got a few, you know. But in this case,
I'd say your secrets are more present. Recent, even,"
she said.

"I don't have any secrets."

"Oh, no?" Landry waited a beat or two—her father
had taught her the effectiveness of the approach—and
watched as his attention caught, then held on her. "Then
what is a big, bad FBI agent doing here on babysitting
duty?"

Chapter 2

*S*ecrets.

The word whispered over and over through Derek's mind, filling up every nook and crevice until he barely knew who he was anymore.

Hell yes, he had secrets. And an endless series of questions that always culminated in the biggest query of all. When had it all gone so wrong?

Six months ago he was a man with a plan. A career he loved. A fiancée he was planning on spending the rest of his life with. And a series of cases that gave him purpose each and every day.

And now he was a glorified babysitter, living with the memories of a child who was still missing, a perp wounded by Derek's own hand and a leave of absence while the FBI investigated it all.

Did he have secrets? Bile choked his throat at the raw truth of that question.

He had a boatload of secrets, and every damn one of them was eating him alive.

"Stay with me, Ace." Landry's sultry voice whispered in his ear moments before her hand came to rest on his forearm. "I have someone I'd like you to meet."

"I haven't gone anywhere."

She cocked her head, the motion almost comical if it weren't for the well of compassion she couldn't fully hide beneath her gentle blue gaze. "You keep telling yourself that."

She turned away before he could respond, and then there was no need when the governor stood before them, his crisp black suit as perfect as his smile.

"Governor Nichols. So lovely to see you again. I so enjoyed catching up at Congresswoman Meyers's home last November."

"As did I, Landry."

Landry made quick introductions and Derek sensed the question that hovered in the air among all three of them.

Who was this man with one of California's favorite daughters?

Was he good enough?

Would he ever be?

"Derek's a friend of my aunt Kate. She's raved about him for years and simply insisted we had to meet."

The governor's handshake was firm and his eye contact direct as he nodded through Landry's introduction. "Kate always gets what she wants."

Landry's arm wrapped around Derek's the moment he was done shaking hands and she squeezed. Hard. "Don't I know it."

Derek took that as his cue, smiling at Landry before turning toward Nichols. "And clearly I'm the lucky beneficiary. A beautiful, dynamic woman on my arm and the endorsement of another dynamic beauty."

"And what do you do, Mr. Winchester?" Nichols's smile was broad, but Derek didn't miss the continued curiosity underneath the polite veneer.

"A little of this, a little of that."

"Derek's got the especially lucky opportunity to travel where his whims take him. Give of his time where he sees fit. And support the causes that are near and dear to him."

Landry's quick description of a wealthy, aimless playboy had the governor's eyes dulling, and Derek chafed at the description.

Sure, he was here on an op, nothing more. But it still stung.

He worked damn hard, for every single thing in his life. None of it had come easy, nor had it come without a price. Long hours. Endless days spent briefing and debriefing, planning and then executing to a precise schedule.

They exchanged a few more pleasantries—and Landry's confirmation of when the organization could expect a check from the governor's office as promised. Only when Nichols walked away did Derek feel Landry relax by his side, her grip loosening, even though she didn't fully pull away.

"Nice job, Slick. Even if you were gritting your teeth through my flowery description of your globe-trotting adventures."

"I have a name, you know."

She dropped his arm, but the husky register of her voice made him feel as if they still touched. Intimately.

"Yes, but then how can I objectify you in my mind? If I use your name, I'll be forced to see you as a person."

He marveled at her words and their distillation of something career abusers inherently understood. Objectify the victim. See them as something separate. Apart. If you don't humanize them, then there's no guilt over your choices—as with Rena and her captor.

"That's awfully deep. And here I thought you had a business degree."

"With a minor in psychology." She patted his arm before reaching for the slim purse she'd laid on their table.

"I'd say you understand more than a few courses' worth."

Those husky notes gave way to a lighter, airier tone. "Ah, yes. The glorious education one receives as an Adair. We can't forget that."

Derek followed her back the way they came, down a long corridor and then through the main lobby. "Sounds lonely."

"At times. Until you hit a point when you don't care any longer." The breezy socialite was back as she handed her valet ticket to the attendant.

Derek marveled at her quick and ready costume changes—the cool, refined temptress from the pool to the excited ingenue on their drive over to the responsible socialite with the governor.

Each one was undoubtedly a facet of her personality, but which one was dominant? Which one was the real Landry Adair?

And when had he begun to crave the answer?

Landry offered up a small "come in" at the knock on her bedroom door. She shoved the Roosevelt biography under her covers and opened the tabloid just as her brother Carson walked in.

She glanced up from a spread on upcoming summer

movies and closed the issue, tossing it beside the bed before Carson could see she had it upside down. "Hey there, big brother."

"Hey, yourself."

Carson limped into the room, the bullet wound that had ended his career in the Marines a permanent presence in his life. Thankfully, so was his new fiancée, Georgia.

She'd worried for him when he first came home, ghosts dwelling in the blue eyes that were a match for her own. But in the past month he'd turned the corner. Their father's death weighed heavily on all of them, but the fact that he'd found something strong and true with Georgia Mason had changed him.

And when you added how they found each other, Carson's journey back to full emotional health was especially amazing.

"I heard you were out and about today."

"When am I not?" She shifted on her bed, making room for Carson's well-muscled form. He might move a bit more slowly than in the past, but he was far from soft. In fact, in some ways, his new physical limitations had only pushed him harder to keep his body in top condition.

"Let me rephrase my point. I heard you were out and about today with Derek Winchester."

"Ah. You mean the babysitter."

Landry let the words dangle there, curious to see Carson's reaction. "The man's damn good at what he does."

"It still doesn't mean I need to be watched over."

"Come on. We discussed this and you said you were okay with it."

They had. And she was.

Until a long, lean warrior arrived at the edge of her pool at eight o'clock this morning. The man messed up her routine and her order. He made her curious. About him. About what had brought him to their door. About what it might be like to kiss him.

And to ignore the fact that their relationship was a fake and pretend for a few glorious moments it was 100 percent real.

Shrugging it off, she tossed a jaunty smile toward her brother. "A girl has a right to change her mind."

"Then if it's that easy, change it back."

"Why have we let an outsider in?"

"So he can see the things we can't. We're too close to it all. We've got absolutely zero perspective, and that makes us vulnerable."

"I'm not too close to anything."

"Oh, no?" Carson stretched out and folded his hands behind his head like a pillow. "You can honestly sit here and tell me you aren't shocked as hell that we might have a brother somewhere?"

"No." *Yes.* She averted her eyes rather than admit the truth to Carson with his all-knowing gaze.

"And you're equally *not* shocked that someone shot and killed our father in cold blood."

"Oh, come on, that's below the belt, Cars."

"No. It's honest." Carson shifted, rolling onto his side. "You know as well as I do this is not only a shock, but it's happening from the inside."

Much as she wanted to argue, Landry knew he was right. The events of the past few months had sent an earthquake through their family. While much of it was a blur at times, she couldn't deny her brother's words.

Underneath it all, everything felt personal. And way, way too close.

First her father's death, shot in his office at point-blank range. Then the discovery during the reading of his will of a kidnapped child from his first marriage. Even their mother's race to Europe smacked of personal knowledge.

Carson's voice dropped. "And you know we can't discard the questions about Noah."

Despite the large rooms and relative isolation each of them had in the various wings of the house, on some level Landry understood Carson's need to whisper.

Their cousin, Noah, had been a part of their lives forever. He was just...*there*. A part of their family. A part of them. Now they all had doubts and reservations since Carson's fiancée, Georgia, asked the one question none of them had ever known to ask.

Was it possible their cousin, Noah Scott, was really their father's missing son, Jackson Adair?

Georgia had seen an old photo years before of her stepmother's father. The old photo depicted a young man, handsome and full of life.

And a shocking genetic mirror of Noah.

Ruby, her stepmother, had lost her baby son, then subsequently her husband. Did they dare get her hopes up that Jackson might have been nearby all these years?

"Please tell me you understand why we need Derek?"

"Of course I do."

"Is that a 'Carson, I understand and will cooperate as you've asked' sort of yes?"

She shoved at his shoulder, the motion doing little to move him. "Yes, it is."

"Good. I've already briefed him. You can give him proper cover in the morning when he begins his investigation."

The words were on the tip of her tongue to argue and let him know she and Derek were going into this as equal partners, investigating *together*, but she held back. She knew Derek hadn't been all that pleased with her request, and she knew damn well her brother wouldn't be, either.

So she held her tongue and smiled. "Of course I will."

Carson lifted up on an elbow to give her a quick kiss on the cheek before rolling toward the edge of the bed. Despite his injury, he moved off the mattress and got to his feet in one swift motion.

"And Landry?"

"Yes."

His hand snaked out before she realized its destination and dragged the thick hardcover out from where she'd hidden it. "Go easy on him. He's one of the good guys."

Carson dropped the hardcover on top of the blankets where it bounced with a hard *thud*, his grin broad and cocky as his hands went to his hips.

That smile brought back memories of their youth, roaming Adair Acres and playing through the endless groves of citrus trees. He'd often fancied himself Peter Pan, his hands perched at his waist as he issued orders for how to fight pirates or manage their skyward flight to Neverland.

There had been a time when Landry thought she'd never see that smile again. And now that it was back, she could only be grateful.

She might not like her immediate circumstances.

But she was glad to have her brother back.

Derek kept his gaze on the pool from his guest-room window, Landry's morning swim as captivating from a distance as it had been up close and personal the day before.

He hadn't intended to be a pervert—and as a lawman who spent his life in pursuit of those who lived up to the moniker, he knew he wasn't—but for the life of him he couldn't turn away from the window.

She was magnificent. Her long body was a vision, the product of discipline and obvious hard work. But it was her mind and the emotions that lurked behind her expressive blue eyes that had him even more fascinated.

He'd replayed the day before over and over, tossing into the early hours of the morning as images of Landry Adair had floated through his sleep-deprived brain.

And for the first time in months, he'd had company through the long night with a memory that didn't end in blood.

With one final glance out the window, Derek pulled himself together and headed for the stables. He knew he'd made a promise to Landry—they'd handle the investigation as partners—but if the suspicions about her cousin were right, her presence would only hinder the investigation.

He slid his wallet in his back pocket, his fingers bereft when a badge didn't follow, and fought the daily swell of battered pride and bruised ego.

He was a federal agent. He knew how to do his job, and he was good at it.

Damn good.

He navigated the large house, the back stairwell into the kitchen the closest to his bedroom. The scent of coffee and fresh muffins assailed him as he hit the bottom step, and he caught a shy smile from the head cook as he stepped into the kitchen.

"Good morning, Mr. Winchester."

"Derek, please, Kathleen. How are you this morning?"

The woman blushed, her obvious surprise that he'd remembered her name highlighting her already-rosy cheeks with a warm blush. "Fine. Fine. I hope you slept well."

"Excellent." The lie tripped off his tongue, and he felt no remorse. To tell the truth would only mar the moment.

"Can I fix you a plate?"

"I'd love to, but I actually wanted to get down to the stables for an early ride. Might I swing a to-go mug of coffee from you?"

The woman blushed once more before quickly busying herself with his request. He used the moment to watch the comings and goings in the large, bustling kitchen. Two additional cooks managed at stations along the wall while a series of maids streamed in and out in the few moments he stood there.

An overall impression of efficiency and expertise pervaded the room, and he marveled at the fact that the home ran without the obvious oversight of the lady of the manor.

Interesting.

Patsy Adair had a reputation for ruling her domain with an iron fist, and the promise of that rule must have extended even to times when she was away.

Was that same personality capable of murder? And the cold-blooded killing of her husband, no less?

While he felt obligated to review every angle, something about it didn't play for him. Why would a woman so determined to keep her place in society risk that place over something as pointless as murder?

Especially cold-blooded, calculated murder in her husband's office.

The power Patsy Adair wielded came from the powerful man she'd married. Killing Reginald would have been tantamount to killing the golden goose.

Kathleen bustled back with his coffee and a wrapped muffin still hot underneath its napkin.

"You shouldn't have."

"I saw you eyeing them yesterday with Miss Landry. I try to tempt her with them every day, but that girl's willpower is greater than my muffins. Please don't break my heart and tell me you can refuse them, too?"

The rich scents of vanilla and blueberry wafted up from the warm muffin in his hand, and Derek shook his head. "No, ma'am. In fact, I was hoping to steal one from you, so getting it fresh out of the oven is an extra treat."

"You enjoy."

Derek took a moment to assess his chances with the sweet woman and decided to go for broke. "Sad things often make people lose their appetite. Landry will come around."

Kathleen shook her head, the light vanishing from her gaze. "I hope so. There's too much sadness here. I left after the holidays to help my sister and her family in Ireland. My niece got married and we made it a family reunion. They were happy times. Then I come back here to nothing but grief and pain."

"I'm sorry. I didn't mean to upset you."

"I'm not upset." The woman dashed at her eyes. "I'm angry. Someone attacks Mr. Adair and leaves him for dead. Then they come after the family. It's not right."

Derek laid a gentle hand on her arm. "The family will get answers and things *will* be right again."

"I hope you're right." She blushed once more, then pasted on another smile before she sent him on the way. Derek couldn't help noticing the smile wasn't quite as bright as when she'd handed over the muffin.

He maintained an easy stride past one of the property's orange groves on his way to the stables. It was only when Derek got closer and saw the man he was looking for exercising a horse in a large paddock that the tension he'd lived with for the past six months returned to his shoulders and stiffened his spine.

If what Carson Adair suspected was true, Noah Scott had been living a lie.

And Derek knew it was his job to uncover the truth.

Chapter 3

Derek waited until Noah was at a stopping point before lifting his coffee mug in a morning salute. "Hello!"

He willed the tension from his body as man and horse swung his direction. The last thing he needed to do was alert Noah he wasn't who he claimed to be. And if the horse got spooked by the subtle tension, Derek could kiss his cover goodbye.

Noah's comfortable smile remained in place before he directed his mount toward the edge of the paddock. "What can I do for you?"

Derek introduced himself, before adding, "I'm a good friend of Landry's."

"Ah yes, the new boyfriend." Noah's smile was friendly and his tone that of an easygoing cowboy. "It was all the kitchen could talk about this morning when I stopped in for coffee."

A strange sensation—like thousands of bees stinging

his face—worked its way across Derek's cheeks and then on down his neck before he ignored it, repressing any sense of embarrassment. "People like to gossip."

"That they do. And I can tell you it's the national pastime here at Adair Acres."

"I'll keep that in mind."

Derek reviewed his approach in his mind, working through the script he'd planned through the long hours of the night. "Landry said I could come down and ride any of the horses. Said to confirm with you who's feeling well and up for a new rider."

Noah's jovial grin grew even broader. "That's her polite way of saying I needed to pick who I want you to ride and also make sure you don't get a crack at Pete."

"Who's Pete?"

"Landry's beloved thoroughbred. Paperwork says he's come down through Seattle Slew's line."

Derek heard the words, even if it took his brain a few minutes to catch up.

Landry Adair had a horse from the same line as a Triple Crown winner? And she selfishly kept him to herself and gave him an ordinary name like Pete?

Maintaining the loose-limbed personality and devil-may-care attitude of an aimless playboy, he smiled and nodded. "I guess I'll have to work on her, then."

"Let me know how that goes. My cousin's not easily swayed."

Cousin. Or half sister.

Without even knowing it, Noah gave him an entrée to discuss the real reason he was here. "You're cousins? Landry didn't mention it."

"Sure are. My mom and her dad are sister and brother."

"So you grew up together?" Derek added a smile he

hoped conveyed a dreamy, besotted quality. "I bet she was a cute kid."

"If all knees and elbows are cute, with a side of bossy territorialism, then yeah," Noah said. "There's a little more than ten years between us so I missed her later years. The stories are legendary of her terrorizing the grooms until they finally put her up on her father's favorite horse."

"Another thoroughbred?"

"Yep. Shared the same sire with Pete."

"Damn." Derek shook his head and tried to imagine a young girl of no more than eight or nine up on a horse designed for speed and endurance, descended from a horse who had those traits in spades. "Where the hell were her parents?"

"Around." Noah said nothing more, and Derek knew he needed to pull back. Whatever loyalties were there were embedded deep, forged over a lifetime. He needed to go slowly.

"She's quite a woman. Clearly that started at a young age."

"That it did. Look. Give me a minute to get Lucky Strike taken care of and I'll get you settled."

Noah dismounted and walked the regal Lucky Strike toward a groom waiting at the edge of the corral. Derek took the moment to observe the exchange, the groom's respect more than evident in the set of his shoulders and the ready smile at whatever joke Noah told.

In moments the man was back, directing Derek toward a long barn equipped with the latest in technology. Electronic signs lit up the walls, detailing feeding schedules, medicine needs, upcoming vet and farrier visits, and general comments around exercise and well-being. The horses he passed in each stall were impeccably groomed and glowed with good health.

Noah's doing?

"You manage this part of the estate?"

"In a roundabout way. I manage most of the agriculture on Adair Acres. But the horses are my passion. So this is where I spend most of my free time."

Derek hadn't been on a horse in years, and he was surprised to find himself anticipating the experience like a kid waiting for Christmas.

"Why don't you take San Diego Sunrise out? Diego needs some time in a big way." Noah pointed toward a horse two stalls down from where they stood. The large bay was a deep brown, the color of the richest dark chocolate.

"Anywhere on the property you'd prefer we don't go?"

"Nah. Enjoy the morning and give him his head for a bit if you will. He hasn't been out for a while. And be sure to give him some time in the alfalfa pasture down on the south edge of the property."

Derek patted Diego's nose, smiling when the horse nudged his palm. "He wants me to butter you up."

"A few well-placed words never hurt, but a trip to his favorite pasture and Diego here will be yours for life."

They worked in tandem, quickly saddling the horse, before Derek pushed his last comment of the morning. "Thanks for the help. This is a beautiful place. It'll be great to see it up close and personal."

"There's something special about Adair Acres. I felt it the first time I came here."

The specific word choice caught Derek's attention, and he cycled quickly through the details Carson had provided in advance. He knew what the family believed about Noah's parentage, but if the man hadn't even been in the States, how could he be the missing Adair heir?

"First time? Haven't you come here your whole life?"

"Nah." Noah added a few notes to Diego's stall via a keyboard. He quickly tapped his way through several screens before turning back toward Derek. "I lived in Europe as a kid. Didn't get here until I was about eight. But I fell in love with this place and haven't looked back."

Was he purposely kept away from the ranch and his real family by his mother? Or was he truly the biological son of Emmaline Adair Scott, Reginald's widowed sister?

Derek reflected on the implications as he maneuvered Diego out of the barn. Noah Scott seemed like a decent, hardworking, stand-up sort of guy.

And whatever love or sense of belonging he felt at Adair Acres was at risk of breaking into a million shattered pieces.

Mark Goodnight glanced at the various materials laid out on his desk and calculated how much he'd need to use to tip Winchester off. He'd already cut out enough letters from magazine covers and newspaper headlines to make a pretty good demand note. All that was left was to glue it together and then mail the note to Winchester at the FBI office.

So damn easy.

It'd be even easier if he could just sneak the materials into the lab and run a few tests on his own, fudging results where he needed to, but a guy couldn't have everything.

Besides, he didn't need everything. He just needed Sarah. And in a few more weeks, he'd have her. He'd already been the world's greatest friend, meeting her every afternoon for coffee and letting her pour her heart out about Derek. How he wasn't there for her. How he made the job his life. And how he couldn't get the disappearance of one small girl out of his head.

What else could she do but leave him?

Mark crooned out loud, his whispered chorus of "of course you needed to leave" a litany that spilled from his lips as he unscrewed the cap on a bottle of rubber cement.

And when *he* solved the case of the missing Rena, Derek's mania would finally be put to rest.

Winchester hadn't been trying to help the girl.

He'd been obsessively destroying her.

And Mark would deliver the proof that put Derek Winchester far away from Sarah. And his job. And everything else he held dear.

Landry let Pete move at his own pace, the fresh morning air whipping past both of them as the thoroughbred thundered over the lush fields of Adair Acres.

Fool. Liar. And freaking Lone Ranger wannabe.

She'd made a deal with Derek Winchester, and a mere twenty-four hours later he'd already disregarded their agreement.

Toad.

Pete's powerful body moved and shifted underneath her, sinewy grace and unleashed speed. The ride matched her mood—wild and untamed—and she hoped like hell Derek Winchester had put on a hazmat suit this morning, because she was about to unleash a rain of fire on his too-fine ass.

She caught sight of Derek and Diego, just where Noah had promised they'd be. The horse grazed in his favorite alfalfa pasture and Derek held lightly to his reins, walking beside the horse at a leisurely pace, bridle in hand.

She applied subtle pressure to Pete's back and he

slowed instantly, the hard race over the grounds calming to a swift gallop. His ears perked up and she could have sworn she felt him begin to prance beneath her as he realized their destination.

Every resident of the Adair Acres barn loved the rich field that lay at the south end of the property. Her father had planted it for the thoroughbred he loved—Pete's brother—and it had become a sort of tradition on the property.

She slowed Pete down even more as they grew closer before bringing him to a halt a few yards from Diego and his traitorous rider.

"Good morning."

"Save it." She dismounted and held up her free hand. "I do not want to hear it."

"Isn't exercise supposed to make you less grumpy? You swam God knows how many laps this morning and just rode hell for leather over the grounds. Where are all your endorphins?"

Whatever she'd been about to say sputtered to a halt at the jovial fellow who stared at her. Where was the pensive bodyguard? Or the FBI agent with hidden, troubled depths? Or even the frustrated playboy wannabe who had to demonstrate a decided lack of ambition to the governor?

She'd seen all those personas yesterday, and wondered how they'd given way to the happy fellow standing in the middle of an alfalfa patch.

"I have plenty of endorphins."

"Could have fooled me."

She felt Pete's tug on his reins and stepped back, unwilling to tease him so close to his treat. She made quick work of removing his bridle, leaving only his halter so he could graze properly.

Or gorge, if he had his way.

As soon as she had him situated, she turned back to Derek. "We made a deal yesterday. I'd do this with you if we were equal partners. And first thing this morning you run away when you knew I wouldn't be looking to come talk to Noah."

"Yes, I did."

She was so taken aback by his words she simply stood there. Did he really think she'd calm down in the face of his honesty?

"Look, Landry. What would it look like if you were with me the first time I tried to get to know the guy?"

"It would look like I was introducing my supposed new boyfriend to my cousin."

"And it would have been polite chitchat before he turned tail and ran to avoid being in the company of the new lovers, in the throes of new, unbridled passion."

She swallowed hard at the image he painted, her mind quickly filling in the heated detail of what unbridled passion actually looked like.

And felt like.

Shaking off the bold images, she forced as wry a tone as she could muster into her voice. "Right. Because I can't keep my hands off you."

"Hey. You said it."

The sheer lunacy of their conversation struck her at the same moment she registered his shockingly huge sex appeal. A worn gray T-shirt stretched over his shoulders and chest, molded to the perfection of his body. Faded jeans followed as she worked her gaze down his body, covering his slim hips and long, long legs.

The man was a vision, and she was increasingly helpless to ignore that fact.

She'd been around the block, and hadn't lived a completely chaste life in her first twenty-six years. She wasn't promiscuous, but she wasn't innocent, either.

And no man she'd ever met made her as *aware* as Derek Winchester.

Energy flowed between them, swift as a raging river, as they stood there in the middle of the pasture. Pete tugged on his lead, pulling her back to the fact that more than a thousand pounds of horse stood behind her.

"Want me to take him?"

"No." She took a step back, the lead once again going slack in her hands. "I've got him. Focus on Diego. He's liable to race off if you don't keep watch."

"Right. Because he's found the equine equivalent of heaven and he's going to race off without getting his fill and then some."

"Just—" She broke off, not sure of what to say. The self-righteous anger that had carried her across the grounds faded in the reality of his words. Her presence would have stood in the way of Derek's initial introduction to Noah.

But it still stung.

She was more than everyone's expectations of her. And for some strange reason she'd thought Derek Winchester had understood that.

Derek moved closer, letting the length of Diego's lead out as he moved. "This field has some pretty fantastic properties for humans, too."

"Oh?"

He took another step closer, one hand closing over her hip while the other held the full extension of Diego's lead. "I'd say it's pretty amazing, actually."

"It's just a grazing pasture."

"No. It's more than that."

She tried to keep up, but the heat of his body was

wreaking havoc on her ability to form a coherent thought. "More? I don't think so."

"It's a pasture with Landry Adair standing smack in the middle of it." That lone hand on her waist pulled her until she was flush with his body. The hard lines of his chest pressed against the sensitive curves of her breasts, and a hard tug pooled low in her belly.

"And if I play my cards right, she might even kiss me."

A question formed on her lips, then vanished as his mouth came down over hers and answered it.

Chapter 4

Landry felt the rigid boundaries of her self-control slipping as Derek's arms wrapped tight around her. Long, luscious moments spun out, one more glorious than the next, as his mouth plundered hers, his hand drifting over her spine until it settled low on her back.

She leaned into the kiss—and the hard man who held her as though she was something precious—and let herself go in the moment.

The long months of fear and worry faded away in the press of a hard male body against hers. The featherlight aromas of citrus and alfalfa mixed with the more potent scents of sweat and leather, all imprinting themselves on her senses.

Life.

It was the one word that kept running through her mind as she leaned into Derek, as taken with the kiss as he was.

This was life.

Raw and needy. Necessary, even.

She vaguely registered Pete's lead in her palm before using her other hand to settle low on Derek's hip. Thick muscles bunched under her fingertips, proof the body she'd sensed lay under his clothes was as taut and well honed as it appeared.

A smile worked its way to her lips, vanishing the moment he reached out with his teeth, drawing the sensitive skin into his mouth. Hot need swirled through her, settling itself low in her stomach, tightening the muscles a few inches below.

The hand at his hips fisted in the material of his T-shirt, and she was about to drag a handful over his stomach to get to the warm skin beneath when his strong hand snapped to her shoulder.

His movements were firm—final—as the moment jolted to a harsh stop and the sensual exploration vanished as if it had never been.

Their connection lost, Landry could only stare up into the dark orbs of his eyes. She didn't miss how his pupils had gone wide with need and arousal, despite the bright sun that shone down on them both.

"That was—" He broke off.

At the increasing evidence of his embarrassment, she took a step back, desperate to get away from the heat that branded her as it shimmered off his body. With long years of practice, she swirled the anger that rose up inside her like a protective shield, cloaking herself from hurt.

"What's the matter, Ace? Cat got your tongue?"

His mouth snapped closed, whatever he was about to say vanishing at her careless tone.

She should have kept quiet. Landry knew she'd regret it later, even as the words spilled forth, but a sad recklessness gripped her with iron claws. With a soft pat on his shoulders, she shot him one of her trademark carefree smiles. "Don't worry. It's obvious we can put on a good show for anyone watching. Our fake relationship should be a breeze."

Without waiting for a response, she tightened Pete's lead in her hand and headed for the stables.

His first year in the Secret Service, Derek and his team had faced a bomb threat at a hotel while on protection detail. Despite working their way through a series of practiced maneuvers as they moved the vice president to safety, he'd never forgotten the sheer rush of adrenaline and the absolute lack of knowledge of what the next several minutes would bring.

Annihilation or safety.

The question had hovered through his mind as they escorted the VP down several long corridors toward her waiting car, a phalanx of men surrounding her in unified timing.

They'd had one goal, one mission.

And they'd executed that mission with flawless grace, their only concern the woman in their protection.

Images of that day still remained, emblazoned on his memories with detailed precision. He'd understood his job before then. He'd known what he'd signed up for and what it meant to lay down his life for another. But until that day, with Kate Adair wrapped in a tight cocoon of protection, he hadn't understood what that vow truly meant.

While Derek knew a kiss in a meadow on a bright spring morning couldn't—and shouldn't—qualify as equally dangerous, he'd be damned if the same thought didn't keep spinning through his mind as he crossed the sweeping property of Adair Acres.

Annihilation or safety.

Although the vice president was no longer his responsibility, her niece was, and Derek recognized the trust Kate had placed in him. Which meant he had no business dragging said responsibility in for a mind-blowing kiss in broad daylight, all while his body screamed with the unfulfilled need to do so much more.

He slipped in the back door of the house, Landry's parting words echoing in his ears.

Our fake relationship should be a breeze.

Yeah. Right.

The sound of voices rose up from the direction of the dining room, Landry's huskier tones mixed with the deeper baritone of her brother. Although Derek sensed the conversation was private from the muted undertones, he was in the middle of whatever was happening here, whether Landry liked it or not. With a resigned sigh, he headed for the entry to the long room, prepared to join in the melee.

"I don't owe you an explanation, Carson." Her direct words spilled into the hallway. "I said I'd go along with it and I am."

"By stomping around here like the spoiled princess of the manor?"

"Oh come now, big brother. I'm simply living up to expectations. You know that as well as I do."

Derek let out a short, discreet cough to announce his presence, and both turned as he walked into the room. Carson and Landry stood close, their similarities as siblings more than evident in their fair coloring.

But it was the matched battle stances that truly marked them as siblings, warriors down to their core.

Whatever he might have been, Reginald Adair had a reputation for being ruthless in going after what he wanted. Stubborn to a fault, he didn't take no for an answer, nor did he back down. It was a trait his children had apparently inherited in spades.

"Am I interrupting something?"

"Would it matter if I said yes?" The quick words snapped at him with the force of a striking cobra. Despite their earlier kiss and his subsequent fumbling, he couldn't quite shake the smile at the fierce expression that only served to heighten the sensuality of those bee-stung lips.

Derek shrugged. "Probably not."

Her bright blue eyes narrowed and Derek saw the light of battle as clearly as if she'd hollered "Charge!"

"Well, then. Since you're not leaving, perhaps you can explain to my brother why you felt the need to introduce yourself to Noah this morning, despite our explicit agreement that we'd manage this little deception together."

"I thought we already worked that out."

"Do I look like we worked it out?"

You look like a woman who's been loved.

The thought gripped him so tightly he was amazed the words didn't actually leak from his lips. Color still rode high on Landry's cheeks, and the faint mark of his morning stubble edged her gorgeous lips in stubborn lines of pink like a brand.

His brand.

"Why don't I get going and leave you two to figure this out?" Carson edged away from his sister, his gaze wary.

"Some ally you are. You're a traitor to the cause."

"Yep." Carson smiled for the first time since Derek

had entered the room, then added a wink for good measure. "See you later."

Landry's moue of disgust did nothing to hide the sultry sweep of her lips, and she turned on a very fine heel to refill her coffee mug.

"I didn't talk to Noah on my own to go against your wishes. I thought I made that clear earlier."

"You did."

Something faint drifted across the gorgeous blue of her eyes. If he hadn't been searching her face so hard, he'd likely have missed it. "You think I was wrong for taking the opportunity?"

"No."

"Then why the attitude?"

Her gaze drifted around the opulent room before she settled her focus back on him. "Noah's my cousin. My family. And he has no idea what we all suspect."

Landry's words stopped him and the momentary amusement he'd felt at her battle stance faded. He knew what it was to ruin someone's life with the truth. Knew even better what it was to have that truth thrust upon you without warning.

Despite that knowledge—or perhaps in spite of it—he pressed his point. "Noah can't know. Not yet."

"Why not? If we ask him, he might be able to assuage our fears. Might be able to give us answers to our questions."

Derek understood her deep desire to keep the truth at bay. Like a hovering specter that turned warm memories cold and settled fear deep in the bone, their suspicions would change the course of Noah Scott's life if they were proven true.

"Or we'll possibly create more questions. What if he

tips his mother off before we have a chance to properly investigate and make our case?"

The mention of Noah's mother, Emmaline, did the trick. Landry's open, almost pleading gaze faded, replaced with stoic resolve. "You think she's guilty?"

"I think we need to evaluate on our own before making suppositions or rushing to judgment."

Her long, slender fingers fisted at her sides. "And you haven't?"

"An investigation based on facts isn't judgment. It's what I do. What I know how to do. If you can't accept that, then maybe my initial thought to work this alone was a better idea."

"Threats, Derek?"

A retort rose up but he held it back, the urge to defend himself fading in memory of the clear hurt in her eyes when she leaped off her horse to confront him earlier.

She *had* been hurt. While he wouldn't have done anything differently, even if given the chance, he wasn't immune to the disappointment he'd seen in the set of her slim shoulders.

Landry Adair was used to being let down. He wasn't sure how he knew that with such bone-deep certainty, but he did. And he'd be damned if he wanted to be yet another person who did the same.

"I don't make threats. And I'm not apologizing again. But now that I've met Noah on my own terms, I have no interest in continuing to work this on my own."

"Oh." The admission was enough to knock the wind from her arguments, and Landry shot him a stoic gaze over her shoulder before picking up a delicate pot of creamer on the sideboard. The dollop she dropped in her cup barely colored the black coffee, and an image of a woman in fierce control of herself struck him with swift fists.

No muffin the day before over breakfast. A spot of cream that was so small as to be invisible. And a fierce battle of wills over her family that she was obviously desperate to win.

Perhaps he'd misjudged the woman who appeared to have everything.

From his vantage point, he was beginning to wonder if she had nothing.

Landry dropped her purse in the backseat of her SUV before she reached for the driver's door. Derek had kept a low profile through the rest of the morning, simply asking her to be ready to take off at lunchtime.

She'd wanted to ask where they were going, but sheer stubborn pride had kept her mouth closed. As a result, she had no idea if the light sweater set and cream-colored slacks were appropriate for their outing or not.

Especially when Derek Winchester sauntered out of the house in another one of his T-shirts—black this time—and low-slung jeans. That same heavy throb from their morning in the alfalfa pasture gripped her stomach and she fought it back, slipping her dark sunglasses quickly over her eyes.

She wouldn't let him see the irrepressible response of her body, which no doubt filled her gaze with ripe appreciation.

And she'd be damned if she worried she was overdressed for whatever outing the infuriating man had planned that he couldn't bother to share with her.

Partners.

The word stuck bitterly in her throat as she climbed into the car.

They were no more partners than her parents had been. Those two loveless souls who'd drifted over Adair Acres, perfectly content to lead vastly separate lives. Reginald and Patsy had known how to turn on the charm and lay it on thick when the social situation warranted it, but the rest of the time they seemed equally happy to ignore each other.

Functional. Cold. And devoid of any sense of passion or need or that bone-deep craving that bonded lovers together.

Was she destined for the same?

Images of her morning kiss with Derek flooded her mind's eye, the thought so vivid she could once again taste him on her tongue. Masculine, with a hint of something smoky like whiskey, tinged with dark coffee overtones. She fought the shiver that gripped her and tightened her hands on the wheel.

Derek climbed into the passenger seat and closed the door, oblivious to her discomfort. *Damn man.*

The walls of the spacious SUV grew tight as his scent surrounded her once more. She'd accepted the feeling of confinement the day before because her sports car was so small, hence the decision to take her boat of an SUV for today's little errand.

So how did he manage to eat up all the space anyway?

Ignoring the zing that lit up her nerve endings, she turned toward him and kept her gaze somewhere around his ear. "Where to?"

"Los Angeles. To my office."

"We're going to the FBI?"

"I want to look into a few things, and it gets us out of the house for a while." He kept his gaze steady on hers and she fought the urge to look away, reminding herself he couldn't see through the dark black lenses of her sunglasses.

"Can't you access your files remotely?"

"I can do it faster and quicker at headquarters. Besides—" He broke off and she caught the sense of something lying just beneath his words.

"Besides what?"

"I want to check in, that's all. I've been out of pocket for a few days and it makes me itchy."

Landry hit the button for the ignition, the high-end model she drove already registering the key in her purse, and shifted into reverse. Despite herself, she was intrigued. By their outing and by whatever else he wanted to accomplish in LA. "What are you looking for?"

"Birth records, for starters. I want to know when and where Noah was born."

The reminder that their hunt centered on digging into Noah's background took some of the wind out of her sails, and Landry couldn't help but eye the large gate that swung closed behind her car after she pulled out of Adair Acres. Two large *A*s sat at the top of the fence, their swirling script as familiar a sight to her as her own signature.

So why did they suddenly appear so menacing? Like a brand, marking the property and all the secrets that hid in its folds?

She shook off the fanciful notion and kept her eyes on the road. The rolling countryside flew by her windows as she traveled the canyon roads she'd grown up on.

"It's beautiful country."

Derek's voice pulled her from her thoughts, echoing what she already knew to be true about the land she called home. "It is. It's so vibrant and lush, and no other place smells quite as sweet."

"You truly love your home."

Heat crept up her neck at his observation. She did love her home and always had. It was a large part of why she'd never ventured all that far, even if it meant living with the stifling expectations of her family.

She'd thought about New York as a teenager, and later fantasized about a flat in London or Paris. She'd even spent a winter on the French Riviera during a college break. But no matter how blue the water, the Côte d'Azur simply had nothing on her little corner of Southern California.

Several thoughts drifted through her mind as she imagined how she wanted to play Derek's question, but in the end she simply settled for the truth. "I do."

"It's good to belong somewhere." She risked a glance at his profile as she took the entrance to the freeway, surprised to see a forlorn expression that turned his masculine features craggy.

But when he turned and caught her gaze, she knew without question there was more beneath his words. "It's good to have roots, Landry."

"What about wings?"

"Sometimes flying's overrated."

His cryptic words smacked of sadness and loss. And as they sank in, the wholly unexpected need to nurture stuck in her chest, tightening her muscles like drawstrings.

She had no right to nurture.

Or question.

Or insert her opinions in whatever had put that haunted look behind his dark, solemn gaze.

They weren't in a relationship. And despite the strange tug of attraction that had been her constant companion since he stood above the pool staring down at her the day before, she didn't know Derek Winchester.

But you do know the feel of his lips and the caress of his hands.

She tamped down the traitorous thought as her car flew down the road, the heavy traffic of the city building with each passing mile. No matter how enticing those few moments in his arms, they were the consequence of a power play, nothing more.

A battle of wills between two stubborn people, testing the other to see how far each could push.

They absolutely were not the quiet moments of a couple in the throes of early attraction, barreling down that steep slide into love.

"At the risk of exposing my deep and abiding love for gritty detective shows, TV really doesn't do it justice." Landry looked around the spacious entrance to the FBI office in LA, doing her level best to fight the mix of awe and excitement.

Derek glanced up from where he signed her in as his guest, a lopsided grin turning up one corner of his mouth. "What were you expecting? Lennie Briscoe sitting at a desk at the corner?"

His reference to Jerry Orbach's character on *Law & Order* warmed her, adding a surprising sense of fun to their hunt for information on Noah. "Maybe."

"What else did you imagine?"

"I don't know." She shrugged before getting into the game. "I guess I thought I might see a crime lord someone nabbed at lunch."

"Naturally. Because crime lords are a dime a dozen."

"Exactly."

"I'm afraid to disappoint, but it looks like we've missed today's crime lord sighting. But I happen to have something even more exciting."

Derek gestured her toward the elevator off the main entryway.

"More exciting than a parasite who preys on the fine citizens of Los Angeles being brought to justice?"

"Better. I've got paperwork. Reams and reams of paperwork."

"A dream come true."

The forlorn passenger who'd ridden in her car had vanished, replaced with a man fully in his element. Derek had tossed a black sport jacket over his T-shirt, and the pressed material only emphasized the width of his shoulders. Which she really wouldn't have noticed—at all— if he hadn't stopped and turned toward her the moment they paused at the elevators, a broad grin on his face.

"I'm sure it is."

They stepped through the sliding doors, his gaze growing speculative. "So detective shows, huh? I'd have pegged you as a reality junkie."

Landry fought a hard snort and simply batted her eyelashes. "You're lucky we're in a place crawling with law enforcement professionals. I'm tempted to hurt you for a comment like that."

"Note to self." Derek mimed flipping open a detective's notebook and jotting down a few lines. "No mention of singers, ladies who lunch or pregnant teenagers."

"Thank you."

"No. Thank *you*." He gestured her toward a large room marked Archives. "I can keep my knowledge of a certain wealthy, home-based executive's wife with extracurricular activities to myself, guilt free."

"The FBI follows them?"

"The FBI follows a lot of people."

Landry maintained a light, breezy air, even as his words struck a discordant note.

The FBI *did* follow a lot of people. And her aunt had thought her current family situation was bad enough to warrant that sort of scrutiny. She knew Aunt Kate was acting in what she believed was the Adair family's best interests, but Landry also knew there was more to it.

An outsider—and a highly trained one at that—could see things others would miss, and Kate was canny enough to recognize that distinct benefit.

If she were smart—if they were all smart—they'd do well to remember that simple fact.

Derek laid a hand on her arm, the warmth penetrating the thin sleeve of her sweater. "You all right? You disappeared there for a minute."

"Don't be silly. I'm right here."

His dark gaze sought hers and held it for a moment before he gestured toward the archive room. "After you, then."

The subfloor hallway was as ruthlessly clean as the lobby, the scents of industrial cleaner and old paper mixing in the thick air. She knew it was silly, but Landry could swear she felt the weight of history pressing in on them as they entered the archive room.

Anxious to will away the oppressive feeling, she sought for humor to diffuse the moment. "You take all your fake girlfriends down here?"

"That all depends."

"On what?"

"If an old FBI subbasement seems sexy or creepy."

She couldn't hold back the light giggle at his words, but before she could answer him, he pulled her farther into the room. "Come on. There's a workstation down here that's not used very much. It'll give us a chance to sit and hunt around for a while."

In moments Derek had them logged into a computer

terminal, the screen awaiting his search query inputs. He'd shed the jacket for comfort, and her gaze was once again drawn to the powerful body beneath the thin veneer of black cotton. Corded muscles roped his forearms, tapering down to firm, capable hands.

Hands that had held her, caressed her and pulled her against his warm frame.

"Noah's thirty-seven?"

The question pulled her from her musings before she nodded, her voice tight when she finally spoke. "Yes."

If Derek heard the distress he ignored it, instead typing in Noah's name, year of birth and parentage into the query field. Even with all their efforts to lighten the mood, Landry couldn't quite vanquish the well of sadness as she watched him type her cousin's name into the search bar.

While their failed kiss had been more the cause of her cool attitude back at the house, she hadn't lied about Noah. The thought of what they were doing—and the consequences for her cousin—was tough to swallow.

Two months before, her father had been ripped from her life, the cruel hand of death dealt by another. If she and Derek discovered proof that Noah was the missing Adair heir, wouldn't they be doing the same in reverse?

Ripping him from the only life he'd ever known? And the comfort of an identity he'd lived with since he was an infant.

On a resigned sigh, she admitted to herself that wishing the truth away—or worse, attempting to hide it— wasn't the answer, either. "You need to add Ruby to your next search string."

"Your father's first wife?"

"Yes. Ruby Townsend Mason."

"Her daughter, Georgia, is Carson's fiancée, right?"

"Georgia's her stepdaughter, but they might as well be related by blood. The two of them are incredibly close."

Again, the pressure of the past few months weighed on her as she thought about the woman who'd come into her brother's life, brightening his entire world and helping to ease the pain of wartime that had scarred him, both physically and emotionally. Georgia was an incredible person, and she'd been raised with an abundance of love and caring. Ruby Mason might not be her biological mother, but she was Georgia's mother in all the ways that mattered.

It was humbling to contrast the relationship to the one she shared with her own mother. As they always did, thoughts of Patsy Adair managed to make her feel sad and stifled, all at the same time.

"I'll include Ruby's information next." Derek's voice broke into her thoughts as he set up another query while the first was running in the background. "It's interesting that it was Georgia who made the connection about Noah."

"She saw an old picture of Ruby's father and was shocked by how much the man resembled Noah."

"Connections." He muttered the word as his fingers flew over the keyboard. Strong. Efficient. Competent.

An entirely unexpected flutter settled beneath her skin and Landry tried to shake off the strange well of attraction. Seriously? When did a man sitting at a computer terminal become sexy?

When he wore a black T-shirt and low-slung jeans like Derek Winchester, that's when.

Ignoring the sexual buzz—especially in light of the fact that Derek seemed to be oblivious to one, his gaze focused on the computer screen—Landry's thoughts returned to Georgia. She knew the suspicions about Noah had been weighing heavily on Georgia's mind.

Was Noah really Jackson?

And could it even be possible he'd been a part of their family this entire time?

Georgia hadn't wanted to get Ruby's hopes up, so instead of reveling in the celebration of her engagement to Carson, the woman was busy keeping secrets from her stepmother.

Landry fought back a small sigh at the realization that yet another layer of deception and mystery permeated her life and the lives of those she loved.

It was further proof that the grounds of Adair Acres held as many old secrets as new ones.

Chapter 5

Derek retrieved the results of their search queries from the printer and briefly toyed with hunting down Mark for an update on the Frederickson case. He'd managed to put some of his seething frustration aside since taking on Kate's request to help the Adairs, but the case wasn't ever that far from his thoughts.

The Bureau-imposed leave of absence hadn't helped.

The case had captured his attention from the start, but the addition of too much time on his hands and a young girl still missing had been agony.

No matter how he worked through it in his head, he always came up with the same answer. He'd had no choice but to discharge his weapon, especially when their suspect—a low-level drug runner who thought he'd increase his income by kidnapping young girls—intimated he had Rena and then moved as if he were pulling a gun of his own.

It had been a race to see who pulled their weapon first, but Derek had beat Mark to the punch and fired. And it was only when he ran to the struggling, bleeding man on the floor that he realized he was unarmed.

In moments, it had also become clear the man didn't have Rena.

One moment Derek was milliseconds from bringing a low-life scum to justice and saving the life of a young girl, and the next he was defending his job to the brass over a botched warehouse raid. He fought the roiling, seething anger that still rose up and grabbed his throat at odd moments. They'd worked so hard. And he knew they were close to finding the girl if he'd only had more time to keep pushing.

Instead, he now cooled his heels while the Bureau worked through its reams of paperwork and protocols. His section chief had been decent about it—and had practically pushed him toward the Adair case when it came up—but he'd still forced Derek to play by the rules and take some time off.

Wounding the main suspect in the kidnapping of a teenage girl was a Bureau no-no, no matter how badly the bastard deserved it.

The rip of paper pulled him back from his thoughts, and he glanced down at the printouts in his hands. The thick stack was crinkled in his fist, several edges torn. Easing up, he forced a sense of calm back into his thoughts. The situation was monumentally unfair, but he was working through it.

And he'd get through it.

"Derek?"

Landry stood over him, an even larger stack of papers in her hand, curiosity riding high in her gaze. "I made a few copies of the files you called up. I'm not sure there's much there but I erred on the side of pulling more so we could sift through it later."

"Good."

She hesitated, that vivid blue gaze roaming over his face as if searching for answers. "Did you find something?"

"No. Nothing yet."

"Well, that's good, then. No evidence points to the fact that Noah's not exactly who he thinks he is. Who he's always been."

"We'll see what leads turn up after we spend some time with the material."

"Of course." Her lush mouth settled into a thin line, and the urge to apologize hit him square in the chest. When the impulse faded, one more powerful rose up in its place.

The desperate need to uncover the truth.

It was the hallmark of his personality, and it had been the driving force of his life, calling him to a career in law enforcement.

Landry settled into the cubby next to him and made herself busy with the stack of printouts. The stiff set of her shoulders hadn't faded, but her focus on the material took some of the edge off. He watched as she typed notes into a small tablet on her lap, and he took the quiet moment to observe her.

She was prickly, yes. And she could turn on the haughty-rich-girl attitude at a moment's notice. But he'd also seen glimpses of another woman beneath those shields.

She was loyal to her family, even though several of them didn't seem to deserve the allegiance. And her thorny demeanor hid a deeply compassionate person.

First her devotion to her children's charity and then her obvious concern over digging into Noah's background.

Landry Adair cared far more deeply than she was likely comfortable admitting.

A sweep of hair framed her face where she'd pushed it behind her ear, and Derek followed the firm line of her jaw. She was a beautiful woman, there was no doubt about it, but there was something else there.

Something rather fierce, if he wasn't mistaken.

Landry Adair had the soul of a warrior. And after spending a few days with her he was more and more sure the people she surrounded herself with were completely unaware of that fact.

Her parents were more concerned with their own lives than the lives of their children. Her oldest brother, by all reports, had been maniacally focused on his career before settling down a few months ago. And her next oldest brother had spent his life in military service. Fair choices for both Whit and Carson, but it would have been all too easy to dismiss their little sister as they went about, focused on their own lives.

With that thought came another—an unbidden memory of Sarah.

She'd been the youngest of several children and had used her role as the baby of the family all too often to get her way. One of their last fights before they broke up had been about what she wanted.

She'd resented his job. She'd hidden it well during their courtship, the subtle disapproval rearing its head only on rare occasions. After they got engaged, though, her attitude had changed.

Resentment over his devotion to his work.

Anger over his long hours.

And bitterness for the victims—missing persons with no one to stand for them—that he worked so hard to find.

The day she left he'd been surprised, blindsided by her abrupt decision. But it was only later, when he tabled his hurt male pride, that he remembered all the signs that had littered the journey of their failed relationship.

While he couldn't let go of his need to see the Frederickson kidnapping through to completion, his memories of Sarah had faded to near nothingness. The wounds still flared up at ill-remembered moments, but the pain of ending his engagement had lost the twin edges of regret and disappointment.

Now there was simply indifference.

"I heard you were down here in the boiler room. And with a beautiful woman, no less."

Mark's voice interrupted his musings and Derek glanced up to see his partner's jovial face. The harsh glare of the fluorescent lights hit his features at odd angles and Derek stood, taking his friend's outstretched hand. "There hasn't been a boiler down here for ages."

"Once a boiler room, always a boiler room."

Derek didn't miss Mark's pointed stare at Landry—or the scrape of her chair as she stood—and he made quick work of introducing the two of them.

"I guess I know why Derek picked the darkest place in the building instead of his desk upstairs." Mark's smile grew even broader, his eyes flashing amusement.

"Why's that?" Landry's polite smile never wavered in return, but Derek heard the notes of steel that lay beneath the polish.

"He clearly wants to keep you all to himself."

"Then Derek and I are on the same page."

Landry settled a hand on Derek's shoulder, the warmth of her fingers at odds with the chilly tone of her voice.

Mark had never been the most suave fellow—and beautiful women made him nervous on the best of days—but his wide eyes and even wider smile had Derek reconsidering the wisdom of bringing Landry here.

Although their office was well integrated, with several female field agents on the team, it was no place for someone he was pretending to romance.

Landry's touch—and the not-so-subtle implication they were a couple—only added to his conviction they should have stayed away.

Mark's eyes widened a bit further before he visibly backed down in the face of Landry's cool reception. "I just wanted to come down and say hi. Give Derek an update on the latest with some of our cases."

"Don't let me stop you."

If the notes of dismissal weren't clear in her tone, her return to her seat and obvious fascination with her tablet did the trick. Mark gestured toward the hallway and Derek followed, resigned to the explanations that would inevitably come when he and Landry reached the car.

Landry focused on her notes and tried to ignore the lingering unease Derek's partner had managed to stir up. She had no doubt Derek trusted him—there was no way you could work that closely with someone if you didn't—but she couldn't shake the sense of dissatisfaction that had registered in Mark's eyes.

Cold, flat and envious.

She'd seen the look often enough in the people her parents associated with. Other society families who didn't have properties that matched the lushness of Adair Acres or business owners who hadn't seen quite the same annual profits that AdAir Corp generated.

Humans liked their boundaries. And they liked it

even more when they were the alpha dog. Landry had sensed—no, she'd known—in mere milliseconds that Derek was the alpha in his partnership with Mark.

"You hungry?"

At the mention of food, Landry's stomach growled as she glanced up from her notes. "Where's Mark?"

"That was a quick visit. He's working a field assignment and had to get back to it."

The statement gave her the opening she was looking for. "Is that a big part of the job? Field assignments?"

"It can be. Depends on what your job entails, but yes, it's a significant part of an agent's duties."

"Is my family considered field duty?"

"No."

The finality of his tone brought her up short. "Your time investigating my family isn't sanctioned by the FBI?"

"I've been given leave, but this isn't an FBI matter."

The husky timbre of his voice wavered on the word *leave* and once again, Landry struggled to understand what was going on. While she'd blithely followed Derek down to the archives earlier, the afternoon had given her new perspective.

The FBI subbasement obviously held the tools they'd needed, but Mark's visit had clued her in that it was a little odd that Derek hadn't even tried to take her past his desk.

"If we're not a field assignment then why are you staying at Adair Acres?"

"It's awfully hard to play your boyfriend from Los Angeles."

"Maybe." She cocked her head and evaluated his sexy, trim form.

Probably, her conscience taunted. Besides, would she really want him a hundred miles away?

"And I'm sure you know best of all, but no one argues with a favor for the former vice president of the United States."

Derek's smile was broad, bordering on cocky, and she gave him credit for the quick save. As answers went, it was effective yet evasive. But as a woman used to digging for the answers that lay underneath what people said, it was the fact that his grin didn't quite reach his shuttered gaze that had her antennae on high alert.

"I would imagine it's a challenge living like that. Always in the field."

"How so?"

"Part of the fun of a job that's always changing is that things are always different."

"Sure." Derek nodded. "I can see that."

"In your case, the scenery changes but the lowlifes never do."

Where she expected that stoic reserve to remain, instead something in the dark depths of his eyes seemed to open. "No. They never do."

Landry wanted to dig further but sensed he'd opened as wide as he was going to. Instead of her normal bullish rush to have things her way, the realization that she might get better information if she bided her time had her nodding. "Why don't we go get that late lunch, then? I know a mean little stall at Farmers Market that makes the most amazing hummus."

"The one by the nut place?"

"Yep."

"Let's go."

She navigated the normal midday traffic as they left

FBI headquarters, excited for a stop at one of her favorite LA spots.

"I have to admit I'm a bit surprised."

Landry turned toward him as she waited for the turn onto West Third. "Surprised about what?"

"I wouldn't have taken you for a Farmers Market girl. The Grove, I can see. High-end shopping and eateries. But its sweet, old-fashioned neighbor is a surprise."

Derek's words struck like swift arrows and she swallowed hard, fighting off the initial urge to offer up a smart-ass remark. Instead, she took her turn at the light and used the moment to marshal her thoughts.

How did they keep coming back to the same place?

No. Correction. How did *she* keep coming back to the same place? *Landry Adair, society girl.*

Although she knew herself well enough to know she'd fastened on her cool, rich-girl attitude from the first moment with Derek, she also knew she'd let it slip more than once.

Was it possible that sense of connection she'd felt hadn't been there at all?

With an indifferent shrug, she answered his question in simple, perfunctory tones. "I like being outside. I like food prepared by hand. This place has it all."

"I always imagined the Farmers Market would be a great first-date place."

Since she'd put on the shield of disinterest, she couldn't exactly pull it right back off, so she kept her voice cool as she maneuvered through the parking lot. "A date?"

"Absolutely. It's casual here but the market has the sophistication of being a part of old Hollywood. Definitely good first-date vibes."

"So how many women have you brought here?" She

put the SUV in Park and turned toward him, intrigued regardless of the shield of disinterest.

"Well, despite the brilliance of my plan, I am forced to admit I've never actually brought a first date here. But Sarah and I used to—" He hesitated before moving on quickly. "I used to come here often."

Sarah?

Landry fought the subtle squeeze of jealousy that he'd spent considerable time here with another woman, firmly pushing the green monster away. Derek wasn't a date, he wasn't her boyfriend and he wasn't a man she wanted to get to know better. They were playing parts, and his background was none of her business.

And if she said it often enough maybe she'd start believing it.

The scents of the market surrounded them as they walked past the vibrant stalls. As usual, Landry nearly changed her mind ten times before she reached the small stand that served the best hummus outside Greece.

Derek put in his order, then gave her his full attention. "You're a determined woman. I'd have stopped several stalls ago and begun working my way here."

"If I tried all those places I wouldn't have room for the hummus."

"Isn't that part of the fun?"

"You might be able to consume mass quantities of sugar- and butter-based deliciousness, but I'm not quite so lucky."

"Oh, I don't know." Derek's gaze turned heated as it flickered below her line of sight. "You work out often enough. Live a little."

Her gaze traveled over his fit physique in return, the

image of a male in his prime stamped in every inch of the large arms that crossed over a broad chest. "Maybe."

"I'm serious. Have a doughnut. Eat a scoop of ice cream. Oooh." He pointed toward an area several counters down. "Or those really awesome crepes at that stall down there are incredible."

"I don't eat those things. And when I do I certainly don't eat them all at once."

"Iron-willed control."

Years of her mother's sharp censure rang in her head. Patsy Adair believed a woman needed to look a certain way: slender to the point of waifishness. Landry had never quite lived up, her tall physique more athletic than her mother deemed fashionable, but she made up for it with ruthless attention to everything that went into her mouth.

"For the record, your first-date skills suck."

Derek shrugged. "So noted."

Their teenage waitress shot him a look across the counter while she finished filling a takeaway tray with their lunch. Landry took the tray the moment the girl set it on top of the counter. Her hands shook with subtle anger as she walked toward an empty table with her food.

She had spent her life since hitting puberty having this argument several times a day. First with her mother, then later with herself.

An Adair had to live up to expectations.

An Adair had to set an example.

An Adair had to be perfect.

And where had it gotten her? Or any of them? With a dead father, a mother who'd run off and a mysterious kidnapping that was still unsolved nearly four decades later.

Perfect? Hell. She'd settle for normal.

* * *

"I can't seem to help myself." Derek set his tray down but stayed standing, willing Landry to look up at him. When she finally did, he saw the misery stamped clearly in her gaze and cursed that damn streak inside him that had to tug line after line.

Landry Adair was a grown woman. She could eat whatever the hell she wanted and it wasn't any of his business. So why had he pushed?

"Can't help yourself with what?"

"Acting like a jerk."

"No, you can't." She tore off a piece of pita and dipped it in her hummus before looking back up at him, her voice softer. "You're an observer by nature."

At the evidence of a softened beachhead, Derek took his seat. "So are you. You watch and notice things. You're always thinking, and your innate intelligence has you processing the world around you very quickly."

Surprise registered itself in the flawless beauty of her face, followed by something he could only call delight. "Since that's one of the nicest things anyone has ever said to me, I'll consider tossing you a bone. If you answer me one question."

"Shoot."

"I can't believe you care that much about what I eat. So what's your question really about?"

On some level his question *was* about the food, but not entirely. "I've noticed your inhuman ability to turn down sugar and it's made me curious."

"Like I said. A lot is expected of me and I don't need to eat bad food anyway." She swirled a piece of pita in her hummus before glancing up. "So what else has you curious?"

"I asked the question because it's tied to a bigger issue in my mind."

When she said nothing, he pushed on. "Why do you care what anyone else thinks?"

"My mother cares, and that's all that matters."

"But she's not here."

"Oh, that's right. She's a killer on the run you're determined to catch."

He laid a hand over hers. "That's not my wish. Not by a long shot."

A sharp sigh whistled through her lips before she laid her food back on the plate. It didn't escape Derek's notice that she kept her other hand beneath his.

"She didn't do it." Again, that sense of something fierce lay beneath her tones, quivering in the hard set of her slim shoulders. "She didn't kill my father."

"Okay." He nodded. "Walk me through why."

Landry had proved herself to be an outstanding partner while they were at the FBI office, providing him with names and dates, various family connections and a history of the Adair lineage, all the way back to her great-grandparents.

She'd even added in a few anecdotes about Kate that had him laughing and seeing his former boss and mentor in an entirely different light.

Maybe she did know something about her mother. Or could at least offer up a few strings to tug that made more sense than what he had right now, which was the simple fact that a wealthy woman had managed to vanish into thin air.

"My mother's complicated on a lot of levels, but very simple in others."

The comment was a surprise—not to mention an interesting place to start—and Derek felt himself pulled into the story. "She's got a reputation for flawless beauty and high expectations of others."

"She does. And there's no one she had higher expectations for than my father."

For the second time in as many hours, images of Sarah filled his mind's eye. Their terse words that led to fight after fight. The seemingly endless tears. And the abject frustration that perpetually marred her features when he was working on a big case.

Rena Frederickson's kidnapping had been the final straw...

"She loved him once. I've always believed that."

Landry's words pulled him from the abyss of memories, an odd punctuation to his thoughts of Sarah. "Sometimes a person is simply unable to be what someone else wants them to be."

"Or sometimes they're trifled with until their love changes into something else entirely."

She slipped her hand from beneath his and reached for her bottled water. "Of course, it's observation only. My mother would never speak of anything as delicate as her pain or her feelings."

"Back to that public image again?"

"But of course."

Derek had spent many years in the FBI observing some of humanity's worst behavior. He'd thought himself well educated on how many ways humans could hurt each other. But sitting here with Landry, a light breeze whipping through the open-air market, he saw yet another facet of pain and loss.

"Do you think she loved your father?"

"With her whole heart. It's the only reason I have

for believing her innocent. Her love for him never truly went away, despite my father's very best efforts to kill all trace of it."

Chapter 6

Landry curled up on the couch in her sitting room. She'd made her excuses when she and Derek had arrived home and hadn't left her room since. A bottle of Cabernet sat, open but untouched, on her small coffee table.

She'd thought to go straight to bed, the shock of the day mixing with the bone-deep weariness she hadn't been able to shake for weeks. When sleep proved elusive, she'd roamed the room on restless feet before sending down for the wine.

Then the wine had arrived and she hadn't wanted that, either. So here she was. Unable to sleep or relax with a drink to think through her problems. Or the endless questions those problems churned up.

What did she come from?

The question had sneaked beneath her defenses after the initial shock of her father's murder had worn off and had gotten louder—like a drumbeat—in the months since.

She'd been honest with Derek. She believed to her core her mother was innocent of killing Reginald Adair. But Patsy had a long line of sins since that fateful night in her father's office, and Landry couldn't explain them away no matter how hard she tried.

And at the top of the list was Patsy's attempts to kill Whit's wife, Elizabeth.

"Who did that?" The words were out before she could stop them, a harsh cross between a mutter and a moan.

Was she really the child of a woman who thought so little of another's life she'd seek to take it? Her mother had claimed it was because she thought Elizabeth was Reginald's pregnant paramour, but even that betrayal didn't excuse her behavior. It only added to the possible body count had Patsy been successful in her attempts.

The knock on her door brought her up short, and Landry briefly toyed with ignoring it before crossing the room. After the wine, she'd left specific instructions not to be disturbed, but maybe her brothers didn't get the message.

Or maybe Derek was back to question her.

Although she'd struggled with his questions earlier, it did matter to her what he thought. Of her family. And more important, of her. With the investigation into her family and their morass of secrets, Landry was fast coming to assume he thought very little.

The knock came again and she resigned herself to the inevitable questions. And promptly burst into tears at the sight of Rachel Blackstone on the other side of the door.

"Hey now." Rachel entered, her arms wide before they wrapped around her in a tight squeeze. "What's wrong?"

Landry hung on for another moment before she pulled back. "How'd you know I needed a friend?"

"I came for the gossip." Rachel closed the door behind them, then pulled Landry in for another tight, side-armed hug. "But clearly I was needed for other reasons."

Landry looked down into vivid green eyes that normally danced with amusement but were now filled to the brim with concern. "What gossip?"

Rachel couched her obvious concern underneath a bright smile and animated voice as she beelined for the wine and poured them both glasses of the rich red. "Hell yes, gossip. Do you really think it would take me very long to find out you spent the day in Los Angeles with a hot hunk of a man who Marcie Willoughby swears—and I quote—'is so movie-star sexy he should be on billboards in his underwear'?"

"I'm... Well... We—"

"Yes?" Rachel smiled, clearly enjoying herself.

"He's not a movie star." Landry managed to get that out, her only coherent thought as her imagination stubbornly stuck a picture of Derek in his underwear in the forefront of her thoughts.

And it was a really good picture. Amazing, really.

"So who is he?" At what had to be a blank stare, Rachel pressed on. "The non-movie-star underwear model."

"You wouldn't believe me if I told you."

Those green eyes softened once more, the humor fading in the reflection of true and lasting friendship. "Try me."

Long minutes later, after Landry had outlined all the reasons Derek had arrived at Adair Acres, she was left with one last, lingering piece of the story.

Rachel refilled both their glasses. "So he's here to investigate your mother?"

"Among other things."

Rachel's eyebrows rose over her glass of wine. "There

are other things? Besides your mother freaking out and fleeing the country?"

Landry took a deep breath and leaped.

"There's suspicion that Noah is really my older brother, kidnapped as a baby."

"Noah?" Color drained from Rachel's normally bright, vivid features. "Kidnapped?"

"I don't want to believe it. And I've told Derek there's no way it could even be possible. Who steals a baby from one woman to give it to another? Which is what it amounts to if he's really my father's son raised by my father's sister as her own."

"But kidnapped?" Rachel set her glass on the coffee table, and Landry didn't miss the subtle shake of her best friend's hands. "News like that will devastate him."

"Rach? You okay?"

Landry watched as her friend visibly pulled herself together. Like a phoenix rising from the ashes, Rachel's initial shock faded as if it never was, morphing into a stoic mask of concern and friendly support.

"Have you told Noah what you suspect?"

"We can't." Again, that heavy weight of suspicion pulled at her with thick, clanking chains of guilt.

"Why ever not? You can't really think Noah's a part of what happened to your father?"

"Of course not. But if it's remotely possible Noah is Jackson Adair, then his mother becomes chief suspect number one."

"Your aunt Emmaline? A kidnapper?"

Landry swirled her wine, the reality of Rachel's question not lost on her. Her aunt had never seemed like a very strong person. She wore her wealth and privilege like a shawl, rarely taking it off. It hardly seemed possible the woman would have had the means or the wherewithal to kidnap any baby, let alone her own brother's child.

"I know it does sound crazy. Which is why we have to be absolutely sure."

"So how is Derek getting around the property and asking questions?"

Landry braced herself for the fireworks. "He's pretending to be my boyfriend."

Rachel's eyes widened, bright green orbs flashing with surprise and—if Landry wasn't mistaken—ribald good humor. "You can't be serious. Are you sure he's not really a movie star and this isn't some zany fifties sex comedy?"

The heavy weight of the day—heck, of the past two months—lightened at the humor she saw in her best friend's eyes. "It does smack of elaborate drama, doesn't it?"

"In spades." Rachel reached for the wine once more, filling them each up and finishing off the bottle. "I guess that means you're going to need to play this whole relationship up."

"Where?"

"Everywhere."

"What's that supposed to mean?" Landry nearly bobbled her glass as Rachel's words sank in.

"It means you need to get sassed up, get that gorgeous man on your arm and get yourselves out on the town."

"Town isn't the problem. Whatever we're dealing with is here at Adair Acres."

"Very practical." Rachel nodded, but Landry didn't miss the twinkle in her eyes. "Let me ask you another question."

"What?"

"Do fake boyfriends come with fake kisses, too?"

* * *

Light breezes blew in from the coast, cooling the valley with that unique blend of sea air and moisture that was so specific to California. Mark punched in the stable code he'd secured from that washed-up track master in LA and stepped into the barn. The stink of animals filled his nose and he held back the urge to gag. He'd be on his way shortly.

The various snorts and whickers of the horses whistled past his ear as he walked the length of the stalls, and he pushed hard against the faint sense of discomfort at their size. He just kept reminding himself they were locked in stalls. Four-legged beasts.

Four-legged *thoroughbred* beasts, of course.

Just like Landry Adair.

He'd known it the moment he'd seen her. Long, coltish legs on a ruthlessly perfect body. Pristine blond highlights she no doubt kept regular appointments for. Cool, assessing blue eyes that could turn a man on or shrivel his parts, depending on what mood she was in.

Oh, yes, Landry Adair was a prize.

He'd kept his ear to the ground and knew Winchester was on the Adair property to work a case as a favor for his old boss. He might be on leave, but the brass would jump for good old Lady Kate, yes siree.

Mark had actually been grateful when he'd realized there was a project afoot. Derek had been up his damn ass, asking about the status of the Frederickson case since he'd been put on leave. Daily updates. Calls at odd times to share a theory on the signs they must have missed, which was why they'd never found Rena. He'd even sent a series of emails with theories he was working on.

Derek and his questions. The bastard was full of them. *Mark, did you file that report?*

Mark, did you do that background check on the run-away's family?

Mark, did you know the perp was unarmed?

A hard shot of fury whipped through him like brush-fire, and Mark pushed it back. He'd set the perfect trap, and soon it would all be over.

Derek would get his.

And Mark would have his position at the Bureau and his happy ever after with Sarah.

A win-win, in every way.

In the meantime, the former veep had conveniently given him a bit of breathing room and Mark was sure he wasn't going to squander it. Since Derek's visit to FBI headquarters hit a little too close to home, he figured it was in his best interest to get down here and create a bit of a diversion.

Mark kept his steps light, his gaze taking in the lush stalls and the signs above each. Feeding timetables. Riding schedules. Vet visits. All the responsibilities that went into managing a barn the size of the one at Adair Acres were divided up across various members of the household and staff.

The cloth bag grew heavy and he shifted it to his other hand, another layer of distaste coating his mouth with harsh metal.

He could do this. And he would do this.

It was just one more step in the destruction of Derek Winchester.

His gaze scanned the boards next to each horse's stall, and he'd nearly cleared the length of the stable when he finally came upon the name Pete. The notes for this horse indicated he had an early-morning ride with one Landry Adair.

Perfect.

Mark made his way to a wall of built-in containers a short length down from Pete's stall. Each was marked with a different horse's name, and he lifted the lid for Landry's horse, slipping it aside. A heavy metal bin sat inside the enclosure, about half full of oats and whatever else horses ate.

He was careful as he worked the top of the writhing cloth bag in his hand, settling his bundle gently on top of the mix of oats. The light shake of a snake's rattle broke the hush of the barn, where it echoed off the metal walls of the can and Mark stood back as the sleek body wove its way out of the thick canvas.

The rattle echoed again, louder this time when the snake bumped into the metal edge of the feed can. Despite his fascination, Mark took a quick step back and closed the lid on the mesmerizing display, deliberately leaving the wood frame slightly askew. His thoughts had already drifted to the surprise that awaited the first person who reached into the can for the horse's feed.

He could only hope it was Landry Adair.

Derek fought the sucking gravity of memories as the nightmare pulled him deeper into his subconscious. On some level he knew it wasn't real. Knew the cool stench of the old warehouse in downtown Los Angeles was a mirage in his mind.

But no matter how hard he willed himself to come out of it, he couldn't shake the need to put one foot in front of the other. Step by careful step.

He only had to take the required steps before he'd find Rena and this nightmare would be over.

Rena. The young girl with the haunting eyes. She'd gone missing the month before, a runaway without any protection or anyone to stand up for her. She'd come to the attention of the FBI through one of the vice cops at the LAPD. The man they believed kidnapped her was an international drug runner with a predilection for taking young girls out of the country.

Derek and Mark had picked up the case and were working it as fast as possible to keep that all-too-common outcome from happening yet again.

The light scrape of a shoe pulled Derek up short, and he motioned Mark to take the far wall. An old door hung at a lazy angle, and when the shoe squeaked once more, Derek pointed toward the closed room.

"On three." He mouthed the words, hardly daring to breathe and tip off their quarry.

Mark nodded and they moved through the door in unison, guns drawn.

Thin, drawn cheeks and several days of unkempt beard covered the man's face, but the perp met the description and photos from the vice squad. Albert "Big Al" Winters. A nickname at deliberate odds with his scrawny frame and small stature.

"Hands!" Derek hollered the standard protocol and knew he needed to keep his focus on the man. But damn it, where was Rena?

His gaze flew around the room, desperately seeking some sign of the kidnapped girl, but other than an old cot and a twin mattress covered in dirty blankets against the far wall, there was no one but the scraggly excuse for a human being who stood before them.

Mark added his directive for a show of hands and Derek moved closer, his gaze drifting from the dime bag on the floor back to the shaking frame of the low-level enforcer they'd been hunting for.

"Where's Rena?" The question fell from his lips in

a harsh bark, a strange, desperate panic clogging his breath.

"Rena who?" The man was partially bent at the waist, his hands still out of sight. A creepy giggle rumbled under his question before his voice echoed in a singsongy chorus. "Rena who? Rena who? Rena who?"

Something cold and hollow filled Derek's chest, replacing the lack of air with something else entirely. Disgust and repulsion, but something more. Something far more insidious.

Bone-deep hatred.

Derek struggled to keep himself in check, the anger a living, breathing thing inside his body. He'd worked so hard to bring an innocent home. Had followed every lead and spent hours tracing her possible whereabouts.

And what did they find instead?

An addict on a bender, so blitzed out of his mind he had no idea where he'd even put the girl. Derek hollered the order for hands once more before Mark's scream echoed off the dingy walls. "Gun! Derek!"

His partner's cry was like an accelerant to flame. The cold burn that lived under his skin burst into a raging conflagration as pure instinct took over.

Gun.

Kidnapper.

Danger.

Derek lined up his shot, intending first to hit the perp's shoulder and then his hand if a second round was needed. Neither was meant to be fatal.

The shot echoed, registering even before the gun recoiled in his hand. The scene swam before his eyes as emotion swirled and panic eddied down to his very core. And like a mirage before his eyes, Big Al had already started moving, lunging toward Mark over the man's battle cry about a gun.

Derek rose straight up in bed, his hands trembling as he squeezed off the imaginary shot. No matter how many ways he played it in his mind—or in his subconscious while asleep—the outcome never changed.

The perp shifted and the shot meant for his shoulder landed in the upper right quadrant of the chest, instantly shattering the collarbone.

Pale light colored the slats of the blinds as Derek fought to come out of the nightmare. With slow, aching breaths he became aware of his body again. The hard set of his shoulders. The sweat that poured down his face. The tight clench of his hands that he gently unfisted.

He was okay.

Deep breath. In. Out.

The department shrink had given him some tools to use when the panic came on, and even though it pained him to do so, he focused on the woman's gentle instructions.

Count backward. Focus on the present. Maintain your breathing.

Step by step, he felt the calm return. Felt the tension ebb from his body. Although he couldn't shake it completely, the worst of it was over, the hard wash of memories fading back to the place in his mind where he kept them locked up.

In.

Out.

With swift motions, he scrubbed his hand over his jaw, the scratchy stubble pulling him firmly back to the present.

He was here. Now. A quick glance around had him remembering he was in one of the guest rooms at Adair

Acres, and the rest of his reality slammed back in one great, gulping wave.

Landry Adair.

The image of perfect features, sky-blue eyes and lush lips skyrocketed through his thoughts. Although he'd done his level best to keep his attraction to her in check, the combination of the early morning hour and the visceral image of her alive and well in his mind's eye had his body hardening beneath the sheets.

She was a looker, he'd give her that. But over the past few days, he'd come to realize the exterior was actually a very small part of who she was. A very enticing part, but a small part all the same.

Landry was sharp, her mind rapidly assessing the world around her. He'd observed her the day before at headquarters, her ability to scan the reams of data they were reviewing both swift and nimble. Yes to this document, no to another. Questions about dates that led them to another search query.

He'd seen her concern for Noah. Knew she was upset about what they might find, yet she stayed focused as they searched for the truth.

And then you went and fouled it up at the market.

With another scrub to his cheeks, Derek got up and walked into the en suite bathroom. He made quick work of his morning routine, the echoes of his lunchtime interrogation still ringing in his ears.

"Why do you care what anyone else thinks?"

"My mother cares, and that's all that matters."

"But she's not here."

"Oh, that's right. She's a killer on the run you're determined to catch."

The food was a prickly point, no doubt about it. Yet he'd pushed anyway, anxious to understand the issue beneath the surface. And wasn't surprised when it circled back to Patsy Adair.

The search for Reginald's missing son had ruled their marriage for over thirty-five years.

What did that do to a woman?

To be married to a man who couldn't move on? Couldn't move past the tragedy? Was it possible she murdered her husband?

Landry refused to believe her mother had done it and had made some fairly persuasive arguments to support her point. None of it changed the fact that Patsy had proven herself willing to take a life with her attempts on Whit's new wife, Elizabeth.

But her own husband?

Derek snatched a fresh pair of jeans and a T-shirt out of his duffel and added a windbreaker after considering the cool California air in the morning. The nightmare over the Frederickson case had him up, and now that his mind was whirling he wanted a place to put all that energy to good use. He'd enjoyed his time on a horse the day before.

He'd saddle up and see if he couldn't puzzle out some of the mystery as he flew over the grounds of Adair Acres on Diego.

Landry walked into the barn, the normal, sweet scent of hay masked by a layer of something sour, like rot in a garbage can. She'd thought to get in early and ride Pete, but at the evidence that something wasn't right, she came to a halt inside the barn.

Did one of the horses get sick?

She stood still for another moment, trying to orient her senses and identify the scent, but the exercise proved futile.

Although early-morning light filtered through the high barn windows, Landry flipped on all the overheads to check each stall. The horses were all awake and alert, their breaths quick as they watched her pass. She greeted each one by name, stopping to pat their noses and stare into their eyes.

Damn, but what had them riled up this morning?

There hadn't been any storms the previous night, and when she'd spoken to Noah yesterday before going up to her room he'd said that every horse had been well exercised.

So what had everyone upset?

She moved from stall to stall, checking each horse while her gaze roamed over their bedding and food supply. Everything appeared to be in order, yet their discomfort was real. Tangible. And if anything, it had gotten worse since she'd walked into the barn.

Diego greeted her with a hard shove of his nose on her hand and she took an extra moment to soothe him before heading for Pete. The large thoroughbred shook his head, his agitation more than obvious when she finally reached his stall. "What's wrong, baby?"

With soft tones, she kept her voice level, crooning to him through the open window of his stall. They were nothing but nonsense words, the sort one would use with a colicky baby, but nothing she tried seemed to settle him.

Even with his nose nuzzling her hand and her cheek pressed to his, that sense of agitation never wavered.

"What is it, buddy?"

When Pete only shook his head and stamped his front hooves, she stepped back.

Landry kept contact with Pete, but allowed her gaze to travel the length of the barn and back. Whatever was going on wasn't obvious, but something had the horses spooked.

She turned on her heel and walked into the small office they kept inside the barn. The three-digit code to the main house was answered immediately, despite the early hour.

"June, this is Landry. Is Noah up yet?"

The woman was sweet and efficient and seemed to sense the urgency immediately. "No, but I can go get him for you."

"Please send him straight down to the stables. Something has the horses agitated and I'd like to have him here."

"Can I send someone else down, Miss Landry? Are you there alone?"

Landry forced a sense of calm into her tone. "I think Noah will be enough. Let him know I'm calling Dr. Walters, as well."

"Of course."

The vet's number was tacked on the wall in bold letters, and she called him next. She'd barely heard the first ring when a loud series of whinnies had her slamming down the phone.

"Hey—" Landry stopped midsentence when Derek's broad form filled the walkway.

"What's going on in here? Why are the horses so upset?"

"I don't know." Sly, panicky fingers gripped her stomach and she fought down the sick ball. "They've only gotten more agitated since I got inside."

"Should we let them out into the corral?"

"I'd like to get Noah here first. And I was about to call the vet." Landry hesitated before she spoke. "Pete seems the worst. Maybe you can help me calm him down. Or between the two of us we can get him outside?"

Derek nodded. "Where's his lead?"

"Everything's in the feed room, stored in cubbies for each of them."

A sense of calm punched through that hot ball of lead, Derek's presence more soothing than she could have ever imagined. How did he know she needed help? Now that he was here, she had to admit she felt a little silly.

Goodness, but she'd spent her entire life around horses. She knew how to handle herself and how to handle the animals. So what the heck had her so spooked?

"Which would you like me to use?" Derek pointed to the large cubby and the various pieces of equipment stacked neatly in the efficient space.

"I'll get the one I like."

She passed Pete's stall on her way to Derek, shocked when the animal shoved his large form against the stall door, an agitated cry escaping his lips.

"Pete!"

Derek pulled her close, his arm wrapped tight around her shoulders. "Has he ever done this?"

"No. I can't imagine what it—"

The sharp, swift shake of a snake's rattle had the words dying in her throat.

But it was the sight of a large, coiled brown body on the edge of the feed bin that had a scream crawling up to take their place.

Chapter 7

Derek pulled at Landry's shoulders, pulling her just clear of the snake's striking range as it fell off the feed bin, primed to attack. Her booted foot got tangled with his and they nearly fell into a heap before he righted them, dragging her back several feet.

"Hold still." Landry hissed the words, her voice barely above a whisper.

"Are you out of your mind?"

"It's startled. Give it a minute to settle. We can't lose sight of it and risk it getting into one of the stalls."

Derek eyed the agitated snake, its body coiled to strike as its dark rattle lit up the quiet of the barn. Even the horses had gone still, their heavy breathing the only sign they were there. "You ever dealt with one of these before?"

Her body quivered under his hands, but she held her ground. She maintained that quiet tone and he marveled that she could manage the thread of calm woven underneath the words. "Not like this. No."

"How are we going to take care of it?"

"We're going to give it another minute to calm down and then you're going to back away slowly behind me and grab the metal shovel from the tack room."

"I'm not leaving you here."

"I'm closer. And my boots go up to my knees if it does decide to strike."

Derek knew his city upbringing hadn't prepared him for this sort of scenario, but he also knew enough about threatened animals to know she put herself in danger.

"I'll stay here and you go."

"Go now. Please." She shoved at his arm. "I can't put the horses at risk. They trust me."

The knowledge that she'd protect the horses at such risk to herself was as maddening as it was humbling. Unwilling to argue any longer than necessary, he took a few steps back, stopping once more when the rattle began to click faster.

"Derek. Hurry."

He kept his steps even, one foot behind the other, as he moved toward the tack room. With each deliberate step, the lingering vestiges of his nightmare rose up, tightening his chest and trapping the air in his lungs.

The predator might be different, but the threat was all too similar.

That familiar anger—the one he'd held on to for the last several months—warred with the lack of air and he ran the last few feet to the tack room.

He'd get there in time. He *had* to.

The shovel was right where Landry said it would be and he grabbed it before rushing back to her.

"On my mark, Landry."

"Derek—"

"Move now!"

She was already in motion as the thin edge of the shovel came down, his aim true. The snake's body continued to move, but the severed head lay separate and no longer a threat.

He reached for Landry and dragged her close. A hard tremor started in his arms and he clung to her, willing the shaking to subside.

"You didn't have to yell, you know." Her terse grumble was muffled against his chest as she pressed her face into his shirt, her arms tight around his waist.

"I wasn't yelling. I was ordering. There's a difference." He'd meant the words as a joke, but the guttural exhale of breath messed up any attempt at humor.

He took the moment to simply breathe her in before he pressed his lips to her head. Images of what could have happened rose up along with a sudden shout.

They pulled back as Noah barreled into the barn, an unbuttoned shirt on over his jeans and boots. "What happened?"

Landry stepped back and pointed toward the now-still rattler. "We had a poisonous visitor arrive last night."

"What? Where?" Confusion grooved sharp lines in Noah's face before he crouched down to look at Derek's handiwork. "Clean work. You got him on the first try."

"I didn't plan to miss." Some measure of equilibrium had returned to his voice, but he still wasn't able to quite hit the casual, humorous note he was going for. "Damn thing fell right out of the feed bin."

"What the hell?" Noah was back on his feet, stomping toward the line of individualized bins. "Where?"

"Right there." Landry pointed toward the bin labeled

with Pete's name. "He was coiled on top of Pete's feed bin."

"I closed that last night. Secured it myself after I fed him."

"So someone else must have pushed it aside."

"No." Noah shook his head. "No. I left pretty late and I checked everything myself. I'd already sent Mac and Wendy on their way."

Noah walked the length of the sealed feed bins, his hands running over the edges.

"Be careful." Landry stepped forward, and Derek fought the desperate need that clawed at him to lay a hand on her arm to keep her still. "Where there's one there could be others."

"Not this time." Noah lifted the lid of Pete's feed bin and reached inside. When he came out, he had a thick canvas bag in his hand. "That snake didn't find its way in here on accident. Someone put it here."

Landry let the wild air whip around her face and willed the events of the morning to fade from her mind. She'd never been as scared as the moment she saw the snake coiled on top of Pete's feed container.

But to know someone put it there?

The powerful body beneath her bunched and moved, all sinew and corded muscle, and she leaned into him, willing the animal to take her wherever he wanted to go.

Away.

Far, far away from whatever threat lurked around her home.

She'd believed herself immune to the same danger as the rest of her family, but now she wasn't so sure. The snake was placed in *her* animal's feed bin. And her schedule wasn't exactly a secret to many people. She

often rose early to go to the barn. Heck, Noah kept updated schedules throughout the barn at all times so they
kept track of which horse needed a workout and who
needed rest.

What if the snake had been meant for her?

And what if someone else had found it instead? She
didn't make it to the barn early every morning. And in
point of fact, Derek had been the one to get to the feed
bin first, searching for Pete's lead.

The cool morning air coated her body. Where it normally invigorated, all she felt was a bone-deep chill that
had nothing to do with the weather and everything to
do with the threat that had suddenly decided to target
her family.

The pasture at the far end of Adair Acres beckoned,
and she added pressure with her legs to slow Pete down.
While she'd love nothing more than to run all morning,
her beautiful boy probably needed a rest.

And no matter how badly she wanted to put it off, it
was time to talk to Derek.

The whistle of the wind faded. Pete reduced his speed,
and she felt his subtle prance as they drew nearer to the
field. The thunder of hooves grew louder and she turned
to see Derek and Diego headed their direction.

Her breath caught in her throat at the picture he made
atop the horse. Even from a distance, she could see the
corded muscles in his forearms and how his powerful
thighs bunched around in the saddle.

She allowed herself a moment of pure feminine appreciation to watch the view.

And wonder how he always managed to catch her off
guard. As though her memory of him never quite competed with the reality of Derek Winchester in the flesh.

Rachel's words from the night before whispered slyly

through her thoughts, and before she knew it, Landry had a very vivid image of Derek in his underwear, splayed across a billboard fourteen feet high.

The man was a vision; there was no doubt about it. But the past few days had ensured that her image of him continued to grow and expand. From his competence at the FBI offices to his pushy lunch conversation at the Farmers Market to his role as protector this morning.

She'd felt his barely leashed strength as he stood behind her in the barn while they dealt with the snake. She'd also recognized his ire when she sent him off to get the shovel. Despite the fear that the snake would strike one of them or the horses, she'd had a moment of pure pleasure, too.

He hadn't wanted to leave her behind.

"That was quite a ride." He pulled Diego into a walk, their pace acclimating to hers and Pete's, and she let the fleeting thought fly off into the breeze.

"After this morning, I'd say it was a well-needed run for all of us."

"No arguments here." As if providing further evidence of his skills, Derek stayed close enough to communicate, but maintained a distance between the two animals. Their morning scare still had the barn's residents skittish, and she appreciated that Derek understood each horse's need for individualized attention.

"You're quite the rider. Where'd you learn?"

"You wouldn't believe me if I told you."

She cocked her head at that, the challenge in his answer too tempting to resist. "Try me."

"College."

"I figured you for a city boy with a criminal justice degree."

"I was both of those things, but I got my degree at a

rural college in Maryland. Equestrian lessons were electives, and I decided to take a class."

"What was her name?"

The question was out before she could stop it. When she was rewarded with an easy grin that suffused his face in carefree lines, Landry was glad she'd asked the question.

"The girl I liked or the horse?"

"Both."

His dark eyes grew reflective, and she saw the years fade away. "Emma was the girl. Harlow was the horse. Both were beauties."

"Harlow?"

"The owner had a thing for old movies. He named all his mares after Hollywood stars. Which, I might add—" his gaze darkened as he glanced at Pete "—is a far more elegant name than Pete."

Landry leaned forward and pressed her lips to the top of Pete's head. "Don't tease my baby."

"Why Pete?"

"Why not?"

"Because he was sired through a Triple Crown winner's lineage."

"All the more reason he should have a normal name."

"Nope. Not buying it."

Although she wouldn't exactly call Derek Winchester an open book, there was an honesty about him she found refreshing. Unlike the society crowd she'd run with her whole life, there was something simple in his direct approach to life.

Add on the fact that he didn't pull any punches—if he had a question, he asked, and if he had an opinion, he stated it—and Landry found herself growing more and more comfortable in his presence.

It was an odd sensation—both the lack of artifice and the fact that she was enjoying it. And it was more than a little unnerving to know she couldn't quite get her footing with him.

What was even more unnerving was realizing that perhaps she didn't want to.

"I never cared about his lineage."

"Didn't you pick him out?"

"In a way. When I showed an interest in riding, my father encouraged it. It was the one thing we could do together, and I loved every minute of it. Being with him, in his orbit, with his full attention focused on me."

"So what changed?"

"When I began to get good at it, my mother stepped in. She felt that riding was an acceptable activity for a young girl of wealthy means and proudly preened to all her friends and acquaintances about my advancing skill. She also felt it would help me keep my weight in check. She pressured my father to get me a spectacular horse."

"So they gave you Pete?"

"My mother went on about it for weeks. How I'd get a fancy horse and show up every family in the county. The more she talked about it, the more I wasn't interested."

"Yet you went along with things anyway?"

"Of course. The good daughter, following her mother's instructions."

While she would defend her mother's innocence until the day she died, Landry had to admit that the last few months since Patsy fled had been freeing. She'd known her mother's ways were oppressive, but it was only with her finally gone that Landry could admit just how bad things had become.

The endless censure and criticism. The prying eyes and leading questions, wondering when Landry's next date was or why she'd stopped seeing that Asher boy. Even Carson's arrival home from the military—injury and all—hadn't shifted her mother's eagle-eyed focus off Landry's life.

"So what happened?"

"My father scheduled an afternoon with the owner of Pete's dam for us to take a look. I'd spent the car ride sullen and irritated and had played 'Let My Love Open the Door' on repeat the whole way."

"Pete Townshend?"

"Yep."

"And then I got out of the car and walked into the stable and fell in love with my own Pete, and that was the end of my complaints."

Derek's eyebrows shot up, a wry grin on his face. "Love opened the door?"

Landry bent down and wrapped her arms around Pete's neck. "I guess it did."

Derek had never been jealous of anyone or anything in his life, but in that moment he had to admit he'd finally experienced the emotion.

And how the hell was a grown man jealous of a thousand-pound horse?

He'd listened to Landry's story, and similar to their lunch the day before, had taken away yet another facet of her life. What appeared perfect and pristine on the surface hid a wealth of anger and frustration.

Who treated their child that way?

While he'd never considered his upbringing much more than average, the more time he spent with Reginald Adair's family the more he realized just how good he'd had it. Two parents who'd loved each other. A sister and brother he still talked to and enjoyed spending time with. And a pool of memories that weren't filled with experiences based on how he looked or what the neighbors might think.

As that thought hit, another followed, and that sense of jealousy faded to nothingness. "I'm glad you had Pete."

"I am, too."

While he'd admired her persistence earlier and her commitment to the animals in the Adair stables, he hadn't fully understood why she'd put herself at risk for the horses.

With the understanding of what the horse meant to her, he saw her actions in a new light. He couldn't quite assuage his frustration that she'd put herself in danger, but it helped to understand it.

"Who do you think left the snake?"

The proverbial storm cloud that had hovered above them all morning finally opened up. He'd spent the ride turning it over in his mind, but he was no closer to an answer. Nor could he come up with a place to start looking for one.

"The one you insisted on charming?" He hadn't quite hit the point where he could be carefree about the morning's events, but he could add a small bit of levity to what was going to be unpleasant territory.

"I did no such thing. I let it calm down."

"You know, it's funny but I remember our morning a bit differently."

"One thing I think we both remember the same way. The bag it was delivered in."

Derek would have found an excuse to get the bag away from Noah if he felt he could have learned anything off the material, but the canvas drawstring tote was a dead end. Bags like that were easily available and could have been purchased at any number of stores.

Landry continued. "What I don't understand is why whoever did this left the bag behind."

"To send a message."

"It's an awfully cryptic one. If you're sick enough to send a snake and someone at Adair Acres was the target, send it to the house. Or put it in the car. Something."

"And risk having a servant find it instead?"

At her sharp intake of breath, he saw the recognition light in her eyes. "Someone could have been hurt."

"I think that was the general idea. But it's not a targeted way to harm someone, which is why I think this was meant more as a message than an actual attempt at doing real damage."

"I have to talk to Whit and Carson, and we need to talk to the staff. Tell them to be on their guard." A hard laugh escaped her lips. "Won't my mother be pleased to come home to half her staff having resigned."

"No one will do that to you and your brothers."

"How can you be so sure?"

He shrugged, the interactions he'd observed over the past few days more than obvious. "They love you. And they don't stay because of your mother. They stay for you and your brothers."

Her mouth drooped in surprise before she firmly snapped it closed. Although he'd only had a few days, it hadn't been hard to size up the dynamics at Adair Acres. Patsy Adair might rule the roost, but her chicks held the true power.

Since he suspected that depth of knowledge would only make Landry feel more guilty about the danger to her staff, he pushed forward with more questions.

"How accessible is the stable?"

"It's open. I mean, we don't always lock it." She pulled

Pete up as they approached a long stretch of field and rose up in the saddle. "Want to walk for a bit?"

He dismounted from Diego and attached the horse's lead to allow him his grazing reward after their hard run. Landry stood a few feet away, her voice gentle as she thanked Pete for the good ride.

A few strands had come loose from her ponytail and Derek watched, mesmerized, as they blew against the soft curve of her cheek. She was a vision. The long, firm body. The porcelain skin. And the innate care and awareness of others that was easy to overlook when she was pulling the princess-of-the-manor routine.

But he had seen it.

Had seen glimpses of the caring woman underneath.

Her love of the horse was one small example. He'd also seen it in her concern for the staff. Her fierce defense of her mother.

Landry Adair was a woman who, by all accounts, had made herself. Out of a loveless childhood and the rarefied air of wealth and privilege, she'd emerged, like Aphrodite on the half shell. Fully formed and fully lovely.

His stomach tightened on a hard knot of need and he willed it back, refusing to allow it any more control over his thoughts.

This was a case.

A *job*.

And he couldn't afford to lose sight of that.

Voice gruffer than he intended, he returned to the morning's incident. "Who knows the stable's open?"

Landry's eyes widened slightly, but if she sensed a shift in the conversation, she said nothing. "Everyone, I guess. But it's not like the property's open. You can't just stroll through the front gates."

"The ranch is nearly 200 acres. All someone needs is

determination and a bit of patience and I'd wager they don't need to use the front gates. An old line of fence or a thick copse of trees and someone could get through."

"Which is why we keep track of the main perimeter of the house and stables, as well."

"The stables, too?"

"Of course. We have hundreds of thousands of dollars of horseflesh in there, not to mention top-of-the-line equipment."

"Do you have video equipment? Eyes on the stables?"

"Yes. It all feeds into the main security system in the house."

He cursed himself for not thinking of it immediately. His thoughts had been so full of Landry while they were still in the barn that he hadn't even looked at the situation through the eyes of a trained operative.

With a hard, swift slap, the same shame he'd known at his failure to protect Rena rose up to knock him down. He was already on leave for one failed attempt at protection. Would he fail Landry, too? And by default, her aunt Kate?

The calming benefits of the hard ride vanished as reality came crashing back in.

His last case was still a disaster.

Adair Acres still held a wealth of secrets and sins.

And Landry Adair was still in terrible danger.

Chapter 8

Landry fought the urge to ignore her work in favor of pacing the small room she used as an office. But she did give herself a moment to simply sit and stare at the wall. And brood.

The room had been her play area as a child, but she'd traded dolls and stuffed animals for bookshelves and a writing desk years ago. The soft cream-colored walls, dotted with vivid prints to add splashes of color, were her sanctuary. But not today.

Maybe because you're hiding.

Her conscience rose up to taunt her and she resolutely ignored it. She wasn't hiding. She was doing work. Good work if the letter she was drafting to the governor would ever get written. A thank-you note for his support and the confirmation that her children's charity had received his promised funding.

So why was her mind filled with Derek? They'd

worked as partners this morning. First in the stable and then after, helping Noah calm the horses and resettle them into their routine. Even their ride had been full of carefree moments as they flew over the grounds of the ranch.

Easy.

The moments had been easy, even with the danger of the morning hanging over them. Sure, they'd need to consider all the angles around the break-in to the stable and put together a suspect list of who might be interested in doing them harm. It was tension-filled work, especially since she couldn't dismiss those she knew completely out of hand.

But they'd agreed to partner on investigating what was happening at Adair Acres. And they had a comfortable camaraderie that was friendly enough. Pleasant, even. If the sexual tension reached up and grabbed both of them every so often, well, she could live with that.

They were working in close proximity to each other.

And then he'd gone and checked out. She'd seen it happen, too. One moment there was a deep smile reflecting from those midnight-dark eyes of his, and then the next he was shuttered and terse. All business with an edge of annoyance.

Landry searched her memory for something she might have said or done, but knew she wasn't at fault. Whatever was going on was his problem.

So why the hell was she upset about it?

Minimizing the window on her computer, she shifted into her email. A few notes from friends. Some names she recognized from another charity whose board she served on. And a note from David Asher asking if she wanted to accompany him on a date.

She tackled David's note first. The decline was easy—

she didn't want to go, and the wedding was the same date they'd planned Elizabeth's upcoming baby shower, so she had an easy excuse. Besides, it was obvious she was a last-minute choice if he was asking her for the following weekend.

"Jerk," she muttered out loud as she hit Send on her politely worded email that dripped social niceties like a sieve.

"Was that directed at me?"

The moment of self-righteous indignation was short-lived as she glanced up to see Derek in the doorway.

"If I said yes would you know why?"

"I've got a pretty good idea."

His admission of guilt was such a surprise she could only sit there, stunned.

"I suspect it has something to do with my grumpy-ass attitude while the horses were grazing."

"What happened?" The question slipped out, and she cursed herself for giving him any leeway at all.

"It's nothing you did, but it's not something I talk about." He moved into the room, his hands shoved in the pockets of his jeans. "Ever."

So much for leeway.

She was used to being shut out. Her parents had no problem leaving their children to fend for themselves emotionally, and her relationship with her brothers had always held elements of the same. The fact that Carson was four years older and Whit seven had contributed, Landry knew.

In fact, it had been only recently that they'd begun to push back some of the walls that had always kept distance among the three of them. But despite their recent movement in a positive direction, the Adairs weren't inherently close, and they weren't particularly adept at sharing their thoughts with one another.

None of it changed the fact that they *were* a unit.

"Since we were talking about something having to do with me, my family and my home, I find it hard to believe I don't have a right to know what set you off."

"That's not why I was upset."

"Then why are you here? You clearly don't feel the need to apologize, and I, for one, have had enough danger and sleuthing for the day. It's time I got productive and got some work done."

Dismissal rang in the air like a school bell, magnifying her guilt at her terse tone.

"When you do have a moment, please come down to the security room. I'd like to show you the tapes of the stables."

"Fine."

"Damn it, Landry—" He broke off and dragged a hand from his pocket to run it over his short-cropped hair. "I just wanted to say it wasn't you this morning. That's why I came in here."

"I know that." The words spilled forth and she knew them for what they were. A deliberate attempt to pick a fight. "What I don't know is this great, huge, magnificent secret you're determined to keep but which you use as an excuse to act like a sullen bastard the moment you get uncomfortable."

"That's not true."

"Oh, no?" She shoved off her office chair, the movement hard enough to push the rolling piece against the wall. "You arrive here at the ranch and you do nothing but ask me questions. Personal questions that are absolutely none of your business and have nothing to do with investigating my family."

"I'm here to help—"

She shut him down, pressing her point. "Then you toss back some excuse about an issue in your past that you don't 'discuss.'"

She made exaggerated air quotes around the word *discuss*, absurdly pleased when the motion acted like an accelerant to the anger already sparking in those midnight eyes.

"Pain and hurt don't give you a right to act like a jerk with a get-out-of-jail-free card. So the hell with you!"

The air stilled around them, her words hovering like a storm cloud. Oddly, all she could think of was their moment earlier in the barn, as they waited for the snake to make its move.

Strike or retreat.

Stay or leave.

Fight or flight.

Derek reached out, his hands fisting over her shoulders as he dragged her close. His mouth came down on hers and his large frame simply consumed her.

And as she lifted her head, accepting the powerful crush of his lips against hers, Landry knew the sweet victory that Derek Winchester stayed to fight.

Late-afternoon sunlight slanted through the room, highlighting the golden hue of her hair like a halo. It was the last thought Derek had—the last coherent one, at least—before the overwhelming need to consume her gripped him with mad, desperate need.

The barely pent-up anger she'd wielded like a weapon channeled into a different sort of battle as they fought each other for control of the moment. Need shimmered around them in thick, humid waves. He tried to catch his breath, but he couldn't seem to drag his mouth away from hers; the urge to devour—to consume whole—was a living, breathing fire inside him.

Derek knew he needed boundaries—knew pushing this mind-numbing attraction for Landry Adair was a mistake—but he could no more walk away than he could stop breathing.

"I want you." He whispered the words against her lips, his hands roaming over her skin, seeking the heated flesh under her blouse.

She smiled up at him, her eyes filled with a wash of feminine power. "You don't say?"

Before he *could* say, her hands were at his waist, dragging his T-shirt from his waistband and up over his stomach. Her hands splayed over his flesh, a sensual brand that had his skin on fire wherever she touched while she ran a series of nipping kisses over the line of his jaw.

Her hands drove him crazy. Her mouth drove him wild. Hell, the woman drove him out of his ever-loving mind.

"Landry—" A hard knock and a strange voice broke the moment.

A wash of awareness slid over Derek and he dragged himself away from the temptation of the woman before him.

"Oh. I'm so sorry to interrupt."

"Elizabeth." Landry smoothed the hem of his T-shirt back into place. She then kept her hands on his waist an extra moment, as if she were ravished in her office every afternoon, before she turned toward the woman in the doorway. "Come on in."

A light blush colored Elizabeth's cheeks, and Derek suspected if the woman could redo the last few moments, she'd have run for the hills. As it were, she made a quick recovery, her voice brisk and all business.

"Whit wanted to do a family dinner this evening. I was stopping in to make sure you'd both be home."

"Of course."

"Good. I'm going to leave a message for Rachel to join us, too," Elizabeth added.

The thought of a family dinner, him and Landry pretending to be a couple, struck Derek as a strange sort of torture. Despite his misgivings, he was obviously in, prepared to see their charade through.

It would also give him an opportunity to observe how the conversation swirled around their near miss in the stables that morning.

"Noah volunteered to be on grill, but I think he may need to fight Whit off for the spatula." Elizabeth's eyes twinkled as her hand hovered over her rounded belly. "Please don't tell me you're going to fight them for a spot at the grill, as well, Derek."

"My talents around food extend to microwaving water and putting bread in the toaster. Whit and Noah can duke it out."

Elizabeth smiled, her grin going wider as she looked at the two of them. "I'll see you later then. Seven on the back porch."

Whit's wife vanished as quickly as she'd arrived, leaving the two of them.

"Why don't we go down to the security room and look at that footage." Landry wrapped her arms around her waist. "I'm sure the snake incident will be a topic of conversation this evening."

Not for the first time, she surprised him with just how in tune with him she was. "I was thinking the same. Tonight will be a good opportunity to observe."

"Noah's already spread the word, and whomever he missed, the staff has caught up by now."

"I'm not so sure about the staff. I think Noah's playing it a bit closer to the vest than that. He pinged me earlier to see if I'd called the police."

"Hmmm." Her vivid expression grew thoughtful. "He sees more than he lets on. He always has. Maybe he's waiting to see what type of response he's going to get from my brothers."

"He also doesn't know why I'm really here. Or that I've got investigative skills of my own."

A haze of worry dulled those vibrant blue eyes. "That part still feels awkward. We all know why you're here, and he doesn't."

"We could tell him I'm investigating your father's murder. Would that make you feel better?"

"No," she said. "Whit, Carson and I agreed how to approach this, and we're all in. My brothers know because they need to. I'm sure Whit told Elizabeth because he tells her everything and the woman is the equivalent of a human vault anyway."

"She was your father's secretary?"

"Yes." Landry hesitated, her voice faltering. "She found him, too."

"She seems to be doing okay with it."

"Day by day. That's what Whit keeps saying, and it appears to be working. Their focus on the baby is probably helping, too."

"The first Adair grandchild."

"For my father's line. Kate's got grandchildren and so does my father's sister Rosalyn."

"Kate's crazy about that baby. I think it's one of the things that helped her survive the shooting attempt on her life."

Landry's gaze grew thoughtful. "What if they're related?"

"What's related?"

"The attempt on Kate last year. The issue now with my father."

Derek thought back to those dark days. The call from Kate's son, Trey, telling him about the attempt on his mother's life. He'd kept close tabs on her touch-and-go situation in the hospital and had followed the news of the case and the ultimate capture of her shooter through his counterpart in the Raleigh field office.

"Kate's shooter was caught."

"But it is strange, don't you think? The danger she and her family faced last year? The problems we're having here?"

"Landry. I know you want to believe this situation isn't that dire, but I can't promise you that. And I won't placate you to make you feel better and inadvertently put you at risk."

"I know." The light still shone through the oversize windows in the office, small dust motes swimming in the air. Only instead of highlighting her hair in a halo, all he saw were the twin expressions of fear and disappointment that filled her face in the afternoon sun.

He owned putting the disappointment in her gaze—there was nothing to be done about it. But he'd be damned if he'd rest until he caught the bastard who'd marked Landry Adair with fear.

The rich scent of cooking meat wafted toward her, and Landry gave herself mental permission to enjoy dinner that evening. A juicy steak, an oversize baked potato and a piece of Kathleen's cream cheese–frosted carrot cake was in her future, and she couldn't wait.

"Another?" Georgia waved a bottle of wine near her

glass, her sharp green eyes bright with merriment, and Landry nodded for the refill.

Landry took a moment to swirl the pretty Cabernet before taking a sip. Although she usually preferred light, crisp whites in summer, the anticipated steak and the fact that Whit had invested in the vineyard made it an easy decision.

"This is amazing. Whit chose well."

Elizabeth smiled at the compliment before shooting her husband a warm, adoring smile. "He did."

"He chose well with you, too."

Elizabeth's eyes widened on the compliment, a light sheen of moisture coating her warm brown gaze as her hand instinctively rested against her expanding belly. "That's lovely."

"It's true."

"Hear, hear," Georgia added with a lift of her glass.

And it *was* true, Landry realized as she and Georgia clinked glasses with Elizabeth's flute of sparkling water. Elizabeth and Whit's relationship had started under the most extraordinary circumstances, but love had found its way. The bond between them was strong, forged even deeper as they awaited the birth of their first child.

She turned a smile on Georgia. "Carson chose equally with you, my dear. He's never been so happy."

Georgia's smile was warm, her gaze full of the happy secrets of new lovers. "Neither have I."

Even with the pain of the past few months, Landry couldn't help but count her blessings. She had two new sisters—women who had brought a renewed sense of family to both of her brothers—and, by extension, her. They *fit*, she thought as she took in her new sisters-in-law. Elizabeth, with her light blond hair, and Georgia, with her sassy red, fit in as if they'd always been there.

And as they sat next to each other and shared a knowing gaze, Landry sensed that the familiar was about to become…sisterly.

"So tell us a bit more about Derek."

Landry kept her voice low, unwilling to risk Noah overhearing. "He's here as we've discussed."

"Oh yes, he's definitely here." Georgia shifted to the edge of her chair. "And he definitely notices *you.*"

Her gaze drifted toward Derek. He'd stayed true to his earlier promise—he hadn't touched the grill—but he had taken up a very manly pose next to Whit, Carson and Noah. All four men held beers and had fallen into easy conversation. Their voices drifted across the patio—a rather heated discussion about the Padres' and Dodgers' chances for the season.

Whit and Carson may have known Derek's real reason for being at Adair Acres, but they'd fallen as easily into the pretend situation as she had.

It shouldn't be this easy.

When her brothers had told her Derek would be joining them, at her aunt Kate's request, she'd been hesitant. Worse, she'd been insulted. Yet Derek had managed to captivate her in a matter of days.

He fit here. And the more time she spent with him, the more she felt that urgent tug that said he fit with her.

As her gaze once more took in the conversation circle around the grill, she couldn't help noticing what an attractive foursome the men made. And she found herself wondering what it would be like to see all of them huddled together regularly.

"Well, isn't that a charming quartet of testosterone." Rachel's voice interrupted her thoughts, and Landry glanced up to see her best friend smirking down at her, a bottle of wine and a fresh bouquet of flowers in hand.

Landry popped up and firmly tamped down the blush that threatened at being caught staring at Derek. "I didn't think you could make it." She gave Rachel a hard hug. "I'm so glad you're here. I thought you had to go up to San Francisco for the day?"

"I got back early, and when I got Elizabeth's message I thought an evening with friends would cap off a pretty good day."

"What happened? It sounds like a toast is in order." Georgia swapped a fresh glass for the flowers in Rachel's hands before gesturing her toward a chair. "Let's hear all about it."

Landry lost herself in the moment, congenial conversation under the fading light of day. Surrounded by friends and her increasing family, a warm, comfortable hum had settled in her veins. Although the past several months had been the hardest of her life, it was humbling to realize the time had brought good things, as well. Two new sisters and a closer bond with her best friend.

And Derek.

Rachel laid a hand on her knee after Elizabeth and Georgia disappeared into the house. "You doing better after last night?"

She knew the conversation would ultimately swing around to the morning adventure in the stable, but Landry was hesitant to ruin the moment of calm. "Better. Last night's girlfriend time went a long way toward making me feel better."

"And things with the underwear model?" Rachel kept her voice low but her gaze ran high with merriment. "I do hope you've gotten to the kissing part."

When Landry didn't say anything, Rachel's eyes widened. "You *did* get to the kissing part. Oh, please throw the single girl a bone here and tell me all about it."

"There's nothing to tell."

"It's the best friend code of honor to point out that if there wasn't anything to tell, you'd have told me already."

"I don't tell you everything."

"You told me on the phone two days ago you had a chip in your nail polish. If that's not the definition of everything, I'm not sure what is."

Landry laughed in spite of herself. "Maybe I was just savoring it for a while."

"That's a better answer."

She was prevented from saying anything by the arrival of Derek and Noah.

"Did you and Whit fight it out for the grill?" Rachel shifted her attention to Noah, her gaze appreciative. Maybe it was the dying light of day or the poolside tiki torches one of the staff had lit earlier, but something in Rachel's gaze caught her attention.

Was it possible? Rachel and Noah?

Landry let the thought swirl, surprised when she moved so quickly to how she and Derek might use that to their advantage in trying to uncover the truth about Noah's background.

Oblivious to her thoughts, Noah grinned broadly, his gaze fully focused on Rachel. "Nah. I left Whit to the grill. It was his and Elizabeth's idea to have a group dinner tonight and I figured the least I could do was let him do the cooking. Besides, I wanted to get the latest details from Derek on this morning."

"What details?" Rachel went on high alert, her eyes darting to each of them.

Landry lifted her glass in a breezy wave. "We had a snake in the stable. It was no big deal."

"Ignore Landry. She said the same thing this morning, and if it was up to her we'd just brush over this."

Noah patted her on the back before he took the seat next to Rachel. "It was serious."

Noah ran down the events of the morning, and every time Landry tried to brush off the incident, Rachel shushed her until she finally stopped trying. Derek took the seat beside her and linked his fingers with hers. The warmth of his hand enveloped her fingers and she squeezed tightly.

She had an ally in this. A partner. And she was quickly coming to appreciate the fact that she wasn't dealing with this alone.

Was that Derek's real appeal? Or was it something deeper?

Yes, the man was devastatingly handsome. And she had a base attraction to him that she simply couldn't deny. But it *was* something more. Something that went beyond sex or even the appreciation that he was there to help her.

Unlike the majority of the men she'd spent time with, she genuinely enjoyed Derek's company. She'd dated plenty, of course. It wouldn't do for Landry Adair, society queen, to be dateless to any event.

But she'd always felt as if she was going through the motions. Living up to expectations instead of spending time with someone she could come to care about.

"Both of you could have been seriously hurt." Rachel's heated comment and lurch across the small conversation area to pull her into a tight hug had Landry dropping Derek's hand along with her train of thought.

As she held her friend in a tight hug, Landry knew Rachel wasn't far off the truth. They could have been hurt by the threat in the stables.

But if she didn't protect her increasingly vulnerable heart, the possibility of physical danger was the least of her worries.

Chapter 9

Derek settled into the ebb and flow of conversation around the table. Although he and Landry had spent time in the hot seat discussing the morning's danger, the group had sensed when it was time to move on to new ground, as well.

Topics ranged from Elizabeth's pregnancy to Whit's expansion of AdAir Corp to an expected new foal Noah was excited about. It was only now when they sat with coffee and after-dinner drinks that Derek realized he'd actually enjoyed himself.

Until thoughts of Rena Frederickson descended like a black cloud. He owed her better than a night spent in carefree conversation while she still sat in captivity somewhere.

"You okay?" Landry's hand floated over his forearm, gentle as the soft evening breeze that blew around them.

"I'm fine." When his voice came out on a strangled whisper, he took a sip of his coffee. "Fine."

Her smile never wavered, but he saw the confusion in her gaze. Knew another moment of sharp guilt that he'd put it there.

Just like Sarah.

The insult vanished as soon as it arrived, but the moment of surprise lingered on. Landry wasn't like Sarah. Aside from the fact that he and Landry had a pretend relationship while he and Sarah had been engaged and planning a wedding, the women weren't the same.

Landry had proven herself a full partner. Even with her concerns about going behind Noah's back, she'd soldiered on. Sarah, in contrast, had simply sat at a distance and bitched at him for his work ethic.

The guilt that had slithered in, dragging up thoughts of Rena, faded as he considered the past few days. The stress of the Frederickson case had been intense, but it was only with a bit of distance that he'd begun to understand how it had taken over his life.

Sarah hadn't been wrong about that.

He cared about his cases, but something about this one had been different. Maybe it was the clues that pointed to a case of heinous debauchery. Or maybe it was just the last straw in a long line of them that had proven how frustrated he was by his work.

No matter how many missing persons he and his team found, there were always more. More individuals who vanished, their lives and the lives of their loved ones ruined by the evil choices of another.

Coming to Adair had been good for him. Prior to his arrival at the ranch, he'd been on top of Mark constantly. Other than their quick catch-up at headquarters the day before, he hadn't been in touch with his partner. Instead, he'd given himself the gift of distance, even without really realizing it. Much as it pained him to admit it, maybe his team lead was right all along.

Distance from the Frederickson case was essential to solving it.

With that, he laid a hand on top of Landry's and squeezed. He pressed his lips to the shell of her ear, pleased when a light quiver hitched her breath. "I am fine."

She nodded. Her mouth opened, then closed again on whatever it was she wanted to say. His gaze searched hers, but she'd shuttered her emotions along with her lips.

Serves you right, Winchester.

Kathleen bustled out of the kitchen, a large cake held up as she navigated the pathway from the back door through the patio. The men leaped up at once but Noah was closest and took the cake from her hands.

Derek used the moment to once again observe Noah.

The man was comfortable here, that was obvious. His quick grin and wink for Kathleen—and her corresponding blush—as he transferred her masterpiece was easy and comfortable. His conversation earlier around the grill was relaxed and carefree.

The man belonged here.

Whether he really was a cousin to the Adairs or their lost half brother remained to be seen, but he was family. Derek could only hope that bond was strong enough to withstand whatever he and Landry discovered.

Noah whispered something in Kathleen's ear that caused a giggle before she swatted at his shoulder. "You're a tease, young man."

Noah sneaked a finger-full of cream cheese frosting from the base of the cake and popped it into his mouth. "And proud of it."

With the cake cut and distributed, everyone returned

to their chairs. Whit had insisted Kathleen join them, but she'd made several excuses and vanished back to the kitchen.

Patsy Adair's lingering influence, no doubt.

Derek let the other impressions come as they would, the relaxed, semifugue state a good way to see if anything new popped. Sometimes the most important things came into clarity when you stopped looking so hard.

Before they sat down to dinner, Landry had whispered her thoughts about Noah and Rachel. Using her observations as a guide, he focused on the two of them. They'd naturally paired off on their side of the table after everyone else took their seats.

Seating arrangements didn't necessarily mean attraction or a relationship, but it did reinforce how natural the two of them looked together.

Could they use that to their advantage?

Rachel knew why Derek was at Adair Acres and the suspicions about Noah's parentage. She could add her observations to the whole and maybe get additional details from Noah about his background and his formative years with his mother in Europe.

"I thought about something earlier." Landry pushed aside her now-empty dessert plate with a pointed stare before she shot him a wink. "How long was our old stable manager gone before Noah took over?"

"A good year at least. I was spending a lot of time in San Diego but I seem to remember Mom mentioning something about how hard it was to find good help." At the realization of what he said, Whit winced and turned toward Noah. "Sorry."

"No offense." Noah's smile was congenial enough. "Not when considering the source."

"You know—" Carson let the thought hang there as

he swirled his snifter glass. "Mom's ignorance might have had another implication. How many people did flow through the stable after Warren retired?"

Whit shrugged. "At least four or five different people. Probably twice that if you add in the usual turnover in support team."

"That many people with access, codes and keys?" Derek picked up on the conversation and filed away a note to himself to check employment records later on his FBI log-in. "That leaves a lot of people with information on how to get on the property. Do you change security codes every time you have turnover here at the ranch?"

"No." Whit shook his head. "We never had a reason to in the past."

"Clearly we have a reason now." Carson muttered the words before he laid his hand over Georgia's.

Derek knew the Adair children were grown adults, but something in Whit's comment stuck with him. Reginald and Patsy had created a cocoon here at the ranch. An environment ruled by wealth and privilege. Despite its obvious dysfunction, the ranch concealed another problem: isolation.

The pristine paradise had kept everyone who lived there separate. And in its seclusion, it had made them all sitting ducks.

Mark scanned his email, surprised when he saw nothing from Derek. He supposed he should be grateful for a few days' breathing room but the sudden lack of communication was as unsettling as it was welcome.

The ball game blared from the TV behind him as he popped open another beer. He knew Derek cared about the Frederickson case. Hell, the bastard had lived and breathed the case like it was oxygen. And now he just abandons it?

Mark took another large swallow of beer and willed the nausea in his stomach to recede.

Derek had been bothering him for months now, and when things finally get moving the jerk goes radio silent.

He reread the fake letter he'd run through the lab. Just his luck, the inconclusive missive caught the attention of a lab assistant who laddered it up to the big boss. What he'd intended to use to simply keep Derek off balance and engaged in the case had turned on him. Their section chief was even questioning if Derek should be taken off leave and brought back in to finish things up.

He needed to get Derek involved again, and then he needed to end this.

Maybe it was just the natural course of things. He had Rena and her supposed kidnapper. Keeping them both holed up was growing tedious, but he'd come this far. There was no way he was letting it all fall apart now.

It was funny, Mark reflected, how the case of Derek's life would be his ultimate demise.

The bastard's interest in Rena Frederickson had been evident from the jump, his attention fully focused on her photo the moment it hit their desks. The poor little kid who looked like one of those sickly orphans you saw in those commercials that begged for a few cents a day to save them.

Derek had taken one look at the kid and had practically fallen on his sword to help her. Late nights. Weekends. Extra lab work and reports as he dug into her disappearance.

He'd gone along at first. The lost kid had become something of a pet project for the office, and his star could only rise by working on it. The mayor of Los Angeles had held her up as what was wrong with criminals and what needed to be stopped in his fair city.

And the big muckety-mucks at the Bureau had seen saving Rena Frederickson as their chance to cozy up to the mayor so he'd buy into their latest terrorism task force requests.

Politics. Life was all about it. And getting what *you* wanted, which was really what politics was when you stripped away the supposed layers of do-gooding and rhetoric, was his end game.

Derek never understood that. All he wanted was to save the kid. And it was his desire to be a freaking hero that had finally given Mark the in he needed to make Sarah his own.

Sarah.

He thought about her sweet body and lush mouth. She'd be his at the end of it all. She'd already let him know she was interested. Once he proved to the world that Derek was hiding behind a do-gooder attitude and had killed Rena's supposed kidnapper in cold blood, Sarah would be fully his.

No more questions that maybe she'd been too hasty. Or hadn't given Derek enough leeway. Nope. She'd see him for the monster he was.

Or, more to the point, the monster Mark was crafting him to be.

Sarah's sweet face faded from his mind's eye as Landry Adair's sexy lips and high cheekbones took its place. Damn, but she was a looker.

It was a real shame she was likely to get caught in the cross fire, but it couldn't be helped. The little present inside the Adair stables clearly hadn't done its job, but he'd thought of a few other diversions, the first of which was set to go off tonight.

With one last swallow of his beer, he got up to go to the fridge and snag another cool one. It was going to be a late night as he worked through the logistics for his next trip down to Adair Acres.

"You need to play this one straight with me." Carson Adair closed the door to the security room with a light click.

Derek pressed Pause on the computer terminal where he'd toggled back and forth between imagery for the past hour and turned to face Landry's brother. The mild-mannered, jovial dinner companion of earlier was gone. In his place was the former marine lieutenant, straight as an arrow and at full attention.

"I promised you from the start I wouldn't keep you in the dark."

"What happened this morning down in the stables? Landry can gloss over it like it was no big deal, but do me a solid and tell me the truth."

"Someone left your sister a rather nasty message. A rattler inside Pete's feed bin along with the bag he was smuggled inside in."

"What if it was left for you?"

"Me?" Derek bobbled the bottled water he'd lifted to his lips. "No one knows I'm here."

"Don't fool yourself. There are eyes and ears everywhere at this place. People know."

"So take me through it. Who would use the off chance that I might be visiting the stables as a way to harm me? And further, that I'd suddenly engage in managing the animal's feeding schedule?"

Carson took a deep breath before dragging his hand over his military-short hair. His bravado noticeably faded before he crossed to a chair behind one of the room's four computer terminals. "She's my sister. I'm supposed to protect her."

"So am I."

The urge to continue—to define what Landry meant to him—was strong but Derek held back. If he couldn't explain it to himself, he'd be damned if he was going to try to define it to her brother.

"You see anything on the recordings?"

"Shadows, but nothing more concrete. You appear to have a ghost."

Carson leaned forward, the bright blue eyes so like his sister's backlit with curiosity. "Take me through it."

Derek spent the next half hour walking Carson through all he'd found. The various images from around the grounds. The perimeter cameras on the front gates. Even the cameras they had throughout the stables. All appeared undisturbed, yet there were swaths of time he couldn't account for on the time stamps.

"Here and here." Derek hit Pause, then toggled backward frame by frame. "You have a quick jump in time, then that small shadow on the screen like something's been covered over or blacked out."

"Hell." Carson leaned closer, his finger sweeping over the screen. "Right there."

"Yep. Looks like it was around three this morning, best as I can tell."

"Nothing matches on the front cameras?"

"Not at all. I've been through the footage several times and can't see anything that looks unusual or has been tampered with."

"Do you think we're dealing with someone already here on the grounds?"

Derek had wondered the same and had kept a mental list since arriving at the ranch. Despite questions, he'd yet to see anyone who seemed suspicious or even overtly strange. "Everyone appears to love the family. And please don't take this the wrong way, but the staff seems positively giddy with your mother out of sight."

Carson grinned at that—his first since walking into the room. "My mother is a tyrant on the best of days."

"Do you think she killed your father?"

Derek let the question roll, curious to see Carson's reaction. The man had walked in loaded for bear—Derek figured he might as well use the cruddy mood to his advantage. When he got a short laugh and an exaggerated eye roll instead he had to reconsider his tactics.

"You'd get a different answer if you asked Whit. Especially since it's his wife my mother did actually go after. But no, I don't think she killed my father." Carson held up a hand. "Don't get me wrong, she's got the chops for attempted murder as Elizabeth can well tell you, but she didn't have it in her for my father."

"That's an awfully big leap. From a possible scenario of playing the scorned wife, ready to take down the mistress and not the husband, too?"

Carson shrugged. "The best I can tell you, it's not my mother. She and my father had a loveless existence, but it was founded on great love. Hers far more so than his."

"Sounds like you, Landry and Whit have spent your lives paying for it."

"Oh, I don't know." The congenial light fled Carson's eyes, replaced with something more somber and solemn. "I'd like to think we've learned from their mistakes and are bound and determined not to repeat them."

Cycles were tough to break—Derek had seen that proven true in the course of his job more often than not—but he had to admit that if anyone was capable of breaking out, it was the Adair children. Both Whit and

Carson had found strong women to share their lives with. And Landry—

He stopped short, his thoughts drifting to the memory of her hand in his, their fingers linked.

She would definitely break the cycle, of that he had no doubt. She was a bright, vibrant woman, beautiful inside and out. Any man would be lucky to have her. To make a life and build a family with her.

"Why don't I let you get back to it, then." Carson stood and extended his hand. Derek appreciated the gesture and took the proverbial olive branch, satisfied he and Carson Adair had crossed some sort of unspoken chasm.

After Carson left, Derek allowed his gaze to drift back to the computer screen. A dark shadow still smudged the center of the image, proof someone had been in the stables and then erased the evidence. A nameless, faceless threat, determined to bring irreparable harm to Landry and all she held dear.

He'd protect her. He knew that with a bone-deep conviction that he didn't question. But recognizing that he'd need to walk away from her when this was all over?

His phone buzzed in his pocket, shattering the morass of thoughts. With a glance at the readout, his responsibilities came crashing back. Responsibilities he'd taken on before Landry Adair came into his life and responsibilities that would be there long after he left her.

He slid his finger along the glass. "Mark? What's going on?"

Landry paced her bedroom, the roller coaster of the day weighing heavy on her mind. Although the danger that started the day was vastly different from the danger that ended it, she had no illusions of just how much trouble she was in.

Death threats were one thing, but a man who managed to get under a woman's defenses and strip her bare was something else entirely.

Damn it, how had he managed to do it?

Derek Winchester was hell on a woman's good sense.

He'd said he was going to spend another couple of hours in the security center before heading to bed. It had been a couple of hours and she hadn't stopped thinking of him since.

Should she go?

Should she stay?

She glanced at the clock, the readout ensuring it was too late to suddenly arrive in the security room as a curious observer. No, a woman who went hunting for a man this late at night had one thing on her mind.

When her body responded in a wave of tingles that centered at her core, she knew the late-night jaunt through the ranch had better be something she was prepared to see all the way through. Not because Derek would expect it, but because she did.

No, she mused. He wouldn't expect anything at all. Derek Winchester was 100 percent gentleman.

The light knock on her door broke into her thoughts, but it was the whispered "Landry" that had her heart beating double time.

"Derek." She opened the door, delight quickly turning to concern as she ushered him in. "What's wrong?"

Lines carved hard grooves into his lean cheeks and she wrapped an arm around his as she walked him toward her small sitting room. "What happened?"

"Rena."

A hard chill gripped her at that single word. A woman's name. How could she have been so stupid?

They hadn't discussed their pasts or their relationships. He'd mentioned someone named Sarah at the Farmers Market and spoke of her as though she was a part of his past, but that didn't mean there wasn't someone else.

Someone who even now waited for him to come home to her.

A hard metallic taste swam in her mouth, nausea threatening the contents of her stomach. She'd allowed her imagination to make something out of nothing.

Forcing a calm she didn't feel, she gestured him toward her sitting area. "What's happened?"

"Rena's—" He scrubbed at his face, his dark eyes going even darker with the tinted circles beneath them. "She's my case. Or was my case. My last one before I had to take a leave of absence."

Unease whipped through her like a summer storm. Here he was, genuinely in pain, and she was too busy working up a good old-fashioned date with the green-eyed monster. Settling them both on the couch, she worked on coaxing the story out of him. "Tell me about her."

"She's young. Just fourteen."

Derek's words struck like freezing rain, and her guilt only grew deeper. Fourteen years old? And part of an FBI case?

She still remembered fourteen. The carefree days, even with an often-unsettled home life. Time split between the mansion in San Diego and Adair Acres, pulled back and forth like a pawn in the demise of a marriage. Despite the frustration of living under the rule of Reginald and Patsy Adair, she'd been safe. Protected. She'd known it then and understood it now.

"After I left the Secret Service, your aunt helped me find my way into the Bureau. Missing persons."

"That must be difficult work." They had spoken briefly about his job on their ride to the fund-raiser in San Diego, but he'd limited his comments and she hadn't probed. "Rewarding, but difficult."

"Mark. The guy you met yesterday. He's my partner, and he and I were working this case of a girl who went missing after she ran away from the projects, likely kidnapped."

As Derek wove the details—a young girl, snatched from her impoverished existence by an international crime lord—she began to get a picture in her mind of exactly what he dealt with day to day in his job. How did anyone handle that? And certainly not for a number of years. How would a person bear up under that sort of strain? And the hopeless reminder of how depraved human beings could be?

"How'd you get her case? Isn't that the jurisdiction of the LAPD?"

"The case fell into our jurisdiction because all signs pointed toward him taking her across international borders."

"Human trafficking."

He nodded. "Unfortunately, yes."

"So why aren't you on the case now?"

The wall she'd observed repeatedly began its descent, and rather than take it personally, Landry used the opportunity to push back. "Oh no. You did that too many times already. I ask for details and you poker up. Why won't you realize I can help you?"

As he'd spoken, their hands had entwined without her even realizing it until he stared down where they were joined. "I can't taint you with this. Or with my failure."

"Excuse me?"

Of all the things he might have said, the idea that he

saw himself as a failure was the very last thing she expected. "How did you possibly fail?"

"I was pulled off the case for shooting the suspected kidnapper."

"So?"

His gaze never wavered, but she didn't miss the hard bob of his Adam's apple as he swallowed. "I was put on a leave of absence. I'm not allowed to work the case any longer. That's a pretty big failure in my book."

"So how do you know about what happened today?"

"Mark's been feeding me details on the sly, and I keep sending him things to look into or different insights I've gleaned from other cases. I can't give this up. I won't give it up. I owe it to Rena to see it through."

While she admired his focus and desire to bring the child home, she struggled with his partner's role in things. "Can't Mark work this on his own?"

"He's been working—"

When Derek stopped midcomment, Landry saw some of her questions reflected in his gaze.

"Of course he can work it on his own. And he does. Is."

"But?"

"He's a good agent, but not the strongest agent we have."

"And if he stays partnered with you he looks better?"

Landry let the question hang there, curious to see what conclusions he might draw.

She'd observed his partner the day they were at headquarters and hadn't been impressed. Thinking back on it, it wasn't simply his strange gaze or slightly odd comments. There had been something more.

"We were assigned together a few years ago. He'd had a big case come in and was riding high on that. My old partner had just transferred to another office. The window of opportunity was open and we clicked well enough."

"Well enough?"

"Well, sure. He's a bit hotheaded and I don't always agree with his leaps in logic, but Mark's a good man. He cares about his cases and goes the extra mile."

The man she'd met didn't strike her as the extra mile sort, but Landry held her tongue. She figured she'd planted enough seeds and would give Derek some time to work things through in his mind. "Do you need to go back to LA?"

"Not tonight. I'll head in tomorrow and meet Mark for lunch. He said they got another note from the kidnapper, this time with more concrete details on where he's keeping her."

Landry knew she was out of her depth, but the pieces didn't fit for her. "I thought you shot him?"

"Wounded him."

"So now he's out and sending notes on his victim's whereabouts?" Something struck her as off about that sort of behavior, but she reminded herself that she wasn't a criminal. She'd heard internet jokes for years that they weren't all that smart, and this latest run of evidence pointed once more to that very fact.

"The lab results are somewhat inconclusive, but they match the MO on the previous notes. And the bastard skipped out on his bail two weeks ago, completely in the wind."

The depth of his knowledge on the latest details in the case only reinforced the fact that he'd been working it on the side. "Is this what had you so upset earlier?"

"Landry...I—"

"Because I'd like to know."

"I couldn't talk about it with you."

"Why?"

He dropped her hands. "I failed at this. You think I want to broadcast that?"

"From where I'm sitting, you failed at nothing. You have a criminal who's eluded you despite what is obviously all your time, effort and energy. How is that failure?"

"You don't understand."

"Then explain it to me."

The same bleak expression she'd seen that morning after their ride once again covered his face in harsh lines. Pain so raw and so deep she wondered if it had a bottom seemed to well up and spill over. "I am my job. I live these cases, determined to bring justice to those who aren't capable of getting it for themselves."

"No doubt one of the many reasons my aunt thinks so well of you."

"I let this girl down. I missed something in the clues and I failed her when I had the chance to take down her kidnapper."

"But you just walked me through it. The man lured you and Mark to that old warehouse and Rena wasn't there."

"She had to be close."

Landry stood, unable to sit still while he paced like a caged animal. "You've lost perspective on this."

Derek stopped at that, all the leashed fury she'd seen in his large frame suddenly provided with a target. "You know nothing about it."

"Oh, no?" Like staring into a mirror, Landry saw her own pain and anger and swirling fury reflected right back at her.

Like hell she didn't know.

"You think I don't know what it's like to live, day in and day out, determined to make the world better and never seeing it happen?"

"I—"

"Let me finish." She kept her hands at her sides, fisted tight for fear she might walk up and slap him if she didn't. "You think somehow because you acted quickly and made the only freaking decision you possibly could under the circumstances that somehow you've failed?

"I live with that every day. If I'd only followed my parents' wishes. If I'd only tried harder to have a relationship with my dad. If I'd only read the signs and understood what was happening around me instead of burying my head in the sand like some clueless society girl, I might have been able to step in and save my father!"

Chapter 10

Sometimes the most important things came into clarity when you stopped looking so hard.

Derek could only stare at the volcano erupting before him, his earlier thought at dinner coalescing into reality. He thought he knew grief—and he thought he'd sensed the depths of Landry's pain—but he obviously knew nothing. She'd hidden it so well and so deep, now that it was out, there was no putting it back where it had lain hidden.

"You can't possibly think you're responsible for your father's death."

"Me. My brothers. My mother. We all are. There was a threat lurking here beneath our noses and we all missed it."

"You can't know that."

"How can't I know that? There was no struggle in his office, he was shot at point-blank range and the security cameras were off for a maintenance upgrade. My father knew his killer."

"Yes, he did." There was no way you could add up that series of facts and believe anything else. "But it still doesn't mean you were responsible."

"Funny you can assume that logic about me yet can't apply it to yourself."

Derek saw how neatly she'd boxed him in. "Rena's my job."

"And Reginald was my father. It's not about logic or reason, Derek. It's about emotion and that's why it's so hard to let go."

She moved closer, and the light scent of honeysuckle he'd noticed during dinner tickled his senses with its sweet overtones. He'd believed the scent had carried from the gardens, but with Landry so near he now knew the sweet scent was her. Fresh and airy, it suited her to a T.

And when she moved closer still, he took another deep breath, filling his lungs with the rich, clean bouquet.

"If I let go, there won't be anything left."

"Or if you let go, you can finally reach for something new."

Her lips pressed to his jaw, and she trailed a line of tender kisses over hard bone. The moment was both tender and erotic, especially when she flicked her tongue over the edge of his chin before continuing a path toward the other side of his face. "Tell me you want me."

"You know I do."

"Tell me there's no one else."

"There's no one—" He broke off, her words like a pinball in his mind. "No one else? Of course there's no one else."

A light blush worked its way up her cheeks, but her gaze stayed level. Determined. "I just wanted to make sure. You…you mentioned someone named Sarah the other day. At lunch."

"Ah."

He stilled, the urge to brush it off warring with the need to be honest. She'd had the guts to ask, and he at least owed it to her to tell her the truth. "Sarah was my fiancée. We've been broken up for a few months now. Another casualty, along with my day job, of Rena's case."

"Oh."

Derek hesitated, then went with instinct. He traced the line of her jaw, his fingers mimicking the same play of her lips mere moments before. "Turns out in the end Sarah didn't want to be a glorified cop's wife."

"That's what she said?"

"In pretty much those words. And, as it turns out, I'm happy being a glorified cop. Or I at least want to be with someone who will support me for as long as I want to be one."

"Why do people want to change the ones they're with?"

Head bent, he pressed his lips to hers, murmuring against their sweet softness. "I have no idea."

"I think—" She broke off, her breath mingling with his before she kissed him fully.

"You think what?"

He felt her smile as it spread against his lips. "I think you talk too much."

Her hands settled at the back of his neck, pulling him closer and deepening the kiss. He allowed himself to be dragged along, into the sweet abyss of need and desire and something incredibly soft and warm that he'd never felt before.

The swirling vortex was all-consuming, and in moments, the sexy banter and lingering kisses had turned urgent. Greedy. And oh, so enticing.

With careful steps, he walked them backward toward the love seat in her sitting room, pulling her on top of him when he felt the plump cushions at the backs of his legs. He fell into the pillows, rewarded with even more softness when her breasts crushed against his chest.

The careful dance they'd maintained between them vanished as the rush of the moment overtook them both. A rich, carnal craving settled into his veins, and Derek felt himself going under, a drowning man without breath who needed only the woman in his arms to sustain him.

An abstract image of a siren on a rock floated through his mind. If the siren was anything like Landry, no wonder sailors crashed to their doom. He'd follow this woman anywhere. And he was fast coming to believe he'd do anything to possess her.

Just as earlier, her hands were like a brand against his skin. Fires flared high everywhere she touched, and he felt the world melting away as Landry Adair became his entire focus.

She had the material of his shirt up and over his head before moving into a seated position on his lap, her hands on his shoulders. "Those are some awfully impressive muscles."

The thin blouse she wore was in his hands and up over her head before she could blink. He took in the strong lines of her body and the shape of her full breasts where they spilled over the silky cups of her bra. "Likewise, Ms. Adair."

A sexy, bewitching smile spread across her lips. "I do believe we've got a mutual admiration society going on here."

He leaned forward and pressed a light kiss to her

chest, flicking his tongue over the generous flesh of her breast. "What I feel is considerably deeper than admiration."

At her sharp intake of breath, he continued his exploration, tracing a path down the silky edge of her bra with his tongue. Her hands stayed firmly positioned on his shoulders. Every time he hit a particularly sweet spot, her palm flexed against muscle like a telegraph of her pleasure.

And when he finally slipped one silky cup beneath her breast and took a nipple into his mouth, he was rewarded with a hard cry of pleasure that filled the air between them.

"Derek." His name floated on the air before her head fell back, her eyes closed as she took pleasure in the moment. The soft light of the lamp beside the bed sheened her skin in a golden glow, and Derek let the moment spin out, the sweetest taste of her on his lips.

His hands stayed firm across her back, holding her in place as he worked the sensitive flesh between his lips. His fingers drifted to the clasp of her bra, anxious to have no barrier between them.

The silky material fell between them and Landry was bared, naked to his gaze. "You're so beautiful."

The words exhaled on a reverent hush as he gave himself a moment to simply look at her.

"Who's complaining about my willpower around doughnuts now?"

A light tease suffused her husky words and he found himself captivated by her sultry gaze. The bright blue of her eyes had turned a vivid indigo, the darkness of her pupils wide with desire.

But it was something else—something that hovered beneath the desire—where he saw the question.

Am I enough?

Anger, honed to a fine point, lit him up inside. What had her family done to her? While her brothers had suffered through the obvious expectations of their father, she was left to her mother's endless criticism.

How could a woman so vibrant—so caring and aware of others—believe she was somehow lacking?

"You're gorgeous, Landry. Inside and out. Nothing will change that. Ever."

He bent his head and took her lips with his, slipping his tongue into her warm mouth. Her tongue tangled with his, drawing him in with the warmest welcome.

It might take time, but he was going to convince this woman of her worth. He believed she knew it—somewhere deep inside her there was a light Patsy and Reginald Adair hadn't been able to snuff out—but he also knew it would take time.

And he was more than up to the task.

Long, lush moments spun out between them, growing more urgent with each passing second. Their touches grew more frantic and their breathing more urgent as they pushed each other onward.

He shifted beneath her, the hot heat of her core driving him wild with the need to make her fully his. And when she reached between them, her hands slipping beneath the waistband of his jeans, Derek knew the deepest satisfaction as her hand brushed against his hard body.

"Well, what have we here, Mr. Winchester?" That teasing note was back, and he fought the groan as her fingers closed around him.

He pressed his forehead to hers and closed his eyes, the wash of pleasure so immense he needed a moment to get himself in check. But when the hints of laughter faded, replaced with a quiet urgency, he knew he was lost.

"Please, Derek. Let me."

He took her mouth once more, his only answer to the warm, willing, generous woman in his arms. His body was already strung out, pushed to the limit with the desperate need for release, but still she urged him on.

"Landry—" He broke off, unsure of himself. He wanted her. With madness that ran so deep he didn't know if he'd ever recover. But he'd also just shared the realities of his life.

Rena.

His forced leave of absence.

His ruined engagement.

All were realities that weren't going to go away if they made love.

"Landry—" He held her still, one hand on her shoulders while the other covered her hand. "Wait."

"Hmmm?" Confusion lit her features as she slowly recognized he had stopped her. "Derek?"

An apology was already springing to his lips when the room plunged into inky blackness.

Landry willed herself to surface from the sexual haze that consumed her. Derek had been so willing—so into the moment—before he halted it.

And now the lights were out?

Despite the fact that her brain was still trying to assimilate all the facts, the irony wasn't lost on her.

Abstractly, she realized the position they were still in and removed her hand from beneath his. His sharp intake of breath as her fingers slid along his length gave her a grim sort of satisfaction.

Why had he stopped her?

She lifted off his lap, her movements stiff as her body still struggled with abandoned desire. Her slacks were unbuttoned and her blouse had disappeared somewhere. She kept one hand on the cushions, reaching for the drawer in the small end table at the edge of the couch.

Her hand closed around a lighter and she pulled out the cool metal, flicking the starter. She focused on the flash of warm light and ignored the heavy cadence of both their breaths. Within moments, the small, fragrant candle she kept on the end table flared to life, illuminating them both in the glow.

She ignored Derek and went to work righting herself. Her blouse was in a heap beside the couch and she slipped it on, regretting the lack of bra but unwilling to spend any more time naked before his gaze.

"I'm going to go down and see what this is about."

"I'm going with you."

"Suit yourself."

"Landry—" His hand closed over her forearm and he pulled her close.

"Yes?"

"I want you. I might be a clumsy ass with equally clumsy timing, but know that as sure as we're both standing here. I want you."

She nodded around the hard lump that welled in her throat, but didn't trust herself to speak.

And then there were no words because Derek had her in his arms, his mouth fused to hers, those same sparks flaring to life as if they'd never been dulled.

When he finally lifted his head long moments later, his voice was husky, stamped with need. "I want you."

He dropped her hand and made quick work of finding his T-shirt and zipping up his jeans. She moved equally quickly, sliding her blouse over her head and fluffing her hair into some semblance of order. She could only hope whoever they ran into in the hallway saw her messy hair and blamed it on bed head instead of passionate kisses on her love seat.

Derek grabbed the squat candle from the end table. "Let's go see what this is about."

They wove their way through her wing, toward the large staircase to the first floor. Landry heard a sharp cry from the direction of the kitchen and picked up her pace. She called out so as not to surprise anyone. "Kathleen?"

"Miss Landry?" Another sharp cry added to the question and Landry raced for the swinging door into the oversize kitchen that was Kathleen's domain.

She gasped and dropped to her knees. "Kathleen! What happened?" Several plates lay shattered a few feet away from their cook's supine figure, her leg trapped underneath her at a funny angle.

"I tripped." The older woman tried to move and another heavy cry fell from her lips.

"Shhh. Shhh now." Landry took her hand, grateful when Derek dropped to his haunches on Kathleen's other side.

"You're going to be okay." His voice was calm and quiet as he set the candle down next to her. "I'm going to leave this here and I'm going to call for help."

He already had his cell phone out of his back pocket and was dialing as he crossed to the far side of the kitchen.

"I was just putting some things away. That's all. Just a few last-minute things before bed."

Landry sat down and wrapped her arms around the woman as she let her talk. She crooned nonsense words, trying to calm Kathleen's obvious shock as she babbled about putting away dishes from the night's dinner.

"I know. I know. You like a clean kitchen before you go to bed."

Voices echoed outside the kitchen door as Carson and Georgia came in, followed closely by Whit and Elizabeth. "What?"

Landry shot her brother a dark look and waved them in. "The blackout scared Kathleen and she tripped."

Her sisters-in-law went to work immediately, Georgia picking up the shattered plates while Elizabeth crossed to the pantry to grab a broom. Whit followed his wife, beating her to the broom and dustpan. "I don't think so, babe."

"I'm pregnant, not disabled," Elizabeth said, obviously disgruntled.

"Let him spoil you, sweetheart." Kathleen waved a hand from the floor before trying to move again.

Landry held her still but figured her ability to key into what was happening in the room was a good sign.

Carson stood on the far side of the kitchen with Derek, their heads bent now that an ambulance had been called. Landry knew without being told that their little pow-wow was because neither thought the blackout was an accident.

There was no bad weather, and the house had a backup generator that kicked in when they did lose power. The pitch black that had descended over Adair Acres was immediate and absolute.

And it put them in jeopardy.

With no backup generator, the house alarm and every bit of security was turned off.

Carson swung the beam of his flashlight across the wall of the security center. The panel that was perpetually lit with blinking lights was dark, snuffed out by their latest power problem.

"There's no way this is a fluke. Someone did this."

"The security center *and* the generator." Derek swung his own beam of light, searching for the circuit breaker he'd seen earlier. "Yeah. Someone's behind this."

"But who? I know we've not been as on top of the employees coming and going, but the security here's good. Top-of-the-line. My father would expect nothing less."

"You and Whit have both dealt with problems in the last few months." Derek found the panel on the far wall and unhooked the thin metal door. "Is it possible they've come back to roost?"

"I find that hard to believe. My mother was behind the danger to Elizabeth, and I took care of the bastard who was after Georgia."

Derek digested Carson's words as he examined the circuit breaker. Even though he wanted to find some other answer for what was happening, Carson wasn't off the mark. The recent threats felt new—and different—from what the Adairs had been living with since Reginald's murder.

It was possible Patsy Adair could have hired someone again, but he had a hard time believing she'd threaten her own daughter. And while obviously scary when they were happening, the threats on Elizabeth and Georgia had been dealt with.

Which left Landry as the current target.

"Only a few people know the reason why you're here," Carson said. "Whit and Elizabeth, Landry, our aunt Kate, and me and Georgia."

"Yet none of this started happening until I got here. Why?"

"I have no idea. You've done a convincing job of making everyone think you're my sister's new boyfriend."

Derek didn't miss the slightly disgruntled tones in Carson's voice but ignored them. Instead, the heated moments in Landry's room came flooding back, filling his thoughts with vivid, erotic images of them together. His already-heated body responded and Derek was grateful for the dark.

He went back to work on the breaker panel, willing his body to calm. But the woman had him in knots.

"I want to go out and look at the generator." Carson disappeared and Derek let out a raw breath. It was only when he turned back toward the unit that he saw a set of lights flash on the server panel connected to the security center. Light illuminated the hallway, and Derek reached for the room switch they hadn't bothered to turn on when they arrived.

Overhead light flooded the darkness, and several beeps echoed from the computer monitors as they rebooted.

Although he'd taken all the requisite training in cybercrime and basic technology courses, he was still out of his depth when it came to all the ins and outs of computer forensics. Mark was a whiz, and he'd depended on him for the heavy lifting when necessary.

Even with his limited knowledge, he knew enough to know the wavy lines growing brighter on the screens were a bad sign. The whirling of sirens dragged his attention from the immediate problem and he vowed to return after they got Kathleen safely to the hospital. He'd give Mark a call and ask him to walk them through correcting it if need be.

He'd nearly left when Noah came barreling through the door, his breathing heavy. "What the hell is going on around here? I heard the ambulance and just saw the sirens. Who's hurt?"

"Kathleen. She tripped when the lights went off. It looks like she broke her leg."

"When did the lights go off?" A puzzled frown crossed Noah's face, his hands on his hips. "I've been down in the stable for the last two hours doing some paperwork and had power the whole time."

"Nothing went out?"

"Nope. I'd still be down there if I hadn't heard the sirens."

Derek's knowledge of electricity was even less developed than his computer skills, but even he knew that was odd. "The power went off up here, along with the backup generator. Doesn't that power the stables, too?"

"Nope. We have a separate generator down there." Noah shook his head but a heightened sense of awareness sparked in his eyes as he let out a sharp expletive. "This isn't an act of Mother Nature. Someone did this."

"On that we're in agreement."

"Just like a snake doesn't magically get into a sealed feed bin."

"No. But like leaving the snake's canvas bag behind, whoever did this left us a clue."

"I don't think I follow."

"The bastard wasn't aware of a backup generator in the stables. Which means we should be able to backtrack through the security feeds from the barn and find out what he did."

"You can do that?"

"I can't. But I think I know someone who can."

Chapter 11

Landry fought the urge to lay her head on Derek's shoulder and instead watched the strange ballet that was a hospital waiting room. Doctors or nurses came in frequently to provide updates to loved ones. She'd watched through the night—had seen the look of hope cross each face, followed by sobering relief or the heartbreaking reality of grief—and had wondered how those kindly souls could keep doing it.

Day after day, caring for those who'd been hurt, sometimes beyond repair.

They'd been fortunate to receive good news of their own—Kathleen was in surgery now to repair her broken leg—but even knowing she'd recover, things had irrevocably changed for their cook.

"She'll be okay. It's a bad break, that's all. They'll fix her up."

Derek had tried repeatedly to reassure her, but Landry

couldn't stop worrying. Kathleen was seventy-one. A break like this would be hard for anyone to recover from, but a woman of her age wasn't going to simply bounce back.

Whit had taken Elizabeth home earlier to rest, and Carson and Georgia had gone off to fetch bad coffee from the vending machine. There had been one other couple in the waiting room who finally left, and she and Derek had the room to themselves.

Tabling her worries about Kathleen, Landry focused on the bigger picture. "The house power and the generator? There's no way both went out at the same time. It smacks of sabotage."

She appreciated when Derek only nodded his agreement with her assessment. Maybe they really had become partners.

In name only, her still-bruised ego bandied back at her.

But partners all the same.

"Noah was down at the stables when it happened. The generator there was untouched."

A renewed wave of panic swamped her as she thought about Pete, Diego and the other occupants of the barn. "What is wrong with me? I didn't even think about the horses."

"There's nothing wrong with you and there was nothing to think about. Noah was with them the entire time and they're safe. And possibly sitting on the clues we need."

"What clues?"

He walked her through his theory—how the fact that the security wasn't breached in the stable meant they might be able to electronically backtrack to the person trying to do them harm. "You know how to do that? Work your way through reams of computer code?"

"No, but Mark does. I'll call him in the morning."

A wholly unreasonable shot of alarm clenched her stomach in a hard knot. Unable to stem the rising panic, she fought to keep her voice calm. "Are you sure about that?"

"Of course. He's good at it, too. It's how he ended up in missing persons."

"Computers?"

"He cracked a major drug ring in the Pacific Northwest, tracking it back to a series of cyberattacks they'd perpetrated."

"That group a few years back? The Rainier Cartel?"

That sting had made the evening news, and Landry recalled the importance of the bust and the positive effect it would have on crime as far south as San Diego.

"Mark did that? The man I met the other day?"

"That was his case. Or he was part of the team on that case. It's how he ended up getting his transfer to Los Angeles."

Landry tried to assimilate an agent capable of cracking down on a problem that large and the man she'd met at the FBI offices the other day and found herself unable to reconcile the two.

The man she'd met had seemed soft and deeply lazy. And not because of hours spent behind a computer, working through layer upon layer of code. No, it was something else.

She respected Derek's opinion, but no matter how hard she'd tried to reframe her image of Mark, her first impression had been of a man who was jealous of those around him.

Perpetually overlooked by the brass and forever angry, convinced it was someone else's fault.

"You don't think all that well of him, do you?"

"I didn't get a good vibe off of him. So. Well. No, I don't."

She saw Derek nod, his gaze considering. "Would you feel better if I called someone else at the Bureau to help?"

"You'd do that?"

"Of course. I trust Mark but I trust you, too. And I've got a few other team members I can call. I'll get one of them to look into this for me."

"Thank you."

The sexual disappointment she'd felt earlier came back in full force, tinged with a layer of sadness.

The two of them were good together.

Their chemistry was explosive, yes, but it was something more. Something that went far deeper than simple attraction. And she'd sensed it from their very first morning ride on the horses.

She and Derek Winchester clicked.

Over the past few months, she'd observed the same sort of chemistry when she watched her brothers and their new wives. She'd been unable to put the sense into words, but it was fascinating to now realize she understood it on a personal level.

"Miss Adair?" Landry was pulled from her musings by the nurse who'd been giving them updates all evening. "Kathleen's out of recovery and in her room. You can go in and see her now."

"Thank you."

"Go ahead in. I'll wait for Carson and Georgia to get back and then we'll join you."

Landry nodded and followed the nurse. The private room they'd requested for Kathleen was only a short way down the hall, and in moments the nurse had ushered her through.

Their sturdy cook, a fixture at Adair Acres since

Landry and her brothers had been small, smiled back at her from the bed. "All this trouble."

"Nonsense. It's no trouble at all." Landry picked up the older woman's hand and squeezed it tight. "All we need to focus on now is getting you well."

Kathleen's tremulous smile fell, tears welling in her eyes. "There's so much to do. So much to be done. Miss Elizabeth's baby shower and keeping everyone in line for when your mother returns."

"Shhh, now." Landry pulled a chair toward the bed, then settled Kathleen's blankets more firmly around her. "You're not to worry about any of this. Georgia and I can finish up the details for the shower, and I know Rachel will be happy to help, too. You're going to focus on getting well and enjoy being a guest. The doctor said you only need to stay for a day and then you should be ready to go home."

Kathleen greeted her with sleepy protests, and Landry could only be grateful the woman would likely remember nothing of the conversation. They'd focus on pampering her for the next few days and getting her settled at home. Whit had already sent her a text saying that he was looking into home health care, and they'd make sure she was taken care of to the best of their abilities.

"How's she doing?" Derek stepped into the room, Carson and Georgia in his wake.

"As well as can be expected. And very upset she hasn't finished all the details for Elizabeth's shower."

"That's the least of her worries." Georgia moved to the other side of the bed and patted a now-sleeping Kathleen's shoulder. "She needs to focus on getting well."

Landry couldn't quite hold back the rueful smile. "I think that will be easier said than done."

"Unless..." Carson moved around to stand next to his wife.

When they all only stared at him, Carson gestured them back toward the lobby. "I've got an idea."

"You're up early." Derek reached for an empty coffee mug off the sideboard in the dining room. Landry sat, pert and perky as a daisy at the table. That delicious honeysuckle scent of hers drifted his way and went a long way toward clearing the early-morning cobwebs from his mind.

They'd finally arrived home at four and said goodbye at the entrance to her room. He'd wanted nothing more than to come in and finish what they'd started earlier, but had gone on to his room after saying good-night, well aware he had no right to finish anything.

Another hour of tossing and turning in bed, thinking about Landry, hadn't gotten him any closer to deciphering his sudden attack of nerves about the shoddy state of his life. Instead, he'd cursed himself for walking away from the woman he was fast coming to believe was the best thing that had ever walked into his life.

"What are you working on?" He pointed toward the tablet at her elbow.

"I'm reviewing the notes I've taken so far from our trip to LA. I want to get your take on them."

"I've got my own notes, but I think I can remember most of them. Let's compare."

She shifted her chair closer to his and another wave of honeysuckle washed over him. Without giving himself time to check the impulse, he leaned forward and pressed his lips to her ear, inhaling deeply.

"You're beautiful."

She stilled, her blue eyes going as soft as a field of bluebonnets. "Thank you."

"I meant what I said last night. I want you. And I spent what was left of last night cursing myself and my damned conscience."

"Would it make you feel better if I told you I lay awake cursing your damned conscience, too?"

A heavy laugh hit him and he couldn't hold it back, the sheer joy of being with her replacing whatever lingering frustration he might have had. Her laughter joined his, quickly capturing both of them in the moment.

Still grinning, he couldn't resist placing another kiss against her ear as their laughter quieted. "Maybe you'll give me another chance."

"Maybe I just will." She pressed a lingering kiss against his lips, the light coffee-flavored taste of her going to his head like the most potent whiskey.

In spite of all that was going on, nothing mattered but being in her orbit. Power outages and snakes and kidnapped babies simply faded away in the reality of her.

"Derek." Her voice pulled him back to the present.

"Hmmm?"

She laid a hand on his shoulder, holding him still. "We need to go through this."

"Maybe you can sit on my lap when we do."

He was rewarded with another giggle before she tossed her napkin at him. "As I was saying."

And then she had the tablet, her tone all business, even if she did keep a hand over his as she spoke. "The first place I started was the immigration records you pulled. My aunt Emmaline was in Europe when my father's son was born. She was pregnant with Noah at the time and on bed rest."

Although he wanted nothing more than to find someplace secluded and finish what they'd started, Derek had to admit she had him at the details. Years of training and natural curiosity had his gaze drifting off her lush mouth and toward the screen of her tablet. "Your aunt never traveled at all?"

"No." Landry tapped on the screen, then pointed toward a section of notes. "Right there. Between the death of her husband and her difficult pregnancy, she didn't travel at all for almost a two-year period, both before and after Noah was born. And even for years after that, her travel was sporadic."

"She was widowed? That long ago? That never made it into Kate's briefing."

"About six months into her pregnancy."

Derek considered that tidbit. On one hand, he could understand leaving it out. The notes had said Emmaline was widowed young. But something in the fact that it happened while pregnant struck Derek as important. Poignant, somehow. "What does that do to a person?"

Landry's eyes narrowed as she considered his question. "Grief is a horrible thing, and it's not logical when it comes."

"No, but to lose your spouse—your support system— at the very moment you need it most?" Derek took a sip of his coffee. "That must have been horrible for her."

"I'd say so." Landry scrolled a bit further in her notes. "It's also another reason why the idea that Noah is Jackson seems so off. Emmaline couldn't have taken Jackson. She was nowhere near him."

"True." Derek reached for her tablet again and scanned the meticulous accounting of dates and had to concede her point. They could have as many suspicions as they wanted, but none of it changed the fact that by all accounts, Emmaline Adair Scott was living a life in Europe, content to stay there and raise her own family. "What else?"

"I also scanned the investigation records quickly. It was almost four decades ago and I didn't spend much time with them, but I'm surprised the police records from North Carolina are so spotty."

"I noticed that, too." Derek had thought the records inconclusive, as well, but he'd taken it a step further and questioned the overall investigative skills of those assigned. It might have been nearly forty years ago, but good investigative technique wasn't only in the purview of those who had computers and smartphones at their disposal.

The cops on the Adair kidnapping had done a terrible job. In one report they have neighbors claiming a car had circled the block several times the day the baby was taken, but no one had followed up on the make or model.

And yet another report had said there was a statewide search, yet Derek hadn't found any proof of much beyond a few door-to-door checks of known offenders out on parole.

None of it made much sense. A child goes missing and the cops do everything they can to bring the child home. The child of a wealthy family goes missing and no one in law enforcement sleeps until they have answers.

Yet Jackson Adair vanished from almost right beneath his mother's nose, never to be seen again, and the case seemed flubbed or misguided every step of the way.

Curious, he waited to see Landry's take.

"I know this isn't my expertise, but the police records seem awfully incomplete."

"Because they are."

Landry was prevented from replying when Noah walked into the room. She recovered quickly, leaning forward and giggling against his cheek, looking for all the world like a woman in a heated flirtation with her boyfriend.

The quick thinking had obviously worked when Noah wiggled his eyebrows in Derek's direction from the spread set out on the sideboard. "I'd ask what you two are up to but I think I can guess."

Landry stood to refresh her coffee and pressed a kiss to her cousin's cheek. "Mind, gutter, Noah. Disengage the two."

He pulled her close in a side-armed hug and dropped a big smacking kiss on her cheek. "You know no one's good enough for my little baby cousin."

Derek fought the wince at Noah's loaded words, especially since the man was oblivious to the conversation he'd interrupted. While Noah fixed his breakfast, Landry flitted around the dining room like a queen bee, keeping things light and easy.

Heck, if Derek hadn't just gone over the data with her, he'd never have believed the two of them were just questioning Noah's parentage.

"The shower's later today. Is your mother coming down from Palm Springs?" Landry asked.

"She wouldn't miss it. The woman's crazy about babies. It's all she can talk about. Especially when it comes to my getting in gear and giving her a grandchild." Noah tucked into a large bagel he'd smothered with cream cheese, the move doing nothing to erase a quick and irritated frown.

"A woman's prerogative."

"As is a man's right to choose when he procreates."

"Touché."

Landry picked at her own breakfast, tearing off a

small piece of toast. "Your mom's picking up Aunt Rosalyn and Uncle Sheldon, isn't she?"

Derek sat, fascinated to see how she manipulated the dialogue.

"Better her than me." Noah visibly shuddered. "Sheldon's getting more and more crochety by the day. It only rivals his all-around general craziness."

"I wish they'd get him to a doctor and have his memory checked." Landry made a small *tsk*ing sound. "Maybe get him some meds. That nasty disposition of his only gets worse with age."

"Well, I for one can't wait to meet your family, babe." Derek laid it on thick, draping his hand over hers and leaning forward to press a quick kiss to her lips. "I think I might have something to do this afternoon."

He shot a pleading look at Noah. "You sure you don't need help down at the stables today? I can exercise the horses. Feed them. Muck stalls."

"You'd take stall mucking over a baby shower?" Landry pretended offense, but he saw the humor lighting the depths of her eyes.

Derek shot Noah a wink before pressing another kiss to Landry's cheek. "Any day, babe. Any day."

Georgia handed her one end of a blue streamer and pointed toward the far side of the living room. "Let's tack it on the end of the fireplace."

Landry unrolled as she walked, twisting the streamer to create an arc of baby blue. "I'm going to be an aunt. Every time I think I have a handle on it, I have a moment when I realize in a few short months there will be a baby here."

"I know. Things have happened so fast, but I can't wait to meet him." Georgia pulled a tab of tape off some contraption she wore on her wrist. "Do you think we're doing the right thing?"

"Elizabeth wanted something quiet at home."

"I mean about Noah."

The quavering voice reached her a moment before a quick, hard sob. Landry dropped her end of the streamer roll and pulled Georgia into her arms for a tight hug. "Come on. What's the matter?"

"I feel like Pandora. I'm the one who made the connection about the picture of Ruby's father and Noah, and now I can't take it back."

"You shared an observation, Georgia. You didn't do anything wrong."

"I know, but that was before I knew him well. And now that I've spent more time with him—" She broke off, another sob spilling from her throat as tears rolled down her cheeks. "I feel like I've set in motion the steps to ruin his life."

"No, no, no. You can't think that way." Landry kept her arm around Georgia's shoulders and tried to comfort her, but even her attempts at soft, soothing words felt flat to her own ears.

Hadn't she felt the same?

Hell, just that morning she and Derek had worked through their notes from the FBI almost beneath Noah's nose.

"I'm not sure what I hate more," Georgia said. "The questions, or the fact that we all think this huge, enormous secret and haven't shared it with him."

"I understand and feel the same way. I know we need answers, but we don't have to like it."

Georgia dashed at the tears that covered her cheeks. "What if we're right?"

"We love him. And if we find out that your suspicions

are correct, then we'll continue to give him all the love and support we have."

As they finished with the decorating, Landry couldn't help wondering if she was being too optimistic. Yes, they would all support Noah no matter what the outcome, but would he want their help once he knew the truth?

Landry slipped on a thin pair of sandals to match the light wrap dress she wore and closed her bedroom door behind her. She felt better after sharing the time with Georgia earlier, even if the guilt over what they were doing increasingly weighed like an anchor.

At least their conversation had reinforced that the others felt as bad as she did.

She loved Noah; she always had. And until recently, with the reading of her father's will and the revelation that he'd had a child from a first marriage, she'd had no reason to view Noah under any light except that of favored cousin.

None of it changed the fact that Reginald and Ruby had spent their lives bereft of their son. Was it possible her father died never knowing his son had actually been nearby his entire life?

The two had always gotten along. Her father had kept his distance—she'd always believed he knew no other way—but it hadn't stopped a bond from forming between them anyway. Their mutual love of horses had shaped much of it, but Reginald had always been a father figure, especially with Emmaline's husband having already passed away.

The doorbell rang, pulling Landry from her thoughts, and she opened the door to see Emmaline, Rosalyn and Sheldon at the door. "Hello! Come in."

Landry braced herself for the onslaught of familial

hugs and the usual banter that accompanied a visit from her father's sisters. Sheldon grumbled about keeping his hat and she deftly ignored him, swooping in for hugs from her aunt Rosalyn and her aunt Emmaline.

As Landry pulled Emmaline close, she wondered who she held in her arms. A sweet, loving aunt who still grieved the loss of her brother so soon after his passing? Or a cold, brittle woman who'd betrayed that brother by taking and raising his only son?

If she had done it, how did she live with herself?

Whit was about to have a baby boy, and Landry held nothing but excitement for the arrival of her new nephew and happiness for her brother and his wife. She couldn't even imagine touching a hair on the new baby's head, let alone taking him away from his parents.

Was she actually related to this woman who possibly felt neither of those things?

Stepping back, Landry let her gaze travel over her aunt. Slender and petite, Emmaline's features were small and birdlike. Her thick brown hair was shot through with gray and she had it pulled into a severe bun.

She hardly looked like a kidnapper.

But what did that really mean?

Afraid to get caught staring, Landry quickly ushered them into the dining room for some refreshments. "Kathleen's been cooking for a week to get ready for this. Please, help yourselves."

Sheldon's eyes lit up when he saw some small pastry-wrapped hot dogs, and he beelined toward them with a speed that belied his age.

"Not too many, Sheldon."

Sheldon waved a hand in Rosalyn's direction. "Don't fuss at me, woman. I'm fit as a fiddle."

"It's a baby shower, not a five-course meal. Make sure you leave some for everyone else."

"We have plenty, Aunt Rosalyn." Landry gave her aunt a good-natured eye roll before leaning in and whispering, "The kitchen knows those are his favorites. Kathleen made sure they cooked extras."

Rosalyn patted Landry's arm. "Such a good girl you are. Reginald had good children."

Landry waved her aunts off toward the living room and the conversation that already hummed with Elizabeth, Georgia and several of Elizabeth's friends. While she wanted to continue her observations, she figured she'd better keep an eye on Sheldon until he'd made a plate or Rosalyn's admonition of vanished appetizers might come true.

So as not to appear as if she was watching him, Landry made a fuss over the table settings and decorations. "How have you been, Uncle Sheldon?"

"Fine. Fine. Fit like I told you."

"Of course you are. I'm so glad you and Aunt Rosalyn could make it to Elizabeth's baby shower."

"Baby?" His head snapped up as he stared at her, his dark brown eyes rheumy with age. "What baby?"

"Whit and Elizabeth's baby. The baby boy they're having in a few months."

He continued to putter his way around the table, muttering to himself the whole time. Although she'd been joking with Noah that morning, her uncle really was worse off than she'd realized.

"Babies. Always talking about babies. Live ones. Dead ones."

The hair on the back of her neck stood on edge and Landry stilled her movements. The stack of napkins in her hands flopped and she dropped several on the table.

Bending down to retrieve them, she forced a calm she didn't feel into her voice. "What dead babies, Uncle Sheldon?"

"The one that died. Right?" He shook his head. "Or maybe it didn't die."

She moved around the table to settle a hand on his shoulder. "What baby didn't die, Uncle Sheldon?"

"Emmaline's baby. He was born sick and we thought he died but then he didn't. Right?"

"Of course. Noah's fine and well, Uncle Sheldon. In fact, he's here. He'll come into the party later and say hi to everyone."

"Right as rain."

"Yes, Noah's fine." She steered him toward the living room, adding a few extra puff pastries on his way through the door to keep him occupied and his mouth busy.

Shock raced through her, slamming her heart against her ribs as Landry fell back against the wall and closed her eyes. Had her senile old uncle just confirmed the truth behind their questions?

And if Emmaline had a baby who died, then who was Noah Scott?

Chapter 12

Derek stayed true to his promise. In exchange for skipping out on spending the afternoon with Landry's family, he helped out wherever he was needed in the stables. The work was sweaty and tiring, but he took pride in the finished product—a stable that positively sparkled.

"We've got an opening if you want it." Noah's grin was infectious when he handed over a cold bottle of water. "You're a natural in here."

"It was time well spent. I can feel my muscles."

"There's something to that, isn't there?" Noah took a seat opposite him in the small stable office, his skin as covered in dirt as Derek's.

Noah's gaze traveled the office walls. "It's something my mother's struggled with." When Derek said nothing, Noah added, "My interest in working here. Taking care of the horses and the grounds. She has some idea that it's beneath me."

"Parents don't understand everything."

"Do yours?"

"I got pretty lucky." Again, he was reminded that his own upbringing was fairly idyllic. But even amid the seeming perfection, there had been holes. "But parents don't always know how to express their feelings. My mother didn't like a woman I used to be engaged to."

He'd deliberately pushed those early days with Sarah out of his mind, but his mother hadn't been crazy about his choice and had made sure he knew about it, too.

"What happened?"

"Let's just say I figured out before it was too late that you can't share your life with someone who wishes you were a different person."

"That's for damn sure." Noah waved his water bottle. "You introduce your mother to Landry yet?"

"Not yet. But soon."

Derek knew he was only playing a part, but suddenly he had a vision of bringing Landry home to meet his parents. The two of them, seated at his mother's dining room table, sharing a meal as his mother trod that delicate balance between being nosy and interested, and his father kept a sweet, supportive smile pasted on his face.

"What about you? You ever get close enough to getting married?"

"Not yet. That's my mother's other bone of contention with me. She hates my job and is upset she doesn't have any grandchildren. She's accused me of being a rolling stone." Noah took a last long swig of his water, a hard laugh bouncing off the stable doors. "I just tell her she's obsessed."

Noah snagged two more waters out of a cooler by his side and tossed Derek one. "So we've mucked stalls all day, groomed horses and even shared nagging mother stories. You going to finally give in and tell me what you really do? Because I find it hard to believe you're a simple, carefree, jet-setting playboy."

"Will I ruin your image of me if I say no?"

"Nah. I figured you from the first. But watching you the last few days and how much Landry digs you have only confirmed it."

"That was your clue?"

"Hell, yeah. The woman's dated far too many jet-setting playboys. They bore her to tears. And you don't."

The door was open—all Derek had to do was step through it. But he liked Noah and respected the life the man had carved out for himself. He didn't like lying to him, but years of FBI training kept him from giving up the charade before he had something concrete to prove or disprove his theory.

"I used to work on Kate's Secret Service detail. When news of what was going on out here reached her in North Carolina, she asked me to come here and keep an eye on things."

"It's a good thing you're here. They need looking out for. I know Carson and Whit would balk at that, but it's true. It's a big part of why I came here after Reginald's murder."

"And now? Why do you stay?"

"The work." Noah's gaze took on a faraway look. "And maybe I'm enjoying getting to know a certain socialite who does far too much work and far too little jet-setting herself."

Rachel.

Landry had sensed something was going on the night before, and he'd gone along with it because in his experience women loved pairing up unattached people. But now, looking for himself...yeah, he could see that extra shot of heat fill Noah's gaze.

Noah crushed the empty water bottle in his hand.

"We should probably get inside and get cleaned up, then. Go visit those socialites who've captured our attention."

"What? We're not dressed for a party."

Derek slapped Noah on the back. "I'm not sure we're dressed to set foot in the house."

Landry was still struggling with Uncle Sheldon's weird comments about dead babies, even though she'd spent the past two hours trying to convince herself otherwise. Maybe she hadn't heard him right. And maybe there was a time-bending space portal to Paris in her backyard, too.

The man might be senile, but he had no reason to make that up. Especially something so specific.

No. He had a memory of something, and she needed to find out what.

The shower was winding down, and the dining room showed the evidence that people had enjoyed themselves. She busied herself combining some of the trays of food, condensing some and emptying others for the kitchen.

"Why are you in here cleaning up?" Emmaline bustled in, her face awash in horror. "That's what the help's for, dear."

"It doesn't hurt to make things a little neater."

Emmaline shooed her hands from the table, gesturing her back toward the living room. "Nonsense. Leave those things."

With her irritation spiking at the end of a long afternoon, Landry nearly snapped out that she was fine, until she thought better of the reaction. "You're right. We've barely had a chance to visit at all. What with Daddy dying I feel like I've been so wrapped up in my grief I haven't even tried to reach out."

Not that her aunt had made an attempt in return, but Landry decided to push it and see where it got her.

"Grief affects us all, darling." Emmaline perched next to her on the sofa. "Speaking of which, I didn't want to say anything in front of the company but how are things with your mother?"

"None of us has heard from her."

Emmaline's eyebrows rose, her lips pursing in distaste. "To think she might have killed your father, then left all of you here to fend for yourselves."

She knew her mother wasn't anyone's favorite. Heck, taking potshots at Patsy was a sport around Adair Acres, the result of long years of personal torture and abuse of all she knew and loved. But something in her aunt's tone had Landry's spine straightening up.

"She didn't kill my father."

Emmaline blinked, her bright blue trademark Adair eyes blank with confusion. "But she tried to kill Elizabeth. I simply assumed she was responsible for your father."

"That's an awfully big leap, Aunt Emmaline."

"Hardly."

She was prevented from saying anything by Rachel's arrival in the living room. Her best friend carried two glasses of wine, and she shoved one off on Landry with a wink before taking a plush chair opposite the couch. "We got all of Elizabeth's amazing gifts situated in her and Whit's wing. The room's nearly done and all these gifts will finish the nursery off."

"They've finished the nursery already?" Emmaline teetered on the edge of the couch. The tart, gossipy woman who'd sat next to her seemed to shrink before Landry's eyes. "Isn't it a bit early to do that?"

"The baby's arrival is only a few months away. I think they want to be prepared."

"Yes, but it seems a bit early to finish everything. What if—" Emmaline broke off as if catching herself. "Well, you kids nowadays. You like to be so prepared."

"Everyone's so excited. A baby on the way." Rachel sighed. "I can't believe how fast it's happened. It's all Noah's been able to talk about."

"My son's been talking about the baby?"

"Oh, yes." Rachel nodded and Landry could only sit there, amazed as her best friend worked her magic. "He's so happy here. And he seems really excited for Whit and Elizabeth."

"You'd never know it when I talk to him. I've been after him for simply years to settle down and give me grandchildren."

"And if he hasn't found the right woman yet?" Landry asked, curious as to the answer. She knew love hadn't been a huge priority in her father's generation, as evidenced by her parents' marriage as well as her aunt's. Although Emmaline's husband had died early in their marriage, she had to wonder if it was a love match.

"Love has its place, but so does moving on with your life. Growing up and having a family. Carrying on your family name." Emmaline's gaze narrowed on Rachel. "You say you've been spending time with Noah?"

"Yes." She nodded, her green eyes sparkling. "He's been helping me with my riding technique. And we've picked up a few rounds of golf at my club. You know how horrible I am, Landry, and if I don't get any better at it I just know they're going to kick me off my position on the hospital board."

Landry picked up on the charade, ready to keep it going when Emmaline interjected. "Do you care for my son, Rachel?"

"Of course. He's a great guy."

"Yes. But are you interested in him?"

"Well, I…" Rachel dropped her gaze, a small, shy smile edging her lips. "I do a bit. I mean, I would like to see it through if he were interested."

Noah's deep voice carried down the hall and Emmaline was prevented from saying anything else. For her part, Landry was near ready to hand Rachel a gold statue, her performance had been so incredible.

Noah stepped into the room, his head still damp from a shower, giving away how he spent his afternoon with Derek.

"Did you just get back from the stables?" Landry asked.

"After putting in a full and honest day's labor with your boyfriend." Noah winked before crossing the room to his mother. "I'm glad you're still here. I wanted to say hi before you headed back with Aunt Rosalyn and Uncle Sheldon."

"Where did they get off to?"

"Sheldon's terrorizing another round of dessert out of the kitchen and Rosalyn's still upstairs oohing and aahing over the nursery. I said hi before I started down."

"What's she going on about? She's got grandchildren. You'd think she knew what a nursery looked like."

"Mother." Noah took her hand in his, his voice gentle. "She's excited for Whit and Elizabeth."

Noah seemed to have a calming effect on his mother, and her acerbic tone faded as they spoke. "Of course she is."

Landry searched her memories for images of Noah

and Emmaline through the years. She had vivid memories of having Noah at the ranch, but her aunt, not so much. Although she had been much younger then, Landry recalled that her aunt had accompanied him on every trip to Adair Acres until he was of age. So why was it so hard to remember them all spending time together as a family?

"I'm going to go up and check on Kathleen. She's still recovering and today took a lot out of her." Landry made her excuses and used the opportunity to escape. She shot Rachel an apologetic smile but her friend's subtle nod assured her she could handle herself just fine.

The walk to the servants' wing took her through the security center, and she was surprised to find Derek in there, his head as damp as Noah's. "What are you doing in here? With the door open, no less?"

She closed it behind her. "What if someone finds you in here?"

"I told Noah I was here at your aunt's request."

Landry pushed herself off the door and took the seat next to him at the line of computer terminals. "Why'd you do that?"

"Because he asked. And I didn't tell him what we suspected about his mother, but I did tell him I was here to keep an eye on you. Kate's orders. He seemed relieved.

"He also figured out I wasn't a playboy globe-trotter."

"What was his first clue?"

Derek pulled her chair closer and closed his hands over the arms, effectively caging her in. "He said it was because you were actually interested in me. And if I was some wastrel globe-trotter you'd have kicked me to the curb by now."

She was as delighted by the observation as she was surprised. Noah obviously saw more than he let on, and the idea that he understood her ennui around the majority of men she'd dated was a bit of a wake-up call.

Perhaps she wasn't quite as hard to read as she thought. Or hoped. "What if he's right?"

"Then I think maybe I should press my advantage."

Derek pulled the chair closer until their knees touched. He closed the remaining distance and pressed his lips to hers, the warmth and security welcome after a day full of unsettling questions.

She sank into the kiss, open and ready for him, and marveled at how quickly she could lose herself in the amazing attraction that lived and breathed between them.

The moments spun out, as tender and sweet as cotton candy, and Landry gave herself the permission to simply sink into the pleasure that flowed so naturally.

A loud *ping* resonated from the desk, and Derek pulled back. "I'm sorry. Really sorry."

"What is it?"

"I'm waiting for some feedback from my contact at the field office. He's been looking into the power outage for me, running a bunch of diagnostics."

"Go ahead. Check it. It's important."

He pressed a quick kiss to her lips. "So are you."

Something warm and gooey settled itself in her chest, pushing out the ice that had settled there earlier while she observed her family.

Derek scanned the text message, then turned toward the computer. "He sent me a file to run on the machines. Are you okay if I do that?"

"Of course."

He grew quiet as he worked, his full focus on his task. Landry watched him, fascinated by the efficient way he moved through each step. Methodical and deliberate, he kept toggling back to his email as he completed each phase of the instructions.

"Two more steps and we should be good. Then John will have a full diagnostic of the machines here."

She let him work, content to simply sit by his side and breathe the same air. Which was as strange as it was wonderful.

"Can you call up your work files from here? Like the databases we looked at in LA?"

"Sure. They run a bit slower since the files are so large, but I have remote access. Why?"

"I'd like you to pull something up for me."

In moments, Derek had a familiar-looking visual coming up on screen. He shifted the image to the large viewing station above them and put in the various queries she requested.

"My uncle made a very strange reference to a baby they thought had died."

Fingers still, Derek shifted his focus from the screen. "A dead baby? Have you ever heard anyone say that before?"

"No, and that's what's strange. I've lived in my family home my entire life and never once have I heard any mention of a family member who lost a child or who almost lost a child." Landry hesitated. "He's also suffering from senility. It's gotten worse over the last few years, but it was fairly obvious today he's not all there."

"They say that more recent memories vanish first. If he's referring to Noah it would have happened when he was in the prime of his life, making very solid memories."

"True."

"What else did he say?"

Landry walked him through all the details of her conversation with Sheldon, curious to see how he used the questions to then shape the search queries he put into the system.

"Is Rosalyn the oldest?"

"Bucannon was actually the oldest. He's Kate's first husband. Then Rosalyn and Emmaline, in that order. My father was a bit of a surprise after they thought they were done having children."

"How many years' difference between him and his sisters?"

"Four or five, I think. I can nose around and find out."

"That's okay. We'll start there and then expand if we need to."

Derek worked through several search strings, the depth of information at his fingertips mind-boggling. "That's a lot of information."

"No one really lives off the grid anymore. They might think they do—or wish they did—but they don't."

"You'd think that would make your job easier. But from all you've said, it doesn't sound like it."

"It's a dimension that's gotten easier. We can learn a lot more about a suspect or a victim. Get a better picture of who they are and how they've lived their lives. But even with the technology, if someone doesn't want to be found, they can often find a way."

"Like my mother."

Mark kicked the dirty pallet at his feet, the bag of bones who lay there snoring like a lumberjack. "Wake up!"

"Wha?" Al grumbled before turning over again.

Mark thought about kicking him again, this time against his ribs instead of against the old mattress he slept on, but held back. The guy was doing a halfway decent job of keeping the kid occupied, and he'd have a hard time doing that with broken ribs.

Rena stared up at him from her spot against the wall. Her dark eyes bored into him with hatred that ran so deep it actually warmed his heart.

He'd done that. Had generated a reaction so hard and so deep she'd never be free of it.

Just like him.

Now all he needed to do was find a way to use it to his advantage.

"You didn't eat again."

"I don't like slop."

"It's fast food. What kid doesn't like fast food?"

"Me, that's who." Her little chin quivered, but the steady hate in her tone never wavered. "I want something fresh from the store. Fruit. Vegetables. Not fake meat."

Mark shrugged and pulled out the burger he'd bought for himself. She could suit herself and pretend she didn't want to eat. He'd leave behind what he bought for her and wouldn't be surprised if she worked her way around to it eventually.

"What do you want with me?"

Rena asked the same question every time he showed up to feed and water her and the dirtbag. He had to admire her persistence, even though there was no way he was risking telling her she was a pawn in a much bigger game.

"It's not about what I want with you. It's about what you can do for me."

"I ain't doing anything for you."

"Sure you are." He wadded up the empty wrapper from his burger and tossed it at her. "Just by being here you're doing something for me."

She stared at the ball of paper where it landed in her lap but didn't make a move to toss it back.

"Why don't you just kill me?"

He had to hand it to her, the kid had ice in her veins. "What fun would that be?"

"You think this is fun?"

"Baseball's fun. Se—messing around's fun. This is necessary. There's a difference."

"Does that mean you'll let me go?"

"I haven't decided yet."

Sure he had, but he wasn't letting her know. The kid could still be useful, and he needed her thinking she still had something to lose. It was basic Victim Psychology 101.

Tired of the chat, he got down to business. "I need you to write something for me."

"What if I don't want to?"

"Then I go over there and kick Big Al a few times until you do."

Her focus drifted to Al, then back to him. The softness he'd seen in her eyes for the older man faded when she met his gaze head-on. "Give me the paper."

"I've been looking into your mother. Nothing's popped yet. We know she used her passport to leave the country, but then the trail goes cold." Derek grimaced at the screen as he typed a few more commands.

"She vanished? Just like that?" Every time she thought she had a handle on the way Patsy betrayed the family, something rose up to slap at her again.

If her mother had vanished, it was because she'd meant to.

And if she'd meant to then that also meant she'd had an escape plan all along.

"Landry?"

"Hmm?"

"You okay?"

She waved a hand. "Sure. Nothing like realizing the woman who gave birth to you is a soulless monster who plotted for some length of time to leave you, never to speak to you again."

With a tight leash on her anger and disappointment, Landry continued. "Emmaline asked about her. Made a big show of acting concerned, but the censure underneath suggested my mother had killed my father."

"Have you prepared yourself for that?" Derek laid a hand against her cheek, tracing the bone with his thumb. "Others are going to think it, too. People with an interest in gossip and innuendo."

"They're already doing it. Why do you think I pared back my charity commitments as far as I have?" She leaned into his hand, the show of support so welcome.

And more needed than she ever could have imagined.

On a sigh, she closed her eyes, the pain of the past few months bubbling up in a witches' brew of frustration, anger and bone-deep weariness. "The thought of being whispered about like that? No, thank you."

"You aren't responsible for your parents' actions. And it would be a shame for those who benefit from the incredibly good work you do to lose out on that gift. Don't let anyone take that away from you."

He was right. She knew he was right. Funny how much it helped to hear it.

A pop-up window appeared on the screen, catching her attention. "Looks like the query's done running."

Derek called up the data, scrolling through key dates and names until he stopped and toggled backward. "There. Look right there."

The tip of his finger rested on the screen and she followed the paragraph he pointed to. "Adair invests in airstrip? What's that about?"

"It's from the late sixties. Your grandfather apparently decided to put some of his vast wealth into an upgrade for the greater Raleigh regional airstrip."

"I was small when he died, but I know he had a plane. Several, as a matter of fact. My father, too. At the risk of getting my snob on, it's sort of table stakes at a certain level. Besides, at the time my grandfather did this, there were few others who could have made such an investment."

Derek continued to scan the article, picking up on key elements. "It says here he wanted a small regional airport that could accommodate larger jets, capable of sustaining intercontinental flights."

"Which makes sense for his business."

"But it also means he had the private means to quickly get to Europe."

"He never made a secret of how much he loved London, Paris, Rome. He and my grandmother were jet-setters in the truest sense of the word, and they spent a lot of time away from home."

"His jets provide opportunity."

"Opportunity for what?"

"Opportunity to kidnap Jackson and whisk him out of the country."

Chapter 13

"Oh, come on. My grandparents kidnapping their own grandchild?"

Landry stood to pace, the momentary quiet vanished in the wave of what they'd discovered. "I know we put standard dysfunction to shame, but what you're talking about is just not possible."

"You've already taken the leap that Emmaline raised Reginald's son as her own. And we know she never left Europe during the time of his birth. How else did she get the baby?"

"I don't—"

He saw it the moment the truth registered. The pacing stopped as a connection painted her face in thoughtful lines. "That's why she was never around."

"Around where?"

"Earlier. I had a thought about when I was a kid. I

always remember Noah being around the ranch during the summer, but memories are fuzzier about my aunt."

"Did she send him here and go off on her own?"

"That's what's so odd. She came for every visit, but after thinking about it, I realized that she was always like this ghost in the background. Present, but sort of hazy and faded. She must have wanted to avoid all of us, especially my father, as much as she could, but she didn't want to let Noah out of her sight."

"She was probably scared your father might figure it out at some point and wanted to be able to run at a moment's notice."

"So why bring him at all? They spent much of Noah's formative years in Europe. They didn't need to be here."

Derek had spent his professional life dealing with the minds of criminals. While their choices often made no sense, there was an underlying sense of logic and order that made perfect sense to them. "Maybe it was guilt? Or a desire to give him some exposure to his father, even if Noah only ever understood his relationship to Reginald as uncle to nephew?"

"That still assumes we're right about this whole thing."

"I want to look into flight plans. The Adair family might have bought off the airstrip but there was no way they'd have been able to hide flight plans, especially internationally. If your grandparents did take the baby, there would be a record of them delivering him to Emmaline."

"Can you pull the plans now?"

"Maybe. The airport's small and I might have to call directly if I can't find it here in our files. Either way, we'll get our hands on the records from the window when Jackson was kidnapped."

Landry leaned back in her chair and swirled gently on the casters. "It's real, isn't it?"

"It appears that way."

"I've hoped. All along I've hoped we were somehow wrong about the whole thing. But if we're not..." She stopped swiveling. "If we're right we're going to ruin everything Noah's ever known. His whole life will not only be a lie, but it will be a lie perpetrated by his mother. Who does that?"

"A desperate woman."

She dropped her head in her hands, her voice muffled through her fingers. "You must think we're monsters. Crazy, insane, evil monsters."

"I don't think that."

Her head popped up, her normally cultured voice ragged, like she spoke around shards of glass. "How can't you think that? *I* think that and it's my family."

"You're not defined by your family, Landry. And neither are your brothers."

If she noticed that he lumped Noah into that category, she said nothing. She just shook her head, the tears that filled her eyes spilling over onto her cheeks.

"Do you know what I thought about today?"

The need to comfort was a living thing inside him, but when he reached for her, she shifted back, rolling away. He ignored the hurt that speared through his chest and focused on giving her what she needed instead. "What?"

"I'm hanging decorations and putting out food for my brother's wife's baby shower and I actually thought about what it would be like if I stole the baby." She waved a hand and rushed on. "Not because I actually want to steal the baby, but because I simply couldn't imagine any scenario where I'd consider that even remotely acceptable behavior."

"Desperate people do desperate things. And you're not desperate."

"But don't you see? This was what I spent my time thinking about at my nephew's baby shower. Not how much he was going to weigh or how many inches or even what day he might make his arrival. I thought about someone taking him. About Elizabeth and Whit spending their lives trying to find him."

She tried to hide her face from him, but Derek wouldn't be stopped this time. With one hand he kept a solid grip on the chair handle and pulled her close. "Landry. Look at me."

Tears had turned her vivid blue eyes into watery pools. The bright vivacity normally found there was nowhere in evidence, replaced by a horrified awareness she couldn't undo.

He knew that look. Had lived with it his entire professional career. It was the haunted look in the eyes of the people he worked so hard to save. That look drove him on, even when he had to pull from the very reserves of his soul to continue a case.

Before he'd felt compassion and an overwhelming sense of duty to restore order and justice to a life. But with Landry it was different.

With her, he wanted to share the burden.

She leaned forward and pressed her lips to his cheek, a kiss of thanks. Of understanding. And of something more...

"Stay with me." Her words whispered, featherlight, where she pressed her lips to his ear.

The secrets that swirled around Adair Acres nearly held him back. He cared for her, and he didn't want to take advantage of her situation. A situation that *would* have a resolution.

Her lips moved once more against his ear. "Make love with me because it's what we both want."

When he hesitated, torn between what he wanted and what he believed was right, she pushed on. "This is what *I* want, Derek. I want you. Forget all the reasons we shouldn't. Be with me. Just because."

He'd felt himself capitulating, but it was only when she said the last words that he knew he was lost.

"Yes."

Just because.

Landry heard the song lyric years ago, and it had always stuck with her. Do something for no reason other than because you wanted to.

She knew making love with Derek would add further layers to an already complicated situation. And sex always complicated things on the best of days.

But oh, how she wanted him.

And in the moment he pulled her close, his lips firm against hers, she knew the sweetest victory. "Yes."

The hands on either side of her chair shifted to her legs as he ran long, lazy strokes over her thighs. She kept her hands on his shoulders, reassured by the ready strength she found there. No matter what happened—and she knew there was so much they still had to navigate—this was absolutely right.

"Let's go upstairs."

He nodded before pressing his forehead to hers. "Let's go."

Their footsteps echoed on the Spanish tiles that made up the broad hallways of the ranch as they navigated the walk from the security center up to her bedroom. She expected that the path would be quiet and solemn, both of them well aware of the step they were about to take, when Derek tickled her ribs on the stairs. She turned into him on a muffled scream. "I'm ticklish!"

"I was hoping so."

He reached for her again, his hands grabbing at her waist to pull her close while he pressed a heavy line of kisses along her neck. The giggle in her throat faded to a hard moan when his fingers shifted up over her stomach before they feathered over one breast.

The thought abstractly crossed her mind that they might get caught, but the house that had been active all day was blessedly quiet and they made it to her room in a tumble of arms and legs as the door slammed behind them.

"Locking this, too."

She could only smile at his proprietary tone. "No one comes in without knocking."

"Let's just say I'm hedging my bets."

"Hedge away." She flicked a hand toward the tie that held her wrap dress together, but he rushed forward, gently removing her hand.

"Let me."

"Hedging your bets again?" The light tease drifted out on sultry tones, and she marveled that she was the one saying the words.

In the past she'd use that tone to manipulate a situation or to get what she wanted. How humbling and awesome at the same time to realize that teasing tone was only an additive to the giving and receiving of pleasure.

"No. Just reveling in the moment."

Then his large hands were on her, his dark, enigmatic gaze engaging hers, and Landry let herself fall. Golden light flooded the room, the tail end of a glorious spring day. The naturally bronze tones of Derek's skin grew darker, a captivating contrast to her own paler skin.

She ran a hand along the thick stretch of muscle that made up his biceps, trailing her finger down over the firm strength of his forearm. "I never did ask about your heritage. Gorgeous tanned skin like this looks natural."

"Cherokee. Amazingly enough, from both my parents. Quite by accident, they each decided to research their heritage and found each other in the stacks at a library in DC."

She smiled at that, the randomness of his parents' meeting juxtaposed with the clear evidence they were meant to be. "Life is funny that way."

"So it is."

"But it also explains a lot. The first morning I saw you riding on Diego, I could see you in my mind, galloping across the plains, the wind whipping your hair as you protected what was yours."

The image had only grown more pronounced as she'd spent time with him. He was a protector. A righter of wrongs. And for tonight, he was hers.

"It's a far cry from law enforcement."

"Oh, I don't know." She ran her fingers over his shoulders, unwilling to break even that simple contact. "Keeping the world safe smacks awfully hard of protecting what's yours. You're just painting on a much broader canvas."

"Thank you." His fingers slipped over the tie at her waist, tugging on the thin string.

She would have responded—would have found something sexy or flirty to say—but her breath caught once more at the reverent expression that suffused his face and turned his gaze dark with desire.

"I want you, Landry. I know your life's been a roller coaster, but I won't hurt you. I *will* protect you. And I promise, I will never hurt you."

"I know." She reached for his hands and glided them down to her breasts. "I trust you. With my body." She pressed a kiss to his lips, the tension in him still as strong as ever.

She sensed his hesitation, knew he struggled with what he perceived as his duty to her and her family. And knew that the only way she could finally convince him tonight was for both of them was to show him.

With a slight wiggle of her arms, she shed the wrap dress and felt the cool material slide down her back. When he shifted his hands to her waist, she reached back and unhooked her bra, slipping from the straps before the material floated on top of the dress.

With one last shift, she ducked from beneath his hands and shed her panties, one last piece of silk following the others.

"With my life, Derek. I trust you."

Whether it was her words or her actions—likely a combination of both—she saw the moment he acquiesced. When he finally acknowledged that what was between them could no longer be ignored.

His hands came around her, urgent and fiercely demanding. Landry allowed herself to be swept up—in the moment, in the man—and gloried when the dam on his self-control burst wide open. He crushed his lips to hers, their tongues dueling a battle for control.

"You're wearing too much." She already had her hands at his waist, material fisted, when he smiled and shifted away.

"I can do it faster."

"A challenge?"

"A fact. And—" The word hung there as he flipped his shirt off, then followed with his jeans and briefs all in one clean sweep. "I'm done."

Laughter, deep and rich, welled up in her throat. She'd expected power and strength when they finally made love, but she hadn't anticipated the laughter. It bubbled in her chest, spilling over in great, glorious bursts.

Derek moved up and pulled her into his arms. The strength of his body wrapped around her, while the proof of his desire pressed to her stomach and indicated how much he wanted her. "Don't you know it's bad form to laugh at a naked man?"

"I'll have to make it up to you." The laughter faded, but her smile stayed firmly in place. She reached between them and her hand closed over the thick length of him. She was rewarded with a sharp intake of breath as he pressed himself into her palm.

She worked his thick flesh in her hands, thrilled when his eyelids dimmed to half mast, pleasure rapidly taking over his self-control. The line of his jaw hardened as she put him through his paces, unwilling to let up.

Unwilling to give him any further opportunity to think.

Only to feel.

Murmured words floated between them. Echoes of need. Of want. And of a powerful desire neither could deny.

Derek gave her a few moments more before he reached down and stilled her movements, his breath exhaling on a hard rush. "You're driving me crazy."

"That's the whole idea." She nipped a quick kiss at his collarbone before drifting her lips along the sensitive line of his neck.

"Actually, you're killing me. Decimating me so I can barely stand."

She smiled against that sensitive skin. "I'll consider that the highest compliment."

Without answering, he twirled her in his arms, then lifted her in one swift move. "There's no way you get to have all the fun."

Landry felt the world tilt, the arms beneath her back and buttocks strong and sure as he carried her toward the bed. He laid her down with gentle movements, the sensation that she was precious quickly overpowering the aura of fun that had gripped both of them.

He treated her as though she was cherished, as though she mattered.

How had she never understood how important that was? Or how desperately she missed mattering to someone?

In their own way, her family loved her. Her brothers were fierce protectors who would do anything for her. But during this past week with Derek, he'd given her a gift beyond measure. He'd shown her what it meant to feel loved.

"What's the matter?"

Unaware of the tears until they spilled over, hot against her cheeks, Landry shook her head. "It's silly."

"Landry?" The haze of passion rapidly faded from his gaze, replaced by a very real concern in those dark depths. "What's wrong?"

"It's nothing. Nothing." She shook her head and tried to dash away the stubborn tears that continued to fall. "I think too much, that's all."

He kept his arm around her but laid them both back on the bed, face to face. "Please tell me what's wrong."

"Nothing. That's the problem. Absolutely nothing is wrong." A hard sob welled up and she tried to swallow it back. "And now I'm ruining this between us."

"You're not ruining anything."

"I'm certainly not helping."

Despite her rising embarrassment, he said nothing, just continued to hold her. She willed the tears back, swallowing around the hard knot in her throat before she spoke. "I'm crying because you look at me like I'm precious."

His arms flexed and tightened before he brought a hand to her chin, lifting her gaze to his. "Because you are. Precious and rare and incredibly special."

"Yes. But—" She broke off, well aware she'd ruined the mood between them and any chance of returning to the sexy, lighthearted passion that had carried them upstairs.

"But what?"

"Until a few moments ago, I'd never realized how rare that was. Or how rare it's been in my life."

"I know this can't make up for it, but you do realize that's their problem? That the inability to show love and affection rests solely on your family? Your mother and father. Your aunt. Your grandparents."

Landry knew he was right. And still the pull of a lifetime of inertia held her back. "I'm a part of that. Descended from that."

"Yet you've made yourself. And you make choices every day that prove you're not like them. From your charity work to your love of animals, you have chosen a different life. A different path."

The lure of what he promised pulled at her, more tempting than she ever could have imagined. "You make it sound so simple."

"Because it is." His gaze never wavered. Where in the past she might have thought that sort of intensity was too much, Landry found herself unable to look away.

"You make me feel things, and I'm not entirely sure what to do about it."

The smile filled his dark eyes first, before it spread to his lips. "If it makes you feel any better, I'm not sure myself."

Whether it was the smile, the words of support or the gentle honesty, she wasn't sure. But as she reveled in the glow of simple understanding, her sadness faded, replaced with a life-affirming need to be with him.

His arms were still locked around her, the two of them curled against each other on the bed. She used their proximity to reach out and run her index finger over his broad chest. His skin tensed wherever she touched, a live wire sparking under her explorations. When she reached a nipple, she ran the tip of her fingernail gently around the flattened edge, gratified by his sharp intake of breath.

"You really do kill me."

"I really do need you alive for this." Feminine anticipation filled her with a buoyant spirit. "Perhaps you could find a way to hold on?"

His hand came up and covered hers, flattening it against his chest. "I'll do my best."

Derek pulled her close, his lips finding hers once more, eager to pillage and plunder the rich depths of her mouth.

Had he ever seen such deep-rooted pain?

The thought drifted through Derek's mind, along with a healthy dose of anger, before he pushed them both away. There'd be plenty of time to analyze later. For now, it was enough to simply be with her. To make love with her and push the demons they both carried to the furthest reaches of their minds. What came before and what would come after had no place in this moment.

No place at all.

Hungry for her, Derek pulled Landry against him,

shifting their positions so he covered her body. She responded immediately, a small mewl of pleasure rumbling from the back of her throat as her long legs came up to wrap around his waist.

Heat assailed him, scorching his skin from the top of his head to the tips of his toes in every place they touched, and it took every ounce of willpower he possessed to remember the small packet in his jeans.

"Damn it." The curse came out on a hard moan and he reluctantly dragged himself from her.

"What's wrong?"

"I need to get something."

Awareness flashed, along with a broad smile. "End table. Top drawer."

He snaked out one long hand, gratified to find the condoms right where she promised. "You're amazing."

"I did a bit of advance planning when I was out running errands for Elizabeth's shower. I thought—" She broke off. "No. I hoped."

The emotions that had threatened earlier swamped him with a heavy sucker punch to the gut, and when he finally spoke, the words were a low whisper. "I hoped, too."

The packet disappeared between her fingers and he lifted up on his elbows to give her room to maneuver. She finished in moments, then guided him into her body, welcoming him home.

Derek stilled and took the moment to watch her as her body adjusted to his. And when he sensed she was ready—when he simply couldn't wait another moment for her—he began to move.

The emotional moments between them gave way to something raw and needy, both of them hungry for com-

pletion. He filled her and with each thrust, felt himself
slipping further and further away.

Here there was no danger. No lurking threats. No unfinished assignments. In this moment, there was only
Landry and the mind-numbing passion that had a grip
on them both.

Her breathing quickened and her cries grew more urgent. He increased his pace, willing himself to hold on
until he sensed she was near peak. And as a hard cry escaped her, her fingers flexed along his back. She pressed
herself to him; he allowed himself to let go.

Chapter 14

Landry listened to the quiet sounds of Derek's breathing and let her mind float in long, lazy circles. She thought about the first morning she met him, his large form staring down at her as she finished her pool laps. Their horseback rides and their day in Los Angeles.

She even thought about the tense moments in the stables as they worked in tandem to eliminate the snake.

Had it really been less than a week? Less than seven days for him to walk into her life and make such an irrevocable place for himself it was hard to imagine life without him?

Her racing heartbeat had begun to slow, but at that thought—spending her life with Derek Winchester—it sped right back up. They'd had sex. Amazing, awesome, incredible sex. And if she had anything to say about it, they'd have quite a bit more.

But sex was different from permanence. He was here

to do a job and when that was over, he'd go back to his life, as would she. The two of them didn't have a relationship. They had a fake arrangement that was in place to expediently deal with whatever wasteland her family had managed to scorch over the past four decades.

Thinking otherwise would open up a world of emotions she would prefer stayed closed.

What she would take away was how he'd made her see herself. The encouragement and support inherent in who he was and how he saw others had given her a boost she didn't even realize she needed. If nothing else came out of their time together, she was grateful for that.

"You do realize your thoughts are louder than a marching band on the Fourth of July."

"Hmm?"

"I can hear you thinking." Derek pulled her close, wrapping his arms around her waist and drawing her back to his front. "And sex that amazing shouldn't include any thinking afterward."

"You're talking, which means you're thinking."

He pressed a kiss to her neck. "My brains have already leached out all over the pillow. I'm simply babbling incoherently until I manage to drum up a thought or two from whatever's still left."

"A woman's mind is never still."

"Pity." He kissed her neck again before snuggling into the crook between her head and shoulder, his hands traveling on a lazy exploration over her stomach before reaching up to cup one of her breasts.

Her earlier thought—to simply enjoy the time together—skipped its way through her mind as his hands worked magic over her skin. But when his thumb pressed over her nipple, shooting sparks to her core, she gave up her resistance.

There'd be time for thinking later.

Right now, there was Derek.

She turned in his arms, giving him better access to her body. He took full advantage, changing the direction of his kisses from her neck to shoulder to chest. When she thought he might drive her mad with the teasing flicks of his fingers in counterpoint to the erotic play of his tongue over her skin, his mouth closed over one nipple and she pressed into him on a hard cry.

Hot, wet suction dragged another cry from the very depths of her as an elemental sort of electricity began to swirl beneath her skin.

That wet heat continued to torment her as his hand drifted lower, back over her stomach before settling between her thighs. His clever fingers pressed against her core, igniting sparks she was helpless to resist. Ruthless, he drove her up, pushing her toward another release so soon after she'd come apart in his arms.

Shocked by her body's readiness, she clung to his shoulders and rode the current. Hard, churning waves buffeted her through the storm of pleasure, but he was her true north throughout. His big, strong body and the safety to be found with him, even as he pushed her toward the most vulnerable moment of her life.

And then she was tumbling, screaming his name, falling into the swirling storm.

Darkness had fallen while they slept and Derek awoke to the disorienting sensation of his phone's muffled ring. He normally slept with it near his head, so it took him a moment to realize it was across the room, tucked in the pocket of his jeans.

He disentangled himself from Landry's warm body,

her small sigh tugging at something deep inside him when she sprawled into his place on the bed.

The muffled phone rang once more before it went to voicemail, and he was tempted to leave it. Ignore whoever lay on the other end and wake Landry back up with an inventive series of kisses...

Heated images faded from his mind as duty stole in like a thief in the night. It might be Mark. Or a lead from his buddy at the office who was looking into the security breach at Adair Acres.

He was here on a job, damn it. How had he forgotten that?

Another glance at Landry, her naked back golden in the moonlit room, and he had his answer.

Landry Adair was the reason he'd forgotten.

She'd gotten into his system like an addictive drug, and now that he'd had a taste of her, there was no going back. No unremembering the moments in her arms. Or the taste of her skin. Or the generous way she shared herself fully in the act of giving and receiving pleasure.

His hand closed around the flat, rectangular shape of his phone and he fought to keep his mind on whatever issue had generated a call at almost eleven at night. He swiped through the screens and hit Voicemail.

Mark's frantic voice barked out words on the message.

He needed to come. Now. To the warehouse they'd staked out early on but thought was empty. The one down past LAX.

A vision of the abandoned space came to mind. The building had been between tenants when they caught wind it might have been a temporary home base for Rena's kidnappers before they moved her out of the country. He and Mark had spent a long week staring at the building's exit points, waiting for proof that their lead was sound.

All they'd gotten for it had been several days of stale coffee and a ten-point spike in their cholesterol levels from too many take-out burgers.

"I think we've found Rena!" The message disconnected on Mark's parting words and Derek moved into action. He knew he owed Landry and her family his attention, but he needed to be there in LA.

Needed to see this through and bring that young girl home.

"What's the matter?" Landry's voice drifted toward him and he turned from where he pulled his pants on. She sat up in bed, the sleep fading from her tone. "Where are you going?"

"I got a call. Well, a message." Images jumbled in his mind and he tried to find the right words to reassure, even as the need to leave as fast as possible gripped him. "Mark. He thinks he's found Rena."

"That's incredible." Landry was up and out of the bed, rushing toward him. She seemed oblivious to her nudity, instead crossing with speed and purpose. "Let's get down there."

"You can't go."

She stilled where she was, on her way to her closet. "Why not?"

"This is an FBI investigation."

"You can't go by yourself."

"Like hell I can't."

"Derek." She grabbed a robe off a hook on the door and slipped into it. "You haven't even talked to Mark. Where are you supposed to go?"

"I'll find it. She's at a warehouse we'd staked out early on."

"And you're just going to go barreling in there? With no backup?"

"Mark will be there."

"Then you're both fools."

Frustration punched holes in his patience and he lashed out. "Let me do my job, Landry."

"I'm not standing in your way. But even I know you can't go there unprotected. And where's your boss in all this? Shouldn't you talk to him first?"

"Mark's been keeping me informed on the side. My boss doesn't know I'm up to speed."

She stood before him, her hand on his arm. "Which makes this seem even worse. Why aren't you following protocol?"

"A young girl's life is at stake."

"So is yours." The gentle, soothing calm faded, replaced by a veritable taskmaster.

"And your coming with me is going to make that better."

"Let me at least drive you to headquarters. You're too close to this. I can get you there and you can call for information along the way."

"And risk having my boss get involved, pissed as hell I've been keeping tabs on this investigation?"

She stilled at that. "So getting the brass involved is less preferable to getting that girl home safely?"

"Yes." He dragged at his shirt, pulling it over his head as he tried to calm his thoughts. "No. No, of course not."

"It's over an hour to the office. Let me drive and you can make plans as we go. I promise I'll stay out of the way. But you can't go alone."

"I can and will."

"You don't have to do this alone. I'm offering help. Not to stop you from doing what's right but to make sure you can do what's right. Why won't you let me?"

Determination lined her features, firmly setting her

jaw. She wasn't going to be swayed, and the more time he spent allowing sparks of rational thought to leach into the urgent need to act, the more he knew she was right.

"You're a civilian, Landry. I can't take you into this."

"For the last time, I'm not suggesting you take me on an op. I'm suggesting you let me get you there so you can prepare for it properly."

He thought to argue—and wanted to—but she'd already walked off and disappeared into a closet so large it looked like another room.

It looked as if he had a ride-along partner, whether he wanted one or not.

Landry kept the pace steady as they drove ever closer to Los Angeles. She knew Derek was still mad—she had a good mad on herself—but she was also pleased she'd worked her way around it.

And she'd done it with honesty and direct action.

She'd spent years watching her parents. Their destructive relationship tactics designed to go behind each other's backs to constantly prove some sort of one-upmanship. It was only now, faced with the moment of actually disagreeing with Derek on something, that she realized just how poor an example had been set for her and her brothers.

There you go again, Landry-girl. Acting like this is some sort of real relationship.

But real or not, the man walked a dangerous path, and if left to his own devices, he'd have gone charging off mindlessly.

The very idea he'd go walking into something completely unprepared bothered her more than she wanted to admit. She knew the situation with this young kidnapped girl had wreaked havoc with his career and, she was increasingly coming to learn, his self-worth.

She had no idea it had damaged his judgment, as well.

"Why is this child so important to you?"

The question slipped out and she risked a glance at his profile as she drove, the oncoming headlights painting his face in a wash of harsh fluorescence.

Derek said nothing and she was almost convinced he wasn't going to say anything when he finally spoke. "I don't know."

"You're willing to risk your life for her. You must feel something."

"It's Rena, yes. I want to bring that child home and give her some quality of life. But it's also the idea of her."

Landry nodded, the underlying meaning of his words a strange echo for her thoughts earlier about Whit and Elizabeth's baby. She knew she'd love her nephew, but with all that was going on, that innocent baby had begun to represent something more.

The restoration of her family.

A new life for them all to nurture and help grow into the next generation of Adairs. A stronger generation, if she had anything to say about it.

"That child stands for all that's not right with the world around us. She's the reason I do what I do and she's the reason I hate that my very job even exists."

"Humans can do terrible things to each other."

"Terrible, horrible things. And as long as they do, it's my job to make sure I can save as many as possible."

His comments matched the very same strains he'd mentioned earlier when he finally told her about Rena. But still, she sensed that wasn't the entire story.

"Isn't there something else?"

"Maybe she's—"

Derek was an action-oriented man—she'd witnessed it several times over the past week—so it was odd to see him hesitate.

"Rena's kidnapping forced me to look at my life differently. Where I was going. What I wanted. Who I wanted to share it with. People talk about cases that are turning points in their life, and this case has been one for me."

"Sarah?"

"Among other things."

"What happened?"

"Hell, Landry!" His voice bounced off the confines of her SUV, even the high-end leather not thick enough to absorb his upset and pain.

She wanted to lash out. Might have even a week ago. But she was a different person now. The woman who had stripped away every defense—every pretense—in this man's presence had changed. And she'd grown into someone who expected the same in return.

A wash of oncoming headlights lit the interior in harsh detail while highlighting a sign indicating they were about thirty miles outside Los Angeles.

Thirty miles until he headed straight into danger.

"Damn it." He shifted in his seat, his large shoulders rocking the back of it as he maneuvered.

"Damn. It." He muttered the words once more before he turned to face her, twisting against the confines of his seat belt. "How can you ask me questions about Sarah when we were in bed an hour ago?"

"It's a simple question."

"No, actually, it's not."

Now it was her turn to shrug. Yes, she wanted to know more about the mysterious Sarah, but she also wanted him to know he had a safe space to share. Whatever had come before they met, Derek had made it more than clear he wasn't in love with his ex-fiancée any longer. Landry knew most women would still find the circumstances a threat, but strangely, she didn't.

"She's a good part of the reason this situation with Rena is so upsetting to you. Whatever else might have come between us this past week, I hope you consider me a friend."

"Of course I do." And then, "I consider you more than a friend."

"So talk to me."

"You are persistent."

"I'm an Adair. It comes with the territory."

"You don't say."

When she made no move to say anything further, he let out a small sigh. "I never saw the signs. Not once until it was too late. I think that's the part I can't quite get past."

She caught the tense set of his body from the corner of his eye. How he shifted against the seat once more, hands clenched into hard fists on his knees.

"Relationships come and go, and while I was planning on making a life with her, it's not the relationship itself I'm upset about." A hard laugh rumbled from his chest. "Which is part of the problem, I'm sure."

"What signs didn't you see?"

"How unhappy she was. How she resented my job. How she quietly and deliberately tried to manipulate me day after day. I was oblivious to it all."

"Relationships are hard. And we all check out from time to time. Sometimes it's easier that way. To let the things you don't like swirl around you while you focus on the other things in your life you can control." She reached out and laid a hand on his arm. "I've dubbed it the Landry Adair Relationship Method. It's been rather effective up to now."

"Don't sell yourself short. I think you've done an incredible job with what you've had to work with." His hand crossed his body to cover hers, the gesture warm and intimate in the darkened car. "Besides. I'm a cop. I should have seen the signs and known how to deal with the situation."

"Ah, yes." She nodded sagely, and purposely pushed bite into her tone. "The Derek Winchester Relationship Method. My profession makes me bulletproof and nothing can hurt me."

"Landry—"

The traffic was light, not a car nearby for hundreds of yards, so she risked a glance his way. "Am I wrong?"

"It's not the same."

"Oh, hell, Derek. It's all the same. Life. Relationships. Human interaction. It doesn't suddenly get easy because you have a certain job or a given amount of cash in your bank account. Life's hard and we all deal with our own fair share of crap."

She slid her hand from his arm, tired of trying to make him see reason. Whatever pain he carried, he was obviously more content to hold it close and allow it to continue eating away at his soul than to get help or share the load.

A dull wash of gray reflected back at them through the windshield as Landry pulled up to a warehouse several blocks down from the one he and Mark had targeted. The dynamics of the area changed block by block, and he knew this corner to be one that was well maintained by the building owner, who also believed in a strong security system. He'd made peace with Landry coming along, but there was no way he was putting her in the line of fire.

An unmarked car sat down the street and Derek knew it to be one issued by the department for sting operations. Even with the seventy-five yards that separated them, the car's inhabitants could be there in a moment if needed.

His gaze drifted over the woman next to him. Strong. Sure of herself. And altogether too determined to have her own way. She'd refused to be shaken off, and he'd already exacted a promise that she'd go straight to a hotel room that had been prearranged and wait for him there.

Anxiety aside, if he were honest with himself, he had to admit her cool head and reasonable logic back at Adair Acres had rung true. The car ride up had given him time to call Mark and work through the details of the operation.

The end of the ride, however, had been a different story.

Was the woman mad?

How could she ask him questions about another woman when he could still feel the heat between the two of them branding his skin? They'd made love for hours and she wanted to know about his ex-fiancée?

Worse, she wanted him to talk about where he'd gone wrong with his relationship. How he'd ignored the signs, or worse, didn't even bother to look at how unhappy Sarah was. Instead, he'd been content to live his life and drag another person along the path of his life choices.

Sarah had hated his life as an FBI agent. Oh, she enjoyed telling her friends what he did, but beyond that, she resented his time in the field. His time away from her.

How had he missed that?

He knew plenty of people who juggled a life in the

Bureau with marriages and families. At one time, he thought himself capable of the same, but now...

Now he wasn't quite so sure.

The Rena Frederickson case had put more into focus than just his career. Maybe that was why, on a visceral level even he couldn't describe, he needed to save this child. For her own life and future, yes.

But somehow she'd become the redemption for his.

"Do you have what you need?"

Landry's voice pulled him from his thoughts. That Zen place he always went to before an op where the things around him faded away, replaced by a focus on what he needed to accomplish. "I've got it all."

His sidearm was in its holster against his ribs, and he knew Mark had an arsenal of backup already with him. With the added men Mark had worked to line up, Derek knew they were set.

"I'm good."

"Then I'll let you get to it."

The limited lighting in this part of town kept the SUV fairly dark, but there was a sliver of moonlight that filtered through her driver's-side door, reflecting off the blond strands of her hair.

Since they'd already agreed she'd wait at one of the luxury hotels downtown, he focused on that simple bit of reassurance. She'd be safe as soon as she drove away. Away from the wash of darkness that had clouded his life for far too long.

"I'll have Mark bring me back to the Bureau when we finish the op and then we'll come to the hotel after we get everything filed. Try to get some sleep as it'll probably be around ten or eleven tomorrow morning before we've got everything wrapped up."

"I'll see you then." She closed the gap between them

and pressed her lips to his. The quiet of the car closed around them like a cocoon, and for the briefest moment, Derek allowed himself to sink into her.

He'd been unable to resist her, but in that moment he needed her with a raw hunger that sent a shiver of fear through his midsection.

When had he gotten so vulnerable?

Landry lifted her head and pressed a hand to his cheek. "Be careful."

Although it was dim, a small swath of light reflected from a street lamp at the end of the block. The angle of the beam framed her gaze and he took the moment to stare into those bright blue depths.

Derek braced for the thinly veiled censure that he was leaving, but all he saw was support.

He slipped from the car, unable to spend another moment waiting. He needed to focus on the op. On the need to protect and defend and finally—*finally*—bring Rena Frederickson home.

Landry drove off as they'd planned and Derek waited, watching the back of the car until her taillights faded fully from view. He'd deliberately selected their stopping point because it put her two simple right turns back to the freeway. She was a competent woman who knew where she was going, and he had to trust she'd find her way.

He'd also reassured himself by punching the hotel address into her GPS, reviewing every prescribed turn on the navigation system in advance.

Landry would be fine. And when he picked her up tomorrow they'd figure out what to do with the rest of their lives.

A hard breath caught in his throat as that image took root.

The rest of their lives.

When had he started thinking about her in terms of something permanent?

And with another dose of reality crashing in, he had to admit it was about ninety seconds after he met her, her blond hair slicked back as she stared up at him from the pool. Even now, he could picture it as vividly as if he were standing there. Sun backlit her features, framing her like a goddess rising from the pool as rivulets of water ran over her face and chest and down her impossibly long legs.

She was beautiful. And in all the moments since, he'd seen how her external beauty was dwarfed by the woman she was inside.

Her care for her family and friends. The focus, attention and devotion she lavished on the charities she was involved with. Even her fierce protection of her mother's name, despite her very real acknowledgment that Patsy didn't deserve it.

Landry Adair was amazing.

And he loved her for all of it.

That sense of vulnerability slapped at him once more but Derek pushed it back. He'd thought himself in love before, only to discover it was a mirage of poor expectations and veiled frustration.

What he had with Landry was different. Her willingness to bring him here was only one example that set her apart. And set apart what they felt for each other.

With one last glance in the direction she'd driven away, Derek shifted his focus inward. He might have just had the revelation of his life, but it was time to do what he'd come for.

There'd be time soon enough to tell Landry how he felt.

The target location was about a hundred yards away

and he kept to the shadows, walking against the outer walls of each building between his drop-off point and the warehouse entrance. He patted the tools in his pockets and sensed the reassuring weight of his gun under his arm and another piece strapped to his leg.

Satisfied with his preparations, he moved on to the next phase. An image of the building's layout filled his mind's eye. Mark said their intel pinpointed Rena on the first floor behind a row of old office cubicles.

Derek kept that image firmly in place and slipped into one of the building's required fire exits. The door had already been identified as a weak spot on their first reconnaissance, and it only took him a few minutes to work his pick tools before a hard snap on the frame finished the job.

A light breeze wafted over his neck, chilling him.

They were almost done.

An eerie stillness descended over him as he moved through the back side of the warehouse, gun in hand. Large, dirty windows filtered what little light was outside, but it was enough to give him a dim picture while his eyes further adjusted to the interior of the building.

The layout was much as he remembered, and he passed several rows of abandoned cubicles. The fabric that lined each cubicle showed its wear, the evidence of rodents chewing through the cloth visible in the frayed fabric and small holes at the base of the various frames he passed as he moved.

When he reached the end of a row, he stilled, doing his level best to orient himself to wherever Rena might be. While he knew there wouldn't be a parade in his honor, he expected some sort of noise, even if it were just the muffled noises of her sleeping.

But no matter how hard he strained, his body still,

he couldn't detect a bit of sound that indicated another human was anywhere in the vicinity.

Another frisson of unease skittered over his skin and he glanced back the way he came. The door had been awfully easy to get through, and the lack of noise persisted. More than the lack of noise, the overarching stillness of the space felt unnatural.

He slipped a small, high-powered flashlight from his pocket and swung it low, illuminating layers of dirt and animal droppings on the floor. The evidence of such filth added a layer of anger over the anxiety and he fought to keep his calm. He'd do Rena no good to get upset now.

There would be plenty of time for anger later.

He kept tight to the cubicle wall and knew he'd pass one more row before he hit the wall of physical offices. Rena would be there.

She had to be there.

On the signal he and Mark had practiced, he tossed a beam up toward an exterior wall of windows, flashing three times. The tomblike stillness wrapped around him as he waited for Mark's response.

Nothing.

He waited, counting off his breaths, then flashed the signal once more.

After several beats, again. Nothing.

An image of Landry wavered before his eyes. She was waiting for him. She expected him to come back. To meet her at the hotel tomorrow morning so they could drive together back to Adair Acres.

Even with the image of her pulling him like a lodestone back the way he came, he pushed himself forward. Toward the wall of offices and the child he knew was there. In life or in death, he needed to go to her. Needed to see for himself.

He stepped forward, his only focus on the office door that sat ajar halfway down the hallway. It was the only reason he stepped into the pool of blood that lay around the scrawny figure of Big Al Winters.

Chapter 15

Time passed in a blur of action and image. Derek dropped to his knees to check for Al's pulse, knowing full well he was too late. The body was still warm, but all evidence of life had drained along with the man's blood.

Derek screamed for help, the remembered protocols flashing through his mind as he hollered out the commands for all clear and victim down, before he searched for the gunshot.

He found two neat, clean holes at the chest and throat.

The shots were precise—and lined up in a familiar pattern—and he stilled a moment to simply catalog the wounds for himself before moving on to the rest of the body.

Al was obviously unarmed and by the look of him, hadn't washed in days. Derek shifted away from the body, determined to investigate the rest of the warehouse. It was only when he glanced down to find himself covered in blood that he stilled.

There was no way they'd recover any additional evidence if he layered the place in bloody footprints.

So he waited.

And watched as Mark came through the door first, gun drawn.

"All clear!" Derek hollered the words, his hands up so Mark would connect the words with the body language. He waited and saw the moment his partner shifted from on guard to aware.

A pained expression filled Mark's face, his eyes dark with worry. "Why the hell didn't you wait for me?"

Derek lowered his arms, his movements slow as the others began spilling in the doors. "Why did you miss my signal? I flashed it several times, just like we arranged."

"Signal? I've been waiting outside for you for the last hour. There was no signal."

Mark was waiting?

Derek ran through the moments when he flashed his light at the exterior windows. He'd made the signal, then waited. Then he'd made it again.

He *knew* he had.

Their team lead, Leo Manchester, came in and took his place behind Mark, interrupting Derek's mental backtrack through the past several minutes. "Winchester. You okay?"

"Fine, sir."

Lines carved deep into the man's face as he held up his free hand in a gesture to stay. His other still held a firm grip on his pistol. "Don't move. Techs are coming right behind."

As several of his Bureau mates flooded in behind Mark and Leo, Derek willed himself to stand still.

And hoped like hell he hadn't just become a sitting duck.

* * *

Landry flipped through the file she'd stowed in her purse, ever hopeful something new would reach out and grab her from the papers. Not that it had so far.

She shook her head, trying to remove the lethargy and cross-eyed exhaustion reams of paperwork could cause in a person. The hours had ticked off the clock with aching slowness, matched only by the tedium of working her way through page after page of government documentation.

She and Derek had reviewed the files they'd printed at the FBI as they'd been able, but always in bunches, stack by stack. When the idea hit her the night before—to lay the papers out in hope of finding a pattern—she'd believed it worth a try.

Now?

She'd finally accepted the fact that she'd spent the better portion of eight hours engaged in a vain attempt to find patterns that simply didn't exist. Add on a vat of black coffee and all she had to show for her time was a case of the jitters and considerably more familiarity with her family tree.

Life events. News clippings. Flight plans.

Each report was yet another piece of evidence defining her family over the past century like a mini film rolling before her eyes.

She reviewed the photo of her grandmother in her Irish lace wedding gown and could picture the same gown where it was preserved behind glass on a dressmaker's dummy in the family house in North Carolina.

A news report announcing the initial public offering of AdAir Corp, her father's proud smile reflecting up at her from the page. The same photo still sat, framed in his old office, a lone hundred-dollar bill set off beneath the image signifying AdAir Corp's first earnings as a public company.

And then there was Jackson's birth announcement, memorialized in a Raleigh newspaper. The notation of his parentage—Reginald and Ruby—and a photo of the two of them leaving the hospital in Raleigh. Some enterprising photographer had expected that the couple might be worth something someday and had camped out to grab the shot. He'd had no idea his photo would become one of the centerpieces of a kidnapping investigation a mere three months later.

Landry rubbed at her arms and dragged the comforter around her shoulders.

Her family records. But were they really the key to uncovering family secrets?

Although her grandmother had died when she was small, she tried to conjure up some memories in her mind. A sleek woman, Eleanor Adair had prized her standing as one of the leading socialites in Raleigh. She'd married into the Adair family to cement that position and ensure she birthed the next generation of Raleigh society.

On the rare occasions they had spent time together, Eleanor had kept them all at a distance. Landry remembered a summer visit when the head cook had sneaked her, Whit and Carson Popsicles and her grandmother nearly fired the woman on the spot for allowing the children on the "good sofa."

Could that vain, vapid woman really be behind it all? Had she stolen from one child to give to another? And to what end?

Landry's gaze fell on the clock and she registered the time. It was ten already?

She'd expected to hear from Derek by now.

The urge to shoot him a quick text was strong but she

had no idea if even the vibration of his phone might alert someone to his presence, so she held back. She vowed to call the FBI in another fifteen minutes if she didn't hear from him.

She sifted through the pile on the bed, digging once more for the articles about her grandmother. The memories of Eleanor had left a funny aftertaste, and she was curious if the woman was as brittle and emotionless as she remembered.

The stack of newspaper announcements she'd placed together earlier—weddings, births, deaths—were in easy reach and Landry flipped through them.

Eleanor's engagement to Baxter Adair. The requisite wedding photos that took up what had to be the entire section of a newspaper at that time. The announcement of Bucannon's birth, followed by Rosalyn's and Emmaline's and then her father's.

She flipped to the last page and found the photos of Emmaline's wedding. Her late husband, Nicholas Scott, stared back from the photo, his hands entwined with Emmaline's.

At the image staring back at her, Landry stilled, Georgia's words coming back to her.

Georgia had believed Noah bore a shocking resemblance to Ruby's late father. A resemblance that was more than evident in photos, which had tipped Georgia off to the possible connection.

And the photo she held in her hand showed nothing similar between Noah and the man everyone believed to be his father. Noah had the Adair blue eyes but he had dark blond hair. No one in the Adair family was blond unless it came out of the bottle, and Emmaline's late husband had dark hair that looked almost black in the photo.

On a frustrated sigh she crossed to the dresser and gave herself a good once-over in the mirror.

It could be a coincidence.

Hair color changed as people aged. Heck, she knew that as well as anyone, since she paid good money for the blond that highlighted her hair. But still…

She twirled a lock of her own hair—dark with blond highlights—and considered the photo on the bed. Noah had a fresh-faced, all-American look about him that didn't mesh with Nicholas Scott's darker European looks.

The connection was skimpy, but it was valid.

Her gaze alighted on one of the other stacks she'd piled up and she dug through, suddenly curious about the birth certificate she'd flipped past earlier.

"Noah, Noah, Noah," she muttered as she worked her way through the stack. "There!"

The birth certificate was in French, the dates reversed in the custom Europeans used. Date first, followed by month and then year.

"Oh, no." Landry scanned the papers once more, her gaze skimming over the dates. "Aunt Emmaline. What did you do?"

Derek sat in the interrogation room, his earlier expectations ringing like a haunting reminder in his mind. He'd been in here for hours, various members of the department taking shots at him with endless questions.

"Walk me through it again, Winchester."

"Damn it, Leo, I've walked you through it. Several freaking times already. Big Al was dead when I got there."

"So how did you end up with all his blood covering you?"

"I came upon him by surprise. You were in there.

You saw how narrow the cubicles were and the position of the body."

Leo shook his head. "You walked into a dead guy? Come on, Derek. You haven't been on leave that long. You know protocol. Procedure."

"And I also know my partner was supposed to have my back and he didn't."

"Yet you went in anyway."

Derek saw the corner he'd painted himself into and focused on his rationale. "Rena's been missing for months now. We owe it to the kid to find her."

"And you owe it to your teammates and yourself to follow the correct procedures designed to keep your ass safe!" Leo slammed his fist onto the table. "Why the hell didn't you wait? Now I've got one of my best agents at the scene of a crime, with a man he's already shot once, gun in hand and blood all over him, and a pattern of bullet holes you're known for."

The adrenaline that had sustained him throughout the long hours of questioning kicked in, drawing on a reserve Derek didn't even know he had. "Excuse me?"

"The bullet holes. The throat and chest. On the vic."

"Yes?"

"It's signature Derek Winchester. All the way back to your days with the Secret Service. Your shots are meticulous."

A terrible cold began to spread through his body, numbing him to his core, and the strange sense of familiarity he had while examining the vic came back to him in full force. "I didn't shoot Al, Leo."

"You had every reason to. You didn't follow procedure. No one was there with you. And the vic bore your signature shot pattern."

"He died at the hands of someone else. All I did was find the guy. And where were you all, anyway?"

"Us?" Derek saw the spark leap into Leo's eyes and knew he needed to tread carefully. When had this gone so far south?

"All of you. Mark wasn't where he was supposed to be. And hell, no one else was where they were supposed to be, either. You guys were parked across from the warehouse and never even showed up until you followed behind Mark."

"We weren't across from the warehouse."

"Of course you were. I saw the department issue when I pulled up."

"What department issue?" Leo pushed forward, his body vibrating with sudden interest. "We weren't there, Winchester."

The cold in his veins receded, replaced by the sudden kindling of anger and betrayal.

Where was Mark in all this?

Mark had given him the intel. Mark had worked through all the logistics with him on the drive up from Adair Acres. And Mark had arranged tonight's drop.

Derek glanced toward the two-way mirrored glass, then caught Leo's eyes. He reached for the notepad at his elbow and scribbled a quick note.

So who was at the warehouse?

Derek was still shaking a half hour later as he sat in Leo's office. He'd finally been given leave to call Landry. A vague sense of shame tugged at him as she was ushered into Leo's office and he tried to push it away.

He hadn't done anything. Yet here he was, stuck in his boss's office waiting for her, unable to leave on his own.

"Derek!" She launched herself at him, her arms wrapping tight around his midsection. She'd asked minimal questions on the phone but he could see that the lack of information had shaken her. Her face was pale and he heard a distinct quaver beneath her words. "What happened? Are you okay?"

"Fine. I'm fine." He leaned in and pressed his lips to her ear. "I'm sorry to do this to you and I'll explain it later, but you need to follow my lead. Nod if you understand."

She pulled back, her eyes wide with concern, but she nodded, the move nearly imperceptible.

"Landry. Let me introduce you to my commanding officer, Leo Manchester."

The two of them worked their way through introductions and it was only when Leo sat behind his desk, his hands folded, that Derek saw the realization kick in as it covered Landry's face in subtle surprise.

She wasn't here for a polite series of introductions.

"Miss Adair. Do you mind if I ask you a few questions about last night?" When she only nodded, Leo pressed on. "I understand you accompanied Derek into the city last night."

"Yes. He's been a guest in my home and when he got the call to come into the city, I told him I'd drive him while he worked on his preparations in the car."

"That was awfully generous of you."

She shrugged, but she never broke eye contact. "I care for Derek. I wanted him to be safe."

"And you thought you could keep him safe?"

"I hardly think a trained FBI agent needs my protection. But I did think he could use the help I was capable of offering, namely a ride."

The two bantered back and forth and, to her credit, she never wavered from her story.

Nor did she back down.

Whatever questions Leo threw her way, she answered back in kind. But it was the last that had Leo stilling in a mixture of surprise and shock.

"Look, Agent Manchester. Perhaps I've been a bit too delicate. Derek and I are in a relationship. We spent last evening together and were, in fact, together when he got the call. I care for him and I refused to see him go alone. Nagged him about it until he gave in, as a matter of fact."

"Were you aware Derek was heading into a confrontation with a man he shot not too long ago? A shooting that was responsible for his current leave of absence from the Bureau."

"Yes, I was."

"Yet you were willing to help him?"

"It was my understanding that Derek's been focused on saving a young girl's life. That's what I was helping him to see through to fruition."

"I think Miss Adair has been rather accommodating, Leo. Are you done with her?" Derek said.

"Actually, I think I can resolve this misunderstanding." Landry laid a hand on his arm. "I don't know why I didn't think of it sooner. My car has the latest in GPS technology. Derek punched in the coordinates for me to the hotel and hit Start on the navigation instructions. There's a time stamp there that should be easy enough to verify."

The slightest smile played about Leo's lips before he nodded. "If we can get your permission on that, I can have a tech check it out and get you on your way." Leo's gaze was pointed. "Both of you on your way."

Derek hadn't managed to shake the vague sense of embarrassed shame that had dogged him since Landry arrived at headquarters, but he'd added frustration and anger to the mix.

What had Mark been thinking?

If Derek were honest with himself, he knew Mark didn't live and breathe the job like he did. Hell, few people lived and breathed the job like he did, and Derek had accepted long ago that wasn't a shortcoming in others.

"You haven't said much." Landry took a sip from a diet soda she'd picked up when they stopped for fast food for the drive back. Her half-eaten burger still sat in the console between them, neatly wrapped.

"I've got a lot on my mind."

"That seems to be going around."

The dry notes of her voice faded into the space between them like dust. "Want to talk about it?"

"Yes, but I want to hear what happened first. I played along with your boss but I want to hear it from you."

"Would you believe me if I said I don't know?"

"Yes."

That one word—sincere and absolute—did more to assuage the roiling storm inside than anything else could have.

She believed in him.

The same clarity that had assailed him as she drove away from the drop site came back once again and he reached for her hand. She linked their fingers, and the physical show of support was as welcome as her simple words.

Words. Actions.

The thought stuck—took root—and Derek turned it over in his mind. Mark's words didn't match his actions. And as he sifted through the past few months in his mind, he realized that Mark's actions had been off for a while.

"Come on, Derek. Walk me through it. Explain it and maybe it will make more sense to you, as well."

The retelling of the previous evening took nearly the entire drive to Adair Acres. Landry had stayed quiet throughout, stopping him only a few times to ask questions. And as they drove through the gates that bore the double *A*s, Derek was surprised to realize how therapeutic it was to talk through the events with someone else.

"Thank you."

"For what?" The afternoon sun was high and she shielded her eyes as she drove down the long, winding driveway.

"You made me walk through it, step by step. Leo was so busy pressing for details it made it impossible to think through the small impressions that mean as much as the large ones."

"There's something else." Landry nodded before pulling into a space near the garages. She turned toward him and took his hands in hers. "Rena wasn't there. I think you need to accept that she might be gone."

The swift sucker punch to the gut had him dragging his hands away as her words stole into his mind like a thief. "We just haven't found her yet."

"Derek. Look at the circumstances. That child's been used as bait, but have you really seen her?"

"Mark's got intel that has put her in each of the locations we've monitored."

"Mark. There you go with Mark again. Why the hell can't you see he's the problem? Did you gather the damn intel yourself?"

"He's my partner. I trust him to gather as much of the information as I do."

"But you haven't gathered anything since you've been on leave. It's been all him."

Derek slammed out of the car, his frustration mounting to the point he needed out of the SUV.

He knew Landry wasn't responsible for the situation he found himself in. He was still figuring out exactly how *he* himself was responsible for all the strange twists and turns that had sent the Frederickson case off the rails. But he also knew he didn't need her poking holes in the things he was sure of.

"I'm on a leave I didn't ask for, playing babysitter, so I've used the resources at my disposal. Namely my partner."

The babysitter arrow was out of the quiver before he could pull it back, and now he had to watch it pierce Landry's chest. Something cold and dark settled in her vivid blue eyes, turning them to ice. "I wasn't aware I was such an imposition."

"Damn it, Landry—" He broke off, well aware he had no excuse for the remark.

Or the bad behavior.

"The remark wasn't directed at you."

She put up a hand as he moved closer. "I'm not interested in talking to you right now."

Her body language was an even more effective deterrent than her words and Derek took a step back.

"I need to take care of some responsibilities this afternoon. I'll see you at dinner."

"Of course." He knew an apology was in order, but he also had the good sense to know it wasn't going to be well received, so he let her walk away.

She'd nearly reached the kitchen entrance to the house when she stopped and turned. "Whatever he once was, that man is not your partner."

* * *

Mark parked the government-issued piece he'd restored in the garage he rented for storage. The thing was a pain to maintain, but it sure did come in handy.

Just like last night.

He'd left the car in a visible place and knew Winchester would take the bait. Backup. *Yeah, right.*

He still couldn't believe how smooth and easy things had gone. The frantic calls, setting up the op. Even dragging Big Al to the warehouse hadn't taken too long. The guy had struggled but he'd managed to subdue him.

Headquarters had taken longer than he'd have liked but all in all, even that went according to plan. Leo had chewed him out for giving Derek intel on the case when the man was supposed to be on leave, blah, blah, blah.

Whatever.

Fortunately the death of Big Al had provided a sizable diversion and the ass whipping had been minimal. His airtight story and the manufactured notes he'd created on the case had helped seal the deal.

Just doing my job, boss. Can I help it Winchester's obsessed with the Frederickson case?

Obsessed was right. And that obsession was going to be the end of Derek Winchester.

He pulled out his phone and hit Sarah's number. The soft strains of her voice lit him up inside, tightening his gut with need. "Did you hear anything? I've been so worried."

"Sorry it took me so long to call. It was a bad night, babe."

"What happened? Is it Derek?"

The ball of need that pulsed for her, desperate to make her his own, morphed into something raw and ugly. "Derek's in trouble, Sarah."

"What happened?"

"He shot the perp. The one we've been after for Rena. Killed the poor sucker."

"What?"

He walked her through his version of the story—the same one he'd shared with the office brass—adding his own concerns about Derek's mental health in this retelling.

"I don't believe it."

"Come on, Sarah. We've talked about this one. Derek's out of control and his vengeance over that kid knows no bounds."

"Has she been found yet?"

Mark imagined his next stop and caught himself before the smile on his face could reflect in his voice. "No. Not yet. Perp keeps playing us with just enough information to get excited."

"And now there's no perp."

Her use of the word was a surprise. Normally she shunned any and all police talk, so the question had him stumbling. "No, there's not."

"What about the people he works with?"

Mark forced a light tone, well aware the seething in his gut would come through if he didn't play his comments correctly. "When did you suddenly get so interested in this case?"

"I'm not. I mean—" She broke off. "I've just had a lot on my mind."

"Want to tell me about it?"

"It's just…I've been so alone lately. And I can't help wondering if I made a mistake."

"Mistake?" A hard bite edged his words and Mark fisted his free hand on his knee, willing the anger out of his voice.

Mistake?

When the hell had she suddenly changed her mind?

"Well, yeah. I mean, I know Derek wasn't there for me but, well, maybe I was too hasty."

"And his mental health? Are you willing to simply overlook that?"

"Ye... No." She wavered before speaking again. "No, I'm not."

"The Bureau's a tough life when you make it your whole life. Derek didn't put you first, and you deserved to be first."

"You're right. I know you're right." Sarah heaved out a heavy breath, her voice stronger when she spoke. "Of course you're right."

"You want me to come over?"

"Not tonight, I'm tired. It was a long day at school and the kids were a bit out of control with spring fever. Want to meet for a movie this weekend?"

"I'd like that."

Mark disconnected after their promise of where to meet. Although their meeting was a bright spot, her sudden softening over Derek was a concern. He was so close with Sarah he didn't have time for her second thoughts.

An image of Derek where he sat under a street lamp, ensconced in the car with Landry Adair, drifted through his mind. He thought Rena was the key to getting rid of Derek Winchester once and for all, but maybe he'd been too quick to judge.

As he climbed in his car, Mark mapped out his next steps. It looked like Rena Frederickson might be getting another roommate after all.

Chapter 16

Landry paced her sitting room, the wine in her glass sloshing from side to side as she walked.

Babysitter?

Was that really how he saw her? How he saw his time here at Adair Acres?

She knew he was disillusioned about his forced time off from the Bureau and the difficulty with his current case, but Derek Winchester had no right.

No *freaking* right.

She took another sip, surprised to see how much she'd drunk already. She wasn't a lush and didn't view alcohol as the answer to her problems, but, well…a girl was entitled to a bit of a wine bender every now and again. Especially when the cause of said bender was a stubborn, gorgeous, pigheaded man who couldn't see past the end of his very strong, attractive nose.

And when had she decided he had a handsome nose?

Landry glanced down at her glass, then resumed her pacing. Maybe she had had a bit more than she'd thought.

"Hi."

The reason for her pacing stood in the arched doorway that set off her sitting room from her bedroom. Her gaze zeroed in on his nose quite before she could stop it.

Yep. Strong, firm and gorgeous. Just like the rest of him.

"Why are you in here? I had my door closed."

"I figured after the way I left things I should take my chances and just come in."

"Well, you can head right back out the way you came and go away."

"I'd like to talk to you."

"I'm not ready to talk to you."

He strolled into the room, looking for all the world like the king of the manor. She saw where he stopped and lifted the wine bottle from the coffee table, holding it up to the light to see how much was still in the bottle.

"You're welcome to what's left."

"Oh, don't let me stop you."

The thread of amusement underneath his words nipped at her heels. "You can stay or you can go but you will not sit here and laugh at me."

"I'm not laughing at you."

"Nor will you be amused at my expense."

"What if I'm amused at my own?"

She stilled, curious. "What?"

"I realized something yesterday and I was too big of an ass to remember to tell you."

Landry wasn't sure if it was the wine or the sudden tension that gripped the room, but she had trouble catching her breath as his gaze lasered on hers. Those dark, fathomless pools gave nothing away. Instead, they dragged her in and under, holding her still in their spell.

"What's that?"

"I love you."

Landry stilled all the way, her body nearly going numb at his words, until her gaze dropped from his to the wineglass in her hand. A wash of emotions—happy, sad, euphoric, angry—slammed into her from every direction and she desperately sought to grab on to one to find some purchase from the storm.

With surprisingly steady movements, she set the wineglass on the coffee table, then whirled on him in a flash.

"You love me? Because you have a damn funny way of showing it."

"I know."

"And now here I am, half drunk on wine and anger, and you try to tell me you love me? Way to ruin it, Winchester! Where are the flowers? The moonlight? The freaking candles!"

She caught the screech in her voice and dropped it as tears balled in her throat. "And why am I yelling at you when you said the most lovely thing?"

A hiccup had her gasping for breath as another hard wave of tears fell. Before she could say anything else, Derek had pulled her up in his large arms, his hands smoothing over her hair."

"Shhh. Shhh, now."

"You told me you love me and I'm ugly crying."

"You're what?"

"Ugly cry—" She broke off and swallowed around another lump of tears. "Never mind."

"You're beautiful. Even when you cry."

"I'm no—"

Her protest was smothered by his mouth, the tight press of his lips simply stealing her breath.

She sank into him, the moment as powerful as he was. As powerful as the feelings that had sparked to life between them in such a short period of time.

How had it happened? As fast as a blink and as powerful as a hurricane.

And so necessary she needed him the way she needed her next breath.

In some dim, distant part of her brain Landry knew she'd made a muddle of this—as had he—but she couldn't find a way past the crazy, desperate need to kiss him back.

He was safe. And he was here with her.

The endless moments back at the FBI office—and the implications beneath Derek's boss's words—had chilled her to the core. Even the anger and frustration that had carried her inside after their fight had been fueled by something more.

Fear.

It consumed her, the reality of what he lived and worked with. The horror of kidnapped children and murdered criminals that now threatened to pull him under, branding him as a criminal, too.

"Landry?" Derek pulled back, his gaze tender as his thumbs grazed over her wet cheekbones. "What's the matter? You were kissing me back and then you just seemed to disappear."

"They think you did it." Her quiet words filled the room, their power louder than a gunshot.

The mouth that had just moved over hers, so lush and rich with passion, firmed into a straight line. "I'll deal with that."

"*You'll* deal with it?"

"It's my damn job, isn't it?"

"And I'm the woman you claim to love."

"Claim?" Another round of flame sparked to life, filling the depths of his gaze. "Do you think I'm lying about my feelings? Using them to manipulate you? Because believe me, I've been there. I've been the one manipulated and I won't do that. Ever."

She saw the hurt as clearly as if she'd struck him, but filed that away for later. They would deal with the lingering specter of his relationship with Sarah, but not now. Not when there was so much more they needed to discuss.

"I think you struggle to share your circumstances at work out of some sense of embarrassed pride."

"Now you're a shrink, too?"

"No, I'm just a woman who can see clearly. And that clarity, along with stubborn, boneheaded comments like the one you just made, make it more than evident you're too close to this."

"And you think you have the answers?"

"I do know I'm as involved in this as you. I'm here, Derek. And I will help you see it through."

"The case is my job. You're my life!"

Raw truth crackled between them and she nearly crumbled right there—nearly gave in and leaped right back into his arms—but something held her back. For once the fear of being alone had faded, overridden by the fear of being with the right person for all the wrong reasons.

"Yet you push me away and compartmentalize that aspect of your life from me." She took a few steps of her own, backing away from the heat and warmth that beckoned her closer. "You say you love me, yet you want me to know my place."

"This isn't 1952, Landry. There is no place."

"Isn't there? You can say your attitude's modern, but it smacks of trying to protect the little woman."

"This has nothing to do with you being a woman. I'm a trained federal agent. It was irresponsible enough of me to bring you into the city last night. To taint you with the stench of whatever is going on with that case. Hell, with my partner, as well."

He dragged a hand over his head and ran his long fingers over the short-cropped hair at the crown. "I don't know who to believe anymore."

"Believe me. And believe what's between us." She moved back into his space and settled her hands on his shoulders, before slipping them up to cup his face. "Believe in us, Derek. Because I love you, too."

The light in the room seemed to change—soften somehow—as his gaze narrowed on her. Moments rich with emotion welled between them, wrapping them up tight, like the warmth of a roaring fire.

He laid his hands over hers before reaching out to pull her close, pressing his forehead to hers.

"Yes." His lips followed the whisper, soft and gentle on her forehead. "Yes."

Once more his lips pressed to hers. And once more, Landry knew the searing ecstasy of being in his arms.

And as the kiss spun out, pulling both of them further and further into the abyss, Landry couldn't help wondering if it was enough.

Derek crushed her against him, willing everything he felt inside into the kiss. How could she possibly think he'd prey on her emotions to get what he wanted?

Once again, the evidence of her family's dysfunction threw a strange, disturbing set of challenges into how they communicated with each other. And he was determined to break down every wall—every single obstacle she could prescribe—to make her see he wasn't the same.

"I want you." Landry's sultry voice banished the thoughts of her family as she ran a line of kisses down his throat and over his chest, easily accessible from the exposed vee of his shirt.

"Landry—" Her name came out on a harsh breath before he pulled her close for another kiss. "It hurts to breathe I want you so badly."

"Then it's lucky for us we're already in my bedroom." She slipped from his arms, walking backward toward the bed.

Although he'd grown up comfortable, Derek knew the Adairs lived in the rarefied air of true wealth and privilege. While he'd seen firsthand the challenges that lifestyle had created, he had to admit a private wing definitely had its uses. "I do like the privacy here."

"That makes two of us."

She already had the thin silk blouse she'd worn up and over her head, and Derek could only stop and stare. Her full breasts pressed against the pale silk of her bra, and his eyes traveled those lush curves before following a path over her trim waist and flared hips.

"Why, I do declare." Landry cocked a hand on one hip, her smile at odds with the delicate Southern drawl she affected. "I believe you're speechless."

"Nearly." He moved in quick, his arms wrapping around her and pulling her flush against his chest. "Fortunately I still have a few other moves at my disposal."

"Talk, talk, talk, Mr. Winchester."

He flicked the hook of her bra, then slid the material off her arms, making quick work of the piece. "Then maybe I should show you."

His mouth closed over her breast and all he heard was his name, echoing on a long, lingering sigh. It was the last word either of them said for a long time.

Derek ran a lazy hand over her shoulders, delighting in the simple feel of having her in his arms. The night before played through his mind on a loop, and the simple comfort of holding Landry close and feeling her heartbeat went a long way toward calming his roiling thoughts.

Not that he was any closer to the truth.

Was Mark really behind the killing of Big Al? Derek turned that one over, the question lingering even as he came up with a dozen reasons why it made no sense. What purpose would killing Al possibly serve? The man was a low-level enforcer. Small potatoes, even if he was in the running for scum of the universe.

Nothing added up.

Derek didn't want to believe his partner was responsible, and not simply from some misguided sense of wanting to be "right." He cared about Mark. Hell, the man was going to be in his wedding before things had gone south with Sarah. They'd been partners for a long time and he trusted the man with his life.

Had Mark gotten himself into some sort of trouble?

As that idea took root, Derek let it flow, itemizing what he knew about Mark's lifestyle. To the best of his knowledge, Mark wasn't dating anyone. He'd never shown signs of having a gambling or drinking problem, but that didn't necessarily mean anything.

"Mark or Noah?"

Landry's sleepy voice whispered over his chest on a warm puff of her breath.

"Hmm?"

"You're lying here thinking about Mark or Noah. I was curious which one."

At the realization he'd forgotten about Noah in the rush to LA and back, Derek struggled to surface from his thoughts. "It's Mark. And I should have my mind on Noah."

"I'd say both are pretty hot priorities." She patted his stomach before shifting so they could face each other. "And if I were being honest, I'd say I was more than happy for you to get your mind *off* Noah for a while."

"I know." He tightened his arms. "Your family's been through enough. I don't want to add to that."

She swirled a soft pattern into his chest with her index finger. "I know you don't. That makes it easier to bear somehow."

Derek laid a hand over hers, holding her palm to his chest. He pressed a kiss to her forehead, determined to give whatever comfort he could.

"So what were you thinking about Mark?"

His sigh fluttered the soft strands of her hair. "That it doesn't make any sense. And that the longer this case has gone on, the less sense it makes. Al, the man who was killed last night, was a low man on the totem pole. A thug, nothing more. Yet he's somehow the mastermind behind some bigger human trafficking ring?"

"How long have you been following this case?"

"A few months," he said.

"So why hang on to Rena so long? She would have been held temporarily, then processed for whatever horrors they'd planned, right?"

"Sadly, yes."

"So why would she still be held captive?"

"I have no idea. But all our intel has suggested there's

been something about this child they've wanted to hold on to."

"But why? To what end?"

Just as during their drive to LA the night before, Landry was engaged in the discussion. Engaged in what he had going on professionally. Engaged in his life. "That's what's so impossible. I don't know."

"Which is why it all comes back to Mark as the conduit of information."

Derek nodded, the truth not lost on him. "Even if he is, it's no excuse for my forgetting about Noah."

"Let's just say I've done enough worrying for the both of us. In my rush to have our first fight, I forgot to tell you what I found."

"Found where?"

"The papers we pulled at the Bureau the other day. I took them with me and spent most of my time in the hotel going through them."

"And?"

"And I don't think I can pretend any longer that my cousin isn't really my brother."

Derek scrambled to sit up. "Why do you think that?"

"Come on." She sat up next to him. "Let me walk you through it and you can tell me if you see what I see."

Landry laid out the papers she'd organized. She pulled the tie of her robe tighter before pointing at the ones on top of the stack. "Take a look, then tell me what you think. I want to see if your interpretation is the same as mine."

Derek picked up the stack and laid each page out, side by side. She stood back to give him time and reached for the mug of coffee she'd had sent up.

Maybe she was being silly. What had seemed like a

lead after staring at pages all night might be nothing. Sleep deprivation had a way of blurring information and blowing things way out of proportion.

"Here." Derek pointed toward the birth certificate and that last thread she was hanging by snapped.

"Yes. That's the one."

Landry sat next to him and pointed out the details. "Right there. I know the dates are written in the European standard of day, month, year. That's why the birth certificate caught my attention. When I looked closer I could see the dates look adjusted."

"February second, 1978." Derek read the form. "That matches his age, right?"

"Yes, but look at the zero before the month. Doesn't it look like a one turned into a zero, written over with dark ink?"

Derek nodded, his gaze scanning the document. "And here, as well." He pointed to the year. "The last seven on 1977 was rewritten into an eight. Even on this photocopy you can see it."

"So they forged government documents?"

"Where would they have gotten a birth certificate in the first place?"

Landry had wondered the same until the truth slammed into her with absolute certainty. "The baby who died. The one my uncle Sheldon was talking about. That's got to be it."

"This is easy enough to verify. I've got my laptop in my room. Let me get it and log in to the Bureau database and we can check the records."

He'd put his slacks on when they had dug into the records, but she couldn't help being fascinated with the play of muscles across his back when he bent down to grab his shirt. Her gaze was drawn to the hard lines of his shoulders, and sparks shot off under her skin.

He was so strong. So capable. Even with the latest events—and she knew his confidence had been shaken by Rena's case—he was still determined to do what was right to see that a young girl got her life back.

As they'd done since the previous evening, her emotions batted between Derek's case and the situation with Noah. And swung right back to Mark.

Was that part of the problem? Had Mark lived in Derek's shadow for far too long?

She'd have believed one of the most elite organizations in the world knew how to weed out problems, but what if Mark had circumvented the system at the FBI? Toed the line just long enough to gain trust before he did damage?

The questions were still swirling when Derek returned with his laptop. She'd nearly put voice to the most pressing ones about his partner when Derek turned the laptop around in his arms. "You were right. Look here."

She leaned forward and studied the original copy of the birth certificate on the screen.

"Scroll top to bottom."

Landry did as Derek asked, taking in the birth records of a child named Noah born to Emmaline and the late Nicholas Scott in December of 1977. "The child in this record was born in December."

Landry picked up the altered birth certificate and held it up to the screen. "Yet my cousin was born on February second of the following year."

"I did a quick search query on a death certificate." He sat on the love seat, the laptop on his knees. "Let me see if it's come back yet."

Concentration limned his features, reinforcing her

earlier thoughts. He was innately competent, likely to a degree he didn't even realize.

Derek Winchester was a man who knew how to take charge. And for a lesser man, that could either be an inspiration or a threat.

An awful, terrible threat.

Landry took the seat next to him and laid a hand on his arm. "Is anything there?"

"The birth certificate on record for everything Noah's ever done states a birth date of February second. Paperwork. Job applications. His driver's license. All say February second."

"That's the date we've always celebrated his birthday."

"So what happened to the Noah Thomas Scott born on December second?"

Chapter 17

Landry knocked on Whit's door, a wash of nausea coating her stomach. The reason Derek was here—the real reason—had been proven true.

Noah was Jackson. All the evidence added up and a simple DNA test would finalize the results.

Not that they needed one.

Derek had done some additional digging now that they knew what they were looking for, and he'd uncovered flight plans from the night of March first, filed when Noah's grandmother flew a transatlantic flight from Raleigh to Lyon, France.

Derek reached for her hand, linking their fingers together. "We will help him get through this."

"I know. We're all committed to that. But—"

Whit opened the door, immediately taking in what had to be somber visages from her and Derek. "Come in."

Elizabeth slipped from the small study that occupied

the far corner of Whit's wing and stood beside him. "What did you find?"

"What Georgia suspected all along. Take a look." Landry handed them the birth certificate as Elizabeth gestured them back into the study.

Derek walked them through everything they believed, then opened up his laptop to outline the flight plan details. Both a departure to France and a return the following evening.

Elizabeth had laid a hand over her rounded stomach in the retelling and hadn't moved since, her fingers splayed over her belly. "Who would do that? And a parent, no less. Your grandmother stole your father's son."

Whit kept his arm around her, pulling her close. Despite all the pain at the evidence of what they'd found, Landry couldn't help the small spark of joy that filled her. Her brother had found love with an amazing woman and they were bringing a new life into the world.

She glanced at Derek's strong jaw and wondered if they'd ever get to that point. She loved him, yes. And she believed he loved her in return. But they still had a lot to work out. His job. Her dysfunctional family. And the truth of his past. While he hid it well, his failed relationship with Sarah had done damage.

And he still didn't see her as a full partner. She gave him all the credit for wanting to—and believing he did— but in the end, he still saw her as a responsibility instead of as an equal. That wasn't how she wanted to live her life. She'd had the bright, shining example of Reginald and Patsy and she knew what an imbalance of power in a relationship did in the long run.

She wouldn't live the same way.

* * *

Derek linked his fingers with Landry's, a small bed-side lamp keeping the darkness at bay as they walked back into her room. They'd stayed late with Elizabeth and Whit, turning the situation over and over until they had a workable solution.

They needed Noah's agreement to take a DNA test. Derek had assured all of them he could get the test done via something as simple as a glass the man had used, but the Adairs were firm in vetoing that approach.

The next step required Noah's full participation.

Georgia had kept a small bit of hair from Ruby's brush in the eventuality of a DNA test, but had kept that news from her stepmother. The risk of getting the woman's hopes up had forced more stealth into the situation than any of them were comfortable with and they refused to do the same to Noah.

He admired the hell out of their approach and re-spected the fact that it was time to tell Noah the truth. What he hadn't quite reconciled himself to was his fu-ture.

It was time to go home.

He'd done the job Kate asked—finding the missing heir—and he needed to move on. Even if a pervasive stain lingered over Adair Acres. Reginald's murderer still walked free and the faceless saboteur who'd used a snake and a blackout as weapons had yet to be caught.

Stay or go?

Derek knew what he wanted to do, but he also knew he needed to get back to his life. Even if Rena Frederickson was never found, there were others who'd go missing.

Others who were already missed.

And it was his job to find them.

He knew returning to LA shouldn't change things with

their relationship, but the reality of distance and his reinstatement in the Bureau would change the dynamics between them. It was only a matter of time before Landry grew tired of his caseload and fieldwork. The travel and the endless hours of not knowing when he'd be home.

Landry fiddled with the edge of her bedspread, her anxiety palpable. "It'll be an early morning. Noah's up at the crack of dawn to get down to the stables and we need to get to him first."

"We'll tell him over breakfast. You'll all be there with him and you're coming clean on what you suspect."

"We're ruining his life." Landry sat down on the edge of the bed. "He went to sleep this evening as Noah Scott and tomorrow we're going to tell him he's Jackson Adair. What kind of people does that make us?"

"The fact that you're this upset and worried about telling him makes you very good people in my eyes."

Derek sat next to her and took her hand in his, the mattress sagging where he sat. He'd recognized it before but it struck him once again how easy it was to be with her. To laugh and love, yes, but to comfort and share the more difficult moments, too.

"That's what will get him through this. You care for him. This is eating you all up yet you're willing to do what's right. You'll do right by Noah, too."

"And what of his mother? Will we just arrest Aunt Emmaline?"

Tension tightened her slim shoulders and he pressed a hand to her back, rubbing light circles. "It's ultimately up to Ruby to press those charges. But at this point I suspect the joy of a reunion will overshadow the immediate need for punitive action."

"He's an adult. Ruby's spent her life missing him. Noah's spent his life thinking he was another man. And

Emmaline's spent her life hiding the truth. What does that do to a person? To all of them?"

"People can grow twisted, Landry. The things they want that they don't have. The dreams they have that go unfulfilled while they're unable to find a new direction or a new goal. The changes life brings, oftentimes that are painful or terribly unfair. It's a thin line to cross before those perceived injuries are seen as punishment instead of what they are."

"Life."

"Exactly."

Myriad expressions tumbled over her face, lining that porcelain skin with any number of concerns. He knew her love for her family. And he also knew the tentative bonds she and her brothers had worked so hard to create since Reginald's death.

Yet all three of them had been in unison when it came to Noah, proving those bonds were stronger than any of them realized. They were a family and the core of that—the core of what made them a unit—would see all of them through the new reality of uncovering the missing Adair heir.

The deep blue of her eyes was nearly purple in the soft light of the room when she turned to him, studying his face. "You see it all. The lowest depths of people's souls, yet you keep on. That's a special gift, Derek."

He waved off her words, uncomfortable with the praise. "It's what I do."

"No." She reached for him, one hand on his shoulder while the other took his hand. "What you do every day. That's real strength. You're brave beyond measure. And you give up your life in service of making others' better. First your willingness to protect my aunt. Now the victims you work so hard for. That's rare, Derek."

Her compliment and the sincerity buried deep in her words touched him on a level he'd never known. Had anyone ever really seen him like that? Understood his need to help others and how it pulsed in his soul, as necessary to his life as the beat of his heart?

Yet she'd seen.

"There are many who would argue it's selfish to those I care about."

"Then that's their shortcoming."

The fresh shoots of love that had been growing for days sprouted deep roots in those quiet moments together. He'd looked for someone to share his life with. Had thought he'd found someone—had believed they'd make a good life—but now that he saw Landry he knew how wrong he'd been.

And just how far he'd missed the mark in all the moments of his life that had come before.

In Landry Adair he'd found a partner and champion. He'd found a woman who believed in him.

The early notes of morning lit up the windows with pale light, visible through a small break in the curtains she'd forgotten to close all the way. She hadn't slept well, and the first signs of morning had her rising from bed, ready to do battle with what lay ahead.

She had another brother.

From the moment her father's will had been read up to now, it was so strange to realize just how monumentally her life had changed.

In addition to a brother, she had sisters now in the form of Georgia and Elizabeth. She had the new reality of a life without her father and—whenever Patsy was eventually caught—likely not her mother, either.

And she had found love.

Derek's breathing was heavy and even where he still lay in bed, and she took a moment to simply watch him as she pulled the tie of her robe around her waist.

Connections.

And they all circled around her father.

Whether the mantle had ever set comfortably on his shoulders or not, Reginald Adair had been the center of AdAir Corp, the heart of Adair Acres and the foundation of their family. Through that connection, Whit found Elizabeth. Carson found Georgia. And they'd all found Jackson.

She turned from the bed and crossed to the window, parting the curtains slightly so she could look out over the grounds. Landry knew she was apprehensive about what was to come. She also knew a strange sentimentality she couldn't quite shake.

It was so odd to reflect on it all now and see how everything had unfolded. Because even in the sad reality of what her aunt and grandparents had done to her father and his family, those connections had been vibrant and strong, iron bands tethering them all together.

Jackson Adair had lived right under their noses, but alive and well. Whatever fear her father and Ruby must have lived with could finally be assuaged. Their baby boy was a grown man.

"You're up early."

Derek wrapped his arms around her from behind, his large body like a shield, protecting her from all that was still to come. "I didn't sleep well."

"It's to be expected. You'll feel better once this is behind you. Once you can begin again as a family."

"Which means you're going to leave."

The statement was out, so simple, really, she hadn't

even realized it was lingering, lying in wait for the perfect moment to leap out.

"I... Well..." His arms tightened before he dropped them and stepped away. "My responsibilities to Kate will be completed."

"And you have a life to get back to."

"You don't have to make it sound like a duty."

"Neither is staying here."

"Landry—"

She wrapped her arms tight around her waist, holding back whatever pain threatened to swamp her. They'd made love. Had even told each other their feelings. But they'd never discussed a future, and it was silly to pretend there was one.

"We can talk later. We need to get downstairs."

That went well.

Landry hadn't stopped berating her impulsive tongue since she reached the dining room. A part of her—the small, petty part—wanted to blame her "state of our relationship" question on sleep deprivation, but she knew that was unfair.

She'd asked because she wanted to know, plain and simple.

And hadn't been prepared for any reaction besides an unequivocal desire to stay.

The large silver urn of coffee that had stood sentinel at the end of the breakfast sideboard for as long as she could remember greeted her as she filled a mug. Landry watched the rich black coffee fill her cup, hot and strong, and wished for a do-over. All at the tender hour of 6:00 a.m.

Maybe if she had enough coffee she might find a way

to put the genie she'd inadvertently unleashed in her bedroom back in the bottle.

She risked a glance at Derek, busy fetching cream from the small fridge the staff kept stocked in the corner. The hard lines of his body had remained stiff as he finished dressing in her room, then left to change into fresh clothes in his own room. He'd donned a buttondown shirt and faded jeans, and she wondered how she could be so attracted to him, even as her thoughts were in a million different directions.

They didn't live that far away from each other. A relationship wasn't out of the question, and it was barely even long distance considering how often she was in LA for her charity work. They could find a way. And if things continued to progress, she could eventually see herself moving to Los Angeles full-time.

Except he hadn't suggested that would be a welcome next step.

The truth slapped at her and Landry busied herself with making a plate of fruit to pass the time until Noah arrived. Just when she thought she couldn't dither over selecting one more strawberry, her brothers' arrival in the dining room ratcheted up the tension several more notches.

"Anyone see Noah yet?" Carson kept his tone casual as he beelined for the coffee, but Landry sensed the notes of unease under the gruff demeanor.

He was a man used to giving orders and expecting them to be followed. Process. Rules. Order. Carson had lived by those principles for his entire adult life. Which made what they were about to do that much harder.

They were about to unleash chaos.

"Everyone's up early."

Noah's voice rang out from the doorway. He looked

comfortable, Landry realized, his usual work outfit of jeans, T-shirt and chambray button-down like a second skin. Yet even if the dress were casual, she knew it was something more.

He was comfortable with who he was. Even the jokes the other day before the baby shower had held more frustration at his mother's insistence on his settling down than any real upset over the matter. He did as he liked and lived as he pleased and by all accounts, Noah liked it that way.

With the truth of his parentage, his life was about to grow considerably more attached, with responsibilities and expectations.

And with the complete annihilation of anything he believed to be real.

"I'm glad you're here." Whit greeted Noah first, slapping the man on the back and gesturing him toward the coffeepot. "Carson, Landry and I have something we'd like to discuss with you."

The pleasant civility ringing out in the Adair dining room had a tense air about it, and Derek kept his position by the French doors that led out to the patio, unwilling to intrude any more than he needed to.

He wasn't a part of the family and they deserved the space to make the proper explanations to Noah. Hell, he was just the evidence man. The keeper of the facts and details that would blow up Noah Scott's world.

Starting with the fact that he wasn't actually Noah Scott.

"Oh?" Noah snagged a mug off the sideboard. "What's going on?"

"We've come upon some information you need to know. About our father."

"What?" Noah stepped away from the coffee immediately, his concern evident as he walked toward his family. "Did you find out something about his killer?"

"No." Carson shook his head. "We found out something about you."

Confusion stamped itself in Noah's gaze—a vivid blue he shared with Landry, Carson and Whit. "Found out something? About me? Like what?"

Landry moved close to him, her hand on his shoulder. At the subtle nods of her brothers, she confirmed what they already knew. "You're Jackson, Noah. You're the one our father spent his life searching for."

"I'm what?" Color drained from his face, leaving a ghostly visage in its wake. "That's ridiculous."

"I know it's hard to believe—"

"You know?" His words were sharp, their bite swift and immediate. "You think you can drop a bomb like that on me and then tell me you *know*? Like you somehow understand?"

"I don't claim to understand, no. But I can empathize that this is a shock to you." She lifted her hand once more but dropped it, her fingers curling into a fist at her side. "A terrible shock."

Noah shook his head, his gaze darting to each Adair in turn. "What could possibly make you think this? I'm your cousin. I've been coming here since I was a kid. There's just no way."

"It may be hard to swallow, but it's true." Landry gestured in Derek's direction. "Derek has the details. The only thing left to do is a DNA test to prove it."

"Details?" Noah's gaze swung from puzzlement to accusation as it landed squarely on Derek. "You've got evidence or something? Is that why you're really here?"

Unwilling to lie any longer, Derek nodded. "That's

why Kate sent me. My expertise is missing persons, and she wanted the Adair heir found. We can do the DNA test but you're Jackson. I know it."

Each word was like a gunshot, and Derek saw how the delivery took Noah apart, piece by piece.

"So it was a lie. The relationship with Landry. Your time down in the barn, buddying up. You were playing me?"

He'd prepared himself for the accusations—knew they'd be a part of Noah's inevitable reaction—but even he hadn't expected how much it would hurt to hear them from a man he'd come to like and respect.

Add on the reference to a fake relationship with Landry and Derek fought to keep his voice level and do the job he'd come to do. "No. It wasn't like that."

"Spare me." Noah stilled before turning on his family. "And all of you. You're in on this. You all knew before I walked in here. Have you been planning this? Plotting to screw up my life?"

Carson stepped forward. "Georgia pieced it together a few weeks ago. After she met you something bothered her. She felt like she knew you. It was only when she remembered a photo of Ruby's father that she put the pieces together. The photo was an image of you."

Landry reached out once more, her voice soothing. "We never meant—"

Noah flung his arm, dislodging the comfort of her touch. "If I meant anything at all to you you'd have told me. Instead, you went behind my back. For what reason? Some misguided sense of protection?"

"We couldn't tell you." Whit hesitated before pressing on. "We couldn't risk your mother vanishing into the wind."

"You think—" Noah broke off at that, landing heavily

in one of the dining room chairs. "You think my mother's responsible?"

Derek stepped forward, effectively taking the burden off Noah's siblings to share the truth. He laid the proof of what they'd uncovered on the table, the flight plan information on top. "Your grandmother was behind it all. She managed the kidnapping and took you to Europe after stealing you from Reginald and Ruby's house."

Noah glanced at the papers before reaching forward to take the top sheet. His moves were ginger, as if he were dealing with a frightened horse, and Derek knew the analogy wasn't that far off. Only now, Noah was the frightened one.

"My mother might not have known who I was. She might have thought I was just a baby that her mother arranged."

"But she was still complicit. Whether she knew beforehand or after, she kept you. There was no way she didn't know who you were."

"But she was pregnant. I've seen photos. Even in the photos from my father's funeral, she was visibly pregnant."

Landry tried once more to touch him and laid her hand on Noah's shoulder. "That baby didn't live."

"This isn't possible. Nothing about this is possible."

"I know this is a lot to digest." Derek took the lead once more, the overt shock and upset in the room in dark contrast to the sun streaming through the windows. "I'd suggest taking a DNA test first. That will give you actual proof and then we can work on next steps from there."

"Next steps?" Noah leaped up at Derek's words, ignoring the papers on the table. "I'm not a project, Derek. Or an FBI file."

"Noah—" Carson reached out but Noah shut him off.

"None of you understands this. You can't possibly begin to understand and I could see past that. If this is true, it's not your fault that you uncovered it. But what I can't see past is that you didn't tell me what you suspected. That you left me in the dark while you played Sherlock Holmes with my life."

Every word hung over the room, noxious clouds of black, before Noah slammed out the door.

They all remained still for a moment, absorbing the reality of what had just happened, when Landry stood up. "Let me go. I'm sure he's at the stables, and we have a special bond over the horses."

"You don't have to go alone," Whit said, already moving to follow her toward the door.

"No, really. Let me try." She glanced in Derek's direction once more before she turned toward the door, the dazed look in her eyes cutting him off at the knees.

He'd known her life hadn't been easy these past months. The death of her father and all that had ensued since had taken its pound of flesh. But what killed him was the sheer absence of hope in her gaze, replaced now with a resigned sense of duty.

The woman he'd come to know was warm, vibrant and full of life.

And the woman who slipped from the dining room looked as if the weight of the world had settled on her shoulders, never to lift again.

The cool morning air whipped around her shoulders as she headed for the stables. Landry's thoughts were a jumble between Noah and Derek, swinging back and forth, one to the other. Her brother needed her, more than ever, and she'd do her best to help him through this trying time.

But she needed Derek. And as each moment passed he seemed to be slipping further and further away.

Or maybe you pushed him away.

The thought she'd tried so hard to ignore wrapped around her with the breeze, whispering in her ear and forcing her to consider her role in what was between them.

She loved him.

After a lifetime desperate for the emotion, it was amazing to see how easily it had planted roots and now lived inside her. And with that love she'd learned something even more significant about herself. Derek's wants were as important to her as her own. Maybe even more so. She wanted what was best for him and believed in supporting him.

So what are you afraid of, Adair?

Grass crunched underfoot as she continued her walk, replaying the morning in her mind. Today was about Noah yet she'd attempted to rush into a conversation with Derek about their future.

Why? To sabotage what was between them?

Or to protect herself from the risk that he might walk away first?

She'd spent so long blaming much of her life on her mother it was startling to acknowledge her own role in what had happened with Derek earlier. *She* had pushed him away. Their focus should have been the meeting with Noah yet she had pushed her fears smack in the middle of their discussion. And when he had been caught off guard, she'd used the moment to pick a fight.

The stables came into view, the tall structure reassuring. No matter how bleak her life had ever seemed, the stable held the key to restoring her equilibrium. She could only hope it did the same for Noah. Or did she need to call him Jackson now? Would he even want that?

Landry sighed and let the thought fade. They'd figure all that out in time. What Noah needed now was their understanding and support.

Then she'd go see Derek and start over. The morning hadn't gone as she planned, but they would get through it. And this time she wasn't hiding behind juvenile emotions that had no place in their relationship.

A wispy cloud floated past her peripheral vision and Landry gave herself a moment to stop and look at it. So simple, a quiet moment enjoying nature.

There was beauty to be found if you looked for it. She could see that now. Even after all she and her family had been through these past months, she could—and should—take a moment to appreciate what she had.

In time, Noah would find the same.

Images of him through the years floated through her mind, as wispy as the clouds. He'd always been as much a brother to her as Whit and Carson. As youngest, she was both family pest and doted-upon sister. She'd been teased to within an inch of her ponytail and championed for whatever she wanted to do.

Yet no matter the circumstance, Noah along with Whit and Carson had always shown a fierce devotion, their concern for her well-being at the heart of their actions.

They were her first loves. She'd spent the past few months determined to help Whit and Carson find their way. Now she'd help Noah do the same. And as she navigated the waters with Derek—no matter the outcome— she knew the Adair men would support her in return.

The welcome scents of the barn greeted her as she stepped through the heavy door. "Noah!"

She strode down the long path toward the back office,

so full of her own thoughts it took several moments to register the anxiety in the horses. Landry stopped, the restless underpinning growing evident just as she heard a loud whinny from Pete's stall.

And felt the distinct kick of adrenaline and fear as Mark Goodnight stepped out of Noah's office.

Chapter 18

Derek refilled his coffee mug, the meaningless action something to pass the time. He'd already drunk enough caffeine to be jittery and on edge, and certainly didn't need any more.

He knew he should be focused on Noah but all he could think about were his clumsy moments with Landry that morning in her room. He wanted to make it up to her—*would* make it up to her—as soon as they got Noah past the upheaval of learning his real identity. He'd already put a buddy at the Bureau on notice for a DNA test and the need for expedited results.

All they needed was Noah's go-ahead.

And then he could focus on the woman he loved. If he'd had any question at all about his future, the past few hours had erased any doubts. He loved Landry Adair and wanted to spend his life with her.

"Did he agree to take the DNA test?" Georgia's

voice interrupted his thoughts, the question giving him a chance to focus on the real reason he was here.

She'd joined Carson shortly after Noah, followed by Landry, had left the room and her husband had filled her in on the details.

Carson shook his head. "He didn't agree to much of anything. And he's worried about Emmaline. You can see it beneath the anger."

"What should we expect there, Derek?" Whit asked. "As you said before, she's complicit in this."

Derek took a seat, happy to have something to focus on. This he knew. Missing persons and kidnapping was his profession and he'd spent nearly his entire adult life understanding the ins and outs of the law.

He also understood the damage individuals could inflict on each other and wanted to prepare them. The shock of the news likely wouldn't assuage Noah's innate need to defend his mother, regardless of the evidence against her.

"We first have to prove she knew. We've all leaped to the conclusion she had knowledge Noah was really Jackson, but it's possible Eleanor could have kept that from her."

"And if she didn't?" Carson's question went straight to the heart of the problem.

"Then Noah hasn't only lost the life he believed he had, but he's lost his mother, too."

At Derek's words, Georgia covered Carson's hand with her own. "I know Ruby's suffered. The pain of losing her son has never faded, even after all these years. And because of that, I struggle to give any sort of excuse to Emmaline. But what sort of madness must that be, to live a sort of half life as a parent? To forever look over your shoulder and know that your child came with a price?"

"What price?" Whit stirred his coffee. "If what we believe is correct, Grandmother stole Jackson from son to daughter. No one was paid."

"It's not the money. She's paid with her soul."

Georgia's words echoed through the room with a grim finality and Derek knew she spoke the truth. No matter how desperately Emmaline wanted to be a mother, the choices made decades ago had to have taken a toll. "Landry mentioned she'd come here, to the ranch, every summer with Noah. But that somehow she'd fade into the background, as if she didn't wish to be scrutinized too hard."

Carson nodded. "Now that you put it that way, I know what Landry means. Emmaline was here, but she wasn't. She just sort of hovered on the fringes."

"Remember the summer she had that fight with Dad?" Whit said.

"What fight?"

"What happened?"

Derek and Carson both leaned forward on that tidbit, their questions overlapping.

"I don't know all the specifics, but it had something to do with AdAir Corp and Aunt Kate's run for VP." Whit rubbed at his chin. "I'm pretty sure that was it. She was upset with how public a figure Dad was with the company. Always throwing lavish parties and doing his level best to get as much PR—even if it was personally related—as he could."

"She didn't like the spotlight on the family, then?" Derek considered Landry's memories along with Whit's, adding another mental tally in the "Emmaline knew" column.

"No. And she hated the spotlight that hit the family once Kate made the presidential ticket and ultimately became VP," Whit said.

"Mom has never liked her," Carson added. "And while that's not saying much, it's the reasons why she didn't like her that have always stuck with me."

"What are those?" Derek pressed Carson, sensing there was yet another level of detail. For all they'd never known about Noah's parentage, it was growing more and more evident there had been signs that all wasn't right, either.

"Mom always felt she was a woman who let the world act upon her instead of making her own choices. Said she had a birdlike countenance that came off weak and needy and way too fragile."

Derek knew circumstantial evidence was just that—more anecdotal than hard fact—but he'd always believed in trusting his gut. By all appearances, the Adairs had borne a traitor in their midst and it was up to all of them to now tread lightly enough to get Emmaline to confess.

"You're all still here?" Noah came back into the room, color high on his cheeks.

"Where's Landry?" Derek was on his feet first, immediate alarm ringing through his system in harsh, clanging waves.

Confusion stamped itself in Noah's blue eyes, still hazy and dull with the news of the morning. "I don't know. I never saw her."

"She came to find you in the stables."

"I didn't go to the barn. I wanted to walk through the orange groves for a while and calm my thoughts. I was afraid of spooking the horses with my bad mood."

The alarm bells that hadn't quieted on Noah's arrival

ratcheted up to a five-alarm blaze. "You never went to the stable at all?"

"No."

"So where's Landry?"

Landry fought hazy memories and the harsh wash of light as she opened her eyes. Pain screamed through her skull and she stilled, focused on breathing through the pain and the sudden panic that gripped her chest.

Where was she?

The air had a dank, heavy smell, like a wet basement or a cave at sea level. She kept her eyelids at half mast and stared at the brownish, water-stained ceiling. Her mind whirled as she tried to piece together where she was.

The anxiety of the morning filled her mind in a wash of memories. The discussion with Derek about their future. She and her brothers' announcement to Noah that he was their long-lost sibling. And the walk to the stables...

Thoughts of her family faded as the reality of what had lain in wait came crashing back.

Mark.

Derek's partner and fellow agent at the FBI was dirty. He'd waited for her to arrive, then taken her—

A sob filled the air and Landry bolted upright at the evidence she wasn't alone. Pain ricocheted through her skull and she held still, eyes closed, willing the agony to subside to a dull roar now that she was upright.

With delicate movements, she blinked open her eyes and stared into a dark brown gaze devoid of hope. "Who are you?"

The child's whisper was raw, as if she hadn't spoken in days, and whatever pain had accompanied Landry upon waking faded against the insistent hum of realization.

"You're Rena."

"How do you know that?"

Fear lit up the dark brown depths of the girl's eyes and Landry tried to quickly reassure her. "I know the man who's been looking for you. He's from the FBI and he wants to bring you home."

"No one's looking for me." The rasp was still there, but her voice now held wisps of bravado. "And the FBI's the reason I'm here."

She knew Mark was responsible, but she hated to think how he'd destroyed any image this child held of law enforcement. So many were working so hard to get her back. Not just Derek, but his entire team wanted to see this child rescued.

"No, sweetie, they're not. They're the ones trying to find you and bring you home."

The heavy metal door to their room swung open and Mark stood in the entryway. Rena pointed toward Derek's partner. "Then why have they been holding me?"

Her pulse spiked once more as adrenaline rushed her system and Landry fought to remain calm. She'd get nowhere if she didn't keep her wits about her, especially since he had the upper hand. Because based on what she knew of the case, Mark had had plenty of time to prepare for whatever it was he had planned.

Derek's partner strolled into the room, the trim cut of his suit at odds with the menace that rolled off him like heat lightning. "Glad to see you woke up. You're surprisingly heavy for a woman with such a hot body."

Landry ignored the insult—only made worse by the leer that traveled over her breasts—and forced a calm bravado she didn't feel into her tone. "What have you done?"

"Isn't it obvious?"

"No, it's not. You're a federal agent. Why are you holding this child?"

"She's a means to an end." Mark walked up and stood over her, that leer morphing into something far more menacing. Madness.

Sheer, utter madness.

"Just like you, Landry Adair."

Derek and Landry's brothers had already raced through the stables as soon as they'd ascertained Noah had never seen her after rushing from the house. Their hurried walk-through past the agitated horses hadn't produced much and he was now back in the estate's security room assessing what he could on the cameras.

The morning's footage clearly showed her walking into the barn and then nothing.

"You find anything?"

"No. Damn it!" He dragged a hand over the back of his neck, frustrated at the evidence that the video feeds had been tampered with once more.

Carson took the seat next to Derek and ran the surveillance footage, his fingers surprisingly nimble and well versed on the keyboard.

"And my contacts at the Bureau haven't gotten any more details on the tampering last week, either. It's like the footage simply evaporated. They've tried tracing it and nothing's worked. All they get are some bouncing shadows that suggest there was footage but it's been thoroughly erased."

"I thought you couldn't do that anymore. Not with digital technology the way it is." Carson tapped a few more keys.

"I thought so, too. And when I say the Bureau team is the best, I mean it. They can do amazing things with the smallest amount of footage. Heck, I saw them re-create an incident off a slivered image from a building's surveillance thirty yards across the street from another building."

"You send them the new stuff from this morning?"

"Yes."

"If they can work with cameras at a distance, what about our neighbor in the sky?"

Derek had his eyes on the screen, willing something to show up when Carson's comment registered. "What neighbor? You've got all the acreage for nearly half a mile."

"I know, but we've also got a cell tower in our back-yard. It's a bit of an eyesore but my father was never one to turn down money. And it ensures we always get out-standing reception here. He camouflaged it in the trees just past the stables."

"Give me a minute."

Derek made quick work of the information and had his Bureau contact on the line in moments. "Can you get at it, Brad?"

The hard grunt and quick tap of a keyboard was all the confirmation Derek received and he knew it was more than enough. In moments, Brad was giving instructions on how to pull up the feed on the house computers.

Derek put him on speaker, then leaned toward the screen, orienting himself to the angle of the cameras. "There, Brad. What's the time stamp on Landry's ar-rival?"

When Brad gave him the same time as the house com-puters, Derek pressed him on. "Good. We're in sync. Go ahead and back it up. Someone got in there and we need to find out who."

Footage whizzed past, nothing visible but the stable

dwelling growing increasingly dark as the time moved earlier and earlier in the morning. As the screen grew darker, Derek worried they'd miss something when an image caught all of them at the same time.

"There," Carson said.

"There it is." Brad's voice smacked of triumph through the speaker. In moments, the man had the image manipulated, using the lights surrounding the barn to maximum advantage. He zoomed in on the individual hovering around the doorway, his gasp evident when a face became visible through his work on the resolution. "I don't believe it."

"I do."

Derek's acknowledgement was grim and devoid of any emotion. Landry had been right all along.

Mark Goodnight was dirty.

Derek worked through the specifics with Leo and Brad as they developed a sting operation. Mark still needed to show up for work, but they couldn't be sure he hadn't created some sort of remote detonation on wherever he was keeping Landry. Brad was given authorization to dig into Mark's files and phone records, but so far he'd found nothing on Bureau assets that was useful.

Although he wanted to leave immediately, the chances were high that Mark was holding Landry in LA. He owed it to Landry's family to fill them in before he left. He kept the updates short, walking them through what he knew of his partner.

Whit spoke first. "And you've never had any signs?"

"None. I've worked with the guy for years." Derek hesitated before the well of grief and regret that threatened to swamp him spilled over. "How couldn't I have known something?"

Elizabeth had been quiet in the telling, her hand on Whit's shoulder, but she moved next to him, her voice warm and soothing. "People know how to hide their true selves and their true feelings. You can't beat yourself up over that."

Derek knew Elizabeth and Whit had cared for each other for a long time, neither admitting to their attraction, but somehow he couldn't see this as the same thing. Their love for each other was something that made each of them better when they'd finally admitted the truth. Mark's deception, on the other hand, was like a cancer, eating away at the core of the Bureau. Hell, at the core of his life.

How much had the man known that he'd never shared? And how much of the recent cases they'd worked had Mark messed with out of sheer spite or ill will? There was no time to go through it now but once this was over—once he had Landry back—he'd find out.

Because he would get her back.

Failure was simply not an option.

Landry had spent the better part of the day calculating what time it was based on the movement of the sun through the windows. Rena had slept off and on and in the child's quiet moments Landry had observed her.

What horrors had this poor young girl seen?

Derek had said she was kidnapped with the intent of using her in a human trafficking ring. Had that happened and Mark rescued her, only to then use her as an expedient resource? Or was Mark a part of that, too?

She shuddered, humbled by a reality she'd never acknowledged before. She'd believed herself well aware of the problems brought on by poverty and lack of opportunity, but did she really have any idea? She'd spent the better part of the past two months feeling sorry for her own personal situation, yet here she sat with a young girl who had nothing.

Landry was entitled to her own grief and pain, but something shifted inside her as the day progressed, one long hour after another.

Reginald and Patsy's inability to love her and parent her in a functional, positive way was on them. She'd done nothing to deserve their lack of care and yet the longer she wallowed in it, the greater disservice she did to herself.

And to Derek.

She'd recognized her error on the walk to the barn, but it was only now, when the risk she might never see him again became all too clear, that she truly understood. Love was a gift. An offering of the heart that shouldn't come with strings. If he wanted to accept her love and share his in return, then they'd figure out their life together.

And if he didn't, then she was still better for having loved him.

Rena cried out from her cot and Landry went to her, pulling her small body close. The child clung to her in sleep, desperate for the comfort and warmth she'd been denied for who knew how long. Landry crooned to her, soothing her with gentle words and soft strokes over her hair.

She let the moments drift, puzzling through the information she already knew. Did she have anything she could use against Mark? Anything she might hold over his head that would get him to at least release Rena?

The loud *thud* of the door woke her, and Landry realized she'd fallen asleep herself while holding the girl. Rena was still wrapped around her but the room was darker than earlier, the light through the window holding the sheen of early evening.

"Get up!"

Rena whimpered awake, her thin arms squeezed tight around Landry's waist. Landry shifted them both to a sitting position, unwilling to cower in the face of Mark's bullying.

Now was the time to get the information she desired.

But as she stared into his eyes, she had to question why he had done this. And how many others had he possibly hurt?

If she could get those details, she might find some way to use them, either to trip him up or to leave some bit of evidence behind for Derek and his team to use.

"You don't have to yell. You're scaring her."

"Kid's been scared for a month."

A month?

A renewed burst of anger filled her chest but Landry held on. "Why did you do this?"

"I rescued her from that human trafficking ring. She should be thanking me and instead all she does is whine and complain."

"Maybe because she's still locked up, away from her family. Her life."

"She's got three squares and a better life here than she would have." Mark's eyes grew dark, the sneer he perpetually wore firmly in place. "But what would you know about that? Miss Overprivileged and Overindulged. Daddy's little princess is now horrified to see the seamier side of things, is that it?"

"The only horror is you. You have a position of honor and bravery and you've thrown it away on some twisted, petty jealousy." The words spilled forth and she refused to hold them back. "What made you crack? Was it the proof that you'll never be as good a man as Derek?"

Mark's face narrowed in anger but he stood his distance. It was curious, she realized. She'd have expected him to strike her for her comments. Instead he stood back, distancing himself.

The impression of cowardice she'd had wasn't far off the mark. Despite his anger and rage, he clearly found it distasteful on some level to exact punishment directly. Other than his rough handling after he'd knocked her out with something in the stable, she was untouched. And she'd gently questioned Rena earlier to find out the girl hadn't been physically harmed throughout her ordeal.

So why was he doing this?

"Winchester's an ass. The office golden boy. Damn protector of the vice president so everyone thinks that makes him a hero."

"He's a good man."

"He's a phony. He acts like he's this big family man yet he never appreciated what he had." Mark slammed a hand over his chest. "*I* appreciated it but could never have it."

Landry stilled as raw fury mottled his face in a vivid red. "What didn't Derek know how to appreciate?"

"Sarah."

"His fiancée?"

"Ex-fiancée." Mark spit the word out on a snarl, the "ex" more significant to him than she ever could have realized.

This was all about Sarah? Mark had thrown his life away—and clearly his sanity—over a woman?

"Does she know?"

"You think I'd taint her with this?" Mark tossed a hand in Rena's direction. "She already thinks brats like Rena take up too much of the job. Too much time and focus and attention. Why would I tell her this?"

Landry couldn't imagine that his subterfuge had come off without considerable time and planning, as well, but she held her tongue. He was obviously riled and now that she had her information, her only goal was to get her and Rena out as smoothly as possible.

"Maybe you would let me talk to her? Sarah."

"Why would I do that?"

Landry forced as much of a bored, rich girl tone as she possibly could into her voice. "I'm the new woman. It'd be easy enough to let Sarah know how right she was and what a good idea it was to walk away."

Interest sparked in Mark's gaze, a small, predatory smile coming to life. "That's not a bad idea."

"Of course it's not."

Mark frowned and Landry nearly thought she'd over-played her hand when she realized his gaze had slipped away from her completely.

He swore, long and low under his breath, before slamming them all back against the wall. "Looks like your good idea is going to have to wait."

"For what?"

"I need to go kill your boyfriend."

The old warehouse in downtown Los Angeles brought back a series of memories Derek had pushed to the back of his mind. On his first sting after he joined the Bureau, they'd uncovered a flophouse for one of the city's major criminal networks.

The warehouse looked abandoned—purposely so—but the place was used as a transition stop. They primarily trafficked drugs, prostitutes and any young girls they were shipping out of the country, but their capabilities far exceeded simple transportation.

Though the building appeared condemned, it had state-of-the-art security and computer capabilities that rivaled NASA.

He and the team had dismantled the place, piece by piece, securing reams of evidence that had put several criminals behind bars for life and had chipped away at a huge portion of the crime ring's cash flow.

After Brad's cursory glance into Mark's files, they'd spent the afternoon digging more deeply through whatever they could get their hands on that Mark might have touched. The time and forced patience had nearly killed him, but Derek knew they had one shot at this.

One shot to get Landry and bring her home.

Whatever game Mark was playing had come to its end. And there in some obscure piece of paperwork, Derek's patience had been rewarded. As soon as Brad snagged the building file, Derek had made the connection.

It had been Mark's one slipup, but it had been enough for them to put the pieces together. The orders on the building had been signed off on by Mark Goodnight. And when they dug into the paperwork behind the authorization, Derek had found what he needed.

His earpiece buzzed, Leo's voice strong and clear. "Eyes on him. Snipers got a view through the windows. Do not engage."

"They see anyone else?"

"Negative." Leo's voice snapped through the line. "Hold your position, Agent Winchester."

Derek had been through it already and knew the protocols. Mark was armed and if they tipped him off, there was no telling what he'd do.

Derek *knew* he needed to wait for the signal.

But all he could imagine was Landry inside, bound up or—worse—hurt and in need of help. In need of him.

So he held his post, standing sentinel against the battered old door on the back side of the building. He kept calm, tracing the building floor plan over and over in his mind. And he thought about all the ways he was going to tell her he loved her.

How he'd hold her close and never let her go. How he was going to ask her to marry him at the first possible opportunity.

He believed they'd see each other again, willing it with everything he was.

Whether it was the heightened direction of his thoughts or the sharp awareness of seeing this through to completion, he didn't know, but he was already on the move when the door behind him opened.

His body flat against the wall, Derek forced Mark to walk through the door to get a good look at him. Those last few steps were necessary and compelled Mark to expose himself in the open. Despite orders and the snipers in easy range, Derek made his move.

He had Mark slammed against the doorframe, wrestling him against the wall. "Where is she? You bastard! I trusted you!"

The words tore from his lips in a hard cry, words he was barely aware of even speaking. Betrayal layered over anger until all he could see—all he could feel—was the steady slam of Mark's head against the outer wall of the building.

Moments flashed in a blur as screams echoed down the sidewalk, his backup on him in seconds, pulling him off Mark.

And then Landry was through the door and in his arms, saying his name over and over.

"You're okay."

"I'm fine. Shhh." Her arms were tight around his shoulders, her lips against his ear. "I'm fine."

Derek clung to her, amazed she was back in his arms. He'd hoped—believed—she would be, but the reality was so much better.

"Derek." His lips moved over her hair and she said his name again before pressing on his shoulders. "Come here. Come with me."

Time blurred in a series of impressions and he fought to stay with her as she reached for his hand. "Come on. I have someone I'd like you to meet."

Landry pulled him back through the doorway, into the dark, dank space of the building. He nearly pulled her back out, unwilling to have her spend even another minute there, when he saw her.

Rena.

Her tall, gangly body was draped in a T-shirt and jeans, her feet bare.

"We found her, Derek." Landry's voice was quiet as she pulled him closer to the young girl. "She's safe."

Derek fell into a crouch before the girl, unwilling to startle her after all she'd been through.

Landry moved to stand next to Rena, her arm draping those slim shoulders. "He's the one I was telling you about. He wouldn't rest until they found you."

Rena glanced up at Landry, trust swimming in her quiet eyes. And then she moved, all arms and legs, and threw herself into Derek's arms. And as he looked over Rena's head, into the eyes of the woman he loved, Derek knew he'd found his partner. The woman who under-

278 *Secret Agent Boyfriend*

stood him. Who accepted him for who he was and who he wanted to be.

And for her, he'd do anything. She was his life. His love.

His forever.

Epilogue

"They caught her." Landry snuggled deeper into her robe and wondered why that statement didn't make her feel worse.

Rachel's eyes widened from the opposite couch. "Your mother?"

"Yep. She's being extradited as we speak, ripped from the arms of her European lover, under investigation for the acts perpetrated against Elizabeth."

"Oh, Landry, I'm so sorry." Rachel moved to sit next to her and laid a soothing hand on Landry's leg. Her eyebrows did shoot up in clear surprise. "But a lover?"

Landry wanted to be angry—knew she would have been even a few weeks ago—but she simply didn't have the time or attention to care about her mother's poor choices any longer. "Apparently she's been seeing Raphael for the last year. She was actually with him the night my father was shot so she's cleared of suspicion there."

"I'm still sorry."

"I'm not. She needs to own up to her part in what happened to Elizabeth." Landry thought over the past forty-eight hours. The rescue in the warehouse. Rena's return to her family. Even Noah's agreement to take a DNA test.

All of it was coming to a resolution, and Patsy's extradition was another necessary chapter closed.

Rachel offered up another soothing pat. "Then we'll agree to bury this in the friend vault and only pull it out from time to time if you need to discuss it."

Landry pulled Rachel close in a hug. "You've got a deal."

They drifted to other topics—namely how they'd both gone overboard purchasing baby outfits—when Noah walked into the room. "I wanted us all to be together for this."

"For what?" Landry watched as her entire family trooped in, with Derek closing the line, an envelope in his hands. His gaze was somber as he sought her out, subdued from the brighter joy that had marked him since they returned from LA.

When he came over and took the seat next to her, his hand closing over hers, she squeezed back. She knew that envelope held Noah's future, and she was glad they would share the moment together.

"I should probably get going." Rachel stood but Noah pressed her back to the couch.

"Please stay. I'd like you to be here."

Rachel nodded, her green gaze solemn. "Of course."

"Derek? Please." Noah took the envelope from Derek, his hands steady as he ripped through the thin seal. "I've had some time to think about what's in here. And I've come to accept that you all did what you thought was best."

"Noah—" Whit halted before adding, "You're our

family. You mean the world to us and you always have. No matter what's in there, we're here for you. We're always here for you."

Noah nodded before his gaze landed on Landry. She reveled in the warmth there and the love, always so evident in his gaze. "I know that. And almost losing Landry was a really crappy way to be reminded of how much you all mean to me, too."

Derek wrapped an arm around her and she moved closer to that protection and, to the very depth of her soul, knew Noah was right. Family—the ones you were born with and the ones you made—were what made life worth living. And in a matter of months, she and Derek would solidify their feelings by marrying and becoming a family of their own.

Noah slid the papers out and Landry marveled at how so few pages could change a man's life. He scanned the top page but it was his words that sent shock waves through the room.

"I'm Jackson Adair."

* * * * *

MAN OF ACTION

JANIE CROUCH

To Anu-Riikka, because you talk me down from
the ledge with almost every single book.
Thank you for listening to me for hours on end
and for offering a fresh perspective when I can't
see clearly any longer. You're the greatest buddy
a writer could have.

Prologue

Andrea Gordon huddled inside her car in the bank parking lot as pandemonium reigned all around her. Cops, SWAT, ambulances and other emergency vehicles she didn't even recognize flooded the area. Blue and red lights flashed in a rhythm that drummed brutally against her eyes. Officers pointed assault rifles toward the building. People ran back and forth.

Just behind the roped-off section, news crews formed the next layer of people, their lights and cords and equipment adding to the chaos.

Beyond that were the witnesses, the gawkers, hoping to catch something exciting. Andrea wasn't sure what would pacify them. A chase? Bullets? A dead body? Smartphones recorded the scene from every angle.

Three men had taken sixteen people hostage after an attempted robbery had gone wrong in a bank just outside Phoenix, Arizona. Andrea would've been one of those sixteen, but she had seen the signs on the robbers' faces when they'd first walked in.

Danger. Violence.

Andrea was only nineteen years old, but she was an expert at spotting the approach of danger. Maybe she should be thankful for all the times she'd had to discern it in her uncle to avoid his fists. Either way, it had gotten her out of that bank before the trouble went down.

The men hadn't come in together, but they were definitely working as a team; Andrea had immediately seen that. It was obvious to her that they weren't afraid to hurt, even to kill. Simmering violence was a vibe she was very attuned to.

Two of the men fairly buzzed with it. Excited about taking money that wasn't theirs and maybe taking a life, too. But it was the third man, who stood completely still and broadcast almost no outward emotions at all, that scared her the most.

She'd waited a minute longer, studying them while pretending to fill in a deposit slip, in case she was wrong. The two hyped-up guys were making their way back toward the bank manager's office. The other man, the scary one, stood against a side wall, a briefcase in his hand. He caressed it with a lover's touch.

He felt her eyes and turned to her, giving a smile so dark, so full of violence, Andrea had turned and nearly run out of the bank. She'd felt his eyes follow her as she left.

She'd been the last one out. Not two minutes after her exit, shots had been fired inside. The robbery soon turned into a hostage situation. Once out, Andrea had hidden in her car, parked in the back of the bank lot, and watched as the police arrived minutes later, then observers, then press.

Andrea would've been escorted back with the observers if anyone had known she was in her car. She'd been so scared at the third man's evil smile, she had literally melted herself into the driver's seat of her vehicle, curling into a ball and protecting her head and face with her arms.

She'd learned long ago that position didn't stop pain, but at least this time it had kept her away from anyone's view. The uniformed officer who had been in charge of security and taping off the parking lot had walked right by Andrea's car without even seeing her in the dimming hours of twilight.

Unfortunately, now she was trapped here since the lot was blocked off by police vehicles. There was no telling how long the showdown could continue with the three men inside. She would need to go find someone who could let her out if she wanted to leave this evening.

Andrea exited her car, kept her head down and walked toward the action, planning to talk to the first relatively nice cop she could find. She didn't want to draw any attention to herself, just wanted to get the help she needed and get out.

When she got to the front line of police officers, Andrea started looking around more. There was a lot of excitement in most of these cops. Some were nervous, a few downright fearful. A couple were bored.

She was easily able to spot the man in charge. He exuded self-confidence and self-importance, even without a radio in each hand and people constantly asking him questions. When he gave orders he expected them to be followed, and he was definitely the one giving orders in this situation. Another man and woman were standing with him. Everything about their faces and body language also suggested confidence, but they were respectful, caring—not power hungry. They stood back slightly, observing.

Drawn by the situation even though she didn't want to be, Andrea made her way toward those people in charge. She was careful not to get in anybody's way or do anything to draw someone's scrutiny, although she expected to be stopped at any moment. When she got close enough to hear the leaders, she stood beside an unmarked sedan, watching them studying and discussing the bank.

She heard the man and woman—the observers—arguing with the man in charge.

"Lionel, deadly force isn't necessary yet," the man stated, quiet but emphatic. "Plus we don't know the exact situation. We have no inside intel."

"This isn't your operation, Drackett," the man named Lionel snapped. He wasn't interested in anyone else's opinions. "Omega isn't in charge here—the Bureau is."

"We're not even sure how many perps are in there, nor how many hostages," the woman said, her voice as calm as Drackett's had been.

"We've got eyes on the building. There's obviously two gunmen holding a room of seventeen people. They've got everyone in one location to keep them in line."

Lionel was wrong. There were *three* men involved. But Andrea imagined the third one with the evil smile just looked like one of the hostages if he hadn't made any obvious threatening moves. With his briefcase and suit he'd blend right in.

And he meant to kill everyone in the building. Everything in his body language and his emotions had screamed violence.

"Neither of those guys have hurt anyone yet. Let us get our hostage negotiator down here to talk to them. Matarazzo is a whiz in this type of situation—you know that." Drackett again. "He can be here within the hour."

Lionel shook his head. "No, I don't need your rich wonder boy. I will handle this the way I see fit. The two gunmen have left the back of the building ripe for our entry. They are obviously camped in the front. They're nervous. I'm not going to wait until they kill someone before I make my move."

Although their expressions changed for only the briefest moment, Andrea could feel the waves of frustration coming off Drackett and the woman he was with. Whatever was going on, it was personal. Lionel all but hated Drackett.

That disdain was going to get everyone in the building killed. She could hear Lionel getting a SWAT team ready to breach the back door.

She was afraid when they did, the third man would make his move. She had to tell the police leaders what she knew. She didn't know if it would make a difference, if they would listen to her at all, but she had to try.

She walked over to Drackett and the woman before she could let herself chicken out. She didn't try to talk to Lionel; she already knew he wouldn't listen to her.

"Excuse me, Mr. Drackett? There's a third man inside that bank. Someone more deadly than the other two you can see."

Drackett immediately turned his focus to her, as did the woman. It was a little overwhelming. Andrea wasn't used to people actually listening to her that intently.

"How do you know?" His voice was clipped but she knew it was because they were running out of time, not because he didn't believe her.

"I was in there. I saw them come in. I'm—I'm pretty good at reading people, their expressions. I could tell something was not right with the three of them. Those two guys." She pointed at the bank doors where the two men could be seen. "And another one you don't know about."

Drackett and the woman met eyes and stepped closer to Andrea. She could tell they had Lionel's attention also, although he didn't turn toward them.

"I'm Grace. Tell us everything, as quickly as you can." The woman touched her on the arm. Andrea fought the urge to flinch even though she knew the woman meant her no harm.

"The two men, the ones with guns, are excited, a little shaky. They're thrilled about a big payoff and perhaps about having to shoot their way out of the situation. They will kill if they have to, but that's not their primary intent."

"And the third man?"

"Evil." Even in the Phoenix evening heat, Andrea felt cold permeate her bones. "He'll kill everyone. *Wants* to

kill everyone. I think he wants to take as many people as possible down with him."

Drackett whispered something to Grace and she eased back and disappeared into the crowds of law enforcement. She was gone too quickly for Andrea to get a read on whether she believed Andrea or not.

"So help me God, Drackett, if you tell me we need to listen to what this child is telling us…"

"This young woman has more actual intel than anyone else here. I'm not asking you to stand down, Lionel, just to listen and make sure you have all the facts before making any big move."

"I'm not going to wait for these gunmen to kill someone before we move in. SWAT will be ready to storm the back door in three minutes. We go then."

Everything about Lionel screamed determination. Andrea didn't even try to convince him; he wasn't going to listen to her.

She took a step back. She had done all she could do. Things inside the bank would play out the way they would play out.

She was about to fade back even more when Drackett looked down at a message on his phone. He turned and walked the three steps so he was standing directly in front of her.

"You. Name. First and last."

"Andrea Gordon." He wasn't angry with her but the abrupt statement had her giving her real name rather than a fake.

"Just wanted to know the name of the person who's going to cost me my career if you're wrong," he whispered. "Go stand back there with that uniformed officer. All hell is about to break loose." He motioned for the officer to come get her.

Andrea walked back with the cop, but when he became distracted with something else, she slipped away. She eased into the crowds. She'd come back for her car another time.

She heard and felt the chaos behind her a few moments later. A shot fired then a bunch of people yelling. She just kept walking, not looking back.

ANDREA WASN'T SURE what had happened in the bank that evening. She'd watched the news the next day and it seemed as if the men had been stopped without any problems. One of the gunmen had been wounded in the raid; the other had surrendered without a fight. All the hostages had left the bank unharmed.

The third man was never mentioned or shown by the media. Andrea accepted that maybe she had been wrong; maybe he hadn't had anything to do with it. But then she thought of that evil smile the man had given her in the bank. Even now it had the ability to make her stomach turn.

Andrea hoped Mr. Drackett and Grace hadn't gotten in trouble because of what she had told them. She'd probably never have any way of knowing, so she put it out of her mind.

Until they both walked in to Jaguar's a couple of hours later.

Andrea was immediately self-conscious. She wasn't on-stage dancing—thank God—but she was serving drinks, and even though the waitress outfits were more concealing than whatever the dancer was wearing, it still left very little to the imagination.

They were obviously here for her. Jaguar's rarely got customers in business suits. Especially suits that screamed law enforcement.

It was too dark for Andrea to read their expressions and body language as well as she would like, but anger radiated off them. This had to be about the bank. They must have gotten in trouble. And now they were here to let Andrea know. She wondered if she was about to be arrested.

"Harry, I need a break. I'll be back in fifteen," she said to her manager.

Harry leered at her the way he always did. "Any more than that and I'll dock your pay." He stepped closer, grasping her chin. "Or we can work out our own way of you paying me back."

He didn't see that Drackett and Grace had made their way up behind him, overhearing his words. Drackett cleared his throat.

Harry pegged them as cops as soon as he turned around. "And by paying me back, I mean working extra shifts," he muttered, going to stand farther behind the bar, glaring at the suits.

"Andrea, could we talk to you outside for a few minutes?" Grace said over the thump of the music.

"Am I about to be arrested?"

Drackett's eyes narrowed. "Why do you say that?"

Andrea shrugged, very aware of how much her clothes revealed. Her skimpy bra was clearly noticeable through the mesh of her top. The short pleated skirt she wore barely covered her bottom, and men often took it as an invitation to run their hand up her thigh.

Andrea had stopped slapping their hands away once Harry threatened to fire her.

She was used to men gawking at her body, but Mr. Drackett's eyes hadn't so much as left her face once since he'd arrived.

"You're angry," she said. It wasn't terribly noticeable in his expression, but she could tell.

Grace was surprised. "I don't think Steve is angry, Andrea." She turned to him. "Maybe we're wrong about her."

Steve shook his head once. "No, she's spot-on. I'm

pissed as hell that she's working in a place like this." He stepped closer to Andrea and she couldn't help but take a step back. He froze. "I'm not angry at *you*, I promise."

Andrea believed him. "Okay."

"But do you mind coming outside with us? This will only take a few minutes."

Andrea grabbed her lightweight jacket and followed them out the side door. "I can't stay out here very long. I'll get fired if I do. I need this job," she said in the quieter, cooler air of outside. Finally she felt as if she could breathe again.

"You were right about the third man in the bank." Grace smiled at her. "You probably saved a lot of lives yesterday. He had a briefcase full of explosives and was just waiting to use them. Was waiting for SWAT so he could take them down, too."

Andrea closed her eyes in relief. At least no one had gotten hurt and these two people hadn't gotten fired.

"Andrea, I'm going to cut right to the chase." Mr. Drackett kept his distance so she wouldn't feel uncomfortable. "We believe you have a gift at reading people's emotions and microexpressions, even when they're only available for a split second."

Andrea wasn't exactly sure what microexpressions were, but she knew she was good at reading people.

"Maybe." She shrugged, clutching her jacket to her chest. "So?"

"I'm Steve Drackett. Grace and I work for Omega Sector: Critical Response Division. We're law enforcement, sort of like the FBI, but without as much red tape."

"And smarter and better looking," Grace chimed in, smiling again. "We're based out of Colorado Springs."

That was all fine and good, but what did it have to do with her? "Okay."

Drackett crossed his arms over his chest. "We'd like you to come work for us."

"What?" Andrea wasn't sure she was hearing right. "Doing what?"

"What you did at the bank. What you seem to be a natural at doing, if we're not mistaken. Reading people."

Andrea's gaze darted over to Grace then back to Drackett. "You don't even know me. Maybe I just got lucky at the bank."

Steve tilted his head to the side. "Maybe, but I don't think so. There are some tests that can help us know for sure. We'll pay for you to fly to Colorado Springs and for all your expenses during testing."

Andrea grimaced. Tests, books, schooling were not her strengths. The opposite, in fact. She looked down at her feet. "I'm not too good at tests. Didn't finish high school."

"It won't be like math or English tests you took in school," Grace said gently. "It's called 'behavioral and nonverbal communication diagnostic testing.'"

Now Andrea was even more confused. "I don't know what that means."

Grace smiled. "Don't worry about the name. The testing will involve a lot of pictures, or live people, and we'll see how accurately you can pick up their emotions and expressions."

Okay, only reading emotions, not words. Maybe she could handle it, but she still wasn't sure. What if she failed?

"Andrea!" Harry yelled from the door. "Time's up."

Steve looked at Harry then back to Andrea. "There are no strings in this offer," Steve said, his voice still calm and even. "You can check us out before you get on the plane, make sure we're legit. Read up about Omega, so you feel safe."

Andrea studied them both. There was no malice in either of them as they looked back at her, just respect, concern and a hopefulness. They legitimately seemed to want her to join them.

"What if I can't do what you want? If I'm not as good as you think?" she whispered.

"Then you'll be paid handsomely for the time you've spent doing the testing," Grace said. "And we'll fly you anywhere you want to go. It doesn't have to be in Arizona."

"Andrea." Harry's voice was even louder. "Get your ass back in here. Now."

"And we'll help get you started in another career. It may not be with Omega, but it doesn't have to be here. This is not the place for you. Why don't you leave with us tonight?" The compassion in Steve's face was her undoing.

She looked back at Harry. He was livid, wanted to hurt her physically, emotionally, any way he could. It seemed as if there had been someone wanting to hurt her all her life.

But Steve and Grace didn't. They wanted to help. She just hoped she didn't disappoint them.

Andrea slipped her jacket all the way onto her body. "Okay, I'll come with you."

There was nothing worth keeping her here.

Chapter One

Four years later, Andrea stood in front of a bathroom mirror inside Omega Sector headquarters. She smoothed her straight black skirt and made sure—again—that her blouse was tucked in neatly before checking her reflection in the bathroom mirror one last time. Blond hair, cut in a sleek bob—the most professional haircut she'd been able to think of—was perfectly in place. Makeup tastefully applied and nothing that would draw attention to herself.

She was about to be fired from her job as a behavioral analyst at Omega Sector's Critical Response Division.

Why else would Steve Drackett be calling her into his office at ten thirty on a Monday morning?

Actually, she could think of a half dozen reasons why he would be calling her in: a new case, a new test, some assignment he needed her to work on or a video briefing where her analysis was needed. But her brain wasn't interested in focusing on any of the logical reasons he wanted to meet with her.

"Steve and Grace both know your background and still want you here," she told her reflection. The scared look didn't leave her eyes. She forced herself to vacate the bathroom and head down the hall. If Steve was going to fire her, there was nothing she could do about it.

No one said hello to her as she walked through the corridors and Andrea didn't engage anyone. She'd utilized this keep-to-herself plan ever since she had realized exactly how important Omega was and the caliber of people they had working here in the Critical Response Division. Ever since Steve and Grace had officially offered her a job four years ago after six weeks of testing.

She may have a gift of reading people, but Andrea didn't think for one minute that she was the sort of person Omega normally hired.

She'd known from the beginning she needed to keep her past a secret. Announcing to her colleagues that she was a runaway, dyslexic high school dropout who—oh yeah—*used to be an exotic dancer* would not inspire much confidence in her. So she'd made it a point not to tell anyone. Not to ever discuss her past or personal life at all. If it didn't involve a case, Andrea didn't talk about it.

Her plan hadn't won her any friends, but it had successfully worked at keeping her secrets. She could live without friends.

Andrea pushed on the door that led to the outer realm where Steve's assistants worked. One of them stood, welcoming and walking her to Steve's office door and opening it. The clicks of Andrea's three-inch heels on the tiled floor sounded more like clanging chimes of doom in her head as she stepped through.

"Hey, Andrea, good to see you," Steve said from behind his desk, looking up from a stack of papers.

She supposed he was handsome, with his brown hair graying slightly at the temples and his sharp blue eyes, but since he was nearly twenty years older than her, she'd never even thought of him in that way. She respected him with every fiber of her being. Not only for getting her out of a dead-end life back at Jaguar's in Buckeye, Arizona, but because of how fair and respectful he acted toward all the people who worked at Omega.

But he was tired. Andrea could tell. "You need a vacation, boss. Some time away from this circus."

Steve put his elbows on his desk and bridged his fingers together, grimacing just the slightest bit. "You know why I don't invite you in here very often? Because you see too much." But his words held no fire. He knew what she said was right.

Andrea nodded.

"Sit down, Andrea. I'm afraid what I have to say might be a little difficult to hear."

Oh my God, he is *going to fire me.*

Andrea took a breath through her nose and tried not to let her panic show. She had known this was a possibility from the beginning. Not just a possibility, a *probability.*

She tried to mentally regroup. Okay, she wasn't the same girl who had left with Steve and Grace from Buckeye. She had managed to successfully complete her high school equivalency degree and even had two years of college under her belt. Yes, her dyslexia made some classes difficult, and she had to take them at a slower pace than most people, but she was making progress.

She could get some other job now. She had money in savings. She didn't have to go back to Jaguar's and let those people paw at her again.

"Andrea."

Steve's tone made her realize it wasn't the first time he'd said her name. She finally forced herself to focus on what he was saying.

"I don't need to have your gift to see that you're panicking. What the hell is going on in that brain of yours?" She could feel waves of concern flowing from him, and it was easily readable on his face.

She rubbed her skirt again. "Steve, I understand if you need to let me go. I've always known that was a possibility—"

"Andrea, I'm not firing you."

"But you said this may be difficult."

"And it probably will be, but why don't you let me finish before you jump to conclusions."

Now Andrea felt the reprimand. She sank back a little in her chair. "Yes, sir."

"I need you for a case."

He really wasn't firing her. "Okay."

"It involves a serial killer. He's been striking in the Phoenix area, with the last woman found dead just outside of Buckeye."

Her hometown. Now his concern made sense.

"And you want me to go there." It wasn't a question.

"I think your ability as a behavioral analyst, plus your knowledge of and history with the area, makes you one of our best chances of stopping this guy as quickly as possible."

She was glad she wasn't being fired, but Steve was right—this was hard. She didn't want to go back to Buckeye. When she'd left there that night with Steve and Grace, she'd never returned. She'd gone back inside Jaguar's to collect her personal belongings and her tips and had told Harry she wasn't coming back.

She'd been glad to have Grace, obviously a cop and obviously carrying a weapon, standing behind her as she did it, because she didn't think Harry would've taken it so well otherwise. As it was, his face had turned a molten red, small eyes narrowed even further. But he hadn't stopped her.

She'd never really explained it all to Steve, but Jaguar's was really just the tip of her iceberg of bad memories when it came to Buckeye. The situation she'd lived through the years before she'd run away from her aunt and uncle's home had been much worse. She still bore a few scars to prove that.

"I know this is hard for you." Steve was studying her carefully from behind his desk.

"Buckeye is not somewhere I'd choose to visit." The understatement of the century.

Steve came around to sit on his desk, closer to her. "Andrea, you're not the same person Grace and I met in Buckeye four years ago. You're stronger, more confident, able to handle the stress of this job, which isn't a light matter."

"Yeah, but—"

"I know you feel like you don't have the same educational background or experience of most of the people actively working cases at Omega. But you have a natural talent at reading people that continues to be honed."

"But—"

Steve wasn't really interested in her arguments. "I can think of a dozen cases, just off the top of my head, where your assistance provided the primary components needed to allow us to make an arrest."

Andrea took a breath. She knew that. Intellectually, she knew all that Steve spoke was the truth. But it was so hard.

"You've got to stop thinking I'm about to fire you every time I call you to my office. I'm not, trust me. I can't afford to lose such a valuable member of the Omega team."

Steve radiated sincerity. Of course, he always had. And she did believe she was part of the team. A noneducated, ex-stripper part of the team, but part of the team.

Okay, she could handle this. She could handle going back to Buckeye.

"Of course, we won't be sending you alone. You and Brandon Han will be working together."

Andrea smiled through gritted teeth, glad that Steve wasn't as skilled at reading people as she was. Brandon Han, as in *Dr.* Brandon Han, with something like two PhDs and an IQ higher than Einstein. They called him "the machine." He was considered the best and most brilliant profiler at Omega.

Not to mention he was hotter than sin. Tall, black hair, with a prominent Asian heritage.

"Do you know Brandon?"

Besides when she'd fantasized about him? "Um, I've never worked any cases with him, but I've met him a couple of times, briefly."

She wasn't sure he would even remember meeting her.

"Great. He'll be here any minute. Then we can go over details and get you guys going today."

BRANDON HAN WAS running a little late for his meeting with Steve but knew his boss would understand. Brandon had just come from visiting the widow and kids of his ex-partner.

Brandon didn't get by to see them as much as he liked, but he knew there were other Omega people checking in on them, also. David Vickars had been a well-liked and respected member of the team. He'd had the backs of many agents over the years, and the Omega family didn't forget their own.

David had died a year ago from a foe even Omega couldn't fight: cancer. He'd worked active duty until a month before he died from an inoperable tumor, then spent his last weeks with his wife and kids.

Brandon and David had been partners for seven years and had been friends for long before that. Brandon hadn't been interested in working with a partner since David died.

But he knew the minute he walked into Steve Drackett's office and saw beautiful, blonde Andrea Gordon sitting in a chair, body language screaming nervousness, that he was about to get partnered again.

Damn it.

Brandon had become quite adept at working alone. He

liked the quiet. He liked being able to work at his own pace, which—no conceit intended—was often quite a bit faster than everyone else's.

"Hey, Steve," he greeted his boss. He nodded at Andrea, but she'd looked away. Par for the course for her. She'd looked away every time he'd ever been in the same room with her.

Drackett stood from behind his desk and shook Brandon's hand. "Let's go over to the conference table to talk about a case."

Steve was moving them to neutral ground, not wanting to pull rank from behind his desk if he didn't have to. He wanted Brandon to agree to whatever was about to be asked without having to force him. If Brandon wasn't mistaken, his boss's friendliness had to do with Andrea. A protectiveness maybe.

"Sure," Brandon agreed amicably. He might as well let this play out.

Andrea stood and joined them. Brandon held out a chair for her, waiting to see if she was one of those women who got offended by the gesture. That would tell him a lot about her.

But she just looked surprised for a moment before taking the chair he held out. He helped slide it in as she sat.

Okay, not afraid of her own femininity and didn't feel that every situation needed to be a struggle of power.

"You've met Andrea Gordon?" Steve asked, glancing at them.

"Yes, a couple of times. Good to see you again."

"Yes, you too," she murmured, voice soft. Sweet, even.

"We've got a serial killer working in the Phoenix area. Three dead so far." Steve handed them both a file.

"Confirmed serial?" Brandon asked, glancing through the file.

"Pretty much as confirmed as these things can get. All

three were women in their early twenties. All were found covered in some sort of white cloth and holding a lotus flower."

"Purity," Andrea muttered.

"What?" Steve asked.

Andrea shrugged. "Lotus flowers are the symbol of purity in some cultures."

"She's right," Brandon said. "And so is the white cloth. Almost like a cleansing ritual."

"Okay, that's something to go on. I'll need you two to leave tonight. The local police department is expecting you."

"Steve, since David…" *Died.* Brandon found it difficult to say the word even now a year later, so he just didn't. "Since David, I've been working alone. That's been going pretty well for me. I think I'm more productive that way."

Brandon turned to Andrea. "I mean that as no offense to you whatsoever."

Some emotion passed across her face but was gone before he—even with all his training—could read it. Frustrating.

"I understand," she said, nodding.

"Brandon, the last murder took place inside the town limits of Buckeye, on the outskirts of Phoenix. That's where Andrea is from. With ritual killings like this, we both know it's usually someone from the area."

Brandon grimaced. He couldn't deny that. Having someone familiar with the area—especially someone with a stellar skill set like Andrea's—would be invaluable.

But still, Brandon didn't want to work with her. Didn't want to be in forced proximity with her for an extended length of time. He glanced over at her but she wasn't looking at him, again. She was studying the pictures in the file, as if she couldn't care less about the conversation going on around her.

Brandon's eyes narrowed. No, he did not want to partner with this woman for a case. He'd discovered over the past year that he liked working alone, but it was more than that.

He didn't trust Andrea. The woman had secrets. Secrets tended to blow up in everyone's faces at the most inopportune moments.

David had kept his illness a secret from everyone for as long as he could. Brandon didn't want to be around secrets anymore.

He especially didn't want to be around a stunningly beautiful woman with secrets. The kind of woman who made him want to toss out his never-mix-business-with-pleasure rule. The kind that made him want to find out all her secrets.

He didn't trust her and she was distracting. She damn well had distracted him every time he'd seen her the past few months. Including today. Her perfect legs in her perfect suit with her perfect hair and makeup. It all distracted him.

He was not a man who liked to be distracted.

Brandon could kill a man a dozen ways with his bare hands, but it wasn't his strength or speed he relied on to get ahead of criminals. He relied on his intellect, his education, his experience to stop the worst of the worst bad guys.

Having Andrea Gordon's distracting presence around him during a serial-killer case was just not going to work.

He leaned back in his chair and feigned a casualness he didn't have. "I just think it's better for me to work alone on this case."

Because he wasn't sure he'd be able to work at all otherwise.

Chapter Two

"She has secrets, Steve. Something she's not telling people."

Steve had already excused Andrea from his office and had told her—much to Brandon's vexation—to go pack for the trip to Buckeye.

"We all have secrets." Steve had moved himself back behind his desk. Evidently time for neutral ground was over. Steve was reaffirming that he was in charge.

"Do you know what they call her around here?"

Steve raised one eyebrow.

"'The ice queen.' She never talks to anyone, never engages anyone. Nobody knows anything about her."

"Just because she's not the life of the party makes her an ice queen? I thought better of you, Han."

Brandon didn't know why he felt the need to so quickly defend himself, but he did. "Not me. I didn't say that or think it, nor any of our inner group. It's just what I've heard some other people say."

"She's damn good at what she does. Next time someone wants to talk trash about her because she's not all touchy-feely, you be sure to tell them that."

"We all know she's good. She's a natural reader. I've never seen anything like it." Brandon held a PhD in interpersonal communication and still couldn't read people's expressions and body language to the extent Andrea could.

"But?"

"No buts about that. All I'm saying is she has secrets."

"She has a past, Brandon. We all do. Hers is a little more bleak than most of ours. If she's got secrets it's because she wants to not live in that past."

Brandon had to admit there was nothing wrong with that.

"I know it hurt you when David didn't tell you about his cancer. To find out then lose him so quickly was tough. It was for all of us."

Brandon got up out of his chair and walked over to the window. "I want to say this isn't about David, but of course that's not true."

"I know he was your best friend too, Brandon."

Brandon nodded without turning around. David had been his best friend since long before they worked together at Omega. David had been his anchor when the darkness of wandering inside the minds of killers had become too much.

"Andrea's the top person for this case, just like you're the top person for this case. There's somebody out there murdering young women and he needs to be stopped before he kills again."

Brandon knew Steve was right.

"Andrea's young, only twenty-three," Steve continued. "She's unsure about her abilities and where she fits in here."

Twenty-three? Something inside Brandon eased. She *was* young. Brandon was only thirty-one, but twenty-three seemed like a lifetime ago. He'd been more unsure about himself then too, so he couldn't blame her.

"You know me, Steve. I like having all the facts going into anything. She's an unknown variable and it gets my hackles up."

"I know some of what she keeps to herself, and although

I am not at liberty to share, what I know about her makes me respect her more, not less. But some of her secrets she's never shared with me. May not have shared them with anyone. That's her choice."

Brandon nodded. As Steve said, everyone had secrets.

"She's damn good at her job and she'll help you find that killer."

Brandon ran a hand over his face. "Okay, you're right. I'll go pack."

"Han, thank you," Steve said as Brandon turned for the door. "I know this isn't easy."

"Like you said, the important thing is getting the killer off the street."

"Going back to that town is not going to be easy for her. I'd appreciate if you'd just keep an eye out for her emotional well-being."

"Anything in particular I should know about?"

Steve shrugged. "It's where she grew up. Faster than most, I would venture."

Somehow Brandon got the feeling there was a huge chunk of information Steve was leaving out, but he let it slide. "Okay, I'll keep an eye out for her as best I can. Is that it?"

"Actually, no."

Brandon didn't even try to refrain from rolling his eyes. "There's more?"

"It's probably nothing, but I wanted to make you aware of it." Steve's tone had turned from concerned to downright serious.

Brandon walked back toward his desk. "Okay."

"Damian Freihof escaped from federal custody thirty-six hours ago."

Brandon filtered his mind for the information, finding it. "He was the guy who planned to blow up those people in that bank in Phoenix, right? What, three years ago?"

"Four. We also think he was responsible for two other bombings, but we weren't able to prove it."

"Do you suspect he's in Buckeye?"

"No. But like you said, the bank he tried to blow up was in Phoenix, pretty close by. He blames Andrea for his arrest."

"Why? Was she even there?"

"She was there, and she was the one who led to his capture, although she was not in law enforcement at the time."

Yeah, because at the time she would've been nineteen years old, if Brandon's math was correct.

"Did you tell Andrea about his escape?"

Steve's hesitation was minuscule, fleeting. Brandon would've missed it if he hadn't been trained to see it. "No, we chose not to tell her. When Freihof went to prison, Andrea was not yet working for us. Plus with two life sentences we didn't figure he would be getting out until he was at least eighty. He escaped during a transfer."

"You think keeping her out of the loop is wise?"

Steve shrugged. "Freihof was mad at pretty much everyone during his case and sentencing, so we didn't—and still don't—give his threats against Andrea much credence. We're not even sure how he got Andrea's name since she wasn't involved in his arrest or trial, but I doubt he's after her now. All she really did was let us know there was a third man in the bank. I don't think she had any idea he planned to blow everyone up and that her info thwarted his attempt."

Another secret. Another potential problem.

"All right." Brandon nodded. "I'll keep my eyes peeled for any extra psychos while we're chasing down our current one."

Steve smiled. "Remember, she's not an agent, just a full-time consultant. She has some physical training, but not nearly as much as you do."

"Okay. I'll keep that in mind."

Steve shook Brandon's hand. "Good hunting. Keep me posted."

Brandon nodded and headed toward the door. This was already more complicated than Brandon liked it. And he knew it was just going to get worse.

BRANDON'S ARRIVAL AT the Colorado Springs Airport three hours later to discover the flight to Phoenix had been delayed due to mechanical issues did not make him feel any better about the start of this case. They were flying commercial since the two Omega jets were occupied with other missions.

Andrea showed up, still looking chic and cool in her skirt and blouse. The ice queen. Brandon wondered if she ever let herself get rumpled. His fingers literally itched with the desire to be the one who did it.

Rumpling Andrea Gordon was such a bad idea.

Brandon had noticed her around Omega for years—it was difficult not to notice someone who looked like Andrea—but he'd been very careful not to allow himself to study her. Not to try to figure out what made her tick and what made her smile or frown. With two advanced degrees in human behavior and communication, not to mention one in law, figuring people out was what Brandon did.

But with Andrea that had seemed a dangerous path to start down.

Then for the past year he'd been so involved in his own issues—David's death, learning how to work alone—that his attraction for Andrea had gotten pushed to the back burner. But now it was sitting down next to him in the airport chair, unavoidable.

"Hello." She smiled briefly at him. "Ready for this?"

Andrea wanted to be professional. Everything about her suggested it, from her prim clothes, to her tasteful makeup, to her perfect hair. Brandon would answer in kind. Professional was better for both of them.

He nodded. "Not quite up to speed yet, but getting there. We're scheduled to meet with the Phoenix and Buckeye police tomorrow. Evidently Buckeye's department isn't equipped to handle a homicide investigation, so Phoenix is helping out."

"Buckeye is small. They don't get many serial killers."

"Let's hope we can stop this one before he kills again."

He found her studying him as he took some files out of his briefcase, her expression a little bemused. "What?"

"Nothing." She shook her head. "You're just…complicated."

Brandon's eyes narrowed. Quite the interesting observation. "Why do you say that?"

She shrugged. "Most people only have one or maybe two main emotions transpiring inside them at the same time. You have more." Her lips pursed. "And they're complex."

He did have more. Brandon knew that about himself. Knew that he compartmentalized in order to be able to get more done, to think about different things without actually dwelling on them.

It was part of what made him a good profiler. His subconscious brain was able to continue to work on certain aspects of a case while his conscious brain focused on something entirely different. Part of it was his own natural ability and intelligence. Part of it came from years of training his brain to do what he wanted.

He also had darkness in him. He could admit that, too. A side of him that knew he could use his intellect and training and experience to commit crimes if he really wanted. And would probably never get caught. It was never too far from the surface, although he never shared it with anyone.

Brandon had never had someone—especially someone

who didn't really know him well—sense the complexity of the emotions inside him. It was disconcerting, particularly because he didn't want her to be able to read him so well.

"Oh." Andrea looked away from him.

"What?"

"Annoyance just swamped out pretty much everything else." She folded her hands in her lap and looked at them.

She thought he was annoyed with her, when really his annoyance stemmed from not having as much control over expressing his emotions as he thought he had. That was the problem with naturals, with people who were just gifted behavioral analysts rather than those who had studied human psychology and nonverbal communication to become experts. The naturals could read the emotions but couldn't always figure out the context.

"Let's just focus on the case, okay?" He handed her a bundle of files. "We pretty much need to be completely familiar with all of this before we meet with the locals tomorrow."

Andrea grimaced. "Okay."

So she didn't like to do her homework. She wouldn't get far solving cases without it. No amount of skill reading people could offset having a good understanding of the particulars of a case.

Brandon began reading through the files. He often found that insight came after the third or fourth read-through, rarely the first.

It didn't take him long to realize Andrea wasn't reading. She was looking at the photographs—the postmortem shots of the women as well as the crime-scene photos—but not actually reading any of the information that went along with them.

When she slipped on headphones and began listening to music or whatever, Brandon felt his irritation grow. Did she need a sound track to make it more interesting? Was death not enough?

Brandon knew different people processed information different ways. Some of his best friends at Omega often got insight on a case while in a workout room or in the middle of hand-to-hand sparring with someone. He should cut Andrea some slack. If she wanted to listen to music and just study the pictures, that was her prerogative.

But damn if it didn't piss him off. It didn't happen often, but she had fooled him. Who would've guessed that under the professional clothes and standoffish attitude rested the heart of a slacker. Brandon took a deep breath and centered himself. It wasn't his fault or his problem if she lacked motivation and self-discipline.

He'd told Steve he preferred to work alone. It looked as if, despite Andrea's attractive packaging, he'd be getting his wish.

Chapter Three

This whole thing was a terrible idea. Going back to Buckeye? Terrible. Going back with the likes of Brandon Han? Even worse. The plane hit some turbulence at thirty-five thousand feet, as if nodding in agreement with Andrea's conclusion.

Brandon didn't want to work with her on the case. He'd made that abundantly clear in Steve's office. She wanted to assume it was her fault, that he knew about her shortcomings and lack of education as an Omega consultant, but forced herself to stop. He'd mentioned liking to work alone. She could understand that, too. Andrea liked working alone, but for different reasons.

Brandon's irritation had been pretty tangible when she'd sat down next to him at the airport. It had just grown as they waited for their flight, first when she'd mentioned him being complicated, then when they were both looking through the case files.

By the time they got on the plane, about an hour after their scheduled departure time, Brandon was hardly even talking to her. He was mad—she had no idea why—and she was awkward—as usual around someone she was so attracted to. Good times.

Andrea tried to pretend she was reading the files when he handed them to her, but she wasn't. She knew better than to even try. Her dyslexia made reading simple books difficult, although she had learned some exercises to help with that. But reading handwritten notes and case files often written in different fonts and sizes—that pretty much just led to a headache and frustration.

She'd had an extra hour at her apartment, so she'd used the special software on her computer to scan a few pages so they could be converted into audio clips. She'd found that listening worked much better for her than trying to read. Unfortunately, she hadn't had enough time to scan all the files as she normally would.

Listening to the files on audio clips had just made Brandon more irritated. Andrea had no idea what to do about that, so she ignored it. She would listen to the clips she had, then spend this evening—all night if she had to—reading through the files in her room, when she was alone and it was quiet. She refused to go into that meeting with the local police tomorrow unprepared.

She didn't want to go back there at all. If it wasn't for Steve asking her to go, Andrea wouldn't have done it, serial killer or not.

Maybe they wouldn't run into anyone she knew. Or maybe the people in Buckeye wouldn't recognize her. She'd gone to great lengths to look nothing like the girl who had worked at Jaguar's. Her blond hair was shorter, cut in a flattering bob; her makeup was tasteful. She'd learned how to dress and present herself in a professional manner.

She doubted her own aunt and uncle would recognize her. Not that she planned to drop in on them. She hadn't seen them since the last time her uncle, in a drunken stupor again, had awakened her with a backhand that had sent her sprawling from her bed to the floor when she was seventeen. Another punch had sent her hurling into a glass table. She'd gotten away from him and hidden that night, wrapping her cut arm in a T-shirt.

The next morning she'd told her aunt, who'd looked the

other way *again* during all the commotion, that she was going to school.

Andrea hadn't gone to school. And she hadn't gone back home. Ever again.

She hadn't gone far, just to the other side of the town she'd only ever known as home, but they hadn't come looking for her. Had probably been relieved that she'd left.

So yeah, no joyous homecoming in Buckeye.

Andrea withdrew into herself as they landed at Sky Harbor Airport. She let Brandon take the lead as they rented a car and headed west on I-10 out of Phoenix, stopping to get something to eat on the way. The stark, flat lands of Arizona were a huge contrast to the backdrop of the Rocky Mountains in Colorado Springs, where she'd spent the past four years.

Coming here was a mistake. Andrea was convinced of it. If she'd been alone, she might have turned around and gone back home.

Home, Colorado Springs. That was her home now.

"Hey, you doing okay?"

Andrea struggled to hide her shock at Brandon's hand on her arm. She didn't think he was going to engage with her for the rest of the trip.

"Yeah. I just… This is hard. I don't think I want to do this."

She could feel his annoyance or coolness, or whatever it was he felt toward her, ease.

"Going back to the place where you grew up can be hard. Is there anyone you'd like to see while you're there? Friends? Family?"

"No, I don't think so. I don't think anyone here will remember me."

He didn't push it and she was thankful. They drove on in silence from the airport west on I-10 before turning south on smaller Highway 85. A couple of miles down they passed her old high school, Buckeye Union. Before thinking it through, she pointed it out to Brandon.

"What year did you graduate?"

She didn't want to tell him that she hadn't graduated, so she told him the year she'd stopped going. Then she realized it might make it sound as if she'd graduated early or something, so she changed it to the next year.

Brandon looked at her with one eyebrow raised, but fortunately, he didn't say anything else about it.

Before she knew it, before she could *stop* it, they were in Buckeye. The town hadn't changed much. They passed the dollar store, one of the town's grocery stores and Buckeye Auto Repair.

She actually remembered Buckeye Auto Repair pretty fondly. They had quite politely not mentioned that it looked as though everything she'd owned was in her car when she'd had to take it in for repairs when she was seventeen.

That was because everything she'd owned *had* been in the car. She'd been living in it at the time. Before she got the job at Jaguar's and made enough money to move into a sparsely furnished, run-down studio apartment.

She was pretty sure the owner of Buckeye Auto Repair hadn't charged her the full price for the repair.

She and Brandon pulled up to the town's one decent hotel. There were a couple of others on the rougher side of town—ones that were rented out by the hour, or the opposite, used to house multiple illegal immigrants in one room. This was a much better choice for law enforcement.

Brandon checked them in, getting rooms right next to each other on the first floor. They grabbed their bags and headed through the lobby and down the hall.

"I'm going to call it a night," Andrea said, slipping the key card into her door. She needed to be alone, away from all her thoughts and feelings about this town. She also needed to begin the painful process of studying the case files before tomorrow's meeting.

"Okay, I'll see you tomorrow. We'll leave at eight o'clock." Brandon turned to his door. "Are you okay?"

Andrea nodded. "Good night." She shut the door behind her without another word, away from Brandon and his brown eyes that saw too much.

Because she wasn't all right. Being back here was worse than she'd thought it would be.

This whole thing was a terrible idea.

THE NEXT MORNING at the Maricopa County Sheriff's Department office, Brandon and Andrea waited in the conference room for the local officers who would serve as their liaisons. The sheriff's department was just a mile or so on the outskirts of Buckeye.

When Andrea had seen what building they were arriving at, her eyes had nearly bugged out of her head. Her skin had turned a concerning shade of gray. Brandon had reached for her hand, and she had clutched his, almost automatically. Her skin was cold, clammy.

A sure nonverbal tell of fright. This building frightened Andrea.

She'd taken a couple of deep breaths and gotten herself under control, releasing his hand. She'd smiled over at him, an expression nowhere near touching her eyes, so nowhere near real. Something about that fake smile nearly broke his heart.

Maybe the whole idea of bringing her back to Buckeye had been a mistake. Her input would be valuable, sure, but Brandon had solved a lot of cases without having an inside person.

Maybe the price of doing this was too high for Andrea. Whatever judgments Brandon had made about her began to dissipate a little. Maybe she just wasn't ready to deal with this.

"Andrea." He'd turned to her from where they sat in the parking lot. "Perhaps this isn't a good idea. It's okay if I need to go in alone."

"No, I'm fine. I just didn't realize we'd be coming *here*, to this building, that's all."

What was here that made her so upset? "You have some history here?"

She took a deep breath. "Not really. This whole town just sets me on edge."

"Are you sure you're okay?" He didn't want her to get inside then panic.

"Yes, I'm fine. I promise." The smile she gave him was at least a little stronger than the shadow of one she'd given him a few moments ago. He touched her hand. It was closer to normal temperature again.

But she looked tired, despite makeup that carefully covered it, as if she had been up most of the night. Maybe she had if the town had this sort of effect on her.

But except for the telltale signs that he was sure only he would notice, looking at her from across the conference table now, she looked like the consummate professional. Andrea wore sharp trousers and a matching blazer, managing to be attractively feminine and coolly businesslike at the same time. The high heels she wore everywhere were the perfect complement to the outfit. Not a hair was out of place in her chic bob.

She may have been scared out in the parking lot, but she was determined not to show it in here. Brandon's respect for her ratcheted a notch. If only she was as prepared for the case as she looked, which he knew she wasn't. Maybe he could help her out if she got stuck, save her any embarrassment.

Two men entered the room, one in his midfifties in a

sheriff's office uniform, one in his early thirties in a suit. Both looked a little tired, frazzled. The older man took the lead. "I'm Lance Kendrick from the Maricopa County Sheriff's Department. Since all three murders took place— or at least the bodies were found—in Maricopa, I'm taking the lead."

"I'm Gerardo Jennison with the City of Phoenix Homicide Unit. We're providing investigative resources for anything which the sheriff's department may not have."

"I'm agent Brandon Han from Omega Sector, as you know. This is Ms. Andrea Gordon, one of our behavioral analysts. She'll be consulting as needed."

As Jennison shook Andrea's hand, Brandon could see his appreciation of her as a woman. Lance Kendrick, on the other hand, studied her pretty intently. Andrea had looked at him when they shook hands, but then glanced away.

Andrea recognized Kendrick.

That wasn't impossible or even improbable. Andrea had lived here her whole life. She probably would've run into members of the sheriff's office from time to time. "Have we met before?" Kendrick asked Andrea.

Her expression remained smooth although she shifted just slightly in her chair. "Maybe." She smiled at him. "Omega works a lot of cases."

A very nice side step. She wasn't offering up that she used to live here or that she recognized Kendrick, so Brandon didn't, either. Her comment seemed to pacify the sheriff's deputy, although Brandon knew that wasn't where they knew each other.

"We have three victims so far," Kendrick said, tone bordering on bored. "All Caucasian females between the ages of twenty to twenty-five. Cause of death was strangulation with a thin rope. The ligature marks were quite clear. All had been restrained—marks on their wrists were obvious, but there was no sign of any other assault, sexual or otherwise. And they all were found outside a church. Different one each time."

Putting the victims outside a church corresponded well with the purity theme he and Andrea had batted around yesterday.

"Any known connection between the victims?" he asked.

"They didn't seem to know each other, as far as we can tell. All lived in Maricopa County, but different parts."

"But two had been arrested for something in the last year or two," Andrea interjected.

Brandon glanced at her discreetly. So she *had* studied the files.

Kendrick nodded. "Different charges, but yes. Brought here for holding, actually. One was arrested for solicitation, one for underage drinking. Neither of them were ever booked or went to trial."

If Brandon hadn't been looking over at Andrea, he would've missed her slight flinch. Had there been some trouble with the law in her past? Was that what made her nervous about this building?

"Occupations were not exactly upstanding, either. Two of them worked at exotic dance clubs somewhere in Phoenix or the surrounding areas. One worked at a diner that is known to be a hot area for solicitation." Jennison grinned slyly at Kendrick.

Kendrick chuckled. "Yeah, I offered to do some undercover work at the clubs, but somehow couldn't clear it with my boss, much less my wife."

Brandon ignored the jokes. He wasn't surprised about the women's occupations. Quite often an arrest record accompanied such jobs.

"What exactly have you done concerning the investigation?" Brandon could hear the tightness in Andrea's tone.

"We've done our due diligence." Kendrick sat up a little

straighter in his chair. "We interviewed employers, canvassed the area for witnesses, ran DNA and searched for any prints."

Jennison interjected. "Look, we appreciate Omega sending you down here, and if you come up with any insight we'd love to hear it. We don't want a killer wandering around loose. But the fact is, none of these women seem to have anyone who cares about them, two have an arrest record and all have employment that is a bit questionable."

Kendrick shrugged. "So basically, we'll do all we can— like Jennison said, nobody wants to let a killer go free— but we're not getting any pressure from the higher-ups to put major resources into this investigation. Unfortunately, these women were pretty much nobodies."

Chapter Four

These women were pretty much nobodies.

No family who cared. Arrest records. Questionable employment.

If the killer had been around four years ago, Andrea might have been one of the victims. Every part of that account described her when she was nineteen, before changing her life at Omega.

She wanted to, but she could hardly blame the cops. Law-enforcement funding was limited. Unfortunately, without family demanding justice, these murders, if not easily solved, would just get pushed to the side.

The only reason Omega had been called at all was because it was obvious the three kills had been performed by the same person. Otherwise Andrea didn't know if the locals would've put any true effort into finding the killer.

They were on their way now to The Boar's Nest, one of three bars here in Buckeye, where the latest victim—Noelle Brumby—had been known to frequent. It was two o'clock in the afternoon, but evidently Noelle had hung out here in the afternoons since she worked nights.

Andrea's weariness pressed against her—reviewing the case files had taken her most of the night—but she pushed it aside. She had made it through talking to Lance Kendrick, who had thankfully not remembered her from her brief run-in with the sheriff's office for underage drinking years ago. She could make it through this.

Walking inside, she thought The Boar's Nest looked just the way someone would expect a small-town bar to look in the middle of the afternoon: dingy, run-down, pathetic. Night hid a lot of sins of this place that sunlight brought out.

The Tuesday afternoon crowd wasn't the most upstanding. Anybody who had a white-collar job, and even most of the blue-collar ones, would not be in this place at this time. The people patronizing The Boar's Nest now worked nights or didn't work at all.

Andrea heard a low whistle as they walked in, but didn't know if it was for her looks or because they were obviously law enforcement. Nobody ran for the exit or stopped any activities suddenly, so at least it didn't appear that anything illegal was happening.

She felt Brandon step closer to her and could see him looking around, obviously checking for any danger. Cops were sometimes not welcome in places like this, although that would not stop her and Brandon from their questioning. Brandon had a weapon, but Andrea didn't. Hopefully he wouldn't need to use it.

Two pool tables lined the far end of the room, with three guys playing on one. A bartender unpacked boxes and put glasses away behind the bar, and a couple sat at a table sipping beers in the corner.

All of them were looking at Brandon and Andrea.

Brandon touched her gently on the back—she knew it was an unconscious habit more than anything else but it still sent a slight shiver through her—and they headed toward the bar.

The bartender looked at them without halting his motions. "Lost or cops?"

Brandon chuckled. "Can't be thirsty?"

"Yeah, you can. And I'll gladly get you something, but I'm still pretty sure you're one of the other two, also."

"You're right—the latter. We're investigating the death of Noelle Brumby."

The bartender stopped putting away the glasses. "Yeah, that was a damn shame. She was a nice girl. Friendly. I'm Phil. I own this bar."

Andrea studied Phil while he talked. He seemed very sincere about liking Noelle.

"Can you tell us anything else about her?" Brandon asked.

"She worked at a…er, gentleman's club closer in to Phoenix."

Allure. They already knew that and would be interviewing people there soon, even though Kendrick and Jennison had also spoken with them.

"Why didn't she work at Jaguar's, do you know?" Andrea was hesitant to bring up her former place of employment in front of Brandon, but understanding why Noelle would drive farther to work at a club rather than work at the strip club here in town might have some bearing.

Both the bartender and Brandon looked a little surprised at her question.

"You from around here?" Phil asked. "You've never been in this bar before. I'm pretty sure I'd remember you."

"I've driven through town a few times." Better to just keep her past out of it.

"Noelle didn't like the owner over at Jaguar's. Had heard some bad things about him. Harry Minkley's his name."

Yeah, Andrea already knew Harry's name. And she was glad Noelle had the good sense not to work for him. Although in the long run, it hadn't helped her.

"Noelle came in here a lot?" Brandon leaned one arm against the bar so he had a better view of the whole place.

"Mostly during the week in the afternoons. Weekends were pretty busy for her, as were a lot of evenings. She hung out with those guys over there. The tall, skinny one's named Corey. Big one next to him is Luke and the other is Jarrod." He pointed back to where the three guys were playing pool. "They knew her better than me."

Brandon and Andrea both turned toward the men. "Thanks for your help," she said over her shoulder.

"Thank you for trying to find the killer." Phil turned back to his unpacking. "I wondered if anyone would bother."

The three younger men—all in their early to mid-twenties—continued to play pool as she and Brandon made their way over. But she could tell they were quite aware of her and Brandon as law enforcement and of her as a woman.

"Hey, guys." Brandon's tone was friendly but firm. "We'd like to talk to you about Noelle Brumby."

Andrea tried to watch all three as closely as she could. Two, Luke and Corey, immediately tensed, but she wasn't sure if that was because of their relationship with Noelle or because they just didn't like cops. The other one, Jarrod, definitely expressed some guilt at Noelle's name, but mostly couldn't seem to get his attention off Andrea.

Andrea tried to classify in her mind the reactions of each man. She wished she could record them and study them multiple times later, but she didn't have that luxury in this situation.

"What makes you think we even knew her?" Luke asked, now holding the pool cue with white knuckles.

"Phil said she hung out with you three a lot."

"Yeah, well, maybe Phil should keep his mouth shut," defensive guy number two—Corey—muttered, not looking up from the shot he was making.

Brandon walked around the pool table so he was standing against the far wall. Andrea understood why he did it, to get a different angle and perspective for reading these guys, but she felt more exposed without him next to her.

"We're trying to find the killer of someone who was your friend. I'd think you'd want to help with that." Brandon was watching Luke and Corey as he made the statement—one meant to cause a reaction. Andrea turned her attention to Jarrod, only to find him overtly studying her, so she looked back at the other two men.

"Some sicko killed Noelle," Luke said. "We don't know anything about it."

Corey was looking more and more uncomfortable. "What's your name?" she asked softly even though she already knew.

"You don't have to answer that, Corey." Luke wasn't too smart.

Jarrod laughed from where he stood against the wall. "You just told her his name, Luke. Dumb ass." Of course, he'd just done the same thing.

"Corey—" Andrea took a step toward the other man "—do you know something? Anything that could help us find Noelle's killer?"

"No." Corey shook his head, not really looking at her. "I don't know anything."

Andrea was about to press further with Corey when Jarrod interrupted.

"Oh my gawd, are you Andrea Gordon?" Jarrod all but gushed. "It is you, right? You were in one of my math classes in high school. I'm Jarrod McConnachie."

Damn it. Andrea knew she might be recognized at some point, but hadn't thought it would be by some guys in a bar in the middle of the afternoon.

Luke tilted his head to one side. "Oh yeah, I think I remember you. You were pretty quiet. But always hot." All three men snickered.

Oh God, had they come to see her dance when she worked at Jaguar's? She'd always worn wigs and enough makeup to give herself an entirely different appearance, but the thought they might recognize her and announce it made her absolutely sick.

"I thought you'd moved away your junior year," Jarrod said.

She hadn't moved away, really just to the other side of town. But she'd dropped out of school. "Yeah, something like that."

"But I still kept seeing your mom and dad around. So then I didn't know what happened to you. A couple people thought you'd died and they just hadn't announced it."

It was good to know a few people noticed she was gone.

"It was my aunt and uncle I lived with, not my mom and dad. But yeah, they stayed here when I left." They'd never once tried to find her, thank God. That last time when she'd fallen through the table, they had probably been afraid they might go to jail. Looking for her wouldn't have been in their best interest.

Andrea should've gone to the police. She knew that now. Knew there were good officers out there—Omega worked with them all the time—who wanted to help. Who would've believed her or at least have thoroughly investigated. But at the time she'd been young and scared and thought all cops were the enemy.

The exact way these guys thought of them, too. She needed to get the questions back on track but had no idea how to do so.

"Well, you sure cleaned up nice," Jarrod said, moving slightly closer. "And you're a cop. I'd be happy to let you cuff me to anything you want."

The other guys chuckled.

"How about if I cuff you and throw you in a cell with a couple of long-term criminals?" Brandon interjected, coming to stand next to Andrea again. "Would that work for you?"

"Look, man—" Jarrod backed off "—I was just trying to say hello to an old friend."

Brandon's eyes narrowed. "Instead, why don't all of you tell us where you were on Friday night between midnight and 4:00 a.m.?"

The body had been found Saturday afternoon, but the coroner put the time of death as late Friday night or early Saturday morning.

"I was at home with my wife," Corey said. Brandon marked it down in a notebook.

"I was in Phoenix at a bar with a bunch of friends," Luke said, giving its name. "We started home after last call." He glanced down before looking up defiantly at Brandon and Andrea.

There was definitely more to that story. Luke's emotions weren't necessarily guilt in a specific sense, but a sort of overall vague sense of shame.

"I was at my house sleeping, after walking home from here. I live off Old Highway 80," Jarrod said, still staring openly at Andrea.

"You live alone?" Brandon asked.

Both the other men snickered. Brandon raised an eyebrow. "What?"

"No," Luke said. "He lives with his mother."

Jarrod turned away, grimacing. "Thanks, Luke."

Andrea couldn't help but smile a little at Jarrod's comeuppance. Especially since his desire to bed her practically oozed from his pores. He wasn't even trying to hide his craving for Andrea.

"Your mom can vouch that you were at the house?" Brandon asked Jarrod.

"Yeah, man. She's always at home. Gets so angry at me whenever I go out."

Probably pretty angry that Jarrod didn't have a job, ei-ther, but Andrea didn't mention that. Didn't want to draw the attention back to herself.

She watched all three men as Brandon got their names and contact information. He explained that, at this point, they were eliminating suspects. Telling the truth now would save them from more trouble later. Although none of them were thrilled at giving the info, none of them re-sisted.

Jarrod tried to talk to her while Brandon spoke with the other men, but she wouldn't engage with him. She'd had plenty of practice being standoffish over the past few years. Shutting him down was easy.

Plus, she wondered if he wasn't trying to get on her good side because he was hiding something.

One thing she knew for sure as she and Brandon left the bar, waving to bartender Phil as they went—all three men they'd interviewed today had secrets. All of them had lied or withheld information in some way.

Chapter Five

They spent the entire next day traveling around Phoenix
and Buckeye, checking alibis, talking to the employers
and colleagues of the women.

As the detectives had said, none of the victims had family who had spoken up. It didn't seem as if they had many
friends, either. The killer had chosen well: women whose
deaths would go relatively unnoticed. Only the ritualistic
placement of the bodies and the symbolic items found with
each victim even clued in law enforcement that it was the
same killer at all.

The killer probably hadn't been able to stop himself
from placing the symbols of purity around the women,
even if he'd intellectually recognized that it could lead to
his demise. The purity rituals had been just as important
to the killer as the kill itself.

The killer was calm, sure of himself—almost definitely
a *he* based on the nature of the crimes and the fact that the
victims were all females. These murders hadn't been done
in rage. There had been no mutilation of the bodies, no
bruising beyond the restraints on the wrists and the rope
marks around the throat.

If he let himself, Brandon could perfectly envision the
rope tightening around the victims' throats. The killer most
certainly would've had them on their knees—an act of re-
pentance, needed before one could be deemed pure.

The killer hadn't been interested in the women sexually—or perhaps he had and wouldn't let himself act on it—only in freeing them from their evil. Cleansing them.

Brandon had been sitting in his hotel room for the past hour, looking blankly ahead. To most people it would've seemed as if he was staring out into nothing, but really he was giving his mind a quiet place to sort through all the data he'd been processing for the past forty-eight hours.

Letting his mind get into the head of a killer.

It wasn't a comfortable place to be, and since David's death, Brandon didn't let himself get in that dark place too often.

Brandon was aware of the dark side of his intelligence, of his nature. Was well aware that immersing himself deep into the thoughts of a killer could leave him tainted by that darkness.

And now there was no one to drag him back but himself. No one to warn him when he was getting too close to the abyss. It was one of the things he missed most about having a partner he trusted.

And speaking of partners, it was time to meet his temporary one. When they'd arrived back at the hotel, Andrea had all but fled into her room. She'd said it was because she wanted to look over some notes from today's interviews, but Brandon knew that couldn't be it. She hadn't taken any notes all day.

She was an enigma. Her work ethic seemed impeccable—she was punctual, attentive and focused—but then she'd do something completely unprofessional like refuse to take any notes.

Even Brandon took notes. He realized a long time ago his brain—all brains—were capable of great things, but they were never infallible. Evidently Andrea thought hers was the exception.

He should be thankful for her flaw. For her reminder

that he didn't want someone like her as a partner. Because if he woke up one more time, his body hard and wound up, dreaming about her—about kissing her and removing all the professional clothes she wore like armor—he was afraid he would act on it.

He needed to keep his distance.

Pulling rank and forcing her to have dinner with him was not helping with that plan. She'd wanted to camp out in her own room all evening, grab some crackers, go over what they'd found. He'd told her they needed to eat real food and could discuss the case while doing so. She put up a bit of an argument, but he hadn't listened, just threatened to bring dinner to her hotel room so they could work there.

That got her agreement.

He moved into the lobby to meet her. They were going to walk a few blocks down the street to the mom-and-pop Italian restaurant. He saw her as she walked in the lobby just moments later. He had changed into jeans and a T-shirt, but she still wore her pants and blazer from the interviews earlier. She looked nice, no doubt about that. But definitely not casual or comfortable. He wondered if she ever looked casual or comfortable, if she ever just let herself relax around anyone.

He couldn't seem to make himself stop looking at her. Damn, he wanted to peel her out of those clothes. To see if there was any fire underneath and disprove the ice-queen theory. To show her that it was okay to *let go* with him. To protect her from whatever demons she was fighting. The sudden overwhelming thoughts caught him off guard.

"What?" she asked at his continued stare.

"Nothing. Just hungry. Ready?"

After walking to the restaurant and ordering, Andrea immediately brought up the case, obviously wanting to offset the chance of talking about anything personal. That was fine with Brandon. He hoped to use this time not only to go over the case, but to give her a lesson in law enforcement about the need to take notes. He wanted to point out how many things she missed by not taking notes and trying to keep it all in her head.

"So what do we know about each of the victims? Let's make sure we haven't missed any details," he said as the waitress brought their salads and they began eating.

Andrea nodded. "Victim one, Yvette Tyler, found two weeks ago. Twenty-one years old, brunette, five feet five inches, 115 pounds. No family. Place of employment— Diamond Cabaret Strip Club in Phoenix."

Her lips pursed the slightest bit with that sentence. Evidently she didn't approve of that career choice.

Brandon continued. "She was arrested last year for drunk and disorderly, and underage drinking, but since she had no record the charges were dropped."

"Yes. Victim two, Ashley Judson, found six days ago. Eighteen years old, worked at a diner west of here in Tonopah on I-10."

"That truck stop is known to be a place for truckers to pick up women, and women to pick up rides, literally and figuratively."

Andrea smiled a little at that and speared another bite of her salad. "Judson had also been arrested for solicitation, no surprise there. Spent a couple of nights at the Maricopa County lockup, too. Charges were dropped because of some technicality."

"And we have Noelle Brumby."

"Yes, twenty-three, blond. Worked at Allure in Phoenix."

She knew her facts better than he'd thought. Maybe he'd misjudged her at the airport when he'd thought she was just skimming over the files.

The waitress brought their main course. Andrea had

ordered chicken Alfredo; Brandon had gotten lasagna. He had to admit, it smelled delicious.

"So give me your opinion of Noelle's friends, the guys at the bar yesterday. Jarrod and the other two."

"Luke and Corey," she murmured, taking a bite.

Hmm. That had been his first attempt to catch her, to use as an example later of why she should take notes. Guess that wouldn't work.

"They're all hiding something," she said.

"Something about Noelle's death?"

She shrugged. "Tied to it, probably yes, although I don't think any of them are the killer."

Interesting. "Okay, tell me what you saw and what you concluded."

"Corey looks most guilty at first glance. Or at least he feels guilty about something."

Brandon had noticed that, also. "Go on."

"I think he was either having an affair with her or was in love with her or both. His guilt probably stems from a lot of things—failure to help Noelle, his feelings about cheating on his wife, not being able to do anything about it now."

"I agree."

She nodded. "And he's scared. That's what initially made me think he might be the killer, but I think he's scared that his wife is going to find out. That the investigation will uncover the affair."

"What about the defensive guy, Luke?" He took a bite of his lasagna. It tasted as good as it smelled. "You think he's hiding something, too?"

"He definitely has no love for law enforcement."

Brandon chuckled; that had been clear enough for a blind person to see.

"He also didn't want us looking into his alibi at the bar."

That was interesting. Something he hadn't picked up on.

He slowed his chewing. "Okay, why do you think that? His alibi checked out today."

She shrugged. "He definitely had a vibe, something he didn't want discovered. After talking to the bartenders today, I think it was probably that he and his friends drove home drunk. They were definitely drinking enough to be drunk, and then according to his own testimony he drove himself home."

A good insight.

She took another bite. "Or his guilt may have been about some sexual shenanigans they got into. Maybe he seduced some girl in the bathroom and feels a little bad about that— I don't know." She couldn't quite keep eye contact with him as she said it.

She couldn't look at him when talking about sex. Maybe he wasn't the only person affected when the two of them were together. Maybe Little Miss Professional wasn't as buttoned-up as he thought.

"Okay, interesting theories."

"But not pertaining to the case, so not important." She frowned and stabbed her pasta with more force than necessary.

"I didn't say that. Understanding—getting inside their heads, their desires—can lead you to the right path. It's not always a direct route, but it almost always helps."

She shrugged. "Only if it's the actual criminal. Otherwise you're wasting time."

"Eliminating someone isn't a waste of time. It's one step closer to the truth."

"Well, I don't think either Luke or Corey are our killer. I think they're up to no good in at least some part of their lives, but not killing."

"And Jarrod?"

"I didn't really get a read off him, one way or another.

He was embarrassed to still be living at home, I know that."

Brandon had gotten a read off Jarrod. Not because of his skill as a profiler, but because he was a man.

Jarrod wanted Andrea. It had pretty much consumed the man's thoughts. That neither cleared him nor made him guilty. His mother had told them that Jarrod was home when they talked to her today, but she had to admit, she hadn't actually been in the room with him during any of the hours in question.

Jarrod could've come home then sneaked back out.

Of course, nothing about Jarrod matched the profile Brandon was developing in his mind. Jarrod wasn't methodical or meticulous like the killer, so Brandon wasn't looking at the younger man as a true suspect yet. However, Brandon still might find reason to arrest him if he kept making moves toward Andrea.

"So did you know Jarrod well in high school?" Brandon wasn't sure why he'd asked, but he knew he wanted to know.

The fork that was carrying food to her mouth stopped and returned to the plate without the bite being eaten.

"No. To be honest, I don't remember him at all."

"He said he was in your math class."

She shrugged, fidgeting slightly in her seat. "A lot of high school was just a blur for me. You know how it is."

Brandon wanted to know more about her. "What clique were you? Sports? Nerd? Punk rocker?"

A ghost of a smile passed her lips. "None, really. I pretty much kept to myself."

Like the way she pretty much had kept to herself the past couple of years while at Omega?

She was pushing her food around on her plate now, not really eating it. Okay, she didn't want to talk about high school. Maybe she had bloomed more in college. That happened. For some people high school had been a miserable experience. Brandon's own high school experience had been nothing fantastic.

But now Brandon found he wanted to know something about Andrea. Something about her as a person. Not about her abilities as a behavioral analyst—hell, he was already completely impressed by just about everything she'd done concerning the case. His plan to teach her about note-taking had just proved fruitless; she'd taught him a lesson about her abilities instead.

But what did he really know about her? Name, occupation, age. Brandon made a living getting inside the minds of others, but he'd be damned if he'd been able to do so with her.

Brandon eased back into info and tactics he'd learned in his basic psychology classes way back in undergrad: get someone comfortable with you if you wanted them to freely share information. The best way to do that was a compliment.

That was easy with Andrea. Her skills were impressive.

"I think everything you've said about the guys tonight is spot-on. You caught a few things I missed." He wasn't faking any sincerity when he said it. "And I like to think I don't miss very much."

He could see the tension ease out of her torso even from across the table. She really didn't want to talk about high school. Maybe it was just being here in town; maybe it was something she never wanted to talk about. Brandon wouldn't push.

He smiled at her. "Steve was right about your abilities. It's impressive."

She smiled back at him, obviously basking in his praise. That was something for him to file away. It confirmed what Steve had told him in his office on Monday. Andrea still wasn't sure about herself and exactly where and how she belonged in Omega.

Which was a shame. Someone with her abilities should rest very comfortably in them. It would make her a better analyst if she wasn't constantly second-guessing herself. Brandon found himself wanting to help her with that.

To make Omega a stronger law-enforcement entity, of course. It had nothing to do with getting closer to the woman sitting across from him, with seeing more of her smiles, seeing her relax and ease into her own abilities.

He forced himself to tear his eyes away from hers and eat the last bite of his food.

He would start on neutral territory.

"So, where'd you go to college? Did you decide to study criminal science or end up going with psychology?" It had been a question he'd had to choose, but had found he couldn't decide, so he'd ended up studying both.

"I, um...I—"

Brandon looked up from his plate and found all of Andrea's tension back. More. She was biting her lip and pulling at her blazer sleeve.

Evidently the subject of college was even worse than high school.

"Andrea—"

She stood up, her chair scraping loudly on the floor. She flinched. "Brandon, I'm sorry. I have to go. I'm not feeling well."

"Just wait and I'll—"

"No. I'm sorry, no—"

She was gone, hurrying out the restaurant door before he could stop her.

Chapter Six

Brandon paid the bill a few minutes later, trying to figure out what had just happened. He replayed the conversation in his mind to see if he'd said anything that could be construed by Andrea as offensive or threatening.

All he'd really done was ask her about high school and college.

Brandon had been studying people long enough to know her behavior signified more than just a desire not to talk about herself. It came back to what he had argued about with Steve in his office.

Andrea Gordon had secrets. And they had to do with this town.

What Brandon didn't know was if he should press or not. Her secrets, whatever they were, didn't seem to get in the way of her doing her job. He had no complaints about the insights she was bringing into the case.

But the man inside him—his basic, most primal man— could not abide that she was hiding things from him. That she had pain, that she needed help, and she would not share that with him. He wanted to force her to tell him so he could fight the battle for her.

Brandon grimaced as he sat back in his chair. He knew himself well enough to know there were parts of his psyche that he didn't allow to break through very often, but were still quite strong inside him.

The part of him he called the warrior.

The warrior kept things very simple, saw only in black and white, right or wrong. Not the shades of gray that his intellect wandered in all the time. The warrior inside was who kept Brandon from becoming a criminal himself.

The darkness and the warrior combated each other.

God knew he came by the warrior honestly. He had literal fighter's blood flowing through his veins from his ancestors on both sides: Japanese samurai from his father's side, Scottish clansmen from his mother's.

The warrior wasn't interested in profiling or studying nonverbal cues. He wasn't interested in what was politically correct or even polite. He was interested in fighting for what was *just*. What was *his*.

Brandon didn't let the warrior side of himself come to light very often. He preferred to use his intellect and reasoning abilities to get things done.

But when it came to Andrea, the warrior kept pushing his way forward.

Well, that was too damn bad, because Brandon wasn't about to let his Neanderthal self run roughshod over this entire investigation. Brandon had to work with Andrea. She was his partner, for however long this case lasted. He would not go demanding answers from her.

Demanding kisses from her.

But he would go find her and make sure she was okay. Let her know he wasn't going to push her to talk about things she wasn't ready to share.

The warrior inside all but growled, but Brandon ignored him, pushing him back down.

Brandon exited the restaurant and walked back up the block toward the hotel. And, just his luck, it was starting to drizzle hard enough to be an annoyance.

He almost didn't see Andrea.

Of course, he wasn't looking for her to be standing on

the edge of the parking lot since she'd left the restaurant ten minutes ago. But she was, staring at a car—an old beat-up Chevy—parked close to the hotel's front entrance.

She wasn't moving, just standing in the rain. Frozen in what seemed to be terror.

Brandon's first thought was that it was Damian Freihof, the would-be bank bomber. Had he found Andrea here? But then he realized Freihof wouldn't be sitting in a car and Andrea wouldn't just be staring at him if he was.

He walked up to Andrea, careful to come at her slowly and from the side so he didn't sneak up on her in any way.

"Hi." He kept his voice even, calm. "What are you doing out here? Everything okay?"

She looked at him then back at the parking lot.

Without being obvious about it, Brandon withdrew his weapon from the holster at his side. Had she seen something to do with the case?

"Andrea." His voice was a little stronger now. "What's going on? Is it something to do with the murders? Did you see something or did someone threaten you?"

She kept staring.

"Andrea, look at me."

She finally turned to him, hair plastered to her head from the rain, makeup beginning to smear on her face.

"I need you to tell me what's happening. Is there danger? Did you see something having to do with the case?"

Andrea's eyes finally focused on Brandon. "N-no. No, there's no danger. I just...I just thought..." He waited but she didn't finish her sentence.

Okay, not an immediate danger and nothing from the investigation. Something from her past, then. He holstered his weapon. There wasn't danger, but she needed help. Especially since she didn't seem capable of taking care of herself at the moment.

"Let's go inside, sweetheart." The endearment slipped out unbidden. "Let's get you out of the rain."

She stiffened. "No, I can't go inside." Her attention narrowed again on the old car parked near the front entrance, under the hotel's overhang. It looked as if someone was sitting inside, but it was too far for Brandon to get any details.

He and Andrea couldn't stay out in the rain—even the desert of Arizona was cold in March. Andrea was already shivering.

The car seemed to be the center of her terror, not the hotel.

"What if we go in the side door?" Brandon pointed to a door nearer to them. It wasn't close to their rooms, but it would at least mean not having to go in the main entrance through the parking lot.

She looked over at the door he referred to and nodded. Brandon wrapped an arm around her slim form and led her to the door. Once inside he kept her in his grasp as they made their way down the hall. She was still shivering.

Warrior or not, there was no way Brandon was letting Andrea out of his sight right now. He wasn't even sure he could let her out of his arms.

He stopped at his room and got his key card out of his pocket. He knew Andrea was in bad shape when she didn't protest him bringing her into his room.

He shrugged off his jacket and threw it over the chair, then helped her take off her soaked blazer and eased her down to sit on the edge of the bed.

He left her for a moment to go get a towel from the bathroom. When he came back she hadn't moved at all, was still sitting, huddled into herself, where he'd left her.

His heart broke a little bit at her flinch when he put the towel around her and began gently drying her hair.

"Shh. I won't hurt you. I just want to make sure you don't get sick." He took a corner of the towel and wiped it across her cheeks in an effort to dry them and also remove some of the makeup that had run down her cheeks. Her green eyes just stared out at him.

Brandon left the towel wrapped around her shoulders and grabbed a chair so he could set it right in front of her. He sat so they were eye to eye.

"Who was that in the car out front?"

He heard the tiny hitch in her breathing. "You saw it?"

"No, I could just see that *you* saw whoever it was."

"That's my aunt and uncle's car. They raised me after my mom died when I was ten."

"And you don't want them to know you're here?"

A shudder racked Andrea. "No. I don't ever want to see either of them again."

She looked away and began rubbing her arm, repeatedly. He looked down and saw scars, multiple small lines all around her elbow. He'd never seen the scars before but then realized it was because he'd never seen her without a long-sleeved shirt or blazer.

Her professional wardrobe was not just an emotional barrier between her and the world; it was a physical one.

As he looked down at the scars again, at her countenance, her posture, a rage flooded him. She had been abused.

He immediately tamped down his anger, knowing she would read it and could take it the wrong way. She needed support right now. Gentleness. Caring.

"They hurt you." His voice was barely more than a whisper, but it wasn't a question.

"They're alcoholics. And whenever they drank... My uncle mostly. My aunt just locked herself in her room."

A tear rolled down her cheek as she looked away from him out the window. She was still rubbing her arm.

"I know they can't hurt me now. I'm older. Stronger. Not the same person who lived in their house."

"All of that is true. Every word."

"And you could arrest them if they tried anything."

She was obviously trying to give herself a pep talk.

He nodded. "I wouldn't hesitate to do so."

"I was so young and stupid. They didn't want me after my mom died, but I didn't have anywhere else to go. I tried to stay out of their way as much as possible. But in a way, I guess I should be thankful for them."

Brandon couldn't think of a single reason why an abuse survivor should be thankful for what she'd been through.

She shrugged. "It's because of my uncle that I learned to read people so well. The situation at home forced me to really study nuances of expressions."

"So you could stay a step ahead of his fists."

She nodded. "But it didn't always work. Sometimes you knew what was coming, but you couldn't escape it."

She was referring to her situation in second person instead of first—distancing herself. It was a coping strategy.

"The situation at home may have helped you hone your skills at a younger age than you would have otherwise," he agreed. "But I imagine your gift at reading people still would be there. You would've always been an extraordinary behavioral analyst—you just wouldn't have known about it until later in your studies."

Suddenly some of her earlier words and actions clicked into place for Brandon. Her defensiveness about college, the reason she had given him two different graduating years for high school.

"You ran away, didn't you?"

She flushed, embarrassed. "Yes. I was about to turn seventeen. My uncle came in, drunk, and pulled me from a sound sleep, throwing me off the bed before beginning to whale on me. I got out, after falling through a glass table. But I never spent another night in that house."

Rage coursed through Brandon. The temptation to go

out there and give her uncle just the slightest taste of his own medicine almost overwhelmed him. But he ratcheted his temper under control.

Andrea needed him here.

"Good for you."

She rolled her eyes. "Sure, except for the fact that I had to drop out of high school. I was never any good at school anyway." She seemed to shrink into herself. "I'm dyslexic, so reading was—still is—hard for me."

Brandon grimaced. Dealing with dyslexia was a challenge for any child. And a child who had no academic or emotional support at home? A setup for failure. He thought about how he had mentally criticized her for not reading the police file at the airport. Now he knew why. Reading it would be difficult enough for her; reading in a crowded place with a bunch of distractions would be nearly impossible.

"Steve Drackett and Grace Parker, the head psychologist for Omega, met me in Phoenix when I was nineteen. I helped them with a bank hostage situation."

Brandon nodded, leaning closer to her and taking the hand that was still rubbing at her scars. He gently ran his fingers along her knuckles, not sure if he was trying to soothe her or himself. He knew about the bank, or at least about Damian Freihof. At this moment Brandon completely agreed with Steve's decision not to tell Andrea about Freihof. Buckeye was hard enough on her without adding the possible threat of a madman.

"They had me do some testing, because Steve was sure I had a natural ability at reading people."

"Behavioral and nonverbal communication diagnostic," Brandon murmured, not letting go of her hand.

"You know it?"

"I'm familiar with it." More than. He'd helped develop the latest, most thorough version of it when he'd been in grad school ten years ago. She'd taken the test he'd helped create.

"So you ran away to escape an impossible home situation and had to quit school. Steve and Grace realized how naturally gifted you were and brought you into the Omega fold."

She glanced down for just a second before looking at him again. "Yes, pretty much."

There was other stuff she wasn't telling him—glancing down rapidly was almost always a tell of hiding something. Amazing that she could read so clearly the emotions and microexpressions of others, but couldn't control them in herself.

But mostly what she felt, what every nonverbal element of her body language and facial expressions spoke for her, was shame.

"I'm not really your typical Omega caliber person, right?" She smiled crookedly, not quite looking him in the eyes. "No education, no training. Can't even read right. Afraid to face an old couple in a car."

Those sentences explained so much about her and her behavior over the past few years at Omega. She wasn't standoffish or an ice queen; she was an abuse survivor. She'd been keeping herself apart so her colleagues wouldn't find out about her past, afraid they would consider her unworthy of being part of the Omega team.

Brandon couldn't stop himself. He let go of her hands to cup her face, gently wiping her still-damp hair back from her cheeks.

"A few people might have thought that at first, but no one would think it now, given your track record with cases."

She just shrugged.

He trailed his fingers down her cheek. The warrior in him happy to have her close, to finally know some of her pain so he could try to protect her. "You have a *gift*. Steve recognized it so thoroughly that he brought you—an unknown teenager—into Omega. And he has never regretted that decision, I'm positive."

"But I don't have any education. Any training."

"You can get both of those if you want it—you have plenty of time. Hell, if I could naturally do what you do? I would've stopped going to school when I was ten."

A ghost of a smile, but at least it was a *real* one. Brandon wasn't sure he'd ever seen anything so beautiful. He got up and sat next to her on the bed so he could put his arm around her. He had to be closer to her.

"I did get my GED a couple years ago," she murmured, leaning into him. "And have taken a few semesters of college courses. But the dyslexia makes it hard."

"Of course it does," he said against her hair, pride running through him. "But you've persevered. You'll take it slow and finish as you're able. With your abilities, getting a degree is no big rush."

Brandon slid them back so they rested against the headboard of the bed. He kept his arm around her for support, but also because he couldn't seem to force himself to put any distance between them. She didn't seem to want it, either.

He wondered how long it had been since someone had just held her like this.

If ever.

He could feel her relaxing into him. Tension easing out of her body.

"I suppose I should go see if my aunt and uncle are still out there. I shouldn't be surprised they heard I'm in town. Gossip runs pretty freely around here." She shrugged. "I don't want to see them. Don't know why they would want to see me. But I guess I've got to face them sometime."

He tilted her face from where it rested on his shoulder

and kissed her. Gently. Tenderly. His passion was there, just below the surface, but he kept it under tight rein—his passion was not the emotion he wanted her to pick up on. She didn't need that.

"Yes, but not tonight. You face them on your time, when you're ready. Not a minute before."

She sighed sinking back into him, nodding. Brandon wrapped his arms more tightly around her, wanting to keep her safe from anything that would ever cause her harm.

Chapter Seven

Andrea woke up with a start, eyes flying open. It was dark. She always slept with a light on, mostly because she didn't want to wake up like this: panicked, braced for violence. She didn't move, but held her body tense, ready to shoot off in whichever direction would get her to safety.

Slowly realization dawned. There was no danger here. The opposite, in fact. She was lying on top of the bedcover, wrapped in Brandon Han's arms.

They'd shifted a little in their sleep; he pulled her more closely to him so that she was draped nearly all down his side. Her leg was even hooked over his thighs.

Like lovers.

The thought of Brandon as her lover sent little explosions of passion barreling up and down her spine. She could think of nothing she wanted more.

She'd told him about her home situation. About not finishing school. About not having the education or background to really be a part of the Omega team. None of it had seemed to matter to him.

Of course, she hadn't mentioned she'd also been a stripper for a period of eighteen months—the worst eighteen months of her life. Some of those girls had thrived on being onstage, being the center of attention, driving men wild. For Andrea it had been an exercise in agony every time.

It was a part of her life she'd just as soon forget. And

she couldn't think of a reason why she would need to tell Brandon, or anybody at Omega, about it.

She wanted to stay here in his arms, to sleep with him, to wake up with him and kiss him in the way she'd dreamed of. And much more than that.

Now that her eyes had adjusted to the darkness, she could see his chiseled features illuminated by the cloudy moonlight floating through the window. Black hair, prominent cheekbones, soft lips relaxed in sleep.

Despite his earlier, gentle kiss and the fact that he held her in his arms even now, Andrea didn't think Brandon was interested in her sexually. He was a colleague, perhaps could even be a friend. His emotions last night had radiated concern and sympathy for her, and even anger directed at her past.

Not passion.

Andrea eased her way back from him slowly. She should leave now. There was no need to have an awkward morning-after when they hadn't really had the fun part of the night before.

She worked herself away from him and out of the bed without waking him. She grabbed the shoes she'd taken off and her blazer from the chair. With one last look at his sleeping form, she slipped out the door.

A FEW HOURS LATER, in the hotel's dining room, Brandon slid into the chair across from Andrea. It didn't take any special reading ability for her to see he was pretty irritated.

"You snuck out in the middle of the night," he said as he added a creamer packet to his paper coffee cup.

Andrea would've thought he'd be relieved, not mad.

"Yeah, I woke up and thought it would be better if I went to my own room."

He tilted his head to the side and studied her.

"What?" she asked.

"I'm surprised you were able to get out without me waking up."

She shrugged. "I'm good at moving very quietly." A skill she'd picked up when not waking her drunk uncle had been a priority.

He still didn't stop staring at her. It was making her uneasy.

"Did you sleep okay?" he finally said. "Yesterday evening was a pretty rough one for you."

Her discomfiture came rushing back. She never should have told him all that stuff about herself. Sure, last night he'd been supportive, but this morning... Maybe this morning he realized what a fraud she really was.

He reached over and grabbed her hand, squeezing it just short of being painful. "Hey, whatever is going on in that mind of yours right now, stop."

"But—"

Now his eyes were mad. "I mean it. The only one thinking bad things about you at this table is *you*. So stop."

"Okay." She took a breath. He was right. She needed to learn to stop her self-sabotaging thoughts.

"So I'll ask you again—did you sleep okay?"

Did he mean before she left his room or afterward? She had slept amazingly in his bed. In his arms. But she probably shouldn't announce that, since he might think she was trying to get an invitation to do it again. Once she'd gotten back to her room the bed had seemed too big, too empty. She'd slept, mostly from the sheer exhaustion of having stayed up nearly all night on Monday studying the case files, but not nearly as well.

"I slept fine. Thanks." Seemed like the safest answer.

She had gotten up a little early to make sure she had time to do her hair and makeup perfectly. She was wearing the suit she knew she looked most professional in. After what had happened yesterday, Andrea had felt the need to show she was as competent and proficient as possible. To Brandon and herself.

"So what's our agenda for the day?" she asked briskly.

Brandon's eyebrow rose at the question. Andrea knew she was probably being a little too sharp, but she had to find a way to get them back on neutral footing.

Thankfully Brandon took her cue.

He sat up straighter. "We need to talk to the rest of victim number two's coworkers at the diner. See if any of them remember Ashley talking to someone in particular, not only that night, but the nights leading up to her murder. Find out if she had any regulars. That might be more difficult since none of them want to admit they're turning tricks on the side."

"It's probably not a regular who killed her since—"

Her sentence was cut off when both of their phones started vibrating.

"Damn it," Brandon muttered, looking down at the email message that had popped up on his phone. "Maricopa Sheriff's Department found another body. Another girl has been murdered."

They were in the car and headed toward the crime scene five minutes later. Brandon called and updated Omega as they drove, promising to give more details as they became available. They didn't have far to drive. The body had been found just on the outskirts of Buckeye, again in front of another church.

Andrea glanced at Brandon. "Just so you know, I don't do crime scenes very often. My talents are with witnesses."

He nodded. "Yeah, I guess dead bodies don't give off many nonverbal cues for you to read."

"Honestly, I haven't really been around any." This was just another example of how untrained she was.

"Hey, a lot of agents try to get out of crime scenes—especially those with a dead body—any way they can. You know Liam Goetz, right?"

Andrea had worked with him and his pregnant soon-to-be wife, Vanessa, on a human-trafficking case a few months ago. He was head of Omega's hostage-rescue team—and had proved his skills rescuing a group of young girls who had been kidnapped and were about to be sold into sexual slavery.

"Yeah, I know Liam." She didn't know him well, but liked the big, muscular man and how caring he was with petite Vanessa, who was now huge with the twins she was carrying.

"He'll be the first to tell you that he doesn't mind putting bad guys in body bags—that man loves his guns—but he will keel over every time he's in a coroner's exam room or there's a body at a crime scene he has to attend."

Andrea laughed just a little at the thought of it.

"Yeah, go head, laugh," Brandon continued, smiling. "You're not the one who has to drag two hundred pounds of pure muscle over to the side to get him out of the way. We've started requesting he not attend any situation where there's a body being examined."

"So I guess you're telling me it's okay if I don't go into the crime scene with you."

"That's up to you. All I'm saying is that there are Omega agents who choose not to. We don't think any less of them for it."

Andrea did appreciate Brandon trying to put her at ease.

The parking lot of the church where the body had been discarded was completely blocked off by police—both Maricopa County and City of Phoenix officers. There was a buzz of excitement in the air.

With a fourth victim, no one could deny this was a serial killer, not that Andrea had any doubts before.

Brandon immediately walked over, showing his Omega

credentials, and began speaking with the coroner. Lance Kendrick and Gerardo Jennison were here also, talking to each other and Brandon.

Andrea hung back. She didn't want to do something stupid like pass out from being too close to the body. Although the thought that Liam Goetz did so made her smile.

Andrea could still see where the dead woman lay from where she stood. Like the others, she was covered with a sheer white fabric and a lily had been placed in her hands. Andrea couldn't tell, but she would guess the woman had been strangled like the others.

Officers were moving all around her, canvassing the area for any clues that might have been left on the ground. Another two were attempting to get fingerprints from nearby surfaces.

When he saw her, Kendrick excused himself from Brandon and Jennison and walked over to her, purpose in his eyes. He'd remembered her; she had no doubt about it. She wanted to run, but knew it was no use.

"You're Andrea Gordon, Margaret and Marlon's kid."

His expression wasn't hostile or even condescending. If anything, it was sympathetic.

"Actually, they're my aunt and uncle, but yeah, my guardians."

"You looked so familiar, but it was so vague I thought it was a case, like you'd suggested."

Andrea shrugged.

"You look a lot different than your mug shot," Kendrick continued.

Andrea clenched her teeth. Was this it? The end of her career? Would Kendrick tell Brandon? Could someone with a criminal record even work for Omega?

"Once I saw that picture I knew where else I'd seen you. Coming in with your mom—well, I guess your aunt—to pick your uncle up after he'd been thrown in holding when he was too drunk to find his way home. Must have happened a dozen times."

Andrea shrugged again, turning away slightly.

"Uncle was a mean drunk, if memory serves. Maybe those nights we threw him in holding we were doing you a favor, I'm thinking now."

They'd been a much better night's sleep, that was for sure, but Andrea didn't say anything.

"There were a lot of screwups where you were concerned, Ms. Gordon. I'd like to offer Maricopa County's apologies, my personal apologies, for that."

Andrea turned back to Kendrick, surprised.

He looked at her solemnly. "Sometimes you can't see the full picture, except in hindsight. The system failed you. But you seem to have done all right for yourself." He gestured at her outfit.

"You mean despite having a record?"

Kendrick smiled at that although there was still a lingering sadness in his eyes. "You don't have a record, Andrea. You got brought in for underage drinking, but were never formally charged. I think the arresting officer just did it to scare you into going straight."

"It worked. I still can hardly drink anything without feeling some panic."

The officer smiled. "Well, there's no official record of your arrest, outside our storage room. So you don't have to worry about that. I'm just sorry no one ever looked further into your situation earlier, before you ran away."

His regret was so authentic it was almost painful.

"Like you said, I did okay for myself. I have a good job where I make a difference."

"And you're very well respected, if Agent Han is anything to go by."

Andrea looked over at Brandon to find him gazing at

her, concern in his eyes. She smiled at him to offer reassurance.

Lance Kendrick made his apologies once again and expressed his happiness to be working with her. Then he left to go deal with things pertaining to the dead woman. Not long after, Brandon made his way over to her, the notebook where he wrote everything down open to details about the case.

"Everything okay? I saw Kendrick over here."

"Yeah, he remembered me. He's a good cop. A little rough around the edges, but he cares."

Brandon nodded. "I got the info about the victim. Twenty-two years old, from here in Buckeye." He flipped a page in his notebook. "Her name is Jillian Spires and she's another stripper. Worked at a club called Jaguar's."

Chapter Eight

Andrea had wisely hung back as Brandon had examined the body with the coroner. As he'd told her, there was no need for her to get close unless she wanted to. If she wanted to get more thorough in investigating, he could ease her into that later when they were back at Omega in controlled circumstances. It didn't need to be while she was standing around a group of people she didn't know.

Or maybe one she did. Brandon saw Lance Kendrick come up to Andrea and had kept an eye on them as they conversed. Now that Brandon knew more about Andrea's past, what she'd survived, he found himself much more protective of her. The warrior was protective of her, as was the intellectual man.

Not even to mention how angry *both* were when he awoke to find her gone. It had been all he could do not to storm down to where she was and demand her return to his room.

To his bed.

But he'd gotten control of himself. An icy shower had helped. By the time he'd made it to breakfast he'd been able to be civil. He'd gotten the warrior tamped down, buried.

But he hadn't been able to stop himself from keeping a close eye on her all morning.

Andrea's conversation with Kendrick had been civil.

Whatever the older man had to say, she hadn't been upset by it.

Or so he had thought. Because when he came over to give Andrea the details about the dead girl, all the color had drained from her face. The police had told him the dead woman had a local address, and she was close to Andrea's age. Maybe Andrea had known the woman personally.

"Hey, are you okay?" He stepped closer and cupped her elbow, moving her so she was blocked from the eyes of the other cops. "You look shaky. Did you know Jillian Spires?"

Andrea closed her eyes briefly. "No. I didn't know her. She must have moved here after I left."

Brandon's eyes narrowed. Her statement was odd. Wouldn't you automatically assume you just hadn't run in the same circles? Buckeye was a small town, but not *that* small. There would certainly be people you didn't know. Why would Andrea assume Jillian had arrived after she'd left?

"Are you sure you're okay?" he asked again.

She shrugged. "Yeah. I'm fine. I'm just— These women are my age. Some of them younger. They may not have a lot of family, but they don't deserve to die like this."

Brandon agreed although he was sure that wasn't the entire situation going on inside Andrea's head.

"Maybe this one will have family. Kendrick will do a more thorough check as soon as they get back to the office."

"So what's our next step?"

"We have a home address and a work address for the club, Jaguar's, where she worked. I figure we should probably start with the home. See if we get any known associates from there."

Her nod was just a little too exuberant. "Yeah, her home is probably our best bet."

Brandon's eyes narrowed slightly once again. There was something off in Andrea's behavior. She was hiding something. He almost started questioning her about it, but then stopped himself.

It could be about what had happened between them last night. Or about being back in this town that held so many painful memories. Or about being at her first homicide crime scene.

There were a lot of reasons Andrea could be a little off. He'd cut her some slack.

"The locals will also be there processing the scene at her home, so it'll be crowded. But we'll see what we can find. Besides, I would imagine her place of employment isn't open at ten thirty on a Thursday morning."

She didn't say anything, just turned toward the car with him. The ride across town to Jillian's apartment was mostly in silence, also. Generally Brandon didn't mind silence. He preferred it to someone filling the car with inane chatter. But he couldn't help but feel as though Andrea was not talking in order to deliberately withhold information.

Privacy was her way, ingrained over the past few years of having to keep totally to herself. Just because he knew about her abusive past didn't mean she was automatically going to start sharing every thought that came through her mind. Which was fine.

Except there was something else going on, he knew it.

They worked through lunch, examining Jillian's apartment. She hadn't been a neat freak, for sure, which made going through her personal belongings more time-consuming. They did find two glasses on the cardboard box that doubled as a coffee table, one rimmed with lipstick, one without. That meant someone besides Jillian had been in here relatively recently. The locals would run prints.

If anything, Andrea got more quiet as they looked through the girl's apartment. Brandon knew this wasn't her area of expertise—objects rather than people—so he didn't really try to draw her into the investigation. She looked around, staying out of the crime-scene team's way. Brandon did similarly.

There were two boxes full of stuff—notes passed in high school, a yearbook, pressed flowers from dances, a few stuffed animals and other knickknacks. Obviously items Jillian cared too much about to give away, although none of it held any value. Andrea picked up the yearbook and began looking through it.

"She graduated four years ago. She's from Oklahoma City." She held out the page that showed Jillian's senior high school picture.

Young, smiling, very much alive.

"That gives us something to go on." Brandon took a picture of the picture with his phone. "She looks different now, but we can still use this picture when questioning people."

"Maybe she has a family." Andrea's face was pinched.

"Maybe. Kendrick will definitely start inquiring there."

After they finished with the apartment, they hit a fast-food place for a very late lunch. As they were finishing, Kendrick called to say the Phoenix coroner was almost ready to go over the body with them if Brandon wanted to attend in case he had any questions. Brandon agreed.

At his words, the heaviness that had befallen Andrea since the discovery of the body seemed to lift a little.

"Um, I don't think I'm up to seeing a dead body twice in one day," she said. "What if we split up? You can head into Phoenix. I'll walk up to Jaguar's—it's only a few blocks from here—and start interviewing the girls as they come in for work."

Brandon nodded. "Yeah, that's a good idea." He trusted Andrea's ability. At the very least she could narrow down who they should talk to more. "They're probably more willing to talk openly with you."

She paled. "Why do you say that?"

Brandon tilted his head to look at her. Why was she reacting so strongly to his statement? "Because you're a woman. You're young. I would think you pose much less of a threat to them."

Andrea smiled, but it didn't reach anywhere near her eyes. "Yeah, absolutely. Good thinking."

Brandon stood. "Okay, I'll text you when I finish at the coroner's office and we can touch base."

They both walked out the door. "I'll just give you a ride, okay? No need for you to walk. The extra two minutes won't make any difference to Kendrick." There was no rush. A dead body wasn't going anywhere.

She tensed for just a second before shrugging. "Sure. Thanks."

Brandon drove the few blocks to the gentlemen's club, *gentlemen* being quite a loose term in this situation. At night he was sure it didn't look quite so run-down and cheap. But right now it just looked like a warehouse that nobody cared about. He felt bad that Jillian had worked here. Felt bad for any women who worked here.

Andrea was staring at the building with as much contempt as he was. Her lips were pale with tightness and her hands pressed against her stomach. For a moment he thought she wasn't going to get out of the car.

"I'm sure the front door isn't open yet. I'll go around to the side. Text me when you're done, and we'll make a plan like you said." Her voice was tight. She didn't look at him.

She was out of the car before he could check that she was all right. She stopped a few feet away, then turned and waved, giving him a slight smile.

Obviously code for: *I'm okay. I can handle this.*

Brandon pulled around and out of the parking lot. Four

days ago he wouldn't have left her here alone. Wouldn't have trusted that she could do the job. Wouldn't have believed she wouldn't miss something. It was that knowledge that kept him driving toward Phoenix. He needed to show he trusted her professional abilities.

But everything in his mind insisted this situation was wrong. That he was missing something obvious. Andrea hadn't been okay all day since they'd arrived at the crime scene.

No, actually, she seemed to have done okay with that, too. It was not until he had told Andrea the dead girl's name that she'd totally withdrawn into herself. Had she known the woman? Her statement about Jillian moving into town after Andrea had left still struck Brandon as odd.

But Andrea had been right, according to the girl's yearbook. Jillian had obviously been in Oklahoma City four years ago, and that was when Steve had brought Andrea to Omega.

So she didn't know the girl.

Then what was the cause of Andrea's reaction? Her *continued* reaction all day, because she certainly hadn't bounced out of it. It had only gotten worse.

Brandon tried to think of exactly what he'd said when he told Andrea the victim's name. As he figured it out, he cursed. Violently.

Andrea hadn't been reacting to Jillian's name. She'd been reacting to the other information he'd given her: Jillian's place of employment.

Jaguar's.

He spun the car around at the first available safe place on the road. He put his phone on speaker and dialed Kendrick.

"This is Lance Kendrick."

"Lance, this is Brandon Han. I have some stuff I'm

looking into and will need to miss the meeting with the coroner."

"No problem. I don't think there's anything much different than the other women. I'll email you his full report."

"Thanks."

"You need help with your lead?"

"No. I'll let you know if we find anything. Andrea and I are headed to Jaguar's now to interview Jillian's coworkers."

"We'll keep each other posted, then."

"Absolutely." Brandon ended the call. Right now he just wanted to get back to Andrea. To figure out what was going on there. Fifteen minutes after he'd left her—pale and tense—in the parking lot at Jaguar's, he pulled back in.

She'd known there was a side door and where it was.

Brandon cleared his mind from every thought. He didn't want to come to the natural conclusion Andrea's actions pointed toward. He walked toward the side door she'd mentioned and entered the building once he found the door propped open. He stood back in the shadows, close enough to hear but not easily be seen.

There was Andrea, surrounded by four different women, all of them crying and hugging her. They all talked over each other, about Jillian's death, the state of the club, how much they'd missed Andrea and how mad they were that she'd just left without telling anyone.

Brandon couldn't force the thoughts away any longer, his brain turned back on full force.

Andrea had been a stripper at Jaguar's.

Chapter Nine

Walking back into Jaguar's had been the most difficult thing Andrea had ever done. She was thankful Brandon hadn't been here to witness it because there was no way she'd be able to explain the terror that swamped her as she made her way to the side door from the parking lot.

How many times had she come through the door in the late afternoon just like this? Her apartment had been only a few blocks away, so she had walked most of the time, a bag full of skimpy outfits, wigs and makeup thrown over her shoulder.

The eighteen months she had worked at Jaguar's had been some of the worst of her entire life. She had hated every second of it. But after being attacked while living out of her car when she couldn't afford anything else from what she made working at a gas station, Andrea had decided her safety was worth more than her pride.

Working here had at least gotten her off the streets.

She hadn't expected anyone to remember her when she came back, or perhaps they would just be able to vaguely place her. After all, she'd pretty much kept to herself here, too. The instant recognition and warm greetings—hugs, in fact, from three girls—had definitely not been expected. A fourth girl, who didn't even know Andrea, didn't want to be left out and jumped into the fray.

At first they'd just held on to her and cried. They'd heard

about Jillian's death and were sad, scared. Then they'd had questions. They all, just as Andrea remembered—one of the few fond memories she had of this place—talked over each other.

"You just left without saying goodbye."

"Oh my gosh, you look so fancy. Like a lawyer or something. Gorgeous."

"Do the cops know who killed Jillian?"

"You're not coming back to work here, right?"

Andrea tried to answer the questions as best she could when they were being fired so rapidly she couldn't figure out who was asking what.

"I work as a consultant for a law-enforcement agency called Omega Sector. We're looking into Jillian's death with the local police."

"You were always too smart to work here." That was Lily. Andrea remembered her. She was kind, sort of scatterbrained.

Andrea shrugged. "I don't know about that. I didn't even graduate from high school. Dropped out."

"You may not have been book smart, but you definitely had an awareness of people. Could tell what they were thinking and feeling. Downright spooky sometimes. I'm not surprised the cops scooped you up to work for them."

That was Keira. She wasn't in the hugging/crying circle, didn't have time for that sort of nonsense. She was two years older than Andrea and had been the closest thing Andrea had had to a true friend while working here.

Keira may have been the closest thing Andrea had had to a friend, ever.

Andrea removed herself from the circle of women and walked over to Keira.

"Hey," Andrea said softly. "I'm sorry I didn't say goodbye all those years—"

She was shocked as Keira pulled her in for a tight hug.

"Don't apologize for taking your chance to jump this ship," she whispered in Andrea's ear. "If you had come back after having a chance to get out, I would've kicked your ass."

Keira grabbed Andrea by the forearms and pushed her back. "Let me look at you. You cleaned up exactly like I imagined you would." She put her forehead against Andrea's. "I'm so proud of you. So happy for you."

"Thanks, Kee. I have a great job."

"And a man who cares a great deal about you."

Andrea laughed. "Um, no. Unfortunately, the job didn't come with that accessory."

"You sure about that? Because there's one tall drink of water over there who can't keep his eyes off you. And his suit says law enforcement, too." Keira gestured toward the side door with her chin.

Andrea felt her stomach lurch and swallowed rapidly. Brandon was here?

"He's just a man, honey. Don't forget that. Ultimately, we hold the power," Keira whispered in her ear before turning to the other girls. "Ladies, I'd like to see you at the bar so we can go over tonight's set. You can talk to Andrea later."

The women murmured disappointment, but followed Keira over to the bar. Andrea finally forced herself to turn around. When her worst fears were confirmed, she closed her eyes.

Brandon stood, the shadows from the doorway casting a bleak hue over his already-dark features. There could be no doubt in his mind that Andrea used to be employed here. There was no other possible interpretation of what had just happened with the girls.

"Andrea."

She opened her eyes, surprised to hear him directly in front of her now. Almost within touching distance.

But not quite.

"You should've told me."

What could she say to that? She just shrugged.

"I thought you were going to Phoenix."

"Kendrick is going to email me the info instead. I had a feeling there would be more action back here."

Andrea gave a short bark of laughter that held no amusement whatsoever. "You definitely got that right."

"How is it even possible you worked here four years ago? I'm not licensed to practice law in Arizona, but I imagine the legal age has to be twenty-one."

Not licensed to practice in Arizona? That meant he had to be licensed to practice in some other state. Plus two PhDs? Andrea rubbed her eyes tiredly with her hand.

"I had a fake ID. You could dance at eighteen, but couldn't serve drinks. I soon discovered I could make a lot more money if I waited tables between my dances. The owner wasn't one to look too closely at the IDs we showed him."

Brandon's lips pursed. Disapproval all but radiated off him. Andrea wrapped her arms around her waist. She couldn't blame him for disapproving. She should've just told him everything up front last night. At least now he understood why she really could never be part of the Omega team.

She'd always known eventually someone would find out about this. She looked around the club, the deep bucket seats around the tables where girls gave individual dances, the stage shaped like a T with three poles. With all the lights on there was nothing sexy about it. Just coldness, hardness, crassness.

Yeah, she'd always known eventually someone would find out about this—the truth Steve Drackett and Grace Parker had always refused to see—and would know Andrea wasn't meant to be part of Omega Sector.

It looked as though Brandon Han had just become that person.

ANDREA LOOKED AS if she might shatter into a million pieces at the slightest touch.

He wanted to wrap his arms around her, to hold her, to assure her that everything would be okay. But the tension in her body language suggested she would reject the physical contact. So he took one step closer, but went no farther. Even then she looked as if she might bolt.

He shouldn't be surprised that Andrea had worked in a place like this, given her history. But try as he might, he couldn't imagine her on the stage. He'd been to his share of bachelor parties, and hell, *college*, so he'd been to strip clubs before. Andrea definitely had the looks and physique to be a dancer.

But nothing he knew about her personality or temperament suggested to him that she would've wanted to work at this place. Not like, say, the friend she'd been talking to, who seemed very comfortable in her own skin and able to easily manipulate the stage and men's desires. Not that it mattered either way.

The psychiatrist in him wanted to fire off a bunch of questions, to understand her psyche, to understand all the circumstances surrounding her working here. Although a lot of it he could probably piece together himself.

"You needed money after you ran away."

She nodded. "I was living in my car, working at a gas station. When I was almost attacked one night while sleeping, I knew I had to do something else. I happened to meet Keira and she told me about this place."

"It's understandable, Andrea. No one would blame you for that choice."

"Yeah, right." She slid by him to walk out the door but stopped when a man entered. Andrea backed up.

"What are you doing in here?" the man—big, greasy, gruff—asked. He turned toward the bar and yelled,

"Keira, what are customers doing in here before we're open, damn it?"

He turned back to Andrea. "We're not open, so you'll have to come back lat—" His eyes bulged and a nasty grin spread over his face. "Wait a minute—I recognize you. If it isn't little Drea all dressed up."

"Hi, Harry." Andrea's voice was small. Her shoulders hunched, and Brandon could see her arms crossed over her stomach in a protective huddle.

This man frightened Andrea.

"You come back to work for old Harry, sweet girl? I hear we have an opening."

Brandon gritted his teeth in distaste. He wished he could arrest Harry for something right now. He hoped he could keep himself from pummeling him into the ground, this man who so obviously threatened Andrea.

The warrior stretched inside him.

"No, I—I..." She was having difficulty getting the words out. Getting any words out.

Brandon stepped up so he was flanking Andrea. His chest was right at her shoulder and he placed his hand on her hip, making sure she could feel him. She wasn't alone in this.

"I'm agent Brandon Han with Omega Sector. We're investigating the death of Jillian Spires. You, of course, are one of our prime suspects." That wasn't true, but Brandon felt no qualms whatsoever about the lie. "We'll need you to provide a detailed written analysis of where you've been for the past seven days."

Harry's mouth fell open, but he stopped leering at Andrea. That had been Brandon's ultimate objective.

"I, um." Harry blinked rapidly and turned his attention to Brandon. "For a whole week?"

Brandon nodded, using his hand on Andrea's hip to guide her behind him. "That's right. Every place you've been. Written down. We'll be back to get it tomorrow and maybe to bring you in for questioning."

Brandon had no doubt that if Harry contacted a lawyer, his counsel would tell him that he didn't need to do any of this. That unless law enforcement was going to formally charge Harry with a crime, he didn't have to do jack squat to cooperate.

But Brandon had a feeling that Harry, with his thinning hair made even more evident by the way he slicked it back, was too cheap to call a lawyer. So let him spend the rest of his evening stewing and writing.

Brandon looked over his shoulder to Andrea, relieved to see at least a little color coming back to her face. "Would you mind telling the ladies that we'll be back tomorrow to interview them? Ask if they could come in early afternoon so we can talk."

Andrea nodded and walked toward the bar.

Harry evidently decided to try the buddy-buddy approach with Brandon. "Even all buttoned up, you can imagine what that one looked like on the stage, can't you?" His grin was slimy. There was no other word for it.

"She's my colleague." Brandon clenched his fists.

"Well, let me tell you, there was something about her up there." Harry had no idea how thin the ice he skated on was. "She wore wigs and makeup, but you couldn't hide those big green eyes. Like a deer caught in headlights every time she was up there. Everybody loved it. Not that they were looking at her face once her ti—"

The warrior inside Brandon broke free. He was in Harry's face in less than a second.

"That woman over there is an important member of a prestigious law-enforcement agency. What she did when you hired her—illegally, I might add, since she was a teenager—holds no bearing whatsoever to her ability to do her job now."

Harry swallowed hard. Brandon barely refrained from grabbing the other man by his dirty T-shirt.

"If I hear one disrespectful word come out of your mouth again about her, I will personally see to it that every person you've ever hired, every license you have to operate and every code involved in running a business like this is investigated. And if there are any problems or discrepancies, you will be *shut down*."

Harry nodded.

"Okay, I told them." Andrea returned and touched Brandon on the arm. He took a step back from Harry. "They'll be ready tomorrow."

Brandon turned to smile at her. He knew she would be able to pick up what was going on between him and Harry and wanted to assure her it was okay. "Harry and I got some things straightened out, too. Isn't that right, Harry?"

"Um, yes, sir. We're all clear. I'll have what you need by tomorrow. Anything to help catch Jillian's killer."

Brandon took Andrea's arm and led her out the door.

Chapter Ten

Andrea was huddled against the car door, as far away from him as she could get in the small rental, as they drove back to town and the hotel. Brandon, despite his training, wasn't sure what to say to her. But he knew it had to be something.

Finally she solved the problem by speaking first.

"I should've told you I had worked at Jaguar's." Her voice was small. Tiny. Ashamed. Part of his heart broke.

Brandon shrugged. "Maybe you should've this morning after we found out Jillian worked there. But before then it was pretty much irrelevant."

She rolled her eyes. "Right. Because no one at Omega would care that I was an ex-stripper."

He pulled the car into the parking lot of the hotel and shut off the engine, turning to her. "If I had been a carpenter or a janitor when I was twenty years old, would it make you think any less of me as an agent now?"

"That's different."

"How is it different? Most of us had a life—some of us had completely different careers before we worked for Omega."

"It's not the same." She clenched her fists.

"Why?"

"I took off my clothes for money."

Brandon took a breath. Damn, he was pissed. And he

knew she would be able to feel it. But his anger wasn't directed at her. He wanted to make sure she understood that.

"What you did was survive a situation most people never have to live through."

"Nobody at Omega is going to care about that."

Maybe it was time for a little tough love. "No offense, but nobody is going to care either way."

That got her attention. She spun her head toward him. "What?"

"You do your job well. That's all anybody at Omega cares about. You are an intelligent, gifted behavioral analyst."

"What I am is a runaway high school dropout, ex-stripper."

She got out of the car, so he did the same. Thankfully the parking lot was mostly empty. She stared at him across the hood of the car. At least there was some color in her cheeks and fire in her eyes. She didn't need sympathy and gentleness. That just encouraged the vulnerable side of her. She needed someone to tell it to her straight.

A friend.

Brandon wasn't sure she'd ever had one. Definitely hadn't had one at Omega. Well, he could be one for her.

He may be a turned-on friend, but he could be a friend.

"You forgot dyslexic."

Her eyes bugged out of her head. *"What?"*

"You're a runaway, dropout, *dyslexic* ex-stripper. Throw in an unfortunate shark attack and you've got yourself a pretty tragic tale there."

Now her eyes narrowed to slits. "Do you think I'm trying to get you to feel sorry for me?"

"No." Although God knew there was plenty to feel sorry for. "But I'm trying to get you to see the truth."

"That my past doesn't matter." Her lips tightened into a line. "You'll have to forgive me if I disagree."

She turned and began walking toward the side entrance of the hotel they'd used last night. Neither of them wanted to have this conversation coming through the main lobby. He jogged a few steps to catch up with her. Amazing how fast the woman could walk, even in heels.

"Of course your past matters. Everybody's past matters."

"That's easy for you to say. Your past is filled with schooling and degrees and graduations. Mine is filled with thongs and sleeping in my car and getting beaten by my uncle."

Brandon stopped her at the door. "Like it or not, our pasts are what make us who we are. But when it comes to Omega, you only want to concentrate on the bad parts of your past."

"That's because they're the most important parts."

"Says you. And you're stuck in your own head."

She started to reach for the door, but Brandon grabbed both her arms. He was gentle, but there was no way she was getting out of his grasp until he was ready to let her.

"You know what else is in your past? Four years of helping Omega solve cases. Saving many lives and assisting in putting a number of criminals behind bars."

She shrugged, looking down. He put a finger under her chin and forced her face back up, ignoring the heat coursing through him.

"Not to mention you dropped out of high school but then got your GED, so I think you can stop using the dropout title. Plus you're actively going to college. At twenty-three, it's not like you're some grandmother going back to school."

He could tell he was getting through to her. Her posture was relaxing, her body angling more toward him.

He wanted her; he could feel it in the tightness throbbing through his body. He wanted to sweep her up in his arms and carry her down to his room like a grand romantic movie. Wanted to make love to her for days until neither of them had strength to move.

But more than that he wanted her to see the truth about herself. How much she brought to the table.

He released her chin when she nodded. She opened the door and they both walked into the hallway.

"It's hard for me to get past. Hard for me to think anyone else could get past it, either, especially at Omega. Best of the best and all that."

"I would argue that your talent, your ability to read people, makes you one of the best. And your past—even the part when you worked at Jaguar's—helped make you into who you are now and what you can do."

"I just wouldn't know how to tell anyone about it."

"Why would you have to? Have you ever been in a briefing where we all sat around talking about our complete history? No. Because that's not what matters. Tell people you waited tables. That was true, also."

"Yeah, I guess so."

He wanted to shake her. Or hug her. Or definitely kiss her, but knew it wasn't the time for that. "You have a natural gift. Everybody knows it, and no one questions it. You don't have to have an origin story to tell everyone."

She laughed a little. "That's good, because I'm not a superhero."

They were at her door. He wanted to say the most important thing before she left. "You don't have to tell anybody anything about your past. Most people won't ever ask, and hardly anyone would care even if they knew all the details."

She nodded slightly.

"But the true issue here, I think, is not even about what judgments people might make if they knew about your shark-attack past and the rest." He tried to keep it light, before making his ultimate point. "The true issue is that if you embrace your past and own it, you'll be forced to stop treating every good behavioral analysis choice you make like it's a happy accident."

Her head jerked up to look at him.

"Embracing, or at least accepting, your past means accepting your present and your future at Omega. It means having to trust people. Not about knowing your past, but about allowing you to make mistakes in your future and not hold it against you."

He kissed her forehead gently, although he wanted to do much more than that. "You hold yourself away from everybody to try to make yourself perfect. Being real, being part of a team, means showing others you're not. And giving them a chance to accept you in spite of that."

He stepped back from her. "The past doesn't have to control your future anymore."

Brandon turned to walk to his room. He heard Andrea's door click and hoped he hadn't said more than he should.

WAS BRANDON RIGHT? Had she kept her distance from everyone these years at Omega not because she was afraid of what they'd think of her past if they knew, but because of her refusal to take the responsibility of her job as a behavioral analyst?

How many times had she called herself a fraud? Too many to count. Was it because it was easier to think of herself as a fraud who got lucky with some of her analyses?

She'd certainly lived in fear the past four years of doing something majorly wrong and getting fired. Of getting fired for no reason at all.

Either way, maybe it was time to stop letting her feelings about the past control her every action. It had stunted her growth professionally, for sure. But it had also stopped her from making any friends.

From having any intimate contact with anyone at all.

All the stuff Brandon had said, she was going to have to sort through. It would take a while. Some of it wasn't correct, but some of it was dead-on.

Especially the part about not letting the past control her future anymore.

She'd hated seeing Harry today. Hated even worse seeing the stuttering idiot she'd become around him. The same with her aunt and uncle in the car yesterday, afraid to face them.

These people were from her past and didn't have any control over her unless Andrea gave them that control.

She was tired of giving control over to anyone or anything else but herself. She'd lived without things she wanted—friendship, companionship—for too long. Let her fear convince her to give them up.

She wanted sex and she wanted it with Brandon Han.

She shot off from where she'd been sitting on her bed, the fading evening sun shining on her through the window. She was out the door and knocking on his before she could let herself overthink it too much.

"Hey," he said to her, his eyes traveling all over her face. "Are you okay? I was afraid I said too much, that I overstepped my bounds—"

Andrea grabbed his tie and pulled his mouth down to hers, stretching up on her toes to meet him. She didn't have far to go in her heels.

She thought for a second he might pull away, refuse, but he didn't. Instead he wrapped an arm around her waist and pulled her rapidly, fully, against him. He spun them around, getting her out of the doorway so he could shut it.

The heat was instantaneous. Overwhelming. It seemed to pool through her entire body. The fact that Brandon obviously felt it too just made the heat increase.

She'd wanted this man for years. She'd been afraid to

show her attraction, to move on it, because of her past, of what he might find out.

But now he knew. And beyond that, damn her past and the hold it had had over her for so long.

He backed her up until she was against the wall, their bodies pressed so close against each other there was no room for anything else. Still, her hands gripped his waist, tugging him closer to her before sliding up his back to link behind his neck to capture him. The heat of his body against hers thawed something that had been frozen in her for far too long.

His lips were the perfect blend of firm and soft. Her eyes slid closed as his large hands came up to cup her face, to take control of the melding of their mouths. Andrea was glad to give over the control. She wanted him to give her whatever it took to ease the hunger that clawed at her every time she saw him.

Brandon kissed his way across her jaw and over to her ear. She couldn't stop the quiet gasp that escaped her when he bit gently on her lobe.

"Are you sure this is what you want, Andrea?" he whispered. She could feel his hot breath against her cheek.

More than anything else she'd ever wanted.

"Yes," she murmured, her eyes still closed, her arms sliding to his shoulders, trying to force his big body closer to hers.

But he held firm. "We can wait. It doesn't have to be tonight."

Her eyes flew open. Had she misread him? Did he really not want her? How could she have been so wrong about something like this?

"Is this not what you want?" She choked the words out.

"Oh, it is very much what I want." He stepped his body up against hers so there was no space between them whatsoever, leaving her no doubt that he did want her. "I'm just trying to be a gentleman."

"I don't want a gentleman. I want you."

He smiled. A wicked, hot smile that had her insides melting.

Then his mouth was instantly back on hers, the kiss harder, more urgent. He licked deep into her mouth and they both groaned. He slid his arm around her waist, pulling her off the wall, closer to his chest, so he could ease her blazer down her shoulders. He tossed it over on the small table where his also lay.

He brought his lips back to hers and began unbuttoning her blouse. "You cannot imagine how many times I've wanted to get you out of the perfectly professional suits you wear."

She smiled against his mouth. "I've had a few similar thoughts about you and those shirts and ties."

"Well, then." His brown eyes were so clear she couldn't look away. "I think we've delayed gratification long enough."

They made quick work of getting rid of the rest of their clothes.

He reached down and crooked an arm under her knees, swinging her up in his arms as though she didn't weigh anything at all and carrying her over to the bed. He laid her gently on it and reached down to devour her mouth again as if he couldn't bear to be away from her lips for another second.

A hot ache grew in her throat as his lips moved down her jaw to her neck and bit gently; her fingers slid into his thick black hair. His lips grew more dominating as his hands moved downward, skimming either side of her body to her thighs and back up, before pulling her tightly to him in a raw act of possession.

He hoisted himself up onto his arms for a moment so he could look down at her body then back up to her face.

"Mine," he whispered fiercely, and she almost didn't recognize him as the controlled, intelligent being he usually was.

It ignited something inside her. A burning she knew only he could ease.

Andrea pulled him closer and forgot about the past, forgot about the future, forgot about everything but the heat and desire between them.

Chapter Eleven

He caught her trying to get back out of bed in the middle of the night. To sneak back to her room.

"Not this time," he murmured, reaching an arm out to hook her waist and pull her back into bed next to him. "No sneaking off."

"I should probably go back to my own room," she said.

"In the morning," he said, snuggling into her neck. "Sleep now."

He held her close, her back to his front, running a soothing hand slowly up to her shoulder, then back down, catching her waist then following the line of her body down to her hip and outer thigh, then back up again.

He wanted her to rest, to relax, to get the sleep she needed. Even before the mind-blowing sex they'd just had, it had already been a pretty overwhelming day. Hell, the whole week had been stressful for her.

The warrior in him wanted to protect her, to keep her in his arms until she got the rest—the peace—she needed. He wanted to hold her and keep her safe from anything that would harm her. But even more he wished he could go back and protect the girl she had been. The one who had been forced to work for the likes of Harry Minkley at Jaguar's just to survive. His teeth ground thinking about it—about her on a stage she hated with men leering at her—but he forced the hand that touched her to remain calm, soothing.

He soon realized she was not relaxing under his touch and definitely wasn't going to sleep.

"What's going on in that head of yours?" he asked against her hair.

"I've never slept with someone before. It's weird. I can't relax."

Brandon tensed. "What? You've never..." Had he heard her right?

"Well, I've...you know...had sex before. A couple times in high school. But it was a quickie and never in an actual bed. At night. Ugh."

She pulled the cover up over her head, embarrassed.

It made sense that she hadn't been with anyone since high school. She'd kept herself so apart from everyone else at Omega, there couldn't have been much chance to find someone she was attracted to.

It hurt him again to think of her alone for all those years. Especially when she hadn't needed to be.

He pulled her in closer to him and wrapped an arm around her waist. He slid his other arm under her pillow so her head rested on it.

"There's nothing to it. You just take a few deep breaths and let your eyes close."

"Sometimes I have nightmares."

"About what?"

"Mostly my uncle. That he is attacking me, hitting me, before I can really get awake and away from him. That was finally the reason I left home. Because I knew eventually he would kill me."

"Somebody should've helped you. A school counselor, a doctor, somebody."

He felt her shrug against him. "I was good at being invisible. And terrible at asking for help."

"The trouble asking for help is still a problem, I see. You need to get better at that."

"Yeah, probably. I'm still pretty good at being invisible. I don't think anyone knows me around Omega."

Brandon laughed outright at that. She turned toward him. "What? I don't ever really talk to anyone."

"That doesn't mean they don't notice you, sweetheart. Most are just too scared to start up a conversation with you. You're known as being…" He cut himself off. He didn't want to hurt her feelings.

"What?"

"A loner. Not someone who wants to socialize with others."

"That's pretty much true, I guess."

"Not anymore. Not once we get back to Colorado Springs." He felt her stiffen. "But we don't have to talk about that right now. Right now you just practice the task at hand."

"Oh yeah? What's that?"

"Learning how to sleep with my arms around you."

"Okay, that I can do."

Brandon held her until he felt the tension ease out of her body and her breathing take on the deeper evenness of sleep. But it was a long time before he could sleep himself.

ANDREA STILL SNEAKED out a little before dawn. She wasn't trying to make Brandon angry. She wasn't even trying to get away from him. She just needed to be by herself. To regroup before seeing him again.

Before seeing his gorgeous brown eyes and striking cheekbones. His thick black hair she didn't know if she'd be able to stop her fingers from running through next time she saw him.

Everything about last night had been perfect. And she wasn't running now. Wasn't scared. Or at least wasn't scared of being close to Brandon. It was just that being close to him—being close to *anyone*—for that long was hard for her. She'd spent a lifetime keeping people at arm's length. That habit wasn't going to change overnight.

Not that Brandon had given any sort of indication that he was interested in anything more than just last night. She wished she had more experience with this sort of situation. She'd known one thing: if he'd awakened this morning and she'd sensed regret from him, it would've broken something inside her that couldn't be fixed.

So maybe she was running a little bit.

After putting on jeans and a shirt, for once not feeling the overwhelming need to look immaculately professional, she headed out to the hotel's small dining room as she had yesterday.

She was hungry. She and Brandon hadn't had much dinner and had expended considerable energy during the night. But first things first: coffee.

The lobby was deserted; she couldn't even see someone working behind the counter. The little dining room was also empty.

But for some reason Andrea felt like someone was watching her. She spun all the way around, but couldn't see anyone, just the shadows from the sun starting to rise behind the clouds. It cast an eerie light in the building.

But she could swear she could feel rage, violence, hatred pointed in her direction. She'd felt them enough from her uncle over the years to recognize the emotions.

Was her uncle here?

She was about to go back to her room, to lock herself in, but stopped. No. There wasn't any reason to be frightened. No reason to go hide somewhere.

There was no one here. Just her own imagination—coupled with not getting enough sleep—that was messing with her mind. This *town* messed with her mind.

And if her uncle and aunt were here, she would deal with it.

She forced herself to get the coffee she wanted, then sat down at the corner table. Her back was to a wall and she could see everything that happened in both the dining room and through the glass into the lobby.

She felt better a couple of minutes later when three guys came walking—albeit quite unsteadily—into the lobby. Maybe that was whose presence she had sensed, although it seemed unlikely. They were all laughing so hard she would be surprised if they didn't wake sleeping guests.

They'd obviously been out all night, were barely sober and were highly amused with themselves. They were college-aged, a little younger than Andrea. Clean-cut, good-looking guys.

"Top of the morning to you, miss," one of them said as the others made a beeline to the coffeepot.

Andrea raised an eyebrow. *Top of the morning?* These guys were definitely still drunk. Normally that would have made her tense, but, although she was wary, she found herself too relaxed after last night to jump back into full tension mode.

"Looks like you fellows had a good time. I'm hoping you didn't drive here just now."

"Oh no," another one said, holding up two fingers. "Scout's honor, we took a cab."

"But we do have to drive home in just a few hours." All of them groaned at that. "They're going to have to send security to drag us out of bed at checkout time."

The third one added a ton of sugar to his coffee and grabbed a Danish. "We've got to pace ourselves, you guys. We're never going to make it through the pilgrimage if we keep having nights like last night."

They all smiled. "But what a night."

"Pilgrimage?" Andrea shook her head. "I'm almost afraid to ask what pilgrimage you guys might be on that has left you in a state like this."

Guy number one eased himself into the table next to her, wincing at the sunlight beginning to come through the lobby windows.

"We went back to a place we heard about on the Devils and Angels Pilgrimage."

Andrea had no idea what that was.

"We go to Arizona State," he explained.

"The Sun Devils," Andrea said. Anyone from around here knew Arizona State's mascot.

"Yes!" The guys were all inordinately pleased that she knew that. They got distracted and started talking to each other about their school's latest basketball endeavors. Evidently the Sun Devils were doing well.

Andrea just went back to drinking her coffee; she wasn't interested in basketball statistics. Honestly, she wasn't interested in these guys at all, but knew they'd leave of their own accord soon.

Finally they remembered she was there and that they'd been in the middle of telling her something.

"Sorry. Anyway, Devils and Angels Pilgrimage. One of the local DJs decided he was going to travel all over Arizona to find the best..." The guy stopped, looking at Andrea, unsure how to continue.

He was embarrassed. Andrea could feel it radiate from him. One of the other guys leaned down and whispered something in his ear.

"The best exotic dance clubs," the first guy continued, obviously relieved to have found a more neutral phrase. "All over the state. Some fraternities are taking part in the pilgrimage, including ours."

"So, what, a different club each week?" she asked.

"Yep." He got a bent postcard out of his pocket and slid it to her. "See, we've done the first six and now have three more to go."

The postcard wasn't too difficult to read since it was

just a list of clubs and dates on one side. A picture of a scantily clad she-devil and angel sitting on the shoulders of DJ Shawn "Shocker" Sheppard on the other.

But what caught Andrea's attention was three clubs on the list. Three of their four dead girls had worked at three of them.

"Do you mind if I keep this?" she asked.

"Sure," the guy said, sitting up straighter and looking at her more carefully. "Hey, are you interested in going to any of the clubs with us? There are always a few women there, even straight ones. I'm Pete. We'd love to have you. It would be a lot of—"

"She's not interested, but thanks." Brandon's deep voice came from behind them. "Or if she is, I'll be the one to take her."

He slid into the chair next to Andrea, kissing her on the way down. "Good morning."

"Morning," she murmured against his lips. Brandon pulled back, but kept his arm around Andrea's chair. The message that she was off-limits was more than clear.

"Yeah, well, we've got to get some rest," the college guys said, instinctively backing away from the threat they could feel in Brandon. "The information on the postcard is also on the DJ's website. It's a whole big thing where people vote and they talk about it on the show. It's pretty wild."

The guys grabbed a few more things to eat and then headed up to their room. Pete winked at her over his shoulder and Andrea couldn't help but smile.

"Things are getting progressively worse with you," Brandon told her as he stood to get a cup of coffee. "Yesterday you sneak out of the bed. Today you sneak out of the bed and have three boyfriends by the time I get to breakfast."

"If it helps, I think only Petey wanted to be my boyfriend." She smiled, a little shocked at herself. She wasn't sure where this ability to make light flirtation was coming from, but it was pleasantly surprising.

Brandon turned and leaned against the counter, crossing his arms over his chest. "I might have to start handcuffing you to the bed so you don't escape."

She grinned. "I believe that would be improper use of your restraints, Agent Han."

The heat in his eyes caused her to blush. The thought of being handcuffed to Brandon's bed sent explosions throughout her body.

She liked knowing this man—with all his brains and degrees—wanted her.

He stood there for a long moment just looking at her. The heat in his eyes never went away, but a soft smile formed on his lips as he studied her.

"What?" she finally asked.

He came back to the table and sat across from her this time, leaning close. "You know, I've seen you in your suits, dressed impeccably professional, and totally naked. Nothing in between."

She felt her face burn. "Oh."

"So seeing you in jeans and a shirt is nice. Relaxed."

She leaned into him. "I feel nice. Relaxed."

And she did, amazingly. She didn't have to worry about her secrets being found out; Brandon already knew them. Even the earlier uneasiness about someone watching her had fled. She was here with him and she was relaxed.

She didn't know how long it would last, but for the moment she was willing to just enjoy it.

Chapter Twelve

"So, what did your boyfriend give you there?" Brandon asked between bites of his cereal.

A number of couples and families were around them now, the romantic mood that had engulfed them broken, but not the easiness.

"Something I wanted to check into. See if the dates lined up." She slid over the postcard with the dates the DJ would be visiting the different clubs. "I noticed they were at Jaguar's three nights ago and at Allure last week."

He took the card to study it. "And at Diamond Cabaret two weeks before that, which would be right around when the first victim was found."

"I know the dates don't correspond with their deaths, but I just thought it was interesting that it was the same order."

Brandon nodded. "Very interesting."

"Do you think this DJ Shawn Shocker has anything to do with it?"

"I doubt he is our culprit. Purity doesn't really look like his thing."

She looked at the back of the card with the picture of the DJ and the angel and she-devil on his shoulders. No, Andrea wouldn't peg him as the killer, either. "So maybe it's someone, like Petey and his friends, traveling around on the 'pilgrimage' with DJ Shocker."

Brandon nodded. "Definitely a possibility. Actually, this could be the biggest break in the case we've had so far. Good job."

She smiled, then looked at the paper again. "It doesn't explain about victim number two, Ashley Judson. She didn't work at a dance club at all, one on or off DJ Shocker's list."

"You're right. But also, there was no one killed from the club that the DJ visited that week."

"What does that mean?"

Brandon shrugged, looking at his notebook. "Let's follow this thread all the way out." He lowered his voice so their conversation wouldn't be overheard by the few people eating breakfast. "Let's say it's a DJ Shocker groupie who's committing our crimes. Someone who is following Shocker from club to club, picking a woman and killing her a day or two later.

"Okay, victim number one, Yvette Tyler, was killed one day after Shocker's stop at Diamond Cabaret. There were no reported deaths after Shocker's stop at Vixen's the next week."

"But victim number two was killed where she worked at the truck stop."

Brandon nodded. "And we know she moonlighted as a prostitute."

"Shocker's group headed to Allure the following week. Noelle Brumby was found dead two days later." Andrea used sugar packets to provide a graphic representation of what she was saying. "And then Shocker was at Jaguar's on Tuesday and Jillian Spires was found yesterday, so killed Wednesday night."

Brandon stood. "Definitely fits. We need to get this to the sheriff's office."

Sitting in Officer Kendrick's office two hours later, Andrea back in one of her professional suits, Brandon could feel frustration pooling all around him. They weren't going to get any help from the locals.

Kendrick had pretty much been ordered to let the case go and release it to the City of Phoenix homicide department. The Maricopa County Sheriff's Department had neither the resources nor the manpower to continue the investigation.

And honestly, except for Kendrick, Brandon wasn't sure they had much of a desire.

The conference call with Gerardo Jennison with the City of Phoenix PD hadn't offered much hope, either. They would offer their labs, coroners, crime-scene investigators and even continue to be a liaison, but they couldn't afford to put much detective and officer manpower on it. Phoenix and Maricopa County in general had bigger problems than the deaths of four women on their hands: they were dealing with unprecedented biker gang wars all along Interstate 10.

Unless something drastically changed, he and Andrea were on their own when it came to investigating. The sheriff's office promised to send out a notice to the owners of the exotic dance clubs in the area, asking them to warn the women working there to be extra cautious.

But that was it. No one else was working full-time on trying to find the killer.

He could feel Andrea becoming more agitated, so Brandon wrapped up the conference call and meeting pretty quickly. He'd been around red tape long enough to know that sometimes you just worked around it instead of trying to go through it. He led Andrea back out to the car.

"They don't care at all," she said, barely out the door. "The deaths of these women mean *nothing* to them."

He walked with her toward the parking lot, stopping by a tree that was at least a little bit away from the main entrance. "I know it seems that way, but I don't think that's true. Money and manpower are finite resources. The department wants to put them both where it's going to help the most number of people."

Andrea ran her fingers through her blond hair. Brandon had never seen her this aggravated before.

"If it wasn't for us, *nobody* would be looking into their deaths. Trying to figure out what happened. Trying to stop it from happening again."

He ran a hand up her arm. "The locals want to help, too. They just don't have the funds."

She turned away from him, looking off into the desert that surrounded them. "What if DJ Shocker had decided to do this stupid tour four years ago? I could've been the one the police found yesterday. And just like those four other women, nobody would've cared about my death. No family members would have stormed the sheriff's office demanding the killer be caught."

Although he knew it was probably the truth, everything in Brandon tightened in rejection at the thought. The thought that she could've died without his ever knowing her.

"Andrea—"

"I care about these women, Brandon. I don't know them, but I care."

He turned her around and folded her into his arms, thankful that she didn't pull away. He needed to have her close to him right now, to know that she was okay.

"I know you do."

"I will stand for them. Find the killer. Stop this from happening to other women. No matter what choices they made in their lives, they didn't deserve to die like that."

"Together. We will stop this guy together."

He could feel her nod against his chest before she took a step back. "I have a plan."

"Okay."

"It involves us both stepping outside our comfort zones a little."

Brandon grimaced slightly. He wasn't sure he liked the sound of this. "Okay."

"We've got four days until DJ Shocker's next club appearance. We'll talk to him, talk to his production crew, see who the groupies are, following from club to club."

He nodded. "Okay, good. I already have an appointment lined up with him this afternoon."

"We'll need to interview those people. See what we can figure out from them."

Brandon nodded. "Yes." So far none of this was out of their comfort zone.

"We know that Club Paradise, on the northern side of Phoenix, is where the party is heading next." She took a deep breath, then continued in a rush. "I'll go undercover. Get a job there as a stripper. Try to lure the killer o—"

"No." The word was out of his mouth almost before his brain had processed what she was saying.

"Brandon, it's a good plan—"

"No."

He could feel the warrior inside him rising up and fought to keep hold of the logical, reasonable side of his mind.

There was no way in hell she was getting up onstage naked in front of strangers and trying to lure out a killer.

No. And no.

He couldn't drag her away and lock her in a room to keep her safe—and away from prying eyes—so he fought to find the logical words to make his case.

"First of all, you're not a trained agent. You don't have the skills or experience to work undercover. Not to mention, what if the killer *does* come after you? You don't have the hand-to-hand or weapons defense training you need to protect yourself."

"But—"

"Not to mention, as someone who holds a doctorate in psychology, I cannot even begin to list the ways it would damage your psyche to go back into a situation like that. To put yourself back into the club scene where you were objectified by men could have a truly damaging effect on your state of mind."

Brandon began pacing back and forth.

"You're just beginning to come out of your proverbial shell, connect with other people—me in particular—and to place yourself back into the exact situation where you found such shame and—"

"Brandon."

"Fear will only set you back emotionally, which is not what…"

"Brandon." She said his name again, but this time she stepped in front of him and touched his cheek, stopping his pacing.

He stared down at her clear green eyes. There were no shadows in them now, as there had been so often in the past. No fear. Just determination.

"You're frightened for me. I can feel it."

He wanted to deny it, to argue that he was just being reasonable—especially if she couldn't seem to be—but he knew it was the truth.

He was terrified at the thought of her doing this. Of the damaging effects it could have on her on multiple levels.

"Thank you," she continued. "For caring enough to be scared for me."

"It's not a good idea for you." He put his forehead against hers. "It will hurt you in ways you're not really considering right now."

"I know it's not the best plan for me. But right now I need to think about whether it's the best plan for Jillian

Spires and Noelle Brumby, and the other women who will come next if we don't stop this guy."

Brandon straightened. Objectively speaking, for the case and stopping the killer, it was actually a pretty good plan. But he still didn't like it one bit.

"But what about you not having training?"

"I was a stripper for a year and a half. I think I have all the training I need."

"No, law-enforcement training. Self-defense training."

"I have some. Drackett required me to have some."

Brandon planned to make sure she had more. Not just for this case, but because Andrea needed to know she could take care of herself, that she never had to be a victim again.

"*Some* is not enough in a situation like this. Especially when you're trying to capture the attention of a killer."

Brandon could feel another plan formulating in his brain. Within just a few seconds he had run a dozen pros and cons mentally and had come up with some plausible alternates to her plan.

"I need to do this, Brandon. It's the best way. You know that."

He held up a finger to get her to wait a moment more as everything fell into place in his mind.

"Fine. But you don't go undercover as one of the main performers. You go under as a waitress. One of our victims wasn't a dancer at all, so that can't be the only link. You'll be able to get up close with the patrons, especially when DJ Shocker is there. See if you can get any readings of anything unusual."

Andrea nodded slowly. "Okay."

"I will also be in the club at all times when you're there. I'll come in as a customer, but under no circumstances are you to leave with anyone except me."

"Okay, that's probably for the best."

"And I'm going to call Steve and tell him we need out

of the hotel and into a rental house. One that has a lot of space in the living room."

"Why?"

"Because if you're going to set yourself up as bait for a killer, I'm going to make damn certain you know more than just *some* defense tactics. We have four days. Anytime we're not interviewing suspects or investigating the case, you're going to find yourself going hand to hand with me."

Chapter Thirteen

"Can't you arrest him for something?" Andrea leaned over and muttered under her breath to Brandon. *"Anything?"*

They'd been in the lobby of DJ Shawn "Shocker" Sheppard's radio station for the past thirty minutes. Unfortunately, because DJ Shocker was doing a live show, they hadn't been able to question him yet. They'd also been forced to listen to his show.

Distasteful would be the most polite word for it. Less polite terms would be *vulgar, juvenile* and *ridiculous*.

"Unfortunately, being an idiot is not currently a crime in this country. So, no, I can't arrest him." Brandon looked as disgusted as she felt.

The radio program catered to college students—men in particular—and the humor was rowdy and raunchy. At least one word every second would have to be bleeped out over normal airwaves, although most of the audience was probably listening to the station over the internet, where no censoring was needed.

Andrea had listened for the past half hour, teeth grinding, as DJ Shocker had attempted to make a case for the banning of all women's sports bras. He'd used every obnoxious tactic from "that's how God would want it" to trying to compare the bras to illegal performance-enhancing drugs.

The entire premise was asinine, but that was the point. DJ Shocker wanted to live up to his name.

They could see him through the large window that separated the waiting room from the radio booth. DJ Shocker wasn't a bad-looking guy. Probably in his late thirties, way too old to be saying the ridiculous stuff he spewed. His show was on the air three hours a day, five days a week. And it was not only one of the most popular radio talk shows in Arizona, but a top-twenty across the whole country. People couldn't wait to hear what he would say next.

Andrea couldn't wait for him to shut up.

He finally did, tying in the topic du jour with his Devils and Angels pilgrimage tour. He invited everyone out to Club Paradise in four days. It would be the focus of much conversation in next week's shows, he promised. Not something any red-blooded Arizonian would want to miss.

The On Air sign finally flipped off. DJ Shocker was finished for the day. He took a moment to talk to his production crew, who'd gotten him through the past three hours. When an assistant came up to him and said something, pointing at Andrea and Brandon, he looked over.

"Hi. I'm Shawn Sheppard," DJ Shocker said as he walked out of the large radio booth, his voice sounding different than it had on air. "Megan told me you're law enforcement?"

"I'm Brandon Han." Brandon shook the hand the DJ offered to him. "I'm with Omega Sector: Critical Response Division. This is Andrea Gordon."

Andrea shook his hand also, although she really didn't want to. At least he didn't come across quite so obnoxious in person. Although he was much shorter than she would've thought. Shorter than Andrea's five feet eight inches. *Much* shorter than Brandon's six feet.

"Has there been another threat against my life?"

Brandon looked over at Andrea. She hid a snicker in a

cough. It was no surprise to her at all that someone would like to get rid of DJ Shocker permanently.

Brandon shook his head. "Not that we're aware of, Mr. Sheppard. Do you get a lot?"

The man shrugged. "Please, call me Shawn. I get a couple a year. Most of them we don't take seriously, although my lawyer has reported them all to the police."

Andrea watched him closely as he said it. He didn't seem to be hiding any fear about the threats.

"No, we're not here to talk about that. We'd like to ask you a few questions about the Angels and Devils Pilgrimage."

Shawn opened a bottle of water. "What about it?"

"Who came up with the idea for a strip-club tour?"

He answered as he led them down the hall toward his office. "My producers and I last summer. Something to do this winter where we could announce the best club around spring break—the end of March. College students make up my primary audience."

Andrea was content with letting Brandon ask the questions. She would just watch and try to gauge Shawn's feelings.

"Would you consider it a success so far?" Brandon asked, sitting in a chair next to Andrea. Shawn sat on a sofa.

"Yeah. Enough that we might do it again, or something similar, next year. The clubs seem to love it—I'm bringing in a lot of extra revenue for them. And I can't complain about the gig." He smiled at Andrea as he said it. She didn't smile back.

"Have you had any problems? Anything weird?"

The DJ's eyes narrowed slightly. "We've had a rowdy bunch sometimes. Once or twice it's gotten a little out of hand. A couple fights. A couple of guys getting a little too fresh with the dancers. Cops were called."

"Were any of these women involved with those situations?" Brandon laid out the pictures of the four victims, shots of them before they'd been killed so Shawn could see how they really would've looked. The DJ studied them.

He definitely recognized the first, Yvette Tyler. Andrea caught his slight change in breathing as well as a stiffening in his posture.

"What's this about?" Shawn asked. "Are these women suing me or something?"

"Do they have reason to sue you?" Brandon asked.

Shawn sat back and rolled his eyes. He was now aware that he was being accused of something here, rather than potentially being the victim as he had first thought. His posture became more defensive, less open.

"Have you heard my show? I offend everyone. I'm surprised there's not a lawsuit every week. Of course, I do have the First Amendment on my side."

"Do you recognize these women?"

"They're all dancers at the clubs, right? But I don't know which was at which. It's all become a blur of pasties and pole dances."

Andrea pointed at Yvette's picture. "But you definitely know her, right?"

Shawn fidgeted. "Look, yeah. She was at one of the clubs a few weeks ago. Cute girl. Sexy. Great dancer. She cornered me in the hallway when I went to use the bathroom. Wanted to do some private dancing with me at home, if you know what I mean."

"And did you go home with her or vice versa?" Brandon asked.

"No. This was business for me. I was a celebrity. Leaving with her publicly wouldn't have been a good idea."

"What about leaving with her privately?"

"No. I didn't leave with her at all. She was irritated at

the time, but when I saw her later after closing, she had moved on to some other guy. Was all over him at his car."

"Did that make you mad? Make you think she was some sort of slut or something?" Brandon asked.

"No. Honestly, I didn't care. I get a lot of women who throw themselves at me, if you know what I mean."

He glanced sideways at Andrea as if he expected her to do just that at any moment. She rolled her eyes.

"You're safe from me," Andrea said.

"What is this all really about? Not me going home with these women."

"No," Brandon said. "Unfortunately, all of these women are dead, Shawn."

"What?" He shot back against the sofa, eyes wide.

As far as Andrea could tell, the shock flowing off DJ Shocker was completely authentic. He had not known the women were dead.

Brandon looked over at her and she gave him a slight nod. He nodded back, agreeing.

"When— What— How did they die?" Shawn looked back at the pictures.

"They were all murdered. Within a day or two of your Angels and Devils tour stopping at their place of business."

Shawn's face lost all color beneath his ginger hair. "Oh my God, are you serious? I'm sorry if I was flippant before. I had no idea they were dead. I swear I didn't have anything to do with this."

Brandon nodded. "We'll need your whereabouts at certain days and times, but we believe you. You're not actually a suspect, although at this time we're in the process of successfully eliminating as many people as possible."

"Okay." He buried his head in his hands. "Sure, sure. I'll provide you with whatever you need."

"Thank you."

Andrea leaned a little closer toward him. Now that he

wasn't acting like a complete jerk, it wasn't so difficult. "Were there any people you remember seeing at all the clubs that showed a lot of interest in these women?"

"There's a number of guys, mostly from competing fraternities, that have come to most, if not all, of the tour stops."

"Do you remember anyone in particular?" Brandon asked.

Shawn thought about it for a long time. "No. I'm sorry. The clubs are pretty crazy and I just wasn't paying attention. More focused on other things." He started to move back into sleazeball shocker mode, but stopped himself. "There were a lot of people around. A lot of women. A lot of guys. I don't remember anyone in particular. I'm sorry."

"Okay. Thanks for your assistance."

"Do we need to cancel the tour?"

"No. As a matter of fact, we think your tour is our best chance at catching the killer."

"Oh. Okay."

Brandon stood and Andrea followed suit.

"We're probably going to be at all your club appearances, from now on. We'd appreciate it if you didn't draw anyone's attention to us."

"Yeah, sure. Whatever will help."

Brandon shook Shawn's hand. The other man looked pretty shell-shocked. Andrea didn't blame him—it was a lot to take in. They left him and walked back out the way they'd come.

"He seemed pretty legitimately surprised," Brandon said, once they were outside.

"Yeah. I think he was definitely authentic about that. He's not our killer unless I'm way off."

"I agree."

They were almost to the car when Andrea turned back toward the building, sure that Shawn or someone from inside was calling them. But she didn't see anyone in the doorway.

But she knew someone was studying them.

"What's wrong?" Brandon asked, coming up behind her.

"Nothing. I don't know. I thought—" She looked around. That feeling from this morning was back. As if someone was watching her.

"What?" She felt Brandon's hand slide down the arm of her blazer. Having him near helped her shake it off. She was overtired. Had been bombarded by too much over the past few days.

Andrea shook off the feeling and leaned into Brandon. "Nothing. I thought I heard someone call me from back at the building. Must be the lack of sleep getting to me. You know any reasons why lack of sleep might have been a problem for me last night?"

Brandon smiled down at her. "Hmm. Maybe. Can't promise that won't happen again tonight."

Andrea hoped so. She would take a repeat of last night any way she could get it.

But there was a lot of work to do before either of them could think about sleeping—or not sleeping.

"We need to go back to Jaguar's so I can talk to the girls. See if they know or remember anything. Warn them to be careful."

"If the killer follows the pattern and keeps going with the tour, then the other women at Jaguar's should be safe," Brandon said.

"Well, we already have one discrepancy with the pattern. Victim number two wasn't a dancer at all. So I don't want to take any chances that the pattern gets changed and the killer comes back to Jaguar's."

He squeezed her shoulder. "Absolutely. Drackett is already making sure that the club owners are aware of the issue. He knows the local police department is also notifying them, but maybe hearing it from two different law-enforcement sources will make sure everyone is taking it seriously."

"Yeah, that's good."

"Are you sure you're okay?"

Andrea looked around again but didn't see anything that made her suspicious. The only thing she needed to be suspicious of was her tendency to see the boogeyman everywhere she looked.

Chapter Fourteen

At nine o'clock the next night Brandon was almost ready to exit his car and enter Club Paradise. Somehow he doubted very much that was what it would turn out to be.

Andrea was already inside, had been there for the past two hours working as a waitress. They'd cleared it with the club manager, "Big Mike," who'd been happy to keep the women who worked for him safe as well as have free help during the Saturday-night rush.

Big Mike, despite his name, was considerate and businesslike, the opposite of Harry Minkley at Jaguar's.

Brandon had been happy to spend a couple of hours putting the fear of God and law enforcement into Harry yesterday as Andrea talked to her friends.

Brandon hated the shadows that overtook Andrea's eyes whenever they were near Jaguar's. The shadows worsened around Harry. There were a number of scenarios Brandon could envision that would make Andrea react that way even four years later. None of them good.

So putting pressure on Harry, even though he wasn't really a viable suspect, was no hardship for Brandon. The man was sweating every corner he'd ever cut—and there were many—by the time Brandon left. Oh, and Brandon said they would have constant surveillance on Harry and Jaguar's for at least the next year.

Brandon rolled his eyes at the thought of how much of

a misuse of funds that would be, how ridiculously expensive, how it would never get approved. But Harry didn't need to know that. Every time someone came in looking slightly uptight, Harry would wonder if the person was undercover law enforcement. Good.

Brandon had watched Andrea interacting with the dancers of Jaguar's—some she'd known before, some she hadn't—and just kept his distance. The women, rightfully, had questions about Jillian Spires's death and Andrea answered them as best she could without giving away important details about the case. DJ Shocker was not mentioned by Andrea, although all the women said how crazy the night had been. Busy, especially for a Tuesday, not normally a great night. They'd all made a lot of money, which had made everyone happy.

None of them could remember any particular guy hanging around Jillian. Of course, there had been men everywhere because it was so busy.

Andrea warned them all to look out for each other. To walk to their cars at least in pairs. To carefully vet anyone new in their lives before trusting them. The women listened to Andrea in a way they never would've listened to Brandon. She was one of their own.

Keira, the woman Andrea had been so friendly with the day before, had come up to them after Andrea was finished and the other girls had left.

She told them that Jillian had been mentioning a new guy in her life. She hadn't given a name, just that it was someone she'd known for a while and that their relationship had recently taken a turn toward the romantic.

It was something to look into and Brandon assured her they would.

"Hey, you won't leave town without coming to say goodbye, right?"

Keira had gorgeous wavy black hair that fell to the

middle of her back. She was shorter and more voluptuous than Andrea's tall slender build. The two of them standing side by side made a striking pair.

"No, the case is far from over."

"Well, I want you to catch this sicko, but no just taking off like last time, okay?"

"I'm sorry, Keira. You were a good friend to me and I shouldn't have done that." Andrea looked down, and Brandon could see her begin to withdraw into herself.

Keira pulled Andrea to her in a huge hug. "Oh, honey, once I found out you'd left with those two cops and you weren't in any trouble, I was thrilled for you. This was never the place you were meant to be."

Andrea wrapped her arms around Keira, also. "You either, Kee. It's time to move on."

Keira slid back and winked at Andrea and smiled over at Brandon. "It's not so bad for me. I know how to work the stage, the whole place. But I got a plan, don't you worry."

"I'm going to be moonlighting over at Club Paradise for the next few days," Andrea told her. "Undercover type stuff."

"Dancing?" Keira's eyes got big.

"No, just waiting tables. We've got reason to suspect the killer might target someone from there next."

"You be careful." She turned to Brandon. "You'll be there looking out for her?"

"Absolutely."

"Good. She's going to need it. She's all tough now, but she won't be feeling so tough when she's in the club. Even working the floor can be brutal. Sometimes more so with the wandering hands."

Brandon felt his own hands clench. The thought of drunk, sweaty men—of *any* men—pawing at Andrea had the warrior clawing to get out. He had to take a deep breath to calm himself.

Keira gave him a knowing smile. "Yeah, you're going to have to keep that under control if you want this undercover mission to work. She can handle it. She handled it for months when she worked here. Can you?"

Brandon hadn't known, still didn't know, as he was walking into the club now.

Club Paradise was nicer—more high-end—than Jaguar's, but in the end it was the same general principle: almost-naked women making themselves pseudo available.

These clubs sold a fantasy—a private dancer fantasy—where it didn't matter what a guy looked like, how short or tall, fat or skinny, skin tones or hairstyles: he got the girl.

For a price.

And only for a three-minute dance.

Although he'd been to a few for parties over the years, strip clubs had never been his thing. He had always found them to reek of desperation from both the men and women, although you could easily ignore it if you wanted to. And obviously many people wanted to.

A woman's naked body, although he could appreciate it, was not ultimately what turned him on. He found a woman's mind, her emotions, her ability to converse, infinitely more attractive.

Take Andrea, for instance. He couldn't deny he was attracted to her blond hair, green eyes, the delicate lines of her face. Her slender body, curved in just the right places, definitely turned him on.

But it was the other things: her obvious intelligence despite having to overcome her dyslexia, her shy smile, her ability at reading people. Those were the things that really attracted him to her.

The thumping sound of the music permeated the entire building. Brandon passed two bouncers who were actively surveilling the club, making sure none of the girls needed to be rescued from any of the men. Their job would get progressively more difficult as the night—and drinking—went on.

It was Saturday night, still relatively early for a place like this, but there were already men sitting around the main stage, where a dancer worked the pole with strength and skill that would rival an acrobat.

A topless acrobat, but still.

Big Mike had reserved a small table for Brandon in a strategic location in a corner near the bar. It wasn't the best seat if you wanted to be close to or watch the dancers, which was fine since Brandon didn't, but it was excellent for watching the rest of the club without looking as if he was doing so.

DJ Shocker's show would be here in three more days. Brandon and Andrea wanted to use her time working here leading up to that to try to identify regulars and people who could potentially pose a threat. Both so they knew who to watch and who they didn't really need to worry about watching when Tuesday rolled around.

Brandon would study behavior patterns: men who looked as though they were observing the girls with a more nefarious purpose in mind. Andrea would use her skills at reading body language and emotions to do the same thing, but from a stripper's point of view.

Sitting at his table, Brandon ordered a vodka tonic from a waitress who came by, smiling. He wouldn't drink it; he needed all his facilities firing at full speed, not dulled by alcohol. Next time around he'd switch it out for a club soda. It would look the same to anyone who happened to be observing.

He hadn't seen Andrea yet, but it was a big place. Big enough that he couldn't watch everything at one time. He had to constantly be looking around in order to see everyone, much like the bouncers. But he had to be much more subtle about it.

He wasn't wearing a suit, of course. Nobody in here was. He was wearing jeans and a black T-shirt, since he knew Club Paradise would just get warmer as the night went on and more bodies were packed inside.

His waitress brought his drink back, smiling, and Brandon paid, tipping generously. Drackett was not going to be thrilled when Brandon's Omega expense report included drinks from Club Paradise.

Brandon saw Andrea as she came out of a room from behind the bar. At first he could see only her shoulders and the side of her head through the crowd. Then a group of laughing guys moved and he could see her completely.

He picked up his drink and gulped it all the way down, alcohol be damned. If he'd had another he would've done the same thing.

This was Andrea as he'd never seen her, hell, would never even have been able to picture her in all her professional button-down suits.

Her shoulders were bare, her breasts cupped in a red corset bustier that cinched her already-small waist. Her black skirt was short, loose, not even reaching to midthigh. He couldn't tell what shoes she wore from where he sat, but knew from the way she towered over everyone that she had to be in heels.

Her hair that had always been perfectly tidy at work was now sexily, skillfully mussed. Her dark makeup gave her eyes a smoldering look.

Brandon wasn't the only one who noticed her. The group of guys that had parted so he could catch a glimpse of her soon saw the gorgeous waitress and made their way over to order more drinks. One put his hand on her waist; another played with a little piece of her hair.

Andrea laughed at something one of them said, then showed them to a table near the stage. All of them were staring at her legs as she walked away to get their order.

When her back was turned to them, one made a crude gesture to another, obviously about what he'd like to do to Andrea.

It took every ounce of willpower Brandon possessed to stay in his seat. What was he going to do, go punch some twentysomething guy in the face because he'd made a suggestive gesture?

Besides, look at what Andrea was wearing. Could he really blame the punk?

Brandon realized that was just as unfair a thought. Andrea was dressed the way all the waitresses here were dressed. It seemed to be a uniform of some sort: corset bustier and flirty skirts. All the girls had them on in different colors.

He hadn't even really noticed the outfit when his waitress had brought him his drink, but he sure as hell noticed it on Andrea.

He leaned back farther in his seat and forced his eyes away from her at the bar. He was here to study potential suspects, for anybody acting out of the ordinary. Not to act out of the ordinary himself.

But he couldn't stop himself from looking as Andrea brought the drinks back over to the guys. As she leaned down to put them on the table, all of their eyes flew to her breasts, hoping, he was sure, that there might be a happy accident with her top. One guy rubbed his hand up and down the back of her knee. Not going far enough up to be trouble, but certainly more intimate than he had a right to be.

Andrea just smiled and shook her head at him, as if scolding a toddler for being naughty. The men paid and she walked away. Their attention turned back to the stage.

Brandon sat back in his chair.

When he had found out a couple of days ago that Andrea had been a stripper, had worked at a place like this, Brandon had thought he was okay with it. He knew how quiet and reserved she was, plus the abuse that had occurred in her past, the desperate situation that had led her to it.

It had made for a very tragic figure in his mind.

What had he thought, that she had just cried all the way through every night she'd worked there? Sobbing and pushing away every man who came near her?

Obviously that hadn't happened. She'd worked the scenario to her advantage. Worked the men. She might have even enjoyed it all, if how she looked tonight—all smiles and flirtation—was anything to go by.

This jarring close-up of her scantily clad past made it a little harder for him to accept.

Brandon sat up and looked away from her again, from her laughs and flirtatiousness with seemingly every man in the room. The warrior snarled, demanding that he remove her from this situation, get her out of here. Prove—to all these men *and* her—she was his and only his.

But Brandon refused. His intellect ruled him, not his body and definitely not his emotions. Not the warrior. He had a job to do. He ignored the darkness that seemed to be waiting like a cavernous pit for him to fall into. And possibly never crawl back out.

No, he would do this job. Find and stop this killer.

Maybe Andrea wasn't the woman he'd thought. The partner, in more ways than one, that he'd been subconsciously hoping for. He'd survive.

Chapter Fifteen

"If a man comes up behind you and has you in a grasp you can't escape from, the most important thing is not to panic," Brandon had said yesterday evening as they went through self-defense moves in the large living room of the house Omega had rented for them for the rest of their stay here.

"Actually, not panicking is always the most important thing," he'd said, then continued to show her how to throw her arms up and then reach behind her attacker in a sweeping motion with her leg to take him down.

"It's not about size—you're never going to get attacked by someone smaller and weaker than you—it's about staying calm, focused and moving quickly."

It was some sort of jujitsu move, he'd told her. He had a black belt in it, as well as Tae Kwon Do. Andrea had always known about his intellectual prowess, but had no idea about the physical. Although she should've guessed after seeing his rock-hard abdomen and well-defined chest while in bed with him.

They'd practiced over and over, Brandon taking the brunt of the fall each time, until Andrea could do it naturally, without having to think about the different steps. Then they'd practiced more because Brandon said it needed to become muscle memory.

She'd finally stopped him by rolling on top of him after she'd swept him to the ground and kissing him.

"I don't think this is how you're going to want to behave during a crisis," he muttered against her lips, but she could feel his smile.

He'd slipped his arms under his head as she'd sat up, straddling his hips, and pulled her shirt over her head. She'd loved how his eyes had narrowed and his breath hissed out of his lips.

"I think I've got that particular attack crisis taken care of. There are some other one-on-one moves I'd like to work on now, if that's okay with you."

"Um…"

She reached back and unhooked her bra, throwing it to the side, and looked down at him, eyebrow arched. "Got any other moves we can commit to muscle memory?"

"I can definitely think of a couple."

Andrea held on to those memories of yesterday evening as the hours dragged on at Club Paradise. The memories of making love with Brandon with her on top, then in the shower, before he'd tenderly held her while they slept. She was getting used to having his arms around her, snuggling into him while sleeping.

She could use his strong arms around her now. It was nearly midnight, she had two more hours to work and the Saturday crowd was getting more rowdy.

Her first steps out the backstage door onto the club floor had brought back memories, all of them bad. The feelings of being exposed, being watched, being thought of as a piece of meat.

The hands that touched her, sometimes innocently, sometimes much less so.

The bouncers were great here, much better than at Jaguar's. She'd already seen one step in at just a look from one of the waitresses. A guy who had pulled her down in his lap didn't want to let go. The bouncer made his way over, and without a word, he offered the waitress a hand to help her out of the guy's lap. He gave a pointed look to the man, again not saying a word. The guy had apologized to the waitress and everything had been fine.

Other waitresses, Andrea noticed, didn't mind the wandering hands of customers. Provided better tips. The bouncers seemed to know who was who.

Andrea still hated everything about it. Being down on the floor was almost worse than being up on the stage. At least onstage there was a distance—you were a performer. Here you were in the middle of the fray.

She'd seen Brandon sitting over at a corner table. She'd wanted to go over there, but didn't. She didn't want to encroach on another waitress's table, plus Brandon seemed to be deep in the study of the club. His face was pinched and focused, almost angry.

So, although she could desperately use a friendly smile from him, she forced herself to look away and do her job.

Survive this night, which had been her motto when working at Jaguar's, was not her job now. Now her job was doing what she could to find a killer.

It was difficult to get a reading of anyone in here. It was too chaotic; her own feelings were too chaotic. Lust was the primary emotion, followed by guilt and greed. Alcohol caused everything to be hazy and people to have emotions they might not normally feel. She felt as if she was trying to filter through solid walls.

She tried to focus and find the emotions of anger, judgment, condescension. The ones the killer was most likely to have. It didn't take her long to realize the biggest place all three were coming from was Brandon's table.

She had to be wrong about that. Maybe Brandon was just using those emotions, channeling them almost, in order to try to find them in other people. Looking for nonverbal clues. She knew he wasn't the killer, but he definitely wasn't happy.

Andrea turned away from Brandon. She had to focus on what she was doing, not on how he seemed to be behaving.

Instead of trying to feel out general emotions for the whole place, Andrea decided to take it table by table.

She carried her drinks, trying to stay a little longer at each table to get a read on the men there.

The killer was icily controlled. What had been done to the women had not been done in a rage or burst of passion. It had been planned. The killer would study his victim. That was what Andrea was hoping to catch tonight. Someone who just didn't quite fit.

The emotions would be cold, not hot. Andrea needed to look beneath the heat of the lust and general rowdiness. She took a breath and centered herself.

The rest of the night went by more easily. She blocked everything from her mind besides trying to find the coldness of the killer. She thought of it in terms of color. Almost everything in the club was red and she was looking for blue.

Once she focused, the things that used to bother her so much when she worked at Jaguar's faded away. The hands that grasped at her leg or waist she ignored. She wasn't here to make tips; she was here to observe. She didn't need to flirt or smile in a suggestive manner. She froze them out and concentrated. These men were nothing to her. She could leave at any time.

She never found what she searched for. She wasn't able to pinpoint any source of contempt or cold calculation. Everything in here just seemed to be what someone would expect from a strip club: drunkenness, rowdiness and a lot of lust.

A little before 2:00 a.m. Big Mike yelled out for last call. Andrea made her way to the back room, taking her tips and splitting them among the other waitresses, slipping the money into their lockers. Her job was done for the night.

She was exhausted.

The last six hours had taken everything out of her. Getting past her fears, getting past the men, getting past it all and focusing despite her feelings. All for nothing.

She wanted Brandon. Wanted his arms around her. Wanted to go to their little house and leave this all behind her. At least until tomorrow night.

The plan was to exit separately so no one would think they were leaving together. Not that she thought anyone was watching her. But it never hurt to be sure.

Andrea stepped out the back employee door to discover it was storming. There were no windows inside Club Paradise, of course, and either the storm had just come up or Andrea had been so focused on finding who might be the killer that she hadn't even noticed if people had started coming in with wet hair. Either was possible.

She stood alone under the small awning covering the door, but it didn't offer much protection from the rain. Brandon should be here soon to get her. He would drive the car, even off the club parking lot if necessary, to make sure no one was watching him, then swing around to pick her up. She wasn't sure how long it would take.

She stood, huddled under the awning, trying to ward off the chill. The doorway was well lit, but the parking-lot lighting here in the back wasn't great, and beyond the lot seemed to be a vast darkness. She shivered.

That feeling was back. The feeling of someone watching her with anticipation and violence, but she was finally coming to realize that feeling was based on her physical exhaustion and emotional turmoil. Like her past, she wouldn't let it control her.

But she couldn't shake it.

She happened to be looking in the right direction—

across the parking lot into the group of trees and cacti that surrounded the outer edge of Club Paradise—when the lightning struck.

She could see the outline of a man in the bright flash. Big, powerful. He wore a black rain jacket with a hood and the water flowed down it. Although the hood hid his features, she knew he was staring right at her.

This man intended to harm her. She had no doubt about it.

She immediately turned back to the door but found it locked. Damn it. Big Mike had told her they locked it from the inside after 9:00 p.m. to keep anyone from sneaking in that way. She rammed her fist against the door heavily, hoping the music was off and someone might hear her.

She turned back to where the man was. He was the killer. He had to be. She couldn't see anything in the darkness.

Was he almost on her? She strained her eyes but couldn't see anything. Dressed in black as he was, it would be difficult to see him in the lot. Lightning flashed again.

He was closer. Oh God, he was closer. He must be walking, taking his time. Which somehow panicked her even more. He was playing a game with her. Was that a knife in his hand?

She pounded again. Nothing. She was afraid to keep her back to him. What if he started to run and pounced?

Should she leave, try to make her way around to the front door? That would require running through some darkened parts of the parking lot around the edge of the building, but it seemed better than sitting here alone with her one jujitsu move and no one opening the door.

She turned, almost certain she would find the big man right behind her, but didn't. Her breath sawing in and out of her chest, Andrea jumped down the side of the small door ledge, keeping her back to the wall so the killer couldn't sneak up on her. She was about to run when she saw Brandon's car pulling around the corner.

It stopped, a beacon of safety standing between her and whoever was out there in the darkness. When Brandon saw she was standing in the rain he got out.

"What's going on? Are you okay?"

"The k-killer." She could barely get the words out and pointed toward the lot where she'd seen the man. "I think he's out there. I saw him when lightning flashed."

Brandon immediately pulled out his weapon. "What? Are you sure?"

Andrea nodded, still trying to get in enough breath to calm her racing heart. "I know he was there."

"I'm going to check it out. You stay by the car."

"No!" There was no way she was letting him go alone, or staying here alone, for that matter. "I'll come with you."

"Andrea, you're not an agent—you don't need to do this."

"Yeah, well, I have a pair of eyes. I'm not letting you go out there with your back exposed."

Brandon nodded. "Fine. Let's drive the car that way so we at least have the headlights helping us."

They got in the car and he reached into the glove compartment, pulling out a gun. "This is a Glock 9 mm. Are you familiar with weapons at all?"

"Some, but only at the range."

"That's better than most." He handed it to her. "Just don't shoot me on accident."

They drove over near where Andrea had seen the man during the first flash of lightning. Brandon spun the car slowly in a semicircle to provide light on a wider area, but they didn't see anything.

"He seems to be gone now. Where did you see him?"

Andrea pointed. "At first it was over near those trees.

Then I was trying to get back inside and when I turned around again he was in the middle of the parking lot."

"That rain is coming down pretty hard out there, but let's see if we can find anything."

She didn't want to go. She wanted to stay inside the safety of the car. She wanted him to stay inside the safety of the car. She reached for his hand and was surprised when he pulled away as if she'd burned him.

She turned to him, but he didn't look at her.

"You can stay here if you want—that's okay."

She shook her head, not understanding exactly what was going on, the emotions that were radiating from him. Maybe, like inside the club, he was just focused. "No, I'll come, too."

They didn't find anything particularly useful. The rain was washing away everything too fast. Brandon did find two footprints right around where the man would've been watching her the first time she saw him. Brandon took a picture with his phone.

"There was definitely someone standing right here since the rain started. A perfect place to be watching the door when the women exited after work."

Andrea felt chilled to her very bones, as if she would never get warm again. The rain had both of them sopping wet, but the cold she felt came from the inside.

"He was coming for me, Brandon. I'm sure of it. I could feel him getting closer. I was about to make a run for the front door when you drove up." She managed to get the words out without her teeth chattering.

Brandon was only two feet away from her but he might as well have been a million miles. He finally turned and looked at her. She felt a slight softening from him before his walls rammed back up in place.

"Let's get you home."

ANDREA TOOK ONE look at herself in the bathroom mirror once they got home and understood some of the reason why Brandon was keeping such a distance. She looked like a drowned rat with too much makeup on.

The dark colors she'd used on her eyes to give herself more of a smoldering appearance at the club were now running down her cheeks. The carefully tousled hair now lay flat against her head in knots.

If she was Brandon she'd stay far away from her, also.

He was on the phone with Omega, or maybe the Phoenix police; Andrea wasn't sure which and really didn't care.

She definitely couldn't deny any longer that something had changed in Brandon since earlier this afternoon, when they'd made love for hours, and now, when he couldn't even seem to look at her.

It didn't take a genius to figure out what had happened. He'd seen her in her "natural" habitat. Had figured out what her life had really been like before. And it hadn't been pretty.

Andrea almost staggered under all the weight she could feel pressing down on her.

This was what she'd known from the beginning. Why she'd always tried to hide her past from everyone at Omega. Because ultimately it was ugly and seedy and lewd.

Brandon had thought he was okay with her past until he'd come face-to-face with it tonight. Obviously, now he wasn't. He hadn't touched her once of his own accord since she left Club Paradise. She couldn't hide from that fact any longer.

He now found her distasteful.

She felt something deep inside her shatter at the thought. Pieces she knew she would never be able to put completely back together.

She couldn't bear to look at herself in the mirror any more. She stumbled over to the shower and turned it on.

Chapter Sixteen

The next morning Brandon was at a loss for what to do or say. It was new for him and not pleasant.

None of what he was feeling was pleasant.

Andrea sat quietly at the table, eating cereal. Was totally engrossed in her cereal as if she'd never eaten it before and it was the most fascinating thing she'd ever seen. Which he was sure had nothing to do with the cereal and everything to do with not having to talk to him.

Cold professionalism from them both.

By the time he had finished reporting the man Andrea had seen to the local police, she had been out of the shower and had enclosed herself in the smaller bedroom.

Not the one they'd slept in together the night before.

He told himself that was better, that they needed the space apart. That it would've been ugly if they'd had a confrontation right then. But part of him wanted to get it out in the open, fight it out.

Part of him wanted answers to how she could seem to enjoy dressing so scantily and flirting with dozens of unknown men all night.

The reasonable part of his brain nagged at him: Hadn't that been the plan? For her to blend in, do the job, get close enough to be able to read the emotions and nonverbal behavior of these men and see if any were acting out of place?

Just why the hell had she needed to seem to enjoy it so much?

Intellectually Brandon could see the unfairness of the direction of his thoughts. But the warrior couldn't. Couldn't seem to get past the short skirt and heels and hanging all over other men.

So he'd left her alone last night. Gotten hardly any sleep himself. And now they ate in silence.

She was dressed in her professional suit once more: pants, a cream-colored blouse and a blazer. Not a single hair was out of place, her makeup tame and tasteful.

But Brandon knew what lay beneath it.

Hell, just about any guy who'd been at Club Paradise last night had a pretty good idea of what lay beneath it.

He was struck again by the unfairness of his thoughts, but damned if he could stop them. He got up for another cup of coffee. He was going to need it to get through this day.

THE ICY PROFESSIONALISM and silence from both of them continued through the morning as they looked over the parking lot and surrounding area of Club Paradise. The local police had met them there to help search the wooded area, but besides a couple of footprints, nothing had come of it.

But standing where the man would've stood showed Brandon that he'd had an excellent view of the back door of the club. If it hadn't been for the lightning, Andrea might never have seen him at all. If he had kept to the shadows, he could've been on her before she'd even been aware of his presence.

It reminded Brandon once again that Andrea wasn't a trained agent and wouldn't be able to fight off an attacker. What he'd taught her hadn't nearly been enough. He needed to show her more, but that seemed highly unlikely given that they weren't even talking to each other at the moment.

They were now headed back to Jaguar's. Keira had called them; she'd found a note she was sure was in Jillian Spires's handwriting. It had some initials on it and part of a phone number.

Keira was waiting for them inside the empty club and gave Andrea a hug.

"How'd it go last night?"

Andrea rolled her eyes. "It was a Saturday night at a club. Some things haven't changed."

"Get any useful info?"

"No," Brandon said.

Keira stepped closer to Andrea, picking up on the tension between the two of them, touching her arm. "How are you doing? Was going back to it as hard as you thought?"

Andrea shuddered just the slightest bit. "Worse in some ways. But I had a job to do and that gave me something to focus on."

"You never should've gone back there." Keira angled her body so she was standing between Andrea and Brandon.

Brandon realized the shorter woman was trying to protect Andrea.

From him.

The thought was preposterous. Why would Andrea need protection from him?

Andrea's smile was soft and gentle as she looked at her friend. "I won't lie. It brought back a lot of the old memories and old fears. But at least I didn't have to call you to come bail me out this time."

Keira hugged Andrea tightly to her, almost motherly. "Well, you know I would have."

Brandon didn't know what the two women were talking about, but he could feel a weight beginning to sit in his chest. Looking at Andrea now with Keira, he realized the icy professionalism she'd had with him since they'd awakened this morning wasn't actually her true feeling. There was pain in her eyes, in her voice, in her posture that he'd missed before.

Missed because it hadn't been there or missed because he'd been too busy with his righteous anger to see it?

All he knew was right now Andrea definitely wasn't the same confidently flirtatious woman who used her body to get what she wanted that he'd seen with the men last night. Nor was she the consummate professional who'd greeted him coldly this morning, then went about her business.

Right now she just looked young. Haunted. Clutching a friendly hand because she desperately needed someone to hold on to.

The weight in his chest got a little heavier.

"But anyway, I got through it," Andrea told Keira. Neither of them were looking at him. "We didn't really gather any useful intel, but hopefully now I should be more ready for tonight and especially tomorrow when DJ Shocker is there. That's what's important."

"You don't have to do it, you know," Keira whispered. "I'll come do it."

Andrea hugged the woman. "Thanks for the offer. But I can't teach you how to read people the way I can. It's just something that clicks in my brain."

Keira shrugged a delicate shoulder. "Okay. Let me know if you change your mind."

"So what did you find of Jillian Spires's?" Brandon asked.

Keira turned so her back wasn't to him and he could be included in the conversation. But he noticed her eyes were neither warm nor friendly when she looked at him, the way they were when she looked at Andrea.

"A note from last week. Evidently someone had given

it to her and she had stuffed it in the drawer by the server's station."

"Why would she do that?" Brandon asked.

Keira rolled her eyes. "Our outfits—even when waiting tables—don't tend to have a lot of pockets or places to stuff paper."

"What did it say?" Andrea asked.

Keira walked a few steps to the bar where she'd placed a napkin that had been folded. "Here."

She handed it to Andrea, but Andrea looked at it briefly and handed it to Brandon, looking embarrassed. "It will take me too long to decipher that."

Because of the handwriting and water stains, the note would be hard for anyone to read, dyslexic or not, but Brandon couldn't find a way to reassure Andrea of that.

Trust me, I can give you a lot more thrills than DJ Shocker ever could. Text me when you get off work tonight. J

It had a phone number, but the last four numbers were unreadable because of liquid that had hit the napkin.

"That was given to Jillian the night DJ Shocker was here," Andrea said.

"Or maybe the night after," Brandon agreed. "Either way, this person would fit our MO. We know he was here for the DJ Shocker show and we know he wanted her attention."

"Will the phone number help?" Andrea asked. "The area code is local for Phoenix."

Brandon nodded. "It gives us something. We'll also get the police department to run this napkin for any forensic evidence, although at this point it's highly doubtful."

"Do you remember her with anyone, Keira?" Andrea asked softly.

"No. I'm sorry. The night with DJ Shocker was crazy. There were a ton of locals here, plus people we'd never seen before." Keira's distress was obvious.

"It's okay, Kee. You can't keep track of everything and watch over everyone. Even though you try." Andrea wrapped an arm around her.

"She was a nice kid." Keira shook her head. "Wasn't shy, like you. She was outgoing. Didn't mind flaunting what the good Lord gave her, if you know what I mean. Even down here waiting tables, she still had a lot of sass. And tended to go home with men from the club, even though we all warned her that was a bad idea."

"Everybody has to go their own way, Keira. You can't be mother to us all."

Keira, of course, wasn't old enough to be mother to any of these girls, was hardly old enough to be mother to a baby. But age had nothing to do with mothering instincts.

Keira gave them a crooked half smile. "I always try."

It was getting late in the afternoon. Andrea said her goodbyes to Keira, both of them needing time to get ready for the night's work. He left them so they could talk privately.

The thought brought the weight back to Brandon's chest. Everything he'd heard from Keira about Andrea did not mesh with the conclusions he'd drawn for himself after seeing her last night.

Maybe he needed to talk to her, to clear the air. To tell her what he was feeling.

Hey, I didn't like that you pranced around for a bunch of men while being so scantily clad last night. I know you were undercover but you didn't have to look like you were so comfortable with it.

Yeah, he didn't come across as a jackass with that thought. The weight in his chest got heavier.

"You ready?" she asked, joining him at the door. He turned and stared down at her.

"What?" she finally asked.

"Nothing. I—" Not knowing what to say, he stopped himself and held the door open for her. Should he try to explain?

He was about to try as they walked outside, even knowing that it probably wouldn't come across well. But she stopped abruptly just a few feet out into the parking lot.

"What's wrong?" he asked, about to reach for his weapon.

"It's my—" She cleared her throat and started again. "It's my aunt. I don't see my uncle."

Brandon took his hand off his sidearm, but didn't relax his guard. He saw the older woman now. She was standing next to the same car that had been parked in front of the hotel on Tuesday.

Despite any coldness between him and Andrea, Brandon knew he would protect her from this.

"You don't have to talk to her," he told her, stepping closer. "We can just leave. Or I'll go talk to her if you want."

He could see the tension outlining Andrea's body. "No, like you said, they can't hurt me anymore. I don't know what she wants."

As Andrea walked toward her aunt, Brandon stayed close to her side. The older woman took a few steps toward them as they got closer to the vehicle. Andrea stopped about ten feet away.

"Hello, Margaret."

No title or anything to insinuate they were family.

"Andrea. You look so beautiful." The older woman moved closer but stopped when Andrea visibly flinched. "So grown-up."

"I have grown up since I was seventeen and left your house in the middle of the night, scared for my life."

It was Margaret's turn to flinch. "Andrea, I'm—"

"Where's Marlon?"

"Your uncle passed away two years ago."

Andrea nodded, obviously not curious how Marlon had died. She relaxed just the slightest bit. That man truly could never hurt her again.

"I don't expect you to forgive me for not stopping him from hurting you. But I am sorry. Sorry I wasn't stronger and didn't stand up to him."

Andrea nodded again. "Thank you for coming by."

Andrea began to walk away but her aunt stopped her.

"One of the ladies from church told me you were in town and working for law enforcement. She said you knew some people here."

Margaret just stared at the building for a moment. He wondered if she knew Andrea used to work there.

The older woman brought her gaze back to Andrea. "I knew I needed to come and make my apology face-to-face while I could. I didn't think you'd talk to me on the phone."

Everything about Andrea's stance clearly said her aunt was right.

"Well, it was nice of you to make the gesture." Andrea turned to their car, obviously finished with the conversation.

Her aunt reached out. "I also have a box of your things. Letters you received and a few items that were in your room that you left behind." She opened the door to the backseat of her car and took out a box that wasn't much bigger than a shoe box. "You used to like horses and collected a couple figurines."

Andrea stopped and turned back to her aunt, her eyes narrowing. "Yes, I remember those."

"They're in here. Please, honey, I know you don't want

anything to do with me, but I wanted you to have these things."

Andrea hesitated for a moment, but then walked over to her aunt. When she reached out to take the box, Margaret put her hands over Andrea's.

"I stopped drinking. Marlon did too a few months before he died. Both of us realized what damage we'd done to you, and I'm so, so sorry. I know we'll never be family again, but I hope someday you'll be able to forgive me."

Andrea nodded again, but didn't say anything. Margaret held her hands so long Brandon took a step closer in case he needed to force Margaret to let go. Brandon's action caught Andrea's attention and seemed to pull her out of whatever place in the past she'd gone.

"Thank you for getting these to me." She gestured to the box while stepping backward, breaking the contact with her aunt.

"I'm so glad you've done so well for yourself," Margaret whispered. "That you were able to overcome everything and rise above it."

Andrea looked at her aunt, then at Brandon. "I'm learning that the people who hurt you are ultimately the ones who make you stronger."

Chapter Seventeen

The people who hurt you are ultimately the ones who make you stronger.

Andrea's words still rang clearly through his head hours later when he sat at the corner table of Club Paradise again.

He and Andrea had left her aunt, returned to the house, and Andrea had gone into her small room. She hadn't said anything to him besides the most basic of answers to his questions about food and particulars of the case. He'd left her at the house to take the napkin Keira had found to the locals for analysis.

When he'd come back Andrea had still been in her room, although there had been evidence that she'd fixed herself dinner. The box her aunt had given her lay unopened on the kitchen table.

They still hadn't said anything but polite phrases to each other as he took her to Club Paradise to get ready for her shift.

The weight in his chest hadn't gotten any less heavy, either.

She'd looked right at him when she'd said the words: *the people who hurt you are ultimately the ones who make you stronger.*

It was now nearly eleven o'clock and he'd been watching the men in the club—watching Andrea—for more than an hour and a half from the same table as last night.

Despite the weight in his chest, he still couldn't stop his anger, his distaste, at seeing her flirt so easily with the men. At seeing her dressed so skimpily again, at knowing *others* were seeing her show off so much skin.

"How you doing there, Agent?"

Brandon's eyes flew to the petite form, dressed in high heels, jeans and a tank top, who plopped down in the chair across from him.

Keira.

Brandon sat back. "Hi. Didn't expect to see you here."

"Thought I'd come out, give a little support to our girl. I know she needs it."

Brandon looked over to where Andrea had crouched down near a low chair so a man in his midforties could give her his order. He noticed the man never took his eyes off her breasts cupped in the bustier. Andrea didn't seem to mind at all that the guy was salivating.

"She seems to be doing just fine on her own," Brandon said to Keira.

Keira's eyes narrowed, but she didn't say anything. A waitress, with *Kimmie* on her name tag, came over to take her order, and when she brought the drink back, Keira took a twenty-dollar bill, rolled it up and stuck it between the other woman's breasts—also visible from the bustier she wore. Keira winked at the waitress and she winked back.

"You into girls?" Brandon asked.

"No. Not that way." She took a sip of her drink. "Just like to support my sisters who work damn hard for their money then a lot of times are rushing to a second job or a family or something else that also requires their time."

Brandon hadn't necessarily thought about it like that, but guessed it could be true.

"Let's take our waitress, Kimmie. She's Andrea's age or a little younger. Maybe twenty-one."

Brandon nodded. "Probably."

"Maybe Kimmie got knocked up by someone who took off. Or has a husband who can't get a job. Or hell, maybe she's always dreamed of being a stripper. Whichever. She finds a job here. Any of that make you think less of her?"

"Not really."

"She comes in every night, smiles at all the guys. It's not hard for the good-looking frat-boy types. Maybe a little more difficult for the old ones or fat ones or ones that sneer at her. But she still does it, because, well, that's how you make a living at this job. Think less of Kimmie now?"

Brandon knew where Keira was going with this, but didn't stop her. "No, I don't think less of her."

"She gets up onstage and takes her clothes off and smiles. She works down on the floor serving drinks and smiles. She smiles. Because this is her job. Giving men something to look at is her job. And she does it well."

Brandon held a hand out in surrender, but Keira continued.

"There are some girls who have to use drugs in order to do it. Kimmie isn't one of those. There are some girls who make some extra money by going out in back and having sex with guys. But Kimmie doesn't do that, either. Because Kimmie's just trying to live—support her family or whatever—off the money she makes at this job. She doesn't give guys come-ons. Doesn't tease them. She just dresses up her admittedly beautiful body in a somewhat revealing outfit and smiles. Nothing more."

Brandon looked over at Andrea. She was smiling. But she wasn't touching any of the men, leading them on in any way. Like Kimmie, she was just doing her job.

Keira leaned over the table toward Brandon. "You got a problem with what Andrea's doing here tonight? What she did four years ago?"

Brandon shrugged. "I didn't think so until I saw her up close and in action. It's hard to watch. Hard to accept."

"Whose hang-up is it?" She gestured toward Andrea. "That sweet girl right there? I don't think so."

Keira took another sip of her drink. "Do you know why she was so popular onstage? Because everyone could tell she didn't really want to be there. Made her seem untouchable yet available at the same time. Guys ate it up."

Brandon shook his head. He didn't want to think about Andrea onstage, and thinking about her being up there when she didn't want to be was even worse, but Keira wouldn't relent.

"You see me? I am what I am. I go up onstage and I'm confident and strong and hot. It's not every guy's thing, but it's enough that I'm pretty popular. Do you think you could make me feel bad about myself?"

Brandon began to answer but she stopped him.

"Let me help you—no. Nothing you could say to me about my chosen profession would make me feel bad about myself. Because I am how I dance—confident and strong. I own my choices and I don't second-guess myself."

Brandon raised his glass in a sort of salute. Everything Keira said was obviously true.

"But you know what I'm not, Dr. Han? It is doctor, right?"

"Not medical, but PhD, yes."

"I'm not kind. I'm not willing to put myself on the line to help other people. I'm not willing to fight through hardships and claw my way up from the holes life tries to throw me in."

"I'm not sure life would be able to throw you in a hole." And he didn't think the other part was true, either.

She shrugged a delicate shoulder and glared at him. "One thing I know—I sure as hell wouldn't be willing to go back and do something that sickened me about myself, that broke my own heart, because it might help a complete stranger."

She pointed across the club where Andrea was talking to another group of men. "But I think we both know someone who did. Who *is*."

Brandon stared at Andrea for a long time. Finally Keira stood up, her drink empty. "It's time for me to get going. I have responsibilities having to do with stuff not here."

"I'll walk you out."

She put a hand out. "I'll be fine."

She walked a few steps before turning back to his table. "I don't know Andrea well. She doesn't let anybody know her well because she's afraid they'll hurt her. But I've seen the way she looks at you. She respects you, has opened herself to you."

Brandon couldn't deny that. Andrea had opened herself to him, in more ways than one.

"Knowing you were here had to make this even harder for her. That you might judge her. Hurt her like other people had. And then you did."

Brandon couldn't deny it. Keira was right.

She continued. "Andrea will eventually come to terms with the fact that she was a stripper. In the greater scheme of things, who the hell cares? It's in her past and it got her through. Someday she'll look back on her past and realize she has nothing to be ashamed of. I doubt when you look back at how you've treated her that you'll be able to realize the same."

HAVING THE FACT that you were a hypocritical jackass pointed out with such crystal clarity was pretty painful.

The image of Andrea, smiling and flirting with other men in a skimpy outfit, seeming to enjoy it? It burned into his mind.

Another image tried to fight its way in, one of Andrea in the rain, cold, needing him. But he pushed it out.

He could admit to himself it was easier to deal with

anger and disgust over stripper Andrea than with the feelings that swamped him over kind, talented, reserved Andrea.

Those feelings scared the hell out of him.

And it wasn't as if he'd said anything to Andrea about how seeing her at the club had made him feel. He wasn't that much of a jackass.

She was in the shower now. It was nearly 3:00 a.m. He was listening to a message left for him by Gerardo Jennison at the Phoenix police department with a report of what they'd found in the woods around Club Paradise today. It hadn't been much.

He sat down on the couch, realizing he'd been pacing. He pushed all thoughts of Andrea away and concentrated instead on the man she'd seen in the storm.

There'd been no sign of him tonight, and neither Brandon nor Andrea had found any persons of interest in the club. If the storm guy was the same one who had killed the other women then his MO seemed to be changing. He wasn't waiting until DJ Shocker's visits to pick his victims; he was hunting before.

Of course, he'd also killed Ashley Judson, victim number two. She hadn't been a stripper at all, just a waitress, although she'd had a reputation for serving up herself for truckers who stopped at her restaurant and were willing to pay the right price. That could certainly seem just as "impure" as the other women, who took their clothes off to make money.

But coming after Andrea didn't really make sense, since it was her first night and she hadn't really done anything "impure," unless the actual women he killed didn't matter, just someone who worked at a strip club.

Brandon sat back and let his mind work, doing what he did best, thinking of all the possibilities. Maybe the storm guy wasn't the serial killer at all. Maybe it was

Damian Freihof. Brandon took out his phone and speed-dialed Steve.

"Damn it, Han, do you know it's three o'clock in the morning?" Steve asked by way of greeting.

"Sorry, boss. We've had a slight update." He explained the situation and what had happened to Andrea.

"Do you think the killer has turned his sights on her?" All traces of sleep were now gone from his boss's voice.

"Not unless he's changed his MO. I was wondering what the latest update on Damian Freihof was."

"It's still an active manhunt, but he was last seen near Midland, Texas."

"That's not out of the realm of possibility for arrival in Arizona."

"True. But it's also a direct route to Mexico, which is a logical place for him to be headed if he wants to get to South America. Plus, we still don't have any reason to think he'll actually come after Andrea. He hasn't had any contact with her since she's been at Omega."

"All right. Sorry to wake you. Keep me posted if anything changes."

"You'll be my first call. How has the undercover work been going?"

"Fine. Andrea jumped back into it like she'd never left. Seems like wearing next to nothing and flirting with total strangers is second nature to her."

There was a long silence on the other end.

"What?" Brandon finally asked.

"You're telling me that Andrea looked like she was having a good time while working at the club?"

"Yeah. She was fine. Happy, even. Why?"

"I must have misunderstood the nature of the club you were infiltrating. This club must be different than Jaguar's, more like a restaurant."

Brandon all but sneered. "No. It was a strip joint. Maybe

a little higher rent than Jaguar's, but there were still mostly naked girls dancing on the stage. And the waitresses' outfits weren't much better. Drunken guys. Groping. You know the drill."

"And Andrea was all right?"

"More than. I'll bet she made a killing in tips. Looked perfectly at home in a bustier and heels. All smiles."

Brandon couldn't get the image out of his mind. It wasn't even the outfit that bothered him so much. He'd gladly have watched her all day in that skirt and top. Would've loved to have peeled her out of it. Under much different circumstances.

It was her actions. Her flirtations, friendliness. The smiles she'd given other men. Touches she'd allowed.

He felt the warrior clawing his way up. He wanted to go and beat down all the men who had dared to touch her. Then pin her to his side and make love to her until she was never even tempted to smile at another man.

Steve interrupted his thoughts. "Wow. She must be better at undercover work than I would've thought. Good for her, for fighting through it to do her job."

"She didn't look like she was doing a job."

"Brandon, if you could've seen her at Jaguar's when Grace Parker and I picked her up there four years ago, you'd be amazed that she could even function tonight, much less do her undercover work well."

"What do you mean?"

"She was all but broken. She hated every minute she worked in that club—it was destroying her piece by piece. Going back into a similar situation has to be overwhelming for her, probably terrifying."

Brandon could feel something clench in the pit of his stomach. Again.

"I'm proud of her for just facing it," Steve continued. "Even if she had only made it for ten minutes, I still would've been proud. To hear that she did so well? Be sure to pass along my official and personal congratulations for a job well done."

Brandon murmured something; he wasn't quite sure what.

"I hope this will help you guys find the killer. Because I'm sure Andrea paid a high personal price getting out there the last two nights."

Brandon managed to say the correct words and end the call with his boss.

That feeling in his gut still hadn't gone away. Still felt like a heaviness pressing down on him. How heavy was the weight?

The exact weight of a judgmental, hypocritical ass.

Someone who had acted completely unprofessional the past two nights and it hadn't been the unseasoned consultant with no undercover experience. She'd done what she was supposed to do. Make nice with the locals and try to get a reading on anybody who might not fit in.

All Brandon had been able to see was the short skirt, revealing top and sexy makeup. Not the capable law-enforcement figure underneath.

Or the very vulnerable woman who had probably needed support from him. Possibly during her time at the club. Definitely afterward.

He'd turned away. Deliberately.

The shower had long since turned off. He realized Andrea hadn't come through the living room at all. Not that he expected her to come say good-night, but she hadn't come to get any food from the kitchen or even a glass of water.

Regardless of her outfit, she'd worked very hard for the five hours he'd watched and some time before he'd arrived. That tray probably would've gotten heavy after a while, and her heels were even higher than usual. That couldn't have been easy on her feet.

Brandon rubbed a hand down his face. She had preferred going to bed hungry and thirsty than to walk by him to get what she needed.

He headed back to one of the two bedrooms this house contained, looking at the one he and Andrea had slept in together two nights ago. They'd fallen in bed after showering, both exhausted by the hours of training and lovemaking. She'd slept in his arms the entire night, and he'd smiled when he'd awakened to still find her there. No running away this time.

But she wasn't in that bed now. It was empty, covers of the king-size bed still undisturbed. He walked over to the other, smaller room that barely fit the single bed, dresser and desk.

There was Andrea sound asleep.

The light in her room was on. Her back was pressed all the way against the wall the bed sat against, one arm resting halfway over her head in a defensive position. Even in sleep she was prepared for someone to strike.

Brandon knew he had added to her psychological need for that posture by his actions. The thought shredded him.

He pulled out the chair from the desk and sat in it, watching her sleep. He wanted to wake her up, to apologize.

He hadn't said anything that an outsider would consider cruel. Hadn't done anything that would seem unforgivable. But Brandon knew how sensitive Andrea was, the emotions she could sense and decipher. She'd known how he felt. His disapproval, his anger. The distaste he'd felt.

God, he would take it all back if he could.

Given some time to process it now, and with the help of both Keira and Steve, he realized he hadn't really been prepared to see her like that. Hadn't really come to grips that she had taken off her clothes for money when she was younger.

But now, sitting here, watching her, he realized he had no right to judge her. He'd been raised by two loving parents, surrounded by two brothers and a sister. He'd been a challenging child, acting out in his younger grades, on a route to trouble. His parents had loved him enough, known him well enough to realize the problem was he wasn't being challenged sufficiently. They'd moved him to a gifted academy, one that allowed him to excel at his own pace.

The course of his life had been set. He'd flourished from there.

Who'd been around to see that Andrea flourished? No one. The opposite, in fact.

She shouldn't have to apologize for how she had chosen to survive. The important fact was that she had. She was already ashamed of it.

He had added to that shame. What did that make him?

He reached toward her to wake her up, tell her all these things, beg her forgiveness, but dark circles under her eyes stopped him. She needed rest. She'd been working hard for days and hadn't been getting enough sleep. The things he needed to say could be said in the morning. They were his burden to carry.

He wanted to at least pick her up and carry her to the bed they'd shared. He wanted to hold her during the night. Be close to her.

But he had to face the fact that she might not want that anymore. She was sleeping peacefully now. For once he would make an unselfish decision concerning her and leave her alone.

She'd scrubbed her face completely clean, making her look so young and innocent and vulnerable that it was almost painful to look at her.

He realized she was exactly those things. Even when she had on a skimpy outfit and a ton of makeup and platform heels, she was still those things: young and innocent and vulnerable.

She had to go back there again tomorrow night—hell, it was so late, it was tonight—but this time he planned to make sure she understood that she wouldn't be going in there alone.

If there was one benefit of having an IQ as high as his, it was that you learned from your mistakes and you learned *fast*.

Chapter Eighteen

Andrea slept later than she had been, but not enough to
wipe the exhaustion from her body. Her sleep had been
plagued by nightmares. First ones that hadn't bothered
her for a while, of her uncle and her life in Buckeye. Then
ones of the past two nights, groping hands and the man
she'd seen in the lightning.

Her heart began to thud just thinking about him.

She forced the thought of it out of her head. She had to
admit she'd been so emotionally piqued getting off work
in the storm that it was possible she'd imagined the whole
thing. Not the man. She had definitely seen the man. But
maybe he hadn't meant her any ill intent at all. Maybe he'd
just been a guy walking across the parking lot and it just
got all spooky-out-of-proportion because of the lightning.

She also didn't want to think about Brandon and how
he obviously now felt about her. She noticed he'd left her
where she was for the second night in a row, sleeping
alone in the small guest bed. He hadn't wanted to be near
her. Hadn't touched her at all since he'd seen her at Club
Paradise.

She threw off her covers and got out of bed, still fully
dressed in sweatpants and a T-shirt. She even had a bra
on. She knew sleeping fully clothed was something she
did when she felt nervous or uncomfortable. A habit from
the days when she'd had to run in the middle of the night

from her uncle. Sometimes she fought the urge. Last night she hadn't.

She was surprised to see Brandon already awake, pulling out the beginnings of breakfast in the kitchen. She stopped in the doorway.

"Hi." His black hair was tousled and his chest was bare. Andrea fought the urge to lick her lips. It was totally unfair that she was this attracted to him when he obviously wasn't attracted to her lately.

"Want some coffee?" She nodded and he smiled at her before turning to get a mug and pour her some.

Her fingers touched his when he handed her the mug. At least this time he didn't jerk away as if he couldn't stand to touch her.

"Thanks." Her voice was husky with sleep. She didn't know what else to say to him.

"I'm going to make some breakfast, okay? I don't think you ate anything last night and you worked pretty hard." He smiled again. "Then we can compare notes, see if we come up with anything."

Andrea was confused by his behavior. This was different from the cold and distant Brandon she'd experienced for the past day and a half.

He was being professional, she realized, something in her sinking. He knew they still had to work together even though he found her distasteful. Their personal relationship was over but he was at least making an effort to make the situation less awkward. She could do the same.

It wasn't the first time she'd put back together the shattered pieces of her emotions. They might not be without cracks, but she knew the glue would hold. Later, after they'd stopped this killer and made sure no more women died, when she was back at Omega and no one was around, then she could fall apart.

While watching him cook, Andrea wondered if Brandon would suggest to Steve that she wasn't Omega material. That he'd seen her in action and she just wouldn't be a good fit long-term.

Maybe it was just time for her to move on altogether.

He brought a plate filled with eggs, bacon and toast and set it in front of her.

"Eat up," he said. "We've got a full day. And night."

She took a bite of her toast and realized how famished she was. He set his own plate down and began eating, also.

Her plate was nearly empty when he asked about last night. She was glad she was nearly done because her food became tasteless. She didn't want to think about last night. Didn't want to face him as she talked about it, knowing what he thought about her. His disgust.

"I wasn't able to pick out anyone in the club who seemed to be acting odd," he said as he took a sip of the coffee. "But then again, I didn't think the killer would actually be there."

"Because you think he follows DJ Shocker in. That he's in the club for the first time that night."

"Maybe not in the club for the first time, but picking his victim then. I was working on a profile last night."

Andrea wasn't sure if he meant while he was at Club Paradise or later while she was sleeping.

"Except for victim two, the truck-stop waitress, all the murders have occurred between twenty-four and forty-eight hours after DJ Shocker's appearance at the club," Brandon continued. "I think the killer picks his victim that night, perhaps the one who is acting the most overtly promiscuous, and comes back to kill her later. But he might come in before, since DJ Shocker's events are so well advertised, to check out potential victims."

"Okay, that's sick, but logical."

"Have you gotten anything over the last couple of nights? Anyone who has seemed out of place?"

She took another sip of her coffee to fortify herself, then looked back down at her plate. She didn't want to eat another bite, but at least it gave her somewhere else to look besides at Brandon.

"It was pretty tough, at first. Filtering through… everything." The barrage of sounds and sights. The unwelcomed touches of men who thought she was cheap. "The first couple of hours of the first night, honestly, I was just trying to survive. Wasn't sure I was going to be able to do it."

"And then what happened?" Brandon's voice was hoarse, almost anguished. She could feel the unhappiness coming from him, but couldn't bring herself to look at his face.

"I don't know. I just had a suck-it-up talk with myself. I had a job to do, and if I didn't, another woman was going to die."

"Sounds like a pretty professional way to think."

For a stripper.

He didn't say it, and she had to admit she didn't even know if he was thinking it. But *she* was.

She still didn't look up from her plate. She took the last bite of her toast that now tasted like cardboard in her mouth.

"Not surprisingly, the overwhelming emotion in the club was lust. Drunken euphoria was a close second. I colored all those in my mind as red and then just ignored them. Guilt—I'm sure more than a few married men were in attendance last night—I colored as green, because I thought that might be worth looking into. Anger and disgust, the key emotions I thought might come from the killer, I tried to color as blue."

"Using colors, that's smart. Did you see any blue?"

"A little." She finally looked at him. "But not from anyone I thought was the killer."

He was too smart not to know she was referring to him. "Andrea—"

She didn't want to talk about his disgust with her. She was holding on by a thin enough thread as it was. She stood up, grabbing their plates.

"You cooked. I'll do dishes. Thanks for breakfast, by the way."

He stood up too and grabbed her wrist gently. "Andrea."

She looked at him, but his face was so intent with something to say she had to look away. She could not do this right now. Not if she had to make it through the entire day and night beyond.

"Brandon, I can't. Not right now. You felt what you felt. Whatever we have to talk about, can we just do it later?"

"Fine. But I'll do the dishes. You go sit. You'll be on your feet enough today. Plus we have another self-defense lesson in fifteen minutes."

She thought about what had happened with the last self-defense lesson, how they'd ended up in bed all afternoon. "Are you sure that's a good idea?"

"As long as there's a killer around, it's a good idea."

That wasn't what Andrea had meant, but she didn't press it. She just left him to do the dishes and went to sit on the couch. The next thing she knew, Brandon was shaking her awake, gently.

"Come on, lazybones. Nap break is over. Time to do some work." She found his face close to hers, smiling, as she opened her eyes.

She touched his cheek before she remembered she wasn't supposed to. But he didn't pull back as she expected. Instead he leaned forward and kissed her on the forehead.

"I must have fallen asleep for a few minutes," she murmured.

"Try two hours."

Her eyes flew open at that. "Are you serious?"

He smiled again. "It's okay. You needed it. But now it's time to work."

He stood and held his hand down to help her from the couch. She stretched and took it.

"Okay, let's go over our bear-hug move first."

They practiced that a few times and Andrea was pleasantly surprised at what she remembered. What her body automatically remembered. Brandon praised her for it, too.

They spent the next hour going over how to twist out of wrist holds, and the most vulnerable points of an attacker she could hit.

The physical activity, focusing on something besides what was going on between her and Brandon, felt good. She found she had a knack for it, because it was somewhat like dancing, ironically. She just had to think of what step came next. And eventually her body knew what step came next without her having to think about it.

"Okay, one more thing I want to teach today. If someone has you on the ground in a choke hold."

He had Andrea lie on her back and he straddled her hips. He gripped her throat with one hand.

"Most of what I've shown you hasn't been dependent on strength or speed, just on basic human mechanics. Joints only turn certain ways. This is more labor intensive on your part. Someone bigger, heavier, is going to be harder to get off you."

Andrea wasn't sure she could do this. Having Brandon this close in this position? If he slid his hand over they'd be in an embrace rather than in combat. But she tried to focus.

Like all the other techniques he'd shown her, he went over the moves slowly at first: trapping his leg with her foot, grabbing his wrist and elbow, hiking up her hips and flipping him over.

She could do it when he worked with her, but once they started going at a faster speed Andrea had trouble.

"What's the problem?" he asked. "You're going to have to move more quickly and fluidly than that for it to work."

Andrea gritted her teeth. She didn't think she could do this—he was too big. And she might hurt him. *And* she really did not want to thrust her hips up against his.

"Look, I'm a little tired. Maybe we should just take a break."

Brandon's eyes narrowed as he looked down at her from where he straddled her hips. "Make me."

"I'm serious, Brandon."

The hand that held her throat squeezed a little tighter. Not enough to hurt or cut off her breath. Just enough to make the threat a little real.

She did what he had taught her but her movements were jerky and halfhearted.

"That's not going to be enough. With this move it's not enough to just go through the correct motions. You've got to have some strength behind it. Some fire."

She tried again but the results were the same.

"That's not enough, sweetheart. You've got to do this move like you've got nothing left to lose."

She tried again, chest heaving in frustration when she couldn't budge him.

"Don't call me 'sweetheart,'" she spit out.

"Why?"

"Because you don't think I'm sweet. You think I'm dirty."

"That's right, sweetheart. I'm the jackass who judged you for doing your job the last two nights. I'm the jerk who turned away from you when you needed me to help anchor you. I'm the idiot—"

Andrea let out a cry and did it. Broke his hold, flipped

her body around so she was on top of him. As he hit the ground his air rushed out with a whoosh.

She threw her head back and laughed. "I did it!" She was amazed at the sense of accomplishment.

She felt Brandon's hands resting on her knees. "Yeah, you did. Good job."

She wasn't ready for him to sit up quickly and wrap his arms around her hips, crushing his chest against hers. He buried his face in her neck.

"How I've acted the last two days, what I thought...I was so wrong, sweetheart."

"Brandon—"

"And you're wrong. I don't think you're dirty. I think you're amazing, beautiful, sweet. Seeing you in the club was hard, I'll admit. But it was *my* problem, not yours. You were doing a job. And did it damn well."

She grabbed his face so she could pull him back. He needed to understand. "When I worked before, I wore just as skimpy an outfit. Less, if I was the one onstage. And when I waited tables, I'll admit I flirted to get tips. Encouraged glances and even some touches. I didn't like it but I did it."

He brought his lips reverently to hers. "You did what you had to in order to survive. Being smart enough to work the system to your advantage is not something to be ashamed of. And I promise, I will never make the mistake of judging you for it again."

"But some of what you felt was probably correct."

"Sweetheart, nothing of what I felt was correct. And you've got to stop letting your own head think it was correct, also."

She sighed. "That's easier said than done."

"I spoke to Drackett and he said to give you his personal and professional congratulations for a job well done."

"You spoke to Steve?"

"Last night. And for the record, I agree with him."

"I thought you'd never want to touch me again. That you found me distasteful."

She felt his arms wrap more strongly around her waist before he used his powerful leg muscles to stand up in one fluid motion while still holding her.

"Trust me when I say, I find you more and more tasteful each day I know you." Keeping her legs wrapped around his hips, he carried her back into the bedroom and proceeded to show her.

Chapter Nineteen

If Brandon could've spent all day in bed with Andrea, he would've. He did his best to apologize with both words and actions, trying to say with his body what he wasn't sure she could hear with his words.

He didn't let himself think too much about why it was so important for him to repair what he'd damaged with her. That would lead to too many questions about the future. About how things could never go back to being the same between them at Omega after this case.

The warrior had the woman he craved by his side. That was enough for now.

But they couldn't stay in bed all day, because they still had a killer to catch.

And they were both pretty hungry despite their breakfast.

Andrea was making sandwiches when Brandon came out of the shower. He could tell by the way she moved across the kitchen that she was feeling lighter, happier. The shadows were gone from her eyes.

He should be surprised that she was more attractive with no makeup and messy hair, dancing around in shorts and a loose T-shirt, but he wasn't. Andrea's natural beauty would always outshine what she could do with makeup and a brush.

She felt his presence and turned to smile at him. "Lunch," she said, handing him a plate.

The silence during their meal this time was easy and light. Unlike before. They were washing dishes together when Andrea caught him off guard with her question.

"Hey, do you know who a guy named Damian Freihof is?"

Brandon stilled. She instantly picked up on his nonverbals, stilling and tensing herself.

"What?" she asked.

"Why do you ask who he is?"

"That box my aunt gave me with my stuff. It contained like fifty letters from a Damian Freihof. I have no idea who that is. I think he's got me confused with someone else and has for a long time. I only opened one letter, but they all had the same name and return address on the envelope."

"Can I see them?"

"Do you know him?"

Brandon wouldn't lie to her. He hadn't thought keeping her in the dark about Freihof was a good idea, although he'd agreed because he'd thought there hadn't been any link between Andrea and Freihof since he went away to prison.

But evidently there were fifty links between them.

Steve had been wrong when he thought Freihof had forgotten about Andrea. He sure as hell hadn't forgotten her if he'd written her that many times.

"Yes, I do know who he is. And you do, too. You just don't know that you do."

Andrea's eyes narrowed and he could see her trying to remember. "Was he part of a case I worked? I can't place the name."

"Damian Freihof was one of the three bank robbers/ hostage takers you helped stop on the day you met Steve Drackett."

He hated how stress began to fill her body again. "The third guy. The evil one."

"He was the one mostly kept out of the original press reports because of the ties he had with some other bombers and terrorist organizations. We were going to try to use him to catch some bad guys even higher on the food chain, but he decided he'd rather serve a double life sentence."

"Well, evidently he decided to make me his pen pal from prison. That's kind of creepy."

"What did the letter you read say?"

She shrugged. "Nothing threatening. Just that he wished he could've gotten to know me better and looks forward to the time we'll eventually spend together." She shuddered. "That's really frightening now that I know who he is."

"I need to send the letters to Omega, if that's okay. Get someone to check them out."

Andrea shrugged. "Sure. I don't want to read them. Why would Omega want them? Freihof is already serving two life sentences. They're probably not going to find much in the letters that will keep him in jail longer than that."

Brandon put his hands on both her arms. "Freihof escaped from federal custody last week during a prison transfer. Nobody knows where he is."

ANDREA COULD FEEL all the blood leave her face. "He escaped?"

"Yes." Brandon pulled her in for a hug and she leaned into him for a moment, needing his strength.

Damian Freihof. That was the name of the face that haunted her dreams over the past four years. She had never forgotten his eyes and the evil that had radiated from him in that bank.

She'd asked Steve about him after she'd gone to work for Omega since she'd never heard anything about him in the news. Drackett had assured her that the third man had been arrested, had just been kept out of the press for national-security reasons.

She pulled back from Brandon. "Steve knows Freihof escaped."

"Yes, and we've been keeping our eyes and ears to the ground for info about him. But Steve didn't think Freihof would come after you."

"Why would Steve even think that was a possibility? Before the letters, I wouldn't have thought it was."

Brandon's lips pursed. "During and after his trial, Freihof mentioned coming after you."

"What?"

Brandon shrugged. "Drackett didn't really take it too seriously. Freihof was in custody and he was mad that he was going to jail for the next eighty years. Steve figured the guy was just running his mouth. He also mentioned wanting to kill some other people."

"Why didn't Steve tell me?"

"Freihof was in jail. You were safe."

Andrea took a step back. "But then he got out of jail. Steve should've told me then."

Brandon held out a hand, entreating. "I agree, and even told him so. But this was right as you were coming back here. Steve felt like you had enough on your plate already."

"Well, the last letters are postmarked as late as two weeks ago."

"That's why we need to get them to Omega and see what we can find from them."

"Does anybody know where he is now?"

"He was briefly spotted in Texas. Probably heading to Mexico."

Andrea thought about all the times she'd felt someone watching her over the past few days.

"What about the lightning-storm guy? That could've been Freihof."

Brandon nodded and pulled her back into his arms. "Yes, it could've been. But he would've been taking a huge chance by coming here after you right now. Steve agrees. He's probably heading south."

"So I don't need to worry about him?" That was definitely not going to happen.

"I won't lie to you. Freihof definitely needs to be worried about. Your safety is something Steve and I will be having a heart-to-heart about when we're back at Omega. I'm not going to let anything happen to you, even if it means moving you in with me." She could feel his kisses in her hair. "I just don't think we have to worry about him right at this moment."

Andrea could feel warmth pooling through her. After the brittle cold that had settled on her insides the past couple of days, this felt wonderful. Having someone really care about her felt wonderful. And Brandon had mentioned Omega for the first time, as if what was happening between them would continue.

The thought was both thrilling and terrifying.

She pulled back to look at him, this man who had brought out so many emotions in her over the past week.

"What?" he asked.

"Nothing. Just thinking about life after this case for a second. Realizing that you know just about every single thing there is to know about me, but I don't know much about you."

"You know that I can be a conceited ass who refuses to see the truth that's right in front of him."

She smiled. "Yeah, but I mean the less obvious stuff."

He reached down and bit at her ear in retaliation, then leaned back against the kitchen counter, pulling her with him. "Okay, what do you want to know?"

"How'd you end up at Omega?"

"I was pretty fortunate when I was growing up. My parents realized early that I needed more intellectual challenge than most kids my age or I started acting out physically. That got me on the right path—graduated high school a little early, then found that studying human behavior interested me most."

"So you got a few degrees in it."

He shrugged casually. "Well, schooling came pretty easily to me when I was interested in the subject matter."

"How'd you jump from the academic world to Omega?"

"My best friend since high school, David Vickars. He and I were pretty different in a lot of ways. He was more of an action man. I always tended to think things through and find the most logical solution. He never even went to college. Got all the education he needed from the army, he told me. Anyway, he started working for Omega eight years ago. Pulled me in not long afterward."

Andrea couldn't see his face, the way he was holding her from behind, but could feel the tension, the sadness.

"You guys were partners."

"Yep. A great team, right up until he died a year ago."

"I'm so sorry, Brandon." She turned in his arms so she could face him.

"Me, too. Dave was a good man. Knew when to bend the rules and when to break them. Knew how to keep me in check."

"Do you need to be kept in check a lot?"

Andrea could see the different flecks of emotion cross over his face: sadness, resignation, fear, anger.

"The difference between you and I, sweetheart, is that you have a crooked past but a sweet, pure soul. I'm the opposite—a perfect past with a crooked soul."

Andrea's eyes flew up to his. "What? No, that's not true."

He tucked her hair gently behind both her ears. "Despite all your talents, I'm not sure you can see it because I keep it buried pretty deep. But I think David knew. He always did. That's why he dragged me with him to Omega."

"Knew what?"

"That I've got a darkness in me somewhere. Everything I learned about human behavior and criminal justice in school? I might have used that to be on the opposite side of serial killing if David hadn't gotten me involved with the right side of the law."

Andrea could tell that what Brandon said was true. Or at least he believed it to be so. "You're excellent at your job."

"I'm fascinated by getting inside the head of a killer and figuring out why they do what they do. What mistakes they might make and catching them."

Andrea had no doubt that the beautiful, brilliant man standing with his arms around her could kill someone and get away with it.

He wouldn't make any mistakes.

"With Dave around it was easy to ignore the darkness, to stay out of my own head and stay in the heads of others. Solve crimes. Fight the bad guys. But this last year it's been more difficult." His voice faded to a hushed stillness.

She realized his current demons haunted him as much as her past demons haunted her. He'd kept them a secret from everyone, just as she had.

"I won't let the darkness overtake you," she whispered.

He stiffened, and she was afraid he was going to pull away, maybe even scoff.

Instead, his arms wrapped tightly around her waist and he pulled her to him in a crushing hug, burying his face in her hair. She could feel his breath against her neck, his heart beating against hers.

They held each other for a long while, their embrace keeping all the demons away.

Chapter Twenty

A call came that afternoon from Lance Kendrick at the
county sheriff's department. They had found the full phone
number from the note Keira had provided.

Jillian Spires had been in contact with Jarrod McConnachie.

Brandon cursed, bringing the receiver down and putting it on speaker so Andrea could hear, too. "Yeah, we
talked to him the day after we arrived in town. He was at
a local bar, The Boar's Nest, with some of his buddies."

"We were talking to him because he was friends with
Noelle Brumby. So that ties him to two of the victims right
away," Andrea said.

"He's also attended at least some of DJ Shocker's club
tour. We found him in some footage," Kendrick informed
them. "So there's another tie-in."

"Damn it," Brandon muttered, rubbing a hand over his
face. "To think we'd been so close to him from the very
beginning."

"Andrea, is it possible the man you saw in the lightning
could've been McConnachie?" Kendrick asked.

She shrugged. "Yes. Jarrod would be the correct build
and weight. It was dark. I was a little freaked out. I didn't
get as much detail as I should have."

Brandon slipped an arm around her shoulders. "What's
the next step, Kendrick?"

"We've got an APB out on McConnachie. As soon as he's spotted, he'll be arrested. We've also got a warrant to search his place of residence, which ends up is his mother's house. This guy is quite the loser, seems like."

Brandon didn't disagree. "Can we meet your men there?"

"Sure. I'm coming, too." He gave them the address, an isolated area just outside of town.

"We'll see you there in a few."

Brandon disconnected the call.

"Jarrod McConnachie?" Andrea shook her head. "I have to admit, I didn't see that. If it's him, he completely fooled me at the bar on Tuesday."

Brandon nodded. "Me, too. He seemed too sloppy and disorganized. Let's go see what we find at his house."

McConnachie's house, or actually *Mrs. McConnachie's* house, was a small ranch outside of Buckeye. It was in surprisingly good shape based on what they knew about Jarrod, who didn't have a job and spent a lot of his time at bars.

Neither Mrs. McConnachie nor Jarrod were home, but a ranch worker who didn't speak much English and looked very nervous when the police showed up let them into the house.

They searched Jarrod's room first. Brandon and Andrea stood to the side observing as Kendrick and his men methodically looked through the room. It was what you would expect a room of someone who was in his midtwenties, yet didn't have a job and still lived with his mother would look like: unmade bed, collection of high school sports trophies sitting on the shelves, clothes strewn all around.

The officers were methodical and neat in their search. There was no need to destroy any property. They searched under the mattress, in all the drawers and thoroughly in the closet. Brandon was impressed by their thoroughness: he didn't see anywhere they would've missed.

They moved into the living room next, then the kitchen with the same methodical search methods but found nothing of substance. They searched through the mother's room and the other bedroom that had been turned into an office.

Nothing that suggested any crimes or linked Jarrod McConnachie to the women.

The ranch hand who had let them in watched nervously as they moved from room to room. Each room was clean and orderly except for Jarrod's, making the search easier. Brandon stepped outside to look around. They weren't going to find anything in the house, at least nothing concrete.

He could hear Kendrick speaking in Spanish with the nervous worker, explaining something about a work visa. The worker was worried about being deported, not being connected to a crime.

Brandon felt Andrea join him outside the door as he looked at the small barn. "I don't think there's anything in the house. We should check the barn." He called back to Kendrick. "Does the warrant cover the entire property or just the house?"

"All of it," Kendrick broke from his Spanish to respond. They all made their way over to the small structure that was beginning to become run-down.

They almost missed the hatch altogether.

Brandon saw it as they were beginning to turn away after searching the barn: a small hatch leading down into a tiny cellar. It was meant as an emergency hideout during a tornado, and unless you knew it was there, it was easy to miss. It was only big enough to fit two or three people and the hatch door was mostly covered by bags of feed.

He opened the door and turned on the flashlight function of his phone, sliding it down into the dark space.

Every law-enforcement officer there, including Brandon, pulled out their weapons as Brandon slowly took the half dozen steps down.

"This is federal agent Brandon Han," he called from the stairs. "I am armed and coming inside. If anyone is in there, make your presence known now."

He waited but no one spoke, so he slowly stepped down. Kendrick stood directly over his shoulder, ready to take a shot. Andrea, since she didn't have a weapon, had done the smart thing and gotten herself out of the way.

Brandon gave himself a few more moments for his eyes to adjust, then rapidly descended the stairs.

No one was in the cellar, but there certainly had been someone there recently.

Pictures of the dead women were all over the boxes that had been placed in the cellar. Pictures of them before they died and right after. There were candles lined all along the walls, as well as a roll of the same white mesh that had been used to cover the women when the police had found them.

This was the killer's preparation room. Might even have been where the killing took place, although getting the bodies up and down those stairs would've been difficult.

Brandon didn't touch anything, just backed out slowly. "Kendrick, call Gerardo Jennison. We need the best crime-scene investigators they've got."

"What is it?" Kendrick asked.

"The killer's preparation room. Jarrod is definitely the guy."

The older man whistled through his teeth before getting on the phone to call for the needed people to work the scene.

Brandon called an officer over to him. "Under no circumstances is anyone to go down there until the CSI people have done their thing. That room is about as pristine as it gets, and we don't want to mess it up."

"Yes, sir," the young officer said.

Brandon looked over at Andrea, shaking his head. "I guess Jarrod fooled both of us."

She nodded. "None of his emotions or nonverbal cues gave him away. I just didn't think he had it in him."

"Me, neither. We didn't give him enough credit."

Kendrick walked over to them. "Crime-scene crew is on their way. And we've got some even better news."

"What's that?" Brandon asked.

"We just picked up Jarrod McConnachie. Idiot went to The Boar's Nest, just like he goes all the time. Guy had no idea we were onto him. They're holding him in a cell back at the sheriff's office."

"Mind if I question him?" Brandon asked.

Kendrick slapped him on the back. "I was hoping you would."

AS MUCH AS Andrea was saddened by the thought of Jarrod—someone she had known in high school and who had seemed friendly—as the killer, she was thankful that his arrest meant she didn't have to go work at Club Paradise that night.

Missing the DJ Shocker circus wasn't upsetting at all. Andrea was ready to retire her bustier and short skirts forever. Those days were well and truly in her past.

She wished she could talk Keira into doing the same, but knew no one talked Keira into anything. She would do it when she was ready.

Andrea was on her way to see her friend now. Brandon had ridden with the local police back to the sheriff's office to question Jarrod. Andrea would meet him there soon. But she wanted to talk to Keira first. Let Keira know that things were better between her and Brandon. She would show her Jarrod's picture while she was there, see if that jogged her memory any.

Hopefully Brandon could get a confession out of Jarrod. That would tie up the most loose ends. And then they'd be heading back to Omega.

Honestly, Andrea wasn't sure what that would mean for the two of them. But she knew, either way, it was time for her to make some changes in her life. Keeping herself distant from everyone at Omega wasn't the way she wanted to live any longer.

She pulled up to Keira's apartment, a small one not far from where Andrea had lived during her time in Buckeye, and knocked on the door. Keira hugged her as she pulled her inside.

"Hey, sweetie, what's going on?" Her hair was up in giant rollers and she had the TV remote in her hand. "I'm just catching up on my television viewing."

Andrea looked, expecting to see some drama or sitcom, but found some sort of wildlife documentary on the TV. Interesting choice.

"Just came to ask if you'd ever seen this guy hanging around Jillian. We think he might be the killer."

Keira took the picture. "Yes. Absolutely yes. More than once. But I don't know his name or how to get ahold of him or anything."

"That's okay. He's already been arrested. His name is Jarrod McConnachie. He and I actually went to high school together before I dropped out."

"Jarrod McConnachie. Bastard." She studied the picture a minute more before handing it back to Andrea. "I'm glad you guys got him."

"Yeah, me too." Andrea looked over at the TV again as Keira put it on Pause. "And I also wanted to let you know that things are much better with Brandon and me."

Keira reached up and patted Andrea on the cheek. "I'm

glad. And I'm not surprised. That man is crazy about you, girl."

Andrea laughed ruefully. "I'm not so sure about that. But we're at least doing better. He apologized for getting upset about me at Club Paradise."

"I'd like to hear more about how exactly he apologized—" Keira waggled her eyebrows "—but I'm sure you wouldn't give me the juicy deets anyway."

Andrea felt her face heat.

Keira laughed. "I thought so. He seems like a good man, Andrea."

"He is."

"And more than that, you're a good woman. Past is past. Future is future."

Andrea nodded and grabbed the shorter woman in for a hug. "I'm learning that. In no small part, thanks to you."

"Good. You're a beautiful, compassionate, intelligent, classy lady. Don't you ever forget that."

Andrea could feel tears brimming in her eyes. "Thank you, Keira."

"All right, enough with all the girl talk. You're welcome to stay here and watch my shows with me until I head into work."

"No, I'm going to the station. Help Brandon question the suspect if I can."

"Then I'll catch you later." Keira winked. "Hopefully not as long as it's been since the last time I saw you."

"I promise."

Andrea said her goodbyes and made her way out to her car. There was no message from Brandon, so evidently nothing new with Jarrod.

Andrea pulled the car out of the apartment complex and began driving north up Highway 85 toward the sheriff's office. She passed Jaguar's, slowing as she did so.

She wasn't going to let that place have a hold over her

life anymore. As Keira had said, past was past. Future was future. Jaguar's belonged in her past. She sped up, leaving it behind her.

She saw a car pulled over on the side of the road a few miles outside of town in the direction of the sheriff's office, smoke billowing from the hood. Andrea slowed, not wanting to put herself in a dangerous situation, but not wanting to leave someone stranded in the desert as it began to get dark.

A plump older lady was leaning over her engine, wringing her hands. No one else seemed to be nearby.

Andrea pulled her car over. The least she could do was offer a ride or to call someone.

"Ma'am? Are you okay?"

The woman—a little heavy and probably in her late fifties—looked over at Andrea gratefully. "Oh, honey, thank you so much for stopping! I was afraid no one was going to come along this road. Something is happening with my engine."

Andrea came to stand over next to the woman. "I don't really know anything about cars. But I'd be glad to call someone for you or give you a ride."

The woman looked vaguely familiar to Andrea, probably someone she had known when she lived here, or maybe even one of Aunt Margaret's friends. But honestly, Andrea didn't want to know. Didn't want to answer questions if the woman did know her from when she was younger.

The woman's primary emotion seemed to be anger, and maybe some firm resolution, but neither of those were unusual, given the circumstances. She could be angry at her husband for not servicing the car properly, or maybe just angry that she'd broken down in the middle of nowhere.

"That's so nice of you, dear." The woman began to walk around to the back of her car. "Can you just come back here and help me carry these cables to the front? I think

I might be able to do what my husband did to it last time this happened."

Andrea followed her, but really didn't want to stick around while the woman tried to fix her car. Andrea would help carry whatever cables, then would offer again to give her a ride or call someone. She couldn't spend hours on the side of the road.

She wanted to get back to Brandon.

She walked back and opened up the trunk for the woman. It was completely empty.

"Um, ma'am, there are no cables back he—" Andrea felt a sharp sting in her neck. She reached up to swat away whatever insect had gotten her.

Almost immediately she began to feel dizzy as the world swam around her.

"What?" She tried to focus on the woman, who pushed Andrea down into the trunk.

"Shame on you." The bitterness in the woman's eyes was clear now, although Andrea couldn't seem to focus on them. "You're just as bad as those other hussies. Leading men astray. You're even worse, since you pretend to be the police, too. But I will make sure you're purified."

The last thing Andrea processed was the trunk closing over her before the darkness pulled her under.

Chapter Twenty-One

Even before going in to question Jarrod, Brandon tried to verify the man's whereabouts during the murders. Jarrod had been at all the strip clubs for the DJ Shocker tour where the dead dancers worked. And sure enough, he *hadn't* been at the tour stop for the night the truck-stop waitress was killed.

Probably because he was too busy killing her.

Jarrod's friends, not knowing Jarrod was in custody or suspected of multiple murders, had given Brandon all the information they had. They'd been glad to talk about the DJ Shocker tour; it had been a hoot for them. They'd all independently backed up each other's stories, with just enough details—but not the same details—for Brandon to highly suspect they were being authentic in their responses.

He wished he had Andrea here to get her opinion on whether the men were telling the truth, but she'd gone to talk to Keira. She'd be here soon and he could at least get her opinion on Jarrod's nonverbal behavior.

Because, despite Jarrod's friends' confirmation of his location at the clubs and even despite what they had found in the cellar at his house, Brandon still had doubts that Jarrod was the killer.

He watched Jarrod through the two-way mirror where he sat in the interrogation room. Everything about the man was unkempt. He had on a wrinkled shirt and dirty jeans. His greasy hair needed washing and he looked as if he'd forgotten to shave for the past four days at least. Not to mention the man had been picked up at the bar he frequented. He hadn't even tried to avoid law enforcement.

Brandon found it difficult to reconcile these aspects of the man's personality with the cold, calculating nature of the purity killer. But maybe it was a disguise. Maybe Jarrod had fooled both him and Andrea, and Brandon's pride just didn't want him to admit it.

God knew he'd been wrong an awful lot this week.

Brandon knew where he would start the questioning: victim number two, Ashley Judson, the waitress who dabbled with prostitution on the side. She was the one who didn't fit in the Angels and Devils tour theory. She didn't dance, wasn't a stripper. If Jarrod had picked all his other victims at strip clubs, what had led him to pick her, also?

Brandon glanced at his watch. Andrea should be here any minute. He would go ahead and get started.

"Hi, Jarrod. Remember me?" Brandon walked in the door and took the seat across from Jarrod.

Jarrod nodded slowly. "Yeah. You're that cop that was with Andrea at The Boar's Nest last week. Why am I here, man? I told you everything I knew about Noelle then."

Brandon wanted answers, but more than that he wanted to make sure Jarrod went to jail for the crimes he'd committed. He certainly didn't want him to get off on any technicalities. He would make sure his questioning fell well within the letter of the law. Having a law degree helped make that easier.

Brandon read Jarrod his Miranda rights.

"Yeah, yeah. They already read me my rights when they picked me up at the bar."

"I just want to make sure you know them. That you can call a lawyer if you want to."

Brandon hoped he didn't want to. A lawyer would stall

every question he had for Jarrod. He prayed Jarrod would think he was too smart to need a lawyer.

"Naw, I don't need one." Jarrod sat back in his chair. "I don't got anything to hide."

Brandon smiled. If Jarrod was a wiser man he would've been wary.

Jarrod wasn't.

Brandon took out a picture of Ashley Judson, victim number two—a candid shot, a copy of one Brandon had seen hanging in the cellar at Jarrod's house. He slid it over so Jarrod could see it.

"Do you know this girl?"

"Um…I'm not sure."

There was no doubt in Brandon's mind that Jarrod recognized her. Even if they hadn't just found that picture *at Jarrod's house*, his nonverbal behavior—looking over to the side and down—was giving him away.

"I think you do know her, Jarrod."

Jarrod shrugged. "Maybe. I know a lot of girls."

"How about these? Do you know any of them?"

Brandon took out pictures of the women—all copies of the ones they had found on Jarrod's property—and placed them on the table one after another.

Jarrod's face seemed to lose more color with each picture he studied.

"What's going on here?" he finally asked.

"Why don't you tell me?" Brandon sat back and crossed his arms over his chest.

"What exactly do you want to know? I know Noelle is dead. And I know I told you I didn't really know her very well, but fine, I slept with her, okay? It was a fling. She was getting off of work and I was bored. But I didn't kill her."

"And what about her?" He pointed to the waitress.

"What? Okay, fine. I slept with her, too." He spread his arms out wide across the pictures. "Great, yes. I slept with all these women. Is that a crime? It's pretty damn freaky that the cops are taking a picture of all the girls I've banged over the last month."

Brandon's eyes narrowed. Either Jarrod was the best actor he'd ever seen, or he didn't have any idea all these women were dead.

"How'd you like these girls, Jarrod? Going to see any of them again? Not Noelle of course, but the others?"

Jarrod shrugged one shoulder. "I don't know. Maybe Jillian. She's pretty hot. A dancer." He pointed at Jillian's picture, the woman who had worked at Jaguar's.

"All of them are dancers, right?"

"Not this one." He gestured to Ashley Judson. "She's a waitress."

Brandon smiled, tilting his head to the side. He doubted Jarrod would notice his smile didn't come anywhere near his eyes. "Yeah, I heard that's not all she does. I heard she has a little business on the side with truckers or whoever's willing to pay." Brandon winked.

"Is that what this is about? You think I paid for sex? I didn't pay Ashley, man. It was completely mutual between the two of us. You can ask her."

It was time to move in for the kill. To see if he could force Jarrod into admitting something. All he needed to do was slip up that he knew any of the girls besides Noelle was dead and Brandon would have him trapped in a lie. Then it would just be a matter of wearing him down.

"No, I don't care about money. But doesn't it bother you that Ashley was a hooker on the side? All these girls you've been with aren't exactly upstanding members of society."

Jarrod grimaced. "I don't care about that sort of stuff, man. The girls were fun. I like fun girls."

"You sure about that, Jarrod? Sure you didn't realize that these girls needed cleaning up? That they were tramps? That this town would be better off without them?"

"What?" Jarrod's face wrinkled.

"You know, maybe they needed to be purified in some way. Help them get on the right track? Find God or peace or whatever?"

Jarrod let out a breath, shaking his head. "Dude. You are starting to sound just like my mom. I'm not into that sort of purity stuff. I like girls who like to have a good time. I'm not looking for someone to settle down with. I keep trying to explain that to her."

Brandon sat up a little straighter in his chair. "Your mom talks about purity a lot?"

"All. The. Time." Jarrod rolled his eyes. "I think I'm going to have to move out of her house. The lectures I get after staying out late… Unbelievable. And if she knew I was going to strip clubs? *Sleeping* with girls from strip clubs? She'd blow a gasket. Not enough prayers that could be said for my soul."

Brandon stood up. They had the wrong man. In fact, there wasn't a *man* at all. Jarrod's mother was the serial killer.

He walked over and buzzed the door to let him out. Surely Andrea was here by now. Brandon realized that having her to talk things through with had become important to him over the past few days. After David, he never thought he'd have that again. Never thought he'd want to.

Andrea wasn't in the observation room, but Kendrick was.

"You get that?" Brandon asked him.

"We're already putting an APB out on her. She's not at their house. We've still got people there."

"Have you seen Andrea?"

"No. She hasn't been here at all."

Something clenched in Brandon's stomach. He reached for his phone and dialed her number, knowing texts weren't great for her. It rang then went to voice mail. He left a message, then called Keira next.

"Glad to hear you aren't a complete ass after all," Keira said by way of greeting.

Any other time he would've joked with Keira, even apologized and thanked her. But not now. "Andrea with you, Keira?"

"No, left about forty-five minutes ago. Said you had the killer in custody. Showed me a picture of him. I recognized him as someone Jillian hung out with."

"He's not the right person. Stay in your house until you hear from me. Get a call out to all the girls at Jaguar's if you can. The killer is still out there."

Keira was silent for just a moment. "Okay. Find our girl, Brandon. And have her call me when you do."

"I will."

Brandon put a call in to Big Mike at Club Paradise to make sure Andrea hadn't gone there to tell him the good news. Mike hadn't seen her.

Brandon tried her phone again. Nothing.

Kendrick reentered the observation room. His face was grim.

"Your rental a white Toyota?" He read off a license-plate number.

Brandon nodded.

"It was found abandoned off Highway 85. The phone you're trying to call was inside."

Chapter Twenty-Two

Andrea fought to claw her way out of the darkness. Her brain didn't want to focus; her eyes didn't want to open. Reality felt distant, fuzzy. Her hands were tied behind her back and she was lying on her side; that much she knew.

She forced herself to be still, to think, to try to figure out what was going on.

She'd been drugged by that lady she'd stopped to help on the side of the road. She forced back nausea as she thought of the woman's face, how it had seemed vaguely familiar.

"I know you're waking up," Andrea heard the woman say from a few yards away. "I didn't give you enough tran- quilizer for you to be out for too long."

Andrea remembered being pushed into a trunk, but they weren't in a car any longer. She opened her eyes in the smallest of slits, trying to keep the nausea at bay. They weren't outside. Somewhere inside, but mostly empty. Maybe a small abandoned warehouse? She opened her eyes a little more and saw where the older woman was sitting.

On a pew. An abandoned church building. It looked as if most of it had been burned in a fire.

Given the nature of the crimes, it made perfect sense that this was where the killer would bring the victims.

"I know your aunt, you know," the woman said from where she sat. "Met her at an AA meeting. Not that I'm an alcoholic, but my son is. I thought learning about AA might help me help him. He needs help. Needs to be shown the right path. He's so weak."

It came to Andrea then. They'd had the right house, but the wrong killer.

"You're Jarrod's mother."

"Yes."

Andrea tried to shake off the mental cobwebs clouding her mind. To think. To find some way to relate to this woman. "He and I went to high school together."

"Before you dropped out. Margaret told me."

"Jarrod is my friend. I know he wouldn't want you to hurt me."

"Jarrod doesn't know what he wants. And all you women keep trying to corrupt him. Lead him astray. It's been my job as a mother to clean up after him. To remove temptation from his sight."

"So you killed the women Jarrod was interested in."

"I removed the harlots who led him astray. All of them tempted him beyond what he could bear. All of them either removed their clothes or had sex for money." Mrs. McConnachie stood up. "All I did was what any other mother would do."

"But you killed them."

She took a step closer. "No. I stopped them from committing any further sins. From tempting any other men like Jarrod and corrupting them."

There was no reasoning with this woman about what she had done. Andrea could feel the sincerity radiating from her. In Mrs. McConnachie's mind, her actions were both logical and just. Andrea needed to use another tactic.

"I didn't corrupt Jarrod. He and I have never been romantically involved."

That stopped Mrs. McConnachie for just a moment. She frowned and looked down at her hands. Andrea realized she was holding a rope. No doubt the same one she'd used to strangle the other women.

Andrea began to slide backward on the floor, away from her.

That was a mistake.

Her eyes narrowed and she stepped toward Andrea.

"No. You work at one of those disgusting clubs. I saw you."

"Mrs. McConnachie, I was working undercover." *Trying to catch you*, but Andrea knew not to say that. "I was trying to stop the same thing you were trying to stop, women from corrupting men."

Mrs. McConnachie stopped again, but then shook her head. "No. Margaret said you two had talked, but you wouldn't forgive her, that you were still angry at her even though she had taken you in to raise when you were younger. You're just as bad as those women who tried to corrupt Jarrod."

Andrea realized the older woman wasn't interested in reason or logic. She planned to kill Andrea. The action was already justified in her mind.

Where was Brandon? Had he realized yet Jarrod wasn't the killer? Andrea had no doubt he would; she just didn't think it would be in time to save her. She had no idea where she was. How could Brandon possibly know?

Andrea scooted away on the floor as Jarrod's mother walked toward her. She tried to think of any of the self-defense techniques Brandon had taught her, but with her arms restrained and body feeling so sluggish because of the drugs, it was difficult to move, much less fight.

Tears filled Andrea's eyes. She was going to die here. Killed, ironically, by the very embodiment of a demon from her past, just as Andrea was starting to truly put the past behind her.

She'd never know what could've been between her and Brandon.

Mrs. McConnachie pulled her up into a kneeling position and quickly wrapped her strand of rope around Andrea's neck, coming to stand behind her. Andrea struggled not to fall over, knowing that would just quicken the strangulation.

"Don't worry. This won't hurt very long. Soon you'll be at peace."

Andrea felt the bite of the rope against her throat, instantly cutting off her air. She couldn't help but struggle although it didn't do any good. Her arms bit against the restraints, she could feel blood, but couldn't get loose.

She tried to suck in a breath but the sound just came out as a hoarse sigh.

"There, there," Mrs. McConnachie crooned. "Don't fight it. Find your peace. That's all you need to do now."

Andrea fought one last time, trying to throw her weight to the side, to not panic as Brandon had taught her to do. But it was no use.

Blessed blackness was overtaking Andrea when the pressure suddenly lessened. She collapsed to her side as Mrs. McConnachie fell to the ground next to her. Andrea sucked life-giving oxygen as she tried to figure out what had happened. Had Brandon found them?

Jarrod's mother's eyes stared blankly ahead as a pool of blood began to surround her on the ground. The woman was dead. Andrea couldn't get her body to the angle she needed to prop herself up. All she could do was barely hold on to consciousness as she struggled to get air through her bruised throat.

"Have you ever heard anything so tedious in your entire life as that woman carrying on?" A foot kicked Mrs. McConnachie's body to the side, then squatted down next to Andrea so she could see his face.

She immediately recognized the evil-laden eyes of Damian Freihof.

This time she didn't even try to fight the blackness as it pulled her under.

THE WARRIOR INSIDE Brandon roared to life. Andrea—*his woman*—was in danger, the most desperate kind of danger. Brandon had to do something about that.

He was turning to go back and demand answers from Jarrod—he didn't plan to be anywhere near so gentle this time—when Kendrick put his hand on Brandon's arm to stop him. He took a slight step back when Brandon turned his ferocious gaze on him.

"What?" Brandon snapped out. Kendrick, whatever good he meant, was standing in his way from getting to Andrea.

No one, not even law enforcement, was going to stop him from finding her. By whatever means necessary.

"Whoa, Han." The man held up both hands in a gesture of surrender. "Before you go in there, I just wanted you to know that a vehicle in distress was called in by a civilian near where Andrea's car was found about thirty minutes ago."

Brandon listened. This could be useful intel. "Okay."

"Lady didn't want to stop because she had two babies in the car, but didn't want to leave what looked to be like an older woman stranded. She doesn't remember the exact model of the vehicle, but it was a black four-door sedan. 'Like something from the '80s,' the woman said."

"I'm going to question Jarrod," Brandon told him. "This may not be pretty. I'd appreciate it if there were no interruptions."

Kendrick shrugged. "Actually, I'm going back out to the McConnachies' ranch, make sure there's no unknown buildings where the mom might have Andrea. I'm going to send our other men out to look around town. I'll call Phoenix police department and see if we can get some help, too."

"Good. Keep me posted."

Kendrick handed Brandon the keys to a squad car, then shrugged, turning away. "And damn if the system that records our interrogation-room interviews isn't on the fritz again."

Brandon nodded curtly. He would thank Kendrick later. After he had Andrea back safely.

He unlocked the interview-room door from the outside so he would be able to get back out, then slipped inside. Jarrod was still sitting there, looking bored, biting unkempt fingernails.

"Does your mother drive a black sedan? Late '80s-ish model?"

Jarrod rolled his eyes. "Oh my gosh, yes. She's had that thing since before I was born. I'm embarrassed whenever I have to borrow it."

Brandon refrained from mentioning that Jarrod was in his midtwenties and should have his own damn car.

"Where does your mother like to hang out, Jarrod?"

"Why?" Jarrod snickered. "You looking for a date? I'm sure she wouldn't be much fun, you know."

Brandon rammed his fist down on the table. Jarrod flew back in his chair, eyes wide.

"What the hell, man?"

"I'll tell you what the hell." Brandon reached down and got the autopsy photographs of each of the dead women. He put them on top of the photographs of when they were alive. "Do you know why you're here, Jarrod? Because every single one of the women you had a fling with over the last few weeks is dead."

Jarrod looked as if he was going to vomit. Color leaked

from his face. "I didn't do this, man. I swear to God, I didn't kill them. I have an alibi, remember?"

Under other circumstances Brandon would have handled a situation like this more delicately, broken the news to him more gently. Jarrod's mom might be a killer, but the woman was still his mother.

Brandon didn't have that kind of time.

"I know you didn't kill them. Your mother did."

Brandon's eyes bugged right out of his head. "What?"

"She must have been following you. She saw the women you hooked up with and killed them the next day or soon after."

"But…but why?"

"You said she talks about purification all the time? These women's bodies were left with purification rituals. Like your mother was cleansing them to send them to the next world or whatever."

The final bit of color left Jarrod's complexion. "She talks about that sort of junk all the time." He blanched as he tore his eyes up from the pictures to look at Brandon where he leaned on both arms against the table. "About needing to clean up the 'riffraff' in this town, to get rid of all those who would lead men down a corrupted path. I think my dad might have cheated on her or something before he died. But I never knew she meant to kill anyone. I just thought she meant starting a petition to close down the local strip clubs or something, you know?"

"Jarrod, I know this is hard. But I need your help *right now*. Another woman's life is at stake. Andrea's."

Jarrod was staring down at the pictures again.

"Where would your mom do this, Jarrod? Kill these women. We've already checked your house and barn. Is there anywhere else on your property?"

Jarrod shook his head numbly. "We don't really own

anything besides the house and barn. Most of the land got sold off when Dad died."

"Okay, then somewhere else? Where does your mom like to go? Where does she hang out?"

Jarrod said nothing, just stared at the pictures. Brandon knew he was losing the other man, shock settling in. That was unacceptable until he got the info he needed.

He reached down and grabbed Jarrod by the collar of the cheap jacket he wore and yanked him out of his chair. Under any other circumstances this sort of manhandling of a witness would be completely unacceptable. This wasn't some action movie where cops could do whatever they wanted with no repercussions.

Brandon didn't give a damn about repercussions.

"Think, Jarrod. Where would your mother go to do these things?" He shook the other man.

"I don't know. She goes to church a lot and some other meetings. I don't really know what." His voice was squeaky.

"No. It couldn't be a place other people are around. Where else? Where would she go if she wanted to be alone?"

Jarrod began to cry. Brandon pulled the younger man's face closer to his.

"Focus, Jarrod. Your mother would need to be somewhere where no one is around. Isolated, to at least some degree. Where. Would. She. Go?" He punctuated each word with a shake.

"I don't know, man, maybe the old church off Highway 85? She always slows down when we drive past. It's where my dad's memorial service was held."

"No, a church is too crowded, even if no service is going on."

Jarrod shook his head. "No, this one burned a few years ago. Congregation decided to build a new church in a more convenient location rather than pay to have that one re-built. The outer walls are still standing but the inside is pretty torn up."

That was it. It had to be.

"Where, exactly?"

Jarrod quickly explained, and Brandon was flying out the door and to the squad car in seconds, praying he wasn't too late.

Chapter Twenty-Three

Brandon parked the squad car and got out of it silently, not wanting to take the chance that Mrs. McConnachie might hear him and panic, hurting Andrea.

But he sprinted because the woman had already had Andrea in her clutches for way too long. Brandon pushed the warrior, who wanted to burst in and *fight*, aside. Logic had to reign right now. Caution. The mental state of Mrs. McConnachie was unknown. He'd radioed for help, but wasn't going to wait for backup to arrive.

Brandon eased his way through a side door that couldn't be completely closed because of burn damage. He couldn't see most of the larger section of the charred church, only the front portion near what must have once been the altar area. Brandon was shocked at what met his eyes.

Mrs. McConnachie's dead body lying on the ground.

Brandon no longer worried about silence or caution. Had Andrea been wounded in fighting the older woman? Did she need medical attention? He was glad it was Mrs. McConnachie on the ground and not Andrea, but where was she?

He burst into the room, looking around, but didn't see her. Had she made her way outside? He began looking between pews, to make sure she hadn't fallen behind one.

He sensed her behind him before he saw or heard her. Brandon turned to find Andrea standing in the aisle between the two rows of pews, as if she was a bride about to walk to her groom.

But in the shadows behind Andrea, Brandon could immediately make out another presence. He knew right away who it was.

"Let her go, Freihof."

"Ah, Agent Han, I see my reputation has preceded me."

"Yeah, your reputation as a sicko. Let her go."

"Come now, Agent Han, I'm sure *sicko* isn't the clinical term. You have too many degrees to be using such common terminology."

Brandon's eyes narrowed, but he played along. "How about 'psychopath with homicidal tendencies and sociopathic and delusional proclivity.'"

"Yes, yes. So much better!" Freihof turned to Andrea, shrugging. "Basically a sicko."

Freihof took a few steps closer, forcing Andrea with him as a shield, coming out of the shadows and into the dim light of the church. Brandon could see the knife Freihof held at her throat, which was covered with angry red marks. Andrea had been strangled.

"Miss Gordon unfortunately fell into the clutches of the crazy old lady there." Freihof gestured toward Mrs. McConnachie's body. "I had to take care of that. Wasn't going to let anyone kill our Andrea."

He kissed Andrea's cheek and she flinched. "Anyone but me, that is. Please take your gun out and throw it to the side, Agent Han."

Andrea tried to move away, but Freihof pulled her back against him, his blade still at her throat. Brandon took his Glock out of its holster and slid it on the ground over to the side. He refused to take a chance on Freihof cutting Andrea's throat. Freihof nodded approvingly.

"I've had almost four years to study you all," Freihof continued. "It's amazing how much one can find out about

Omega Sector if he tries, both by electronic and flesh-and-blood sources. Not to mention, your organization has put a lot of people behind bars. A lot of *angry* people."

"What do you want, Freihof?" Brandon asked. He needed to get Andrea away from Freihof's blade.

"C'mon, Agent Han, play along. I'm just trying to impress you with my knowledge. I know Steve Drackett is your boss and was there the night I was arrested. I know a great deal about some of your colleagues, a Liam Goetz and Joe Matarazzo. More than that."

Brandon tried to figure out the other man's endgame, in order to get ahead of him, but couldn't see it. "Great, Freihof. I am thoroughly impressed at your mental database of Omega Sector."

Freihof smiled and shook his head back and forth like a giddy child, taking a few steps closer with Andrea. "I know. I'm showing off. It's annoying, I'm sure."

He had figured the man was a psychopath, but Brandon hadn't realized just how intelligent he was. Freihof's size and strength were also impressive. He'd obviously spent some of his time in prison working out and bulking up.

Freihof was dangerous in every possible way.

"Okay." Brandon took a step closer, arms outstretched. "Honestly, I am pretty impressed. Your escape. Finding us. Knowing so much about Omega. You're definitely more advanced than most of the criminals I face."

"Thank you, Dr. Han. It means a lot that you would say that."

"Now tell me what you want, and let Andrea go."

Brandon purposefully did not let himself look at her. He didn't want to give away how much she meant to him, plus couldn't trust himself to be able to focus if he saw she was about to fall apart.

Andrea was strong. She could handle it. He had to believe that. He did believe it.

Freihof's knife stayed at her neck. "What I want? Do you mean long-term or short-term?"

"Either."

"What I want, what I plan to do long-term, is take Omega Sector apart piece by piece. Destroy you guys from within until the whole organization falls apart. And keep Andrea here by my side as a plaything while I do it."

Over Brandon's dead body. "Some grandiose plans you got there. How about short-term?"

"Short-term, I plan to sit Miss Gordon down right here at this pew—oh, please don't get me started about the church symbolism—and give her a little gift."

Freihof did as he'd spoken and sat Andrea down, awkwardly because her hands were restrained behind her back, on the pew next to him. Brandon watched in horror as he took out a small explosive device with a twine loop and wrapped it like a necklace around Andrea's slender neck. He took her hands and secured them to the arm of one of the pews with a zip tie.

Brandon could see the three-minute countdown blinking out at him brightly.

"I know we're running out of time and the rest of this rinky-dink town's police force will be here soon, so I'm going to start this timer," Freihof continued in a conversational tone. "That will give you three minutes to finish me off and get back to your love here, Dr. Han."

"Don't turn that thing on," Brandon said through clenched teeth. "How's she supposed to be your long-term plaything if you blow her up?"

"I've found you have to be flexible in your plans, Agent Han. Besides, I don't foresee any problem with me being able to take you in three minutes—it will give us both motivation to do our best work, right? Neither of us wants Andrea in little pieces."

Freihof pressed a button that started the countdown.

2:59, 2:58, 2:57…

"I have a feeling you're going to wish you'd spent less time in the library and more time in the gym, Dr. Han." Freihof's eyes were complete evil.

Brandon allowed himself to look at Andrea just for a moment. A single tear fell from her green eyes. Then he looked down at the explosives attached to her neck.

2:51, 2:50…

Freihof was wrong. Brandon wasn't going to wish he'd spent more time at the gym. He stood up straighter, immediately knowing what he had to do. For the first time in his entire life, Brandon didn't even try to keep the darkness inside him at bay. He let the cold, intellectual side of himself be pushed to the side.

As the warrior inside broke free.

He could feel his mind emptying, a complete and utter focus overtaking him. Intellect would not win this battle; the warrior would.

The warrior fighting for his woman.

He saw Freihof's eyes narrow briefly—the man realized his mistake too late—before Brandon flew at him at a speed he wasn't expecting. Freihof still had the knife, and Brandon felt its sharp sting, but it seemed to be at a distance.

Freihof was bigger, stronger and had a weapon. But Brandon fought like a man with nothing to lose.

Because he realized what the warrior inside him had known all along: if he lost Andrea, he lost everything.

The blows between him and Freihof were brutal and coarse. The countdown around Andrea's neck left no room for strategy, no room to dance around each other.

Brandon felt perverse pleasure as Freihof's nose broke under one of his punches, but then felt the burn as the man's knife found his side. Again.

The moves he'd practiced so recently with Andrea

helped him face the bigger man. He heard the snap of Freihof's arm and the man's grunt of pain when Brandon used a move he had just been showing her yesterday.

The only thing the warrior would allow his intellectual side to do was keep track of the time. Without even having to look, Brandon knew the exact second of the counter.

1:02, 1:01, 1:00…

As Freihof fell to the ground, Brandon threw punch after punch at the man's head and torso. Brandon knew at that point he would win the fight.

But he also knew he would pay a heavy price. He could feel himself becoming light-headed from blood loss, although he'd since kicked Freihof's knife away.

0:19, 0:18, 0:17…

He had Freihof in the hold he wanted. One that would subdue him into unconsciousness in a matter of seconds.

"You're running out of time, Han." Freihof wheezed. "Are you going to choose her or me?"

He was right. Brandon didn't even hesitate. He let Freihof go and ran over to Andrea.

0:10…

He had no idea how to disarm the bomb; all he could do was get it off her and away from them, praying it would not have enough power to bring the entire building down on them.

0:06, 0:05…

He slipped it off her neck and threw it as far as he could toward the back corner of the church. He snatched the knife lying beside Freihof's unconscious form and cut through the zip tie and most of the thin twine that bound Andrea's wrists. That was all he could do.

He grabbed her and slid them both under a pew, wrapping himself around her to protect her as best he could, tucking her head into his chest.

A moment later the explosion shook the entire building and nothing could be seen but darkness.

EVERYTHING IN ANDREA'S body hurt. Her shoulders, her throat, her ears. But she was still alive.

The building hadn't collapsed, but given the state it had already been in before the explosion, Andrea wasn't sure how long it would stay standing.

"Brandon, are you okay? I think we need to get out of here."

She nudged him with her shoulder. He had pulled her close to protect her, but now his arms were lying limply by his side. The bonds that held her wrists were looser and Andrea tugged at them for release. Seeing Brandon lying so still gave her a burst of strength.

She bit her lip in agony as her shoulders moved back into a more natural position.

"Brandon?" More panicked now, she brought her cheek up to his mouth to see if she could feel his breath. Yes, breathing. But when she looked down at his body all she saw was blood.

Too much blood.

She tried to stop the bleeding with her hands, but his shirt was so soaked she couldn't even figure out where the wounds were.

"This is the Maricopa County Sheriff's Department," Andrea heard someone call out. "Is anyone in here?"

"Yes," she yelled as loud as her hoarse voice would allow. "Back here."

She waved her hand, but then immediately brought it back down to his wounds.

Too much blood.

"Here," she called out again. Flashlights pointed in her direction as she called out. "I need help." Her voice completely gave out with that last word.

Out of the corner of her eye, something caught her attention. Freihof. She turned and he gave her a tiny wave and evil smile before running silently out the side door.

Andrea wanted to communicate with the police officers who were making their way through the rubble to get to them. To tell them about Freihof, but she literally could not get the words out.

Besides, she didn't care about Freihof when Brandon's blood was seeping out of his body under her. He still wasn't conscious.

She bent back down to say in his ear as loudly as her voice would allow, "Come on, Brandon. I need you. I've had two serial killers almost get me today and we're not going to let them win. You fought for me. You beat him for me. Fight for *you* now. *For us.*"

She kissed him. His lips, his forehead, his cheeks.

A paramedic as well as two police officers came and took over life-saving duties. Andrea didn't want to let Brandon go but knew more qualified people needed to take over. She watched it all as if she was in a daze.

But when they rushed Brandon into the ambulance, Andrea found her spirit and fought to stay with him. She wasn't letting Brandon out of her sight. A paramedic stopped her at the ambulance door.

"I'm sorry—you can't ride here."

"I have to," Andrea croaked out, but the words came out soundless. She could feel herself begin to panic. She couldn't leave Brandon alone.

She felt someone take her arm. "I'll drive you," Kendrick said. "Consider it the beginning of restitution for all the times we let you down when you were younger."

Andrea nodded. She knew she should say something, couldn't anyway, so she just got in the car with Kendrick. Her eyes never left the ambulance the entire time.

Chapter Twenty-Four

Fifteen hours later—the longest fifteen hours of her life—
Brandon was safely out of surgery. Andrea was still watching over him. Keira had brought her a change of clothes,
much needed since hers had been covered in Brandon's
blood. Andrea had talked with her friend for a while, still
a difficult task due to the damage to her throat. Keira had
contacted Steve Drackett for Andrea so he could be updated.

The doctors had done a full scan of Andrea after
Kendrick brought her in right behind Brandon. She'd been
very fortunate, they'd told her, that although she had extensive bruising and swelling, none of her neck muscles
had been ruptured, nor did there seem to be any permanent damage to her larynx.

Ironically, if Freihof hadn't stopped Mrs. McConnachie
when he had, the damage would've grown exponentially
greater every second.

Kendrick assured her that every law-enforcement officer in Arizona was looking for Freihof even as they spoke.
Somehow that didn't reassure her. But she wouldn't let it
worry her right now. Right now she was focused on Brandon.

He had *fought* for her.

Andrea had realized, of course, when he had been
teaching her the self-defense moves, that Brandon knew

how to handle himself. He was a trained agent, so he would know hand-to-hand combat moves.

This had been more than that.

When Freihof put that explosive necklace around her neck, Andrea had not believed there was any way Brandon would be able to fight and beat someone with the size and cunning of Freihof—who had a *knife*—in three minutes. Some things were just not possible.

She'd watched as Brandon had turned into something else before her eyes. In one second a myriad of conflicting emotions had radiated from him: concern, anger, worry, pain. He'd been thinking of multiple different angles and scenarios to tip the situation in his favor, his powerful mind working in overdrive.

In the second Freihof had turned on the explosives countdown, Brandon's powerful mind had been completely shut down. Every emotion he'd been projecting had stopped. Focus and determination had taken its place.

The intellectual genius had been replaced by a dark warrior. And the dark warrior had achieved the impossible: defeating Freihof before the time had run out.

He had *fought* for her. No one in her life had ever fought for her.

Andrea held Brandon's hand as he slept. Soon his family would be here and she'd be relegated to the waiting room. But for now he was hers to protect.

BRANDON'S BRAIN WOKE UP before he could force his eyes open. That happened a lot. He was processing before he was fully awake.

But for some reason he seemed to be processing more slowly than usual. Frustrating. He forced himself to relax, not opening his eyes. To listen, to remember, to piece it all together.

His first awareness was of the pain. It seemed to radiate from everywhere in his body. Everything hurt so much he couldn't seem to figure out where his central injuries had occurred.

He heard the beeping of machines, distant talking farther away. He was in a hospital. The fight with Freihof, the knife, the explosion… It all came back to him.

"College just wasn't for me," a deep voice was saying. "I had better things to do with my time. Things that provided a much more rounded education, if you know what I mean."

Joe Matarazzo. Brandon knew his friend and fellow agent's voice.

Brandon tried to open his eyes but it was more difficult than he'd thought. The pain wanted to pull him back under.

"You're bad." It was Andrea's sweet voice, but different. More throaty. Hoarse, but damn if it didn't still sound sexy to him. He could feel his hand resting in hers.

"My friends say I'm audacious." Brandon could hear the smile in Joe's voice. "I had to look that up to see what it meant, because of the lack of college education and all. Ends up that 'coming from a billionaire family and sleeping with every available woman in a three-state area' is actually the very definition of *audacious*."

Andrea laughed. "Yeah, well, I'm a high school dropout ex-stripper. I think that might one-up you."

Had Andrea just made a joke about her past?

Joe's bark of laughter was friendly and kind. "Well, then you and I probably ought to run off and get married right now."

Now Brandon opened his eyes.

"Nope, she's taken." He raised their linked hands.

Joe smiled. "Hey, bro. You gave us a scare for a minute."

Joe said some other things, but Brandon only had eyes for Andrea. She was here. She was safe. She was at his side.

Joe cleared his throat. "I can see that you and your lady need some time, so I'll be back in a while."

Joe made his way out the door. Brandon appreciated the other man's tact.

"Hey," Andrea whispered, leaning over him so she was a little closer.

It cost him considerable effort, but Brandon reached up to bring her lips down to his. He couldn't go another second without feeling her sweetness against him.

"Are you okay?" he asked against her mouth.

"Yes. You were the one who was hurt, fighting Freihof."

"Your voice sounds different."

"That was actually Mrs. McConnachie's doing. Freihof saved me from her so he could kill me himself." He felt her shudder. "But the doctors think my voice should fully recover. And there is no permanent damage. You, on the other hand… Multiple stab wounds, concussion, dislocated shoulder. You're very lucky, all things considered. One of the stab wounds missed your kidney by a couple of centimeters."

"But you're okay." That was all Brandon could remember about his fight with Freihof. The knowledge that if he failed, Andrea would suffer. He couldn't allow that to happen.

She kissed him again. "I'm perfectly fine."

Thank God. He hadn't allowed it to happen.

"But Freihof got away. Kendrick assures me they have a statewide manhunt going for him."

Brandon's teeth ground. As long as Freihof was free Andrea wouldn't be safe. "Does Steve know?"

"Yes. I think that's why Joe is here. He said he was just passing through on another case, but I think Steve sent him to keep an eye on us in case Freihof came back."

Brandon nodded. "We'll get him, sweetheart. I promise."

Andrea smiled. "I know."

"I heard you make a joke about being a stripper with Joe. That took a lot of guts."

Andrea gave him a shy smile. "Given his past, mine didn't seem so bad. Plus, Joe's easy to talk to. He makes everything seem okay somehow."

"That's why he is so good at his job as a hostage negotiator. Everybody loves to be around him."

"Well, I just love to be around you," she whispered.

"Good, because I don't plan on letting you out of my sight."

Her past didn't make any difference to him except in how it had formed her into the beautiful, intelligent, gutsy woman she was. All Brandon cared about was their future.

A nurse entered the room. "Mr. Han, your family is here."

"Okay, you can let them in."

Andrea stood up. "I'll go wait in the waiting room or find Joe."

Brandon didn't let go of her hand even for a second. "No. Like the nurse said, my family is here." He pulled her down for a kiss. "That includes you, sweetheart. From now on."

Her soft smile balanced out the darkness inside him and appeased the warrior inside.

She was his.

* * * * *

UNDERCOVER HUSBAND

CINDI MYERS

Chapter One

"I was told you're the ones who can help me."

The soft, cultured voice as much as the words caught the attention of Bureau of Land Management special agent Walt Riley. The Ranger Brigade headquarters in Black Canyon of the Gunnison National Park didn't get many visitors, and certainly not many women as beautiful as the one standing on the opposite side of his desk now. Slender, with blond hair worn piled on top of her head, she spoke with an air of command, as if she was used to overseeing a corporation or running board meetings. Everything about her—from the designer sunglasses to the diamonds glinting at her earlobes to the toes of her high heels—looked expensive, and out of place in this part of rural Colorado, where jeans and boots were the most common attire for men and women alike.

Walt stood. "What do you need help with?" he asked. He selfishly hoped she wasn't merely a lost tourist or someone who needed a camping permit or something that was better handled by the park rangers in the office next door.

She opened the sleek leather satchel she had slung over one shoulder and pulled out a sheaf of papers and handed it to him. At first glance, it appeared to be some kind of legal document. "What is this?" he asked.

"It's a court order awarding me custody of my niece, Joy Dietrich." She removed the sunglasses and he found himself staring into a pair of intensely blue eyes, their beauty undimmed by the red rims and puffy lids, evidence that Miss Cool and Collected had, very recently, been crying. "I need your help getting her back from the people who have kidnapped her," she said.

This definitely was more serious than a camping permit. Walt dragged a chair over to his desk. "Why don't you sit down, Ms.—?"

"Dietrich. Hannah Dietrich." She sat, crossing her long legs neatly at the ankles. There was nothing particularly revealing about the gray slacks and matching jacket she wore, but she still managed to look sexy wearing them. Or maybe it was only that Walt had always had a thing for blue-eyed blondes.

"Wait here, Ms. Dietrich," he said. "I'm going to get my commanding officer and you can tell us your story."

He strode to the back of the building and poked his head around the open door of Commander Graham Ellison's office. The FBI agent, who still carried himself like the marine he had once been, broke off his conversation with DEA agent Marco Cruz. Elsewhere in the office or out in the field, officers from Immigration and Customs Enforcement, Customs and Border Protection, and Colorado State Patrol worked together to fight crime on thousands of acres of public land in the southwest corner of Colorado. Walt, one of the newest members of the Ranger team, had jumped at the opportunity to be involved in the kind of high-profile cases the Rangers were becoming known for. A kidnapping would definitely qualify as high-profile. "Something up, Walt?" Graham asked.

"There's a woman out here who says she needs our help recovering her kidnapped niece," Walt said. "Before I had her run through the whole story, I thought you might like to hear it."

"Who does she say kidnapped her niece?" Marco, one of the senior members of the Ranger Brigade, had a reputation as an expert tracker and a cool head in even the tensest situations. Walt hadn't had a chance to work with him yet, but he had heard plenty of stories from others on the team.

"We haven't gotten that far yet," Walt said.

"Let's hear what she has to say." Graham led the way back to Walt's desk, where Hannah Dietrich waited. If the prospect of being confronted by three lawmen unsettled her, she didn't show it. "Ms. Dietrich, this is Commander Graham Ellison and Agent Marco Cruz."

"Hello." She nodded, polite but reserved. "I hope you'll be able to help me."

"Why don't you tell us more about your situation?" Graham pulled up a second chair, while Marco stood behind him. Walt perched on the corner of the desk. "You say your niece was kidnapped?"

"In a manner of speaking."

"What manner would that be?" Marco crossed his arms over his chest.

"I think it would be best if I began at the beginning." She smoothed her hands down her thighs and took a deep breath. "I have—had—a sister, Emily. She's six years younger than me, and though we have always been close, in temperament we're very different. She was always carefree, impulsive and restless."

Nothing about Hannah Dietrich looked restless or impulsive, Walt thought. Even obviously distressed as she was, the word she brought to mind was *control*. She controlled her feelings and she was used to being in control of her life.

"About a year ago, Emily met a man, Raynor Gilbert," Hannah continued. "He was working as a bouncer at a club in Denver that she used to frequent, and they became lovers. She found out she was pregnant, and they had plans to marry, but he was killed in a motorcycle accident only a week after Emily learned she was expecting." She paused a moment, clearly fighting for composure, then continued.

"My sister was devastated, and acted out her grief with even more impulsive behavior. I wanted her to come live with me, but she refused. She said she wanted a different life for herself and her child. She attended a rally by a group that calls themselves the Family. Their leader is a very handsome, charismatic man named Daniel Metwater."

"We know about Metwater." Graham's expression was grim. Metwater and his "family" had a permit to camp in the Curecanti National Recreation Area, adjacent to the national park and part of the Rangers' territory. Though Metwater had recently been eliminated as the chief suspect in a murder investigation, the Rangers continued to keep a close watch on him and his followers.

"Then you are probably aware that he recruits young people to join his group, promising them peace and harmony and living close to nature," Hannah said. "His message appealed to my sister, who I believe was looking for an excuse to run away from her life for a while."

"When was the baby—Joy—born?" Walt asked.

Her eyes met his, softening a little—because he had remembered the child's name? "She was born a little over three months ago. Emily sent me a letter with a photograph. She said the baby was healthy, but I know my sister well enough to read between the lines. I sensed she wasn't happy. She said things had been hard, though she didn't provide any details, and she said she wanted to come home for a visit but didn't know if the Prophet—that's what this Metwater person calls himself—would allow it. I would have gone to her right away, but her letter gave no clue as to where she was located. She said the Family was moving soon and she would write me again when they were settled."

"Did she usually contact you via letter instead of calling or texting or emailing?" Walt asked.

"Apparently, one condition of being a part of this group is giving up electronic devices like computers and cell phones," Hannah said. "I don't know if all the members comply with that restriction, but Hannah was very serious about it. Shortly after she joined the group, she wrote and told me we could only communicate through letters."

"Did that alarm you?" Graham asked.

"Of course it did." A hint of annoyance sharpened Hannah's voice. "I wrote back immediately and tried to persuade her that a group that wanted its members to cut off contact with family and friends had to be dangerous—but that letter came back marked Return to Sender. It was months before I heard anything else from Emily, and that was the letter informing me of Joy's birth. In the interim, I was worried sick."

She opened the satchel once more and withdrew an

envelope. "Then, only two weeks after the letter announcing Joy's birth came, I received this." She handed
the envelope to Walt. He pulled out two sheets of lined
paper, the left edge ragged where the pages had been
torn out of a notebook.

"'I'm very afraid. I don't think anyone can help
me,'" Walt read out loud. "'If anything happens to
me, promise you will take care of Joy.'" He looked at
Hannah. "What did you do when you received this?"

"I was frantic to find her. I hired a private detective, and he was able to track down Metwater and his
followers, but they told him there was no one in the
group who fit my sister's description and they knew
nothing. Look at the other paper, please."

Walt handed the first sheet to Graham and scanned
the second sheet. "Is this a will?" he asked.

"Yes. It names me as Joy's guardian in the event of
Emily's death. I was able to have a court certify it as
legal and grant me custody."

"How did you do that?" Graham asked. "Without
proof of your sister's death?"

"I was able to find proof." She brought out another
envelope and handed it to the commander. "Here are
copies of my sister's death certificate, as well as a birth
certificate for her daughter."

Graham read the documents. "This says she died
in Denver, of respiratory failure." He frowned. "Did
your sister have a history of respiratory problems?"

"She had suffered from asthma off and on for most
of her life, but it was well controlled with medication.
She never had to be hospitalized for it."

"Do you have any idea what she was afraid of?"

Walt asked. "Did she specifically say that Metwater or anyone else threatened her?"

Hannah shook her head. "She didn't. But I know my sister. Emily was a lot of things, but she wasn't the nervous type and she wasn't a drama queen. She was truly terrified of something, and I think it had to do with Metwater and his cult."

Walt scanned the will again. His attention rested on the signatures at the bottom of the page. "This says the will was witnessed by Anna Ingels and Marsha Caldwell."

"Marsha Caldwell was a nurse at the hospital where Joy was born," Hannah said. "She left when her husband was transferred overseas, so I haven't been able to talk to her. And I wasn't able to determine who Anna Ingels is."

"Maybe she's one of Metwater's followers," Walt said.

"Except that most of them don't use their real names," Marco said. "It makes tracking them down more difficult."

"But not impossible," Graham said. He shuffled the papers in his hand. "This birth certificate says your niece was born in Denver. Have you talked with anyone there?"

"The hospital wouldn't give me any information, and the PI wasn't able to find out anything, either." She shifted in her chair, as if impatient. "When I talked to the local sheriff's office, they said the area where Metwater is camping is your jurisdiction," she said. "All I need is for you to go with me to get Joy."

"You haven't tried to make contact with them on your own?" Graham asked.

She shook her head. "The private detective I hired paid them a visit. That's when they refused to admit they had ever known Emily or that Joy even existed. He told me the conditions in their camp are pretty rough—that it isn't the place for an infant." She pressed her lips together, clearly fighting to maintain her composure. "I don't want to waste any more time. I thought it would be better to show up with law enforcement backing. I know this Metwater preaches nonviolence, but my sister was genuinely afraid for her life. Why else would she have made a will at her age?"

"It doesn't seem out of line for a new parent to want to appoint a guardian for her child," Marco said. "Maybe she was merely being prudent."

"One thing my sister was not was prudent," Hannah said.

Unlike Hannah herself, Walt thought. He certainly knew how different siblings could be. "May I see the birth certificate?" he asked.

Graham passed it to him, then addressed Hannah. "Do you have a picture of your niece?"

"Only the newborn photo my sister sent." She slipped it from the satchel and handed it to him. Graham and Marco looked at it, then passed it to Walt.

He studied the infant's wrinkled red face in the oversize pink bonnet. "I don't think this is going to be much help in identifying a three-month-old," he said.

"We can go to Metwater and demand he hand over the child," Graham said. "But if he refuses to admit she even exists, it could be tougher."

"You can't hide an infant for very long," Hannah said. "Someone in the camp—some other mother, perhaps—knows she exists."

"What makes you think Metwater's group has her?" Marco asked. "It's possible she ended up with Child Welfare and Protection in Denver after your sister's death."

"I checked with them. They have no record of her. I'm sure she's still with Metwater and his group."

"Why are you so sure?" Walt asked.

Her expression grew pinched. "Take another look at her birth certificate."

Walt studied the certificate, frowning.

"What is it?" Marco asked.

Walt looked up from the paper, not at his fellow officers, but at Hannah. "This says the child's father is Daniel Metwater."

HANNAH HELD HERSELF very still, willing herself not to flinch at the awful words. "That's a lie," she said. "Emily was pregnant long before she ever met Daniel Metwater, and I know she was in a relationship with Raynor Gilbert. I have pictures of them together, and I talked to people at the club where he worked." The conversations had been excruciating, having to relive her sister's happiness over the baby and being in love, and then the grief when her dream of a storybook future was destroyed by Raynor's death. "They all say he and Emily were together—that he was the father of her baby. A simple DNA test will prove that."

"Yet the court was willing to grant you custody of the child?" Graham asked.

"Temporary custody," she said. "Pending outcome of the DNA test. Believe me, Commander, Daniel Metwater is not Joy's father. Her father was Raynor Gilbert and he's dead."

"Let us do some investigating and see what we can find out," Graham said. "But even if we locate an infant of the appropriate sex and age in the camp, unless Metwater and his followers admit it's your sister's child, we won't be able to do anything. If some other woman is claiming to be the infant's mother, you may have to go back to court to request the DNA testing before we can seize the child."

She stood, so abruptly her chair slid back with a harsh protest, and her voice shook in spite of her willing it not to. "If you won't help me, I'll get the child on my own."

"How will you do that?" Walt asked.

"I'll pretend I want to join the group. Once I'm living with them, I can find Joy and I'll leave with her."

She braced herself for them to tell her she couldn't do that. Their expressions told her plainly enough that's what they were thinking—at least what the commander and Agent Cruz thought. Agent Riley looked a little less stern. "You've obviously given this some thought," he said.

"I will do anything to save my niece," she said. "I had hoped to do this with law enforcement backing, but if necessary, I will go into that camp and steal her back. And I dare you and anyone else to try to stop me."

Chapter Two

Daniel Metwater and his followers had definitely chosen a spot well off the beaten path for their encampment. After an hour's drive over washboard dirt roads, Walt followed Marco down a narrow footpath, across a plank bridge over a dry arroyo, to a homemade wooden archway that proclaimed Peace in crooked painted lettering. "Looks like they've made themselves at home," Walt observed.

"They picked a better spot this time." Marco glanced back at Walt. "You didn't see the first camp, did you?"

Walt shook his head. While several members of the team had visited Metwater's original camp as part of the murder investigation, he had been assigned to other duties.

"It was over in Dead Horse Canyon," Marco said. "No water, not many trees and near a fairly popular hiking trail." He looked around the heavily wooded spot alongside a shallow creek. "This is less exposed, with access to water and wood."

"Their permit is still only for two weeks," Walt said.

"There's plenty of room in the park for them to move around," Marco said. "And Metwater has some kind of influence with the people who issue the permits. They appear happy to keep handing them out to him."

A bearded young man, barefoot and dressed only in a pair of khaki shorts, approached. "Hello, Officers," he said, his expression wary. "Is something wrong?"

"We're here to see Mr. Metwater," Marco said.

"I'll see if the Prophet is free to speak with you," the man said.

"I think he understands by now it's in his best interest to speak with us," Marco said.

He didn't wait for the young man to answer, but pushed past him and continued down the trail.

The camp itself was spread out in a clearing some fifty yards from the creek—a motley collection of tents and trailers and homemade shelters scattered among the trees. A large motor home with an array of solar panels on the roof stood at one end of the collection. "That's Metwater's RV," Marco said, and led the way toward it.

Walt followed, taking the opportunity to study the men and women, and more than a few children, who emerged from the campers and tents and trailers to stare at the two lawmen. More than half the people he saw were young women, several with babies or toddlers in their arms or clinging to their skirts. The men he saw were young also, many with beards and longer hair, and all of them regarded him and Marco with expressions ranging from openly angry to guarded.

Marco rapped on the door to the large motor home. After a few seconds, the door eased open, and a strikingly beautiful, and obviously pregnant, blonde peered out at them. "Hello, Ms. Matheson." Marco touched the brim of his Stetson. "We'd like to speak to Mr. Metwater."

Frowning at the pair of officers, she opened the door wider. "I don't know why you people can't leave him alone," she said.

Walt had heard plenty about Andi Matheson, though he hadn't met her before. Her lover was the man murdered outside the Family's camp, and her father, a US senator, had been involved in the crime. She was perhaps the most famous of Metwater's followers, and apparently among those closest to him.

"We need to ask him some questions." Marco moved past her. Walt followed, nodding to Andi as he passed, but she had already looked away, toward the man who was entering from the back of the motor home.

Daniel Metwater had the kind of presence that focused the attention of everyone in the room on him. A useful quality for someone who called himself a prophet, Walt thought. Metwater was in his late twenties or early thirties, about five-ten or five-eleven, with shaggy dark hair and piercing dark eyes, and pale skin that showed a shadow of beard even in early afternoon. He wore loose linen trousers and a white cotton shirt unbuttoned to show defined abs and a muscular chest. He might have been a male model or a pop singer instead of an itinerant evangelist. "Officers." He nodded in greeting. "To what do I owe this pleasure?"

"We're looking for an infant," Marco said. "A little girl, about three months old."

"And what—you think this child wandered in here on her own?" Metwater smirked.

"Her mother was a follower of yours—Emily Dietrich," Marco said.

Metwater frowned, as if in thought, though Walt suspected the expression was more for show. "I don't recall a disciple of mine by that name," he said.

Walt turned to Andi. "Did you know Emily?" he asked.

She shook her head.

"What about Anna Ingels?" Walt asked.

Something flickered in her eyes, but she quickly looked away, at Metwater. "We don't have anyone here by that name, either," Metwater said.

"I asked Miss Matheson if she knows—or knew—of an Anna Ingels." Walt kept his gaze fixed on Andi.

"No," she said.

"Asteria, you may leave us now," Metwater said.

Andi—whose Family name was apparently Asteria—ducked her head and hurried out of the room. Metwater turned back to the Rangers. "What does any of this have to do with your missing infant?" he asked.

"Her aunt, Hannah Dietrich, came to us. She thinks her sister's child is here in this camp," Marco said. "She has legal custody of the baby and would like to assume that custody."

"If she believes this child is here, she's been misinformed," Metwater said.

"Then you won't mind if we look around," Walt said.

"We have a number of children here in the camp," Metwater said. "But none of them are the one you seek. I can't allow you to disrupt and upset my followers this way. If you want to search the camp, you'll have to get a warrant."

"This child's birth certificate lists you as the father," Marco said.

Metwater smiled, a cold look that didn't reach his

eyes. "A woman can put anything she likes on a birth certificate," he said. "That doesn't make it true."

"Are you the father of any of the children in the camp?" Walt asked.

"I am father to all my followers," Metwater said.

"Is that how your followers—all these young women—see you?" Marco asked.

"My relationship to my disciples is a spiritual one," Metwater said. He half turned away. "You must excuse me now. I hope you find this child, wherever she is."

Walt's eyes met Marco's. The DEA agent jerked his head toward the door. "What do you think the odds are that his relationship with all these women is merely spiritual?" Walt asked once they were outside.

"About the same as the odds no one in this camp has a record or something they'd like to hide," Marco said.

"It does seem like the kind of group that would attract people who are running away from something," Walt said.

"Yeah. And everything Metwater says sounds like a lie to me," Marco said. He turned to leave, but Walt put out a hand to stop him.

"Let's talk to those women over there." He nodded toward a group of women who stood outside a grouping of tents across the compound. One of them stirred a pot over an open fire, while several others tended small children.

"Good idea," Marco said.

The women watched the Rangers' approach with wary expressions. Walt zeroed in on an auburn-haired woman who cradled an infant. "Hi," he said. "What's your baby's name?"

"Adore." She stroked a wisp of hair back from the baby's forehead.

"I think my niece is about that age," Walt said. "How old is she? About three months, right?"

"*He* is five months old," the woman said frostily, and turned away.

The other women silently gathered the children and went inside the tent, leaving Marco and Walt alone. "I guess she schooled you," Marco said.

"Hey, it was worth a try." He glanced around the camp, which was now empty. "What do we do now?"

"Let's get out of here." Marco led the way down the path back toward the parking area. They met no one on the trail, and the woods around them were eerily silent, with no birdsong or chattering of squirrels, or even wind stirring the branches of trees.

"Do you get the feeling we're being watched?" Walt asked.

"I'm sure we are," Marco said. "Metwater almost always has a guard or two watching the entrance to the camp."

"For a supposedly peaceful, innocent bunch, they sure are paranoid," Walt said. What did they have to fear in this remote location, and what did they have to protect?

Their FJ Cruiser with the Ranger Brigade emblem sat alone in the parking lot. Before they had taken more than a few steps toward it, Walt froze. "What's that on the windshield?" he asked.

"It looks like a note." Marco pulled out his phone and snapped a few pictures, then they approached slowly, making a wide circle of the vehicle first.

Walt examined the ground for footprints, but the

hard, dry soil showed no impressions. Marco took a few more close-up shots, and plucked the paper—which looked like a sheet torn from a spiral notebook—carefully by the edges. He read it, then showed it to Walt. The handwriting was an almost childish scrawl, the letters rounded and uneven, a mix of printing and cursive. "'All the children here are well cared for and loved,'" he read. "'No one needs to worry. Don't cause us any trouble. You don't know what you're doing.'"

He looked at Marco. "What do you think?"

"I'm wondering if the same person who left the note also left that." He gestured toward the driver's door of the cruiser, from which hung a pink baby bonnet, ribbons hanging loose in the still air.

"I'M SURE THIS is the same bonnet that's in the picture Emily sent me." Hannah fingered the delicate pink ribbons, the tears she was fighting to hold back making her throat ache. "Whoever left this must have wanted to let us know that Joy is there and that she's all right." She looked into Walt Riley's eyes, silently pleading for confirmation. The idea that anything might have happened to her niece was unbearable.

"We don't know why the bonnet was left," he said, his voice and his expression gentle. "But I agree that it looks very like the one in the picture you supplied us."

"What will you do now?" She looked at the trio of concerned faces. Agent Cruz and their commander had once again joined Walt to interview her at Ranger headquarters. She had broken the speed limit on the drive from her hotel when Walt had called and asked her to stop by whenever it was convenient.

"We're attempting to obtain a warrant to search the

camp for your niece," the commander said. "We've also contacted Child Welfare and Protection to see if they've had any calls about the camp and might know anything."

That was it? When she had come to the Ranger office for help, she had expected them to immediately go with her to the Family's camp and take the child. When they had insisted on visiting the camp alone, she had held on to the hope that they would return with Joy. But they had done nothing but talk and ask questions. They seemed more interested in paperwork than in making sure Joy was safely where she belonged. "What am I supposed to do in the meantime?" she asked. "Just sit and wait?" And worry.

"I'm sorry to say that's all you can do right now," Agent Riley said. "Rushing in there on your own won't do anything but put Metwater and his people on the defensive. They might even leave the area."

"Then you could stop them," she said.

"On what grounds?" the commander asked. "So far we have no proof they've committed any crime."

"They have a child who doesn't belong to them, who isn't related to them in any way. A helpless infant." A child who was all she had left of her beloved sister.

"If they do have your niece, we don't have any reason to think they've harmed her or intend to harm her." Agent Riley reclaimed her attention with his calm voice and concerned expression. "The children we've seen in camp look well cared for, though we'll verify that with CWP."

"You're right." She clenched her hands in her lap and forced herself to take a deep breath. "Patience isn't one of my strong suits." Especially when it came to a baby.

So much could go wrong, and could anyone who wasn't family watch over her as carefully as Hannah would?

"Go back to your hotel now," the commander said. "We'll be in touch." He and Agent Cruz left, leaving her alone with Agent Riley.

"I'll walk you to your car," he said.

"You didn't have to walk with me," she said, after they had crossed the gravel lot to the compact car she had rented at the Montrose airport. A brisk wind sent dry leaves skittering over the gravel and tugged strands of hair from her updo. She brushed the hair from her eyes and studied him, trying to read the expression behind his dark sunglasses.

"I wanted to talk to you a little more. Away from the office." He glanced back toward the low beige building that was Ranger headquarters. "Having to talk to a bunch of cops makes some people nervous."

"As opposed to talking to only one cop."

"Try to think of me as a guy who's trying to help."

"All right." She crossed her arms over her stomach. "What do you want to know?"

"I'm trying to figure out what Daniel Metwater stands to gain by claiming your niece is his daughter," he said. "Understanding people's motives is often helpful in untangling a crime."

"I imagine you know more about the man than I do. He's been living in this area for what, almost a month now?"

"About that. Is it possible your sister listed him as Joy's father without his knowledge?"

"Why would she do that?"

"You said she was one of his followers. He refers

to himself as a father to his disciples. Maybe she was trying to honor that."

She studied the ground at her feet, the rough aggregate of rocks and dirt in half a dozen shades of red and brown. She might have been standing on Mars, for all she felt so out of her depth. "I don't know what my sister was thinking. As much as I loved her, I didn't understand her. She lived a very different life."

"Where do you live? I haven't even asked."

"Dallas. I'm a chemist." The expression on his face almost made her laugh. "Never play poker, Agent Riley."

"All right, I'll admit I'm surprised," he said. "I've never met a female chemist before. Come to think of it, I may never have met a chemist before."

His grin, so boyish and almost bashful, made her heart skip a beat. She put her hand to her chest, as if to calm the irregular rhythm. "My job doesn't put me in contact with very many law enforcement officers, either." Impulsively, she reached out and touched his arm. "You'll let me know the minute you know anything about Joy? Call me anytime—even if it's the middle of the night."

He covered her hand with his own. The warmth and weight of that touch seeped into her, steadying her even as it made her feel a little off balance. "I will," he said. "And try not to worry. It may not seem like it, but we are doing everything we can to help you."

"I want to believe that." She pulled her hand away, pretending to fuss with the clasp of her handbag. "I'm used to being in charge, so it's not always easy to let someone else take over."

"Let us know if you think of anything that might be helpful."

"I will." They said goodbye and she got into her car and drove away. For the first time since coming to Colorado, she wasn't obsessing over Joy and Emily and the agonizing uncertainty of her situation. Instead, she was remembering the way it felt when Agent Walt Riley put his hand on hers. They had connected, something that didn't happen too often for her. She had come into this situation thinking she was the only one who could save her niece. Maybe she wasn't quite so alone after all.

WALT SPENT EVERY spare moment over the next twenty-four hours working on Hannah's case. Though he prided himself on being a hard worker, the memory of Hannah's stricken face when he had last seen her drove him on. The afternoon of the second day, the Ranger team met to report on their various activities. Everyone was present except Montrose County sheriff's deputy Lance Carpenter, who was on his honeymoon but expected back later in the week, and Customs and Border Protection agent Michael Dance, who was following up a lead in Denver. After listening to a presentation by veteran Ranger Randall Knightbridge on a joint effort with Colorado Parks and Wildlife to catch poachers operating in the park, and a report from Colorado Bureau of Investigation officer Carmen Redhorse on an unattended death in the park that was ruled a suicide, Walt stood to address his fellow team members.

After a brief recap of Hannah's visit and his and Marco's foray into Metwater's camp, he consulted his notes. "I've gone over the documents Ms. Dietrich supplied us. We couldn't lift any useful prints from the letter or the will. Nothing on the note that was left at the camp, or the bonnet, either. I contacted the Denver hospital where the baby was born—the hat isn't one of theirs. They think the mother probably brought it with her, and they can't give out any information on patients. We're trying to reach the nurse who was one of the witnesses on Emily Dietrich's will, Marsha Caldwell. She is reportedly living in Amsterdam now, where her husband recently transferred for work, but I haven't gotten a response yet. We haven't had any luck locating the other witness, Anna Ingels."

"I talked to a contact at Child Welfare and Protection and she had nothing for me," Carmen said. "They did send a social worker to visit the camp a couple of weeks after Metwater and his group arrived here, but they found no violations. They said all the children appeared to be well cared for."

"And I don't guess they noted any baby crawling around with no mother to claim her," Ethan Reynolds, another of the new recruits to the Ranger Brigade, quipped.

"We got word a few minutes ago that the judge is denying our request for a warrant to search the camp," Graham said.

The news rocked Walt back on his heels, as if he'd been punched. "What was their reasoning?" he asked.

"We didn't present enough evidence to justify the search," the captain said. "At least in their eyes. The judge feels—and this isn't the first time I've heard this—that the Ranger Brigade's continued focus on Metwater and his followers is tantamount to harassment."

"This doesn't come from us," Randall said. "Ms.

Dietrich came to us. She's the one who made the accusations against Metwater. We weren't harassing him. We were following up on her claim."

"And we found nothing," Graham said. He looked across the table and met Walt's steady gaze. "As long as Metwater and his people deny the baby exists, our hands are tied. There's nothing else we can do."

Chapter Three

Protests rose from all sides of the conference table after Graham's pronouncement. "We need to go back to the judge and try again," Michael Dance said.

"I can talk to Child Welfare and Protection," Carmen said. "Ask them to take another look."

"Unless we have CWP on our side, we're not going to get anywhere with this," Randall Knightbridge said.

Walt raised his voice to be heard over the clamor. "There's still something we can do, even without a warrant," he said.

Conversation died and everyone turned to look at him. "What do you have in mind?" Marco asked.

"I think we should do what Hannah suggested and infiltrate the group." Walt said.

"You mean, send someone in undercover to determine if the baby is really there?" Carmen asked.

"And maybe find out what really happened to the child's mother," Walt said. "Hannah said her sister was afraid for her life—maybe there's more to this story that we need to find out."

"It's not a bad idea," Graham said. "I've thought of it before, if only to get a better sense of what Metwater is up to."

"It could backfire, big time," said Simon Woolridge, tech expert and Immigration and Customs Enforcement agent. "If Metwater figures out what we're doing, he could take it to the press and gain a lot of traction with his claims that we're harassing him."

"He won't find out," Walt said. "Not if we do it right."

"By 'we' you mean who?" Graham asked.

Walt squared his shoulders. "I could go," he said. "I've done undercover work before."

"They'd recognize you," Marco said. "We were just at the camp this morning."

"I'd dye my hair and grown out my beard, and dress differently. They wouldn't recognize me as the lawman they saw one time."

"How are you going to know you found the right baby?" Carmen asked.

"Hannah Dietrich could come with me. I could say she's my sister."

"That won't work," Simon said. "You two don't look anything alike."

"Say she's your wife," Randall said. "From what we've seen, couples sometimes join Metwater's Family together."

"I could do that," Walt said. "If she agrees."

"You heard her," Marco said. "She'll do anything to save her niece."

"Talk to her," Graham said. "See what she says. But she has to agree to follow your lead and proceed with caution. And if you get in there and learn there's a real danger, you get out. No heroics."

"Yes, sir." He didn't want to be a hero. He only wanted to make things right for Hannah and her niece.

HANNAH HAD LOST the plot thread of the movie playing on the television in her hotel room an hour ago, but she left it on, grateful at least for the background noise that helped to make the room a little less forlorn. She glanced toward the porta-crib and the diaper bag in the corner of the room and felt a tight knot in her chest. Had she been naive to believe she would be bringing Joy back here last night, before heading back home to Dallas today? Now she was trapped in this awful limbo, not knowing when—or even if—she would see her niece.

A knock on the door startled her. She punched the remote to shut off the TV and moved to the door. A glimpse through the peephole showed Walt Riley, dressed not in his khaki uniform, but in jeans and a white Western-cut shirt. With trembling hands, she unfastened the security chain and opened the door. "Has something happened?" she asked. "Do you have news?"

"Hello, Ms. Dietrich," he said. "Can I come in? There are some things we need to talk about."

"All right." She stepped back and let him walk past her into the room. She caught the scent of him as he passed—not cologne, but a mixture of starch and leather that seemed imminently masculine.

He crossed the small room and sat in the only chair. She perched on the edge of the bed, her stomach doing nervous somersaults. "Were you able to get the warrant to search the camp?" she asked.

"No." He rested his hands on his knees. Large hands, bronzed from working in the sun, with short nails and no jewelry. "The judge didn't feel we had sufficient grounds to warrant a search. Metwater has complained we're harassing him, and the court is taking that complaint seriously."

"What about Child Welfare and Protection? Would they support you? Or go to the camp to look for Joy?"

He shook his head. "CWP says there aren't any problems at the camp. They would have no reason to be there."

She felt as if she had swallowed an anvil. The weight of it pressed her down on the bed. "What am I going to do now?" she asked.

"We've come up with a plan."

She leaned toward him. "What is it?"

"It's your plan, really. We'll send two people in, posing as a husband and wife who are interested in joining the Family. That will give us the opportunity to determine, first, if there is even an infant matching the description of your niece in the camp, and if her mother is there or not. We also hope to determine the circumstances surrounding your sister's death."

"I want to go. I want to be the woman."

"We're not talking a quick overnight visit," he said. "It could take weeks to gain their trust and learn anything of real value."

"I've taken a leave of absence from my job. I have however much time it takes."

"You said you're a chemist? Is your employer willing to let you off work indefinitely?"

"I'm very good at my job and I've been there a long time. I have savings and not many expenses. And when Joy comes to live with me, I intend to take family leave to spend time with her." She hoped that would give her enough time to adjust to being a mother—something she had never planned on being, but now wanted more desperately than she had wanted almost anything. "I want to do this, Agent Riley. I want to help find my niece."

"If you do this, you have to agree to follow the direction of the male agent who would be posing as your husband," he said. "You can't take any action without his knowledge and you have to agree to abide by his decisions."

She stiffened. "I'm not used to other people making decisions for me."

"Obviously not. But in this case it would be vital. As law enforcement officers, we're trained to put together a case against someone that will stand up in court. If Daniel Metwater and his followers have kidnapped your niece, or if they had anything to do with your sister's death, we want to be sure we can build a solid case against them that will lead to a conviction."

What he said made sense, and she had always been good at following rules, as long as she saw a good reason for them. "All right. I can respect that," she said. "Who is the male agent?"

"That would be me."

She sat back a little, letting the words sink in. Relief that she wouldn't have to work with a stranger warred with the definite attraction that shimmered between them. She didn't need to be distracted right now. She had to focus on Joy, and the future they were going to have together. But what choice did she have? If she refused to work with Walt Riley just because she could imagine sleeping with him, wasn't she being foolish, and maybe even a coward? They were two adults. Surely they could control themselves. In any case, he had given no indication that he felt the same attraction to her. "All right," she said. "What do we do next?"

"Why don't we start by going out to dinner?"

Yet again, this man had caught her off guard. "Are you asking me on a date?"

"If we're going to pass ourselves off as husband and wife, we need to know more about each other and get comfortable in each other's presence."

He was right, of course. "All right."

He stood and held out his hand. When she took it, he pulled her up beside him. "Why don't you start by calling me Walt?"

"All right. Walt." It wasn't so hard here, in the intimacy of her hotel room, to think of him by his first name. A simple and strong name, like the man himself. "You should call me Hannah."

"It's a nice name."

"I think so. I don't understand why so many of Metwater's followers feel compelled to take new names."

"It could be the symbolism of starting over, taking on a new identity," he said. "It's also a convenient way to make yourself harder to track down if you're wanted for a crime, or have something else in your past that you don't want to come out." He held the door as she walked through, then followed her outside. "Did your sister take a new name when she joined the group?"

"I don't know. She never mentioned it." She glanced over her shoulder at him. "I feel terrible that I don't know more about what my sister was doing in the last months of her life. A year ago, I would have said I knew her well, but so many times now, she feels like a stranger to me. It's depressing. You'd think if you could know anyone well, it would be a sibling."

"I think we're most surprised when family members behave in unexpected ways," he said. "It feels more personal, I guess. More like a betrayal."

"Yes." He opened the passenger-side door to his Cruiser and she climbed inside. He put a hand on her shoulder, as if making sure she was safely settled before he shut the door behind her. Again, she felt that current of connection with him. She hadn't felt anything like that—or rather, she hadn't allowed herself to feel it—for a very long time. Maybe losing Emily had made her more vulnerable. Or finding Joy. So many things in her life felt out of control these days, it shouldn't have surprised her that her emotions would betray her, too.

THERE WERE DEFINITELY worse ways to spend an evening than sitting across the table from a beautiful woman, Walt thought, once he and Hannah had settled into a booth at a local Italian place. More than one male head had turned to watch Hannah walk across the room, though maybe only Walt saw the fatigue and worry that lurked in her sapphire-blue eyes. He wished he had the power to take that worry and fatigue away from her.

"Tell me about yourself," he said, once they had placed their orders. "How long have you lived in Dallas?"

"Ten years. I took the job there after I got my master's at Rice University in Houston."

"So you're beautiful and brilliant. I'm already out of my league."

She sipped her iced tea and regarded him over the rim of the glass. "I don't know about that."

"Trust me, it's true," he said. "I have a bachelor's

degree from the University of New Mexico and was solidly in the middle of my class. And while I'm sure there are a few professions less glamorous than law enforcement, patrolling the backcountry of public lands is about as far away from a corporate suite as you can get."

"Your job doesn't sound boring, though."

"You might be surprised how boring it can be sometimes. But mostly, it is interesting."

"What drew you to the work?" She relaxed back against the padded booth, some of the tension easing from around her eyes.

"I like the independence, and I like solving puzzles. And maybe this sounds corny, but I like correcting at least some of the injustice in the world. It's a good feeling when you put away a smuggler or a poacher or a murderer." His eyes met hers. "Or a kidnapper."

She rearranged her silverware. "Do you think this will work? Our pretending to want to join up with them?"

"It's the best way I can think of to learn what really goes on in their camp. I figure you can get to know the women—especially the mothers with children. I can talk to the men. We might be able to find Anna Ingels—the woman who witnessed your sister's will. If your niece is there, someone will know it and eventually they'll let something slip."

The waiter delivered their food—ravioli for Walt, fish for her. They ate in silence for a moment, then she said, "Have you done anything like this before?"

"You mean undercover work?" He stabbed at a pillow of ravioli. "A couple of times. I posed as a big-game hunter to bring down a group of poachers. And I did a few drug buys, things like that."

"Did you ever have to pretend to be married to someone?"

"No. That's a new one. Does that worry you?"

"A little. Not you, I mean—well, I've never been married before."

"Me either." He laid down his fork and wiped his mouth with his napkin. "Before we get too far into this, are you engaged? Seriously involved with someone? Dating a mixed martial arts fighter who's insanely jealous?"

Her eyes widened. "No to all of the above. What about you?"

"I don't have a boyfriend either. Or a girlfriend."

She laughed. "Really? That surprises me."

"Does it?"

"You're good-looking, and friendly. I wouldn't think you'd have trouble getting a date."

"No, I don't have trouble getting dates." He took another bite of ravioli, delaying his answer. "I'm new to the area," he said. "I transferred from northern Colorado just last month."

"And?"

"And what?"

"And there's something you're not saying. I heard it in your voice."

Was he really so easy to read? He searched for some glib lie, but then again, why shouldn't he tell her? "The last woman I dated seriously is now married to my younger brother."

"Ouch!"

"Yeah, well, he's very charming and untroubled by

much of a conscience." The wound still ached a little—not the woman's betrayal so much as his brother's. He should have seen it coming, and the fact that he hadn't made him doubt himself a little.

"So that's what you meant when you said you understood about thinking you knew a family member well, and turning out to be wrong."

"Yep. Been there, done that, got the T-shirt."

"That must make for some awkward family dinners," she said.

"A little. There are four of us kids—two girls and two boys. For the sake of family harmony, I wished the newlyweds well and keep my distance."

"It was just Emily and me in my family," she said. "I think it took my mom a long time to get pregnant again after me." A smile ghosted across her lips. "I still remember how excited I was when she was born. It was as if I had a real live doll of my own to look after. After our parents were killed in a car crash when Emily was nineteen, all we had was each other. We were inseparable, right up until I went away to Dallas to work. And even after that—even though we lived very different lives—I always felt we were close." She laid down her fork and her eyes met his. "I blamed Daniel Metwater for taking her away from me. After she joined his cult, I seldom heard from her. What kind of person encourages someone to cut off ties with family that way?"

"We haven't been able to learn a great deal about him, other than that he's very charismatic and seems to be offering something that some people find attractive." He wanted to take her hand, to try to comfort her, but resisted the temptation. "There are probably experts in this kind of thing who could tell you more than I can."

"He calls his followers a family—as if that could substitute for their real families."

"Maybe this undercover assignment will give you some of the answers to your questions," he said. He picked up his fork again.

They ate in silence for a while longer, until she pushed her plate away, her dinner half-eaten. "I've been thinking about what you asked me," she said. "About what Daniel Metwater stood to gain from keeping Joy and claiming her as his own."

"Did you come up with something?"

"It's not much, but Emily had a trust from our mother. An annual stipend now, with the bulk coming to her when she turned thirty in two years. Under the terms of the trust, it automatically passes to any children she might have, and can be used to pay living and educational expenses in the event of her death."

He considered this information, then shook his head. "Metwater supposedly has money of his own."

"That's what I understood from the research I did." She took a sip of tea. "I told you it wasn't much."

"Still, having money doesn't mean he might not want more. And we don't have any idea what his financial picture is these days. Maybe he made some bad investments, or being a prophet in the wilderness is more expensive than he thought it would be."

"I keep coming back to her last letter," Hannah said. "Emily sounded so frightened—I thought maybe that so-called Family was holding her prisoner."

"The death certificate said her cause of death was respiratory failure."

"I know. She died in an emergency room. Someone dropped her off—they don't know who. And people do die of asthma, but I can't help thinking—what if they were withholding her medication, or the stress of traveling with this group brought on the attack?"

"It would be tough to prove murder in either case."

"I know." She sat back and laid her napkin beside her plate. "And none of it will bring Emily back. I have to focus on what I can do, which is to raise Joy and take the best care of her I know how."

A light came into her eyes when she spoke, and her expression changed to one of such tenderness it made Walt's chest ache. "You already love her, don't you?" he said.

"Yes." That fleeting smile again. "And that surprises me. I never thought of myself as particularly nurturing, but this baby—this infant I haven't even met yet—I already love her so much."

"If she's in Metwater's camp, we'll find her," he said.

She surprised him by reaching out and taking his hand. "I believe you," she said. "And if I have to pretend to be someone's wife temporarily, I'm glad it's you."

He gave her hand a squeeze, then let it go before he gave in to the temptation to pull her close and kiss her. As assignments went, this one was definitely going to be interesting, and a little dangerous—in more ways than one.

Chapter Four

Two days later, Hannah studied herself in the hotel mirror, frowning. She wished she had taken more of an interest in drama club in school—she might have learned something that would come in handy now. The only advice Walt had given her was "Stick as close to the truth as possible and only lie when absolutely necessary." So she was going into camp as Hannah Morgan—her mother's maiden name—and she was a corporate dropout looking for a more authentic life.

She had dressed as Walt had instructed her, in a gauzy summer skirt, tank top and sturdy sandals. She wore no makeup and had combed out her hair to hang straight past her shoulders. Silver bracelets and earrings completed the look—definitely not her normal style, which tended toward plain classics, but that was all part of playing a role, wasn't it…dressing the part?

A knock on the door interrupted her musing. She checked the peephole, but didn't recognize the rumpled-looking man who stood on the other side. Then he shifted so that the sun lit his face, and she sucked in a breath and jerked open the door. "I didn't recognize you at first," she said, staring at Walt. Several days' growth of beard darkened his jaw, giving him a rough—and definitely sexy—look. His hair was streaked blond and tousled and he wore jeans with a rip in one knee, hiking boots and a tight olive-green T-shirt that showed off a sculpted chest and defined biceps. A tribal tattoo encircled his upper right arm. Looking at him made her feel a little breathless.

"What do you think?" He held his arms out at his sides. "Will they still make me as a cop?"

Slowly, she shook her head. "No, I don't think so." *A biker or a bandit or an all-around bad boy, maybe, but not a cop.*

"You look great," he said. "I didn't realize your hair was so long."

She tucked a stray strand behind her ears. "I usually wear it up. It gets in the way otherwise."

"Are you ready to go? Marco just radioed that our contact is at the laundry."

She smoothed her sweating palms down her thighs and took a deep breath. "Yeah, I'm ready."

She collected the backpack into which she had stashed a few essentials and followed him across the parking lot. But instead of a car or truck, he stopped beside a motorcycle. The black-and-chrome monster looked large and dangerous. "We're going on that?" she asked.

He patted the leather seat. "I figured the Harley fit the image better. I've got a small tent and some other supplies in the saddlebags and trunk." He handed her a helmet. "Put this on."

She settled the helmet over her head. It was a lot heavier than she had expected. "Does this belong to the Rangers?" she asked, fumbling with the chin strap.

"No, it's my personal bike." He fastened the strap

for her, a tremor running through her as his fingertips brushed across her throat. But he gave no sign that he noticed. He straddled the bike, then looked over his shoulder at her. "Get on behind me. Put your feet on the foot pegs."

Feeling awkward, she did as he instructed. "I've never ridden a motorcycle before," she said.

"Don't worry. Just hang on." She started as the engine roared to life, the sound vibrating through her. The bike lurched forward and she wrapped her arms around him, her breasts pressed against the solid muscle of his back, his body shielding hers from the wind. She forced herself to relax her death grip on him, but didn't let go altogether. He felt like the only steady thing in her world right now.

She tried to focus on the task ahead. Apparently, several women from Metwater's group came into town once a week to do laundry. The plan was for Walt and Hannah to meet them and turn the talk to the Family. They would express a desire to join the group and ask for an introduction. Walt had explained that interviews with some former group members had revealed this was how new members were often acquired. And Metwater had bragged on his blog that he didn't have to recruit members—they came to him voluntarily after hearing his message.

The laundry occupied the end unit of a low-slung building in a strip center not far from the campus of the local college. Though Metwater's three followers were the same age as many of the students who lounged on chairs between the washers and dryers or gathered in the parking lot, they looked somehow different. Their bare faces were pink from exposure to the sun, and their long skirts and sleeveless tops were faded and worn. One of the women had a baby on her hip, and Hannah couldn't keep from staring at the child, who wore a stained blue sleeper and had a shock of wheat-colored hair and plump, rosy cheeks.

"That's a beautiful baby," she said, forgetting that they had agreed she would let Walt do most of the talking.

"Thanks." The woman, who wore her light brown hair in two long braids, hefted the child to her shoulder, her eyes wary.

"How old is he?" Hannah asked. "Or she?"

"He's almost seven months," she said.

Hannah realized she had been staring at the child too intently. She forced a smile to her face. "I'm Hannah," she said. "And this is my husband, Walt. A friend told me she had seen you all doing your laundry here sometimes, so we came here hoping to meet some members of the Family."

"We've been reading the Prophet's blog," Walt said. "His message really spoke to us. We were wondering how we could go about joining the group."

The baby's mother looked over her shoulder, toward where the other two women were filling a row of washers. "You should talk to Starfall," she said. "Starfall! Come talk to these people."

Starfall had curly brown hair and a slightly crooked nose, and the beginnings of lines along each side of her mouth, as if she frowned a lot. She was frowning now as she approached them. "What do you want?" she asked.

"We wanted to know how we could go about joining up with the Family," Walt said. He took Hannah's hand

and squeezed it. "We've been reading the Prophet's writing and we really like what he has to say."

"Is that so?" Starfall addressed her question not to Walt, but to Hannah.

She licked her too-dry lips and tried to remember something from Daniel Metwater's blog, which she had read repeatedly since Emily had announced she was joining his group. "We're tired of the shallow commercialism and focus on materialism so rampant in the modern world," she said. "We want to be a part of the community the Prophet is building—close to nature and working for the good of one another."

"It's not just a matter of camping in the wilderness for a few weeks," Starfall said. "You have to agree to contribute your resources for the good of all. And you have to work. Everyone in the Family has a job to do."

"We're not afraid of work," Walt said. "And we wouldn't expect the Prophet to take us in and provide for us without us contributing. We have money to contribute."

Starfall's unblinking gaze was starting to make Hannah nervous. She moved closer to Walt, her shoulder brushing his. "Can you arrange for us to meet the Prophet?" she asked.

Starfall's expression didn't soften, but she nodded. "You can follow us to camp when we get ready to leave here."

"Is there anything I can do to help?" Hannah asked. She turned to the first young woman. "I could hold the baby for you."

The woman put one arm protectively around the child. "He's happier with me."

"Wait for us over there or outside." Starfall pointed to the corner of the laundry.

"Come on, honey." Walt took her arm and led her to the grouping of chairs. "You need to rein it in a little," he said under his breath. "She thinks you want to kidnap her kid."

"I just wanted to verify it's really a boy. Don't you think he looks small for seven months?"

"I have no idea. I haven't spent a lot of time around babies."

She slumped into one of the molded plastic chairs grouped against the back wall. "I haven't either. Before I left to come here I read everything I could find on babies, but there's so much information out there it's impossible to absorb."

"Most new parents seem to manage fine." He patted her shoulder. "You will, too."

She studied the trio of women sorting laundry across the room. "What kind of a name is Starfall?"

"I'm not sure where Metwater's followers get their names," he said. "Maybe Metwater christens them."

"If Emily took a new name, maybe that's why no one recognized her when you asked about her."

"It's possible." He squeezed her hand. "We'll try to find out."

Odd that holding his hand felt so natural now. If he was really her husband, it was the kind of thing he would do, right? But it annoyed her that she was settling into this role so easily. She was a strong woman and she didn't need a man to make her feel safe. And she couldn't afford to lose focus on her real purpose here—to find and care for her niece.

She slid her fingers out of his grasp. "I think we

should come up with a list of reasons Metwater would want us as part of his group. It makes sense that he wouldn't want a bunch of freeloaders."

"From what little we've seen, men seem to leave the group more often than women," Walt said. "So he's always in need of extra muscle."

Her gaze slid to his chest and arms. He had muscle, all right. She shifted in her chair. "It doesn't look as if he has any shortage of young women followers. I should think of something to make me look like a better possible disciple. I supposed I could offer up my bank account."

"I'll admit that would probably be an inducement, but I doubt you'll need it."

"But I ought to have something to offer," she said. "Maybe I could say I was a teacher and I could teach the children. That would be a good way to get to know the mothers, too."

"It would. But babies don't really need school yet. I think Metwater will want you in his group because you're just his type."

"His type?"

"Beautiful."

She stared at him, a blush heating her face. Not that she was naive about her looks, but to hear him say it that way caught her off guard. She glanced at the women in front of the bank of washers, noting that they were all young, slender and, yes, quite attractive. "Are you saying Metwater favors beautiful women?"

"From what I've heard, he's got a regular harem around him all the time. The Rangers did a rough census of the group when they first moved onto park land, and there wasn't anyone out there over the age of forty, and most of them are a lot younger. Two-thirds of the group are women and a number of them are, well, stunning." He shrugged. "You should fit right in."

He probably meant that as a compliment, but his words made her uncomfortable. "I really don't like being judged by my looks—good or bad," she said. "It's something I've had to struggle against in the scientific community my whole career. There are plenty of people out there—plenty of men—who still think a pretty blonde can't possibly be smart."

"I don't think you're dumb—not by a long shot," he said. "I'm just telling you what I've observed about Metwater. If you know what you're getting into, maybe you can use his predilections to your advantage."

"You mean, pretend to be the dumb blonde so he'll be less likely to suspect me of being up to something?"

"That's one way to approach it."

She crossed her arms over her stomach. Playing down her intellect and playing up her looks went against everything she believed in. But if it would help her find Joy and bring her home safely... "I'll think about it," she said, and stood. "Right now, I'm going outside to get some fresh air."

WALT WATCHED HANNAH walk away. She nodded to the three Family members as she passed, but didn't stop to chat. He settled back in his chair, chin on his chest, pretending to nap, though he kept an eye on the three women. Hannah was ticked off about his comments about her looks. He was only stating fact, and trying to give her a hint at what she might be in for.

Not that he intended to let Daniel Metwater lay a finger on her. One more reason he was glad they had decided to pass themselves off as husband and wife instead of brother and sister. He couldn't count on the Prophet not to go after a married woman, but it might slow him down. Walt didn't intend for the two of them to be in the camp any longer than necessary. With luck, they would find Hannah's niece within a day or two and get out of Dodge.

"We're ready to leave now, if you want to follow us."

Starfall hefted a large garbage bag he presumed was full of clean laundry and started out the door. Walt hurried to catch up. "Let me take that," he said, and carried the laundry the rest of the way to the battered sedan she pointed out.

Hannah joined them beside the car. "Do you need help with anything else?" she asked.

"No." Starfall slid into the driver's seat and turned the key. "Just try to keep up."

She was already pulling out of the parking lot when Walt and Hannah reached his motorcycle. "I think she's purposely trying to lose us," Hannah said as she pulled on the helmet.

"No chance of that." He put on his own helmet and mounted the bike. "I already know where the camp is." She climbed on behind him and he started the engine. "It's going to be a rough and dusty ride once we reach the dirt roads. Nothing I can do about it."

"Despite what you might think, I'm not some delicate flower who withers if I have to deal with a little dirt," she said. "I'm tougher than I look."

He heard the steel in her voice and sensed it in her posture as she sat up straight behind him. Only her hands tightly gripping his sides gave any clue to her nervousness. He remembered the matter-of-fact way she had laid out her story in the Rangers' office, with no tears or pleadings. As much as he found himself wanting to look after her, she was a woman used to looking after herself, and she wasn't going to let him forget it.

Starfall obviously wasn't concerned about speed limits, as she drove fifteen and twenty miles over the posted speeds all the way into the park. Only when they turned onto the first dirt road did she slow down, in deference to the washboard surface of the two-track that cut across the wilderness.

The landscape that spread out around them was unlike what most people associated with Colorado. Though distant mountains showed snowcapped peaks against an expanse of turquoise sky, the land in the park and surrounding wilderness areas was high desert. Sagebrush and stunted pinyons dotted the rolling expanse of cracked brown earth, and boulders the size of cars lay scattered like thrown dice. Though the terrain looked dry and barren, it was home to vibrant life, from colorful lizards and swift rabbits to deer and black bear. Hidden springs formed lush oases, and the roaring cataract of the Gunnison River had cut the deep Black Canyon that gave the park its name, a place of wild beauty unlike any other in the United States.

Walt had to slow the Harley to a crawl to steer around the network of potholes and protruding rocks, and to avoid being choked by the sedan's dust. Even if he hadn't already known the location of Metwater's camp, the rooster tail of dust that fanned out behind the car hung in the air long after the vehicle passed, providing a clear guide to their destination.

By the time he and Hannah reached the small parking area, the women had the car unloaded and were preparing to carry the bundles of clean laundry over the footbridge. Without asking, they left two bundles behind. Walt and Hannah took these and fell into step behind them.

The camp looked much as it had on his visit four days before, people gathered in front of trailers and tents, others working around picnic tables in a large open-sided shelter with a roof made of logs and woven branches. A group of men played cards in the shade of a lean-to fashioned from a tarp, while a trio of children ran along the creek, pausing every few steps to plunge sticks into the water.

"There are a lot of people here," Hannah whispered.

"A couple dozen, best we can determine," Walt said.

A man stepped forward to take the bag of laundry from Starfall. "Who are they?" he asked, jerking his head toward Walt and Hannah.

"They want to join the Family," she said.

The man, who looked to be in his late twenties, wore his sandy hair long and pulled back in a ponytail. He had a hawk nose and a cleft in his chin, and the build of a cage fighter or a bull rider—not tall, but all stringy muscle and barely contained energy. He looked them up and down, then spat to the side. "I guess that's up to the Prophet," he said.

He and Starfall walked away, leaving Walt and Hannah standing alone on the edge of the camp. Hannah moved closer and he put his arm around her. "What do we do now?" she asked.

"Let's go talk to the Prophet."

"Where is he?" she asked.

"What's your best guess?" he asked.

She surveyed the camp, taking in the motley collection of dwellings, from a camper shell on the back of a pickup truck with one flat tire to a luxurious motor home with an array of solar panels on the roof. "My guess is the big RV," she said.

"You get an A." He took his arm from around her. "Come on. Let's see if the Prophet will grant us an interview."

No one said anything as they headed toward the motor home, but Walt could feel dozens of eyes on them. No one was rushing to welcome the new converts with open arms, that was for sure. Was it because they were waiting to take their cue from Metwater? Or had the Prophet instilled suspicion of all outsiders in his followers?

They mounted the steps to the RV and Walt rapped hard on the door. After a moment it opened and Andi Matheson answered. Andi—or Asteria, as she called herself now—had had more contact with the Rangers than anyone else in camp, but she showed no sign of recognition as she stared at Walt. "Yes?"

"We'd like to see the Prophet," he said. "We—my wife and I—" he indicated Hannah "—are big admirers of his and would like to join the group."

She nodded, as if this made perfect sense, and held the door open wider. "Come in."

The interior of the RV was dim and cool, the living room filled with a leather sofa and several upholstered chairs. Andi indicated they should sit, then disappeared through an archway into the back of the vehicle.

Walt sat on the sofa and Hannah settled next to him. She was breathing shallowly, and he could almost feel the nervousness rolling off her in waves. He gripped her hand and squeezed. "It's going to be okay," he said.

She nodded, and didn't pull away.

"The woman who let us in is Andi Matheson," Walt said, keeping his voice low.

Hannah nodded. "I read about her online. She's the daughter of someone famous, right?"

"Her father is Senator Pete Matheson—though right now he's serving time for murdering an FBI agent."

"She's obviously pregnant," Hannah said. "Is Metwater the father?"

"No," Walt said. "That would be the man the senator killed."

Hannah's face softened with sympathy. "How terrible for her."

"She seems to have settled in nicely with Metwater," Walt said.

There wasn't a clock in the room, so he had no idea how long they waited, though he thought it might have been as long as ten minutes. "What's taking so long?" Hannah whispered.

Just then, Andi reappeared from the back of the RV. "The Prophet will see you," she said.

Walt and Hannah stood and started toward Andi. She held up a hand. "He doesn't want to see you together," she said. She turned to Hannah. "He wants to interview you first. Alone."

Chapter Five

"I don't think—" Walt began, but Hannah interrupted him.

"I don't mind talking with him by myself." She assumed what she hoped was an eager expression. "It would be a privilege to meet the Prophet." Was that laying it on too thick? Probably not, for a man who had the nerve to refer to himself as the Prophet.

Andi turned to Walt. "You can wait outside," she said. "I'll call you when it's your turn."

Walt turned to Hannah. "If you're sure?"

"I'll be fine." After all, it wasn't as if Metwater was going to do anything with Andi right here and a bunch of other people around. And it wasn't as if she hadn't had experience fending off fresh men. Even if Metwater was the lecher Walt had made him out to be, Hannah could handle him.

Walt left, then Andi put on a broad-brimmed hat and headed for the door also. "Where are you going?" Hannah asked.

"The Prophet wants to speak with you alone," she said, and left, the door clicking shut behind her.

Hannah hugged her arms across her chest and walked to the window, but heavy shades blocked any view out—or in. She took a deep breath, fighting for calm. She shouldn't be afraid of Metwater. Walt was close by if she needed anything. She needed to keep her head and use this opportunity to learn as much as possible about the Prophet, and about Emily and Joy.

"Please, have a seat. I want you to be comfortable."

She turned and stared at the man who spoke. Metwater—and this had to be Metwater—was almost naked, wearing only a pair of low-slung, loose lounge pants in some sort of silky fabric. The kind of thing she'd seen Hugh Hefner wear in old photographs. At the thought, she had to stifle a laugh.

"Please share what you find so amusing." Barefoot, he moved into the room with the sensual grace of a panther, lamplight gleaming on the smooth muscles of his chest and arms and stomach. Curly dark hair framed a face like Michelangelo's *David*, the shadow of beard adding a masculine roughness.

All mirth deserted her as he moved closer still, stopping when he was almost touching her, so that she could feel the heat of his body, smell his musk and see the individual lashes that framed his dark eyes. He stared at her, crowding her personal space, stripping away her privacy. She found it impossible to look away from that gaze—the hypnotic stare of a predator.

"What amuses you?" he asked again, his voice deep and velvety, seductive.

"I laugh when I'm nervous," she said. "I never thought I'd get to meet you in person." This much was true. She had never really wanted to meet the man she blamed for her sister's death. Even if Metwater hadn't killed Emily, Hannah believed her sister wouldn't have died if she had stayed near her real family instead of joining up with this pretend one.

"There's no need to be nervous around me." He took her hand and led her toward the sofa. She forced herself not to pull away. Better to let him think she was under his spell. He had the kind of personality that would enchant many women. She could see how Emily, pregnant and feeling alone, mourning the loss of her fiancé and the future she had planned, might fall for someone like this. She would revel in the attention of someone so charismatic and seemingly powerful. She wouldn't have seen through his charm the way Hannah did.

She slid her hand out of his grasp and sat up straight, hoping her prim posture would put him off a little. The dimples on either side of his mouth deepened and he leaned toward her. "Tell me why you're interested in becoming a member of my family," he said.

His family. Not "our family" or "the family", but something that belonged to him. "My husband and I want to build a life that focuses on essentials—what's really important." That was a quote straight out of his blog.

"Why not do as so many others have done and set up a homestead on your own, or sell everything and take to the road?" he asked. "You could sign up for missionary work overseas or join a religious order. Why come to me?"

"While we believe in spirituality, we don't belong to any particular religion," she said. "And we want to work together with a like-minded group with an inspiring leader." Because, obviously, it was all about him.

"We don't have many married couples here," he said. "We discourage it, in fact."

"Why is that?" She knew he wanted her to ask the question.

"I see marriage as an outdated construct," he said. "And it's a distraction. How can you pledge loyalty to the Family as a whole when you've already pledged yourself to one other person? A single person is much freer to follow the dictates of her heart."

"So you require your followers to be single?" she asked.

"Not at all." He brushed his fingers across her shoulder. "I merely see it as a preferable state."

She shifted, putting a few more inches between them—the most she could manage.

"How did you learn about me?" he asked.

Walt had instructed her to say she had discovered the Prophet's blog online and that had led to the two of them reading everything they could find about him and his disciples. But she couldn't pass up the chance to learn more about his connection with her sister. "A friend told me about you," she said. "Before she left to join your group. I'm hoping she's still here. I would love to reconnect with her."

"What is your friend's name?"

"Emily Dietrich."

His expression didn't change, but something flickered in his eyes—a darkness he quickly masked. "Your friend told you she was going to join the Family?"

"Yes. I'm sure that's what she said. She attended a rally where you spoke and was convinced you offered exactly what she was looking for, for herself and her baby. Is she here? When can I see her?"

He took her hand again, holding on tightly when she

tried to pull free. "When was the last time you spoke to your friend?" he asked.

"About six months ago, right before she left to follow you." *Stick to the truth as much as possible*, Walt had told her.

"Your friend must have changed her mind," he said. "She never came to me. At least, no one using the name Emily Dietrich has ever been a member of my family."

He sounded sincere, but the flash of irritation she had seen at the first mention of Emily's name told her he was lying. He had recognized the name, and didn't like that she had brought it up. "How odd," she said. "I wonder what happened to her?"

"Does it change your mind about joining us, knowing your friend isn't here?" he asked.

"Of course not," she said. "You asked how I learned about you, and it was through her. I was hoping I'd get to see her again, but she isn't the main reason we're here. It's because we believe in everything you teach and we want that kind of life for ourselves."

"Do you know what it means to be a part of a family?" he asked.

"Well, I suppose…" She hesitated, trying to remember what he had said about this in his writings, but she was drawing a blank. "Family members look out for and support one another," she said. "You try to live in harmony and act in a way that's to the benefit of everyone, not simply yourself."

"True." He nodded. "As a part of my family, I would expect you to put the needs of the group ahead of yourself. We purposely separate ourselves from the outside world in order to focus on perfecting our union. While I would never forbid you to be in contact with relatives and friends from your old life, most people find as they immerse themselves in the day-to-day life of the Family, they are less and less inclined to want to be with others who don't share our sense of purpose and our views."

She tried to look thoughtful. "I can see that," she said.

He rubbed his thumb up and down the third finger of her left hand. "You said you were married. Where is your ring?"

She stared down at her empty fingers. She and Walt had spent hours going over all the details of coming here. Why hadn't they remembered a ring? "We don't hold with the trappings of society. We don't need a band of precious metal to seal our vows to one another."

He gave her hand a final squeeze—so hard she winced—then released his grip on her and sat back. He was no longer the seducing lover, but the practical businessman. "What resources do you bring to the group?" he said. "Everyone must contribute for the good of the whole."

"We have some money, from savings and from selling some things to pay for our trip here," she said. "And I enjoy working with children. I can teach the older ones and help care for younger ones."

"What about your husband? What does he do?"

They had rehearsed this. What had Walt said? "He was a carpenter. He's very good with his hands."

"Oh, is he?" Why did the words sound so sarcastic? "You'll have to provide your own shelter and clothing," he said. "Everyone here has to earn his or her keep. You'll be expected to embark on a course of study until you prove yourself ready to join us."

"What will we study?" she asked.

"Whatever I deem necessary." He rested his hand on her shoulder, a heavy, possessive touch that had her fighting her instinct to pull away. "I will personally instruct you on what you need to know to be a good disciple."

"Walt and I will look forward to learning more," she said.

"It's important for you to maintain your individuality, even though you are married," he said. "I consider you and your husband two separate candidates for inclusion in our group. Not everyone earns full acceptance as a member of the Family. You'll come to see the benefit of this as part of your teaching."

"Do you ever kick anyone out?" she asked. "I mean, if they do something that upsets the harmony of the group?" Had Emily done something to upset him? Is that why she had been so afraid?

"We punish when necessary. Our justice is not the justice of the world. We answer to a higher power."

"What does that mean?" It sounded as if he thought he was above the law, free to act in whatever way he wished. No wonder Emily had been afraid.

"You'll learn as part of your training." He took her hand and pulled her to her feet. "Come. It's time for you to meet your future sisters and brothers."

"What about Walt?"

"Don't worry about him. I'll see that he's taken care of."

She wasn't sure she liked the sound of that. He had made it clear he didn't think too much of marriage—and the implication was that he preferred to focus on her and leave Walt out in the cold. She definitely didn't like the possessive way he held her hand—she had al-

ways resented men who tried to take over and drag her
around like some pretty ornament who was supposed to
smile and look nice, but not express too many opinions.
She managed to pull her hand from his grasp. But she
hastened to soothe the affront that flashed in his eyes
with a smile and flattering words. "I'm thrilled you've
taken such an interest," she said. "I never dreamed I'd
be so privileged as to study with you personally."

He put one arm around her and pulled her close.
"You and I are going to be good friends," he said, and
pressed his lips to her cheek. "Very special friends."

WALT DIDN'T HAVE to spend very long in the Family's
camp to confirm a few things the other Rangers had
told him about Daniel Metwater. The Prophet had surrounded himself with mostly young people and mostly
women. Beautiful women. Every woman Walt encountered was strikingly attractive. Hannah would fit
in perfectly with the rest of Metwater's harem—the
thought made Walt's jaw tighten. He told himself if she
was a trained officer, instead of a civilian, he wouldn't
be so agitated about her being in that RV alone with
the self-proclaimed prophet. The sooner they learned
what they needed to know about Hannah's sister and
niece, the sooner they could get out of here.

He could feel the other Family members watching
him as he stood outside the RV, the sun beating down,
making him sweat. He wiped his brow, then strode
over to the card players. They looked up and watched
his approach, expressions wary. "Hey," he said, nodding in greeting. "My name's Walt. My wife and I are
hoping to join the Family."

The stocky, bearded man who had greeted Walt

and Marco when they had previously visited the camp looked him up and down, but gave no indication he recognized him. "I saw you ride in," he said. "Nice-looking bike."

"Nice-looking wife, too." A lanky blond laid his cards facedown on the blanket they were sitting around. "The Prophet will like her."

A couple of the other men snickered. Walt ignored them. "Good to meet you."

He offered his hand to the blond, who shook it. "I'm Jobie. This is Emerson." He indicated the man next to him, who wore black-rimmed glasses and a panama hat. "That's Kiram." He nodded to the bearded man.

Walt acknowledged each man in turn. Emerson offered his hand to shake, but Kiram only regarded him coolly.

"The camp looks pretty nice," Walt said. "It's a good location, you've got time to play cards, nobody hassling you."

"It's okay." Kiram laid aside his cards also and nodded to an empty space across from him. "Have a seat."

"Thanks." Walt lowered himself to the blanket. "How long have you been following the Prophet?" he asked.

"A while."

"Kiram's been with the Family practically from the beginning," Jobie said. "You got any cigs?"

"Sorry," Walt said. "I don't smoke."

"Smoking isn't allowed in camp," Kiram said.

Jobie scowled at him. "I didn't say I was going to smoke it in camp."

"I guess there are a lot of rules you have to follow," Walt said. "I know I read on the Prophet's blog that he doesn't allow guns in the camp or anything." An injunction Walt had ignored. He considered the pistol he wore in an ankle holster as one more way to protect himself and Hannah out here in the wilderness.

"There are rules," Kiram said. "It wouldn't say much about a group that preaches peace to have us all walking around armed."

"I can see that," Walt said.

"Was it your wife's idea to join up or yours?" Emerson asked.

"We decided together," Walt said.

"My girlfriend talked me into it," Emerson said. He nudged his hat farther back on his head. "We thought it would be cool living together with a bunch of people who thought the same way we did, communing with nature, hanging out in the woods and living off the land."

"And is it?" Walt asked. "Cool, I mean."

Emerson glanced toward Kiram, who was studying him, expressionless. "Sometimes," he said. "I guess no life is perfect. My girlfriend likes it well enough."

Jobie leaned toward Walt. "The thing you need to know about this place is that the women run the show. Well, the Prophet runs everything, but mostly, he runs the women."

"So you're telling me a woman can get away with anything around here," Walt said.

Jobie shook his head. "Even the women have lines they can't cross," he said. "If they displease the Prophet, then they're out of here. Doesn't happen often, but sometimes…" His voice trailed away and he picked up his hand of cards again.

Though the words weren't particularly ominous,

something in Jobie's tone sent a chill up Walt's spine. "A girl I went to school with used to talk about joining up with the Family," he said. "I wonder if she ever did. Her name was Emily Dietrich."

"A lot of people here take on a new name," Jobie said. "Or they just go by one name."

"This girl was blonde, with blue eyes. Really pretty." Which essentially described Hannah. The picture Hannah had shown him left little doubt that the two were sisters.

Jobie and Emerson looked at each other. "Was that the woman who was here in the spring for a while?" Jobie asked. "It kind of sounds like her."

"That wasn't her." Kiram didn't look up from his cards when he spoke, but Walt sensed the man was focused on the conversation.

Jobie shrugged. "Guess not, then. Maybe she changed her mind about joining up. I'd probably remember her if she had. There aren't that many of us, and I tend to remember the women, especially." He grinned.

"What happened to the woman who was here in the spring?" Walt directed his question to Kiram.

Still holding his cards, Kiram stood. "If you want to get along here, you need to learn not to ask so many questions," he said.

He walked away. Walt turned to the other two. "What's his problem?"

"He's got a point," Emerson said. "Asking questions is a good way to get into trouble around here."

"What kind of trouble?" Walt asked.

The two exchanged looks. "The Prophet punishes the disobedient."

"What kind of punishment?" Walt pressed.

"Just keep your mouth shut and you won't have to find out." Jobie nodded toward the motor home. "Here comes your wife."

Hannah exited the RV with Metwater at her side. The Prophet had one arm around her shoulders. She was smiling, but Walt sensed tension. "Everyone, I have an announcement to make," Metwater said.

Everyone around Walt put aside whatever they were doing and moved toward the RV. Even the children stopped playing and ran to their mothers' sides to stare up at Metwater. It was as if he had brainwashed them all into thinking he really was a prophet, Walt thought, as he pushed through the crowd to the bottom of the steps. Hannah met his gaze, but Metwater ignored him.

"I'd like you to meet a new candidate for membership into the Family," Metwater announced, in a deep, rich voice that carried easily over the crowd. He smiled at Hannah and squeezed her shoulder. "I think we'll call you Serenity."

"Oh." Her smile faded. "I really prefer my own name," she said.

"Serenity suits you," he said. He turned back to the crowd. "Say hello to Serenity, everyone."

"Hello, Serenity," they chorused.

Hannah frowned, but said nothing. Walt mounted the steps, brushing aside the one man who moved forward as if to stop him. He moved to Hannah's side and put his arm around her.

"This is Walter," Metwater said. "He came to us with Serenity."

"Hannah is my wife," he said. "And it's Walt, not

Walter." His grandmother was the only one who ever called him Walter.

The dreadlocked blond who had taken the laundry bag from Starfall ran toward them, a little out of breath. "The cops are back," he said.

Metwater looked over the crowd, to the path that led into camp. Sure enough, Rangers Michael Dance and Lance Carpenter were making their way down the trail. Obviously, Carpenter had made it back from his honeymoon and Dance had returned from Denver, but what were the two officers doing here?

Dance and Carpenter stopped at the edge of the clearing and looked the crowd over. Walt took Hannah's hand and tugged her toward the steps, planning to melt into the background. He figured his fellow officers were savvy enough not to give him away, but he didn't want to risk anyone—especially Metwater—picking up on any subtle cues that they knew each other.

"We've had a report of a young woman who went missing from Montrose a couple of days ago," Dance said. His voice didn't have the orator's tones of Metwater, but it carried well over the crowd. "A witness thought they saw her hitchhiking near here and we wondered if anyone here has seen her." He consulted his phone's screen. "She's described as five feet six inches tall, with short black hair, olive skin and brown eyes. Her name is Lucia Raton."

"We don't know anything about this missing girl," Metwater said. "Why would you assume we would?"

"She might have left her home intending to join your group," Lance said. "Or if she was lost, she might have wandered to your camp looking for help."

"These are the only people new to our camp," Metwater said. "And as you can see, neither of them fit your description of this girl."

Walt realized that Metwater was pointed to him and Hannah, and that everyone—including the two Rangers—had turned to look at them.

Lance frowned. "Hey, Walt," he said. "What are you doing here?"

Chapter Six

Hannah tightened her grip on Walt's hand. Nothing like having a cop call you out to arouse suspicion in a group of people you were lying to. Walt had tensed up and was all but glaring at the Ranger.

"I think these are the two who stopped me and gave me a ticket day before yesterday," he said. His glower looked real enough to Hannah—he was probably furious at his coworkers for blowing his cover.

The taller of the two Rangers nudged his partner. "Should have figured his type would show up with this bunch," he said.

Hannah saw the moment the first Ranger—his name badge said Carpenter—clicked to what was going on. He moved to stand in front of Walt. "Do you know anything about this missing woman?" he asked. "Maybe you gave her a ride on your bike?"

"I only have room for one woman on my bike," Walt said, and pulled Hannah closer. "You remember my wife, Hannah, don't you, Officer?"

If Carpenter was surprised to learn that Walt suddenly had a wife, his sunglasses helped hide his reaction. "She's not the kind of woman a man forgets," he said. He held up his cell phone, which showed a picture of a round-faced, dark-haired woman who couldn't be very far out of her teens. "Have either of you seen this girl?"

Hannah shook her head.

"Why do you people automatically assume we're responsible for anything that goes wrong?" Metwater moved in behind them. "We are a peaceful people and you've never found any evidence to contradict that, yet you continue to harass us."

"In this case, Lucia's parents found your blog bookmarked on her computer." The taller officer, Dance, joined them. He focused on Metwater, avoiding looking at Hannah or Walt.

"That doesn't make us guilty of anything," Metwater said.

"No, it doesn't," Dance agreed. "But we're talking about a missing woman. We have to check out every possible lead. We're questioning a lot of people, and you're one of them."

"So, you don't know anything about Lucia Raton?" Carpenter asked. "You haven't seen her or heard from her?"

"No, I haven't." Metwater spread his arms wide. "Look around you, officer. The camp isn't that large. It's not as if someone could sneak in here without my knowing about it."

"Do you get people stopping by often, wanting to join up?" Dance glanced at Hannah.

"Occasionally," Metwater said. "My message touches people. They want to be a part of what I'm building here."

"What exactly are you building?" Carpenter

frowned at the haphazard collection of tents, shanties and trailers.

"A community of peace and cooperation."

Were they really as peaceful as Metwater wanted everyone to believe? Hannah wondered. Metwater's charisma could only go so far in controlling his followers. Did he use other methods to keep everyone in line—methods that had frightened Emily, and maybe even led to her death?

"Let us know if you hear or see anything that might help us find this woman," Dance said. "Her family is very worried."

Metwater inclined his head, like a king deigning to notice a subject. Dance and Carpenter left. Walt took Hannah's hand. "Come on," he said. "We'd better find a place to set up our tent."

WALT HADN'T TAKEN a step when a strong hand gripped his shoulder. "What was that all about?" Metwater asked, his voice a low growl.

Walt played dumb. "What was what all about?"

"That officer recognized you. He greeted you by name."

"He was just giving me a hard time, the way he did when he gave us that ticket. You know how those cops are."

Metwater's eyes narrowed. "I would have thought the Rangers had better things to do than to give out speeding tickets."

"I guess he just wanted to hassle me—the way he did you."

Metwater nodded, though the suspicion didn't leave

his eyes. "Tomorrow you can begin your training," he said.

"Training?" Hannah didn't look happy about this prospect.

"I will instruct you in preparation for you being accepted as full members of the Family," Metwater said.

"Okay." Walt hid his annoyance at the prospect. All he wanted was to find Hannah's niece and leave. He couldn't say if Metwater was guilty of breaking any laws, but Walt disliked pretty much everything about him, from his snake-oil salesman charm to his glib new age pontificating.

"It's time to eat," Metwater said. He took Hannah's hand in his. "We'll share a meal and gather by the fire. You can begin to learn our ways."

Walt moved to Hannah's side and took her other hand. Now that they were embedded with Metwater and his group, he realized he would need to add another job to his list of duties. In addition to locating Hannah's niece and finding out more about her sister's death, he would need to keep a close eye on his pretend wife, to keep her out of the Prophet's clutches.

IT WAS AFTER ten before Walt and Hannah had the chance to break away from the group. Dinner had consisted of decent stew and bread. Afterward, everyone had gathered around a campfire to witness what Metwater explained was a spiritual dance but what looked to Walt like two scantily clad women performing for Metwater. The man himself stayed glued to Hannah's side until the evening's festivities ended. "You're welcome to stay in my RV," he told her as she and Walt prepared to leave. "You'll be much more comfortable there."

Walt bristled and was about to remind Metwater that Hannah was his wife and therefore her place was with him when she stepped between them. "Thank you," she said, with a sweet smile for Metwater. "That's so considerate of you, but I'll be fine in the tent with Walt." Then she took Walt's hand and led him away.

"He's got a lot of nerve," Walt fumed. "Propositioning you with me standing right there."

"It wasn't exactly a proposition," she said. "And there's no need for you to go all caveman. I know how to look after myself."

"Sorry." He winced inwardly, realizing how the words he had almost said would have sounded to her. It wasn't his place to tell her where she belonged— even if they had been truly married. "He just rubs me the wrong way."

"He knows that and he uses it to his advantage."

They retrieved the tent and two sleeping bags from the motorcycle. "We should set up away from everyone else," Walt said. "Less chance of being overheard or spied on."

"Do you think Metwater suspects something?" she asked.

"I think he's the type who suspects everyone. I'm no expert on groups like this, but I've done a little reading. The best way for one man to control a group of diverse people is to have a team of enforcers whose job is to report back to the leader about what everyone else is up to. Those people get to make sure everyone else obeys all the rules and doesn't get out of line."

"Who are Metwater's enforcers?" she asked.

"I met one guy who fits the bill," Walt said. "A big, bearded man who goes by the name of Kiram. Apparently he's been with Metwater a long time, and the others seem wary of him. There are probably one or two others."

"What happens if someone breaks a rule?" she asked.

"I don't know. But I intend to find out." They had reached the edge of the camp, at a point farthest from Metwater's RV, and farthest from the trail that led into the clearing. Walt shone his flashlight on a large, leaning juniper. "How about here, under this tree?" he asked. "We'd be out of the way and have some shade in the daytime."

"Sure." She unzipped the tent bag and pulled out the stiff bundle of green-and-black polyester. "Why did that officer, Carpenter, call you out this afternoon?" she asked. "He could have ruined everything."

"Lance just got back from his honeymoon. And Michael was on assignment in another part of the state." He began fitting the shock-corded tent poles together. "My guess is the missing persons call came in and they decided to check out the camp without checking in with headquarters, and no one had briefed them. It worked out okay, though. I think Metwater believed my story about the ticket."

"What do you think this training is going to consist of?"

"I don't know, but maybe we'll get lucky and won't have to endure it for long." He laid aside the completed poles and looked at her. "What happened in the RV this afternoon after I was escorted out?" he asked.

She made a face. "He asked how we heard about

him, why we wanted to join up—about what you'd expect."

"Did he make a pass at you?"

She laughed.

"What's so funny?" he asked.

"It's just not a question I expected."

"Well, did he? He was certainly leering at you enough."

"No, he didn't make a pass at me. Not exactly."

"Did he or didn't he?"

She shrugged. "He put his arm around me. He said he thought marriage was an outmoded concept."

"He would just as soon get rid of me and have you stay to be one of his faithful female followers."

"Are you jealous?" She wasn't laughing anymore— instead her blue eyes searched his, making him feel a little too vulnerable.

"I'm not jealous," he said. "But I don't trust Metwater. He clearly has a lot of beautiful women hovering around him, and I think he sees you as another one."

"No chance of that," she said. "I've never been attracted to men who think they're God's gift to women."

What kind of man are *you attracted to?* he wondered, but pushed the thought aside. He didn't have the best track record with women and he ought to be focusing on the job at hand. "I don't trust all his talk of living peacefully and promoting harmony," he said. "That's not the impression I got when I talked to some of the men."

"What did you find out?"

"They didn't say anything specific, but they hinted that people who didn't follow Metwater's rules—or people who asked too many questions—were punished."

"He said something to me about punishment, too," she said. "That they had their own rules and answered to a higher power—which I interpreted as another way of saying he thinks he's above the law. Did you get any idea of what kind of punishment they use? He wouldn't tell me."

"The men I was talking to wouldn't say, either. And they changed the subject when I tried to find out more. But when I mentioned Emily, I got the impression at least a couple of them knew who I was talking about, though they pretended not to."

"You asked about Emily?" She clutched his wrist. "What did you say? What did they say?"

"One of the men said he thought she had been here in the spring. Does that sound about right?"

"Yes. That would have been about the time she left home to follow Metwater. The first letter she sent me arrived in May." She bent and began threading the poles into the channel across the top of the tent. "I asked Metwater about her, too."

He froze. "I thought we agreed you weren't going to say anything about her."

"I couldn't pass up the chance to learn about her. I didn't say she was my sister—I told him she was a friend."

"What did he say?"

"He said he'd never heard of her. But I think he was lying."

"I'm going to try to find out more, but we have to be careful asking questions." He slid the pole into the other channel of the tent, and together they tilted the structure upright. "You try to make friends with the women and find out what you can about your niece—though you realize she may not be here."

"I know. But I feel like she is."

He began hammering in stakes to secure the tent. "You can go ahead and go inside and get ready for bed," he said. "I'll join you in a minute."

"All right." She crawled into the tent and zipped it up after her.

Walt pounded the stakes in with a mallet, hitting them harder than necessary, working off some of his frustration. He needed to get a grip on his feelings before he crawled into that tent to spend the night with Hannah. He had thought pretending to be her husband would be just another undercover gig, one that he would handle professionally. But being this close to her, seeing Metwater leer at her, had triggered something primitive in him—a possessiveness and desire to protect her that caught him off guard.

Now they had a long night ahead of them in a small tent. He couldn't let himself be the man who was attracted to a smart, beautiful woman. He had to be a cop with a job to do—and that job didn't include letting emotion get the better of his good sense.

HANNAH HUDDLED IN a sleeping bag on one side of the tent and waited for Walt to come in. She had changed under the covers, wishing she had opted for sleepwear that wasn't quite so revealing. At the time she had packed, she hadn't been thinking about the fact that she'd be spending the nights alone with Walt. She had pictured them sleeping in a cabin or a travel trailer, not a small tent with only inches separating them.

The tent zipper slid open and Walt crawled in, flashlight illuminating the interior. "Comfortable?" he asked.

"It's not too bad," she lied. She had never slept on the ground like this before—had never realized it could be so hard.

He crawled to the other sleeping bag and began removing his boots. Boots off, he pulled his shirt off over his head. She closed her eyes, but not before she caught a glimpse of his lean, muscular body and felt the instant jolt of arousal.

The light went out and darkness closed around them, so that Walt was only a denser shadow across from her, though in the small space she could hear his breathing, and take in the spice-and-sweat scent of him. She felt the heat of his presence beside her, more intimate somehow than if they had been touching. The idea made her heart race, and she kneaded her hands on her thighs, listening to the sounds of him finishing undressing— the lowering of a zipper and the soft hush of cloth being shoved down, then the crisper rustle of the sleeping bag as he crawled inside. "At least we don't have to worry about it getting really cold at night," he said.

"I've never been camping before," she said.

"Never?"

She shook her head, then realized he couldn't see her. "I guess I've always been a city girl."

"It can be fun," he said. "I've spent the night in a tent in some beautiful spots all over the country."

"I guess it's different when you're by yourself," she said. "Not with a group like this, with other people all around you."

"Camping's nice with one other person," he said. "The right person."

"Did you and your girlfriend go camping?" she asked.

"Once. She didn't like it. Maybe that should have been my first clue things weren't going to work out."

"Relationships are hard," she said. "We don't always know who to trust."

"Sometimes the hardest part is trusting yourself."

"What do you mean?" She rolled onto her side to face him. She could almost make out his features in the dim light.

"I didn't pay attention when my gut told me something was off between me and my girlfriend," he said. "I didn't trust my own instincts, but I should have."

"I guess we all doubt ourselves from time to time," she said. She certainly wasn't one to give advice on handling relationships. She'd done a lousy job of that in her own life. She hadn't even been able to keep her own sister close, much less a lover.

"You're doing great so far," he said. "Just keep it up and we'll get out of here as soon as we can." He rolled over to face the wall. "Good night."

"Good night," she said, but didn't close her eyes. Even though she longed to find her niece and leave Metwater's camp as soon as possible, she was going to miss Walt. She was going to miss lying beside him like this, pretending that in another life, they might have been a real couple, camping together because they wanted to, not because circumstance had forced them together into a relationship that felt so real, but wasn't.

"SERENITY!"

Hannah and Walt were shaking out their sleeping

bags the next morning when they turned to see a pale woman moving toward them. Her hair was so blond it was almost white, and despite the intense sun here in the wilderness, her skin seemed almost devoid of color. Even her eyes were pale, a silvery gray that added to her ethereal appearance. "My name is Phoenix," she said. "I came to fetch you to come help us prepare breakfast."

"Call me Hannah. I prefer it." She rose and brushed off her skirt. "I'm happy to come and help."

Phoenix turned to Walt. "You can gather firewood. Now that we've been here awhile, the best wood is farther away and harder to haul."

"Sure." He rose also. "I'm happy to help."

"It's your job to help if you want to be one of us." Phoenix grabbed Hannah's hand and tugged her, with enough force that Hannah stumbled, then had to hurry to keep up as Phoenix led her back toward the center of camp.

"She's right. Your job is to work for the good of the Family."

He whirled to find Kiram standing behind the tent, next to the tree trunk. He held a long-bladed knife— the kind hunters used for skinning animals. How long had he been lurking back there, listening in on Walt and Hannah's conversation? Walt forced himself to remain passive. "I thought no weapons were allowed in camp," he said.

"This knife is for ceremonial purposes," Kiram said. "And I use it for hunting." He moved away from the tree and walked around the side of the tent, studying it. "Why did you decide to camp back here, far away from everything and everyone?" He stopped beside Walt—close enough to lash out with that knife.

Walt bent and picked up the mallet he had been using to drive in stakes. He felt better with a weapon of his own, feeble as it might be against the knife. He didn't want to risk drawing the gun he wore in an ankle holster unless he absolutely had to. "We're newlyweds," he said. "We like our privacy."

"There's no such thing as privacy in a camp like this," Kiram said. "There's always someone watching you, listening to you. Before very long, everyone will know all your secrets."

Walt knew a threat when he heard one. He met Kiram's cold stare with a hard look of his own. "What's your secret?" he asked. "Why do you feel the need to sneak around in the woods with that big knife?"

"I already told you it isn't a good idea to ask too many questions." Kiram thrust the knife into the scabbard at his side.

"You told me, but you didn't tell me why. Questions can be a good way to learn things I need to know."

"People who ask questions have to be punished," Kiram said. He looked Walt up and down, as if taking his measure.

"I guess that's for the Prophet to decide, not you."

"The Prophet decides," Kiram said. "Then I do his will." He shoved past Walt, then paused a few steps away and looked back. "You didn't ask me what I was hunting."

"Why should I care what you do?" Walt said.

Kiram grinned, showing crooked bottom teeth. "I hunt rats. It's my job to keep them under control." He turned back around and strode away, leaving Walt to stare after him, gripping the mallet at his side, cold sweat beading on the back of his neck.

Chapter Seven

Hannah let Phoenix drag her to the center of the camp, where three other women were already working at two long picnic tables set up beneath a shelter fashioned of logs and branches. One table served as a prep area for the morning's meal, while the other table held two propane-fueled cooking stoves, on which bubbled two large stockpots full of oatmeal. "This is Serenity," Phoenix said by way of introduction. She handed Hannah a paring knife. "You can peel the potatoes." She indicated a ten-pound bag of potatoes at the end of the table.

"Call me Hannah," Hannah said.

"The Prophet named her Serenity," Phoenix said, and moved to stir one of the cooking pots.

"He must like you, if he gave you a name already." Starfall said. Tears streamed down her face from the onions she was chopping. She nodded to the pregnant woman across from her—Andi Matheson. "This is Asteria. And the redhead over there is Sarah."

"It's good to meet you," Hannah said. "And I am flattered that the Prophet would give me a name, but I don't feel like a Serenity. I'm just—Hannah."

"I don't care what you call yourself, as long as you

peel those potatoes." Phoenix added salt to the pot and stirred. "We need them to fry up with the onions."

Hannah picked up the knife and a potato. "Does everyone eat all their meals together?" she asked.

"Usually," Starfall said. "It's more efficient that way, and it fosters a sense of family." She swept chopped onion into a bowl and picked up another onion.

"We take turns cooking and watching the children," Asteria said. "The work is easier with more people to do it."

"I love children," Hannah said. "How many are there in camp?"

"Gloria has a five-year-old son," Asteria said. "Starfall has a son, who's seven months old. Solitude has a three-year-old, too. A boy. Zoe has six-year-old twins. And Phoenix has a fourteen-year-old daughter and a baby girl."

"My husband and I knew this was a good place to be when we saw so many children," Hannah said. The word "husband" sounded odd to her ears, but it was easy enough to say, even though she had never thought of herself as very good at lying.

"That's a good-looking man you have," Sarah said.

"Um, thanks." Hannah wasn't sure how to respond to this comment. Walt was handsome, but it wasn't as if she could claim responsibility for that. "He's a good man." She thought that much was true, at least.

"Maybe he'll be one of the rare ones who stick," Starfall said.

"What do you mean?" Hannah dropped a peeled potato into the empty pot Asteria had set in front of her and picked up another.

"A lot of guys don't adapt well to life in the Family," Asteria explained. "We have a few who have been here awhile, but a lot of them end up leaving after a few months or weeks because it's not what they expected."

"It's not a lifestyle for everyone," Phoenix said. "But the Prophet changes lives. I'm proof of that." She moved one of the pots off a burner and set another in its place.

"Mom, I need a bottle for Vicki." A lanky teenage girl, her long brown hair in pigtails, raced up to Phoenix. Dressed in shorts and a T-shirt, she looked like any other young teen, except for the baby on her hip. The infant, dressed in a pink sleeper, gurgled happily as the girl hoisted her up higher.

"Give me a minute." Phoenix added salt to the pot in front of her and tasted.

"She's been really fussy," the girl said. "I think she's hungry."

"All right." Phoenix set aside the spoon she'd been using to stir and walked to the row of coolers along the shadiest side of the shelter.

Hannah moved around the table to where the girl stood. "I'm Hannah," she said. "I'm new here."

"I'm Sophie, and this is Vicki." Sophie hitched the baby up again. "Well, her name's really Victory, but no one calls her that, except the Prophet."

"How old is she?" Hannah had to restrain herself from reaching for the infant, who kicked her little legs and waved her chubby arms, letting out a wail of protest.

"Almost four months. Would you like to hold her?"

Before Hannah could even form an answer the girl was putting the baby in her arms. Hannah cradled the child against her, patting her back and delighting in her chubby sweetness. The child quieted and stared up at Hannah with wide blue eyes.

Emily's eyes. The recognition hit Hannah like a slap. She touched one finger to the tiny dent in the baby's chin. Hannah had a dent like that in her own chin.

"She must like you. She's not usually that good with strangers." Phoenix had returned and stood at Hannah's elbow, a baby bottle in one hand.

When she leaned in to take the baby, Hannah's first instinct was to hold on tight. She could run away, find Walt and they could leave on his motorcycle. They could reach Ranger headquarters before anyone would have time to pursue them.

Logic—and probably all the lectures she had endured from Walt and his boss about needing proof that any child she found in the camp really was Emily's baby—made her reluctantly release the child to Phoenix. "You don't breast-feed?" she asked as the child latched on to the bottle.

Phoenix frowned at her. "I couldn't. I got sick right after she was born and lost my milk."

"I'm sorry," Hannah said. "That was a terribly rude question. I'm just so curious about anything to do with babies these days."

Phoenix's expression softened. "I understand." She smiled down at the baby. "I never thought I'd have another little one and now I have her. She's been a special blessing in my life."

Hannah clenched her jaw, fighting back the questions she wanted to ask. Who was this baby's father? When had she been born? Where had she been born? Did Phoenix know a woman named Emily? Instead, she held her tongue and returned to peeling potatoes, her mind working furiously. She had to find a way to prove that little Vicki wasn't Phoenix's child, but Emily's. Maybe Phoenix had taken over care of the baby because no one else was available at the time of Emily's death. Hannah was grateful to her if that was the case. But if that was so, why pass the baby off as her own? And surely she hadn't taken in the baby without Daniel Metwater's knowledge. So why had the Prophet lied about having Joy with him?

"Did you hear what those cops said about that missing girl?" Sarah heaved a large watermelon onto the table and plunged a knife into it.

"She never should have left camp," Asteria said. "She would have been safe here."

Hannah almost dropped her potato. "You mean the girl the police were looking for was here?"

"For less than a day." Starfall scraped the last of the chopped onions into a pot. "The Prophet told her she couldn't stay, since she was underage, and she left."

"Why didn't anyone tell the Rangers that?" Hannah asked.

"One thing you need to learn if you stay here is that we don't speak to the cops," Starfall said. "It's one of the Prophet's rules."

"But if it would help them find her, why not say something?" Hannah asked. "Her poor parents must be worried sick."

"It won't help her, and it will only focus unnecessary attention on us," Starfall said. "The point is, she's not here now, and no one in the Family had anything to do with her disappearance, so the cops should look elsewhere instead of hassling us."

"Don't you go saying anything to anyone," Phoenix said. "It will only cause trouble. You don't want to start out like that."

Why would any reasonable person want to be a part of a group that hid evidence from the police? Hannah thought, but she only nodded and went back to peeling potatoes. She would have so much to tell Walt tonight—not only this bit of news about the missing young woman, but that she was sure she had found her sister's baby. All she needed was a little proof.

WALT SET OUT with Jobie and a guy who introduced himself as Slate to gather firewood. They had one hand ax and a rusting bow saw between them, and apparently Jobie and Slate had never been Boy Scouts, because they seemed to have no clue what actually made good firewood.

"I don't think that rotten stuff is going to burn very well," Walt said as Slate tugged at a fallen tree trunk that was so rotten it was growing a healthy crop of mushrooms.

The log crumbled as soon as he tried to lift it. "Guess not," he said, and straightened.

"Do you do this every day?" Walt asked.

"Pretty much," Jobie said. "We keep telling the Prophet if we had a chain saw we could cut a bunch at once and not have to work so hard, but he says the noise would draw the wrong kind of attention."

"Yeah, the cops have already got it in for us," Slate said. "They're always around here hassling us."

"Why do you think that is?" Walt asked.

"Because they're suspicious of anyone who colors outside the lines," Slate said.

"We don't bother anybody and we ask the same of them." Jobie tugged on the end of a branch that lay beneath a tree and held up a four-foot length of juniper. He grinned and added it to his pile.

"What do we need all this wood for, anyway?" Walt asked. "Do the women cook over a fire?"

"They mostly use the camp stoves for cooking," Jobie said. "But every night after supper we have a campfire. Sometimes there's singing or dancing, like last night. Sometimes the Prophet has a message for us, and sometimes there's a ceremony."

"What kind of ceremony?" Walt asked.

"Oh, you know, like when new members join or if the Prophet has had a vision that tells him we need to perform some kind of ritual."

"You mean like saying prayers or something?"

"Not that, so much," Slate said. "Cooler stuff. Once we did fire walking, and another time everyone had to bring something to burn that represented stuff they were letting go of."

"The Prophet is really big on letting go of the past," Jobie said. "Like, if you've made mistakes or whatever, none of that has to hold you back now."

"That's what makes being part of the Family so great," Slate said. "Nobody judges you based on what you did before. You start over clean. That's why I chose the name I did. I'm a clean Slate."

Walt had read Metwater's writings about new beginnings and fresh starts. But he wondered if those teachings might not have a special appeal for people who wanted to get away with bad behavior with no consequences. Simply join up with the Prophet and all your sins are forgiven. You could get away with anything—maybe even murder.

Walt figured this wasn't the time to share his skepticism about the Prophet's message. "I guess that takes lots of firewood," he said.

"Yeah." Jobie swung the ax ineffectually at the spindly branch of a pinyon. "The Rangers think we relocated our camp because our permit expired, but really, it was just that we ran out of firewood."

Walt joined in their laughter and led the way to the next clump of scrubby trees. He estimated they were about a mile from camp, in a part of the Curecanti wilderness that he had never visited. Probably very few people came to this roadless site. "Do you ever run into wild animals out here?" he asked. "Bears or mountain lions or anything like that?"

"Sometimes we see coyotes," Jobie said. "And lots of rabbits."

"We've found other weird stuff, though," Slate said. "An old junk car, shot full of holes. A whole skeleton of some big animal, like a horse or something."

"Once we found a sofa, just sitting out in the middle of nowhere," Jobie said. "We hauled it back to camp and Kiram has it in this shack he built."

Walt pushed through a tangle of tree branches and vines and emerged in a small clearing, no larger than the average living room. A wall of green surrounded it, with a circle of blue sky high overhead. No shot-up car or skeleton occupied the space, but a different kind of oddity that sent a cold chill up Walt's spine. "Is that a grave?" he asked, pointing to the mound of disturbed earth, a makeshift cross at its head.

Chapter Eight

"The Prophet is not going to like this." Jobie shook his head as the three men stared at the grave in the middle of the clearing.

Walt studied the area around the burial site. There were no clear footprints, and the soil had settled some, though he couldn't tell if the grave had been dug in the past few days or the past few weeks. No plants grew on the surface of the mound, and the wood on the cross was new enough the cut edges were still fresh. "We need to notify the Rangers," Walt said. "They'll want to investigate."

"Cell phones don't work out here," Jobie said. "So none of us have them."

"We'll have to talk to the Prophet," Slate said. "It's up to him."

Walt started to point out that the grave was on public land and it wasn't up to Daniel Metwater to decide whether or not it should be reported, but he didn't waste his breath. "Come on," he said. "Let's get back to camp."

They gathered up the firewood they had collected and Walt led the way back toward camp. Kiram met them at the edge of the clearing. "What took you so long?" he asked.

"We have to talk to the Prophet," Slate said.

"He doesn't like to be disturbed before dinner," Kiram said.

"He's going to want to know about what we found while we were looking for wood," Jobie said.

"What did you find?" Kiram asked.

"We'll tell the Prophet," Walt said. He pushed past the bearded man, dropped his load of wood beside the fire ring then strode toward Metwater's RV. Jobie and Slate hurried to catch up with him, Kiram following, his face like a thundercloud.

Metwater opened the door before Walt could even knock. "Is something wrong?" he asked, letting his gaze drift over the four men who gathered on the steps of the RV.

Jobie, Slate and Kiram all looked at Walt. "We found a grave while we were looking for firewood," he said. "It looks pretty fresh."

"Whose grave?" Metwater asked.

"The marker didn't say," Jobie said—as if this was a perfectly reasonable question.

"We need to notify the Rangers," Walt said. "They can determine who's in the grave."

"Maybe it's that girl the cops were looking for," Jobie said.

"If the grave is hers, I'm sure the police will find it before long," Metwater said. "We should stay out of this."

"It's too late for that," Walt said. "We found it and now we have to report it."

Metwater put his hand on Walt's shoulder and

looked into his eyes, his expression that of a father dealing with an unruly—and perhaps stupid—child. "You aren't a part of that outside world anymore," he said. "Here in the Family we don't concern ourselves with the world's evil. That is for others, not us."

"You can't divorce yourself from responsibilities that way," Walt said.

"That's exactly what we're doing, living here in the wilderness," Metwater said.

"Wilderness supported by taxpayer money. You're happy enough to take advantage of that."

Metwater shook his head. "You have a long way to go toward gaining the understanding necessary to be a true member of the Family," he said. "Your wife is much more in tune with our purpose than you are."

"And you know that from talking with her for what, twenty minutes?"

"Women are much more intuitive about these things than most men. It's one of the reasons they are so drawn to my teachings."

And it has nothing to do with naked muscles and flowing hair, Walt thought cynically. "You can't let that grave go unreported," he said.

"That's exactly what we will do," Metwater said. "Although I will meditate on the problem and if I receive different guidance I will act on it." He clapped a hand on Walt's shoulder. "Come. We are having a special meal to welcome you and Serenity to the fold."

"Her name is Hannah," Walt said, reluctantly falling into step beside Metwater, since the alternative seemed to be wrestling with the man, which probably wouldn't go over well with Kiram and the others.

"But you and she are starting a new life here. Serenity suits her. She strikes me as someone who is looking for peace in her life."

Hannah was looking for her missing niece—but maybe Metwater wasn't so far off track. Maybe having the baby in her life would bring Hannah more peace of mind, and ease some of her grief for her sister. Walt wanted to help her find the baby, and the closure adopting her niece might bring.

In order to do that, he had to walk a fine line between doing anything that might blow his cover or anger Metwater to the point where he threw them out of camp, and continuing to uphold his duty as a law officer.

They reached the camp's outdoor kitchen, where most of the residents were already lined up awaiting the meal. Jobie and Slate took their places in line, while Kiram hovered near Metwater. Was he some sort of bodyguard, or simply awaiting more orders from the Prophet?

Kiram looked over and caught Walt watching him. Certainly there was little peace and love in his eyes. Walt spotted Hannah and started toward her, but Kiram grabbed his arm. "Don't get any ideas about sneaking out of camp to go to the police," he said, keeping his voice low. "Try it and you will be punished."

"I'm trembling in my boots," Walt said.

"You should be." He gave Walt's arm a shake, then released his hold. "And remember—you won't be the only one hurt." He turned to Hannah, and the icy hatred in his eyes chilled Walt to the bone.

"WHAT'S WRONG WITH YOU?" Hannah asked when she finally cornered Walt at their tent after supper that evening. They hadn't been able to exchange more than a few words during the day, constantly surrounded as they were by Family members who were either eager to welcome them, curious to know more about them or both. After breakfast, they had both been assigned to work teams to clean up, and after that had been a speech—or more like a sermon—from Metwater. Though Hannah could admit he was a charismatic speaker, she was too focused on Walt to pay much attention to Metwater's message. He sat across from her with a group of men, scowling at the Prophet as if the man had just kicked his dog.

The afternoon was taken up by more work. Hannah stayed with the women and did her best to avoid Metwater. She spent most of her time with Phoenix, taking every opportunity to hold the baby, growing more and more sure that this was her sister's child. She was relieved to finally have the chance to be alone with Walt again after supper, to tell him all she had learned.

"I have to find a way to sneak out of here for a few hours tonight without anyone noticing," he said.

The thought of him leaving her alone here sent a spike of panic through her. "Why do you have to leave?" she asked.

He glanced around. "Let's not talk out here." He unzipped the tent flap. "Inside. And keep your voice down."

She crawled into the tent ahead of him and sat cross-legged on one of the sleeping bags he had unrolled. He moved in after her, zipping up the tent behind him. "Why do you need to leave?" she asked, her voice just above a whisper.

"When I was out gathering firewood this morning with two other men, we found a grave."

"A grave? A *person's* grave?" Her voice rose on the last word and he gripped her hand.

"Keep your voice down," he said.

She nodded, then, realizing he probably couldn't see her, said, "Okay, but what are you talking about? You found someone buried out here in the middle of nowhere?"

"I don't know what's in the grave, but I need to get word to the Rangers so they can investigate."

"You don't think it was from some pioneer ranching family or something?" she asked. "I mean, wasn't some of the parkland private land at one time?"

"This wasn't like that," he said. "I'm pretty sure it was more recent. Much more recent."

A chilling thought struck her and she gripped his hand more tightly. "That girl the Rangers are looking for?"

"I don't know," Walt said. "It's a possibility."

"The women I was working with this morning said she was here—in camp," she said. "But that she left after less than a day. Metwater supposedly sent her away because she was too young."

"I'll be sure and let the Rangers know when I talk to them. If Metwater and his followers are lying about not knowing her, I have to wonder what else they're covering up."

"The men you were with—do they know about this grave?"

"Yes. They saw it, too. Two men, Jobie and Slate. We told Metwater when we got back to camp and he refused to go to the police, or to let us go."

"He can't keep you from telling them," she said. "We came here voluntarily. He can't make us stay."

"He thinks he can."

Something in his words ratcheted her fear up another notch. "Did he threaten you?"

"He didn't, but a man named Kiram did. He's the guy I told you about—Metwater's enforcer. He said if I tried to leave, I would be punished." He took her other hand. "He said you would be, too. In fact, instead of me leaving and coming back, I'm beginning to think we should leave together and not come back. Maybe this undercover op was a bad idea."

"No, we can't leave." She pulled her hands from his. "Not when we're so close to finding Joy and learning what happened to Emily. In fact, I think I've already found Joy."

"What? Where?" He shifted toward her.

She took a deep breath, trying to organize her thoughts, but all that brought her was his scent, distracting and sensual. Heat curled through her, and the space inside the tent suddenly seemed too intimate. If she leaned over just a little, they would be touching, and her skin tingled in anticipation...

"Do you think one of the children in camp is your niece?" Walt prompted.

"Yes. The woman who came to get me to help with breakfast this morning—Phoenix—is a little older than some of the rest of the women here, maybe in her early forties. She has a fourteen-year-old daughter, Sophie. But she also has a baby. A little girl, about four months old."

"Why do you think this baby is Joy?"

"Phoenix isn't breast-feeding her. She's using formula. She told me she wasn't able to breast-feed, but I think she's lying."

"Lots of women use formula. It doesn't mean the baby isn't hers."

"No, but I held this baby. I looked into her eyes. They were Emily's eyes. The same shape—the same color." She wished she could see his face more clearly, to judge if he believed her, but the light was too dim to make out his features.

"What color are Phoenix's eyes?" he asked.

The question caught her off guard. She tried to bring Phoenix to mind, to remember her eyes, but she couldn't. "I don't know," she admitted.

He took her hand again, gentle this time. His voice was gentle, too, when he spoke. "I know you want to find your niece, and that you have good reason to believe she's with Metwater. But you can't let your natural biases lead you into a mistake. Think about how much pain it would cause Phoenix if this baby really is hers, and not Joy?"

She wanted to insist that she knew this baby was Emily's daughter, but the part of her that relied on logic instead of emotion told her that everything he said made perfect sense. "Then we have to stay here and look for proof," she said. "If I make friends with Phoenix, and with Sophie, maybe I can persuade them to tell me the truth about the baby."

"I still have to let the Rangers know about the grave we found."

"Of course." She slid her hand from his and clenched it in her lap. "I'll be fine. After all, it's nighttime. Everyone will be sleeping."

"Stay in the tent. I should be back before morning." He moved toward the door.

"Let me come with you to the bike," she said. "I can serve as a lookout until you get safely away." And she wanted to prolong the time before he left her alone.

"All right. We'd better go now. The sooner I can get away, the sooner I'll be back."

They crept through the darkened camp, keeping to the edges, skirting any lights that still shone outside tents or trailers. Walt held Hannah's hand, and she took comfort from his strong grip pulling her along, his sure steps guiding hers as they moved through the darkness.

They found the bike where they had left it, on the edge of the parking area. Walt had cut tree branches and draped them over the motorcycle to hide it from curious eyes. He quickly pulled these away and pushed the bike toward the road. "I won't start it until I'm farther from camp," he said. "If anyone comes to the tent looking for me, tell them I'm asleep."

"I will."

"And take this." He pressed something hard into her hand.

She looked down at a knife—similar to the one she had used to peel potatoes this morning. "I palmed it at dinner," he said. "It's not much, but I didn't feel right leaving you defenseless. You can keep it in your pocket."

"All right." She slipped the knife into the pocket of her skirt, where it rested, heavy and awkward, a reminder of the danger they might be in here, but an even stronger reminder that Walt was looking out for her, even when he couldn't be with her. The knowledge shook her—she had spent so many years alone.

She was used to looking after herself, so what did it mean that knowing he was on her side felt so good? She looked toward the road, a faint pale strip in the light of a quarter moon. It would take Walt more than an hour to reach a good phone signal he could use to report his find—an hour traveling over rough, narrow roads in pitch-blackness. An unseen pothole, an animal running out in front of him—or one of Metwater's men in pursuit—and he might never reach his destination at all.

"Be careful." She took hold of his arm and leaned toward him, intending only to kiss his cheek. But he turned toward her and their lips met, and she realized this was what she had wanted all along—what she had wanted in that dark, intimate interlude in the tent. He brought one hand up to caress her cheek and she angled her mouth under his. He kissed the same way he did everything—with a quiet strength that moved her more than Metwater's overt seduction ever could. The brush of his unshaven cheeks abrading her skin sent a shiver of arousal through her, and she leaned in closer, wanting to be nearer to him, wanting this moment to never end.

But at last he pulled away, though his hand remained on her shoulder, steadying her. "I'll be back as soon as I can," he said. "Stay safe."

"You, too." Reluctantly, she stepped back, one hand to her mouth as if to preserve the memory of his kiss. She watched him as he walked away, pushing the motorcycle, until he was out of sight, disappearing into the darkness. Then she crossed the bridge back into camp.

She retraced the route they had followed back to the tent, seeing and hearing no one. The few lanterns that had previously been lit were out now, plunging the compound into silent blackness. Hannah felt her way from tree to tree, wishing she had thought to bring a flashlight with her. She let out a sigh of relief when she spotted the tent, by itself on the edge of the camp.

She had almost reached the safety of that shelter when someone clamped a hand over her mouth and dragged her back against him. She kicked out and tried to struggle free, but the unseen man held her fast. "Where is your husband now?" a voice growled in her ear. "And why isn't he here to protect you?"

Chapter Nine

Walt estimated he had walked the heavy motorcycle the better part of a mile before he dared climb on and start the engine. It roared to life, echoing in the midnight stillness. If anyone in camp heard him and figured out what was going on, he would be long gone before they could come after him.

He raced the bike as fast as he dared over the rough washboard road, barely maintaining control of the big machine as it bounced over the rugged dirt track. His headlight seemed to scarcely penetrate the inky blackness, illuminating only a few yards in front of him. More than once eyes glowed from the brush alongside the road—coyotes or foxes or other wild creatures observing his passing.

He tried not to think of what might happen to Hannah while he was away. Instead, he focused on the memory of that goodbye kiss. Working with her on this undercover op, he had grown close to her in a very short period of time. Even though they weren't married, at times he felt that close connection to her—or at least, what he hoped the connection between a husband and wife should feel like.

The kind of connection he had wanted with his former girlfriend, but had clearly never had. Looking back, he remembered how stunned he had been when he learned she was seeing his brother. But he saw, too, how part of him wasn't surprised she had betrayed him. Wanting someone to love you deeply wasn't the same as having that love be a reality. It was a lesson he had had to learn the hard way.

So why was he even thinking about love and Hannah in the same breath? As beautiful as she was, and as close as he felt to her at times, she was here to find her niece. She wanted to return to her home in Texas and start a new life with the baby—nowhere in that plan did he see room for a backcountry cop. He was doing it again—wishing for a relationship that couldn't exist.

It was almost two in the morning when he finally reached the paved highway that led toward Black Canyon of the Gunnison National Park and Ranger Brigade headquarters. He raced the bike over the blacktop to the headquarters building and let himself in with his key, then dialed the commander's number on the office line, more reliable than cell service out here.

Ranger Brigade commander Graham Ellison didn't sound groggy when he answered the phone. "Ellison. What's up?"

"It's Walt Riley, sir. There's been a development near Metwater's compound that you need to be aware of." He explained about the grave and its approximate location, as well as Metwater's stricture against reporting it. "I took a chance, sneaking out of camp," Walt said. "I need to get back as soon as possible."

"Wait there at headquarters. I'll have someone there

in half an hour or less. We need you to show us the area on a map and fill in some details."

"Yes, sir." He hung up the phone and settled in to wait.

KIRAM WRENCHED HANNAH'S arm behind her back, hurting her. "I'm going to uncover your mouth," he said. "But if you cry out, I'll break your arm."

She nodded to show she understood and he removed his hand. "Let me go," she said.

"Where is your husband?" he asked.

"He's asleep in the tent."

"I was just there. He isn't there."

"Maybe he got up to go to the bathroom." She began to struggle again, frantic over what he might do to her if she didn't get away. He started pulling her toward the parking lot—toward the deserted road and the empty wilderness, away from the rest of the camp, where there were people who might help her. "What are you doing?" she asked. "Where are you taking me?"

"I warned your husband what would happen if he disobeyed the Prophet's orders."

"I don't know what you're talking about. Let me go. Help!"

The savage jerk he gave her didn't break her arm, but it hurt enough that she gasped in pain. "You're making a mistake," she said. "Let's go to the Prophet now. I'll prove to you that you're making a mistake." She had no idea what she would say to Metwater, but demanding to see him would at least get her back to the camp, where surely someone would help her.

Kiram stopped. "You want to see the Prophet?"

"Yes. He's the leader of this camp. If he thinks I need to be punished, I want to hear it from him."

"Fine. We'll go to him." He turned and headed back toward camp, still gripping her arm. She had to run to keep from being dragged. The clearing in the midst of the tents and trailers was empty and silent, the only light from the dying coals of the bonfire they had gathered around earlier. Metwater's motor home was dark and silent also.

Hannah slowed her steps as they neared the RV. "The Prophet won't like being awakened," she said.

"You should have thought of that before your husband disobeyed him." One hand gripping her arm, he raised the other hand to knock on the door of the motor home.

Hannah didn't wait for someone to answer Kiram's knock. She had no intention of going into that RV with him—not in the middle of the night, with no witnesses around to notice if the two men decided to make her disappear altogether. She slipped her hand into the pocket of her skirt and gripped the knife Walt had given her. As her fingers closed around the blade, she summoned all her courage. She was doing this for Joy, she told herself. For Emily.

She jabbed the knife hard into Kiram's shoulder. He yelped and released her, and she ran to the far side of the dying bonfire. Snatching a smoldering branch from the fire, she brandished it in one hand, the knife in the other. Then she began to scream. "Help! Someone help me, please! Kiram attacked me! Help!"

As she had hoped, heads poked out of the tents and trailers surrounding the area. Kiram clutched his shoulder, blood trickling between his fingers. "She stabbed me!" he roared, and started toward her, his face a mask of rage.

"Only because he attacked me first. Look at the bruises on my arm if you don't believe me."

No one moved to help her, but none of them went back inside, either. Kiram glared at her. The light outside the motor home went on and the door opened to reveal Daniel Metwater, clad only in pajama pants, scowling at them. "What is going on?" he asked.

"The new man, Walt, left tonight," Kiram said. "I'm sure he went to the police."

"Of course he went to the police," Hannah said. "There's a fresh grave out there, not far from camp, and the police are looking for a missing woman. Her family is probably beside themselves, trying to find her."

"We don't have anything to do with that," Metwater said.

"Trying to hide it makes you look like you do." Hannah slipped the knife into her pocket but kept hold of the smoldering branch. "And the fact that Walt went to tell someone about the grave doesn't give Kiram any right to attack me."

Metwater turned to Kiram. "Did you attack her?"

"I warned her husband if he disobeyed your orders and left the camp, they would have to be disciplined." He lifted his hand from his shoulder. "And she stabbed me."

"When a man puts his hands on a woman against her will, she has a right to defend herself," Hannah said.

Murmurs of agreement rose from the crowd of onlookers. Metwater held up a hand. "Part of being a member of the Family is agreeing to abide by my rules," he said.

"One of your rules is that women are to be treated with respect."

Hannah turned to see who had spoken. Phoenix stepped into the circle of light from a lantern that hung outside her tent. She cradled the baby in her arms. "If Kiram attacked Serenity in the darkness, when her husband wasn't there to defend her, that isn't treating her with respect."

"What about respect for me and my role of carrying out the Prophet's will?" Kiram growled the words. At that moment, he reminded Hannah of a wounded bear.

Everyone was focused on Metwater, as if he really was some king or Old Testament prophet who had authority to rule their lives. Hannah realized she was holding her breath in anticipation, as if she believed he had power over her, as well. Had Emily stood before him like this, waiting while he decided her fate?

Of course, all she had to do was declare she had had enough of this nonsense and walk away. But doing so would end her best chance of finding out what had happened to Emily and her baby. She shifted her gaze to where Phoenix stood, cradling the child. That baby might be Joy. Hannah couldn't walk away until she knew for sure.

"Tomorrow, after Serenity's husband has returned, we will hold a council," Metwater declared. "At that time, we will decide the appropriate response to their willful and disobedient behavior." He fixed his gaze on Hannah. A shiver crept up her spine. Did no one else see the malevolence in those dark eyes? "Until tomorrow, I put you in Phoenix's care. She will watch over you."

"I don't need a guard," Hannah said.

Metwater's smile held no warmth. "But clearly, you do."

Phoenix crossed the clearing to Hannah's side. "Come on," she said. "I'll fix a comfortable place for you in my trailer." She leaned closer, her voice so soft Hannah scarcely heard her words, and she was sure no one else could. "You'll be safer with me than alone in your tent—just in case Kiram gets any ideas."

Hannah glanced at Kiram, who was still glowering at her. Her aching arm reminded her of how easily he could overpower her. She nodded. "Thanks," she said. She wouldn't think of this time as imprisonment. She would use the opportunity to get to know Phoenix and her baby better. Maybe this would be the key to learning the truth she needed to know.

MEMBERS OF THE Ranger team started showing up at headquarters within half an hour of Walt's call—Lance Carpenter arrived first, followed by Michael Dance, Ethan Reynolds and the commander. Walt had made coffee and they helped themselves to mugs before settling down to consider the case. "Sorry for almost blowing your cover out there yesterday," Lance said as he settled at the conference table across from Walt. "We should have checked in with the commander before we headed out there."

"It worked out okay," Walt said. "Now Metwater and the rest think I'm as disgruntled with the cops as they are."

"Tell us more about this grave you found," Commander Ellison said, settling into the chair at the head of the table.

"It looks fairly recent, though I'm no expert," Walt

said. "It was in a small clearing, not visible until you were right up on it, about a mile from camp, at least that far from any road."

"And you're sure it was a grave?" Michael asked.

"It was an oblong mound of earth, maybe two feet wide and four feet long, with a homemade wooden cross at one end. No writing on the cross. No footprints on the surrounding ground. The dirt had dried out and settled a little, but no vegetation was growing on it, and the sawed ends of the cross were fresh, not weathered." He sat back in his chair. "And Metwater was very annoyed when I told him I intended to report it."

"What was his argument against doing so?" Ethan asked.

"It would bring law enforcement into camp again."

"What is he afraid we're going to find?" Lance asked. "He sounds like a man with something to hide."

"Do you think he knows anything about the missing woman—Lucia Raton?" Graham asked.

"Hannah spoke to some Family members who said she came around wanting to join the group," Walt said. "Metwater supposedly sent her away because she was too young."

"And they didn't bother to mention this to us," Michael said. "I think this warrants questioning him again. Maybe we should bring him in."

"Let's see what we find in the grave first." Graham sat back in his chair. "We'll get a team out there at first light, though we'll have to wait for a forensic anthropologist to excavate it properly. That could take a while, depending on where he or she has to come from. If it's Denver or Salt Lake, it could mean an extra day's wait."

"You should at least get someone out there to guard

the site," Walt said. "Now that Metwater knows I know about this, if he is involved somehow, he may try to destroy evidence."

"We'll do that," Graham said. "What else have you learned?"

"Metwater preaches a message of peace and love, but he's set a lot of rules for his followers. He's got at least one guy, calls himself Kiram, whose job is to enforce the rules. He threatened me—and Hannah—if I came to you."

"Threatened you with what?" Lance asked.

"Nothing specific. I told Hannah I'd feel better if she came with me tonight," Walt said. "I gave her the opportunity to call off the operation altogether, but she wanted to stay and see it through."

"Any news about her sister or the baby?" Ethan asked.

"Everyone denies knowing anything about the sister, but I think they're lying," Walt said. "There's a woman in camp who has a little girl the right age to be Hannah's niece, but we don't have any proof she isn't the woman's child. Hannah thinks if she makes friends with the woman, who goes by Phoenix, she can find out more."

"We'll give it another day or two, but if either of you feel at any time that you're in danger, get out of there," Graham said. "If this bunch really is responsible for Lucia Raton's death, we don't want to give them a chance to add to the body count."

"When I described Hannah's sister to some men in the camp, one of them told me she sounded like a woman who was there in the spring," Walt said. "Hannah said Metwater reacted to the name, though he denied knowing Emily."

"Before I forget, we managed to get hold of Marsha Caldwell." Marco leaned back to snag a notebook off a desk. "The nurse who witnessed Emily Dietrich's will."

"What did she say?" Walt asked, tensed on the edge of his chair.

"She remembered Emily—described her as a sweet young woman with a beautiful baby. Caldwell said Emily didn't strike her as particularly fearful. She came to the hospital with another woman—the Anna Ingels who also witnessed the will. She thought Ingels was a friend or maybe an older relative."

"Did you get a description of Ingels?" Walt asked.

Marco consulted his notes. "Nothing really useful. Medium height, late thirties, blond hair and light eyes."

That description could fit a few of the women in camp, but it wasn't specific enough to zero in on anyone. "How could she say Emily wasn't fearful when she wanted Caldwell to witness a will?"

"She said it wasn't the first will she had witnessed," Marco said. "Apparently, labor and delivery is traumatic for some women. She said it makes them aware of their own mortality. Add in the responsibility for a new life, and a will outlining who should care for the baby in the event of the mother's death is a sensible response."

"So she didn't think Emily was afraid someone was going to kill her?" Walt asked.

"She didn't think so, no."

Was Hannah wrong, then? Had her sister died of an unfortunate bout of ill health, and Metwater had nothing to do with it? So why was he trying to hide the child—assuming Phoenix's baby really was Hannah's niece, as she asserted? He shoved back his chair. "I had better get back to camp," he said. "Even though I don't think Kiram would be foolish enough to try anything, I don't like leaving Hannah there too long."

"You may be in the best position to learn what happened with Lucia Raton," Michael said. "Whatever evidence you can find could be crucial to making a case."

Walt nodded. As long as Metwater and his people saw Walt and Hannah as prospective members who were interested in the Prophet's teachings, they were more likely to let down their guard and reveal information that could help solve one or more crimes. Provided Walt could hold on to his cover long enough and get back in Metwater's good graces after disobeying orders and coming here tonight. He was going to have to do some fast talking to do so, but maybe Metwater's desire to keep Hannah around would work in their favor. "I'll try to learn as much as I can," he said.

Graham walked with him to the door and shook his hand. "We'll be back in camp after we've searched the grave. We'll let you know what we find then."

"By that time, I hope Hannah and I are ready to leave. Everything in camp looks innocent enough, but something about the whole setup rubs me the wrong way. Metwater is up to something—we just haven't figured out what yet."

Chapter Ten

Hannah spent a restless night on a sofa on one side of the travel trailer Phoenix shared with her daughter Sophie and the baby. Worries over where Walt might be and what he might be doing competed with nightmares of Kiram or Daniel Metwater leering over her to prevent sleep. Had Walt made it safely to the road? What would the Rangers do with the information he gave them? Was the grave that of the missing young woman? Who had killed her and put her there? Had Kiram merely been trying to frighten her when he had grabbed her earlier, or had he really intended to hurt her? Had Emily suffered a similar fright, which had eventually led to her death?

She tried to distract herself by focusing on the baby. Little Vicki slept in a porta-crib next to Phoenix's bed, and Hannah could just see her from the sofa. The child slept peacefully, fist in her mouth, clad in a pink fleece sleeper. Hannah fought the urge to take the baby from the crib and cuddle her. But that would only awaken Phoenix and the baby and arouse suspicion. And it wouldn't really tell Hannah anything, only satisfy her longing to hold the child in her arms.

Phoenix awakened at dawn to tend to the baby.

Hannah sat up on the sofa, a blanket wrapped around her, and watched as the older woman prepared a bottle of formula. "Would you like to feed her while I get dressed?" Phoenix asked.

"Yes." Hannah held out her arms and took the child, who stared up at her with sleepy eyes. Vicki took the bottle readily and Hannah settled back to marvel at the baby's sweet perfection. Sophie got out of her bunk and came to sit beside her.

"She eats like a little piglet," the girl said, letting the baby latch on to her index finger.

"She's always had a healthy appetite." Phoenix emerged from her bedroom and joined them. "I'm grateful for that."

"Would you think I was terribly nosy if I asked about her father?" Hannah kept her eyes focused on the baby, though she braced herself for Phoenix's answer.

"The Prophet is her father," Phoenix said, unflustered by the question.

"Oh. I didn't know."

Phoenix removed the now-empty bottle from Vicki's mouth. "I'll take her now," she said, and raised the baby to her shoulder and began patting her back. "He's the father to all the children here," Phoenix said. "If not physically, then certainly spiritually."

Sophie made a face. "He's not my father," she said.

"Now, Sophie," her mother said.

Sophie turned to Hannah. "My father is a musician in San Francisco. But we don't see him much." She shrugged. "It's okay. He's kind of messed up."

"Sophie, why don't you run ahead to help Starfall and the others with breakfast," Phoenix said. "Serenity and I will be along soon."

"She doesn't like it when I talk about my dad," Sophie said, standing. "She and the Prophet are big into forgetting the past, but I don't see how anyone can really do that, do you?"

"Sophie!"

"I'm going." Grinning, the girl skipped from the trailer.

Phoenix settled onto the sofa beside Hannah. "I'm sorry about that," she said. "I guess Sophie is a little young to understand all the spiritual concepts the Prophet is trying to teach us."

"You mean, about forgetting the past."

"Maybe not forgetting." She laid the baby across her lap and began removing her diaper. "But putting it behind us. She and I made a fresh start when we came here. It's time to look forward, not backward." Her eyes met Hannah's. "We all have things in our past we would like to not dwell on."

"Yes. But the past shapes us," Hannah said. "We are who we are because of it."

"I would rather not remember the pain," Phoenix said. "I want to focus on the future." She fastened the baby's diaper and smiled down at the child. "Let's go to breakfast," she said.

"The Prophet said last night you were in charge of me," Hannah said as they made their way through camp toward the outdoor kitchen. "Does that mean you're my guard? Will you get in trouble if I leave?"

"Think of me as your companion." She hooked her arm in Hannah's. "I'm watching out for you and helping you. There's no need for you to be alone."

"My husband will be back soon," she said, resisting the urge to pull away from the other woman.

"He'll be assigned a companion, as well. The two of you will be kept apart until the council."

Hannah stopped. "Why?"

"It's for your own good," Phoenix said. "So that you can think more clearly, and so that you will be fairly judged separately and not as a single unit. His crimes don't have to reflect on you."

"Walt hasn't committed any crime," Hannah said. "He did the right thing, notifying the police about that grave."

Phoenix's gaze shifted away, and her mouth grew pinched. "Disobeying the Prophet is wrong," she said. "He has good reasons for all of his decisions. If you want to be a part of the Family, you need to realize that." She took Hannah's hand. "Come on. We'll be late for breakfast. You'll feel better after you eat."

Hannah tugged her hand free, but walked beside Phoenix to the cook tent. She left her with the other women and got in line for oatmeal and dried berries, then found a seat on a bench next to Sophie. "Did you and Mom have a fight about something?" Sophie asked.

"Your mother thinks my husband should be punished because he disobeyed the Prophet, even though he was doing the right thing," Hannah said.

"It's a big deal to disobey the Prophet," Sophie said. "It almost never happens."

"Who was the last person to break one of his rules?" Hannah asked.

Sophie dug into her bowl of oatmeal. "We're not supposed to talk about it."

"I didn't know the person, so what could it hurt?" Hannah said. "Maybe by telling me who they were and what they did, you could help me not to make the same mistake."

Sophie considered this. "It was a girl called Freedom. Well, that's what the Prophet called her. I don't think it was her real name."

"What did she do that was so wrong?" Hannah asked.

"She wanted to run away."

Hannah set aside her own spoon, a cold hollow in the pit of her stomach. "I thought anyone was free to leave here whenever he or she chose."

"Most people are. But Freedom had a baby, and all children belong to the Prophet. So she could have left, but she would have had to leave her baby behind."

"No mother would do that," Hannah said.

Sophie shrugged. "I guess she wanted to leave badly enough that she did."

Hannah stared at the girl for a moment, letting this information sink in. "You mean, she left the Family, and didn't take her baby with her?"

Sophie ducked her head. "I shouldn't have said anything. Please don't tell Mom. I'll get in trouble."

"I won't tell her, I promise." Hannah covered the child's hand with her own and lowered her voice to a whisper. "That's why you have Vicki, isn't it?" she asked. "She was Freedom's baby."

Sophie nodded. "Please don't tell."

Hannah squeezed her hand. "I won't. I promise." Freedom must have been Emily. Vicki—Victory—was Joy. And she belonged to Hannah now. Not Phoenix or the Prophet or anyone else.

WALT HALF EXPECTED to be met in the parking area outside the camp by Kiram and a crowd of angry Family members, but the lot was vacant, only the chattering of a scolding squirrel greeting him. He parked the bike, covered it with the branches he had cut earlier and crossed the bridge into camp. Jobie met him at the other side, a staff in one hand, a breakfast burrito in the other. "Hey," he said by way of greeting. "You missed all the excitement with your wife and Kiram last night."

Walt froze, one hand automatically reaching for the service weapon that wasn't at his side. "What happened with Hannah and Kiram?" he asked, his mind racing. If that thug had hurt Hannah…

"She says he was manhandling her and she called him on it and made a big fuss in front of the Prophet and everyone." He took a bite of his breakfast and chewed.

"Was he hurting her?" Walt asked. "And why?"

"He said she needed to be punished because the two of you were disobeying the Prophet's orders." He shrugged. "One of his jobs is to keep people in line, but he has a rep for taking things too far. A couple of other women have complained, but I guess the Prophet has let him get away with it until now. No way he could ignore the stink your wife was making last night, though."

Good for Hannah, Walt thought. "What did the Prophet do?"

"He sent Serenity off to stay with Phoenix and told Kiram to leave her alone. There's going to be a special council tonight to decide what your punishment should be for breaking the rules and leaving camp to go to the police."

Let them try to lay a hand on him or Hannah and see

how far they got. Walt started to push past Jobie. "Her name isn't Serenity, it's Hannah, and I need to see her."

Jobie tried to block him and Walt raised his fist, as if to take a swing. Jobie took a step back. "Hey, chill, dude! I was just going to tell you it's a good idea to play it cool. Kiram is still really ticked about being called out in front of the whole camp, so it would be smart to steer clear of him until tonight."

What he wanted was to confront Kiram right now and maybe pound his face for laying a hand on Hannah, but doing so would be letting emotion take the lead instead of using common sense. "What happens at these council meetings?" he asked.

"The Prophet usually gives a talk, then each side gets to present their case, then the Prophet makes a ruling." He shrugged. "He'll probably just have everyone involved do some kind of community service like pick up trash or build a new shelter. It's no big deal."

"Where is Hannah now?"

"She's eating breakfast with Phoenix and Sophie. She's fine."

"I still want to see her." He started forward once more and this time Jobie stepped aside to let him pass.

Conversation stopped abruptly when Walt walked into the open-sided shed that served as the Family's dining hall. Kiram looked up from his seat at the end of one of the long wooden picnic tables and glared at Walt, but remained silent. Everyone else stared, some openmouthed with avid curiosity, others avoiding his gaze, clearly fearful. Walt spotted Hannah, sitting next to a young girl, and started toward her. She rose to meet him and, without speaking, he took her arm and led her away from the shelter.

The murmur of conversation rose again behind them. Hannah gripped his arm. "How did it go?" she asked. "Are the Rangers on their way?"

"They're sending a team out to investigate the grave, then they'll want to question Metwater and others in the camp."

"That won't go over well," she said, glancing back toward the tables. Kiram had moved from his seat and stood at the edge of the shelter, watching them.

"They need to explain why they lied about Lucia Raton having been in camp," Walt said. "And why Metwater was so insistent I not report the grave to law enforcement."

"Some of the people here feel the police are invading their privacy with all their questions."

"It's our job to invade people's privacy, if that's what it takes to solve a crime."

"I know." She patted his arm. "But I see their point, too. Not wanting the police here doesn't make them guilty of anything."

"Maybe not. But lying is almost always suspicious." He smoothed his hand down her arm and she winced. "What's wrong?" he asked, immediately tensed. "Are you hurt?"

"Just a little bruised where Kiram grabbed me." She rubbed the arm. "He caught me walking back toward our tent after you left last night."

"Jobie told me you called him out in front of a crowd and that Metwater ordered him to leave you alone."

"Yes. Kiram says he was acting on Metwater's authority, but I'm not so sure. I think he's just a bully." She glanced over her shoulder at the glowering young man. "I'm probably his least favorite person right now."

"He's my least favorite person, so that makes us even." He glared at Kiram. The man was going to be trouble, but Walt would wait to deal with him. He turned back to Hannah. "You're sure you're all right?"

"Yes." She took his arm and led him farther away from the crowd. "Better than all right," she said. "Phoenix's daughter, Sophie, admitted this morning that the baby isn't her mother's. She belonged to a Family member who called herself Freedom. I'm sure she means Emily."

"How did Phoenix end up with the baby?"

"Sophie said the mother, Freedom, wanted to run away. The Prophet said she could leave, but she would have to leave her baby behind, because all children belong to him or some such nonsense." She frowned. "Phoenix told me Metwater was the baby's father, but I know that isn't right. But apparently, he claims to be the father of all the children in the camp, whether he actually is or not."

"So what happened when he told her she could leave but he would keep her baby?" Walt asked.

"Sophie said Freedom left anyway, and Phoenix was given the baby to care for. But I know Emily wouldn't have left the baby behind. Not voluntarily."

"It sounds as if Sophie doesn't know Emily—if Freedom really is Emily—is dead," Walt said. "Maybe she wasn't told because she's still a child."

"Or maybe no one was told because Metwater didn't want anyone to know about his involvement in her death. Emily died in Denver, when the Family was already living here on park land. It would have been easy enough to bring the baby back from Denver after Emily died and tell everyone the mother had abandoned her."

"Maybe Emily left, intending to come back, and died before she could," he said.

"Emily would never have abandoned her baby. Never." Hannah's voice shook and she sounded on the verge of tears.

Walt took her by the shoulders. "It's okay," he said. "Keep talking with Phoenix and Sophie and see what else you can learn. There's still a chance the baby belongs to some other woman and not your sister."

"Vicki is Emily's baby, I know it." She clutched his arm. "Why can't we just take the baby and leave now? The DNA tests will prove I'm right."

"We need to stay as long as we can and learn as much as we can," he said. "We may never have a better opportunity to find out not just what happened to your sister, but to Lucia Raton."

She looked stubborn and Walt braced himself for her arguments. He was prepared to tell her that she could leave with the investigative team when they showed up to question Family members about Lucia, but that he needed to stay behind to gather more information. While Hannah had a court order granting her temporary custody of her sister's child, they needed a positive identification of the baby before Hannah could take her. And as long as Daniel Metwater claimed to be the child's father, and his name was on the birth certificate, he could fight Hannah in court to regain custody of the baby.

Hannah changed the subject. "There's supposed to be some kind of meeting this evening to decide our fate," she said. "I'm guessing after the cops descend on camp, everyone will vote to throw us out."

"They might," he said. "We'll have to work hard to persuade them that we're sincere."

"Do you really think the grave you found belongs to that poor girl?"

"I don't know. We'll have to wait and see."

"I've never been very good at waiting," she said. "I've always been the type to make a decision quickly and follow through." She stared at the ground between their feet. "That hasn't always worked out well for me."

"I'm more deliberate, but that doesn't mean the decisions I've made have always been the right ones," he said.

"Serenity!"

They looked up to see Phoenix hurrying toward them, a worried expression on her face. "Is something wrong?" Hannah asked. "Is Vicki okay?"

"We're fine." She stopped in front of them, a little out of breath. Up close, Walt noted the fine lines at the corners of her eyes and the deep furrow between her eyes. Hannah was right—Phoenix did look closer to forty than thirty—older than the majority of Metwater's followers. How had she ended up with the group? "You need to come with me now," Phoenix said to Hannah. "I'm supposed to watch over you until the meeting tonight."

"Surely the Prophet won't be upset about me talking with my husband," Hannah said.

"Sometimes when two people talk together a lot, away from the group, it can look like they're plotting," Phoenix said. "It sets a bad example."

"Is that one of the lessons the Prophet teaches?" Walt asked.

Phoenix glanced at him. "The Prophet teaches many

lessons," she said. "Some of them have saved my life." She took Hannah's hand and laced her fingers with the younger woman's. "Let's go. You said before you enjoy working with children. You can help me with that job this morning."

She started to lead Hannah away. "What about me?" Walt called. "What am I supposed to do until the council this evening?"

Phoenix looked over her shoulder at him. "Someone else has been assigned to watch over you," she said, then ducked her head and hurried away.

Walt heard heavy footsteps behind him. He tensed, prepared to defend himself if necessary. The new arrival said nothing.

"Kiram, I've got a score to settle with you," Walt said, turning around.

"If I ever catch you away from camp, believe me, we'll settle that score," Kiram said. "For now, you're to come with me."

"What if I refuse?" Walt asked.

"I'd be fine with you leaving camp right this minute," Kiram said. "But the Prophet wants to see you. He has a proposal for you—one you ought to listen to."

"The Prophet wants something from me?" Walt asked. That was a new twist. "What is it?"

"Come with me and find out. I'm hoping he wants me to take you out and beat you to a pulp, but then, I seldom get so lucky."

Chapter Eleven

"Where is Kiram taking Walt?" Hannah tried to pull away from Phoenix when she saw Kiram lead Walt away.

"Your husband will be all right." Phoenix was stronger than she looked and almost yanked Hannah off her feet. "You'll see him tonight, after the council. In the meantime, you can help me with the children. That's our job for the day."

"This isn't right," Hannah said, reluctantly falling into step beside Phoenix. "We shouldn't be separated like this."

"It's for your own good," Phoenix said. "After all, you have to think for yourself, even though you're married. And remember—whatever punishment the Prophet decides for you, it will make you a better person in the end."

"Have you ever been punished by the Prophet?" Hannah asked.

"When I first came here, yes. But I needed to learn an important lesson, and I was grateful for it later."

"What did you do that you needed to be punished for?" Hannah asked. The older woman looked so serene and devoted to Metwater. Hannah couldn't imagine she had ever done anything to displease him.

"That is all in the past and we don't talk about the past," she said. "Come, let's get the children. You'll feel better when you're with them."

Sophie was waiting with the other children, and a duffel bag filled with balls and stuffed animals and other toys. While Sophie and her mother organized the children into play groups, Hannah took charge of Vicki. She was an easygoing baby, seldom fussy, happy to be held and admired.

"You're so good with her," Phoenix said, coming to sit at the picnic table beside Hannah. "Do you have children?"

Hannah couldn't hold back the gasp that escaped her. "Wh-why would you ask that?" she stammered. "If I had children, they'd be here with me."

"Not necessarily. They might be with their father, or a grandparent. Not every child lives with her mother. Sometimes that isn't even the best thing."

Hannah clutched the baby more tightly. "No, I don't have any children." It wasn't a lie. Not really.

"Sophie lived with my parents for a while," she said, her expression calm as she watched her daughter. "I wasn't able to take care of her, so I signed over custody to them. One of the best things about coming here is that she's able to be with me again."

Were Phoenix's parents really happy that she was living in a trailer in the middle of nowhere, following a self-proclaimed prophet? Hannah wondered. Then again, maybe Phoenix's folks were in poor health, or simply tired of taking care of the child. It wasn't Hannah's place to judge. "She seems very happy here," she said.

"She doesn't like the Prophet, but I hope in time she'll understand his wisdom."

"Do you really think he's wise?" Hannah asked.

She smiled serenely. Or was her serenity merely a kind of naïveté? "The Prophet saved my life. I owe him everything. Apollo, what is that in your mouth? We don't eat bugs." She jumped up and hurried to persuade the little boy to spit out his find. Hannah cradled the baby and studied the other woman. Surely she didn't mean that Daniel Metwater had literally saved her—rescuing her from drowning or pulling her from a burning car? Following the Prophet had clearly sent Phoenix's life in another direction—away from a bad situation or wrong choices?

Phoenix returned. "How long have you and your husband been married?" she asked.

"Not long. A few months." Hannah hoped her response sounded natural. She wasn't used to lying, though she agreed that in this case, it was necessary.

"I thought about marriage a couple of times, but it never happened," Phoenix said. "Just as well, since I never stayed with any man very long." She laughed. "Good thing, or I wouldn't have met the Prophet."

"Are you and he, well, lovers?" Hadn't Phoenix hinted as much, when she said Metwater was the baby's father? Or had she said that because she believed Emily and Metwater had been a couple?

Phoenix's smile struck Hannah as a little smug. "I've enjoyed the Prophet's attentions from time to time," she said. "He tries to spend special time with each of his female followers—it's really a privilege." She patted Hannah's arm. "I'm sure your turn will come."

Hannah shuddered. She had no intention of enjoying any such "attention" from Metwater. "I doubt my husband would appreciate that."

"Oh, he'll come around in time. After all, marriage is such an outmoded concept."

Hannah recognized Metwater's words. "I think two people pledging to love each other and care for each other for the rest of their lives is timeless," she said. "An ideal that never goes out of style."

Phoenix wrinkled her nose. "But how many people actually live up to that ideal?"

"A lot whom I know," Hannah said.

"And no one I know."

Before Hannah could come up with a suitable answer, the baby began fussing. Hannah shifted and tried to comfort the infant, but her fussing soon grew to wails. "Let me take her." Phoenix reached for the baby. "Maybe she needs changing."

As she took the child, one sleeve of her loose peasant blouse pushed up, revealing several lines of thin, dark scars on her forearms. "What happened to your arm?" Hannah asked.

Phoenix flushed and quickly yanked the sleeve down and cradled the child. "It's nothing. I'll go get a fresh diaper," she said, already heading toward the trailer. "You watch the children."

A chill swept through Hannah, as if someone had opened a door that should have been left closed. She wished she was home, with Joy safe and the future not so uncertain. There were too many secrets in this particular family.

"I WANT TO know what you told the police."

Daniel Metwater didn't waste any time getting to the point when he hauled Walt in front of him. At least the Prophet was fully dressed today, in faded jeans and a white button-down with the sleeves rolled up. He sat in an upholstered chair in the living room of the RV like a man on a throne. Walt still thought he looked out of place here in the backcountry—like the kind of man who, instead of taking a five-mile hike to see the sights, would order a flunky to take the hike for him and report back.

"Why do you want to know?" Walt asked.

"Lose the attitude," Kiram said, and punched Walt in the shoulder.

Walt turned on him. "Hit me again and you'll be sorry," he said. "You can't shove me around the way you did my wife."

"Leave us, Kiram," Metwater said.

Kiram's face reddened and he worked his mouth as if trying to come up with a response. But when Metwater fixed him with a stare, the bearded man bowed his head and stormed out. Walt waited until the door closed behind him before he spoke. "Hannah has bruises on her arms where Kiram roughed her up last night," he said. "I'm not going to stand for that." He had every intention of filing assault charges against Kiram, though he hadn't discussed it with Hannah yet.

"Kiram can be a little intense in his zeal to protect the Family—and to protect me," Metwater said.

"He's a bully. If you don't rein him in, I will."

"I can take care of Kiram."

"Keep him away from me—and away from Hannah."

Metwater hesitated. Walt was sure he was going to say something about Walt needing a minder until tonight's council meeting, but after a tense few seconds, he relented. "I'll tell him to stay away."

"See that he does."

"I didn't bring you here to talk about Kiram. I want to know what you told the police."

"I told them the truth," Walt said. "That I was out looking for firewood and found what appeared to be a fairly fresh grave. They agreed it was worth checking out, especially with a young woman missing."

"No one in this camp had anything to do with that unfortunate young woman's disappearance," Metwater said.

"I've learned she was here in the camp, yet you lied when the Rangers asked if you had seen her before."

"Who told you that?" Metwater demanded.

Walt leaned against the wall that separated the RV's living area from the rest of the space, arms crossed in a deliberately casual, some might have said disrespectful, pose. "Why does it matter if it's true?" he countered.

"Because of you, officers will be disrupting our lives with their questions," Metwater said.

"No. They'll be doing that because you lied to them and tried to conceal what could be evidence of a crime. Guilty people behave that way."

"Or people who value their privacy," Metwater said.

"Sometimes it's the same thing." Walt had to force himself not to smirk. He was enjoying this too much.

"When the Rangers arrive, I want you to talk to them," Metwater said.

Walt hadn't seen this coming. "Why me?"

"Since you're the one who went to them, they'll be

more likely to trust you. Tell them we had nothing to do with the grave you found or the woman who disappeared."

Walt straightened. "You tell them. I'm not your official spokesperson."

"I have more important things to do than waste time talking with the police," Metwater said.

"Such as?" Walt looked around the trailer. "Writing blog posts and preaching sermons can't take that much of your time."

Metwater stood and moved closer to Walt. They were about the same height, and had no trouble looking each other in the eye. "Why did you come here?" Metwater asked. "I don't believe it was because you want to be one of us. You have no respect for our way of life."

Sticking to his cover required Walt to lie and pretend to be a fan of Metwater and his philosophy, but after the better part of two days in camp, he didn't have the stomach for it. As long as he didn't reveal he was a law enforcement officer, sticking closer to the truth should be safe. And it might even nudge Metwater into revealing something useful. "I came here looking for a friend," he said. "She disappeared a while back and her family is worried about her."

Metwater lifted one eyebrow. "Lucia Raton is a friend of yours?"

"Not her. I'm looking for Emily Dietrich."

"Your wife's friend from school." Metwater nodded. "You think she was one of my followers?"

"She was pregnant. Her fiancé was killed and she became one of your followers. She was living with your followers the last time her sister heard from her."

"Her sister, your wife."

Walt didn't let himself react. "Why do you say that?" he asked.

"The resemblance is there."

"So you do know Emily?"

"I knew her. But she was only with us a short time."

"What about her baby?"

Metwater turned away. "I can't help you there."

"Can't—or won't?"

"You may leave now," Metwater said. "I'll see you at the council tonight."

"Tell me what happened to Emily Dietrich," Walt said.

Metwater sat and looked up at Walt, his expression calm. "I can't tell you what I don't know," he said.

Walt wanted to grab the man and shake him. But all that would probably achieve was a beating by Kiram and friends, and possible assault charges himself. "I'm going to keep asking questions," he said. "I'm going to find answers."

"I can't stop you," Metwater said. "But you might not like the answers you find. Sometimes it's wisest to let the dead rest in peace."

"What makes you say she's dead?" Walt demanded. "You do know something, don't you?"

Metwater's gaze shifted away and he waved his hand dismissively. "I was using a common figure of speech. If I said 'let sleeping dogs lie' you wouldn't think I was calling your friend a dog, would you?"

"I'm not buying it," Walt said. "You know something, and I'm going to find out what it is."

"Don't waste any more of my time." Metwater left the room. Walt stared after him. The Prophet was going to be on guard now that he knew he was being watched, but that wouldn't keep Walt from finding out the truth.

When Walt emerged from the trailer, Hannah was waiting for him—along with Kiram. Walt ignored the bodyguard and addressed Hannah. "I thought you were with Phoenix." Before she could answer, Kiram stepped between them. "You aren't supposed to be together until the council meeting tonight," he said.

Walt studied the other man for a long moment. Kiram was clearly devoted to Metwater and his rules, but if the two of them hung around much longer he had no doubt one of them was going to lose his temper. "The Prophet has decided I'll be okay on my own." He nodded toward the door of the motor home. "If you don't believe me, go ask him."

Kiram looked from Walt to the motor home and back again. "You're trying to trick me."

"No trick," Walt said. "Go on and ask him. It's not as if you can't find me easily enough if it turns out I'm lying."

Kiram glared at Walt, then stormed up the steps and knocked. After a moment, he was admitted. Walt took Hannah's arm. "Let's get out of here," he said.

Hannah pulled him around behind the RV, out of sight of the rest of the camp. "When Phoenix went inside her trailer to get a diaper for Vicki, I walked away," she said. "I was getting worried about you. What did Metwater want?"

"He wanted to know what I told the police. And he wanted to know why we're here," he said. "He wasn't convinced we're true believers."

"What did you tell him?"

"The truth—or part of it. I told him we came here looking for Emily."

All the color left her cheeks and she released her hold on him. "What did he say?"

"He said she was here for a short time, but he didn't know what happened to her—or to her baby."

"Do you believe him?"

"Do you?"

"No." She glanced around, then pulled him farther into the woods, away from the campsite. "I think the people here are lying to us about a lot of things," she said. "And some of the things that might be the truth make me very uneasy. I think we should take the baby and get out of here as soon as possible."

She was still pale, and her hands shook as she smoothed back her hair. "What's got you so upset?" he asked.

"Phoenix told me Metwater has slept with most of the women here. She said she'd slept with him—that it was an honor. She said my turn would come—it doesn't matter that I'm married. Or, you know, that he thinks I'm married."

He smoothed his hand down her arm, trying to comfort her. "I'm not going to let him hurt you," he said.

"I won't be alone with him again," she said.

"Agreed. What else did Phoenix tell you? Did you learn anything more about Emily or Joy?"

She shook her head. "She only talked about the Prophet, and how he changed her life. And she said she had to give custody of Sophie to her parents for a while, but joining up with the Family made it possible for her to have Sophie with her again. But that didn't make a lot of sense to me. Would grandparents really turn over their granddaughter to live with a wandering bunch of modern-day hippies?"

"Maybe they would if they thought it was best for Sophie and for Phoenix."

"There's something else that's bothering me. Not anything Phoenix said, but something I saw."

"What is it?"

"You know how she always wears long sleeves?"

"I hadn't noticed."

"I had. All the other women wear tank tops or short sleeves—it can get pretty warm here during the day, especially in the kitchen. But Phoenix always stays covered up to her wrists. But this morning, when she reached for the baby, her sleeve pushed up and I saw that she has scars." She traced a line on the back of her arm, from elbow to wrist. "Thin lines. I wondered— could it be from drugs?"

"Maybe," Walt said. "Have you noticed any signs that she's using now?"

"No. I don't think she is. She says Daniel Metwater saved her life—do you think he means he helped her get off drugs?"

"I don't know."

She looked back toward the camp. "I don't like it here, and I can't shake the feeling there's a lot going on we don't know about. But maybe it's also possible that Metwater is doing some good, at least for some people."

"I guess no one is all good or all bad, but I still don't trust him."

"When can we leave and take Joy with us?"

"Soon," he said. "When the Rangers get here, I'm going to request a court order for us to take the baby into temporary custody, until a DNA test confirms her identity."

"Will they be able to get it?"

"I think so. In the meantime, I'd rather stay here to make sure they don't try to leave with her."

"I won't let them take her away," Hannah said. "When will you hear from the Rangers again?"

"They can't open up the grave until a forensic anthropologist can be on site. That might take a day or two. They'll want to see what's in there before they question anyone in the camp."

"In the meantime, we've got this council tonight," she said. "What do you think they'll do?"

"I think they'll make a lot of noise and try to scare us," he said. "Just remember they don't have any authority over us."

"That doesn't mean they won't try to hurt us—that they didn't hurt Emily, or Lucia."

"Serenity!" Phoenix raced up to them, her face flushed and out of breath. "There you are," she said, gasping. "I thought you had run away."

"I had to see Walt," Hannah said.

Phoenix glanced at him, then took both Hannah's hands in hers. "You shouldn't keep breaking the rules," the older woman said. "It will only go against you at council tonight."

Hannah pulled her hands free. "I won't blindly obey arbitrary rules that don't make sense," she said.

"Without rules, there's only chaos," Phoenix said.

"But rules have to have a larger purpose than merely controlling people," Walt said.

Phoenix shook her head and grabbed Hannah's

hands again. "Please come back with me," she said. "Or I could get into trouble."

This time, Hannah didn't pull away. "All right," she said. "But Walt has to come with me."

"Where's Kiram?" Phoenix asked. She looked around as if she expected the bearded young man to pop out from behind a tree.

"The Prophet and I talked and he agreed I didn't need a babysitter." Walt put his arm around Hannah again. "Hannah and I can stay with you this afternoon," he said. "And we'll try to keep out of trouble."

"Tell me another one," Phoenix said. "Men like you have trouble written all over them."

She turned and started walking away. Walt and Hannah followed. Hannah leaned in close. "She's right," she whispered. "You do look like a man who wouldn't shy away from trouble."

"Is that such a bad thing?" he asked.

"Oh, not at all." She squeezed his arm. "I'm beginning to think it's a very good thing."

THEY RETURNED TO Phoenix's trailer, where Sophie sat at the small table, surrounded by books, and Vicki played on a quilt on the floor. Hannah moved past Phoenix to scoop the baby up from the floor. "This is Vicki," she said, turning to Walt.

"Hey there, cutie." A huge grin split his face and before she could protest, he was lifting the baby from her arms and cradling her against him. Vicki stared up at him in wonder, then reached up one chubby hand to pat his cheek. "What do you think, little one?" he asked. "Do I look like trouble to you?"

Hannah's stomach quivered and her knees felt unsteady. The sight of this tough, rugged man being so tender with the baby stirred her emotions. Walt was trouble all right—a big disruption to the smooth path she had laid out for herself. She needed to focus on getting Joy safely home and building a stable life for the two of them. She didn't see how she could do that without Walt's help. But it had been so easy to move from wanting his help to wanting more.

"What are you studying?" Walt asked. Still cradling Vicki, he had moved over to the table and was looking down on the books scattered around Sophie.

"It's my homeschool correspondence course," she said. "It's supposed to be Introduction to Algebra, but I'm all confused."

"Maybe I can help." He leaned over her. "What are you having problems with?"

"You definitely need to have children soon." Phoenix moved to Hannah's side. "He's great with them."

"Yeah, he is." Judging from Sophie's smiles, his explanation of algebra was helping her, and Vicki seemed more than content to gaze up at him and gnaw on his thumb.

"Tell me about Vicki's mother," Hannah said, hoping she wasn't making a mistake asking the question.

Phoenix stiffened. "I'm Victory's mother."

Hannah squeezed the other woman's hand. "You've done a wonderful job of caring for her, but I heard her birth mother was a young woman who called herself Freedom."

"Who told you that?" Phoenix looked toward the table, where Walt now sat beside Sophie.

"In a camp this small, there are no secrets," Hannah

said. "Someone told me that when we first came here. What can you tell me about Freedom?"

"She was a troubled young woman who was looking for peace," Phoenix said. "She hoped to find it here, but she had a hard time obeying the rules." She sighed. "She was a lot like you in that respect—always wanting reasons, not willing to simply be and accept."

"You really think she was like me?" Hannah had focused so long on the differences between her and her sister that she hadn't considered all the ways they might be alike.

"She wasn't as lucky as you in love." Phoenix's gaze shifted to Walt. "She said the man she had been engaged to marry was killed. She needed the love of a family to surround her and her baby, and she hoped to find that here."

"What about her own family?" Hannah's voice was strained from the tears she was fighting to hold back.

"She never talked about them. Sometimes it's easier to turn to strangers than to family—families know all your mistakes, and that can make them harder to put behind you."

And you know all your family's mistakes, which can be harder to forgive, Hannah thought. She recalled the last argument she had had with Emily, before her sister left to join Metwater's group.

She pushed the painful memory away. "What happened to Freedom?" she asked.

"She left us. It was for the best, since she wasn't happy here."

"But how could she leave her baby behind?" Hannah asked.

"I don't know," Phoenix said. "It struck me as out

of character, but when people are desperately unhappy, they don't always act like themselves."

"Mind if I join you?" Walt returned to the living area.

"We were just talking about Freedom," Hannah said.

Phoenix frowned. "You told him?" she asked Hannah.

"He's my husband. Of course I told him." How easily the lie flowed off her lips. The longer she was with Walt, the easier it was to imagine him as her partner—which was crazy, considering how little time she had known him. Being thrown together like this, with the underlying current of danger, was obviously getting to her.

"What happened the day Freedom left?" Walt asked.

"She went with the Prophet to Denver," Phoenix said. "He was speaking there and he asked her to go along. He wanted to spend more time with her, to try to persuade her to stay with the Family."

"I thought he had told her she should leave," Hannah said. "That he was punishing her for wanting to run away."

Phoenix nibbled her thumbnail. "Well, yes, he had told her that, but he wanted to give her one more chance. He thought the trip to Denver, just the two of them, would help him persuade her to stay."

"She didn't take the baby with her?" Hannah asked.

"No. She left Victory with me." She took the child from Walt, who didn't protest. "I've taken care of her practically since she was born."

"Did the Prophet say what happened while they were in Denver?" Walt asked.

Phoenix smoothed the baby's curls. "He said Freedom decided to stay in the city and he came back without her."

"That didn't strike you as odd?" Walt asked. "That she didn't come back for her baby?"

"I thought she would, at first," Phoenix said. "But then…" She shrugged. "The Prophet said her mind was made up and he wasn't able to stop her from leaving. He doesn't keep people here against their will."

"So he would have been fine if she had taken Vicki with her when she left?" Hannah asked.

Phoenix stood. "I think the baby needs changing," she said, and disappeared into the back room before they could protest.

"Mom says the Prophet would have changed his mind about making Freedom leave her baby behind if she had come back for Victory." Sophie looked up from her books. "She refuses to believe he would ever do anything cruel."

"What do you think?" Walt turned to look at the girl.

She shrugged and doodled in the corner of her notebook. "I think people do cruel things all the time. Why should he be different?"

A knock on the door interrupted them. Hannah looked toward the back of the trailer, but Phoenix didn't emerge. The knocking persisted.

"I'll get it," Sophie said, but Walt got to the door before her.

He opened it and Agent Marco Cruz moved past him into the room. "I'm looking for a woman named Phoenix," he said. "We have questions for her related to the disappearance of Lucia Raton."

Chapter Twelve

Walt bit the inside of his cheek to keep from blurting out the questions Marco's announcement brought to mind. Of all the suspects Walt might have singled out as having something to do with Lucia's disappearance, Phoenix wouldn't have even made the list.

At Marco's words Phoenix emerged from the back bedroom, her face even paler than usual. She took one look at the officers, then thrust the baby into Hannah's arms and bolted for the door, but Michael Dance stepped in behind Marco and caught her. "Calm down, ma'am," he said, leading her back to the sofa. "We just need to ask you some questions."

"What is this about?" Sophie had moved from her place at the table and stood behind the two officers, eyes wide with fear.

"Hannah, maybe you should take Sophie and the baby and wait for Phoenix outside," Walt said.

"No." Hannah cradled the infant to her shoulder and beckoned Sophie to her side. "I won't leave Phoenix alone with three strange men." She glared at Walt, as if she blamed him for this turn of events. "Can't you see she's terrified?"

"Why don't we all sit down?" Marco moved farther

into the room, while Michael stayed by the door. Phoenix wrapped her arms across her stomach, as if trying to make herself as small as possible. "Ma'am, do you want your friends to leave?" Marco asked.

Phoenix raised her head to look at Hannah. "I want Hannah to stay," she said.

"If Hannah stays, so do I." Walt crossed his arms over his chest.

"I'll take the baby," Sophie said. She reached for the infant and Hannah surrendered her. Then Sophie turned and fled from the trailer, shoving past Michael and slamming the door behind her.

Marco brought a chair from the table and set it in front of the sofa where Phoenix and Hannah now sat next to each other.

"What is this about?" Hannah asked. "Are you charging her with some crime?"

Walt frowned at her and shook his head. She needed to be quiet and let the Rangers do their job. But she looked away from him.

"Ma'am, before we start, I need to know your real name," Marco said.

"My name is Phoenix."

"That isn't the name you were born with," Marco said.

She glared at him. "Phoenix is my name."

Marco consulted his phone. "But weren't you born Anna Ingels?"

Hannah gasped. Walt recognized the name, too— Anna Ingels was the other witness on Emily Dietrich's will.

"Anna is dead," Phoenix said. "I left her behind when I came here."

Marco took something from his shirt pocket and

handed it to her. "Isn't this your driver's license?" he asked. "The picture is yours and the name is Anna Ingels."

Walt leaned over to peer at the picture, which did indeed look like Phoenix. It was a Colorado license, showing an address in Denver, with an expiration date two years from now.

Phoenix clutched the license. "Where did you get this?" she asked.

"Our forensics team found it, along with some other items belonging to you, in a grave in the woods not far from here," Marco said.

Walt sent his fellow agent a sharp look. *What else did you find in that grave?* he wanted to ask, but knew he would have to wait for the answer.

Phoenix bowed her head. Hannah put her arm around the older woman and rubbed her shoulder.

"Why don't you tell us how your license ended up in that grave?" Marco said, his tone gentle.

"I buried the license, along with some clothes and books and other things," Phoenix said. "Anna's things. Part of my old life. I have a new life now. I'm a new person. I didn't need those reminders of what I used to be."

"What did you used to be?" Marco asked.

She raised her head to meet his gaze, her face a picture of misery. "I'm not that person anymore. The Prophet saved me. He changed me. I don't have to think about that life anymore," she said.

"We ran your license," Marco said. "You have a criminal record for possession of heroin and prostitution."

That explained the tracks on her arm, Walt thought.

And maybe why she had lost custody of Sophie temporarily.

"That was Anna. It wasn't me. I'm not like that anymore."

"There's no crime in starting over," Hannah said. "And no crime in burying some old clothes and papers."

Marco ignored her and leaned toward Phoenix. "When did you bury those things?" he asked.

"A couple of weeks ago," she said. "The Prophet had a vision that we should divest ourselves of anything from the past that was holding us back. Some people burned items, or boxed them up and mailed them to their families. I held a funeral to say goodbye to my old self, and buried everything that belonged to Anna." She smiled and the light returned to her eyes. "It was wonderful—like being reborn. I truly was a Phoenix, rising from the ashes of my former self."

"Tell us about Lucia Raton," Marco said. "When did she come to the camp?"

Phoenix sighed. "The Prophet said we shouldn't talk about Lucia. Especially not to the police."

"Lucia is missing," Marco said. "She could be dead. I need you to tell me about her. When was she in camp?"

The lines on Phoenix's forehead deepened. "I don't know. We don't keep track of time here." She looked around the trailer. "I don't even have a calendar."

"Guess. How long ago was she here?"

She considered the question a moment longer. The sound of someone laughing somewhere outside drifted through the open window, along with hammering—ordinary sounds of life in the camp in sharp contrast to the surreal atmosphere inside the trailer. "I buried Anna's things when the moon was full," she said. "Lucia was here a few days after that—maybe a week."

Marco typed the information into his phone. "How long was she here?" he asked.

"Only a day. Less than that, really. She didn't spend the night."

"You're sure about that?" Marco asked.

"I'm sure. The Prophet told her she had to leave because she was underage. She was only seventeen." Her expression grew troubled. "I hope she's okay. She seemed like a sweet girl—a little defiant and confused, but that's part of what being a teenager is about, isn't it?"

"Did you spend a lot of time with her while she was here?" Marco asked.

"No. She came around and introduced herself to me and some other women who were preparing dinner, but we didn't really talk."

Marco took something from his shirt pocket and held it out to her. It was a plastic evidence bag that contained a necklace—a locket on a blackened silver chain. "Do you recognize this?" he asked.

Phoenix shook her head. "It doesn't look familiar."

Marco pressed a catch on the side of the locket and it opened to reveal a photograph of a man and woman. "Who is that?" Phoenix asked.

"Read the inscription," Marco said.

She leaned closer and read. "'To Lucia. We love you. Mami and Papi.'"

"So the locket belongs to Lucia Raton?" Hannah asked.

"Her parents described it when they listed the things

she was wearing the last time they saw her." Marco returned the evidence bag to his pocket. "Are you sure you don't remember it?"

Phoenix shook her head. "No. I only saw her for a few minutes."

"Was she with anyone else when she came here?" Michael Dance spoke for the first time from his position by the door. "Was there anyone she hung out with while she was here?"

"Not really." Walt sensed her hesitation; Marco must have, too.

"What is it?" Marco asked. "Was there someone she spent time with here?"

"Easy offered to give her a ride back into town," she said.

"Who is Easy?" Hannah asked before either of the officers could speak. "I haven't met anyone here by that name."

"He's not a member of the Family," Phoenix said. "He just visits sometimes. He delivers groceries or gives people rides if they need to go somewhere and don't have their own car. Sometimes he runs errands for the Prophet."

"What kind of errands?" Walt hadn't meant to speak, but he couldn't keep the question back.

Phoenix shrugged. "I don't know. He buys stuff he needs or takes him to the airport when he flies somewhere to give a talk."

"When was the last time you saw Easy?" Marco asked.

"A few days ago. I don't remember." She shifted. "What does any of this have to do with me? I'm sorry the girl is missing, but I can't help you."

She looked up as the door to the trailer opened. Michael whirled to face the newcomer, one hand on the duty weapon at his side. Daniel Metwater stepped into the trailer. His hair was wet and he smelled of soap. He wore the same loose linen trousers he usually favored, and a flowing tunic of the same white linen. Walt thought of it as his official Prophet uniform. "What is going on here?" Metwater demanded, taking in the scene.

Marco stood and faced the newcomer. The door was still open and Sophie, carrying the baby, slipped past the officers and joined her mother on the sofa. The girl must have summoned the Prophet to help her mother. Kiram followed her, taking his place behind Metwater, his expression sullen, as usual. The small trailer was too crowded, and the air fairly crackled with tension. Walt thought of the gun in his ankle holster and hoped he wouldn't have to use it. He took a step closer to Hannah, prepared to shove her to the floor if bullets started flying.

"We're investigating the disappearance of a young woman who visited your camp shortly before she disappeared," Marco said.

"We had nothing to do with that," Metwater said.

"Why did you lie to us about having seen Lucia Raton?" Michael asked. "What are you trying to hide?"

"She was here for only a few hours," Metwater said. "And she was fine when she left here."

"Then why lie?" Marco asked.

"I'm entitled to my privacy. And you're trespassing in my home. You need to leave."

"This is public land," Marco said. "You are camping here because you have a permit, but that doesn't give you the right to exclude anyone—especially not officers of the law who are conducting an investigation."

"Why didn't you want us to know about the grave in that clearing?" Michael asked.

"I don't have to answer your questions." Metwater looked sullen, and less handsome and in-control than usual. "You need to leave."

Marco ignored the order, deliberately turning his back to Metwater to face Phoenix once more. "We found Lucia's locket in the grave with your belongings," he told her. "Can you explain how it got there?"

IF SHE WAS feigning shock, she was doing an amazing job, Hannah thought as Phoenix stared up at Marco. "That's impossible," she said. "I buried those things before Lucia ever visited the camp."

"Is there anyone who can confirm that?" Marco asked. "Anyone who helped you with the burial?"

She shook her head. "No. I did it alone. It was important that I do it alone."

"Did you tell anyone what you planned to do?" Marco asked. "Could someone have followed and seen you?"

"I only told the Prophet," Phoenix answered. "And why would someone have followed me?"

Hannah hated seeing the other woman so distressed. "Did you find anything else in the grave that belonged to Lucia?" she asked.

"The forensics team is still sorting through their findings," Marco said.

"You're wasting your time here," Metwater said. "You need to leave."

"We'll go, after we've questioned Mr. and Mrs. Morgan." He motioned to Walt and Hannah. "If you two will come with me, please."

Kiram moved to block the door. "Why do you want to talk to them?" he asked.

"We think it's a little suspicious that they showed up here about the time Lucia disappeared," Marco said.

Even though she knew the words were a lie, Hannah felt a tremor of fear. How much worse must Phoenix feel, being accused by these men who had so much power to destroy her life? She squeezed the older woman's hand, then stood and prepared to follow Walt and the others out of the trailer.

A hand on her shoulder stopped her. Metwater moved close to her—too close. His gaze locked to hers and he smoothed his hand down her arm in a possessive way that sent a shiver up her spine. "Don't be too long," he said. "You have to prepare for tonight's council."

Walt took her hand and tugged her toward the door. They followed Marco and Michael a short distance away, down a path that led into the woods along the creek. The noise of the water rushing over the rocks was a soothing contrast to the tension knotting tighter inside her with each passing minute.

"You're on the wrong track here," she said when the two lawmen stopped and faced her and Walt. "Phoenix couldn't have had anything to do with Lucia's disappearance. She's not the type to harm someone else."

"I got the impression she would do just about anything for Metwater," Marco said. "You heard her—he saved her life."

She looked at the ground, unable to think of a response. Phoenix did have a blind spot when it came to the Prophet.

"How did that locket get in the grave if she didn't put it there?" Walt asked.

"Don't know." Michael leaned against a tree, his posture relaxed. "What do you make of her story about burying her past?"

"I believe it," Walt said. "It's the kind of thing Metwater would preach. They're very big into rituals and ceremonies around here."

"What is this council he mentioned?" Marco asked.

"Some kind of meeting to decide on the appropriate punishment for me disobeying Metwater's orders and going to you guys to report the grave," Walt said.

"Punishment?" Michael asked. "What kind of punishment?"

"I don't know." Walt turned to Hannah. "Have you heard anything?"

"Phoenix said it will probably be extra work or something like that—something to impress upon us the importance of putting the Family ahead of ourselves. We have to prove we're serious about our intentions to become one of them."

"How serious are you?" Marco asked. "Why not just leave now? You've probably learned all you're going to learn at this point."

"We know Phoenix's baby is really my niece," Hannah said. "She told us this afternoon—right before you arrived—that the baby belonged to a woman who called herself Freedom. And Phoenix's real name on my sister's will proves she was at the hospital when the baby was born."

"There's still the problem of Metwater's name as the father on the birth certificate," Walt said. "He can fight any attempt to gain custody."

"Not if we have a DNA test proving paternity," Hannah said. "And not if we prove he was involved in Emily's death." She turned to Marco. "Phoenix said Metwater took Emily to Denver with him and came back without her. He told everyone here that she had left—she had abandoned her baby. Why would he lie about her having died in the hospital, unless he had something to do with her death?"

"He lies about a lot of things," Michael said. "But in most cases, lying itself isn't a crime."

"Why didn't you ask Phoenix about the will?" Hannah asked.

The two officers looked at each other. "We were so focused on the search for Lucia we weren't thinking about your sister's will," Marco said.

"Were you able to get the warrant for the DNA test on the baby?" she asked.

Another look passed between them. "Not yet," Marco admitted.

"I can't leave camp without the baby," she said.

"Taking her without the court order could backfire if Metwater decides to press charges," Walt said. "Child Welfare and Protection has already indicated they're on his side. They could ask the court to award temporary custody to Metwater, pending the outcome of the DNA test, and while we're waiting on results, he could leave the area with the baby."

"I won't risk it," Hannah said. "I have to stay here until I can legally take her away."

Michael straightened. "We'll push harder for the court order. In the meantime, see if you can find out anything that would link Metwater to Lucia's disappearance."

"We also need to find this Easy fellow and interview him," Marco said. He clapped a hand on Walt's shoulder. "Let us know if you discover anything useful. And try to stay out of trouble."

"Right," Walt said. He took Hannah's arm and they walked silently back to camp. She fought the urge to lean into him, to let his presence shield her from the anxiety coiling inside her. Maybe it was seeing Phoenix so frightened, or maybe this was simply the emotional side effect of digging so deeply into Emily's last days, but she felt overwhelmed and a little out of control. As if sensing her struggle, Walt put his arm around her. "It's going to be all right," he said. "It will all be over soon."

Chapter Thirteen

"Phoenix is waiting for you," Kiram told Hannah as she and Walt approached Phoenix's trailer. "She will help you prepare for tonight." He motioned to Walt. "You come with me."

Walt started to protest, but Hannah interrupted. "It will be all right," she said, repeating the words of comfort he had given her. She kissed his cheek. "I'll see you soon."

Much as she would have liked to stay with Walt, she would learn more from Phoenix without him there. She made her way back to Phoenix's trailer and found her laying an assortment of supplies on the table—soap, paints, hair ribbons and a simple white garment Hannah suspected was sewn from a bedsheet. "What is all this?" she asked, surveying the array.

"This is for tonight." Phoenix smiled at her. "You want to look your best for the council." She picked up the soap. "First, bathe with this. Then we'll do your hair and makeup."

The soap was obviously homemade and smelled astringent—not the moisturizing bar Hannah preferred. But she didn't argue, and walked with Phoenix to the outdoor shower someone had built, utilizing a plastic drum to store water that was heated by the sun. After a quick soap and rinse, they walked back to the trailer, where Phoenix seated Hannah at the table and began combing out her hair, humming to herself.

"I told the officers I thought you were innocent," Hannah said after a moment. "I'm sure you didn't have anything to do with that girl's disappearance."

"I have faith they'll learn that soon enough." She picked up a ribbon and began braiding it into a section of Hannah's hair.

"When I heard your real name—your old name—I realized it was familiar to me," she said.

Phoenix's fingers stopped moving. "Did we know each other before?" she asked, her tone puzzled.

"You were one of the witnesses on Emily—Freedom's—will." She waited for Phoenix to ask how she knew about the will, but the other woman merely went back to braiding Hannah's hair.

"She asked me to sign some papers for her, so I did," Phoenix said. "A nurse from the hospital was there and she signed, too."

"Why did she decide to write a will?" Hannah asked. "What was she afraid of?"

"Oh, she wasn't afraid. Not exactly."

"But she was upset about something?" Hannah prodded. "Why else would she be so anxious to have a will that she wrote it right there in the hospital?"

"She had had a fight with the Prophet. That upset her."

Hannah turned to look at her. "A fight? What about? Did he threaten her?"

"The Prophet doesn't threaten—he disciplines. And

only because we need it. Just as a loving father disciplines his children."

Hannah could guess where those words had come from. "How did he discipline Emily?" she asked, stomach cramping in anticipation of the answer.

"I don't know. And I don't know what they argued about, either. That was between Freedom and the Prophet."

"I don't think an adult has the right to 'discipline' another adult," Hannah said.

"You just don't understand because you haven't experienced it." She picked up another ribbon and began braiding another section of Hannah's hair. "For instance, when I first came here, I was still trying to get off heroin. The Prophet locked me up in his motor home and looked after me while I went through withdrawal. He wouldn't let me leave, even though I tried to run away. Some people might have seen it as cruel that he kept me prisoner that way, but he saved my life."

"Emily wasn't a drug addict," Hannah said. She took a deep breath, reining in her anger. "She was a grieving young woman with a new baby. She didn't need to be punished for anything."

"I'm sure the Prophet had his reasons," Phoenix said. "I've never known him to be wrong."

Hannah turned to face her once more. "Do you think he's going to punish me for Walt going to the police?" she asked.

Phoenix brushed a lock of hair from Hannah's forehead. "He likes you. I can tell by the way he looks at you. You're going to be one of his favorites. Whatever he does, it will only be because he cares for you."

Hannah felt sick to her stomach at the words. She

didn't want Daniel Metwater's brand of caring. She had to find a way to safely leave here, and to take Joy with her. *What about Walt?* a voice in the back of her mind whispered. *Will you take him with you, too—or leave him behind?*

"I'M NOT GOING to walk out there in front of a whole camp full of people naked." Walt folded his arms and glared at the scrap of cloth Kiram was holding out for him to put on.

"Everyone else will be dressed this way," Kiram said. "It's to show we have nothing to hide from each other."

Walt took the loincloth. He definitely wouldn't be able to hide a weapon in this getup. He would bet Kiram and Metwater's other "bodyguards" would be wearing their knives along with this primitive excuse for a Speedo. But he didn't see any way to get out of wearing the thing if he wanted to avoid raising further suspicion. "I'll wear it," he said. "But I'm putting my regular clothes back on as soon as this is over."

Kiram shrugged. "What did those cops want with you and your wife?" he asked.

Walt had been waiting for this to come up. "They asked if we knew the missing girl—if we had ever met her or seen her or knew anything about her."

"What did you tell them?"

He pretended to examine the loincloth. "We told them the truth—we didn't know anything."

"Seems like they could have asked you all that when you told them about the grave site."

"Yeah, well, they didn't." He stuffed the loincloth

into his pocket. "I guess I'll go back to my tent and change."

"You can change at my place." He pointed to the shack behind them.

"What do I do with my clothes?"

"Leave them here. They'll be fine with me."

And Kiram would be going through his things as soon as Walt was out of sight. "Okay." He headed for the shack. He'd have to find a hiding place for his gun while he was at the council—someplace Kiram wasn't likely to look.

He stripped off quickly, folded his clothes and left them on the end of Kiram's cot. He thought about hiding the weapon under the bed, but ended up stashing it behind a rafter overhead. In the dim light, it would be almost impossible to see. Then he took a few minutes to poke around in the room. Kiram had a small collection of manga novels and another of porn magazines, stashed in a wooden crate that served as his bedside table. He had a wardrobe of mostly shorts and cargo pants and T-shirts; a toolbox with an assortment of screwdrivers, wrenches and a hammer; and a dartboard with only three darts. A sagging, faded sofa sat against one wall.

Walt eyed the footlocker that sat at the end of the cot. He wished he had the time to check the contents of it, but he didn't dare risk it right now.

The door opened and Kiram stepped in. "What's taking so long?" he asked. "You'd better not be messing with my stuff."

"It took me a while to figure out how to get this thing on." Walt snapped the waistband of the loincloth, which was a little too breezy for comfort.

"Come on, let's go." He stepped aside and motioned for Walt to move ahead of him.

A soft drizzle had begun to fall—enough moisture to make everything damp and uncomfortable, but not enough to get them really wet. The murmur of voices drifted through the trees, swelling as they neared the center of the camp. A bonfire blazed, flames bright against the surrounding blackness, popping wood sending out showers of sparks like fireflies. It looked to Walt as if everyone in camp had gathered, most dressed in the same kind of faux-native garb he and Kiram wore. The crowd parted as he followed Kiram to a spot by the fire, and he looked across the circle and saw Hannah with Phoenix and Sophie.

For the briefest moment, he couldn't breathe, as if he had forgotten how. Her hair was down, spilling around her shoulders in a mass of tiny braids threaded with purple and pink and blue ribbons. She wore a simple sheath which, though it covered her from her collarbone to just above the knees, did nothing to hide her feminine curves. If anything, it made him more aware than ever of his attraction to her. He wanted her, yes, but he also wanted to protect her and champion her and work alongside her.

Kiram prodded him in the side. "Close your mouth and stop gaping," he said. "You'd think you'd never seen your wife before."

A clap of thunder shook the air and a murmur swept through the crowd like a wave, and the mass of people parted to reveal Daniel Metwater striding toward the fire. Walt wondered how long he had waited in the background for that thunderclap to announce his entrance—he doubted it was merely coincidence. Like most of the other men he, too, wore a loincloth, revealing muscular legs and the body of someone who spent a lot of time working out. His chest and face were painted in primitive symbols rendered in red, white and black—his eyes circled in white, a black streak down his nose, and more lines on his cheek and chin. It reminded Walt of a poor copy of an African tribal mask he had once seen in a museum. The effect was eerie, firelight flickering on his familiar, yet not familiar visage.

Metwater raised both hands over his head and the crowd quieted. "Thank you all for gathering with me tonight," he said, his voice booming in the sudden silence. "Thank you for recognizing the importance of coming together as a family, and of working as one to build something beautiful—something the outside world doesn't understand."

Walt recognized the technique—build cohesiveness in a group by pitting the members against an outside enemy—a mysterious "them."

"We are here tonight to consider the fate of two who have petitioned to join us," Metwater continued. "Serenity—" He gestured to Hannah. "And Walter."

Walt was sure the use of names neither he nor Hannah preferred was deliberate, another way of saying *I'm the one in charge here.* "They have expressed a desire to become part of our family, but their actions show they yet lack the discipline and commitment required to build a strong unit," Metwater said.

Walt caught Hannah's eye across the circle. She gave him a half smile, then made a face at Metwater. *Attagirl.*

"I have spent much time in meditation on their fate, and I have received a vision."

Walt watched the faces of those around him as they listened to Metwater. They stared fixedly at him, some almost trancelike as his words rose and fell, his voice having the rhythm and cadence of a hypnotist. He was good, Walt had to admit. But if you had to trick people into listening to you, how good of a leader could you really be?

Metwater spent some time describing his vision— something to do with a figure all in white—an angel— coming to him with a tablet, on which was written the solution to their problem. Were people really buying this? Apparently so, as they began to murmur and nod their heads in agreement.

Suddenly, Metwater reached out and grabbed Hannah's hand and yanked her to his side. Walt hadn't even realized he had lunged forward until Kiram pulled him back. The blade of Kiram's knife pressed to his throat. "I wouldn't make another move if I were you," the bearded man said.

Walt probably could have fought off the other man. He'd been trained in self-defense and was confident of his abilities. But he couldn't fight off a whole camp full of men, and the way this bunch was hanging on Metwater's every word, if the Prophet had commanded them to kill Walt, they wouldn't have hesitated to fall on him like a pack of rabid dogs.

Hannah tried to pull away from Metwater, but he held her fast. She settled for glaring at him. Clearly, she hadn't fallen under his spell like so many others. "My vision told me to welcome Serenity to our fold with open arms," Metwater said. "She has a true gentle spirit and will be an asset to us. With proper guidance, I believe she will come to be a revered and respected member of the group."

Hannah's expression didn't soften. Walt imagined she was grinding her teeth to keep from reminding Metwater that her name wasn't Serenity and she wasn't interested in his guidance.

"As of tonight, Serenity will live with me and I will take personal responsibility for her education and training."

A murmur rose from the crowd. Phoenix clapped her hands together, apparently thrilled. Hannah paled and tried, in vain, to pull away from Metwater. *That does it*, Walt thought. They were leaving tonight. He wasn't going to give Metwater a chance to "educate" Hannah, whatever form that might take.

At last Metwater handed Hannah off to Phoenix again. "Now to the question of Walter," he said. The crowd shifted to stare at Walt, who glared back.

"I fear, and my vision confirmed, that he does not have the proper spirit of cooperation that would allow him to be a valued member of our group," Metwater said. "He has shown a blatant disregard for our rules and an unhealthy defiance."

Or maybe just a healthy skepticism that you would have anyone's benefit but your own in mind, Walt thought.

"For the good of the Family, Walter must be banished," Metwater declared.

"No!" The cry came from Hannah, who was being held back by Phoenix and another woman.

"Fine by me," Walt said. "I'll leave tonight." And he

would be back before morning with a team of Rangers to free Hannah and arrest Metwater for kidnapping.

Metwater ignored him. "In order that he may learn a valuable lesson, and have time to reconsider his rebellious attitude, he will undergo a trial."

"I've had enough of this nonsense," Walt muttered.

Kiram took a firmer hold on him. "Don't try anything," the bearded man whispered.

Metwater turned and strode toward him. There was nothing natural in his movements—he was a performer on stage, playing to his audience. He stopped in front of Walt. "You will be taken out into the wilderness. From there, you can make your own way back to the world. You are never to come here again."

"I have my bike," Walt said.

"No. I have your bike." Metwater smiled. "Or rather, you are leaving it behind for your lovely wife."

"You can't do this," Walt said.

"If you could speak with others who have tried to defy me, you would learn that I can." He turned his back on Walt and crossed the circle to Hannah.

"I won't stay with you," she said. "I'm leaving with my husband."

"I am your husband now," Metwater said. "And your father and your brother and all you need." The words were beyond cheesy, but the frightening thing was, Metwater had managed to brainwash these people into believing them. He took Hannah's hand and held fast when she tried to turn away.

Walt shoved aside Kiram's hand, not caring that the knife grazed his arm, drawing blood. "Let her go!" he shouted.

His eyes met Hannah's, and behind her panic he saw

Chapter Fourteen

Hannah couldn't believe this was happening. Up until now everything about the evening—from the ridiculous dress-up clothes to Metwater's bombastic speech—had seemed like a silly game. It hardly seemed credible that anyone could get away with things like kidnapping and banishment in front of a crowd of people in this day and age.

But they were in an almost roadless wilderness area, far from other people and laws and even cell phones. That isolation—and his followers' willingness to be hypnotized by his words—gave Metwater more power than he might otherwise have had.

But she wasn't going to allow him to have power over her. "Stop!" she shouted, as two men carried Walt's inert body away from the fire, into the darkness. She kicked and clawed at the men who had moved in to help the women contain her, but they only tightened their hold.

"Serenity! Hannah! You need to calm down." Phoenix grasped her hand and patted it, her face twisted in concern. "You don't need to get so upset."

"They hurt Walt," she said, fighting a mixture of rage and dismay.

"I'm sure they didn't." Phoenix squeezed her hand. "He'll be fine. Meanwhile, you've been given a great honor."

Hannah stared at her friend, confused.

"You're going to live with the Prophet." Phoenix stroked her hair. "He rarely takes such an interest in anyone. It's really a privilege."

Hannah winced. "He can take his privilege and stick it where the sun doesn't shine!"

"Freedom was the same way when he chose her," Phoenix said. "Don't make the same mistake she did and fight with him. In the end it will only do you more harm than good."

"He did this to my sister?" Hannah stared at her. "He forced himself on her?"

Phoenix looked flustered. "I don't know about your sister. I was talking about Freedom."

"Freedom was my sister," Hannah said. "Her name was Emily Dietrich, and her daughter's name is Joy. I have Joy's birth certificate, and the will you witnessed. I know."

Phoenix shook her head, as if trying to clear it. "Have you seen her? Spoken to her? Did you ask her why she left her baby?"

"She didn't leave her." Hannah was crying now, tears streaming down her face, even as the two men who held her dragged her toward Metwater's RV. "Emily couldn't come back to her baby because she's dead," she said.

"I don't understand," Phoenix said.

"My sister—Emily—Freedom—is dead," Hannah said. "She died in Denver, when she went there with the Prophet. I believe he killed her."

Phoenix stopped at the bottom of the steps leading to the motor home's door. "That isn't possible," she said. "He told us she had left."

"She would never have left her baby," Hannah said. "You know that."

"I don't—" Phoenix began.

"Come on." One of the women had opened the door to Metwater's RV and held it while the men dragged Hannah backward up the steps. They must have heard what she told Phoenix, but they showed no reaction. "You don't want to keep the Prophet waiting," the woman said.

They dragged Hannah into the RV, which appeared to be empty. If Daniel Metwater was there, he wasn't showing his face. They shoved her into a room and the lock clicked behind her. She stood for a moment, catching her breath and taking stock of her surroundings. The room contained a futon and a single chair. One window. She dragged the chair over to the window, climbed up on it and tried to force up the sash. It wouldn't budge.

"You won't get out that way."

Metwater stood in the doorway. He had removed the paint and the loincloth, and changed back into his loose linen trousers. "The window is nailed shut from the outside," he said. "And there's mesh over the pane so you can't break the glass." He moved closer to her and held out his hand. "Come down from there and let's talk."

He led her to the futon and pushed her down, then sat beside her. "You're even prettier than your sister," he said.

"What did you do to Emily?" she asked.

"I tried to help her, but she wouldn't accept my help." His smile sent a cold shiver through her stomach.

"She didn't need your help," she said.

"You say that because you want to believe that you were all she needed. But if that had been true, she wouldn't have left you and come to us."

His words were like a knife to her heart. No matter how long she lived, she would never stop believing she had somehow failed her sister. "What did you do to her?" she asked. "Why did she die?"

"An unfortunate accident," he said. He reached for her and she pulled away.

"I want to know what happened in Denver," she said. "Why did my sister die alone?"

He sat back, his expression hard. "I took her to the hospital. There was nothing else I could do for her."

She shivered, struck by his coldness. "You could have stayed with her. She was probably terrified."

He said nothing.

"Why did you lie and tell everyone she had run away?" she asked.

"There was no sense upsetting the rest of the Family. I don't believe in dwelling on negatives. What's important is the future." He reached for her again, but she pushed him away.

He scowled. "You're upset," he said. "But I can be patient—for a while." He stood. "We'll talk again in the morning."

"What did you do with Walt?"

"I didn't do anything," he said.

"That's how you operate, isn't it?" Anger made her bold. "You have other people do your dirty work for you."

"Go to sleep," he said. "We'll talk in the morning."

He shut off the light and closed the door. Her instinct was to run after him, to pound on the door and shout for him to let her out. But no one would pay any attention to her, least of all Metwater. She sank onto the futon and glared at the shut window. She had to figure out a way to get out of here. She had to find Walt, and together they had to get Joy and take her to safety.

She thought of Emily, trapped in this same room, missing her baby and desperate to escape. She hadn't been lucky enough to get away. Maybe she hadn't been strong enough. But Hannah would be strong enough for both of them. She would take care of her sister's child. Failure wasn't an option.

WALT CAME TO lying flat on his back in the darkness. He was wet and cold, and something hard was digging into his spine. Groaning, he shoved himself into a sitting position and wiped dripping water out of his eyes. It was raining—a steady drizzle that ran in rivulets across the rocky ground around him. He could make out little in the darkness, except that he was somewhere away from camp, presumably in the wilderness.

He was still wearing the stupid loincloth and was barefoot. He wouldn't get far in this country full of rocks and thorns in such a state of undress. Of course, before very long he'd probably die of hypothermia, what with the rain soaking him and nighttime temperatures in the fifties. Or he'd starve or die of thirst, since the rainwater would dry up in a matter of hours once the sun rose. Metwater was counting on that. It was a good way to kill someone without actually having to pull the trigger. If the body was found later, Metwater could always claim Walt had wandered into the wilderness on his own.

But he didn't have to get far—he only had to get back to camp. He wasn't going to die out here. He would rescue Hannah, recover his clothes and his bike, and head back to Ranger headquarters. Then Metwater would discover how hard paybacks could be.

He struggled to his feet, swaying a little, dizzy from the pounding in his head. He ran his fingers over the knot at the back of his skull, his hair sticky from what he imagined was drying blood. He took a few steps, wincing as rocks dug into his feet. He stumbled over something—a log or a boulder—and fell, hitting the ground hard and cursing loudly. The only answer was the steadily falling rain.

This wasn't going to work. It was too dark to see where he was going. He'd have to wait until it was light. Then he could take his bearings and determine the most likely route back to the camp. Otherwise, he might break his leg or stumble over a cliff. He wouldn't be any help to Hannah, lying at the bottom of a ravine.

Moving carefully, hands outstretched like a blind man, feet shuffling along, he made his way to a tree and huddled at the base of the trunk. Knees drawn up and arms wrapped around his legs, he tried to warm himself. Distraction—that was what he needed. He just had to stick it out here a few more hours. He started by thinking of all the ways he would make Metwater and Kiram pay for their treatment of him and Hannah. He had compiled a long list of possible charges against them, from kidnapping and assault to fraud and violating the county burn bans.

The idea was satisfying, but it couldn't keep his

thoughts from straying to his chief worry—not fear for his own life or concern that he might not find the camp again, but worry for Hannah. He felt physically ill, knowing she might be in danger and he was out here, powerless.

She's tough, he reminded himself. *She isn't afraid to stand up to Metwater. She's smart, too.* She was the most amazing woman he knew, and out here in the darkness, with nothing between him and his feelings, he realized he had fallen in love with her. It wasn't something he had intended to happen, but there it was. He'd lost his heart to a woman who lived in another state, who was focused on making a new life with her orphaned niece and who clearly had no room in her life for an ordinary cop.

HANNAH MOVED THE chair from the window and wedged it under the bedroom doorknob. She'd have to remove it eventually, but at least Metwater wouldn't be able to come into the room while she slept.

If sleep were even possible. She lay down on the futon, her mind racing with thoughts of her sister, of Joy, of Metwater—and of Walt.

Where was he right now? Had Kiram taken him out into the desert and killed him? Or left him to die? Her throat constricted and she swallowed tears. How had the lawman come to mean so much to her in such a short time? He wasn't like any of the other men she had known—he didn't try to change her or expect anything of her or judge her choices. He didn't need her for anything, yet when she was with him she felt stronger and smarter and more confident. Time spent with him seemed better than time spent alone—and that had never been the case with anyone else.

Her breath caught, and she sat up in bed. Was she falling in love with Walt? Was that even possible when she had known him such a short time? She didn't want a man in her life—didn't need one. She had work and Joy and so much going on. How could that leave any room for a relationship?

She tossed and turned until the window changed from a square of black to a square of silvery gray. She returned to the window and stood on tiptoe to see out. No one moved out there at this hour. Not that she would expect to see anyone at any time of day, really. The back of the RV looked out onto a choked mass of trees and underbrush that bordered the creek.

She shoved at the window sash again, and scowled at the wire mesh that covered the glass. If only she was strong enough to throw up the sash despite the nails. Would it help if she had listened to her friends and taken up weight training?

A scraping noise outside the RV made her freeze. Heart racing, she rose on tiptoe again and took a look outside. A scream stuck in her throat as a figure loomed up on the other side of the window. She jumped back, then sagged with relief when she recognized Phoenix. The other woman held up a hammer, then used it to pry the nails from the sill. Moments later, the sill shot up and Phoenix leaned her head in.

"I couldn't sleep," she said. "I've been thinking about what you said—about your sister. Do you think the Prophet really killed her?"

Hannah wanted to suggest Phoenix help her get out of the RV without Metwater knowing, and then they could have this discussion, but she couldn't be sure whose side the other woman was on. She was such an ardent fan of the Prophet that the odds seemed about even that she would alert him of any attempt Hannah made to escape. Better to try to win her over to Hannah's point of view. She moved closer to the window and kept her voice low. "I don't know. She died in the hospital emergency room, of an asthma attack."

Phoenix looked thoughtful. "I remember she had an inhaler she used. She said she was going to get her prescription filled while she and the Prophet were in Denver."

"Maybe he didn't let her fill it."

"Why wouldn't he? I mean, it wasn't as if she used it very much at all."

"No, but stress can make asthma worse. If she and the Prophet were fighting, she would be stressed."

Phoenix frowned. "But that doesn't mean he killed her."

"No. But he left her at the hospital alone." Hannah struggled to hold back her anger. "And he lied to you and everyone else here about what happened to her."

"That's what troubles me most," Phoenix said. "Why would he do that?"

"I don't know. Help me down, will you?"

"I'm not sure I should help you leave."

"I don't want to be here. The Prophet is holding me against my will. Do you think that's right?"

Phoenix hesitated so long, Hannah began to despair. Maybe she should rush the window and try to move past the other woman. "He's not going to like you leaving," Phoenix said. "He'll probably send Kiram and others after you. They might even try to hurt you."

"I know. They might already have hurt Walt. But I have to risk it. I can't stay here."

"All right, I'll help you," Phoenix said. "But wait just a minute. I'll be right back—I promise."

Before Hannah could protest, Phoenix shut the window and climbed down the ladder. By the time Hannah had the window open again, Phoenix had laid the ladder on the ground and left. Hannah moaned softly. The sun was already higher in the sky. She had no idea if Metwater was an early riser, but what if he was and decided to pay her a visit?

THE RAIN SLACKED off and Walt fell into a doze. When he woke again, stiff and cold, the sky was pale with the first hint of dawn. Standing, he pushed out of the underbrush and studied his surroundings. Nothing about this area looked familiar. Maybe if he had been on the job longer he would be more familiar with the wilderness backcountry, but his work thus far had kept him mostly in the national park and along roads. Before him spread a landscape of brown dirt, red and gray rock, and clumps of gnarled trees and sagebrush.

He tried to retrace his steps from the night before, and found the place where Kiram had left him, drag marks in the mud clearly showing where the bearded man had dumped him. Following the drag marks, he came to the impression of tires, showing where Kiram had parked his vehicle. The treads led away from the parking spot in a clear path across the prairie.

Heart pounding, Walt moved faster, trotting now, ignoring the pain in his feet as he followed the faint impressions in the mud. With a little luck, he'd be able to follow these tracks all the way back to the road, and from there to the camp.

An hour later, just as the first hints of pale blue were showing in the sky, Walt crept into the woods on the outskirts of camp. Moving stealthily, seeking cover behind trees and the random piles of junk that had accumulated among the trailers, tents and shacks, he peered out at the center gathering area. No one was moving about yet. A tendril of smoke rose from the remains of last night's bonfire, and the air smelled of wet ashes and earth.

Satisfied that no one was about, he made his way to his tent and quickly dressed. His only shoes were in Kiram's shack, along with his gun. Not wanting to be unarmed, he crept to the camp kitchen and found a knife. Suddenly ravenous, he ate some bread and cheese he found, then stuffed his pockets with several energy bars. Then he headed for Metwater's RV.

Barging into the motor home would be a bad idea. Reports he had read at Ranger headquarters indicated Metwater owned at least one firearm, and Walt couldn't be sure the Prophet was in the RV alone.

Alone except for Hannah. Walt needed to find out where she was, then make a plan for freeing her. He crept around the motor home, listening for any sign of movement inside. Most of the windows were too high up for him to see into, and he couldn't tell much about the layout of the vehicle. He thought the bedroom or bedrooms were to the left of the door, but he couldn't be sure.

He stood at the back of the RV, considering his next move, when a voice from behind him made him freeze. "Walt! You're not supposed to be here."

Slowly, he turned and stared at Phoenix. She stood at the far end of the RV, paler than ever in the early-morning light. And was that a bow and arrow she had trained on him?

HANNAH LEANED HER head against the windowsill and listened for any signs of movement in the other parts of the RV. If she heard anyone coming, she would jump out the window. Maybe she'd get lucky and wouldn't break any bones.

She wasn't sure how many minutes had passed when she heard voices outside. She looked toward the end of the RV where they seemed to be coming from and gasped as she recognized Walt and Phoenix. He was standing with his hands over his head, and Phoenix was pointing something at him. Hannah craned her neck for a closer look and gasped. Was that a bow and arrow?

THE BOW AND arrow Phoenix held looked crude, but effective. Walt had no doubt the arrow could do serious damage, especially at such close range. "I'm here to help Hannah," he said.

"Phoenix, what are you doing?"

Walt didn't dare turn around, but he recognized Hannah's voice behind him. Phoenix shifted her gaze to over his shoulder. "He's not supposed to be here," she said.

"No, I'm supposed to be dead," Walt said. "Kiram took me out into the desert and left me to die of exposure or thirst or whatever it took."

"How did you get back?" Phoenix asked.

"He was too stupid to realize his truck would leave

tracks in the fresh mud. As soon as it was light enough, I followed his trail back to camp."

"Could we discuss this later?" Hannah asked.

Phoenix lowered the bow, and together she and Walt hurried to the window where Hannah waited. He spotted the ladder and propped it against the RV, then together he and Phoenix helped Hannah climb out.

She wrapped her arms around his neck. "I was so worried about you," she said.

He held her close, unable to let go. "Are you okay?" he asked, studying her face.

She nodded. "I am. Especially now." She turned to Phoenix. "What are you doing with that bow and arrow?"

"Some guys made them a while back to hunt rabbits. They didn't have any luck but since you said you were leaving camp, I thought you might want one. You know, for self-defense."

"Is that why you left—to get something to help me protect myself?"

Bright color flooded Phoenix's normally pale cheeks. "I wedged the front door of the motor home shut. If the Prophet saw you escaping, I wanted to slow down his pursuit."

Hannah moved from Walt's arms into Phoenix's. "Thank you," she said, and kissed the older woman's cheek.

"We need to leave before everyone wakes up," Walt reminded her.

"First we have to get Joy—Vicki." She squeezed Phoenix's arm. "She has to go with us."

"No!"

Walt flinched at Phoenix's loud cry, and looked around to see if anyone had heard.

"Yes," Hannah said. "Emily—Freedom—wanted me to have the baby. She said so in her will."

"If the Prophet finds out I gave her to you, he'll punish me." Phoenix looked on the verge of tears.

"Then tell him I stole her."

Phoenix shook her head, tears streaming down her face. Walt clenched his jaw, hating how helpless he felt. He wanted to tell Hannah to leave the baby—that they would come back for her later. But he might as well have told her to leave her right arm behind. She wouldn't go without the child, and he wouldn't go without her, so they were stuck at an impasse.

"Mom, we have to give Vicki to her."

Sophie stepped from the edge of the woods, the baby cradled on her shoulder. The girl was barefoot, dressed only in a thin cotton nightgown.

"Sophie!" Phoenix cried. "What are you doing here?"

"I saw you take the bow and arrow from under the bed and I wanted to know what you were doing." She moved closer. "You always said you would give Vicki back to Freedom if she came for her," she said. "If Hannah is her sister, she's the next best thing."

Phoenix touched her daughter's cheek, then laid her other hand on the baby's back.

"You always said children belonged with family," Sophie said.

"I did, didn't I?" She turned back to Hannah. "You're not lying to me, are you?"

"Everything I've told you is the truth," Hannah said.

Except that she and Walt weren't really husband and wife, he thought, but what bearing did that have on any of this?

Phoenix handed the bow and arrow to Walt, then

took the sleeping infant from Sophie and put her in Hannah's arms.

Sophie slipped the diaper bag onto Hannah's shoulder. "Some of her things are in here, including some bottles of formula and some diapers."

"Thanks," Hannah said, and patted the girl's hand.

"Take good care of her," Phoenix whispered.

"I will," Hannah said. "And thank you—for being my sister's friend, for taking care of her baby and for helping me. You're a good woman, Phoenix."

She said nothing, but took Sophie's hand and turned away. "I'll light a candle for you," she said.

"Wait!" Hannah called.

Phoenix looked back over her shoulder.

"You should come with us," Hannah said.

"No." Phoenix took a step back. "This is my home. This is where I belong."

"But what if someone tries to hurt you?" Hannah asked. "Because you helped us?"

Phoenix smiled. "I'm sure that won't happen. We're safer here than we would be anywhere else."

Walt could see Hannah didn't believe that, but he doubted she would ever convince the older woman she was in danger. Phoenix still believed in the Prophet, despite everything that had happened. "We'll stay in touch," Hannah said. "We'll make sure you're all right." She would ask the Rangers to keep an eye on mother and daughter—to make sure no harm came to them.

WALT SHOULDERED THE crude bow and arrow, then took Hannah's hand. "Come on," he said. "We'd better go."

"I can't wait to get out of here," she said, hurrying along beside him.

"We have to stop by Kiram's place first," he said.

She balked. "Why do we have to go there?"

"I have to get my shoes—and my gun."

She glanced down at his bare feet. "Are you sure it's worth the risk?"

"We won't let him see us. You can hide somewhere nearby while I go inside."

She tucked the blankets more securely around the baby. "Let's get it over with, then."

They found a spot in the woods away from the camp but close enough to give them a view of Kiram's shack. People were beginning to emerge from some of the other trailers and tents, but there was no sign of life around the makeshift dwelling. Walt was beginning to wonder if they had missed the bearded man. "Maybe I should see if the place is empty," he said.

"No." Hannah's fingers dug into his arm. When he turned to look at her, she fixed him with a fierce gaze. "I almost lost you to that bully once," she said. "I don't want to risk it again."

Her words made him feel a little unsteady, as if reeling from a punch. He wanted to demand she explain what she meant, but now didn't seem the right time. Instead, he covered her hand with his own and nodded. "All right. We'll wait a little longer."

Just as he turned back to the shack, the door opened and Kiram emerged. As usual, he wore the knife at his waist. He looked around him, then headed away, toward the center of the camp, where other Family members were gathering for breakfast.

As soon as he was out of sight, Walt rushed forward. He took cover around the side of the shack for a moment, catching his breath. No one shouted or gave any other sign they had seen him. Quickly, he moved to the door and slipped inside.

He went first to the rafter where he had hidden the gun, and breathed a sigh of relief when he found it still there. He checked that the weapon was still loaded, then tucked it into the waistband of his jeans. His shoes were also where he had left them. He put them on, then looked around to see if he had missed anything. Moments later, he rejoined Hannah. "Let's get the bike and get out of here," he said.

"Do you think it's safe to take the baby on the motorcycle?" she asked as they made their way along the creek toward the parking area.

"It's not the safest choice," he said. "But I don't think we have any other option."

"No. I don't suppose we do."

On the way to the parking area, he dumped the bow and arrows into the brush. "I appreciate Phoenix looking out for you," he said. "But I'm more comfortable with my service weapon than those."

"I guess a gun would be more reliable," Hannah said. "Though I hope it doesn't come to that."

They emerged on the edge of the gravel parking area. As usual, the area was empty. They kept to cover until they came to the place where Walt had left the bike, camouflaged with branches. He peered into the thick underbrush and saw a few loose branches on the ground, but no bike.

"I don't see it," Hannah said.

He swore under his breath and kicked at the dirt, where the imprint of the motorcycle's tires clearly showed. "It was here," he said. "Someone took it."

"Metwater wanted it," she said. "He must have hidden it away somewhere."

"That would be my guess." Add theft to his list of charges against the so-called prophet.

"What are we going to do?" she asked.

"We start walking."

"That's right. You can turn around and walk back into camp." The underbrush behind them moved and Kiram emerged. Though Kiram still wore his knife, he aimed a pistol at Walt. "Start walking," he said. "Or I'll take a great deal of pleasure in shooting you."

Chapter Fifteen

Walt stepped in front of Hannah and the baby. He had to give them a chance to get away. Metwater wanted Hannah, but Kiram hated Walt, and Walt could use that fact to his advantage. "What's with the gun?" he asked. "I thought you were a peace-loving guy focused on spiritual matters."

"Shut up and start walking." Kiram motioned with the gun toward camp. The way he was waving the weapon around made Walt think he hadn't handled guns a lot—or at least he hadn't been trained to handle them safely. Which made him more dangerous, but less likely to be a really good shot.

Walt reached back and took Hannah's hand. "We'll come quietly," he lied. "Just allow us one more kiss before you tear us apart again." Before Kiram could respond, he pulled Hannah close and kissed her soundly on the mouth. She stiffened, then melted into his arms. He would have liked to prolong the moment, to savor the feel of her lips on his. But they didn't have a moment to lose. With his back partially shielding her from view, he moved his mouth to her ear.

"When I give the word, run," he said. "I'll be with you as soon as I can."

"Yes," she whispered.

He released her and turned to face Kiram once more. "Get going!" the bearded man shouted.

"I'm going." He took two steps toward the other man, then launched himself at Kiram's legs, sending him flying. "Run!" he shouted, and prayed that Hannah wouldn't hesitate to flee.

Kiram grunted as he landed hard on his back, but he kept hold of the gun. By the time he sat up, Walt had drawn his own weapon. Kiram fired, but the shot went wild. He rolled to the side as Walt fired, so that the bullet struck him in the shoulder, instead of the chest. Kiram's eyes widened in shock. He dropped his weapon and clutched at his shoulder, where blood blossomed, seeping through his fingers.

Walt kicked Kiram's gun away as loud voices approached. The others in the camp must have heard the shots. "Help!" Kiram shouted. "He's getting away!"

Walt didn't wait to hear more. He took off in the direction Hannah had fled. He had run several hundred yards, away from the road and the camp, when he heard her call his name. "Walt! Over here!"

He found her huddled in a thick growth of scrub oak, the baby clutched to her chest. "Are you all right?" she asked, her expression pale and stressed.

"I'm okay." He crouched in front of her. He needed to touch her, to reassure himself that she really was okay. He smoothed her hair back from her face. "What about you?"

"I'm okay." She put one hand to his cheek. "I heard gunshots and I was so worried."

"Kiram fired on me, and I shot him."

"Is he dead?"

"No. I hit him in the shoulder, but he should recover."

"As long as you're safe." She pulled his mouth down to hers and kissed him hard, as if trying to drive away all fear and doubt. He gripped her shoulders and returned the kiss, not holding back any of the emotion he felt. He didn't care that this thing between them was impractical and poorly timed and likely doomed—he was going to enjoy it now, for whatever time together they had.

Voices rose in the direction of camp and he pulled away. "We'd better go," he said. "The more distance we can put between us and Metwater's followers, the better."

He stood and helped her to her feet. The baby began to cry. "I need to change her diaper," Hannah said.

"Hurry." He looked over his shoulder, the way they had come. Though he couldn't see anyone headed toward them, Metwater's enforcers were bound to pursue them as soon as they got the story from Kiram. When he turned back to Hannah, she had laid the baby out on the blanket and removed the old diaper, which she placed in a plastic bag and stuffed in the diaper bag. "I guess we can't count on help from anyone in camp," she said.

"Some of them, like Phoenix, might want to help, but I think Metwater has most of them firmly under his thumb. I don't think we can risk it."

She nodded and fastened the new diaper around the baby, who kicked her feet and babbled. Walt smiled and held out his finger for her to grip. "You're going to be a great mom," he said.

She stared at him. "Do you really think so?"

Clearly, his answer mattered to her. He patted her shoulder. "You already love her, and that's what's most important."

Nodding, she rewrapped the blanket and zipped shut the diaper bag. "What do we do next?"

"We head for Ranger headquarters." He stood and helped her to her feet. "We'll have to travel cross-country. Metwater's people are likely to be looking for us along the roads."

They set out, trying to stay in cover as much as possible, alert to any sounds of pursuit, which didn't come. The sun climbed overhead, the day already hot. Walt wished he had thought to bring water. The creek that ran alongside Metwater's camp was the only water source he knew of around here and they couldn't risk detouring back that way. But it should only take them a few hours to reach the main road. From there they might be able to catch a ride to Ranger headquarters or into Montrose. They could call for help from there.

They paralleled the road leading away from the camp, but the going was slow, the ground rocky and uneven. Every hundred yards or so they had to detour around a pile of boulders or a dry wash or an expanse of cactus. All signs of the previous night's rain had vanished, the ground dry as powder beneath their feet, the air heavy with the scent of sagebrush and cedar.

Though they kept out of sight of the road, the rumble of passing traffic reached them, and dust clouds from the passing cars rose up in the air. "Do you think it's Family members looking for us?" she asked.

"I can't think who else it would be." Walt followed yet another dust plume with his eyes. "These roads normally get hardly any traffic."

"Maybe one of the Rangers will stop by the camp and someone will tell them we're gone," she said.

"We should have headed toward the grave site," he said. "The forensics team might still be working there. I don't know why I didn't think of that before."

"It was too close to camp," she said. "It's probably one of the first places Metwater will look. And you don't even know if anyone is still there."

"No." He wasn't even sure he could find the grave site now—not without returning to the camp as his starting point, and that was far too risky.

They had walked only an hour or so when he noticed Hannah limping. "What's wrong?" he asked, stopping. "Are you hurt?"

She grimaced. "Blister."

"Let me take the baby." He held his arms out and after a moment's hesitation, she handed the child over.

He settled the infant into the crook of his arm, a warm weight. She smiled up at him and he smiled back, enchanted.

"She's just like her mother," Hannah said. "Emily could always charm any man."

"You're pretty charming yourself," Walt said.

"Ha! I'm a lot of things, but charming is not one of them."

"All right, what about—alluring."

Pink warmed her cheeks, but she said nothing, merely set out walking again.

He caught up with her. "Why does that catch you so off guard?" he asked. "Me saying you're alluring?"

"Because I'm not," she said.

"You can't pretend you don't know I'm attracted to you. And you're attracted to me."

"I don't want to be."

He recognized truth when he heard it. "I get that, but I don't understand why."

She glanced at him, then went back to focusing on the ground. "You don't have to understand."

"But I want to."

She said nothing, only quickened her pace. He lengthened his stride to keep up with her. "When I first met you, I thought I had you figured out," he said. "I saw a smart career woman, someone used to being in charge. You became the guardian of your dead sister's baby and you threw yourself into preparing for motherhood the way you would any other project."

She said nothing, so he kept talking, refusing to let her silence shut him out. "You had probably researched all the best products and techniques, maybe arranged for child care, found a pediatrician, furnished a nursery. You had a plan for what things would be like when you got back to Texas."

"Is there something wrong with that?" she asked.

"Nothing. Except then we started working together and these feelings grew between us and I'm not a part of your plan."

"I can't be in a relationship right now."

"Why not? You don't think you can love that baby and me at the same time? People do it every day."

"I'm not every person," she said.

"No, and that's why I love you." He grabbed her hand, stopping her and turning her to him. He waited for her to rebel, to tell him he couldn't possibly love her, she didn't love him, they lived in different states, the whole situation was impossible…

Instead, she stared at him, eyes wide and shimmering with tears. "You can't love me," she said.

"Why not?"

"Because you don't know me. You don't know the awful things I've done."

"Awful things? What awful things?" A chill crept into his chest as he studied her grave expression and read the mixture of pain and fear in her eyes. Had he misjudged her so badly?

Tears were streaming down her face now. She turned away, hugging her arms across her body. Walt shifted the baby to his other arm and moved up behind her, caressing her shoulders. "I can't believe you've ever done anything so awful it would change the way I feel about you," he said.

"Emily knew. It was one of the reasons why she ran away."

"But she gave you her baby. That must mean she forgave you."

She nodded. "Yes. Yes, I think she forgave me."

"Tell me," he said. "You need to tell me or we'll both always wonder what would have happened if you had."

She sniffed, but a fresh wave of sobs shook her. He handed her his handkerchief and waited while she dabbed at her eyes and blew her nose. "I had a baby once," she said.

He blinked. He had never expected this. She had a baby? When? With whom? But none of those questions spoke to the pain in her eyes. "What happened?" he asked.

"I was nineteen. I had just started college and I had a...a fling. Nothing serious. When I got pregnant the guy freaked out. We both agreed we couldn't raise a child, so I decided to give the baby up for adoption."

"I'm sure that wasn't an easy decision. But it doesn't make you a bad person. You gave someone else who badly wanted to be a parent the chance to do so."

"It was the hardest decision I ever made." She drew in a ragged breath. "I chose an open adoption, because I wanted to know what happened to my child. Everything went well. The couple was very nice. Then, when she was three months old, little Madison died."

Another sob shook her. He gathered her close and held her tight. "I'm so sorry," he whispered, stroking her hair.

"They said it was crib death—just something that happens sometimes. But I can't help thinking, if I had been there, I could have kept her safe. If I had taken care of my own child, that wouldn't have happened."

"You can't know that," he said. "Terrible things happen sometimes, for no reason."

"I know. That's what the counselors I saw said, too. But it's haunted me. It made me believe I didn't deserve to be happy. I threw myself into my work because that was something I could control—something that didn't depend on emotion and chance. And then Emily gave me this second chance to be a mother." She smiled down at Joy, who lay sleeping in his arms.

"You're going to be a great mom to her," Walt said. "I believe that."

"But I can't take any chances," she said. "I can't let myself be distracted. Not even by you."

He could argue that he wouldn't be a distraction—that he could help her with the baby and everything would be all right. But he wasn't the one whose baby had died. He wasn't the one who was suffering.

And he couldn't think of any argument that would change her mind. Only time and experience could do that. She stepped away from him and he let her go. "Just know you're not alone," he said. "I will be there for you if you need me."

Her expression grew less bleak. "Thank you," she said. "That means a lot."

"Thank you for trusting me with your story," he said. "Hearing it doesn't change how I feel about you. If anything, it makes me admire you all the more."

"How can you say that?"

"You suffered something terrible. But you didn't let it defeat you. You came out the other side. I've seen the kind of courage you have and now I know some of what's behind it."

She studied his face, as if searching for something there. "I never met anyone like you," she said.

"I hope that's a good thing."

The baby woke and began to cry. Hannah took the child from him. "She's probably hungry," she said. "We should stop and feed her."

He looked around, then led the way to the meager shade of a stunted pinyon. Hannah settled herself against the trunk and pulled out a bottle of formula for the baby. Walt sat beside her and tried not to think about how thirsty he was.

A loud vehicle passed on the road a quarter mile distant, the rumble of an exhaust system with a hole in it echoing across the empty landscape. "Why are they pursuing us like this?" Hannah asked.

"Because Metwater knows we'll go to the police,"

Walt said. "We'll tell them about him kidnapping you and assaulting me, stealing my motorcycle, lying about your sister—all the things he's done. That will lead to more digging into his activities. My guess is that an investigation will turn up more crimes—things he doesn't want us finding out."

"He's built a little kingdom out here and he thinks he can control everyone in it," Hannah said. "He thought he was safe."

"He wasn't able to control us," Walt said. "And that's made him angry—and dangerous."

"How much longer before we reach somewhere safe?" she asked. She stowed the bottle and zipped up the diaper bag, then rested the baby on her shoulder and patted her back. She looked so comfortable and natural with the infant—he started to point this out, but then thought better of bringing up what was obviously a painful topic.

"We've only got another hour or two to walk and we should be able to flag down a car," he said. "Once we're in the park, there will be more tourist traffic. Someone will help us."

"I hope so." She held up her hand and he pulled her to her feet and they set out walking again.

They hadn't gone far when they came to a deep gash in the landscape—a narrow, rocky ravine. Walt peered into the shadowy, brush-choked canyon. "It's too steep to climb down into and out again," he said. "Especially with the baby."

Hannah shielded her eyes and peered down the length of the ravine. "It looks as if it goes on for miles."

"We'll have to walk up to the road. There's a culvert and a bridge there."

Hannah drew back. "Is that safe?"

"We can hear and see cars approaching from a long way off," he said. "We'll hide until we're sure the coast is clear, then make a dash for it."

They turned and followed the ravine up toward the road. As they drew closer, the rumble of an approaching vehicle sent them diving for cover behind an outcropping of pocked rock. Heat radiated from the scarred red granite, but the ground on its shady side still gave off a damp coolness.

Walt peered over the top of the boulder and watched a faded brown Jeep move slowly past. A bearded man sat behind the wheel; Walt was sure it was Kiram, but was that even possible, considering how recently he had been wounded?

When the vehicle had passed, they moved forward again. The bridge over the ravine was a plank affair one lane wide, laid over a rusting metal culvert. No railings separated traffic from the chasm below, and only a single orange reflector on a post marked the beginning of the bridge.

"It didn't seem this narrow when we were on the motorcycle," Hannah said.

"All we have to do is walk across it and we can move away from the road again." Walt held out his hand and she took it.

Their feet made a hollow sound on the wood planks, but the bridge was solid underfoot, and only about twenty feet across. Halfway across, the baby began to fuss and squirm. Hannah stopped and shifted her. "Her diaper's soaking," she said, feeling around one chubby leg. "No wonder, considering the way she sucked down that bottle."

"You can change her in another couple of minutes," Walt said. Standing out here in the middle of the bridge felt too vulnerable. The hair rose on the back of his neck, and he couldn't shake the feeling they were being watched. A hot wind ruffled his hair and he squinted across the prairie, his unease growing.

"What was that noise?" Hannah looked up from tending the baby.

Walt didn't have to ask "what noise?" He heard it, too—the low rumble of an engine turning over. He pivoted toward the sound, and saw what he hadn't noticed before—an old wooden corral, the boards forming the sides almost obscured by several decades' growth of sagebrush and prickly pear cactus. The corral made the perfect hiding place for someone in a vehicle to park and watch the bridge and wait.

The driver wasn't waiting anymore. His vehicle—a faded brown Jeep—shot out from the screen of boards and brush, headed straight for the bridge, and Walt and Hannah standing in the middle of it.

Chapter Sixteen

Hannah froze, transfixed by the sight of the Jeep barreling toward them. She was like someone in a dream, wanting to move but unable to do so.

"Climb down!" Walt tugged on her arm. "Over the side. Into the culvert." He pulled the infant from her and dragged her toward the edge of the bridge. He dropped to his stomach and pulled her down alongside him. "Go!" he urged.

She swung her legs over the side, clinging to the edge of the bridge, the boards shaking as the Jeep hit the bridge, the roar of the engine filling her ears. The baby clutched to his chest, Walt swung down beside her and dropped to the ground. She released her hold on the bridge as the Jeep thundered over them.

She hit the ground hard, the breath jolted out of her, but managed to roll into the culvert. Walt helped her to her feet and shoved the baby into her arms. "Get behind me," he said, drawing his gun and moving into the shadows.

Tires skidded on gravel as the Jeep braked to a halt. Car doors slammed and footsteps crunched. Hannah shrank into the deepest shadows, heart thudding so hard in her chest she had trouble drawing breath. Walt guided her into the middle of the tunnel formed by the culvert, into a corner formed by wooden bracing. He settled her into this hiding place, then turned, his back to her, shielding her with his body. She stared over his shoulder toward the opening at the end of the culvert, a circle of bright light like a spotlight, blinding in its intensity.

Each footstep overhead seemed to echo through the tunnel. Obviously, their pursuers were making no attempt at stealth. The movement above stopped. "We know you're in there, Walter!" Kiram shouted. "Come on out and we'll go easy on you."

Walt remained silent, still as a cornered stag—or a waiting lion.

Two heavy thuds signaled that their two pursuers had dropped into the ravine—one on either side of the culvert. Hannah stiffened. They were trapped now, caught between the two.

Walt reached back and squeezed her hand. The gesture shouldn't have calmed her, but somehow it did. Without uttering a word, he was letting her know he had a plan. She had to trust him.

She took a deep breath and squeezed back. *I trust you.*

A shadow darkened the opening to the tunnel—the silhouette of a tall, muscular man. "You can't escape now," Kiram said. "We've got you cornered."

He raised his right arm, and Hannah recognized the silhouette of a gun before it melted into the shadow of his body. But he was aiming it at the opposite side of the tunnel from where they were standing. He hadn't yet seen them. They were hidden in the deepest, darkest recesses of the tunnel, and his eyes, attuned to the brightness outside, hadn't been able to make them out. The man at the other end of the tunnel wouldn't be able to see them either, especially since the wooden support completely blocked them from his view.

Kiram took a step into the tunnel. Walt would have a clear shot at him now. Didn't Kiram realize this? Or was he so sure of his own superior position that he wasn't thinking? But would Walt fire? As soon as he did so, he would give away their position to the other man.

"It's too late to save yourself," Kiram said. "I promised to kill you and I will. But you can save the woman. The Prophet wants her and the baby safe and alive. Give yourself up now and I promise to take them to him. Try to take me and…well, I can't help it if they get caught in the cross fire, can I?" He took another step toward them.

The shot was a loud, echoing explosion in the metal culvert. Hannah choked back a scream and sank to her knees, her body arched over the baby, who began to wail. A second shot followed the first, then two more in rapid succession. Head down, eyes squeezed tightly shut, Hannah couldn't tell where they came from.

Her ears rang, and the smell of gunpowder stung her nose, but even half-deaf, the scuffle of retreating footsteps was clear. Opening her eyes, she turned to see Walt racing toward the far end of the tunnel. Before he had reached the end, an engine roared to life overhead, and tires skidded as the Jeep raced away.

Walt returned to her, the gun still in his hand. "Are you all right?" he asked.

"Yes." She started to rise, and he bent to help her. "What happened?" she asked.

"I'm going to check on Kiram," he said, and left before she could say more. Too shaken to move, she leaned back against the support and held her breath as he moved slowly toward the slumped figure at the tunnel opening.

She knew Kiram was dead by the heavy, sack-of-cement way his body rolled over when Walt nudged it. Walt knelt and put a hand to the bearded man's neck, then eased the gun from his grip and tucked it into his belt. He took something else from the body, then returned to her side.

"Here." He pressed something heavy into her hand. "He was wearing this on his belt."

She realized she was holding a water bottle, and hurried to twist off the cap and drink. The cool, sweet water flowed over her tongue and tears stung her eyes at the sheer pleasure of it. She forced herself to hold back from drinking it all and passed it to him.

"The other man got away," she said, when Walt had finished drinking and re-capped the bottle.

"Yes. He'll tell the others we're in this area. We need to move quickly."

"Why did he come after us?" she asked. "I thought you shot him back at the camp."

"I wounded him, but it obviously wasn't enough to stop him. His shoulder was bandaged, but my guess is he hated me enough that he was determined to find me. That kind of emotion can lead people to do incredible things."

"But he didn't stop us," she said. "He won't stop us."

"No, he won't." He started to lead the way out of the culvert, but she took hold of his arm, turning him toward her.

"What—?" She cut off the question, her lips on his, her body pressed against him. All the fear and anxiety and the giddy relief of simply being alive and with him at this moment coalesced in that kiss. All the passion she felt for him but was afraid to put into words found expression in the melding of her body to his.

He wrapped his arms around her, crushing her to him. There was no hiding her body's response to him, or his to her. Heat and hunger and need washed over her like a wave, and she moaned softly as he caressed the side of her breast and lowered his mouth to nibble the soft underside of her jaw. Every kiss, every caress, reached past the barriers she had erected long ago and touched some vulnerable part of her deep inside, coaxing her to let go a little bit more, to surrender. To trust.

He rested his forehead against hers, his breathing ragged, his voice rough. "This isn't the best time for this," he said.

"I know." She rested her palms against his chest. "We have to go. I just…I wanted you to know how I felt."

"I got the message, loud and clear." He wrapped both hands around her wrists and kissed the tips of her fingers, a gesture that set her heart to fluttering wildly.

Then he released her, and she wanted to cry out, but instead bit her lip and bent to pick up the baby, who smiled up at her with such an expression of happiness that tears stung her eyes. Talk about an emotional roller-coaster ride! The last thirty minutes had taken her through almost every feeling imaginable.

They moved out of the tunnel, the light momentarily blinding them after so much time in the shadows. Joy wailed, and Hannah rearranged the blanket to shade her face. "We'll stick to the ravine," Walt said. "It'll be rough going, but we'll be out of sight of the road."

Navigating the ravine was akin to negotiating an obstacle course. Uprooted trees, boulders the size of furniture, loose gravel and tangles of thorny vines necessitated frequent detours and stumbles. After a short distance Walt took the baby so that Hannah had both hands free to steady herself as she climbed up boulders and teetered along downed tree trunks. She stumbled often, scraping her hands and muddying her skirt. But she plowed doggedly on. As difficult as this was, at least they weren't out in the open, where anyone looking for them might easily spot them.

They had been walking less than an hour—and covered maybe half a mile—when the roar of approaching vehicles made them freeze in midstride. "It sounds like at least two of them," Walt said.

"Are they on the road?" Hannah asked, straining her ears.

As if to answer her question, the engine sounds faded, followed by crunching gravel, then the engines revved with a different pitch than before. "They turned off the road," Walt said. "They're headed this way."

He turned and continued moving up the ravine. "What are we going to do?" she asked, hurrying after him.

"As long as they stay in the vehicles, they can't see us down here," Walt said. He reached out a hand to pull her up over a large section of dead tree that was wedged across the ravine. "As long as they don't stop and get out, they're just wasting gas racing around up there."

"How did they find us so quickly?" she asked.

"They might have radios."

The engine noises faded again, and car doors slammed. Hannah looked up, and wished she knew what was going on up there.

"We'd better find a place to hide," Walt said.

They moved farther down the ravine, losing their footing often on the rough ground, but pressing on. The ravine forked and Walt led her down the narrower branch, which was scarcely wide enough for them to walk side by side. This channel was more deeply eroded, but less clogged with debris, though tree roots reached out from the bank like bony fingers, snagging at their clothing and hair.

"In here." Walt indicated a place where the bank was undercut behind a snarl of tree roots, forming a recess. Hannah balked, staring at what was really a mud-lined hole in the ground. It looked like the perfect home for spiders, snakes and who knew what else.

"Come on," Walt urged. "We have to hide before they decide to search here."

He was right, and there was no sense being squeamish. She followed him into the niche. He handed her the baby, then pulled the tree roots and a couple of loose branches to cover their entrance.

Sunlight filtered through the network of limbs and branches that formed one wall of their shelter, dappling their faces and making the niche a little less threatening. Hannah settled back into an almost-cozy spot and took out a fresh diaper and a packet of wipes. At least she could make Joy more comfortable. She stashed the dirty diaper in a plastic bag and stuffed it into the diaper bag, which she used as a kind of pillow at her back.

"Here." Walt handed her a protein bar. "Dinner."

"Thanks. You think of everything."

"Yeah. I really know how to show a woman a good time." He unwrapped a bar for himself. "Take this out-of-the-way bistro. You can't imagine how exclusive this place is."

"And it's so romantic." She laughed, and he grinned and rested his hand on her knee. "Anyplace with you seems romantic to me."

She debated kissing him again, but the narrow confines of their hideaway—not to mention the baby on her lap—made that difficult. So she settled for lacing her fingers in his and soaking in the feeling of contentment that filled her. She was dirty, hungry, thirsty and exhausted, terrified of the killers who hunted them, and confused about what lay ahead for her and Joy. But all of those worries and fears faded into the background here beside Walt.

They shared the last of the water, munching in companionable silence while straining their ears for any sound from the searchers overhead. "It doesn't sound as if they've come this way," Walt said after a while. "They probably didn't expect us to get this far. They might even suspect we went another direction."

He shifted to turn toward her. "What happened last night?" he asked. "When Metwater took you to his RV?" Tension radiated from him, as if he was bracing for bad news.

"Nothing, really," she said. "He seemed to think I ought to be flattered that I'd been singled out for attention from the great and mighty Prophet." She made a face. "The guy has an ego bigger than his biceps."

"So he didn't try to force himself on you?"

"He intended to keep me prisoner until I came around to his way of thinking." She sighed. "I think that's what he did with Emily. At least, Phoenix told me he had moved her in with him a week or so before she died. Taking her with him to Denver was a special privilege—maybe an attempt to persuade her to give in to his demands. I think the stress of the whole ordeal, and being without her baby, brought on her asthma attack. Plus, Phoenix told me she had run out of her inhaler prescription."

"It would be tough to prove murder, though if what you say is true, he could have definitely contributed to her death."

"I know. But then, why lie and say she had run away instead of telling people she had died?"

"Because he didn't want to upset the rest of his followers?" He put his arm around her. "We may never know. Though when I bring in Metwater, I intend to ask him."

She settled against him, her head on his shoulder. "Knowing you care means a lot."

He kissed the top of her head. "I do care."

Yes. And she cared for him. But if caring were enough, her baby never would have died. She had made a mistake then, trying to do the right thing. She couldn't afford to make another mistake.

DESPITE THE DISCOMFORT of her surroundings and the lingering fear for their safety, the sleepless night in Metwater's RV, coupled with the physical hardship of fleeing across the wilderness, overcame Hannah's attempts to stay awake, and she sank into a deep slumber.

She woke to Joy's cries the next morning, sunlight streaking down from above. Next to her, Walt stirred.

"I'm going to go up and check things out," he said. "See if it's safe for us to move on."

He moved out of their shelter, and she took advantage of his absence to spread out the contents of the diaper bag and organize them. She had one more bottle of formula, which she would feed Joy this morning— and only two more diapers. No more water or food for her and Walt. But surely this morning they would reach safety. They couldn't be that far from the highway after they had walked so much yesterday.

A shower of dirt signaled Walt's return. "Everything's quiet up here," he said. "I think it's safe to go."

"Let me change Joy," she said. "She can have her last bottle while we're walking."

"I don't suppose you've stashed any coffee in there," he said, eyeing the diaper bag.

"I wish. I guess all the coffee shops up there are closed?"

"Every one of them." He waited while she finished diapering the baby, then reached down to help them out of their hiding place.

She groaned as she put weight on her cramped limbs. "I think every bone in my body hurts," she said.

"We'll have to complain to management about the mattresses in this place," Walt said.

They climbed out of the ravine and she paused at the top to stretch and breathe in the fresh, clean air, which smelled of sage and wildflowers. After spending so much time out here, she would never look at the wilderness as barren again. "Which way do we go?" she asked.

Walt turned in a slow circle, taking in the surrounding landscape. The land was gently rolling, and devoid of any sign of human habitation. Only scrubby prairie and the occasional rock uplift defined the empty expanse. Hannah had hoped to see a road, but no such luck. "Does anything look familiar to you?" he asked.

"Everything out here looks the same to me," she said.

"Me, too."

His grim expression alarmed her. "Are you saying we're lost?"

"I'm saying I'm not sure which way we should go to find the road."

She turned to look behind them, at the ravine they had just climbed out of. "Can't we just follow this back to the BLM road, then parallel that to the highway?" she asked. As much as she hated the thought of backtracking, it would be better than wandering aimlessly in the middle of nowhere.

"We could. If we knew which ravine to follow." He indicated the network of half a dozen similar ditches that spread out in every direction.

"I don't remember those," she said. "When we were down in there, there was only one way to go, at least, after we took the fork off the main channel."

"There were other forks," he said. "Now I'm not sure which one we should take."

She looked down into the chasm again. The thought of repeating the torturous crawl of the day before made her want to sink to her knees and weep. But she was stronger than that. "Do you know which direction the road was from Metwater's camp?" she asked.

"East," he said.

"The sun rises in the east, so we can walk that direction," she said.

"Except we don't know where we are in relationship to Metwater's camp," he said.

"So you're saying we're lost."

He squinted up at the sky. "Yeah. I guess I'm saying we're lost."

The words seemed to bounce up against her brain, refusing to sink in. After all they had been through, this couldn't really be happening. "You work out here," she said. "Don't you have some idea of where we are?"

"I've only been on the job two months," he said. "And it's a lot of territory. It would take years—decades—for any one person to know it all."

"So what are we going to do?" She hated that they were in this situation—and she hated that she was looking to him for answers. She wasn't the kind of person who depended on other people. She was used to solving her own problems. But this wasn't a chemical formulation that needed tweaking or a budget item she needed to finesse. She had nothing to draw on to get them out of this jam.

"Right now, I think we've got an even bigger problem to worry about," Walt said.

"What are you talking about?" What could be bigger than being lost in the middle of nowhere?

"If I'm not mistaken, we've got a prairie fire headed this way."

She turned to follow his gaze and gaped at the line of leaping orange flames that filled the horizon.

Chapter Seventeen

Walt stared at the line of flames inching toward them, the lessons from a wildland firefighting course he had taken as part of his training repeating in his head. The wind was pushing the fire in this direction, and there was nothing to stop it, and plenty of dry tinder to feed it. Firefighters carried flameproof shelters which—sometimes—could save their lives if they were overtaken by an out-of-control burn, but he and Hannah didn't have anything like that.

He took hold of her arm. "We have to get back into the ravine," he said. "If we're lucky, it will divert the flames, or they'll pass over it."

She didn't hesitate or argue, merely wrapped the baby more securely and started half climbing, half sliding into the ditch they had only recently climbed out of. "Try to find the cave where we spent the night!" he shouted after her. Already the roar of the fire was growing louder, like a jet engine revving for flight. The wind blowing toward them carried the scent of burning wood—like the world's largest campfire.

He caught up with her at the bottom of the ravine and together they scrambled over boulders and branches, watching for the opening to the undercut that had sheltered them last night.

"There!" Hannah pointed to the place where they had pushed aside a knot of tree roots as they had exited their shelter.

"Hurry!" He took the baby from her and started up the slope. The fire was almost upon them, a hot, shrieking turbulence created by the flames sending debris flying, branches and even whole trees exploding into flames like hand grenades going off as the sap superheated inside the bark.

He shoved the baby, who was crying now, into the mud-lined shelter, then reached back to haul Hannah up by both arms. He pushed her into the opening, then crawled in after her, shielding both her and the child with his body, his back to the world above that was already being consumed by flames.

Hannah crouched over the infant, whose wails rose over even the sound of the inferno, a siren song that seemed to intensify his own fear and anxiety. He wrapped his arms around Hannah and buried his face against her neck, breathing in deeply of her sweet scent, trying to block the acrid stench of smoke. She gripped his arm, fingers digging into his flesh. The roar of the flames was even louder now—he winced as the heat intensified, searing his back. It was growing harder to breathe, and the baby's wails silenced. He slid one hand beneath Hannah's to touch the child, reassured that she was still breathing.

Hannah coughed, and he held her, then gave in to spasms of his own. But as the pain in his chest eased, he opened his eyes and realized the roaring of the blaze had faded, and light was once more seeping into their shelter. The heat had lessened, as well. Hannah turned her head and her eyes met his. "Is it over?" she asked.

He eased back a little, and then a little more, until he was able to stick his head out to survey the ravine. Smoke curled from a smoldering tree branch and white ash scarred the rocks around it, but the fire hadn't descended to the bottom of the ravine. He retreated into the undercut once more. "Let's wait a few minutes for things to cool off a bit, but I think we're okay," he said. "How's Joy?"

"She's fine." She cradled the infant to her, tears streaming down her face. "I was so scared, but thanks to you, we're all okay."

"I didn't do anything," he said. "And for what it's worth, I was terrified, too."

She wrapped her arms around him. "I might have made it without you, but I'm glad I didn't have to try," she said.

They waited half an hour, then climbed out of the ravine, emerging streaked with soot and ash to a landscape filled with the blackened skeletons of trees and exploded rock. Smoke curled from the ground, and they walked carefully, trying to avoid hot spots. Walt moved in front of Hannah to break the trail, and she gasped.

He glanced over his shoulder at her. "What's wrong?"

"Your back!" She pointed, then covered her mouth with her hand. "It's burned."

He hadn't noticed anything until that moment, but when he reached around and felt along his ribs he winced at the sudden, searing pain. "Your shirt is almost burned away," she said. "You let that happen and you never said a thing."

"I had other things on my mind." He faced forward again. "It doesn't matter. We have to get out of here."

"But where are we going?" she asked.

"Away from the fire."

A droning sound overhead made them both look up. When Walt recognized the helicopter, he raised both hands to wave, ignoring the pain in his shoulders as he did so. Hannah took the blanket from around the baby and waved it also. The chopper dipped lower, and they could clearly see the pilot. He circled them, and then slowly descended to a spot about two hundred yards away.

By the time Walt and Hannah reached the helicopter, the pilot had shut down the engine and climbed out to meet them. "What are you two doing out here?" he asked.

"It's a long story," Walt said. "I'm Agent Walt Riley with the Ranger Brigade. Can you take us to Ranger headquarters?"

"Whoever you are, you need to get out of here. Climb in." The pilot walked around to the door of the chopper. "I'll radio this in once we're airborne. Headquarters is never going to believe this."

"I DON'T BELIEVE THIS." Commander Graham Ellison frowned as an EMT bandaged Walt's blistered back. "When Metwater's people told us you and Hannah had left, we suspected something was up, but not that you'd been trapped in that wildfire."

"Which the fire investigators now say was deliberately set." Carmen joined the group clustered around Walt, Hannah and the baby.

"When Metwater's goons didn't succeed in tracking us down yesterday, he probably thought the fire would be a good way to finish us off." Walt winced as the EMT tightened the bandage.

"That's crazy." Hannah looked up from feeding the baby. "They could have burned down their own camp."

"They were probably counting on the road and the creek to serve as a firebreak," Marco said. "And the prevailing winds were in their favor."

"Metwater is already claiming he knows nothing about anything," Graham said. "And he's telling anyone who will listen that you murdered Alan Saddler—aka Kiram—in cold blood."

"He was trying to kill us!" Hannah stood, unable to rein in her outrage.

"I'm sure the investigation will prove that," Graham said. He turned to Walt. "Until that plays out, you're probably going to take a beating in the press. Metwater has his lawyers working overtime, filing charges."

"But he'll have to submit to the paternity test the court ordered, right?" Hannah asked. Soon after they had arrived at Ranger headquarters, she had learned the court order for the DNA test to determine the baby's identity had come through.

"He will," Graham said. "We won't let him off the hook on that."

The EMT pressed the final bandage in place, then stepped back. "You need to have a doctor check that out ASAP, but I'm guessing you're going to need a couple of weeks off to heal," he said.

"Good idea," Graham said. "You lie low and let us handle Metwater."

"He assaulted me, kidnapped Hannah and he stole my bike," Walt said.

"I've got your bike in my garage," Michael Dance said.

Walt scowled at him. "What are you doing with my Harley?"

"When we showed up at Metwater's camp, looking for you, I spotted it tucked behind one of the shacks," Michael said. "I decided I'd better take it in for safe-keeping before it disappeared altogether."

"Don't let him fool you," Marco said. "He just wanted to ride it."

"It's a sweet ride," Michael said, grinning.

"Metwater didn't try to stop you?" Walt asked.

"He told us you had just left it there when you decided to take off," Marco said. "That's when we knew he was lying about what happened to you. You wouldn't abandon the Harley."

"What about Lucia Raton?" Hannah asked. "Have you found her?"

"Not yet," Carmen said. "But we found a witness who saw her after she supposedly left Metwater's camp, so that seems to let him off the hook."

"For now," Graham said. "As for the rest, the assault charges are going to be tough to make stick, especially with Metwater making a stink about Kiram's death. And the kidnapping—" He looked at Hannah.

"He held me against my will," Hannah said. "But we'll probably have a hard time finding anyone except Walt who will testify to that."

"We'll see what we can do." Graham touched Walt's arm. "As of now, you're on medical leave. Get your back seen to, then go away somewhere and try to relax. Avoid the press."

"But I don't—" he started to protest, but Hannah took his other arm and he fell silent.

"Why don't you come to Texas?" she asked. "I could use some help settling in with Joy."

She didn't blame him for the doubt in his eyes. After all, she had wasted a lot of time protesting that things would never work out between them. But those moments in the fire, when they had been so close to death and he had been willing to risk everything to save her and Joy, had made her see how foolish her fears had been.

Aware of the others watching, she leaned closer to him and lowered her voice. "Please? I've decided I was right that first day I came in here—you really are the one I want to help me."

Her cheeks burned as he kissed her on the lips. His coworkers broke into applause and she pulled away, laughing. "Is that a yes?"

"It's a yes," he said. "Play your cards right and I might even stick around longer than two weeks."

"I always was a good card player," she said, a thrill running through her. She'd never been a big gambler, but right now she was willing to risk a lot to be with the man she loved.

Epilogue

Carmen Redhorse looked up from her computer terminal and smiled at the little family that had just walked into Ranger headquarters. Out of uniform and toting a baby carrier, Walt Riley was the picture of a suburban dad. The woman beside him, Hannah, had lost the pinched look that had haunted her before and now glowed with the happiness of a woman in love.

"I just stopped by to clean out my locker and my desk," Walt said, setting the carrier on a chair by the door.

"How's the back?" Carmen asked. She came over to admire the infant, who babbled and flailed her arms, chubby cheeks framing an adorable baby smile.

"It's fine," he said.

"He's got some scars," Hannah said. "But I think he's almost proud of them."

"Good for his macho cred," Carmen said.

"Where is everybody?" Walt asked.

"Marco and Ethan are at training, Michael and Lance are trying to track down a guy who's been stealing rare plants from the park, Simon is in court, the commander and Randall are at a meeting in Montrose, and I'm holding down the fort here."

"What's the latest on Metwater?" Walt asked.

"Not good," Carmen said. "The DA says we don't have enough evidence to prosecute him for anything. Lucia Raton is still missing, so the fact that her locket was found sort of near his compound doesn't mean much. Anything we have any proof for, like the assault on you, Metwater blames on Kiram, whom he says was acting without his authority or knowledge."

"Right." Walt looked like he wanted to punch someone.

"At least we proved he isn't Joy's father," Hannah said. "He has no claim on her."

"He probably contributed to your sister's death, though we'll never prove it," Walt said.

"Let it go," Hannah said. "I am."

"We're still watching him," Carmen said. "He's going to make a wrong move one day and when he does, we'll catch him."

Walt nodded. "You're right." He looked at Hannah. "And so are you. I'm going to move on."

"So you're really abandoning us for Texas," Carmen said.

"The Dallas County Sheriff's Department has an opening, so I'm going to give it a try."

Carmen turned to Hannah. "Are you sure you're ready for life with a Harley-riding cop?"

Hannah shook her head. "No more Harley," she said. "He sold it."

Carmen put a hand to her chest in a pantomime of shock. "You sold the Harley?"

Walt's cheeks reddened. "Yeah, well, you can't strap a car seat on the back of a motorcycle."

"This must be serious," Carmen said.

Hannah slipped her arm through Walt's, smiling at him with the indulgent look women in love shared. "Yes, it is."

Carmen caught the flash of the diamond on the third finger of Hannah's left hand. "How did I miss this?" She grabbed the hand for a closer l ook. "Nicely done, Agent Riley," she said. "Have you set a date?"

"We're thinking in the spring." He grinned.

"Congratulations," Carmen said. "You almost make me believe in true love."

"Hey, I was a skeptic, too," Hannah said.

"She just had to meet someone tough enough to call her bluff," Walt said.

"Someone who showed me I could trust myself." She squeezed his hand and Carmen felt the pressure around her heart. Why was it some people found love easily and some—like Hannah and Walt—had to fight for it?

The answer didn't really matter, she decided. In the end the prize was all that mattered, not how you came to win it.

* * * * *

Start your free trial now

We Love Romance
with MILLS & BOON

Available at
weloveromance.com

JOIN THE
MILLS & BOON
BOOKCLUB

* **FREE** delivery direct to your door

* **EXCLUSIVE** offers every month

* **EXCITING** rewards programme

50% OFF
YOUR FIRST
PARCEL

Join today at
Millsandboon.co.uk/Bookclub

MILLS & BOON

HEROES

At Your Service

Experience all the excitement of a
gripping thriller, with an intense romance
at its heart. Resourceful, true-to-life
women and strong, fearless men face
danger and desire - a killer combination!

MILLS & BOON
MEDICAL
Pulse-Racing Passion

Set your pulse racing with dedicated, delectable doctors in the high-pressure world of medicine, where emotions run high and passion, comfort and love are the best medicine.

JAMES MACDONALD ... *Raptor* is his first book and it received a Royal Society of Literature Jerwood Award for Non-Fiction in 2011.

Praise for *Raptor*:

'Lockhart puts the rapture back in the raptor. This is in-the-moment writing, raw in beak and claw … *Raptor* rips at its words, turning them into exquisite portraits of the utter wild'   PHILIP HOARE

'Lockhart's soaring debut is a perfect synthesis of travel writing and natural history … He laces vivid prose with illuminating facts to explore his own colourful experiences without shifting focus from the birds themselves …'   *Financial Times*

'If you publish a book on birds of prey in the tumultuous wake of Helen MacDonald's prizewinning *H is for Hawk*, you expect comparisons. James Macdonald Lockhart can relax. His book is outstanding … His facts are couched in unusual and resonant contexts … The writing is beautifully precise'   *Sunday Times*

'Lockhart's prose is usually so intimate, urgent and visceral as to make his darkly resonant ruminations almost unfailingly gripping'   *Independent*

'A hymn in praise of living, soaring, terrifying grandeur ... Lockhart's exquisite, poetic language is a sensuous delight without sacrificing scientific accuracy. *Raptor* is, quite simply, a tour de force'   *Daily Mail*

'A wonderfully modest presence in his own narrative ... Lockhart has mastered an engaging present-tense prose that brings out both the birds' ecstatic gifts of flight but also the tragedy and triumph of their predatory life-style'   *Observer*

'Nothing prepared me for the sustained brilliance and intensity of this book ... Warm, intimate, full of wonder and delight in the ways the birds revealed themselves, and a passionate coming into being of his greatest mentor'   *Caught by the River*

'Lockhart's understanding of raptor ethology shines. His journey – intercut with passages by Victorian ornithologist William MacGillivray – flings us into skies where a hobby "concertinas" the air, or a marsh harrier's ruff gives it the air of an Elizabethan grandee'   *Nature*

'A lovely, poetic book'   *Herald*

'His efforts to see all the 15 species of breeding raptor in Britain make for an enviable series of encounters; they are made riveting by his exquisite way with words ... The writing at times is as good as anything we have on the subject to date'   *Country Life*

RAPTOR

A JOURNEY THROUGH BIRDS

JAMES MACDONALD LOCKHART

4th ESTATE • London

4th Estate
An imprint of HarperCollins*Publishers*
1 London Bridge Street
London SE1 9GF
www.4thEstate.co.uk

First published in Great Britain by 4th Estate in 2016
This 4th Estate paperback edition published in 2017

1

Copyright © James Macdonald Lockhart 2016

James Macdonald Lockhart asserts the moral right to be
identified as the author of this work in accordance with
the Copyright, Designs and Patents Act 1988

A catalogue record for this book is
available from the British Library

ISBN 978-0-00-745989-6

Internal illustrations taken from *A History of British Birds Vol. III*
by William MacGillivray (William S. Orr and Co., 1852).
Illustration of William MacGillivray © The Natural
History Museum/Alamy Stock Photo

Printed and bound in Great Britain by
Clays Ltd, St Ives plc

FSC
the responsible management of the world's forests. Products carrying the
FSC label are independently certified to assure consumers that they come
from forests that are managed to meet the social, economic and
ecological needs of present and future generations,
and other controlled sources.

Find out more about HarperCollins and the environment at
www.harpercollins.co.uk/green

Contents

By the term Raptores may be designated an order
of birds, the predatory habits of which have
obtained for them a renown exceeding that
of any other tribe …

WILLIAM MACGILLIVRAY,
A History of British Birds, Volume III

I

Hen Harrier

Orkney

It begins where the road ends beside a farm. Empty sacking, silage breath, the car parked amongst oily puddles. The fields are bright after rain. Inside one puddle, a white plastic feed sack, crumpled, like a drowned moon. Then feet up on the car's rear bumper, boots loosened and threaded, backpacks tightened. Wanting to rain: a sheen of rain, like the thought of rain, has settled on the car and made it gleam. When I bend to tie my boots I notice tiny beads of water quivering like mercury on the waxed leather. Eric is with me, who knows this valley intimately, who knows where the kestrel has its nest above the burn and where the short-eared owls hide their young amongst the heather. We leave the farm and start to walk along the track towards the swell of the moor.

Closer the fields look greasy and soft. The track begins to leak away from under us and soon the bog has smothered it completely. We are amongst peat hags and pools of amber water. Marsh orchids glow mauve and pink amongst the dark reed grass. The sky is heavy with geese: greylags, with their snowshoe gait, long thick necks snorkelling the heather. You do not think they could get airborne; they run across the moor beating at the air, nothing like a bird. And with a heave they are up, calling with the rigmarole of it all, stacking themselves in columns of three or four. They fly low over the moor, circling above us as if in a holding pattern. When a column of geese breaks the horizon it looks like a dust devil has spun up from the ground to whirl slowly down the valley towards us.

Late May on a hillside in Orkney; nowhere I would rather be. It is a place running with birds. Curlews with their rippling song and long delicate bills and the young short-eared owls keeking from their hideout in the heather. And all that heft and noise of goose. When the greylags leave, shepherding their young down off the moor, following the burns to the lowland lochs and brackish lagoons, then, surely, undetectably, the moor must inflate a little, breathing out after all that weight of goose has gone.

We find a path that cuts through a bank of deep heather. It leads up onto the moor and the horizon lifts. I can see the hills of Hoy with their wind-raked slopes of scree and the sea below with its waves like the patterns of the scree. This morning the sea is a livery dark, creased with white lines that map the movement of the swell. It looks as if the sea is full of cracks, splinters of ice.

Wherever you turn on Orkney the sea is at your back, linking the islands with its junctions of light. It is not enough that the islands are already so scattered. The sea is always gnawing at them, looking for avenues to open up, fractures in the rock to prise apart. The sea up here has myriad ways to breach the land. It showers the western cliffs with its salty mists and peoples the thin soils with its kin: creeping willow, eyebright, sea thrift, sea plantain, all plants that love the sea's breath on them.

It is a trickster sea that comes ashore with subterfuge. Orkney children once made imaginary farms with scallop shells for sheep, gaper shells for pigs, as if the sea, like a toymaker, had carved each shell and left it on the shore, waiting for a passing child. And at night selchies dock in the deep geos and patter ashore in their wet skins to slip amongst the dozing kye.

I arrived on Orkney in the dregs of a May gale. Low pressure swelling in from the Atlantic, hurting buildings and trees in their new growth, ransacking birds' nests. Rushing across Scotland and speeding up over Orkney as if the gale had hit a patch of ice. The hardest thing of all up here, I'd heard, was learning to endure the wind, worse than the long winter darkness. It is a fidgety wind, rarely still, boisterous, folding sheds and hen houses, raking the islands' lochs into inland seas.

This morning the wind still has a sinewy strength. Lapwings are lifted off the fields like flakes of ash. Eric is telling me about the valley. He is alert to the slightest wren-flick through the heather, seeing the birds before they arrive. When he speaks the wind gashes at his words, gets inside them. The hill is shaking with wind. We pass the kestrel's nest and Eric points out a clump of rushes on the hillside where a hen harrier is sitting on her eggs. She is invisible on her bed of rush and ling. Her eggs are pale white, polished, stained with the colours of the nest material. If you could see like a hawk you would notice her bright yellow eyes, framed by a white eyebrow on a flat owl-like face. The face made rounder by the thick neck ruff that flickers bronze and almond-white like the ring around a planet.

Then Eric is leaving and I don't feel I have thanked him enough. I watch him descend the moor, walking quickly along the gleaming track towards the farm and the car like a skiff bobbing amongst the lit puddles. After he has gone there is a sudden rush of rain. But the wind is so strong it seems to hold the rain up, stops it reaching the ground, flinging the shower away, crashing it into the upper slopes of the hill. Only my face and hair are briefly wet; the rest of me stays dry, as if I'd poked my head into a cloud. I have never seen rain behave this way. Months

4

later I came across a list of beautiful old Orkney dialect words for different types of rain and wondered which described the behaviour of that wind-blown shower: *driv, rug, murr, muggerafeu, hagger, dagg, rav, hellyiefer* ... A *rug*, perhaps, meaning 'a strong pull', rain that was being pulled, yanked away by the wind.

I had not thanked Eric nearly enough. For a walk like that will have its legacies, store itself in you like a muscle's memory. Walking up through layers of birds, Eric explaining the narrative of the moor, where last year's merlins hid their nest, where cattle had punctuated the dyke and damaged the delicate hillside. Till we reached a fold in the hills, the 'nesting station', where the hen harriers had congregated their nests, and we could go no further.

I know of other walks, like the one with Eric that morning, where their legacy is precious and defining, walks born out of that experience of guiding or being guided. My great-grandfather, Seton Gordon, in the early summer of 1906, when he was only twenty, walked into the Grampian Mountains with his boyhood hero, the naturalist Richard Kearton. That walk began with Gordon telegramming Kearton with the news he had found a ptarmigan's nest, one of the few birds, Gordon knew, that Kearton had never photographed. Kearton packed hastily and rushed to catch the next train to Scotland. Early June, travelling north through strata of light; a 600-mile journey from Surrey to Aberdeenshire, where Gordon met Kearton off the train at Ballater. They decide to climb the mountain at night to avoid the heat of the day, setting off in the dusk, the smell of pine and birch all around them. Kearton is lame (he was left permanently lame after a childhood accident) and has to walk slowly, stopping often to rest. They toil up the mountain through the thin June dark, Kearton bent like a hunchback under the huge camera he is carrying (the heaviest Gordon has ever seen). At 1.45 a.m. a redstart's song spurs them on.

They reach the snowfield beside the ptarmigan's nest at 6 a.m. The sun is up and bright, the short grass sparkles. Kearton assembles his camera on its tripod and begins, cautiously, to crawl towards the sitting bird. She is a close sitter, Gordon reassures him, and if he stalks her very slowly she should sit tight. The next few moments are so precarious: Kearton exposes a number of plates and after each exposure he edges a little closer towards the ptarmigan. He stops when he is just nine feet away. He can hear his heart thumping in his chest. One last exposure, that's it! He is close enough to see the bird breathing and the dew pearled across her back.

Seventy years later, the year before he died, Gordon was still able to recall that walk, writing about it in an article for *Country Life* magazine. The details of that day still fresh and resonant: the brightness of the sun that morning, the dew along the ptarmigan's back, the cost of the telegram he sent to Kearton (sixpence).

Richard Kearton's photographs of birds, taken at the end of the nineteenth century (many with his brother, Cherry Kearton), were to my great-grandfather what Gordon's own photographs of birds are to me, jewels of inspiration. I grew up surrounded by Gordon's black and white photographs of birds: golden eagles, greenshanks, gannets, dotterels ... peering down at me from their teak frames. I liked to take the frames off the wall, wipe the dust from the glass, then turn the pictures over to read the captions Gordon had written on the back of each print:

- Female eagle 'parasoling' eaglets. The eaglet is invisible on the other side of the bird.
- The golden eagle brings a heather branch to the eyrie.

Whenever I have moved house the first pictures I hang on the new walls are two small photographs Gordon took, one of a jackdaw pair, black and pewter, the other of a hooded crow in its sleeveless silver waistcoat. Under a cupboard I keep a great cache of Gordon's photographs in an ancient marble-patterned canvas folder. You have to untie three string bows to open the folder, and every time I do so a fragment of the canvas frays and disintegrates. My young children like to open the folder with me, and the process of going through the photographs with them – identifying the birds and mammals – has become a lovely ritual. The photographs are beautiful. I am still amazed that anyone could get so close to a wild bird as Gordon did, and photograph it in such exquisite detail. In one photograph, taken in 1922, a golden eagle lands on its nest with a grouse in its talons as a cloud of flies spumes out from an old carcass on the eyrie, as if the landing eagle has triggered an explosion. There is a stunning photograph he took of a pair of greenshanks just at the moment the birds change over incubation duties at their nest. One bird steps over the nest, ready to settle, as its mate pulls itself off the clutch of four eggs. The timing of the photograph, to capture the precise moment of the changeover, is extraordinary. The patterning on the eggs matches the patterns down the greenshank's breast as if one has imprinted – stained – the other.

Along with Richard Kearton and another wildlife photographer, R. B. Lodge (both important influences on Gordon), Gordon was in the vanguard of early bird photography in this country. Cycling around Deeside in the first years of the twentieth century with his half-plate Thornton Pickard Ruby camera with Dallmeyer lens, Gordon took many exceptional photographs of birds and the wider fauna of the region. Upland species were his speciality: snow bunting, curlew, red-throated diver, ptarmigan ... Many of these photographs he published in the books he wrote. Twenty-seven books in all, the bulk of them about the wildlife and landscapes of the Highlands and Islands. His books take up a wall of shelving in my house; greens and browns and pale silver spines, embossed with gold lettering: *Birds of the Loch and Mountain*; *The Charm of the Hills*; *In Search of Northern Birds*; *Afoot in the Hebrides*; *Wanderings of a Naturalist*; *The Cairngorm Hills of Scotland*; *Amid Snowy Wastes*; *Highways and Byways in the West Highlands* ... I love their Edwardian-sounding titles, the earthy colours of their spines, the smell and feel of the books' thick-cut paper with its ragged, crenulated edges.

Of all the birds that Gordon photographed and studied, the golden eagle was the one he came to know the best. Eagles were his abiding love, his expertise. He published two monographs on them: *Days with the Golden Eagle* in 1927 and *The Golden Eagle: King of Birds* in 1955. Both these studies, particularly the latter, went on to influence and inspire a subsequent generation of naturalists and raptor ornithologists. I often come across warm references to Gordon's golden eagle studies in the forewords and acknowledgements of contemporary works of ornithology. His two golden eagle books were also a huge influence on me. I read them many times when I was a teenager. They set this book gestating.

And then there's my own version of Gordon's walk with Kearton. A family holiday on the Isle of Lewis. I am fourteen or fifteen. In the photos from that week we are sitting on the island's vast, empty beaches, our hair washed out at right angles by the wind. Family picnics: brushing the sand off sandwiches, a lime-green thermos of tomato soup. In the background, sand dunes, a squall inside the marram grass, a blur of gannet flying west.

One day out walking on the moors I discovered something momentous. I had been following a river into the hills and as I came up over the watershed I noticed a small loch lying in a shallow dent of the moor. Wherever there is a depression in the land on Lewis, water gathers. It patterns the island intricately, beautifully. From the air much of the land looks tenuous, as if it is breaking apart, a network of walkways floating on black water. The loch I came across – a lochan – a small pool of peat-dark water, like a sunspot against the purple moor. In its centre, rowing round and round, beating the lochan's bounds, a red-throated diver with its chick. I was mesmerised. They are beautiful, rare birds that I had read about but never seen. I sat down in a bank of heather above the loch and watched the bird's sleek outline, the faint blush of her throat. Always the sense in her stream-lined shape that, sitting on the water, she was not quite in her element, that once she dived, like an otter, the water would transform her. But I had to get back – needed to get back – and tell someone. I raced over the moor and gasped out my discovery to nodding, distracted faces.

Except for Mum. She was interested. She wanted to hear more about what I had found, got me to show her in a bird book what the diver looked like, listened when I explained how its eerie, otherworldly call was supposed to forewarn of rain. And the next morning it rained but Mum and I walked across the moor to the lochan where I had found the divers. And so I became a guide, leading my mother up the river and over the rise in the moor, and in doing so felt something Gordon must have felt guiding Richard Kearton up the flank of the mountain through the night. Me walking far too fast in my exhilaration, almost running over the peat bog, Mum calling me to slow down. Reaching the lochan: the two of us sitting down in the heather, catching our breath. Mum asking if she could borrow my binoculars.

* * *

Where Eric left me became my home for the next two days. I walked up the valley in the early morning, looking for the print my weight had made in the heather the day before; not recognisably my shape, more like a shallow quaich scooped out of the heather as if snow had slept there and in the morning left and left behind its thaw-stain on the ground. The heather held me almost buoyant in its thickness. I settled down in it like a hare crouched in its form, felt the wind running over my back.

Rummaging through Orkney's deceased dialects I borrowed a handful of words besides those I had found to describe the different kinds of rain. Loaned words to help me navigate the land. I liked the ways, like a detailed map, they attended to the specifics, to the margins of the landscape around me. *Cowe*: a stalk of heather, which the wind swept like a windscreen wiper across my view of the moor; *burra*: hard grass found in moory soil; *gayro*: the sward on a hillside where the heather has been exterminated by water. And this word – a lovely gift – which described perfectly my form in the heather, *beul*: a place to lie down or rest.

To reach my *beul* on the moor I had to pass through different zones of birds. Each species seemed to occupy its own layer of the valley as if it adhered to an underlying geology of the place. Oystercatchers over a layer of marl, curlews spread across a bed of sandstone. All of these territories seeping, blurring into each other along fault lines in the moor. For a long time I struggled to get a hold of the birds. There was so much movement amongst them, so many birds to keep track of. I began to draw Venn diagrams of the birds' locations and their movements across the moor till the pages of my notebook were filled with overlapping water rings. Gradually I came to see this small patch of moorland as the meeting point of several territories. There were four species of raptor alone breeding in the heather around me – kestrel, hen harrier, merlin and short-eared owl – and these birds' interaction with each other, and with the large population of breeding wader birds, the curlews in particular, held me captivated over the two days I was there.

Trespassing, ghosting through all these territories like blown fragments of white silk, were the short-eared owls. The focus of their territory was a shifting area that moved around the location of the young owls as they dispersed through the deep heather. Sometimes I passed close by the owlets, hidden from me, calling loudly to their parents for food. Their high-pitched *keek* drilled through me as if I was passing through a scanner. Then the adult birds appeared beside me. They arrived suddenly, quietly, like shapes congealed out of mist. They flew very close, hovering just above my head. Pale white underwings marked with black crease lines as if in places the wings were beginning to thaw. Their faces a deep snow-cloud grey. Black eye-bands, like masks, which set their bright yellow eyes deep in their cupped faces. Always, as the owls hung above me, a sense of being watched and of their gaze penetrating through me. Beautiful in their buoyancy. Wing-tippers, possessed of twisting grace, flickering low over the moor like giant ghost moths.

I never expected to see so much so soon on this journey. I had set off fully expecting to be frustrated, to not find many of the birds I was looking for. But Orkney gave me so much time with its birds of prey, spoilt me utterly in that respect, so that every stage along my journey since has harked back to the time I spent on the islands.

There was an old charm used on Orkney which was supposed to heal deep cuts to the skin. To initiate the cure you had to send the name of the wounded person to the local enchanter or witch-doctor (the Old Norse term was *vǫlva*, meaning a wand carrier). The *vǫlva* would then add some new words to the patient's name, as if they were sprinkling ingredients into a recipe. This word-concoction was then chanted repeatedly until, through some telepathic alchemy, the wound was healed. The charm worked even though the *vǫlva* performing it might be several miles away from their patient. After I left Orkney – and was many hundreds of miles away from the islands – I often wanted to send word back to the place, hoping the islands could perform their charm on me once more and help me find the birds I was searching for, just as they had gifted them to me while I was there.

How does a hen harrier live? It swims over the land as a storm petrel hugs the surface of the sea. It flies so low that sometimes it seems to be stirring the grass, its long legs trailing through the heather like a keel. A slow, tacking flight: float then flap. Then a twisting pirouette and it has swung onto a different tack, following another seam through the moor as if it is tracking a scent. It is like watching a disembodied spirit searching for its host, like a spirit twisting and drifting in the breeze. The harrier rides the swell of the moor, clinging to the contours for cover, creeping up on its prey and surprising it with a sudden burst of speed. The moment before it swoops, the harrier stalls, adjusts its angle a fraction – kestrel-like – then drops suddenly to the ground, talons reaching, seizing through the deep grass.

Up on the moor a cold wind has found me, poking me for signs of life. It sets me shivering in my bed in the heather. A male hen harrier is taking his time, twirling a thread over the hill. He is the colour of smoke and lavender, glaucous. He has not killed. The female is up from her nest agitating him, calling repeatedly, pushing him away from the nest site, chivvying him to go and hunt. The male slips away down the valley towards the sea. Later in the morning, when he returns, flapping heavily up towards the moor, he seems brighter, sea-gleamed, as if the sea has dressed him in its brightness.

I stay with the female harrier expecting her to quickly settle on the nest. Instead, what happens next is startling, unexpected, one of those remarkable encounters that Orkney shared with me. She began to gain height, drawing herself up to just above the horizon. Then a pause as she floated there as if in a new-found buoyancy, as if on the apex of a thermal. Perhaps the thermal had a vacuum

14

like a lift shaft running through its centre. Whatever it was, a route through the air opened up to her like a narrow channel – a lead – opening through pack ice. For she saw it, drew her wing tips back behind her, and plunged down through the opening in a beautiful corkscrew dive. At the last moment, before she crashed into the heather, swooping up again, rising above the moor, clearing the horizon, then leaning and tipping over into another dive. She was dancing! A mesmerising skydance, repeated over and over again, making a pattern in the air like the peaks and troughs of a frantic graph. I paused from watching her only to wipe the condensation from the lenses of my binoculars. Then I immediately fixed back on to her display. Was she signalling to the male, or simply flexing her flight muscles after a long stint on the nest? For twenty minutes she scored the air, and held me there.

The hardest thing to do was to leave the moor in the evening. I walked down through the restless geese and kept turning round in search of one last glimpse of the hen harriers. Sometimes I would follow a male harrier down off the peat moss and watch him quartering the marshy borderland between the fields and the moor. Much of Orkney's moorland has been reclaimed by agriculture. Only the difficult land remains as moor, but even this is sometimes coveted: there are hills on Orkney with strips of neat green fields dissecting the moor. In places it looks like the hills have been scalped. But in the borderlands between the moor and the fields there seemed to be a tussle between the two spheres so that it was unclear which was reclaiming the other. What had been tidied from the fields seemed to have been swept to these edges. And hen harriers thrived in these places, hunting voles along these tangled, unkempt margins.

I met hen harriers in unlikely places on the island. Far away from the moors, around the backs of houses, through the engine-ticking quiet of a farmyard. The birds seemed to slip easily between spheres, between the hills and the farmland below. In an evening field behind a white hotel, I watched a great commotion of oystercatchers and curlews dive-bombing a female harrier. She was slow and huge amongst the shrill wading birds, like some wandering beast come down out of the hills to forage.

Driving across the hill road to Harray in the early evening, I came down off the moor towards a farm and there was a male hen harrier swimming in a pool of wind. I stopped the car and watched him swirl through the farmyard, low over a hedge and into a back garden. He drifted up over a washing line and, for a moment, seemed to join the garments there, a blue-grey shirt flapping in the wind.

This morning the wind has shed some of its weight. The curlew's song has more reach. A male harrier is coming in from the west, lucent against the heather. He is flying more quickly than usual, keeping a straight line, heading for the nest that sits in the lap of a hill amongst thick tussocks of moor grass. Now the female is up and rising to greet him, rushing towards the male. She is so much larger than him, her colours so markedly different, her tawny browns set against his smoking greyness. For centuries the male and female hen harrier were thought to be a different species, and this morning she might have been a larger hawk about to set upon the smaller male. But, at the last moment, she twists onto her back beneath the male and their talons almost brush. The male releases something from his feet and she seizes and catches it in mid-air. All of this happens so quickly and the movement is astonishing for its speed and precision. I cannot make out what it is the male has passed to her but the female has flipped instantly upright again and is rising towards the male once more. Again, at the last moment, she twists onto her back but this time nothing is passed between them. I'm puzzled why she repeats the manoeuvre like this. Perhaps the male still has something in his talons? But I am lucky to witness it again, it is like an unexpected echo and gives me the chance to replay the whole extraordinary exchange. I stay with the female and watch her drop into the heather, where she begins to feed.

Why do hen harriers make this beautiful, acrobatic food pass? When she is incubating, then brooding and guarding the young at the nest, the female is dependent on the male to provide food for her and the chicks. Later, when the chicks are closer to leaving the nest, she will resume hunting. But until then the male must work overtime to provide for the brood and his mate. Polygamous males, common on Orkney, are required to ratchet up their hunting, providing for two, sometimes three, separate nests (the record on Orkney is seven). Nesting in tall dense vegetation on the ground, the food pass is the most efficient way of securing the exchange of prey whilst also distracting from the precise location of the nest, the pass often taking place some distance from the nest itself, which helps to avoid drawing its attention to predators. I wonder if the female ever drops the pass from the male. The hen harrier is so supremely agile, their long legs have such reach, it seems like the male could lob the most awkward pass at his mate and she would still pluck the prey out of the air with all the time to spare.

On Orkney, the Orkney vole (twice the size of the field vole found on the British mainland) is a crucial prey species for the hen harrier. The relatively high numbers of hen harriers on the islands (on those islands in the archipelago that have voles) is attributed to the abundance and stability of the vole population. Many hen harriers overwinter on Orkney and voles are the principal reason these birds are not forced to migrate further south. In addition to voles, young curlews and starlings are frequently taken on the islands, as well as meadow pipits, skylarks and lapwings. Rabbits, too, are predated by the larger female harrier. Where voles are absent, hen harriers are able to breed as long as there is an abundant supply of passerine birds. But on Orkney, and over much of the hen harrier's range, avian prey is, on the whole, secondary in importance and preference to voles and other small mammals, so much so that a scarcity of voles can impede the hen harrier's breeding success. In Gaelic the hen harrier's name is *Clamhan luch* (the mouse-hawk).

Midday and the moor is quiet, the slackest time of the day. The harriers are sitting tight. At Lammas time, under a full moon, people used to go up to the moors on Orkney to cut the stems of rushes to use as wicks for fish-oil lamps. And they went to the moors to gather the wiry cowberry stems to twist into ropes. The moors were a busier landscape than they are today, more interacted with. There was a steady trafficking of peats from off the moors: all the different grades of Orkney peat, peats that smelt of sulphur when they burnt, heavy *yarpha* peats with the moss and heather still on them, peats that burnt too quickly and left behind a bright creamy ash in the hearth. Geese (an important part of the economy on Orkney right up till the mid-nineteenth century) were brought down from the moors when they became broody and taken into people's homes. Most houses on the islands were designed to accommodate the geese, with a recess cut into the wall beside the hearth where they were lodged to incubate their eggs in the warmth.

I get up to stretch my legs and go for a wander through the network of peat hags. I liked the notion of geese being 'let in' to people's homes, of the architectural twist made to houses to accommodate the birds. In the Hebrides, if someone had an especially lucky day, it was said that they must have seen the *Clamhan luch*. In Devon the hen harrier was known as the *Furze hawk*; in Caithness the *Flapper*; *Hebog llwydlas* (the blue-grey hawk) in Wales;

Saint Julian's bird in South Wales; in the English Midlands the *Blue hawk* ... We ought to let these birds back in. Today you can count the number of hen harriers nesting in England on your hand. And each year lop another finger off. They are not where they should be and their absence in the English uplands is shameful, a waste. A landscape devoid of hen harriers is an impoverished one. Hen harriers do predate red grouse – young grouse and weaker adult stock are the most vulnerable. But management of grouse moors and protection of hen harriers should not – does not need to – be incompatible. We need to let the harriers back in. Because a bird like this can change the way you see a landscape. Because (I promise you this) these birds will astonish you with their beauty. I wish others could see what I saw over Orkney, how the harriers made a ballet of the sky. I wish more people had the chance to see how the black wing tips of the male hen harrier are offset – made blacker – by his pearl-grey upper wings.

Some of the peat hags are so deeply cut into the moor it is like walking through a trench system. I can move across a flank of the hill without being seen. Except, of course, the short-eared owls have seen me. One of the adult birds has swum over to hover above my head. I can see the flickering gold and black patterns of its plumage, the gold like a dusting of pollen over its feathers. I sit down on the peat bank while the owl's shadow grazes over me. Earlier, I watched one of the owls and a male hen harrier hunting over the same patch of moorland. The owl seemed to hold something back. At least, the owl was not quite as fluid as the male harrier, who appeared to give himself over completely to the wind, like an appendage of the wind, sketching its currents and eddies, its tributaries of warm air.

Later: the moor is woken by a loud clapping noise. I peer over the trench and an owl is spiralling downwards, 'clapping' his wings together as he descends, signalling, displaying to his mate, bringing his great wings down beneath him as if he were crashing a pair of cymbals, whacking the air to show how much he owns it.

I follow the line of an old fence across the hill. Beneath one of the fence posts I find a small pile of harrier pellets. They look like chrysalids, parcels of hair wrapped around hints of bone as if something were forming in there. I can make out the tiny jawbone of a vole with a row of teeth along its edge, like a frayed clarinet reed.

The quiet ran on through the early afternoon. I hadn't expected this, that the moor could shush itself and doze in the day's thin warmth. How does a bird that was once seen as a harbinger of good fortune in the Hebrides become so reviled? Three hundred and fifty-one hen harriers are killed on two estates in Ayrshire between 1850 and 1854; one keeper on Skye kills thirty-two harriers in a single year in 1870; another, on the same island, accounts for twenty-five hen harriers in 1873. An article on Highland sports in *The Quarterly Review* of 1845 illustrates the attitudes of the day:

Hawks of all sorts, from eagles to merlins destroy numbers [*of game*]. The worst of the family, and the most difficult to be destroyed is the hen harrier. Living wholly on birds of his own killing, he will come to no laid bait; and hunting in an open country, he is rarely approached near enough to be shot: skimming low, and quartering his ground like a well-trained pointer, he finds almost every bird, and with sure aim strikes down all he finds.

Though not so *difficult to be destroyed* as this article posits. The hen harrier, in fact (as Victorian game-book records testify), made an easy target: a large, slow-flying, ground-nesting bird with a tendency, amongst the females especially, to be fearless around humans when defending their nest. Female hen harriers are not unknown to dislodge hats, even scrape a person's scalp with their talons, should they venture too close to the nest.

A male harrier drifts along the horizon. He lands on a fence post and begins to preen. The fence follows the horizon and the harrier, perched there, is silhouetted against the backdrop of sky. He glimmers there. Then he drops, pirouettes, hesitates a few feet above the moor and lunges into the grass. It is a quick, purposeful drop, not like the half-hearted pounces I have seen. I know straight away he has killed. I can see him in the grass plucking, tearing at something. After this, he feeds for several minutes. Then he is up and carrying the prey in his talons, flying direct to the nest site. And there is the female rising, making straight towards him.

My last day on the islands. I decide, reluctantly, to leave the Orkney Mainland and its hen harriers and travel to the southernmost isle in the archipelago, South Ronaldsay. I have heard about a place on the island called 'The Tomb of the Eagles', a Neolithic chambered cairn overlooking the cliffs at Isbister. And, well … the tomb's name is enough to make me want to visit.

Late morning and I am walking out across the fields towards the cliffs at Isbister. The heath shimmers in the warm air. In the distance, a broken farmstead surfaces out of the heath like a whale. When I find the tomb I lie down beside the sea pink and begin to crawl along the narrow tunnel that leads into the tomb's interior. Inside, it is a nest of cool air. The stone walls are rent with algae sores, green and verdigris capillaries. I make my way to the far end of the tomb and duck into a side chamber; it has a moonscape floor, sandy, strewn with pebbles. I sit down inside the cell with my back against the rock.

In 1958, Ronnie Simison, a farmer from South Ronaldsay, was walking over his land looking for stone to quarry for use as fence posts. He walked along the sea cliffs at the eastern edge of his farm. Below him fulmars were nesting on sandstone ledges, a seal was berthing in Ham Geo, curlews moved amongst marsh orchids and eyebright. Perhaps it was the pink splash of sea thrift that caught his eye and drew him to the arrangement of stones the weather had recently exposed, a grassy mound peeled back to reveal a sneak of wall. A spade was fetched and Simison began to dig down beside the wall. As he dug the stones spilt things about his feet as if his spade had disturbed a crèche of voles. He picked each object up and laid it out beside him on the grass: a limestone knife; a stone axe head; a black bead, polished and shiny, that stared back at him like an eye. Then his spade had found an opening and darkness was spilling out of a doorway like oil. He fumbled in his pockets and pulled out a cigarette lighter, stretched his arm into the darkness and flicked the lighter's wheel. The bronze shapes he saw flickering back at him must have made him nearly drop the lighter. Certainly, the story goes, Simison ran the mile back across the swaying grassland to his home where, breathless and sweating, he picked up the telephone and called the police.

Inside the tomb I can hear a curlew trilling above the heath. I crawl back down along the tunnel and out into the bright sea glare. My trousers are covered in dust from sitting on the cell's floor and, as I walk along the cliffs, it looks like my legs are smoking as the breeze cleans the dust from my clothes.

The darkness Ronnie Simison's spade had cut loose from the mound that summer's evening was 5,000 years old. The mound was a Neolithic chambered cairn, and staring back at Simison when he sparked his lighter into the dark hole was a shelf of human skulls, resinous in the flickering light. There might have been a second or two when Simison mistook the bones' bronzed colours for a cache of treasure before he realised what they were, grabbed his spade, and ran.

When the tomb came to be excavated, amongst the human bones it was discovered that there were many bones and talons belonging to white-tailed sea eagles. In all, seventy sea-eagle talons were found and, in some instances, the birds' talons had been placed beside the bones of human individuals (one person had been buried with fifteen talons and the bones of two sea eagles). It is estimated that there were thirty-five skeletons of birds of prey in the tomb and of these two-thirds belonged to sea eagles.

The sea eagle was clearly a bird of totemic significance for the people living in that part of Orkney at that time. Presumably the bird performed some sort of funerary or shamanistic role for the community, perhaps in accompanying the dead on their journey to the afterlife, perhaps in assisting shamans in their magico-religious ceremonies. The importance of birds in shamanistic rituals is well known and there are archaeological examples from different cultures around the world of birds being involved in ceremonial and mortuary practices. In Alaska archaeologists unearthed a grave from a proto-Eskimo settlement at Ipiutak in which an adult and a child had been interred alongside, amongst other artefacts, the head of a loon (a species of diver). Strikingly, the diver's skull had lifelike artificial eyes (carved ivory for the white of the eye inlaid with jet for the black pupils) placed in its eye sockets. It's possible these ivory eyes served as a prophylactic to ward against evil (some human skulls from the settlement also contained artificial eyes). Equally, the eyes may have been placed in the diver in recognition of the belief amongst circumpolar peoples that the loon, a totemic bird for these cultures, was a bird with the power to both restore sight and also assist shamans with seeing into – and travelling through – different worlds.

In the museum a mile from the tomb some of the skulls have been given names: 'Jock Tamson', 'Granny', 'Charlie-Girl'. Beside the skulls there were pieces of pottery, fragments of bowl decorated by the imprint of human fingernails. The nails had scratched the wet clay and left a pattern like a wavy barcode around the bowl's rim. I picked some of the sea-eagle talons out of their case and held them in my palm, running my fingers over their blunted points. They were smooth to touch, like polished marble, their creamy colours flecked with rust.

The human bones, in contrast to the eagle and other animal bones in the cairn, were found to be in poor condition, noticeably bleached and weathered. This weathering suggests that the human dead were excarnated, given 'sky burials', their bodies exposed to the elements on raised platforms to be cleaned by natural decay and carrion feeders like the sea eagle. Besides the eagle bones, which were by far the most numerous, there were also bones of other carrion-feeding birds inside the tomb: two greater black-backed gulls, two rooks or crows and one raven. Once the excarnation process had been completed, the human skeletons – their bones scattered by carrion birds and bleached by the sun – would have been gathered up and interred inside the tomb.

That the sea eagles were involved in the excarnation of the human dead on Orkney is almost certain given that the bird is such a prodigious carrion feeder. Excarnation: the separation (of the soul) from the body at death, the opposite of incarnation, where the soul or spirit is clothed, embodied in flesh. Excarnation is not just a method for disposing the dead (to excarnate means to remove the flesh). It was also, for some societies, the process by which the spirit or soul could be released from the flesh. Tibetan Buddhists believed that the vultures summoned to a sky burial were spirits of the netherworld come to assist the soul on its journey to its next incarnation. In parts of the Western Highlands of Scotland it was unlucky to kill seagulls because it was believed the birds housed the souls of the dead. For what better, more natural place to rehome the soul – the restless, fidgety soul – than a bird, whose shape and movement, whose own restless flight, could be said to resemble the soul? Perhaps the Neolithic peoples of Orkney believed something similar, that when sea eagles, this great totemic bird, cleaned the bodies of their dead, the person's spirit, which after death still lived on inside the flesh, was taken in by the eagle. The spirit or soul transmigrated to the bird, lived on inside the bird. Human and eagle fusing – literally, ceremonially – each one inhabiting the other.

II

Merlin

The Flow Country

Aman is walking south from Aberdeen to London. The night before he leaves his home in Aberdeen he dreams of birds, row upon row of birds perched in their glass cases in a locked museum. He walks along the museum's deserted corridors, his footsteps scurry ahead of him. He wants to slow the dream, to pause and study every specimen. When he looks at a bird he looks inside it, thinks about the mechanics of it, how it works, the map of its soul. But the sterility of the place makes him itchy and the dream begins to tumble into itself as it rushes towards its closing. The birds wake inside their cabinets and start to tap the glass with their beaks. The noise of their tapping: it is almost as if the birds are applauding him. Then some of the cabinets are cracking and the birds are prising, squeezing through the cracks. A mallard drake cuts itself on a shard of glass and he sees its blood beading black against the duck's emerald green. Then birds are pouring past him and the museum's roof is a dark cloud of birds. And he – William MacGillivray – is flickering awake.

It is 4 a.m., a September morning in 1819. William MacGillivray is twenty-three, fizzing, fidgety within himself. He writes: *I have no peace of mind*. He means: he is impatient of his own impatience. Often he is cramped by melancholy. In his journals he checks, frequently, the inventory of himself; always there are things missing and the gaps in his learning gnaw and grate. Travelling calms him, it gives him buoyancy, space to scrutinise his mind. And so he walks everywhere, thinks nothing of a journey of 100 miles on foot through the mountains. He recommends liniment of soap mixed with whisky to harden the soles of restless feet. His own feet are hard as gneiss, they never blister.

He is not unlike a merlin in the way he boils with energy. He once watched a merlin pursuing a lark relentlessly over every twist and turn. The pair flashed so close to him he could clearly see the male merlin's grey-blue dorsal plumage. The tiny falcon rushed after the lark, following it through farm steadings, between corn-stacks, amongst the garden trees.

He lives his own life much like this, restless, obstinate, plunging headlong after everything. Not unlike a merlin, too, in the patterns of his wanderings, seasonal migrations. Leaving his home on the Isle of Harris to walk – at the beginning and end of every term – back and forth to university in Aberdeen, sleeping under brooms of heather, in caves above Loch Maree. Most of what he knows about the natural world – in botany, geology, ornithology – he has learnt from these walks. He can name all the plants that grow along the southern shore of Loch Ness. Often his walks digress into curiosity. He will follow a river to its source high in the mountains just to see what plants are growing there. Other times he eats up the distance, 40–50 miles in a day. If he stops moving for too long it's not that his mind begins to stiffen, rather that it trembles uncontrollably.

And now this long walk to London. Because: his mind is a wave of aftershocks and he is desperate – has been desperate for weeks – to be away from Aberdeen, to be out there on the cusp of things. In his house in the city he is tidying away his breakfast, crumbs from a barley cake have caught on his lip. Then a final check through the contents of his knapsack. He calls his knapsack *this machine*. It is made of thick oiled cloth and cost him six shillings and sixpence. Inside the *machine*: two travelling maps, one of Scotland, one of England; a small portfolio with a parcel of paper for drying plants; a few sheets of clean paper, stitched; a bottle of ink; four quills; the *Compendium Flora Britannica* … He picks up the knapsack; its cloth is stiff with newness, like a frozen bat. For a while he tries to knead the stiffness out of the straps. His hands smell like a saddler's.

Five a.m. Outside in the street the light is like smoke, pale the way his dream was lit. He thinks about the dream, the brightness of the egrets in the grey rooms of the museum. Which way is it to London? It doesn't really matter, he has no intention of taking the direct route. London is 500 miles as the crow flies from Aberdeen, but before he has even crossed the border into England he will already have wandered this distance, following his curiosity wherever it leads him. There are things he needs to see along the way, plants and birds to catalogue, places he has never been. Also, he is reluctant to leave the mountains too soon. He knows that once he descends out of them, on the long haul to London, the mountains will wrench at him terribly. So he pulls his long blue coat over his back and starts walking into the deep mountains to the west of Aberdeen. Already he feels his mind thawing; in his journal he writes, *I am at length free.* By the time he staggers into London, six weeks and 838 miles later, the blue of his coat will be weathered with grey like the plumage of the merlin that brushed past him in pursuit of the lark that day.

There are fifteen breeding diurnal birds of prey found in the British Isles. This list does not include boreal migrants – bearing news from the Arctic – like the rough-legged buzzard and gyrfalcon, or rare vagrants such as the red-footed falcon, who occasionally brush the shores of these islands. Neither does it include owls. For they are raptors too; that is, a bird possessing acute vision, capable of killing its prey with sharp, curved talons and tearing it with a hooked beak, from the Latin *rapere*, to seize or take by force. But owls belong to a separate group, the *Strigiformes*. And although the change of shift between the diurnal and nocturnal birds of prey is not always clear-cut (as I experienced with short-eared owls on Orkney), owls require a list of their own; they are such a fascinating, culturally rich species, they need to be attended to in their own right.

Acute vision is a distinguishing characteristic of raptors. Just how acute is illustrated by this vivid description of a golden eagle recorded by Seton Gordon in *The Golden Eagle: King of Birds*:

Four days later I had an example of the marvellous eyesight of the golden eagle. The male bird was approaching at a height of at least 1,500 feet. Above a gradual hill slope where grew tussocky grass, whitened by the frosts and snow of winter, he suddenly checked his flight and fell headlong. A couple of minutes later he rose with a small object grasped in one foot. It was, I am almost sure, a field-mouse or vole. Since he had caught his prey at an elevation well above that of the eyrie, he was able to go into a glide when he took wing and made for home. When he had grasped his prey he had torn

from the ground some of the long grass in which his
small quarry had been hiding: during his subsequent
glide, as he moved faster and faster, the grass
streamed out rigidly behind him.

Avian eyes are huge in relation to body size, and this is
especially the case in birds of prey; many raptors have
eyes that are as large, often larger, than an adult human's.
The foveal area in the retina of birds of prey is densely
packed with photoreceptor cells. A human eye contains
around 200,000 of these cells; the eye of a common
buzzard, by comparison, has roughly one million of
these rod-and-cone photoreceptors, enabling the
buzzard to see the world in much greater detail than we
can. Images are also magnified in a raptor's eye by
around 30 per cent. The birds' eyes are designed much
like a pair of binoculars: as light hits the fovea pit in the
retina, its rays are bent – refracted – and magnified onto
the retina so that the image is enhanced substantially.
Birds of prey see the whole twitching world in infinite,
immaculate detail.

All fifteen of the diurnal birds of prey breed in these
islands, though some in very small numbers. Many are
permanent residents. The osprey, hobby, Montagu's
harrier and honey buzzard are summer visitors. All are
classified within a single order, the *Accipitriformes*, and
subdivided into three suborders. *Accipitridae*: the soar-
ers and gliders, the nest builders, distinguished by their
broad 'fingered' wings; so: hawks, buzzards, eagles, kites
and harriers. *Pandionidae*: with its solitary member, the

34

osprey – a specialist – the hoverer-above-water, the feet-first-diver after fish. *Falconidae*: the speed merchants (whose nests are scrapes or squats): kestrel, merlin, hobby, peregrine; fast, agile fliers with pointed wings, capable (though not all of them do) of catching their prey in the air.

Pandionidae
Osprey

Accipitridae
Honey Buzzard
Red Kite
Sea Eagle
Marsh Harrier
Hen Harrier
Montagu's Harrier
Goshawk
Sparrowhawk
Buzzard
Golden Eagle

Falconidae
Kestrel
Merlin
Hobby
Peregrine Falcon

Fifteen birds of prey, fifteen different landscapes. A journey in search of raptors, a journey through the birds and into their worlds. That is how I envisaged it. The aim simply to go in search of the birds, to look for each of them in a different place. To spend some time in the habitats of these birds of prey, hoping to encounter the birds, hoping to watch them. Beginning in the far north, in Orkney, and winding my way down to a river in Devon. A long journey south, clambering down this tall, spiny island, which is as vast and wondrous to me as any galaxy.

Rain over the Pentland Firth. The cliffs of Hoy streaked with rain. The red sandstone a faint glow inside the fret. The low cloud makes the cliffs seem huge, there is no end to them. We could be sailing past a great red planet swirling in a storm of its own making. I am on the early morning crossing from Stromness to Scrabster. Light spilling from slot machines; the bar opening up; breakfast in the ferry's empty café. Through the window: an arctic tern, so beautifully agile, it seemed to be threading its way through the rain's interstices. Then a couple from Holland come in, hesitate when they hear themselves in the café's emptiness. They have been walking for a week through Orkney and their faces are red with wind-burn. They hunch over their breakfasts and I see how we do this too: mantle our food, like a hawk, glower out from over it. We are passing The Old Man of Hoy and all three of us shift across to the port side for a better view. We see the great stack in pieces, its midriff showing through a tear in the cloud. Then the rain thickens like a shoal and The Old Man, the cliffs of Hoy, dissolve in rain.

The way I'd pictured it, back home, doodling over maps, Orkney would be all hen harriers. Then the ferry, the train from Thurso, a request stop and stepping off the deserted platform into the blanket bog of the Flow Country. Then the vast, impossible search for merlins. I knew the birds were out there somewhere, not in large numbers, but I had seen a merlin once before, a skimming-stone, hunting fast and low far out on The Flows, the peaks of Morven, Maiden Pap and Scaraben on the southern horizon, a patch of snow on Morven's north face like the white dab on a coot's forehead.

All of that happened as best it could. On the crossing over from Orkney I thought of home – ached for it – for my family there, and thought of the fishermen out of Wick and Scrabster who, should they dream of home, hauled in their nets and headed back to harbour, not willing to tamper with a dream like that. I shared a taxi with the Dutch couple from Scrabster into Thurso. They were tired and polite and wanted to pay, Orkney's wind still rushing in them. They sat in the back of the cab, their faces glowing like rust.

Waiting for the train at Thurso, a slow drizzle, the rails a curve of light, glinting like mica in the wet. The last stop, as far north as you can go. Buffers, then a wall and then another wall because, if you did not stop, the train would slip like a birthing ship down through Thurso's steep streets, past her shops and houses and out into the frantic tides of the firth, rousing wreckers from their sleep who go down to poke about the shore like foraging badgers.

Then the warmth of the train, people steaming in their wet clothes. The start of my long journey south. All the staging posts between the moors of Orkney and the moors of Devon lying in wait for me. Reading the maps of each place obsessively, thinking the maps into life, imagining their landscape, their weather. The more I read the maps the more I imagined the possibility of raptors there. That hanging wood marked like a tide line above the valley: perfect for red kites. That cliff on the mountain's south face: surely there must be peregrines there ... The train now pulling away from the north coast. A last glimpse of Orkney shimmering behind us in her veil of rain. Her harriers grounded, hunched under the dripping sky, feathers beaded with rain. The mark I'd made in the heather beginning to fade. Time on the train to reproof my boots, because the place I'm heading for, the next stop on my journey south, hints in its name that I should really be donning waders, flippers, a bog snorkel ...

'Flow', from the Norse *flói*, a marshy place. The Flow Country, or The Flows as it is usually known, is the name given to the area of West Caithness and East Sutherland covered by blanket bog (literally bog 'blanketed' by peat). It is one of the largest, most intact areas of peat bog in the world, extending to over 4,000 km². Flick the noun into a verb and you also have what the landscape wants to do. The Flows want to flow, to move. The land here is fluid, it quakes when you press yourself upon it. The Flows is the most sensitive, alert landscape I know. A human cannot move across it without marking – without hurting – the bog. The mire feels every footprint and stores your heavy spoor across its surface. But it is a wonder you can move across it at all. There are more solids found in milk than there are in the equivalent volume of peat. The bog is held in place only by a skin of vegetation (the acrotelm), predominantly sphagnum, which prevents the water-saturated lower layer of peat (the catotelm) from starting to flow. And, oh, how it wants to flow! Think of the bog as a great quivering mound of water held together like a jelly by its skin of vegetation and by the remarkably fibrous nature of the peat. Think of that great mound breathing like a sleeping whale. For that is what it does. The German word is *Mooratmung* (mire-breathing). It is the process by which the bog swells and contracts through wet and dry periods. The bog must breathe to stop itself from flowing away.

As it breathes the bog changes its appearance. Unlike a mineral soil where the shape of the land is determined by physical processes, the patterns and shapes of the bog are continually shifting; peat accumulates and erodes, the bog swells and recedes. Occasionally, after exceptionally heavy rain, the water in the bog swells to such a volume that the peat, despite its great strength, can no longer hold the mound together. So the bog bursts, hacking a great chunk of itself away. In Lancashire in the mid-sixteenth century the large raised bog of Chat Moss burst and spilt out over the surrounding countryside, taking lives and causing terrible damage, a great smear of black water blotting out the land. Huge chunks of peat which were carried down the river Glazebrook were later found washed up on the Isle of Man and as far as the Irish coast.

The train follows the river Thurso. Herons in their pterodactyl shadows. The river so black it could be a fracture in the earth's crust, an opening into the depths of the planet. Passing Norse farmsteads, *Houstry*, *Halkirk*, *Tormsdale*. The Norse language here flowing down from Orkney and spreading up the course of the river. Flagstone dykes marking field boundaries. Sheep, bright as stars against the pine-dark grass, disturbed by the train, cantering away like brushed snow. Then the train is crossing an unmarked border, a linguistic watershed, the last Norse outpost before the Gaelic hinterland of the bog, a ruined farmstead with a Norse name, *Tormsdale*, peered down on by low hills, each one attended to by its Gaelic, *Bad á Cheò*, *Beinn Chàiteag*, *Cnoc Bad na Caorach*. The last stop, as far as the Norse settlers would go. Because if you didn't stop here you would wander for days adrift on the bog before you sank, exhausted, into the marshy *flói*.

'Bog bursts', 'quaking ground', 'sink holes' ... I am trying to pay heed to the dramatic vernacular of the bog, checking my boots are well proofed, my gaiters are a good fit. I must remember to check and recheck compass bearings against the map, must remember to tread carefully over this landscape. Because once, I nearly lost my brother in a peat bog.

Another family holiday, another peaty, midge-infested destination. This time, the Ardnamurchan peninsula,

Scotland's gangplank, the jump off to America. My brother was six or thereabouts and we had been to the village shop, where he had bought a toy car. More than a car, it was a six-wheeled, off-road thing. Orange plastic like a street lamp's sodium glare, round white stickers for headlights, a purple siren on the roof. My brother took it everywhere. And lucky for all of us he had the car with him on a walk up the hill one afternoon, holding the toy out in front of him, chatting to it, running through some imagined commentary, when he dropped, as if down a hole, into what looked like nothing more than just a puddle. The bog had got him. And he was struggling, sinking into the mire. But his instinct was to protect the car, to stop it getting muddy. So he held it out in front of him and by holding his arms out like that he stopped himself sinking any further and we leant over and hauled him out, oozing with black peat, like some urchin fallen down a chimney.

The train glides across the flow. Fences beside the track to hold the drifting snow. Tundra accents: greylag, skua, greenshank, golden plover. Wild cat and otter's braided tracks. Sphagnum's crimson greens. Red deer, nomads in a great wet desert, stepping between the myriad lochans. Mark the deer, for they can blend into the backdrop of the flow as a hare in ermine folds itself against the snow.

Then the train is pulling into Forsinard, where the Norse language has flanked around the bog and found an opening to the south through the long, fertile reach of Strath Halladale. And halfway down the strath met and fused with Gaelic making something beautiful. *Forsinard*: 'the waterfall on the height'. *Fors* from the Norse (waterfall); *an* from the Gaelic (of the); *aird* from the Gaelic (height). Clothes still dank with Orkney rain, smelling of rain, I stepped down off the train, crossed the single-track road, and walked out into the bog in search of merlins.

What else does he have in his knapsack, his machine? He has taken it off while he pauses to rest at Banchory, 23 miles out of Aberdeen. He leaves the road, sheds his coat and washes his hands and feet in the river Dee. He notices how people's accent here has slipped away from Aberdeen, a softening in the tone, a slower pace to it, as if the dialect here still carries a memory of Gaelic. And sure enough, a little further up the road he passes two men on horseback talking in Gaelic. He speaks Gaelic himself, has considerable knowledge of Scots and its many dialects. All along his journey he passes through the ebb and flow of dialect. Every mile along the road accents are shaved a fraction. Often he struggles to make himself understood. He might follow a seam of Gaelic like a thin trail through the landscape until it peters out on the outskirts of a town.

What else is in his knapsack? Two black lead pencils; eight camel-hair pencils with stalks; an Indian rubber; a shirt; a false neck; two pairs of short stockings; a soap box; two razors; a sharpening stone; a lancet; a pair of scissors; some thread; needles. In a small pocket in the inner side of his flannel undervest there is nine pounds sterling in bank notes. One pound in silver is secured in a purse of chamois leather kept in a pocket of his trousers. In all, ten pounds to last him through to London.

That first day he walks as far as Aboyne, 30 miles from Aberdeen. That night, at the inn, he writes in his journal until the candle has burnt down. He writes a long list of all the plants he has seen that day, both those in and out of flower. He dreams again of the museum, the place obsesses his dreams. But this dreaming is inevitable because the museum is the reason he is making this walk to London. He has heard that the British Museum holds an astonishing collection of beasts and birds, of all the creatures that have been found upon the face of the earth. And he *must* go to London to see these things. There are gaps in his knowledge, in the survey of himself, he needs to fill. As a student at Aberdeen he studied medicine for nearly five years, then, in 1817, switched to zoology. Since then he has devoted himself completely to studying the natural world. Linnaeus and Pennant have been his guides but now he has reached the point where he needs to set what he has learnt of the natural world against the museum's collection. He wants to check his own observations and theories against the museum's. Above all, he wants to see the museum's collection of British birds. Birds are what stir him more than anything. He is anxious to get there, to get on with his life.

* * *

The way I'd pictured it, back home planning this journey, was a neat transition: Orkney's hen harriers followed by merlins out on The Flows. Instead, on Orkney, merlins had darted through my days, led me astray across the moor in search of them. Then, not far out of Forsinard, in a large expanse of forestry, the first bird I saw was a male hen harrier, a shard of light, hunting the canopy.

Before I set out on this journey I had planned to try to look for each species of raptor in a different place, to dedicate a bird to a particular landscape, or rather the landscape to the bird, to immerse myself as much as I could in each bird's habitat. But the plan unravelled soon after I lay down in the heather on Orkney and a jack merlin, a plunging meteor, dropped from the sky, wings folded back behind him, diving straight at a kestrel who had drifted over the merlin's territory. It was astonishing to see the size difference between the birds, the merlin a speck, a frantic satellite, buzzing around the kestrel. He was furious, screaming at the kestrel, diving repeatedly at the larger bird until the kestrel relented and let the wind slice it away down the valley.

I stayed with that jack merlin for much of the day. Sometimes I would catch a flash of him circling the horizon or zipping low across the hillside, full tilt, breakneck speed. The sense of sprung energy in this tiny bird of prey was extraordinary, a fizzing atom, bombarding the sky.

Once I tracked the merlin down into a dusty peat hollow below clouds of heather. I marked the spot and started to walk slowly down the moor towards him.

Grandmother's footsteps: every few paces I froze and watched him through my binoculars. At each pause the colours of his slate-blue back grew sharper. Even at rest he was a quivering ball of energy, primed to spring up and fling himself out and up. Relentless, fearless, missile of the moor, you would not be able to shake him off once he had latched on to you. There are stories of merlins – like William MacGillivray's account of watching a merlin pursuing a lark amongst farm steadings and corn-stacks – where the falcon is so locked in on the pursuit of a wheatear, skylark, stonechat, finch or pipit (the merlin's most common prey species) it follows them into buildings, garages, in and out of people's homes. Even a ship out in the Atlantic, 500 miles west of Cape Wrath, became, for a week, a merlin's hunting ground. The crew reported that the merlin – on migration from Iceland – hitched a ride with them, chasing small migrant birds all over the ship, darting across the gunwale, around coiled hillocks of rope, perching on the bright orange fenders.

They don't always get away with it, this all-out pursuit; merlins have been known to kill themselves, colliding with walls, fences, trees. Merlins need the space – the sort of space there is on The Flows – to run their prey down. They do not possess the sparrowhawk's agility to hunt through the tight landscape of a wood.

I am still playing grandmother's footsteps with the merlin, but I do not get very far before one of the short-eared owls overtakes me and swoops low over the merlin, disturbing him, dusting him, so that he flicks away out of the peat hollow and lands again further down the slope. I mark his position. This time he has landed on a fence post. There is a burn running down towards the fence and I drop into it and use its depth to stalk closer to the merlin. I crawl quietly down the burn and, when I poke my head up again over the bank, the merlin is still there and I am very close to him. He is looking up at the sky, agitated. His breast is a russet-bracken colour, his back a blue-grey lead. That's it: he is gone. The female is above us, calling to him, a sharp, pierced whistle. And then I see the merlin pair together. She is a darker shape, a fraction larger. In his description of the merlin, William MacGillivray picks out the distinction between the male and female's dorsal colouring brilliantly. The male's upper parts he describes as a *deep greyish-blue*; the female's as a *dark bluish-grey*. But now I cannot make out any difference between the pair. Both the male and female merlin are gaining height, moving away from my hideout in the burn, pushing themselves into speed.

They were beautiful distractions, those Orkney merlins, pulling me after them, away from the hen harriers I was supposed to be watching. And throughout my journey, at every juncture, different species of raptor, inevitably, moved through the places I was in. So, hen harriers spilt out of Orkney and, like the Norse language, followed me across the Pentland Firth; merlins flickered through many of the moorland landscapes I visited; buzzards were present almost everywhere I went, however much I tried to convince myself they might be something else, the something that was eluding me –

goshawk, honey buzzard, golden eagle ... Every buzzard I saw made me look at it more carefully.

Quickly the map I had imagined for my journey became a muddled thing, transgressed by other birds of prey, criss-crossed by their wanderings. And though each staging post was supposed to concentrate on a single species, I loved it when I was visited, unexpectedly, by other birds of prey. I liked the sense that the different stops along my journey started to feel linked up by the birds, I liked the ways they set my journey echoing. Sometimes I came across a bird of prey again far from where I had first encountered it: a merlin on its winter wanderings in the south of England, an osprey on the cusp of autumn refuelling on an estuary that cut into Scotland's narrow girth.

The great Orkney ornithologist Eddie Balfour discussed, in one of his many papers on hen harriers, the minimum distance harriers nest from each other (hen harriers, notably on Orkney, will often nest in loose communities). But in a lovely afterthought to this, like a harrier pirouetting and changing tack, he touches on the optimum distance between nests as well, the distance beyond which breeding stimuli would diminish, neighbourly contact become lost. Extending the thought outwards from hen harriers living in a moorland community, he imagines larger raptors, golden eagles, with their vast, isolated territories, living, in fact, like the harriers, within a single community that extended across the whole of the Highlands, each nest within reach of its neighbour, like a great network of signal beacons.

I was fascinated by this idea of a community of raptors extending right across the country. It touched on my experience of re-encountering and being revisited by birds of prey as I journeyed south. Balfour's idea also seemed to challenge the notion that many birds of prey were solitary, non-communal predators, inviting the idea that even a species we perceive as being fiercely independent, like the eagle, still belongs to – perhaps needs – a wider community of eagles. It got hold of me, this idea, it got hold of the initial map I had sketched for my journey and redesigned it. Instead of moving from one isolated area of study to the next, from Orkney to the Flow Country and so on, I started to see myself passing through neighbourhoods – through communities – of raptors, the boundaries of my map – the national, topographic, linguistic borders – giving way to the birds' network of interconnecting, overlapping territories. A journey *through* birds.

The first bird I see as I am walking through the forestry above Forsinard: a male hen harrier, hunting the sea of conifers. And I could still be on that hillside in Orkney, except, what has changed? The bird, the bedrock, remain the same, but the sky is different here, not always rushing away from you as it is on Orkney. The wind is not as skittish here, the vastness of the land seems to stabilise it, give it traction. On Orkney I wonder if the wind even notices the land. And what else has changed, of course, are the trees that no more belong out here on the bog than they do on Orkney, where trees don't stand a chance against that feral wind. But still there are conifers here planted in their millions, squeezing the breath out of the bog. And today the male harrier is hunting over the tops of the trees just as I watched the Orkney harriers quartering the open moor. It is the same procedure except here, over the forestry, he is looking for passerine birds to scoop out of the trees. It is fascinating to watch the harrier hunt like this, as if the canopy were simply the ground vegetation raised up by 20 feet.

To begin with the newly planted forests would have been harrier havens, just the sort of scrubby, ungrazed zones they like to hunt, ripe with voles. But all of that is gone once the trees thicken and the canopy closes over, suffocating the bog. Greenshank, dunlin, golden plover, hen harrier, merlin, birds of the open bog, are forced to move on, or cling on, as this harrier was doing, trying to adapt to his changed world. Recently, hen harriers – always assumed to be strictly ground-nesting birds – have been observed nesting in conifer trees where the plantations have swamped their moorland breeding grounds. Hopeless, inexperienced nest builders, little wonder their nests are often dismantled by a febrile wind.

But this harrier I am watching over the forest still has its nest on the ground. From my perch on the hillside I draw a sketch of his movements over the trees. Meandering, methodical, he covers every inch of the canopy. I watch him drift above the trees like this for half an hour until (I recognise it from Orkney) there is a sudden shift in purpose to his flight. He stalls low above a forest ride, hesitates a fraction, then whacks the ground with his feet. I make a note of the time: 14.50: he lifts from the kill and beats a heavy flight direct across the tops of the trees; there is the female harrier rising towards him; 14.51: the food pass; 14.52: the female keeps on rising, loops around the male; 14.53: she goes down into a newly planted corner of the forest. The trees are only a few feet tall here and I mark the position of her nest: four fence posts to the right of the corner post, then 12 feet down from the fence.

The hen harrier is the bird that brought me to William MacGillivray. The moment came when I was meandering, harrier-like, through books and papers, field notes and anecdotes about hen harriers. Then I read this passage from MacGillivray's 1836 book, *Descriptions of the Rapacious Birds of Great Britain*:

Should we, on a fine summer's day, betake us to the outfields bordering an extensive moor, on the sides of the Pentland, Ochill, or the Peebles hills, we might chance to see the harrier, although hawks have been so much persecuted that one may sometimes travel a whole day without meeting so much as a kestrel. But we are now wandering through thickets of furze and broom, where the blue milkwort, the purple pinguicula, the yellow violet, the spotted orchis, and all the other plants that render the desert so delightful to the strolling botanist, peep forth in modest beauty from their beds of green moss. The

golden plover, stationed on the little knoll, on which
he has just alighted, gives out his shrill note of
anxiety, for he has come, not to welcome us to his
retreats, but if possible to prevent us from
approaching them, or at least to decoy us from his
brood; the lapwing, on broad and dusky wing, hovers
and plunges over head, chiding us with its querulous
cry; the whinchat flits from bush to bush, warbles its
little song from the top-spray, or sallies forth to seize
a heedless fly whizzing joyously along in the bright
sunshine. As we cross the sedgy bog, the snipe starts
with loud scream from among our feet, while on the
opposite bank the gor cock raises his scarlet-fringed
head above the heath, and cackles his loud note of
anger or alarm, as his mate crouches amid the brown
herbage.

But see, a pair of searchers not less observant than
ourselves have appeared over the slope of the bare
hill. They wheel in narrow curves at the height of a
few yards; round and round they fly, their eyes no
doubt keenly bent on the ground beneath. One of
them, the pale blue bird, is now stationary, hovering
on almost motionless wing; down he shoots like a
stone; he has clutched his prey, a young lapwing
perhaps, and off he flies with it to a bit of smooth
ground, where he will devour it in haste. Meanwhile
his companion, who is larger, and of a brown colour,
continues her search; she moves along with gentle
flappings, sails for a short space, and judging the
place over which she has arrived not unlikely to yield

something that may satisfy her craving appetite, she flies slowly over it, now contracting her circles, now extending them, and now for a few moments hovering as if fixed in the air. At length, finding nothing, she shoots away and hies to another field; but she has not proceeded far when she spies a frog by the edge of a small pool, and, instantly descending, thrusts her sharp talons through its sides. It is soon devoured, and in the mean time the male comes up. Again they fly off together; and were you to watch their progress, you would see them traverse a large space of ground, wheeling, gliding, and flapping, in the same manner, until at length, having obtained a supply of savoury food for their young, they would fly off with it.

Attentive, accurate, warm and intimate, you cannot help but feel MacGillivray's delight at being out there amongst the birds. The degree of observation: the way he records the hen harrier's flight, the detail in the landscape, the description of the moorland flowers and moorland birds. It felt to me like the work of an exceptional field natural-ist; the writer seemed to notice everything. And I wanted to read more, had to read more. Felt a kinship there, at least in the way MacGillivray responded to the birds. He caught the hen harrier's beauty in his careful, graceful writing.

* * *

I walk through the middle of the day across the bog. Anything that breaks the horizon draws you towards it. The house is so far out on the flow it is like a boat set adrift. Not long abandoned, the building sagging, tipping into the bog. A portion of the corrugated-iron roof torn back, exposing timber cross-beams. Rock doves blurt out of the attic. Outside the house there is a bathtub turned upside down; four stumpy iron legs sticking upright, like a dead pig. In one of the rooms: a metal bed frame, a mattress patterned with mildew, blue ceramic tiles decorating the fireplace. A dead hind in the doorway, the stench of it everywhere. Deer droppings piled against the walls as if someone had swept them there.

MacGillivray often slept in places like this on his long walk to London. One night, on the outskirts of Lancaster, tired and wet, he stumbled upon a large, misshapen house in the dark. He went inside and groped his way around till he had made a complete circuit of the rooms. There was no loft, not even a culm of straw to bed down in, but earlier he had tried to sleep under a hedge and the house, despite its damp clay floor, was preferable. So he slept behind the door in wet feet with a handkerchief tied around his head, woke to a mild midnight to peep at the moon and walk up and down the floor a bit. Then slept again with his head on his knapsack to wake at dawn and walk down to the river to wash his face.

But that restless night on the outskirts of Lancaster comes much later. It is only five days since MacGillivray set out from Aberdeen and he is still in Aberdeenshire, crossing the Cairngorms on route from Braemar to

the pools are shallow, two or three feet deep, though occasionally one would sink its depth into blackness. Water horsetail grew in some of the shallower pools, bell heather and cotton sedge along the banks. Around the edge of the pools were great mounds of sphagnum moss built up like ant hills. I pushed my arm into one of them, losing it up to my shoulder in the moss's cool dampness, sphagnum tentacles crawling over my skin. Some of these mounds had been perched on by birds, wisps of down feather left behind, the imprint of the bird's weight on the soft moss.

Hours I spent out there on the bog, and so many distractions on the way to the mountain, so much water to weave around. At one point, I gave up and slithered otter-like between the lochans, swirling up clouds of peat particles when I dived into the pools. And somewhere out on the flow a great boulder – just as the abandoned house had done – drew me towards it. A huge lump of rock, 20 feet high, jettisoned by the retreating ice. There was a solitary mountain ash growing up through a crack in the rock like a ship's mast. I clambered up the boulder and found, on the slab's flat top, a plate of bones. I had discovered an eagle's plucking perch, bones strewn everywhere, on the slab and in the heather around the base of the boulder. Amongst the bones there was a red deer's hoof, its ankle still clothed in grey hide.

It was mid-afternoon by the time I reached the mountain and climbed up to the corrie. I sat down with my back against a rock, listened and waited for the merlins.

A corrie is the mountain's cupped ear. It is a contained space away from the rushing noise of the tops, an amphitheatre of silence. You walk into it and enter an enclosed stillness where everything is suddenly closer, amplified, the raven's croaking echo, the golden plover's whistle. I was glad to be out of the wind. I thought, if merlins were here, their calls would sound cleaner, sharper, and hopefully I could track them more easily by listening out for the birds. But, something about the quiet stillness of the corrie, the release from the rushing wind out on the flow … when I sat down beside the rock, I fell asleep and when I woke the corrie had grown cooler, thicker with shadow.

Later I heard another rumour, a sure bet this time, a place where merlins nested year after year. The site was a deep cut through the flow where a burn wound down towards the river. I walked there across the glittering bog, light finding and lifting pools into pools of light. Near the burn I found signs of merlins everywhere: chalk-marked boulders – perches, lookout posts – patterned white by the birds' excretions.

There are some neighbourhoods of the moor that draw merlins to them time and again. It is difficult to identify what it is about a location that has so much appeal, but availability of prey and suitable nesting sites play a crucial role in the land's capacity to draw in raptors. In his pioneering study of merlins in the Yorkshire Dales published in 1921, William Rowan observed nineteen different pairs of merlins return to the same patch of heather every year for nineteen years. Each spring there was always a new influx of birds because each year, without fail, both the male and female merlin were killed by gamekeepers on their breeding ground and their eggs destroyed.

It was enough for keepers to set their traps on top of a merlin's favourite lookout boulder. No need to even camouflage the trap: the merlin's fidelity to certain perches always outweighed the bird's mistrust of the sharp jaws of a trap. Rowan used to plead – even tried to bribe – the keepers to spare the merlins. He had watched grouse quietly foraging bilberry leaves right in front of the adult merlins at their nest, so he knew that merlins posed no threat to grouse. But a few days before the grouse season opened the keeper would go out early with his gun and clear the moor of hawks of every shape and size. And every year another sacrificial pair of merlins arrived to plug the gap. Rowan wondered where they came from, this surplus tap of merlins, replenishing the same patch of moor year after year. What was it about that clump of heather on the side of the fell that had such a pull on the birds? Rowan identified a few characteristics of the place, of merlin nests in general: a bank of deep, old heather; an expansive view from the nest site of the surrounding moorland; a number of lookout boulders above the nest ...

But it is hard to see the land as the birds must see it, to feel a place as they must do. I am always looking for clues in the landscape, trying to anticipate the birds from the feel of a place. The ornithologist Ian Newton observed that, when he was studying sparrowhawks in South West

Scotland, he could glance inside a wood and tell straight away if its internal landscape was conducive for sparrowhawks. Eventually, after you have spent time amongst the birds, once you have settled into their landscapes, you can walk through a wood or sit above a moorland burn and think: this is a good place to be a hawk, I could be a hawk here.

I keep well back from the burn and settle myself against one of the boulders. The rock is limed with merlin droppings and I think, of all the things that draw a merlin down onto a particular bank of heather, these white-splashed boulders, like runway lights, must guide the birds in, signalling that this is a good place for them, signalling to the birds that generations of merlins have bred here.

Then – my notebook records the time – 10.30: 'Heard male merlin calling and turned to see him just above me. He gained height and then flew fast, dropping to ground level and skimming out across the bog, a smear of speed …' I try to keep up with him but he is rushing so low against the ground, eventually the haze and fold of the moor fold him away. I try to pick him up again, but the vast acreage of sky, the speed of the tiny bird … I have lost him.

That was the pattern for much of the day. There were long absences when the merlin was hunting far out on the flow. I caught the occasional flash of him through my binoculars when he glanced above the skyline, followed him as he tumbled downwards and levelled out over a great sweep of the bog. Sometimes I was impatient to follow him out across the flow, to try to intercept him out there. But I knew that would be hopeless, I could never follow a bird so absorbed in its own speed. Gordon would have kept still and waited. Rowan would have kept still; I thought of William Rowan, his night-long vigils in the cramped hide on Barden Moor, buried in tall bracken, so close to the merlins' nest that, when he lit a cigarette to help ward off the flies that infested his hide, the smoke drifted over the female merlin, parted round her, making slow eddies of itself as the falcon bent to feed her young.

You have so little time to take in what you see of merlins. Their world is glimpsed in snatches of blurred speed. I was lucky on Orkney to have spent time beside a merlin who paused long enough for me to notice the russet plumage of his breast. But the merlin seen rushing past you in a bolt of speed is just as beautiful. At times, from my perch above the burn in the Flow Country, watching the male merlin coming and going, it felt like I was in a meteor storm. Always I heard him calling first, then scrambled to pick him up just in time to glimpse his sharp-angled wings and his low rush up the burn. On one approach, I heard the male call and the female answered him, a high-pitched *cheo*, *cheo*, *cheo*. As she called (still out of sight) I noticed the male suddenly jink mid-flight as if he'd tripped over a rise in the moor. Then it looked as if he had grazed, scraped something – another bird – because there was a small explosion of feathers beneath him. And just at that moment I saw a second bird rising from under him and realised it was the female (who up till then I had not seen) meeting the male there, receiving prey from him.

Later, when the moor was quiet, I walked up to the spot where the merlin pair had met. When the female gathered the prey from the male she must have scuffed it, loosening feathers from the dead bird. There was a dusting of feathers across the site where the food pass had taken place: down feathers snagged in the heather and in the cotton grass. How else could two birds of such charged intensity meet except in an explosion, a fit of sparks? I picked up some of the loose feathers and lined my pockets with them. Then I walked on up the burn, following in the merlin's slipstream.

Golden Eagle

Outer Hebrides

Before the long walk to London, before university in Aberdeen, before birds had entered his life, William MacGillivray learnt to shoot a gun. The first shot he fired – his uncle supervising, leaning over him, telling him to keep the butt flush against his shoulder, to anticipate the recoil – he blasts a table, hurries up to it afterwards through the bruised air to inspect the splintered wood.

Getting his eye in, his uncle nodding, encouraging. With the second shot, he brushes a rock pigeon off the cliffs, flicking the bird into the sea. His third shot hits two pigeons simultaneously, sets them rolling like skittles. Recharging his gun with buckshot, peering over the cliff, searching for the pigeons bobbing in the thick swell. *Let the barrel cool, William.* His uncle saying this and as he says it MacGillivray tests the barrel with his finger and flinches at the heat, and in that instant the gun worries him, becomes something more physical, and his shoulder wakes to the ache of the recoil. So by the time he fires the fourth and fifth shots he is too wary of it, of the power of the thing, his body squinting, flinching when he squeezes the trigger. And he pulls the shots wildly. His uncle lightly ribs him at this: *You even missed the mountain!* Some hours later, when the barrel has cooled, when his anxiety has cooled, MacGillivray fires the gun again. This time he hits and kills a golden eagle.

The first time I fired a gun? I must have been the same age as MacGillivray was, ten or eleven, staying at a friend's house on a farm. We drove out with his father one evening in a pickup truck, bumping slowly along the side of a wood, scanning the brambly undergrowth. At first I could not find the rabbit, though my friend kept pointing to it, only a few feet from the truck; puffy, weeping eyes, hunched in on itself. A crumpled, shuffling thing. It had not noticed us. Its eyes looked like they had been smeared with glue. A mixy, his dad said; here, put it out of its misery. He turned the engine off, draped an old coat over the open window, a cushion for me to lean the rifle on. Then, like an afterthought, as if he felt it would stop the gun shaking in my hand, he pulled the handbrake up; its wrenching sound like a shriek inside the truck.

So MacGillivray waits for the ache in his shoulder to subside. Then sets about gathering what he will need to shoot the eagle: a white hen from his uncle's farmyard, some twine, a wooden peg, a pocketful of barley grain, newspapers, the gun. He walks out of the farm and up the hill. When he reaches the pit that has been dug into the side of the moor, he ties the hen's leg to the twine and fastens the twine to the wooden peg. He pushes the peg into the ground, sprinkles some of the grain beside the hen and primes the gun with a double charge of buck-shot. Then he retreats to the pit with its roof of turf. When he enters the hide it is as if the moor folds him into itself. He can keep an eye on the hen from a peephole cut into the wall of the pit. He starts to read the newspapers. Rain seeps through the roof and the damp paper comes apart when he turns it. He finds himself rolling scraps of news-paper into balls of mush in his palm until it looks as if he is holding a clutch of tiny wren's eggs. Outside he can hear the hen shaking the rain off itself.

He is dozing when he hears the hen scream. He scrambles to the peephole and there is the eagle fastened to the back of the chicken. The eagle is so huge it has shut out the horizon with its wings. The hen looks as if it has been flattened. MacGillivray hurries to pick up the gun, takes aim, and fires. But he has overloaded it with shot and the recoil shunts him backwards, the butt smashing into his cheek. He cannot see what has happened – if he has hit anything – as smoke from the gun has engulfed the eagle and the chicken, so he pushes through the heather doorway of the hide and rushes up to the target. The shot, he sees, has entered the side of the eagle and killed the great bird outright. The hen, amazingly, is still alive, trying to hobble away. So this is an eagle, he thinks; it is *nothing wonderful after all* … Gun in one hand, hen in the other, he throws the eagle over his back and brings its legs down on each side of his neck. Then he sets off back down the hill, wearing the huge bird like a knapsack.

Eagles started to make themselves felt while I was searching for merlins in The Flows of Caithness and Sutherland. There was the eagle's plucking post – that huge flat-topped boulder, littered with bones – I came across far out on the bog. Now and then, too, I saw eagles – often a pair – rising high over the mountains to the west. It was hard not to act on these sightings, to stay on the flow and not follow the eagles into the west. Once, watching the male merlin rising above the burn, in the far distance, perhaps a mile away, I saw an eagle circling high over the moor. I liked the symmetry in that moment, lining up the smallest raptor in these islands with the largest. A telescopic projection, the merlin's wingspan magnified onto the rising eagle, pointing the way to the next stage of my journey. So I left the merlins above their burn in the Flow Country and followed that eagle into the west, to spend a week amongst the mountains of Lewis and Harris, William MacGillivray's stamping ground, the place where he shot the golden eagle on that morning of steady drizzle.

What became of the white hen and the eagle that he shot? When MacGillivray came down off the hillside with the eagle slung over his shoulders the whole village came out to greet him. It looked, at first, as if he was carrying a bundle of heather on his back. *Surely the boy could not have shot an eagle?* MacGillivray's uncle proud as punch, one eagle the fewer to worry his lambs. And because then MacGillivray knew no better, because birds had still to enter his life, he did not count the eagle's quills, did not measure its bill, did not dissect it to see what it had eaten. Instead, the eagle was dumped on the village midden. The hen, miraculous escapee, lived on, reared a brood, was then eaten.

The villagers call MacGillivray *Uilleam beag* (Little William). He comes to live among them, on his uncle's farm on the Isle of Harris, when he is three years old. Before Harris, before he acquires his Gaelic name, there is not much to go on. MacGillivray's father, a student at King's College in Aberdeen, leaves soon after William's birth in January 1796, joins the army and is killed fighting in the Peninsular Wars. MacGillivray's parents are not married and his mother, Anne Wishart, is never mentioned again. So his birth is a hushed, awkward thing and the boy is bundled away to be brought up by his uncle's family on their farm at Northton in the far south-west corner of Harris. When he is eleven, MacGillivray leaves the farm for a year's schooling in Aberdeen before enrolling at the city's university. Always returning from Aberdeen by foot to Harris for the holidays; a journey of over 200 miles, walking across Scotland's furrowed brow, at ease within his solitude, hurrying to catch the Stornoway packet out of Poolewe, back home across the Minch.

After a day of rain and fuming cloud I found the eagles hunting at first light. I saw their shadows first, moving fast over outcrops of gneiss, the grey rocks glancing in and out of shade. The rush of their shadows betrayed the eagles; only storm clouds move that fast over the land. They were a pair and hunting low over low ground at the north end of the glen. I climbed a tall boulder, an uprooted molar, and perched on its flat top to watch.

The sun that morning was out of all proportion, suddenly huge and close. And what that sun did to the eagles … It found their hunting shadows and, as it rose, lengthened them like ink spills along the bottom of the glen. It found and lit the crest of gold down the back of the eagles' necks in a clink and flash of bronze. And it lasted only a few seconds. But you hardly ever see that in a golden eagle, you are never close enough to see the bird's golden hue, to the extent that you wonder how the bird got its name at all, when most of the time all you see is a great dark bird which MacGillivray knew simply as the Black Eagle. But there it was below me, the huge bloodshot sun finding and lighting up the delicate golds brushed into the eagle's nape.

Bird of silence and the clouds, what sort of hunter are you? We tend to exaggerate you out of all proportion. Stories of you driving adult deer over cliffs, lifting human babies when their mother's back is turned, fights to the death with foxes, wildcats, wolves … In the city where I work there is a swinging pub sign with an image of an eagle, talons clasped around a human child, flapping heavily, bearing the infant away through the cobalt blue. You must forgive us our silliness, our intolerance. For when we meet you your sheer size is dizzying. Seton Gordon once mistook a golden eagle for a low-flying aeroplane. Even MacGillivray, who so often saw eagles in the Outer Hebrides, was stunned when once, at the edge of a precipice, a huge golden eagle drifted off a few yards in front of him while a great mass of cloud rolled over the cliff. MacGillivray was close enough to almost touch the eagle and so struck by the bird's presence, he shouted out from the top of the cliffs: *Beautiful!*

In reality a golden eagle could never lift something as heavy as a human baby, let alone a child. Even a mountain hare often needs to be dismembered, a lamb broken in two, before an eagle can carry a piece of it away. Gordon once wrote to a Norwegian lady after he heard about a radio broadcast she had made recounting her experience of being carried away by an eagle as a child. Gordon wrote to the woman asking if he could quote her experience in his book. She replied saying that she might consider his request on payment of a £25 fee.

Up on the bealach there is a movement along the ridge to the west: long-fingered wings, an eagle gliding just a few feet above the ridge. Then another eagle joins it: the male, noticeably smaller than the female.

Close up, when he was observing eagles from a hide – as Rowan did with his merlins – Gordon could tell the difference between the male and female golden eagle by the compact tightness of the male's plumage. But at a distance it is hard to distinguish between the sexes until the pair come together, and then the size difference is obvious, as it is with many other raptors, particularly the falcons, hawks and harriers, where reversed size dimorphism (when the female is larger than the male) is a characteristic of the species, in contrast to non-raptorial birds where the male is usually the larger. Some of the male golden eagles MacGillivray saw over these mountains appeared so small he thought for a while that another distinct species of eagle existed in the Outer Hebrides, yet to be identified, cut off from the world in these remote hills.

Reversed size dimorphism is most pronounced in those raptors that hunt fast, agile prey. So, for example, the greatest size difference between the sexes is found in the sparrowhawk, where the female is nearly twice the weight of the male. By contrast, there is far less size variation between the sexes in those raptors that are insectivorous or feed on slow-moving prey, and no difference at all in carrion-feeding vulture species. Female raptors must substantially increase their fat reserves in order to breed successfully. This increase in weight does not equip them well to pursue and catch their quick, elusive prey. However, male raptors (those that hunt avian prey especially) must remain as small and light as possible in order to hunt successfully to provide food throughout the breeding season for the female and their brood. Size dimorphism is reversed in many birds of prey because the male cannot afford to become too big; he needs to maintain an efficient size and weight in order to hunt efficiently. The female can afford to become bigger because, during the critical breeding season, she does not hunt as prolifically as the male. This hunting respite allows her to lay down sufficient fat reserves to produce and then incubate her eggs. There is the additional advantage that the female's larger size better equips her to defend the nest against predators.

What a strange grey beauty these mountains have (MacGillivray compared them to *a poor man's skin appearing through his rags*). The land scraped bare, the moor a craquelure of gneiss. The warm rocks smoking in the rain. Like the earth must have been when it was raw and molten-new.

This morning I am watching a pair of golden eagles gliding low over the mountain into a strong headwind. Then they turn, so the wind is behind them, and drift away across the tops. Not once do I see them flap their wings. Wind-dwellers, they are at home inside the wind, can fly into a headwind as easily as they can fly out of it. There are accounts of eagles holding themselves motion-less in wind so ferocious that men could not stand upright and slabs of turf were ripped from the rock and flung hundreds of yards.

I climbed after them. I wanted to try and follow this pair, to be up at the same height as the eagles, to be amongst them in their world, meet them as they skirted low across the ridges. For hours I walked along the tops of the mountains, red deer coughing their alarm barks at me. I sheltered from the wind in shallow caves amongst the boulder fields, sipping from my thermos, waiting for the eagles, daydreaming about finding MacGillivray's unknown species of eagle, his ghost eagle, undiscovered for centuries, the coelacanth of these Hebridean moun-tains. Spend long enough looking for eagles and you could be forgiven for being haunted by them. Sometimes I have gazed and gazed at a dark shape against the rock convinced it is an eagle, summoning that shape into a bird. Gordon once watched a pair of golden eagles fly into a passing cloud and followed their dim outlines through the depths of white vapour as though, he wrote, *they were phantom eagles, or the shadows of eagles.*

From one of my shelters I see the male golden eagle again, briefly, gliding back along the ridge towards me. Then he turns and shoots out over the deep glen with its black loch full of rushing clouds and now the reflection of an eagle rushing through those clouds.

* * *

Sometimes the hunt begins at a great height. Prey is picked out over a kilometre away – a rabbit cropping the machair, black grouse sparring at the morning lek. Wings are drawn back and the eagle leans into a low-angled glide. At the last moment, wings open, tail fans and talons thrust forward. Stand under the path of an eagle stooping like this and the sound of the wind rushing through its wings is like a sheet being ripped in two.

Golden eagles can also take birds such as grouse on the wing, pursuing the grouse in a tail chase. But eagles need a head start, they need to build up a substantial head of speed, coming out of a stoop for instance, to be successful in overtaking and seizing such a fast bird as the red grouse. Eagles often hunt in pairs, contouring low over the ground together and sometimes even pursuing prey together on the wing. They also, occasionally, hunt on foot, poking about for frogs, young rabbits hiding in the undergrowth.

More often, an eagle hunts only a few feet above the ground, patrolling the same airspace as the hen harrier and short-eared owl. Several times I have watched golden eagles (and once a pair of eagles) hunting like this, glancing over the land, hugging the contours, looking to trip over prey unawares. Stealth is a critical factor in the golden eagle's ability to catch prey. The bird's traditional upland prey across its northern European range, grouse and hares, are equipped with supreme agility and speed, and more often than not this speed enables them to escape a golden eagle. It's a wonder such a large bird could catch anything by surprise ... But when you watch an eagle hunting low across the hills it is hard to keep track of the bird. It blends its dark brown plumage against the hillside and clings to the peaks and troughs of the moor. Glide – pause – drop – strike.

I hang above the deep glen watching the surface of the loch. From my perch on the mountain I can see the wind moving across the water. Blocks of colour, like leviathans grazing inside the loch, shunt into each other, black into grey into blue. The surface ripples as if rain were fretting it. Then, two new shadows pass across the water: both eagles are now hanging over the glen and – I hear it first – a raven is beating out from the cliff to harry them.

I am used to the size of ravens. Besides buzzards they are by far the largest bird I see around my home. I often hear the raven's loud guttural croak as I hang the washing out, and I was glad to hear that call again up here in the mountains. But I had not expected the raven to be so shrunk beside the eagles. This great black bulk of bird I was so used to seeing and hearing, dominating the skies over my home, was utterly dwarfed, reduced to a speck of a bird, buzzing irritably around the eagle pair. I noticed how hard the raven had to work to keep up with the eagles. Either eagle could step away from the raven simply by folding its wings slightly and easing out of earshot of the raven who flapped and croaked, scolding after them. When the eagles pulled their wings back behind them like this, they grew falcon-like in their shape, tidying those great wings away, a split-second change of gear from soar to gliding speed. One of the eagles mock-swooped at the raven, suddenly rushing at it, effortlessly catching and overtaking the raven and then, at the last moment, glancing away.

No bird is so modest in its speed. There is not the impression of speed with golden eagles as there is with the more obvious sky-sprinters, the hobbies and merlins, who appear to live their lives through speed, though Gordon thought that the golden eagle was the fastest bird that flies, utilising its weight in a long glide to gain tremendous acceleration. Gordon once watched a male eagle descend to the eyrie from the high tops carrying a ptarmigan in one foot. The eagle was travelling so fast in its descent that it overshot the nest, rushing past it, before it swung round and was carried back up to the nest by its impetus. Gordon wrote that the speed of that eagle's dive was quite breathtaking and he calculated that the bird must have been travelling at around 2 miles a minute. An aeroplane pilot flying down the east coast of Greece recorded being overtaken by a golden eagle while the aircraft was travelling at 70 knots. As the eagle passed the plane at a distance of 80 feet the bird turned its head to glance at the aircraft before it eased past it at a speed, the pilot estimated, of 90 mph.

But usually it is difficult to gauge an eagle's speed and it is easy to think, because of its great size, that it is a heavy, laboured flier. Not until you see it glide over a wide glen in a single gulp or overtake a covey of ptarmigan flinging themselves down through a smoking corrie do you have a sense of what speeds a golden eagle is capable of achieving.

I watched the eagle pair and the raven skirmishing above the loch for fifteen minutes. The raven threaded between the eagles, barking at them, but it seemed half-hearted in its efforts to drive the larger birds off its patch, and there was almost a harmony in this dance, in the interaction between eagle and raven. The eagles seemed unconcerned by the raven jostling amongst them. Sometimes the eagles stole away from the raven and entered their own whirling dance, gliding towards each other and then a last-minute rush of speed as they sheared past, wingtips almost touching. Each time the eagles rushed at each other like this I was sure they were bound to collide, before the last-minute wing adjustment and the pair glanced past each other through the tightening air.

MacGillivray is awake, unable to sleep, running through the inventory of himself. Tomorrow he is planning another visit to the mountains on the border of Lewis and Harris, where he will be amongst friends, where his days will be overseen by eagles, where his unknown species of eagle shimmers on the edge of things. He sits up all night preparing for the trip. He was only in the mountains a few weeks ago but he wants to return to write – to finish writing – a poem. It has been nagging at him all winter, this poem. And he needs to go back to the mountains to get the details of the scenery right. The sense that he has too little material from his first trip to write the thing has been mithering him for months. But more than the poem this trip to the mountains is really about him trying to settle himself, to find a sense of resolution. He writes in his journal:

> The chief cause of all my disquietude is the want of resolution …

He needs to calm himself with purpose:

> At present I cannot help looking upon the vicissitudes of life with a kind of terror … If I had resolution, I should not despair …

And when he despairs his anxiety boils over and he turns his frustration mercilessly on himself:

> … such is the fickleness of my mind, that my whole life, hitherto has been nothing else than a confused mass of error and repentance, amendment and relapse … I am truly ashamed of myself, not to say anything worse …

But before he can begin his walk there is this long unquiet night ahead and all he can do is check the inventory of himself once more, rehearse his daily rituals, as if he were checking the contents of his knapsack:

- Rise with or before the sun.
- Walk at least five miles.
- Give at least half a dozen puts to a heavy stone.
- Make six leaps.

- Drink milk twice a day.
- Wash face, ears, teeth and feet.
- Preserve seven specimens of natural history
  (whether in propria persona or by drawing).
- Read the chapter on Anatomy in the
  Encyclopaedia Britannica.
- Read the Book of Job.
- Abstain from cursing and swearing.
- Above all procrastination is to be shunned.

Then it is dawn and MacGillivray is leaving for the mountains. He wants to reach Luachair, the tiny settlement at the head of Loch Rèasort where his friends live, before nightfall. But it is not the best of starts: he misjudges the tides and the great sands at Luskentyre are covered when he reaches them. Shortly afterwards, he loses his way in the mist and rain halfway up the ben.

North, then west, then north again, tacking up through the island. Tarbert to Aird Asaig, through the glen above Bun Abhainn Eadarra, up to the head of Loch Langavat. Lately the island does not recognise itself. People tipped out of their homes, the hills planted with sheep. And the villages all along the west coast of Harris, the machair lands at Nisabost, Scarista, Seilebost and Borve, all of them waiting to follow suit. Dismantling their homes, taking the roof beams with them to the new lives set aside for them on the island's east coast, a land so pitted with rock *not even beasts could live there*. Blackface sheep leaking out into the abandoned hills and glens, and so many of them now that, in the moment it takes to turn your back, it sometimes looks as if snow has crept back after the hills have thawed.

One night, descending the hill of Roneval, MacGillivray is spooked by a strange fire flickering on the hillside. He creeps to within a hundred yards of it but then holds back, skirting around the flames through the dark, convinced that the fire had been kindled by sheep stealers, rustling the sheep partly out of anger, partly to alleviate their hunger. *Dear Sirs, we are squatting under revolting conditions in hovels situated on other men's crofts* ... One hovel = two rooms = twenty-five people crammed to the rotten rafters in there. The people's situation beggars all description, the poverty just unimaginable; the shores scraped bare of shellfish, nettles, brambles ... uprooted and eaten, scurvy seen the first time in a century.

At the head of Loch Langavat, struggling through snow and snowmelt, MacGillivray turns north-west for Loch Rèasort. He has not eaten anything since he set out in the morning dark from Northton. Each bog, each bank of snow, seems to swell before him. But once he clears the watershed between Rapaire and Stulabhal, it is a long downhill glide to Luachair. There! He can see the thin glimmer of Loch Rèasort, the mountains are shutting down its light. Two hours after dark he reaches the house of his friends, opens the door, calls out a greeting to them.

* * *

Now I am looking down into the glen with its loch shaped like a rat. If I could bend down from this height and pick the loch up by its long river-tail it would squirm and wriggle beneath my grip. I'd heard of golden eagles doing that to adders, lifting the snakes and carrying them off in their talons as the snakes writhed and contorted in the air like a thread unravelling there. And more exotic things than snakes are sometimes taken by eagles. The lists of prey recorded are eclectic: grasshopper (Finland), pike (Scotland), tortoise (Persia), red-shafted flicker (USA), dog (Scotland, Estonia, Norway, Japan, USA), goshawk (Canada), porcupine (USA) … More hazardous, perhaps, than even a porcupine was the stoat that an eagle near Cape Wrath was once seen to lift, the eagle rising higher and higher in a strange manner then suddenly falling to the ground as if it had been shot. The stoat had managed to twist its way up to reach the eagle's neck, where it fastened its teeth and killed the bird. Or the wildcat that an eagle was seen to lift in West Inverness-shire: the cat was dropped from several hundred feet and the eagle later found partly disembowelled with severe injuries to its leg.

The golden eagle is capable of predating a wide spectrum of birds, mammals and reptiles, and yet where possible they are essentially a specialist predator, feeding on a narrow range of prey items common to the eagle's mountain and moorland habitat. Golden eagles adapt to become a more generalist predator when their usual prey is scarce. In the Eastern Highlands of Scotland 90 per cent of golden eagle prey is made up of lagomorphs (mostly mountain hare, but also rabbits) and grouse (both ptarmigan and red grouse). In the Outer Hebrides their diet is more varied because their usual moorland prey, hares and grouse, are scarce here. So, in the Western Isles, rabbits, fulmars and, in winter, sheep carrion make up a high percentage of the eagle's diet. Grouse and hares are also less common in the Northern and Western Highlands than they are in the east, and consequently the eagle's diet in these regions is also varied, with deer carrion becoming important in winter. But as a general rule, carrion, despite its availability, tends to be much less significant in the eagle's diet through the bird's nesting season, when live prey are preferred, and tend to be easier to transport to the nest than bulky carrion items.

I settle down above the glen with my back against a boulder and keep watch. I can spend hours like this, waiting in the margins for the chance of birds. But today it is a long wait and I can feel the wind drying out my lips. I am just about to give up and move on when I see two golden eagles flying low down a steep flank of the mountain. Their great wings pulled back behind them, their carpal joints jutting forward almost level with the birds' heads. They cling so close to the side of the mountain they could be abseiling down the incline. An adult bird and a juvenile, the immature eagle with conspicuous white patches on the underside of its wings. All the time the young bird is calling to its parent, a low, excited *cheek cheek cheek*, the sound carrying down into the glen, skimming across the loch.

Both birds are only 100 feet now from where I am sitting. Through my binoculars I can see the lighter-coloured feathers down the adult's nape and the yellow in its talons. The juvenile's calling is growing more persistent, rising in pitch. Then the adult eagle drops fast into the heather with its talons stretched in front of it. At once the youngster is down beside its parent. Something has been killed there. The adult eagle rises and starts to climb above the glen. The young bird proceeds to dip and raise its head into the heather, wrenching at some-thing. I stay with it, watching the young eagle feed. When it has finished it remains in the heather, carefully preen-ing its left wing. Each time the young eagle lifts its wing there is a flash of white in the plumage like an intermit-tent signal from the grey backdrop of the mountain.

I realise I have witnessed something special, a juve-nile golden eagle learning to hunt. The immature bird was clearly still reliant on its parents for food, but it was now piggybacking, tagging along while its parent hunted down the mountainside. The young bird flew so close to the adult, it must have seen the prey in the heather – whatever it was – at the same time as the adult eagle.

I remain watching the juvenile for the next twenty minutes and twice it lifts off the side of the mountain and lands again. Each time it lands it thrusts its talons hard out before it at the last minute as if practising its strike. The adult bird comes back into view again and the young eagle shoots up to meet it, circling its parent, crying repeatedly with its begging call, *ttch-yup-yup, tee-yup*. I have a very close view of the adult eagle as it swoops low across the cliff in front of me. Its tail is a dark grey colour, like the gneiss beneath it.

It all comes to a head, this gutting of the island from the inside out, when MacGillivray and his uncle are summoned by the laird to decide the fate of his uncle's farm at Northton. The laird's factor, Donald Stewart, is there, whom MacGillivray does not care for, whom he calls a wretch of a man. Donald Stewart, who is as ruthless as the sea, who will clear the bulk of the people from the west coast of Harris by 1830, who will even plough the graveyard at Seilebost till skulls and thigh bones roll about the ground like stones. And now Stewart has his eye on the farm at Northton, which is the finest farm in the country. So MacGillivray's uncle has been duly summoned to the big house at Rodel for this meeting – the Set, as it's known – and MacGillivray goes along to support him, to steady him, just as his uncle steadied MacGillivray when he was learning to shoot a gun all those years ago. The pair of them enter the house at Rodel where Stewart and the laird, MacLeod, are holding court at a large table, and before MacGillivray and his uncle have even sat down they are told that his uncle has lost the farm, that it has already been decided and would he like to bid for a different farm instead? What happens next is truly wonderful: MacGillivray's uncle, distraught and silent, listens, Stewart seethes and listens and MacLeod squirms and listens and gulps at his snuff, while MacGillivray stands up and harangues them, boiling over with indignation at the injustice, at Stewart's duplicity, at MacLeod's promises to him about the farm. MacGillivray is like the sea that night in January when the wind picked up the water in whirlwinds of agitation. He is furious with MacLeod and Stewart, but most of all he is furious with Stewart, who he knows is really behind all this, the wretch. And when he has finished fuming at them, MacGillivray sits down and there is a long silence. Stewart sits in cowardly silence and MacLeod, who is also a coward, gulps prodigiously at his snuff. Then MacLeod nods and it's settled and the farm is his uncle's for another year at least. The rent is set at £170, the meeting is over and MacGillivray and his uncle are both leaving and making straight for the nearest public house.

Seton Gordon once helped a golden eagle cross back over from death. He found the eagle hanging off a cliff in upper Glen Feshie. The bird's foot had been almost severed by the jaws of a trap which was fixed to the top of the cliff. Gordon and a companion quickly haul the eagle up the rock. They are shocked by how light the bird is, how many days it must have been hanging off the cliff. They carry the eagle, so weak it does not struggle, to some level ground. Very reluctantly, Gordon amputates the leg at the break. They wait and then watch the eagle as it starts to flop its way along the ground towards the precipice. Gordon's friend shouts at him to catch the bird before it is dashed to its death, but he is too late and the eagle has reached the edge of the cliff. It wavers there and they are sure it is going to fall to its death. But then the eagle tastes the icy uprushing current of wind, opens its broad wings, and rises.

The story of birds of prey in these islands is the story of the birds' relationship with humans. The nature of that relationship is integral to understanding the history and the current status of raptors in the British Isles. The status of golden eagles in the Outer Hebrides today is linked to the events that precipitated the meeting between MacGillivray, his uncle and the laird that day in April 1818. In particular, the eagles' current status is linked to the work of the factor, Donald Stewart, who wanted to evict MacGillivray's uncle and who went on after that meeting to clear the people from the west of Harris in the 1820s and 1830s to make way for his sheep. For the legacy of those clearances – the way those events have impacted the landscape of these islands – is still felt by the eagles today. The sheep that replaced the people brought, through poor husbandry, a ready supply of carrion to the hills, enabling golden eagles to live at high densities in these mountains. At the same time the intensive grazing pressure the hills were put under by the flocks (and more recently the large red deer population) produced, eventually, a degraded landscape, stripped of heather, of nutritional quality, and in turn denuded of its native herbivores, grouse and hares in particular. There have been dramatic declines across the region of grouse and hares, the golden eagle's natural prey. And whilst golden eagles can live at high densities in these mountains, they do not breed as well here. Live prey – its nutritional value – is critical to the breeding success of golden eagles; the birds breed better where live prey still thrives, as it does, for example, in the Eastern Highlands. The legacy of those clearances from MacGillivray's time is still felt, their impact on the land has been as dramatic as the ice.

I miss so much compared with them. Gordon, for instance, on the side of Braeriach, finding the perfect impression of a golden eagle's wings, like the imprint of a fossil, in the freshly fallen snow. MacGillivray: noticing how the currents in a channel are lit by different shades of brightness from the moon. Gordon: watching the aerial display of a male golden eagle, noticing that his neck seemed thinner than the female's and that the male's wings appeared larger in proportion to the body. MacGillivray: noticing the component parts of a raven's nest: heather, willow twigs, the roots of sea bent and lady's bedstraw ... MacGillivray: not noticing that the eagle he shot and slung over his back fitted him like a cowl, clung to him, its spirit clung on to him.

IV

Osprey

Moray Firth

Travelling north, early spring: the osprey's trajectory. March wakes a restlessness in the birds. Ospreys begin to part their winter quarters, leaving their roosts in the mangrove swamps of West Africa. Staggered departures, a slow release of birds. One morning rising higher than usual on the thermals above the palm-fringed coast, turning north instead of west in a mêlée of mobbing gulls.

What does that restlessness feel like in the bird, that longing to leave? It must be overwhelming. The muscles needing to work, tense for work. The pull of the north, the prospect of all that light, dragging at the bird like a rip tide. A thickening of need in the birds to be gone. The journey – the awful journey – thousands of miles across the Sahara, the Bay of Biscay, is not the point. It is getting back to spar and mate and claim a patch. Back to the deceiving north, still shuffling spring with winter.

The first ospreys make land off the south coast of England towards the end of March. Coming in over Poole Harbour, perhaps, up towards Rutland Water. The land below is lit by seams of water. Over the Lancashire Plain there is snow in the plough furrows and the crease of tractor prints, lighting the fields' veins like a sonogram. Crossing the Southern Uplands, past Tinto Hill, over the Clyde and the cold flanks above Arrochar. Reaching Loch Linnhe, the bird swings north-east and tracks along the watery motorway of the Great Glen. Between Loch Oich and Loch Ness the earth curves just enough for the osprey – the fish-hawk – to catch its first glimpse of the Moray Firth and the huge expanse of Culbin forest, the sea-black wood.

I am reading all I can about ospreys. Of all the dismal stories: the perceived threat to fishponds, the blanket intolerance ... The whole of England, Ireland and Wales rid of ospreys. Gone from England by the middle of the nineteenth century (though mostly by the end of the eighteenth). In the north of England the last known breeding attempts came at the end of the eighteenth century at Whinfield Park in Westmorland and the crags above Ullswater. A pair bred on Lundy in 1838 and on the north coast of Devon in 1842. The last known English nest site was at Monksilver in Somerset in 1847. By the beginning of the twentieth century there were only a handful of eyries dwindling in the Highlands. Lochs named after the osprey (*Loch an Iasgair*: the loch of the fisher) now outnumbered the birds themselves. And the osprey's rarity hurrying its demise: egg collectors hunting down the beautiful, valuable eggs. A last-minute rally to try to halt the inevitable: barbed wire is draped beneath the remaining eyrie trees, one nest is even given police protection. But the thieves stop at nothing: a man swims across a freezing loch at night, six inches of snow on the ground, clambering up the island's slippery castle ramparts to reach the nest, swimming back across the loch holding the eggs above the water, his accomplice hauling him in with a rope. Coming out of the black loch like that, his arms held above his head, he looks like a narwhal rising through a blowhole in the ice.

Two years earlier, May 1848, in north-west Sutherland, the egg collector Charles St John waits by the shore of Loch an Laig Aird while his companions go to fetch a boat. There is an osprey's nest on an islet in the loch and St John can just make out the white head of the female sitting on her eggs. He will write later that he is sorry for what he does next. Before the boat arrives, before they row out to rob the nest, the osprey rises and flies across the loch towards St John. When she comes into range he raises his shotgun and fires. Her wings are so long that when she tumbles to the ground it looks like a windmill has come unhinged and its blades are spinning, falling towards him. She falls slowly like an ash tree's rotating keys.

Late one May I headed north into the Highlands through a day of immense heat. Water-borne, water-navigating, following the course of the rivers, the Spey and then the Findhorn, travelling deep into osprey country. Rounding the Cairngorms, snow like a ferrule on the caps of the mountains.

I parked on the edge of Culbin forest and began to walk through the trees. Skin prickling with heat. Bronze-coloured pine seeds, like drops of resin, sticking to the sweat on my arms as if a vambrace was growing there. The forest quiet, sleeping off the day's heat. Wood ants turning over the dead pine needles. Cowberry plants beneath the trees, glossy leaves, bright amongst the granite-dark pines. Slender, silvery rowans like waymarks in the pine-gloom. The forest floor rippling, moving under the ant-pannage.

Ninety years ago Culbin was a restless desert, a vast area of shifting sands. A place so unlike anywhere else in Britain that at the end of the nineteenth century it became home to a population of Pallas's sand grouse, a species usually found in the deserts of central Asia. Culbin was known as 'Britain's Desert', large enough to lodge in the imagination, a place where history shuffled with mythology: skeletons excavated by the shifting sands were either travellers who had lost their way in its expanse or an ancient race who had lived and foraged along the shingle ridges.

I walked for an hour through the forest and came out of the trees onto the shore of Findhorn Bay. I swam and cleaned the heat from my skin. Mute swans glided past then rose and flew in low, heavy-wingbeat processions across the water. Herring gulls in their different shades of age. Oystercatchers in their black and white synchrony. The bay loud with birds, busy with wings, squabbles, tern-twisting flight. I waded back through the shallows and dried myself in the warm air. Late afternoon, I pitched my tent just inside the trees. From there I could lean out of the tent flaps and take in the whole sweep of the bay.

Autumn 1694, a violent snow-globe shake: a great storm blows in from the west. Sand pours down from the dunes and sweeps over the fields of Culbin like an avalanche. The sand rushes towards the men working in the fields. Ploughs are abandoned, sheaves of barley smothered. Everything is sealed in sand: orchards, cottages, the mansion house ... Whatever blocks the way is engulfed.

The sand has been working towards this for years, encroaching further and further east, deleting the land as it went. Sixteen seventy-six: the Culbin harvest is abandoned when the fields are drenched in sand. Year on year the estate keeps shrinking. The farms blotted out: Dalpottie, Laik, Sandifield, Middlebin. If you wanted someone to disappear to a remote spot the locals used to wish them, *Gang to Dalpottie!*

Culbin was destroyed in a single night, transformed into somewhere unrecognisable. The following morning the people woke in darkness, their windows and doors banked up with sand. There had been no warning, the storm coming out of nowhere, the sudden, rapid devastation. An act of God, they said: punishment meted out to an irresponsible landowner. After the storm the owner petitioned parliament to be exempt from cess (land tax), citing that the best three parts of his estate had been destroyed and what little remained was daily threatened by the dunes.

Then he is there, an osprey hovering over the bay. I am sitting at the edge of the forest, feet dangling over the crest of a dune. I found him a darker shape, hunting above the gulls, a high-hanging poise, a stillness there, so unlike the garrulous banter of the gulls. Long dark wings. Hovering, scanning, a kite-kestrel, 100 feet above the water. Then he drops, checks, hovers again. Then his drop tilts and gathers into a dive. In the last seconds, talons are thrown out in front of him to part the water and the osprey submerges in a great crashing plunge. A heartbeat later, he is rising, hauling the length of his wings out of the sea. Airborne, 10 feet up, he pauses, and what happens next is quite beautiful: he shakes the water from his feathers and a mist of droplets shivers off him like welding sparks.

I have never been so close to an osprey. I had watched one before, further south, in the Ochil Hills, in a buzzard-tangle over a reservoir. I heard the buzzard calling, looked up lazily thinking it was two buzzards sparring. But no, not a buzzard: look at the long, long wings, the carpal joints, angled sharp as Cuillin peaks. The buzzard was mobbing the larger bird, thumping down towards it, sending the osprey twirling and tumbling to avoid the buzzard's jostling bulk. For days after that encounter: wonder and exhilaration, to finally see an osprey, to grasp and store its shape.

He comes closer to the shore, drifting towards my seat on the dunes. I can see the black strip across his eyes. Head tilted downwards, reading the water. This time, when he dives, he is so close I hear the splash, a great cymbal crash of water and bird. I watch the talons go in and then come out again, clawing, empty: a miss. That grip! One fiftieth of a second is all it takes to clamp around the fish. The outer toe reversed so the fish is held in front and behind, clamped tight in the foot's sandpaper vice.

A grip like that would surely lead to speculation, stories, myths ... And sure enough there are fishermen's tales of osprey skeletons found embedded in the back of fish too big to lift, fish who pulled the birds under, drowned them in the inky black.

There are stories too of young ospreys in the nest forced by their mother to gaze at the sun until the one that blinks first and weeps is dispatched, thrown out of the nest like some brutal Spartan ritual. And there are tales of fish turning their glistening bellies up, sacrificing themselves to the osprey as she cruises over their lake. For how else do you explain a bird so exemplary, so adept at plucking fish from out of the depths at will?

I watch him fall from a great height. Beneath him: a thimble-thin bay that fills and empties with grey, colloid water. At the last minute, before he enters the water, feet are flung forwards ahead of him. As he lines the fish up between his feet it looks as if his beak is reaching to touch the tip of his talons like somebody stretching to touch their toes. Then the splash! So close, this time, it almost wet me!

The turning point, the moment when ospreys returned to these shores to breed once more. When – how – did that occur? Some say they never completely disappeared, that a pair bred on in the quiet of the Caledonian forest. Gordon notes in his book *In Search of Northern Birds* that a pair of ospreys were seen beside a Highland loch in May 1938. One of the birds landed in a tree beside its mate with a fish, a good sign that they may have been nesting in the area, though Gordon is not so sure, suspecting the birds had simply paused a while on their migration to Scandinavia. And there were other sightings over the years, from Galloway to Ross-shire. An osprey was sometimes seen flying high over Loch Arkaig, one of the last places ospreys nested before they became extinct as a breeding species (1916 is regarded as the last year that ospreys bred successfully in Scotland, on Loch Loyne, Glen Garry). The few who knew of them kept their secret close, looked out for the birds each spring. Migrant birds were seen on passage to Scandinavia and small offerings must have been made to the gods by those who witnessed these migrations, willing the ospreys to rest a while longer, to stay. And in 1954 a pair did stay and raised two young from a Scots pine tree at the south end of Loch Garten. But word leaked out and in the following years the birds' eggs were frequently stolen. The turning point came in 1959 when the RSPB took the decision – a brilliant, bold decision – to advertise the ospreys' presence to the world. A public observation post was set up, telescopes trained on the nest. And visitors in their thousands streamed in to see the birds.

The burden of care for the ospreys became a public concern. The press reported the success or failure of breeding. Recolonisation was tentative, incrementally slow. By 1966 there were three osprey pairs in Scotland. Egg thieves still menaced, cutting through razor wire, climbing trees at night with the same determination as their forebear who had swum across the freezing loch with his stolen clutch. The thieves drastically hampered the progress of recolonisation, havocking the breeding season like a May gale. That awful journey, thousands of miles across the Sahara, the Bay of Biscay, for nothing. Once a nest had been robbed the ospreys would often build a 'frustration' nest somewhere nearby; too late in the season for rearing young, going through the motions, a grief nest. Volunteers monitored nest sites around the clock, number plates of suspicious cars were reported to the police. Some of the thieves were caught, some scared off. In 2000 a detachment of Marine Commandos dug themselves in for the night around an eyrie that had been repeatedly robbed. The following morning the Marines ambushed two thieves prospecting beneath the nest and marched them away to the police.

Egg theft is waning now, though not extinct. Custodial sentences, cultural shifts have seen to this. And ospreys are returning and returning; over 200 pairs breeding in Scotland and reaching, spreading out to England and to Wales, returning to their place-names in the landscape.

After the devastating storm of 1694, the sands that had covered Culbin continued to shift. Things that had been buried were suddenly revealed again. The chapel and the dovecot appeared like mirages adrift on the dunes before the sands shook and covered them once more. Trees emerged thinner, their trunks tapered where the sand had moved around them. On one occasion a chimney from the manor house peeked up out of a dune like a periscope. Whoever it was who came across the chimney there did what anyone else would have done, they clambered up the stoss, the windward slope of the dune, peered into the dark mouth of the flue and called out a greeting, *Hello down there ...* Whatever it was that called back at them from the bowels of the great house was surely more than just an echo. Otherwise, why did the man flee, terrified, careering down the side of the dune in a cascade of avalanches, the dune falling after him, repairing itself, smoothing over, as quickly as the man's tumbling descent gashed at the sand.

And once, or so the story goes, the tops of the laird's old orchard were revealed. And the trees blossomed so the sand became a quilt of pink and white. And in the

And in between there was always the osprey. A noise like an intake of breath above my head and there he was coming in off the forest into the glare of the bay. Once I found him hovering high above the trees, so high up and so far away from the water I did not think he was hunting. But then a pause, a fracture in the hover, and he dropped into the narrow channel that links the bay with the firth. Splash! He rose with a fish grasped in his talons, the head of the fish facing the direction of flight, reducing wind resistance; a slight curvature, as if the fish was turning its head, where the talons gripped it.

Iasgair (the fisher); *Iolair-Iasgair* (the fisher eagle); *Iolaire an uisge* (the eagle of the water) ... The osprey has also been called the 'mullet hawk' as, in Scotland, grey mullet are so often taken by the birds. But in addition to mullet any fish that hunt or swim near the surface can be predated by ospreys: pike, carp, bream, trout, grilse, roach and perch ... In their tropical West African wintering grounds the variety of fish taken must be extensive.

Sometimes the osprey called as he flew, skimming over the treetops above me. *Chee-yup*, *chee-yup*: the first note, *chee*, long and slow. I looked up through the trees and there he was, directly above me, gliding over the rim of the forest, his white breast a drifting moon, a spotlight passing over me as I shrank down among the pine roots.

Often I found him between elements: on the cusp of the forest and the sea; coming out of a dive, ascending from the water back into the air. And I found myself drawn to these margins, looking for him there, poking about the shallows of the bay or sitting on the edge of the forest where the pines had lost their footing and fallen, like the man fleeing the ghostly echo, down the face of the dunes.

The lull of the afternoon, watching the tide glut the bay. No sign of the osprey. A distant clicking through the trees: another pine cone falling, skittering down through layers of branches. But the noise is persistent, nearly rhythmic. I crawl to the edge of the dune leaving a spoor of myself trailing through the reindeer lichen. The shoreline is a waxy yellow colour, bright with gorse flowers. Bare-footed, I feel the sharp bite of wood ants objecting to my toes. I roll away from their nest and peer down from the dune. Bloody ants! My feet are stinging from their bites ... In amongst the wrack two hooded crows are lifting shell-fish a few feet into the air then dropping the shells onto the rocks to crack them open. The crows barely break into flight, more a hoist, a ballet-lift, then hover, release: crack.

Sometimes crows called me out of the trees, their cauldron-croak more noisy than usual. I would go to stand on the edge of the forest and there would be the osprey coming in off the bay again. The crows rising towards him, a buffeting escort.

In poor light above the murky bay I watch the osprey hanging in columns of air. Astonished by how high he is above the water, mesmerised by his flickering hover. I stay with him through the long evening. The tide begins to slip. The patterns in the mud look like the bumps and grooves, the gyri and sulci, of a cortex.

* * *

They planted ten million trees across the dunes to try to stabilise the coast, fixing the sand with a thatch of brash to stop the young trees from being smothered. Still, some were smothered and some trees have half their height buried underground. As the brash rotted it formed a layer of humus, but it is a thin layer and only an inch down my finger finds cool black sand.

One evening I walk through the forest to its northern edge and lie down in the marram grass overlooking the firth. Spread out across the tidal flats are long poles sticking up out of the mud. They look like the remnants of a forest, a ghost forest, overwhelmed by the sea. Gulls perch on the top of the poles like lit bulbs. Later I discover the poles were erected during the war to frustrate enemy gliders from landing in a feared invasion from occupied Norway. I wonder why they have never been removed, but they do not seem out of place in this place of verticals, where a church steeple can suddenly emerge out of the sands, shellfish and pine cones fall and crack, ospreys tilt and dive.

Charles St John, the Victorian collector who shot the osprey near its nest in north-west Sutherland, recalls an incident when he was fishing on a bright summer's evening on the river Findhorn. St John describes hearing a sound *like the rushing of a coming wind*. Yet it was a still evening with barely a breeze and so he shrugs the noise off and continues to fish. A few minutes later he notices that the slack water he is standing in is suddenly sweeping against his feet. He turns to look upstream and sees the terrifying sight of the river rushing towards him *in a perpendicular wall of water, or like a wave of the sea, with a roaring noise, and carrying with it trees with their branches and roots entire, large lumps of unbroken bank, and every kind of mountain debris*. There has been a downpour in the Monadhliath mountains some hours, perhaps days, ago and now the legacy of all that rain is about to hit him. St John has just enough time to grab his fishing gear and run for his life, scrambling up to the safety of a rock above the flood.

That sand can behave like this too, that it can be as destructive as water, that it can flood and ruin like water, is hard to grasp. Yet sand has its own fluidity and can shape and mould objects as water can. Charles St John observed that the stones which the Findhorn rolled down from the mountains to the river's lower reaches were *as rounded and water-worn in their appearance as the shingle on the sea shore*. The trees planted at Culbin which were submerged by the shifting sands emerged again thinner, their trunks tapered where the sand had moved around them. One traveller describes being out in Culbin during a sandstorm, a pressure of weight on his body dragging him down, as if gravity had been increased, his pockets, shoes, clothes, eyes, nose … filled, saturated with sand. Sand pours from his clothes like water, he is nearly washed away.

Even the mighty river Findhorn is forced by the sand to change its course. One year the mouth of the river is blocked by such a mound of sand the Findhorn has to shift itself to find another way through to the sea. Birch trees, like snow poles marking a buried road, still line the route of the old river. In the forest, pools of water appear each winter along the course of the extinct Findhorn, remembering it, as if the forest almost dreamt the river back to life.

Sea Eagle

Morvern Peninsula

The shepherd brings MacGillivray a sea eagle he has shot. The day before, the shepherd had dragged the carcass of a horse up to the spot where, as a boy, MacGillivray tethered his uncle's white hen to a post and lay in wait with his gun. The horse is all ribs and strips of tattered skin. There is a drag-line across the moor where the weight of the horse has dented the heather clouds.

The ribcage perched on the brow of the hill like that looks as if a boat is being built up there. You would not know the hide the shepherd conceals himself in from all the other heaps of stones. And if you glimpsed, from a distance, the shepherd busy about the carcass, charging his gun, then disappearing inside the pile of rocks, you might have thought you'd seen a ghost up there, or spied the entrance to some fairy broch.

It is a fine specimen the shepherd brings him. MacGillivray starts to skin the eagle's head and feet. Its skin is covered in long soft down. *Haliaeetus albicilla*; White-tailed Eagle; Sea Eagle; Cinereous Eagle; Erne; *Iolaire chladaich* (the shore eagle); *Iolaire suile-na-grein* (the eagle with the sunlit eye). MacGillivray gives it the name *An Iular riamhach-bhuidhe-ghlas*, with his idiosyncratic Gaelic spelling, which at times has thrown me off the scent trying to follow him through the Gaelic place-names in his journal. And for several hours I find myself struggling to translate this name, picking over *The Essential Gaelic–English, English–Gaelic Dictionary*, trying to navigate MacGillivray's spelling … The best I can do with the translation: 'the eagle with the yellow-grey markings', or 'eagle brindled with yellow and grey'. Unless what the shepherd has actually brought MacGillivray is that other species of eagle, that unknown fugitive eagle of the Harris hills, and this was MacGillivray bestowing on the bird its Gaelic name.

* * *

I have begun to lean on William MacGillivray more than I ever thought I would. If I find myself grounded, my journey on hold, held up by work and family and everything else that must come first, if I find myself away from the birds for too long, I've learnt to rely on MacGillivray, his journals, his books, especially his first book, *Descriptions of the Rapacious Birds of Great Britain*, which I carry everywhere, heavy as a brick inside my backpack. And if I become lost, if, as often happens, I cannot for the life of me think how I'm going to find these birds, I've learnt that it's best to revert to MacGillivray, to his writing. And there's always something there – in him – that gets me going again, keeps me heading back out there to search for the birds.

One evening, as I drove home from work, a buzzard slipped from a squat winter hedge in front of my car. I flinched. The bird was huge and close, filling the windscreen, rushing towards me. I was sure I was going to hit it. But at the last minute the buzzard tilted, flipped up, skimmed over the top of the car, cleared the adjacent hedge and dropped down into the field beyond. I see buzzards almost daily along that stretch of road but they had never brushed so close to my car. What would I have done if I had hit the bird? Pulled over, picked it up? But then, what could I have done with its body? I could not just discard a bird so beautiful. And as I drove on I thought of MacGillivray as a boy dumping the golden eagle he had shot on the village dungheap. And only a few years on from that and birds had entered his life, come to possess him, so much so that he cannot relate to his younger self, cannot think what possessed him to discard the eagle. And now the shepherd is bringing MacGillivray this dead sea eagle because he – MacGillivray – has sent out word that he is looking for specimens to study and before he knows it he seems to have become the depository for all the dead raptors in Scotland. He wants to study these specimens because he wants to understand how the birds work and because, above all, he wants to find a new way – a more accurate way – of describing and identifying birds.

All those hours spent sifting through the dead. His desk lit with the bit parts of eagles, oesophagus, stomach, intestines … For, *it must be obvious*, MacGillivray wrote,

> that a bird is not merely a skin stuck over with
> feathers, as some persons seem to think it, but an
> organised being, having various complex organs and
> faculties, the description of all of which is necessary
> to complete its history.

So the eagle's stomach is no less important than its bill. And this is what distinguishes MacGillivray's work as an ornithologist, his attention to this detail, his insistence on studying and describing every aspect of the bird. And in this way he advocates a new way of seeing the birds, of looking at them so intently that when he is watching a sea eagle perched like a sentinel on the great sands at Luskentyre, he looks beyond its white-fanned tail, the huge, heavy bill, into the pulse and texture of its form, to draw an extraordinary word map of the bird:

Sea Eagle

Bill nearly as long as the head, very deep, compressed, straight, with a long curved tip ... Stomach large, compressed, oblong, slightly curved, the muscular coat very thin; the two central tendons small and thin ... the inner coat soft, without rugæ. Pylorus with a valve formed of three projections. Intestine very slender, nearly uniform in diameter until towards the extremity, when it is considerably dilated ... Eyes large, overhung by a thin projecting eyebrow; eyelids edged with bristly feathers ... Head broad, rather large; neck rather long and strong; body full and muscular, of great breadth anteriorly; wings long ... The cere and bill are pale primrose-yellow; the iris bright yellow; the tarsi and toes gamboge; the claws bluish-black. The general colour of the head, neck, breast, back, and upper wing-coverts, is pale greyish brown, the hind part of the back passing into wood-brown; the belly and legs are chocolate-brown, as are the lower tail-coverts and rump-feathers, some of the upper tail-coverts being white. The primary quills and alula are blackish brown; the base of the primaries and the greater part of the secondaries tinged with ash-grey. The tail is white, but a small portion of its base is deep brown.

I think how lucky I am when a bird such as that roadside buzzard flares suddenly through my day. Those encounters that come out of nowhere, that sear you with their proximity, their unexpected beauty. That sea eagle, for instance, that lived out its life in captivity in the gloom of the old library at Edinburgh University who one evening, as MacGillivray was passing, jolted itself momentarily out of tameness, reached out a leg and clutched MacGillivray's shoulder with its talons. MacGillivray said the eagle did no material damage but I wonder if it was MacGillivray's own aura of passing wildness that made the erne relapse into its wilder self. That wildness that caught up with MacGillivray and shook him periodically, which was not really a wildness, as such, but a fever to be gone, to be elsewhere, out there among the birds.

My journey south was not a fluid thing. There were stops and starts, overwinterings, snatched moments to pick the journey up again. One place that snagged me, kept hoicking me back time and again, was the Morvern peninsula in the West Highlands. So often I returned to walk around its long coast looking for *Iolaire chladaich* (the shore eagle), I realised, unintentionally, I had walked almost the whole way round the peninsula. And then, of course, there were gaps in my circumnavigation which niggled at me, drew me back again to try and complete the circuit.

I went to look for sea eagles in Morvern more out of instinct than any real certainty I would find the birds there. I thought perhaps there might be an overspill of sea eagles from the neighbouring Isle of Mull, which holds the highest breeding density of the birds in Scotland. And really it would have been easier to have gone to Mull, easier to look for the birds there. But, stubbornly, I wanted to try and find the eagles with difficulty, to come across them, if possible, unexpectedly, to immerse myself in the birds' landscape, and wait for them there. I don't especially recommend this approach. Morvern battered me like no other place on this journey. Orkney's luck deserted me, the sea eagles were elusive, the midges voracious. But I got fixated on the idea of trying to find sea eagles there, of walking around Morvern's largely trackless perimeter. I became as stubborn as MacGillivray did on his long walk to London, wanting to complete the journey on foot, despite his hunger and exhaustion, despite the passing stagecoaches which could have scooped him up and whisked him on to London and the British Museum.

But for all the battering my muscles took in Morvern, the homesickness and midge bites, I was glad to be walking in such a remote place, sleeping out in deserted bays, sheltering in the birch and oak woods, waiting for a glimpse of the shore eagle, scanning every tree for the bird's tall grey shape, willing every rock along the shore into flight.

I spent many hours in the steep-sided gullies that carried the burns down from the mountains into Loch Linnhe and the Sound of Mull. Corridors of beauty: primroses the colour of an erne's cere; marsh hair moss and wood hair moss; the slender light of silver birch; grey-green lichen, delicate as filigree, covering every branch and twig like a mist. A cuckoo on a fence post – a hawk mirage – confusing me in my raptor stupor. A buzzard coming in across the sound from Lismore, waking gulls from their roost. When the cliffs rose too sheer, I skirted round them, using the gullies as avenues into the mountains, moving from the shore to the high tops, from sea eagle to golden eagle.

One night, lying in my tent on the loneliest shore in Scotland, I heard footsteps on the shingle, something disturbing the stones, a heavy crunch. Then the sound of pebbles rolling over each other as they fell away down the steep shingle bank. I unzipped the flysheet and stepped out onto the grassy sward. Twelve feet from me stood a red deer hind, long grey neck, ears pricked up, snorting, huffing at me, huge in the drained light. Later, I woke to the sound of the whole shingle bank collapsing around me and stepped out to see a large herd of deer passing my tent in the half-dark, hooves clattering the stones. I watched their black shapes wade into the deep bracken above the wrack line until only their heads and tall necks were visible and the herd floated away up the mountain's lower slope.

One of the things I learnt from my visits to Morvern was how impatient I could be, always wanting to peer around the next headland to look for sea eagles there, fixated on the idea of circumnavigating the peninsula. I was like my teenage self scampering over the moor on Lewis, impatient to show my mother the lochan with its red-throated diver. But I knew I was trying to cover too much ground on Morvern, knew I needed to slow things down and concentrate on looking for sea eagles in a smaller area of the peninsula. So I went back to Morvern one more time to try and steady myself with patience – Gordon's eagle-watching patience – and wait for the sea eagles in a place where I felt they might come to me.

The plan was this: to curb my impatience, to stop myself eating up the distance, I would lock myself into a small uninhabited island in Loch Sunart off Morvern's northern edge. I would wade across to the island at low tide then pull the tide up behind me. The island – Oronsay – would be my lookout post, my home for several days, a place to wait and wait and watch for sea eagles.

A slippery crossing over the rocks between Doirlinn and Torr a' Choilich, like walking over the backs of sleeping seals; a tidal channel, a sea-moat, the seaweed ankle-deep. Then: bluebells, bracken shoots, a fringe of stunted oaks and I am scrambling up the island's rocky eastern slope. Oronsay: what a giddy, youthful feeling, a whole island to myself to explore. But first things first, looking for fresh water and walking all around the island that afternoon and finding only brackish trickles and slug-gish pools amongst the reeds, tiny streams with the shortest of lives, done for by the sea before they can get going.

And finding too, that afternoon, crumbled houses with nettle floors and window sockets looking out towards the hills of Ardnamurchan. And one house still with its chimney stack in place, its high gable end, still angled like a house, not yet collapsed, not yet rounded off by years of wind like its neighbours were. How on earth did anyone make a living here in this rocky, brackeny place, the island virtually gnawed to its core by the sea ...

That night I pitch my tent above a small bay on Oronsay's northern shore, between an otter's whistle and a cuckoo's call. All night it rains and I listen to the slack burn behind me coming alive beneath the yellow flag irises. The rain on the tent keeps me awake and I stay up reading about Oronsay's ghosts:

There was yet another eviction on the estate of the late Lady Gordon of Drimnin, and as this was a particularly hard case, which took place only about fifteen years ago, we feel in duty bound to refer to it as showing how completely the Highland crofter is in the power of his landlord, and however unscrupulous the landlord may be in the present circumstances there is no redress. The circumstances are as follows: About forty years ago, when the sheep farming craze was at its height, some families were removed from the townships of Auliston and Carrick on Lady Gordon's estate, as their places were to be added to the adjoining sheep farm. The people were removed to the most barren spot on the whole estate, where there was no road or any possibility of making one. They had to carry all manure and sea-ware on their backs, as the place was so rocky that a horse would be of no use. Notwithstanding all these disadvantages, they contrived through time to improve the place very much by draining and reclaiming mossy patches, and by carrying soil to be placed on rocky places where there was no soil. During the twenty-five years they occupied this place their rents were raised twice. Latterly, with the full confidence of their tenure being secure, they built better houses at their own expense, and two or three years afterwards they were turned out of their holdings on the usual six weeks' notice, without a farthing of compensation for land reclaimed.

In the morning the island is drenched and heavy. The bay smells of bog myrtle and rusting kelp. Crawling out of the tent I startle an oystercatcher who peels away across the water, calling loudly. It is cold this morning and I work quickly to make tea and porridge. It has stopped raining but there is still so much moisture in the air my woollen mittens are soon damp and I have to keep wiping the lenses of my binoculars.

I spend the rest of the day perched on Oronsay's headlands, scanning the length of Loch Sunart. North across to Risga, Glenborrodale, Eilean Mòr. East to Carna with its hill still being worked on by the rain. West to Ardmore Point on Mull, to the rocks of Sligneach Mòr and Sligneach Beag. Further west, the outlined hills of Coll. Waiting, scanning every inch of shore.

The account I read last night of the people evicted from Auliston and Carrick, that *particularly hard case*, was recorded by the Napier Commission (the royal commission set up by the government to assess the conditions of crofters and cottars living in the Highlands and Islands) when its commissioners arrived in Morvern in August 1883. Because the place the Morvern crofters referred to in their evidence as *the most barren spot on the whole estate* was unnamed, it took me a while, and some more digging, to realise they were referring to Oronsay, a place *where there was no road or any possibility of making one*, a place *so rocky that a horse would be of no use.* The people from the townships of Auliston and Carrick were removed to Oronsay and then, in turn, removed from the island they had worked so hard to make habitable, picked up and herded on again.

– What became of the people of Oronsay?
– One of those who was in Oronsay was the last delegate, another is in Glasgow, he removed to Glasgow, and two or three are on the adjoining estate of Mr Dalgleish, Ardnamurchan.
– The club farm was abolished, and the people had to go?
– Yes.
– Who has it now?
– A large farmer.
– What is his name?
– Donald McMaster.
...
– As I understand your statement, the people were removed for the benefit of the sheep farm, and you may say for the benefit of the estate?

- And for the benefit of themselves.
- But the people were not made the judges of their own benefit?
- They were not asked in the first place.
- What I want to arrive at is this, the people were virtually and substantially removed for the benefit of the estate, in order that this sheep farm, or some other part of the estate, might be more profitably administered and held; in removing the people did the proprietor, in consideration of their number and poverty, and the difficulty of obtaining other places, make them any allowance or gratuity?
- Not to my knowledge.

And here is the rain again, coming down off Beinn Bhuidhe from the south, crossing Loch na Droma Buidhe, then rushing at me as I crouch, hunker down on Oronsay's headlands. All I can do is turn my back and wait for the rain to clatter over me.

- Is there any use in beating about the bush; is it not the fact that those people were removed solely and entirely because they were in the way of sheep?

Some of the things I see that day: cormorant, greylag, skua, tern, black-backed gull, ringed plover, great spotted woodpecker, sandpiper, raven, pipit, hooded crow, heron after heron after heron beating low across the loch. And do not see: the buzzard I hear calling in the woods above Doirlinn, the pine marten whose scat I find lying on a mossy boulder, the erne, the sea eagle, the eagle of the shore.

What sort of bird is it that taps MacGillivray on the shoulder in the dusk of the old library in Edinburgh? A robber baron, a pirate, a sluggish vulture of lakes and fjords ... Much of the time the sea eagle is perched – cormorant-like – on a rock or tree beside the shore. Except, not like a cormorant at all, because if you see the eagle's great bulk on an islet in the loch it looks as if a person is standing there, not a bird at all. Their sheer size: nothing prepares you for that.

Diet: anything, really ... Fish snatched from the shallows, a low glide above the water, pause, a brief hover ... then talons taste the water, seize and grip the fish and the sea eagle is beating its great wings, heaving itself into height. For such a large bird the agility with which the sea eagle plucks fish from just below the surface is astonishing. Wing tips might brush the water as it struggles to rise, but the sea eagle does not immerse itself in the water as the osprey does, there is none of the splashing crash of the osprey as it plunges after fish.

Shetland fishermen used to anoint their bait with sea-eagle fat believing this would bring them luck, such was the great bird's fishing prowess. And just as bait smeared in sea-eagle fat could make all the difference to the day's catch – and a dream of home was all it took to haul in nets and head for home – so the fishermen of the Northern Isles had to tread carefully around language, using their own sea language when they were at the *haaf* (the fishing). Everyday things – pigs, rabbits, fish, the minister – had to be skirted round, ducked under, referred to aslant. So the fishermen could not, for instance, call the birds they saw from their boats by their real names, as to do so would be to tempt ill luck. Cormorant, puffin, sea eagle … all names that were taboo and could only be spoken of in code like a distorted echo of each bird's call. A defiant language of the sea, of kennings and circumlocutions, rooted in Old Norse, holding out against the tide of language from the south. And when they spotted a sea eagle soaring above their boats bobbing in the thick swell off the cliffs of Hoy and the cliffs of Fetlar and Noss, the fishermen would refer to the bird in their strange sea language, calling the sea eagle *Adnin* or *Clicksie* or (my favourite) the *Anyonyou*.

Besides fish, the sea eagle will take shore birds, moulting geese, injured wildfowl, young kittiwakes. A hunting sea eagle will spark the shore birds into the safety of flight, unlike a passing peregrine, whose presence grounds everything. Also: hares, rabbits, occasionally a hauled-up sleeping seal. Sea eagles will pursue gulls – even ospreys – to make them spill their catch. MacGillivray wrote they were especially fond of dogs. And of course carrion: sea eagles have a great propensity for carrion and the birds (described in the chronicles as the 'grey-coated eagle') were often observed cleaning up the aftermath of Anglo-Saxon battlefields, rehoming the souls of the dead.

Though not so vulturine, not so sluggish as we tend to dismiss it for being. Male sea eagles, when providing for their young, have been seen to almost kill at will, swooping repeatedly at diving birds, harrying ducks, cormorants, auks, tracking an eider drake's bright tracer under water as the eider keeps on panic-diving, plucking it from off the water when the duck is too exhausted to dive again.

MacGillivray came at the sea eagle, of course, through observing its anatomy and behaviour, showing how the sea eagle is a convergence of other birds – gull, skua, vulture, osprey – tracing the way these birds gradually form a passage into each other. And in his own way MacGillivray was anticipating Darwin, observing in his studies of birds of prey how the different species had grown alike, evolved to equip their rapacious lives, whilst their anatomies retained the blueprint of their separate origins.

So, part skua, part vulture, part osprey. Above all, perhaps, a cousin of the osprey, in the way the sea eagle can pluck a fish from the shallows, the way that horny spicules line the soles of its feet to help it grip the fish, the way their Gaelic names intermingle – *Iolaire uisge* (eagle of the water) for the osprey/*Iolaire chladaich* (eagle of the shore) for the sea eagle. And above all like an osprey in the way their stories – their melancholy histories – converge. The sea eagle driven out from the great English river estuaries, from its refuges on Lundy, Shiant and Hirta, from the Lakeland crags and the cliffs of Jura. So by 1914, when Gordon is writing his chapters on the osprey and sea eagle for his book *Hill Birds of Scotland*, he is drafting both birds' obituaries. The last reported nesting of a sea eagle occurs on Skye in 1916. And then there is one, a lone female sea eagle – an albino bird – haunting the cliffs of North Roe in Shetland.

When it comes, the end is a hurried thing. The shepherd on Harris tells MacGillivray that he believes the sea eagle to be far more common than the Black (the Golden) eagle. So it's as if the sea eagle falls through a plughole in the sky, to go from being so numerous (in some districts more numerous than the golden eagle) to that lone Shetland female bird in the space of seventy years. It seems that the sea eagle took the greatest share of blame as a lamb killer (more so than the golden eagle) from the new breed of shepherds, jealous of their flocks, that took over the townships of Oronsay, Sornagan, Carraig and Auliston and all the green lands of Morvern and beyond.

The sea eagle, too, proved an easier scapegoat – more easily reached along the shores – than the golden eagle with its skulking ways deep in the mountains. Carrion laced with strychnine was a favoured method for getting rid of the birds. Burning peats were lowered down the cliff to set fire to nests. Failing these, the shepherd would put out some bait then fold himself into a hide of stones to lie in wait with his gun.

And a dead sea eagle fetched a good bounty. In Orkney, a hen from each house in the grateful parish was paid to the person who killed an erne. Ten shillings was the going rate on Skye. The bird's parts had their uses too: apart from the fat which fishermen coveted, the sea eagle's long broad wings would serve as a useful broom. On cleaning days, peering through an open doorway, women could be seen moving back and forth like injured birds, dragging a great broken wing across the room.

28 June 1914, North Roe, Shetland

The artist George Lodge is walking across the hills of North Roe with two companions and the watcher James Hay. It is a day of wind and wet mist that drives across the hill. They struggle to keep up with Hay, who moves like an antelope across the tussocks and deep moor grass. The party is making for the Red Banks where the last resident sea eagle in the British Isles can be found. Hay tells them that she is an albino specimen and has lived here going on thirty years. For a long time she was paired with a mate, but they bred for the last time in 1908 and shortly afterwards the male departed. Since then the female has lived out here on these cliffs alone.

They see her from a long way off, a white spot on the rocks below the old nest. As they approach she flies off and out across the bay and they do not see her again for the rest of that day. She looks as white as a gull when flying. Lodge makes an oil sketch of the nesting cliff. He works for an hour and a half but the weather is awful and after a while he is too cold and cramped to continue, so he packs up his easel and heads homeward.

30 June 1914

Very windy today. The party heads back out to the Red Banks in search of the sea eagle. She is nowhere in sight when they get there and it is too windy to paint, so Lodge makes a pencil sketch instead. The nest looks like a mass of rubbish and is hard to distinguish against the backdrop of rocks. He notices a hooded crow mobbing something round the corner of the cliff. His friends go to investigate and out flies the eagle pursued by several hoodies. He has a good view of her as she passes in front of him, notices that her primaries are not white but appear to be a light brown.

10 July 1922
Eight years later. Lodge is back on Shetland and making for the Red Banks to look for the albino sea eagle. Hay tells him that she has not been seen since 1918. On the way to the old nest site the route is blocked by a burn in spate and Lodge has to trek for two miles before he can cross it. Finally he finds a place to ford the burn and heads back downstream until he reaches the cliffs where he made the sketches in 1914. There is now not a trace of the old nest.

There is a rumour on Shetland that the eagle was shot in 1918, though no one knows what happened to the body. Lodge crouches down out of the wind and scans the cliff face. He cups his hands either side of his mouth and calls out to the cliffs, listens to the pause, the ricochet, the dissipating distorted echo:

Anyone there
Anyonyou
Anyonyou

After the sea eagle has gone the land feels emptier. All those place-names in the evicted landscape. *Earnley* (the wood of the erne); *Arncliff* (erne's cliff); *Creag na h-Iolaire* (eagle's rock); *Cnoc na h-Iolaire* (eagle's hill). And after that lone white female is shot in Shetland in 1918 there are decades of emptiness. But then, in parallel with the osprey, the sea eagle starts to re-emerge into some of these emptied spaces. Young birds are brought over from Norway in the mid-1970s and carefully, painstakingly, reintroduced to Scotland's coasts. Their numbers are still small and like all large birds of prey they are slow breeders (slow to reach breeding age, slow to rear their young and rarely raise more than two chicks per year). But sea eagles have returned and they are gradually spreading along these shores, reanimating the rocks and hills and woods that were named after them.

Besides my visits to Morvern I made trips to other places to look for sea eagles. Recently the birds have been reintroduced to Scotland's east coast and I went to seek them there along the Tay estuary and made several midwinter visits to Loch Leven, where the eagles are sometimes drawn in cold weather by the large flocks of wildfowl that gather on the loch. Occasionally I caught distant glimpses of the eagles but always they were a long way off, crop-filled, static, sitting on a rock or at the top of a distant tree. It bothered me, my lack of any really good time spent watching the birds. I wanted very much to observe how they flew, to study their shape in flight, to watch them hunting. I had to try one more time. So I went back again to the West Highlands towards the end of June and this time focused on a small area further up the coast from Morvern where I spent several days watching the shoreline for sea eagles. I was so glad that I went back.

Early morning, looking down from the cliff at the narrow sound below. The tide is rising and the narrows are a frantic squall of whirlpools and standing waves. It looks like the sea is coming to the boil. A huge volume of water is being squeezed through the channel and the narrows bubble over under the pressure. The air is a cauldron of gulls, swirling above the rushing tide, feeding on the fish being pushed with the tide through the sound. Black-backs, herring gulls, common gulls, cormorants, the white wing-flash of a great skua, a lone gannet … There are dozens of seals too feeding amongst the gulls, snorting, slapping the water with their tails. The morning is so still I hear the seals huffing and whacking the surface long before I reach the cliff. And the noise of the seals is so loud at first I think it is being made by much larger beasts, as if a pod of whales were surfacing there. Some of the seals drift very close, slow black shapes through the clear water beneath the cliff. There are so many seals I could hop from one to the other like stepping stones across the narrows. In places where the tide is running fastest there are seal–gull skirmishes, thefts and squabbles in the thrashing water.

A slight rise in the noise from the gulls, like an increase in pitch of their agitation, and there is the sea eagle flying up the channel. He is following the shoreline, slow shallow wingbeats, but moving quickly. Brown and grey like a red deer's winter coat. Long-fingered primaries fray his wing tips. The most striking thing about his flight silhouette is his long thick neck and the neck is elongated by his huge yellow bill. In flight he is not as outrageously large, nor as cumbersome, as I had expected. There is speed and agility there and he twists easily through the swirling cloud of gulls. His short tail seems to check his size in flight, it gives his shape a squatness (much as a buzzard's tail does). So what you see is mostly wing and neck (unlike a hawk in flight where what you notice is the long narrow tail). It is when he is shadowing a herring gull, or being mobbed by a hooded crow, that the sea eagle comes into his scale. He swamps these smaller birds with his size and the great width of his vast, broad wings sinks home.

I am overjoyed to see him. After all those days spent walking around the coast of Morvern, sleeping out with Oronsay's ghosts ... A chance, at last, to spend some time watching – properly observing – a sea eagle. The conditions are perfect: clear and bright and the eagle appears to want to linger here, where the fishing is good. I have found a seat above the cliff, a mossy cushion amongst the heather where I can look down on the whole sweep of the narrows and scan the woods and rocks on either side.

The gulls have brought the eagle here. And it is the gulls that announce his arrival through the change in pitch of their squabbling. If I cannot locate the eagle I learn, over the coming days, to wait and listen out for the gulls' signal that he is approaching. It is the gathering of the gulls as the tide starts to swell and push through the narrows that ushers in the sea eagle. He is here because he is an opportunist, a fisherman, a scavenger; he is here because of the gulls. The way the eagle interacts with the gulls – the dynamics of this relationship – is fascinating to watch and I am quickly caught up in the drama of it.

Most of the time the eagle is perched near the top of a young larch tree overlooking the sound. He sits up there and I sit opposite him on the other side of the narrows. What is most conspicuous when he is perched like this is his dun grey head and neck. I can also see his heavy yellow bill and there is a flash of yellow a little further down where his talons lock around a branch of the tree. If I lose sight of him – if I have to rest my binoculars to clean the lenses or if a seal-slap below the cliff distracts me – I can usually pick the eagle up again on his perch by scanning the trees for the pale yellowy light his head and bill emit. I can see now why MacGillivray gave the sea eagle that peculiar Gaelic name, *An Iular riamhach-bhuidhe-ghlas* (the eagle brindled with yellow and grey). Those are the bird's colours (the mature adult bird's colours) precisely. He sits up there on the tree, very tall, his head and neck glowing faintly like a dim harbour light. His long wings folded and hanging down behind him make him taller, lengthen his back. The top of the young tree is bent under his weight.

Then he is up and has latched on to a gull. When he leaves his perch there is nothing awkward in the way he detaches his great bulk from the tree. He just steps off, huge wings outspread, launched at once into a low, fast glide across the water. Why does he select this particular gull? What is it about this gull that makes it stand out from all the others churning and squabbling over the narrows? There must be something that gives this gull away, a weakness, a vulnerability, a visible fish-bulge in its crop, something that signals to the eagle that it is time to leave its lookout perch and give chase.

What follows is a shadow dance. The eagle latches on to the gull and proceeds to follow it everywhere. His victim is an adult herring gull, a large bird in itself, but utterly dwarfed by the sea eagle's heavy presence. The eagle does not attempt to attack the gull, simply looms over it like a dark cloud, stalks the gull for as long as it takes, staring down the gull, until the gull can take no more of this thing that is so large and overbearing that its wings block out the sun, locking the gull in a permanent shade.

When the gull finally relents I see it drop something, a tiny morsel of bright fish. And in an instant the sea eagle has shifted into something altogether else. It defies its bulk, its size, its ponderous, sluggish reputation and transforms itself into a bird I did not anticipate. The eagle twists into a burst of speed and swoops down after the gull's spilled catch, but when the gull drops the fish, eagle and gull are too low above the water, and despite his sudden rush of speed there is not enough time for the eagle to intercept the fish. He sees that he will not reach it in time and already, before the fish has even hit the water, the eagle has given up, pulled out of his dive, and is beating back towards his pine-tree perch.

When I check again the eagle is up and flying across the narrows towards me. I sit very still watching him loom and grow through the binoculars. I have a fine view of his long neck and pale nape. He keeps coming straight towards me. I wasn't expecting this … what is he doing coming so close? Surely he has seen me? At the last minute – whoosh – he banks upwards, above my head and lands on a rock on the hillside behind me. His head and the shouldered tops of his folded wings are silhouetted by the backdrop of blue sky above the hill. Straight away a hooded crow is swooping down at the eagle's head, dive-bombing him repeatedly. Each time the hoodie swoops at him the eagle flinches, recoiling his long neck from the attack. It is the raptor's curse, this relentless mobbing; gulls and corvids, especially, are the raptor's bane. Mobbing is their way of saying: *We can see you, we don't fear you, we don't want you here* … The hoodie will not leave the eagle alone. The crow keeps on haranguing him until the eagle has had enough. And he is up again, flying back across the sound to find a quieter perch.

The next time I see him he is harassing a gull, breathing down its neck, following the gull's every twist and turn. The gull does not show any hint of panic. It is unhurried by the eagle's pursuit and does not try to shake the eagle off. They reach a sort of equilibrium, a resignation that the dance just needs to be seen through to the end when the gull must jettison its catch if it's to get the weight of eagle off its back. So they go like this for five minutes until, at last, the gull spills its catch, and this time I see it is a large fish and I follow it as it falls through the air sparkling in the sun and watch it hit the water with a splash. The eagle flexes into speed and shoots after the falling fish but once again the drop-gap is too shallow and he does not have time to catch the fish before it hits the water. Once the fish is in the water the eagle makes no attempt to retrieve it.

The gulls are still here in numbers, working the narrows. The eagle sits on his pine perch watching them. When he is up amongst the gulls I notice how clean and bright his white tail is. It is very noticeable, this flash of white across the tail, whiter than the gulls themselves. Seven herons come croaking up the sound. After them, flying in the opposite direction, a small flock of guillemots, in tight formation, skimming the waves. When I turn back from the guillemots to the shore the eagle has gone from his perch. I look up and see he is climbing high above the sound. Two thousand, 2,500 feet … What is he doing up there so far from the gulls and the fishing? Then I see there is a gull up there with him, trying to outclimb him. The gull is just a speck. The eagle looks like the gull's swollen shadow. For ten minutes they turn about each other in the high air. I keep my binoculars fixed on them waiting for the moment – there it is! – the fish is dropped and this time they are so high up and the fish has so far to fall, the eagle has all the time in the world to flick down in a sudden charge of speed and pluck the fish from the sky.

In the slack tide of the afternoon I walk over the hill behind the cliff. Taking my time, trying to refocus the scale of my gaze from the eagle to the small and near-at-hand. Meadow pipits and grasshopper warblers are out on the hill. Everywhere there is the rapid trilling sound of the warblers and the speckled breasts of the pipits. I meet a dragonfly on the path, as long as my hand, clinging to a thick blade of moor grass. The dragonfly is motionless, undeterred by my shadow. It does not even flicker when I kneel down beside it and place my camera just an inch away to photograph the bright yellow-black traffic-signal stripes along its abdomen.

On the other side of the hill I reach a deer-fenced forestry plantation. A pair of buzzards are calling and swirling above the trees. I follow the buzzards into the wood and find a track that starts to drop steeply down towards the sea. At the high point of the track I pause to scan the canopy for the buzzards again when a huge bird – nothing like a buzzard – flies across the clearing right in front of me. It is the sea eagle, circling just above me and so close that, if I were to climb this stumpy pine, I could reach up and feel the downdraught from his wingbeat. In a quarter of a mile I have gone from dragonfly to meadow pipit to buzzard to sea eagle, as if I were walking through layers of magnification.

I stand very still in the middle of the track and the eagle circles above me, low over the trees. He comes around in a wide arc and as he turns to face me he suddenly flinches and veers to the side, as if swerving to avoid me. He banks awkwardly into a different angle of flight. His huge wings push down under him and the wing tips almost touch each other beneath his body as he pushes and hauls himself away from me.

I saw the moment when he saw me. He was close enough for me to see his left eye as it clocked me standing in the middle of the track. In that instant, I saw how the shock of my shape triggered something in him and caused the sea eagle to flinch and reel away.

In the early evening I am back above the cliff to catch the rising tide. The gulls and seals are there working the narrows. I have not been there long when I hear that sudden shift in tempo from the scolding gulls, and there is the sea eagle beating up the channel. This time he is flying very low above the water, much lower than I had seen him in the morning. What strikes me, too, is the speed and line of his flight: he is heading straight for something. He rises a foot or two, still flying in the same direction, accelerates, then drops down again towards the water. His wings pull back behind him as if he is about to land, both feet push out in front of him and his talons brush the water scooping out a glint of fish. Then he is pulling up and away from the sea and this time gulls are mobbing *him*, rollicking around him, trying to tip the eagle from his catch.

I keep my binoculars fixed on the eagle. The gulls are frantic around him, the noise of their calling has ratcheted up another level. They coil around the eagle as if trying to bind him in a giant knot. But the eagle seems oblivious, he sticks to his course, beating steadily away across the sound, and the gulls begin to dwindle in his wake. Once he has shaken off the gulls the eagle begins to circle over the lower slopes of the mountain. It looks as if he is hunting there, foraging over the ground, and I am puzzled: he has his fish, why is he not returning with it to the nest? Then I realise he is not foraging, he is climbing. He has been looking for a thermal to take him up the side of the mountain and very slowly he is spinning upwards, gaining height. If I drop my fix on him whilst he is flying against the mountain's backdrop I find it hard to pick him up again, the mountain's browns and greys fold the eagle into it. But once he clears the summit and his shape is set against the sky, he is the only black dot up there for miles and I can follow him easily as he keeps on rising. At around 4,000 feet he suddenly turns and shoots away to the south in a steady downwards glide. He has chosen the path of least resistance: once he has gained sufficient height it is a downhill glide and he can cover the distance back to the nest (which must be several miles away) in a matter of seconds.

What a wonderful thing to witness, the sea eagle taking a fish from the water like that. I thought the eagle would revert to harassing the gulls as he had during the morning shift. And it was as if he had spied that fish from a long way out, the way he stuck to such a straight course flying fast and low up the narrows. Here was a bird that kept dismantling my preconceptions of it. In an instant the sea eagle was capable of shifting into astonishing poise and speed and skill.

I am back on the cliff early the next morning. I do not want to miss a beat and I spend most of the rest of the day watching from my mossy seat above the cliff. In the late morning a large school of dolphins comes into the bay, gulls sprinkled above them, drawn by the fish the dolphins are herding. There are so many dolphins, the water churns around them as they travel, and there is such a ferment of gulls following the pod, it looks like a weather front is moving up the channel.

Much of the time the eagle is perched on the shore, or more often at the top of the larch tree. Each time he returns to his perch he approaches the tree from very low down, at the last minute swooping up to the top of the tree, wings labouring, hauling him up the last few feet. He makes several long-distance glides from the tree low across the water, as if he has spotted something just below the surface from a long way out. Most of these flights are aborted and he heads straight back to his perch. Occasionally he lands back on the tree facing the wrong way and has to hop himself around to face the water. When he does this the branch he is sitting on shakes beneath him. Before he settles into his perch he pulls his tail up behind him and it flashes white, once, twice across the sound towards me.

On one occasion he catches something close to the shore, though he is too far away for me to see what it is. Perched on the shore he is camouflaged, his brown body blending into the wrack line of rusty kelp, his pale grey head becoming just another rock. It is hard to keep track of him when he is on the shore like this. I think I have him, refocus the binoculars, then see that all the time I have been staring at a rock ... It is at times like this that he *is* his Gaelic name, *Iolaire chladaich* (the shore eagle).

Sometimes a solitary gull finds the eagle at his perch and there follows an endless round of mobbing. If the gull comes too close (which it doesn't often) the eagle raises his bill towards the gull, extends his long neck to jab it away. But the gull does not relent. It's as if it is locked into a flight path, swooping down at the eagle, persistently, rhythmically, loop after loop, in a shallow curve above the eagle's head.

VI

Goshawk

Scotland–England Border

Here is MacGillivray approaching the Border, walking into autumn through Kirkcudbrightshire, hair a little sun-bleached, shoulders calloused from his knapsack's weight. Muddy splash marks rise up his coat, a crescent pattern to the mud spots like an offshore reef.

It is almost a month now since MacGillivray left Aberdeen on his higgledy walk to London and he cannot put off leaving Scotland any longer. I have (can I say this?) grown envious of his feet, he never seems to complain about them. But are they really immune to all that pummelling: Aberdeen to Fort William, 161 miles; Fort William to Glasgow, 134 miles ...? Seldom more than two meals a day, though he sometimes sounds as if he would like to live off less:

> Bread and water will do very well for the greater part
> of my journey, for many a better man has lived a
> longer period than will be allotted to it, on worse
> fare ...

But his poor feet, surely they are beginning to ache? In Morvern my feet turned a strange crinkled yellow, the skin softened like margarine (how I wished I had followed MacGillivray's recipe and bathed them in whisky and liniment of soap ...). The only time I hear MacGillivray grumble is when he is bitten by bed bugs in Glasgow. He burns up in a fever, can barely open his left eye, and a tumour swells on his cheek to the size of a hen's egg. How he wishes he could have exchanged that bed in Glasgow for a couch of grass on the side of Cairngorm ... And now he is so wary of the blighters he sniffs the air of every inn for the bugs' peculiar coriander scent, combs his mangy rooms with a pin, prising the bugs from their daylight hiding places, the seams and chinks of bedposts, the gaps beneath the skirting board, till his pin holds its own length in wriggling bugs, like a keeper's gibbet or the shrike's thorn.

I managed little better with bugs in Morvern, beating my own world record for parasitic ticks, each night lying in the tent, inspecting my skin by torchlight, extracting the ticks with tweezers one by one. Once, in desperation, I tried smoking a pipe to ward off midges, but smoking it was eye-watering misery: I could not get any draw on the tobacco and kept having to relight it, coax and suck it back into life like a damp bonfire. MacGillivray recommended decocting tobacco for the treatment of bed bugs. Either tobacco, or Irish lime sprinkled across the floor. Once, staying at a London inn, he was so tormented by bugs biting his face, neck, arms, back and legs, even the crown of his head, that he resorted to using candle tallow to rub against his skin where he had been bitten.

Glasgow to Portpatrick, 99 miles; Portpatrick to the Border, 107. Expenditures: half the ten pounds he set out with from Aberdeen, the remaining five tucked in a small pocket in the inner side of his flannel vest, though he is certain he won't need all of it. London from the Border at a steady trot, twenty shillings should cover it. *Bread and water* (repeat the mantra!): *better men have lived on worse.*

Five hundred and one miles clocked since he left Aberdeen a month ago. Bearing up pretty well, the swelling from the bug bites going down, a touch of homesickness now and then (he had it in Fort William when he came into the orbit of the Isles). But doing well, considering: on budget, feet enviably robust, approaching the Border, heading south.

* * *

Early morning above the forest, a smoky winter light. The wind starting up, stirring rooks and jackdaws into plumes of soot. A sparrowhawk, skimming the canopy, rises to meet a woodpigeon. No intent to the flight, it just goes up to have a look. The pigeon flinches and the hawk dives back towards the trees. Then a pair of ravens are up, clearing their throats, a glint of brightness, like polished mahogany, in their thick beaks. The ravens sound different here, their voices dampened by the trees. Nothing like the raven in the Outer Hebrides, jostling with the golden eagles, its call cleaned and sharpened by the cliffs, carried down the glen by loch and gneiss.

Everything about this morning feels slow and hushed. The muted ravens, the mushy light, even the sparrowhawk's pigeon-jink had none of the hawk's usual quickfire dash. There are mornings like this when the forest feels cold-blooded and everything in it seems to take an age to limber up.

Then crows are crossing the forest in twos and threes, ambling, tugging at each other. A buzzard circling to the right of me. A goshawk displaying a long way off. The goshawk is too far out and I cannot get any feel for the bird, any purchase on it. Other than I notice it is roughly the same size as the buzzard, though not as dark and not as compact, not as rounded in its shape. Occasionally I pick up flashes of white showing on the goshawk's plumage. The buzzard is circling, rising through figures of eight. The goshawk is flying slowly a few feet above the treetops. A slight, sudden rise as if the hawk meets an updraught and just as quickly it is dropping out of the rise and landing on a tall pine tree.

Through my binoculars I flick between the perched goshawk and a felled area of the forest about a mile away. The clearing saddles a ridge, a whale's back rising above the shallow valley. I keep drawing back to the clearing, studying it, thinking … if I head up there, that would be a good place to be, that would be a good place to watch for goshawks. Up there, I might get closer to the birds as they find the lift of breeze above the ridge. So I take a compass bearing, drop down into the forest, and make towards the clearing.

Saturday 2 October, 1819. Three miles from Newton Stewart, MacGillivray comes across an outlier from the south, a specimen of trailing tormentil, on the edge of its range, huddled beneath a hedge. He has never seen the plant before in the north and it dawns on him that he is running out of Scotland. He is aware too of how, daily, the light is leaving the land, in the jaundiced grass out on the heath, in the withered bracken. Very few plants are in flower now and sometimes it feels, as MacGillivray approaches the Border, that he is walking in step with autumn as it moves through the land from north to south, snuffing out each flower in turn along his route. He passes through a field of wild carrot, scarlet pimpernel and corn woundwort and picks some of the carrots to crunch as he walks. When he brings the carrot roots up to his mouth it looks, for a moment, as if he has grown a pale yellow beak like the juvenile choughs he saw feeding amongst cattle dung on Barra.

His pockets are stuffed with all the specimens of plants he has gleaned along the way, all his curious digressions. There hasn't been time to press them all and so many plants are lodged in the nooks and crannies of his clothing it looks like they are sprouting from him. The man on horseback MacGillivray passed in the dusk outside Castle Douglas must have thought he had been overtaken by a scarecrow as he watched the figure stumbling ahead of him, wisps of foliage trailing from his cuffs. He is still uncertain how to answer people who stop to ask him about the plants. On one occasion, walking along with a bunch of cuttings in his hand, a woman stopped and peered at him:

– Is that yerbs?
– Yes.
– Ow! That's rushes.
– Yes, it is a kind of rush (It was Hard Rush).
– Fat's this?
– I don't know the English name of it.
– Are you gaun ti' drink affin't?
– No I don't intend to put it to any medical use …

MacGillivray wrote that he left Scotland on his walk to London *without regret*, that Scotland was *too wide a word* for him, that it was the Isles and mountains that really claimed him. But I wonder, did he not feel less sure-footed as he stepped from Dumfriesshire into

Cumberland, did that specimen of trailing tormentil not remind him that much of what lay ahead was unfamiliar to him? And besides, once MacGillivray crossed into England he pelted through it at such a rate, head down, a beeline for London, none of the meandering diversions that Scotland steered in him.

All that walking in circles around the Morvern peninsula, I needed to straighten out. So, when I reached the border between Scotland and England, I decided to follow it and walk along a stretch of its line in the deep goshawk forests above Kielder. I spent the days following broken dykes and firebreaks through the trees, crisscrossing burns and cleughs and sikes. Each firebreak in the forest felt like an avenue for goshawks, every tree along every ride and clearing I scanned for that heart-thumping goshawk meeting. For several days I hesitated over the Border like this, dipping my toes in and out of England. Sometimes I found myself zigzagging, leap-frogging back and forth across the line for mile after mile. In the evening returning to my tent pitched on the boundary, my head dreaming in Scotland, my legs hanging over the Border, pointing south.

Waking on the hillside, and being woken by a sound like a stream gurgling beneath me: red grouse, starting up the day, calling through the heather, their calls burbling under my ear. Fog this morning and the forest has stepped off into whiteness. I go in search of the trees, walking across sphagnum humps, tussocky reed grass, the fog condensing on the sharp reed blades and spiders' webs. In a boggy alley on the side of the fell I find a bloom of grouse feathers, neatly plucked, lying in the heather. I search for the carcass but find nothing. Goshawks are fastidious about preparing their prey, can spend over an hour plucking a pigeon, feathers growing in a ring around the hawk as it works. Afterwards the hawk can feed for an hour, sometimes two. The pile of grouse feathers looked like raptor's work, too neat for a fox.

I fumble through the mist and finally reach the trees. Along the forest's rim I pass through different belts of roe-deer droppings, some fresh from the night before, wet, shiny black, others much older-looking, parched and crumbling. Inside the trees and the forest is dripping with fog-dew. It is dark among the pines with a sense of heavier darkness just out of reach. Beyond the trees there is a brightness inside the mist which seeps a little way into the trees then quickly dissolves in the gloom. Rackways, where thinnings have been removed, wander into the forest then peter out. Deer paths blend into the rackways then veer away again like branch lines or capillaries. I follow one deer track deeper into the forest. Something is glowing up ahead through the trees and I wind towards it like a moth. It is some sort of relic of the Border line, a strange arrangement of standing stones and cairns, gnomish monuments, draped in a moleskin of green lichen that glows almost fluorescent amongst the pines.

* * *

Planting began at Kielder in 1926 and it soon became the largest man-made forest in the country. Sitka and Norway spruce, the Sitka darker, bluer. Scots pine and Lodgepole pine, a redness, like lava, in the fissures of the old Scots pine bark. Bright clumps of larches amongst the pines. Few native trees remain: sallow willow in the valleys, birch in the narrow cleughs, alders along the river banks and on the river's islands of silt.

Wind can havoc a plantation like this. Shallow roots on wet, clay-like soil made the trees especially vulnerable. Early thinning in the forest proved disastrous, letting the winds in to roam through the blocks of trees, yanking at their weak roots, toppling the pines like dominoes. You see the same phenomenon – the same vulnerability – in goshawk feathers. If a hawk becomes stressed through lack of food or, as is sometimes the case in birds trained for falconry, through psychological stress, the bird's growing feathers record the period of distress as a pale line, a band of weakness across the vane. These lines are known as 'fret marks', records of distress, as when a tree logs a period of drought-stress through a narrowing of its growth rings. Feathers with stress marks are vulnerable to breaking along these weakened points. As with the thinning of the forestry plantations, once one feather breaks there is less support for the remaining weakened feathers and these can swiftly follow suit, impeding the hawk's survival, its ability to fly and hunt effectively.

* * *

But the reality is there is no lost world beneath the reservoir. Nothing is revealed when they start to drain it, nor is it drained completely. Every stone of every farmhouse, every tree trunk, was removed when the reservoir was constructed in the 1970s. What was there before the valley flooded – the community of hill farms – was entirely erased. I had just assumed that the remnants of that community would still be there beneath the reservoir. It took a call to the Northumbrian Water Authority to set me right. They told me about the careful disbandment of the farms and houses, the way every tree was uprooted to avoid them later floating to the surface. I wanted to believe that there were still relics down there, signs of what had been drowned in the valley, that the tops of buildings might briefly emerge during a drought, just as they poked up through the shifting sands of Culbin. Instead, every decade, when the waters are lowered, all that is revealed is a vast absence.

Mid-morning and the fog is beginning to peel. Where are you, goshawk? What am I searching for? A chimera, a rumour? A space inside a fir tree where light seeps through, a patch of silvery lichen across a branch ... There are so many things to deceive and delude you when you are searching for – aching to see – the birds. How many buzzards I must have willed into goshawks! How many times I have tried to conjure a hawk out of absence. Even the discarded beer cans I spotted from a distance lying beside the Bells Burn, just over the Scottish side of the Border, were grey and hawk-shaped enough to briefly glint in my imagination, until I was close enough to tell them for what they were and could see how their tin had weathered to a murky silver.

Behind the beer cans, on the opposite bank of the burn, stood a large ring of lichen-crusted stone: a 'stell', a circular walled sheep enclosure, 5 to 5½ feet tall, 30 feet in diameter, a purpose-built snow shelter where flocks could seek refuge from the drifts. I rested inside it for a while, brewed tea, cleaned the glass on my binoculars. The stell was a beautiful construction, remarkably intact. Its wall had been built (as all the walls along the Border are) with two walls leaning towards each other, the gap between them stacked with the *chatter* of smaller stones, both walls then bound together with longer *thruft* stones that reach through the *chatter* like ribs. Built, as well, to be flexible, to bend and sag as the soft ground gives way beneath the wall's weight.

Tree pipits are squabbling amongst the timber brash beside the stell, their sandstone breasts streaked with black rain. The birds bounce from stump to stump like charged electrons. They drop so rapidly to the ground, it's as if they are sucked there through a vacuum. Their descent to the safety of the tangled brash is so sudden it is not really a descent at all, more like a vanishing act.

I cross the valley floor and start to climb through the trees towards the ridge. Buzzards are up hunting the valley. When I reach the top of the ridge I turn west and follow it till I reach the felled clearing. Acres of forest open up beneath me. A crow is calling from its perch on a thin bark-stripped pine trunk. I see it watching me as I enter the clearing and hide myself amongst the brash and stumps.

The next few hours are a dizzying experience. After days spent looking for goshawks and finding only their absence, the birds are suddenly here and all around me. First, there are the usual outriders, buzzard and raven. Two ravens, displaying, tumbling, corkscrewing above the ridge. Three buzzards, calling – also displaying – above my head, twisting, diving, rushing down towards the forest. Then, lower than the buzzards, 30 feet to my right, flying just above the tops of the clearing's remnant trees, a goshawk's blue-grey back. The hawk swings over and hangs huge above me so that I nearly fall over backwards straining my neck to watch it. I can see the contour patterns on its chest, the darker band of feathers round its eye, the white stripe along its eyebrow.

The next one is inside the trees, moving in and out of view. A large shadow flying through the trees, as if they were parting to let it through. Suddenly swinging up to land on a branch. I cannot see all of the bird because it is perched behind a curtain of leaves. There is just a hint of grey shoulder and folded wing, an unevenness of colour inside the trees.

A goshawk spends most of its time perched, blended into a tree. Absence or agitation can sometimes betray the presence of a goshawk: an absence of corvid nests (or successful nests) suggests a goshawk is in residence in a wood, as if the hawk has pulled in an exclusion zone around it. But this absence can just as quickly flip into mobbing agitation, crows furious with fear and ancestral spite, yelling to the wood, to the wind, to the whole world: *Here is a hawk*.

Most birds of prey wear the mobbing with indifference until it becomes so persistent that they are forced to move on. There is an account of one juvenile goshawk being killed by a flock of 200 hooded crows. But mobbing a larger predator is full of risk and there are many more accounts of the harassed raptor suddenly turning and seizing their pursuer. One goshawk I read about was seen joining a raven in mobbing a sea eagle only for the eagle to turn and stoop on the hawk, catching it in its talons. Occasionally, rarely, the hawk becomes the mobsman: Eurasian eagle owls (one of the few species to predate goshawks) have this effect on most raptors. These apex predators are not tolerated by other birds of prey, to the extent that eagle owls are sometimes used as decoys to lure in birds such as goshawks and ospreys for ringing purposes.

Female goshawks are faster in flight, the males have more agility and acceleration. The females are all low-geared power, gulping up the space. Males are slalom-ers, threading through the trees, twisting after prey.

Often a kill starts from a standstill, an ambush along a quiet forest ride, dropping from a perch, accelerating into a passing pigeon or a noisy undulating woodpecker. Sometimes a goshawk will stalk its prey, tree-creep, pausing to listen and check its bearing on prey that the hawk may be able to hear but not yet see. Woodland raptors (hawks and owls for instance) hunt with their ears as well as their eyes. Folds in the land, hedges, walls: all are used as cover to take prey by surprise. Not the leisurely contour-hugging of a harrier's flight, more a dash along a ditch, everything done at hawk-speed. A flock of pigeons feeding in an open field is approached from a low glide, skimming the fields. Then, when the flock breaks and scatters, the goshawk is beating, bursting out of the glide, rushing at the stragglers.

Above all pigeons. Also: corvids, grouse (especially the displaying males of woodland grouse), squirrels, rabbits, pheasants, though lifting a bird as heavy as a pheasant is a struggle. Occasionally other raptors are predated by goshawks: kestrels, sparrowhawks, honey buzzard broods … There are records of everything from domestic cats to birds as large as common buzzards. Even male goshawks must tread warily around the larger female gos, which, recent studies suggest, is becoming larger, the size dimorphism between the male and female goshawk widening in certain localities across the birds' range. Where the goshawk's traditional prey, woodland grouse, have grown scarce, the hawks have shifted to different prey species, evolving in size to adapt to this change. The male goshawks becoming smaller to pursue swifter more agile prey; the females, in turn, switching from woodland grouse to hares and growing larger, evolving to better tackle the hares with all their strength and speed and risk.

A hare must rarely pose a risk. But there is the unfortunate goshawk I read about who grasped a hare in one foot and tried to halt the hare's momentum by seizing a clump of vegetation with its other foot. The hare cried out with its witchy screech but its powerful legs kept moving, charging onwards. The hawk instinctively tightened its grip on both hare and plant and the bird, apparently, was torn apart by the force of the hare's momentum ...

Above all, too, a bird of woodland and woodland edge zones. But the goshawk does not need so much deep forest as we tend to assume. Spinneys, scattered copses, neglected churchyards will do fine. Even city parks, playgrounds, just so long as there is a tree in which to build its heavy nest. Some central European cities now have established populations of goshawks (Berlin has around ninety pairs), where the hawks can be seen hunting magpies, blackbirds and feral pigeons through the parks and streets.

Even – of all the treeless places – Orkney, where MacGillivray had reports from his contemporaries of goshawks *not unfrequently* being seen. And, amongst the many bones of sea eagles that spilled from the tomb on South Ronaldsay, as well as the remains of gulls and corvids they also found the bones of a goshawk. What was a goshawk doing way up there on Orkney miles from any wood? Why would a goshawk, along with all those other birds, be interred in the burial chamber at Isbister? Some of the birds – the gulls and corvids – are carrion feeders like the sea eagle and may have also played their part in excarnating the dead. Goshawks will sometimes eat carrion, though are not renowned for it. But all the

At Dumfries MacGillivray goes in search of Robert Burns's grave. He wanders about the town in the dusk looking for the churchyard. Struggling to find it, walking round in circles, he almost gives up and heads back to the inn. But then the thought strikes him, he cannot possibly pass up the opportunity to pay his respects to the poet. So he wanders on and at last sights the kirk-yard. The gate is locked so he scrambles over the wall and drops down into *a wilderness of tombs*. Burns's tomb is locked with a sign from the magistrate warning that he will throw anyone in jail who is caught climbing the wall. *What*, thinks MacGillivray, *have I to do with restraint? These walls were not intended to exclude me, for the memory of the poet is dear to my heart, and I could not injure his monument.* So he climbs the railings, sits down on the steps of Burns's tomb, and bursts into tears.

It is nearly dark now and MacGillivray spends the next hour on the steps of the tomb in a muddle of grief. He feels that the poet's memory is dearer to him than any living being. He doesn't know why this is, only that there is a kinship, a recognition there. It is not that Burns is also a child of nature, rather that MacGillivray feels acutely Burns's own misfortunes and his untimely death. He tries speaking to God, who he has not spoken to for half a year. Afterwards he feels a soft melancholy, for often, he writes, *there is a stage in the paroxysm of grief which to me is highly pleasing*. Then it is past: MacGillivray climbs out of the tomb, back over the ceme-tery wall and drops softly down into the street.

* * *

It was not always easy to follow the line of the Border accurately. This middle stretch of the boundary is so detached and abandoned, swallowed by forestry. Left to its own devices the line behaves strangely here. It jinks and doubles back on itself, rushes off at sudden, unexpected angles across the hill with no thought to topography. I trace the Border line between Deadwater and Hobbs' Flow on my map. Deadwater, Foulmire Heights, Bloody Bush … the place-names do their best to ward you off. Even Hobbs' Flow comes with a warning from the great explorer and chronicler of the Border, James Logan Mack:

> In a wet season the passage of the Flow should not be
> attempted, and even in a dry one the traveller is not
> free from the risk of being engulfed in the morass.
> While I have crossed it twice in safety, I do not advise
> that this route be followed, and he who ventures into
> such solitude should keep to the west and circle
> round on higher ground.

If you went on the run from justice in Scotland or in England, this is where you ran to, the Debatable Grounds, the Batable Lands, the No-Man's-Land that straddles sections of the Border. A place which neither nation could agree on, a refuge, a place to flee to. *Batable*: contentious, discorded lands. To *bate*: the austringer's term for an untrained, skittish goshawk when it tries to flee the wrist. *Batable*: the reason this middle section of the Border above Kielder behaves so strangely, jinking, doubling back on itself, given to sudden unexpected flights. Maps from the eighteenth and nineteenth centuries describe much of this area as 'Disputed Ground', uncertain, feral places, tending to bate, to flee the authorities. The courses of streams that marked this section of the Border were often diverted, dykes ploughed up in the night, lines erased, land appropriated. It takes a surveyor to referee such disputes, to compromise, to mark a boundary so esoterically with little or no thought to topography. Only a surveyor could create such sharp angles, draw such straight and unexpected lines across the hills.

I climb along the flanks below Deadwater Moor. *Deadwater*: still water, water with no movement; a watershed, between east and west, between the North Sea and the Solway. Also, a watershed for language, above all dialect. Just as in the Flow Country where Norse and Gaelic met and barely recognised each other, the Anglo-Scots border cuts language markedly in two. The distinction between dialects on either side of the Border is abrupt, like nowhere else. MacGillivray felt this when he stopped in Carlisle to ask the way and found the dialect so completely altered:

- When thou comes to the corner, though maun keep to the right, and when thou comes to some houses they will show thee.
- I thank you.
- Welcome.

I treated the Border as the most porous of things, to be breached constantly on my walks along it. But language – dialect – slams up against it, reflects the presence of a boundary along almost all of it. The whole district is rife with dialect isoglosses. Within the space of a mile or two you can go from being a *scarecrow* to a *flaycrow* to a *crowbogle* to a *tattiebogle* ...

The Batable Lands had their own rules. From sunrise to sundown they were treated as common ground where livestock from either nation could be grazed. Anything left overnight – cattle or goods – was fair game and could be taken or destroyed. If property was built inside the area it could be burnt down and any people found inside the building taken prisoner. From time to time the district would be settled and in turn provoke the authorities to clear the people out again. This was the objective behind the Treaty of Norham of 1551:

> Debatable Ground should be restored to its old
> condition, according to usage, that therefore all
> subjects of either realm living in it or having houses
> there were to remove with wives, children, goods
> and cattle by the Feast of St. Michael the Archangel
> next, any found there after that date to be expelled by
> the Wardens and punished according to law.

But always there was a drift of people returning to fill the vacuum, fugitives, rebels, the dispossessed. As quickly as the Debatable Lands were cleared they were colonised again.

* * *

Goshawks went the way – the same ways (and at the same time) more or less – the osprey and sea eagle went. Bounty schemes, vermin lists, clearances ... When they began to return in the 1960s goshawks did so more quietly, more secretively than the sea eagle and osprey: falconers releasing – sometimes losing – goshawks to the wild. A slow trickle of imports and escapees, the latter often trailing jesses into their new lives. The birds are well established now in certain districts, especially the Anglo-Welsh and Anglo-Scots borderlands, but there remain areas, debatable grounds, where goshawks are expelled before they have arrived, sink holes, briefly colonised before they are cleared out again.

My last hour in the forest. The buzzards have returned, the raven too. Late afternoon, light going around the edges of the clearing. The raven steadies out above the treeline and starts to rise and fall in peaks and troughs. Then a goshawk is calling and lifting up from the dark trees to the left of me. This hawk has been calling on and off for much of the day. I am glad to see her. She is much larger than the male goshawk that flew over earlier. Wings held straight and stiff, she flies around the rim of the clearing then crosses in front of me. Slow wing strokes: glide, flap.

VII

Kestrel

Bolton

Late October on the outskirts of Bolton, everything drenched in mist. The town below me in a sump of fog. Rush-hour buses sliding down the hill, tail lights like fading fire ships in a haar. I cross the main road and skirt around the back of a pub. Dormant extractor fans, a yellow drum of cooking oil, starlings in the beer-garden grass, very black in the pale light. Behind the wheelie bins, a five-bar steel gate, an electric strap fence hooked to the gate's straining post. The white strap runs out across the field, 3 feet off the ground, undulating, held up by yew-green plastic pegs. I climb the gate and the metal rattling sound it makes spooks the starlings into flight, black shots through the mist as if the birds were punching holes in it. Beyond the gate a field of deeper mist, the ground bumpy with horse dung, a grey fur on the dung like frost. The strap fence branches off at right angles from itself, demarcating the field into tiny paddocks. The field is full of docks, small thin rabbits bolt from under their blotched leaves.

Another crossing point, another border post. The switch is so sudden here, from town to moor: the end of a street, a sliver of no-man's-land, gorse and bramble, a wet field overrun with rushes. Then I am climbing up onto the crumbling, hacked-at moors. Farms perched on the edge of huge quarries, deep bowls of mist. A peregrine down there somewhere, I can hear it calling from the quarry workings.

Above the quarry, a large field sculpted by landfill, buried and smoothed over, its surface pitted with rubble, glass, tight balls of burnt plastic. Damp sheep on the landfill, muddy Herdwicks, hooves clacking against bits of brick. Across a ditch and the next field is soaking wet. A stunted, windswept holly along its edge, remnant clumps of heather rolled up against the windward side of the dyke, rushes in the peaty hollows. Snipe are here, bursting out from under me in rapid, jagged flight. And from out of the mist a wonderful sight: a large flock of lapwings, thirty birds, rising from the soft field with such lightness, swooping over the moor, flickering black and white. I keep on disturbing them in the mist, dislodging the flock, watching it rise and settle again further up the field like a thrown sheet coming to rest over a bed.

Then something large is heading towards me out of the mist. A tall heavy shape and I think it must be a horse made skittish by my presence in the fog. It is trotting towards me and I am worried that it will not see me in time, that it will rear up and bolt in fright. But when it steps out of the mist and is almost on top of me, the shape and movement are wrong. Not a horse at all: nothing like a horse. What on earth … an ostrich! Of all the places, in the middle of this boggy field above Bolton, striding out of the mist, skidding to a halt in front of me. Thick neck, head tilting down, peering at me. Its huge brown eyes blink. Then it wheels around, its feet slap a puddle left by a tractor print, and it strides back up the hill into the mist. Something about the bulbous shape of its body, the loose straggling feathers, reminds me of huge buzzard nests I've seen, like a nest on stilts. So now, I think, I have the avian extremes of my journey: the tiny wren that bobbed around my heather lookout on Orkney, to this escapee ostrich, fugitive giant of the West Pennine Moors.

I left MacGillivray in Carlisle, asking directions for the road south.

- When thou comes to the corner, though maun
  keep to the right, and when thou comes to some
  houses they will show thee.
- I thank you.
- Welcome.

Beneath the sandstone glow of Carlisle castle
MacGillivray goes into a bank and exchanges his five
Scotch notes for English ones. He searches among the
back streets for cheap lodgings but there is nothing available and no one will give him change for one of his notes.
So he heads out of the city along the Keswick road. It is a
shock how sudden the dark comes on, there is so little
preamble. MacGillivray arrived in Carlisle at five o'clock
with no sense that the day might be dissolving. By seven
he is out on the road to Keswick and there is not a trace
of daylight left. The night is so assertive now.

He does not say why, but the next inn refuses him
lodging. Though his appearance cannot have helped: he
looks so tattered and road-weary, like some wandering
scarecrow come down out of the north. Half a mile on he
comes to another inn and it's, *No beds here, mister*. But
he orders supper anyway because by now he is exhausted,
has not eaten a thing all day except for a twopenny cake.
But here is a new difficulty which he could not have seen
coming: the innkeeper can give MacGillivray change for
his note but she cannot accept a Bank of England note.
And no, it's no good that MacGillivray only exchanged it
at the bank in Carlisle a few hours ago. She is very sorry
and her husband is sorry too, you do sound like an honest

fellow but, you see, there are Bank of England forgeries circulating through Cumberland and, you must understand, they have been cheated once before and resolved to never take a Bank of England note again. It is too much, this small injustice, and MacGillivray hears himself almost yelling that he is hungry and tired and can scarcely proceed upon his journey. And, yes, you do seem like an honest fellow, really, and they are very sorry, but it will not do. So MacGillivray is back out through the door and trudging along the road. And something about the rhythm of walking once more – reverting to what his muscles know – calms him. But it does not alleviate his hunger and he is brittle with tiredness. It is cloudy with slivers of moonlight showing between the clouds. The road has narrowed to a lane, tall hedges loom up on either side. The lane is exceptionally muddy and MacGillivray is soon wet to his ankles. He notices, when the lane sinks beneath the hedgerows, that he is walking through a seam of shadow and he sees how the night's gradient can change so quickly as he passes through pools of darker, cooler air. Crossroads keep bisecting the lane. Soon he is sure he is on the wrong road and has to knock on the door of a house to ask directions. Further on he comes to another inn. But it's no beds here, mister, and, sorry, but we can't let you sleep in the outhouse either and the cook has gone to bed and so it's out the door again, first turning on the left, then right, then straight ahead to the common. Another crossroads, another farmhouse. The door is shut. MacGillivray finds himself swaying in the centre of a quiet farmyard, a cart shed in front of him. So he goes into the shed, climbs up onto the cart and lies down. Then he notices steps up to a loft, so he climbs up and there are rushes and wattlings plus a bit of scruffy mat he has carried up from the cart. Unhooks his knapsack, punches it into a pillow, lies down on the rushes, drapes the mat over his legs, tries to sleep. At midnight his wet feet wake him with cold. Puts off his shoes, wraps his feet in the mat. Then sleep of sorts till he is woken by people moving below in the farmyard, feeding the horses and poultry. Descending the hayloft, back down into the muddy lane. He seems to have passed beyond hunger into a dizzy weakness. He is, by now, covered in grime as if a carriage had splattered him with mud as it hurtled past on the road. And he must have slept on his hat because it is so crumpled it will not be coaxed back into shape. Two miles down the road and he enters a public house. Breakfast at last: tea, bread, butter and eggs. And MacGillivray does something which is unlike him and which racks him with guilt for days to come. He waits until he's finished his breakfast before he presents, nonchalantly, his Bank of England note. Both the innkeeper and his wife, inspecting it, prodding it, shaking their heads. Sorry, but if you had a Scotch note instead ... they would be happy to give change for that. But a Bank of England note: no, we simply cannot take the risk, would rather forfeit the shilling for your breakfast. And they show MacGillivray great kindness, this couple, and say that it does not matter and he is welcome to the bread and eggs. Still, he leaves them feeling a little guilty, a little sly he had not mentioned the pesky notes up front. He makes a vow not to be so dishonest again. Outside the inn he can see Carlisle cathedral in the distance. The hills of Scotland are rinsed in mist. It is eleven o'clock in the morning. The mud on his clothes is starting to dry and flake.

Kestrel

There it comes, advancing briskly against the breeze, at the height of about thirty feet, its wings in rapid motion, its head drawn close between its shoulders, its tail slightly spread in a horizontal direction, and its feet concealed among the plumage. Now it sails or glides a few yards, as if on motionless wings, curves upwards some feet, and stops short, supporting itself by rapid movements of its pinions, and expanding its tail. In a few seconds it flies forwards, flapping its wings, shoots off to a side, and sails, then rises a little, and fixes itself in the air. On such occasions it is searching the ground beneath for mice and small birds, feeding or reposing among the grass. Having discovered nothing, it proceeds a short way, and again hovers. In a few seconds it wheels round, flies right down the wind at a rapid rate, to the distance of some hundred yards, brings up, and hovers. Still nothing results, and again it glides away, bearing up at intervals, fixing itself for some seconds in the air, and then shooting along. When about to hover, it rises a few feet in a gentle curve, faces the wind, spreads its tail, moves its wings rapidly, and thus balancing itself keenly surveys the ground beneath. The range of the tips of the wings at this time is apparently about six or eight inches, but sometimes for a few seconds these organs seem almost, if not entirely, motionless. The bird has once more suddenly drawn up, and is examining the grass with more determinate attention. It slowly descends, fixes itself for a moment, inclines a little to one side, hovers so long that you may advance much nearer, but at length closing its wings and tail, falls like a stone, suddenly expands its wings and tail just as it touches the ground, clutches its prey, and ascending obliquely flies off with a rapid and direct flight.

How does a kestrel hover the way it does? It is a movement of such precision and control. The falcon holds itself in the air like a star you could navigate by. The bird is standing still, walking into the wind. Its head, its eyes are fixed to the ground beneath. Every minute adjustment of its wings and tail is made to keep the head in place. It is astonishing it can keep its head that still despite the wind which flings itself at the bird's light frame. And really – more accurately – the kestrel is not hovering but balancing itself, pushing itself against the wind so that the force of the wind is cancelled out by the momentum of the bird's flight. The kestrel is held in place, pinned by the interplay of wind and flight. If it is pushed back a few millimetres by the wind the falcon stretches its neck to keep its head in place. It adjusts to the rise or fall in the wind's speed by alternating between glide and flap.

To hunt like this the kestrel needs the wind to hold it up. But if the wind is too strong, it becomes difficult to hover effectively, even more so when there is no wind at all. The kestrel can hover on a windless day, wings flickering, winnowing the air. But it is expensive – inefficient – to keep this up. So when the wind is not right or, in winter, when energy is precious, a kestrel hunts by other means than hovering. Sometimes it resorts to piracy: dive-bombing short-eared owls to make them spill their catch. But more often the kestrel will revert to hunting from a static perch, a hedgerow, tree or telegraph wire. A beetle can be spotted clambering through the grass from a perch 50 metres away, starlings foraging amongst cattle are clocked at 300 metres. It is less successful, this method of hunting, because the falcon cannot cover as much ground. But, especially in winter, static hunting conserves crucial energy. In spring and summer, when the male kestrel needs to work overtime, more often than not he reverts to aerial hunting.

After the ostrich and the field of mist I climb higher up onto the moor, but it is hopeless up here as I can see very little in the fog. A kestrel could not hunt in this. Occasionally the mist shifts enough for me to see a flashing red light from a television signal mast on the summit of the hill. The narrow road leading to the mast is cracked and split where frost has picked at it. I head down off the hill and follow a path pebbled black with sheep droppings. A few sheep cross the path ahead of me, smudged identification marks sprayed onto their backs, the turquoise dye corposant on their wool. On the lower slopes there is a brightness building inside the fog. Then suddenly I am out: the mist has ended like a stratum of the moor and I can see the wooded slopes above Rivington and a great stretch of the Lancashire Plain opening up below.

Of all the birds of prey the kestrel flares the most with light. In Gaelic she is the *Clamhan ruadh*, the red hawk. *Ruadh*: a less true red than the bolder, purer red of *dearg*. *Ruadh*: the coppery red of fox and rust and a roe deer's summer pelt. The male kestrel is the brighter red, his brightness offset by his beautiful pearl-grey head and tail. The female lacks this grey but both have black wings from the carpal joint down to the tip which accentuates the ochre colour of their back and upper wings. The female's red is thinner, browner, more chestnut-coloured. Often, when the falcon banks to glide away, you catch that blush of colour down their back and wings. Sometimes, when the sun brushes a kestrel's back, the bird's feathers glint with brightness.

One night in July 1913 a huge blaze is spotted on the side of the hill above Rivington. Lord Leverhulme's wooden summer home is on fire, burning through the night. A few hours earlier, the suffragette Edith Rigby had walked around Leverhulme's property checking nobody was inside. When she was sure the house was empty she broke a window and poured paraffin through the hole, felt the trapped heat of the day spill out of the house when she smashed the glass. The place was tinder-dry, the pitch-pine walls warm to touch. Later, a night breeze licked up the fire, and from across the valley flames could be seen pouring out of the hillside. At her trial Rigby said:

I want to ask Sir William Lever whether he thinks his property on Rivington Pike is more valuable as one of his superfluous homes occasionally to be opened to people, or as a beacon lighted for King and Country, to see that here are some intolerable grievances for women.

I walk on down the hill's shoulder. Around the 1,000-feet contour point, on the western edge of the hill, there is a large levelled area cut into the side of the moor. This is the spot where Leverhulme's house stood. The area is matted with reeds and thick tussocks of grass. There are hints of concrete, like puddles, in amongst the grass. The flatness, the concrete undercoat, make the place feel like a neglected car park. No trace of the house, as if it had been swept clean away. Except, I find some black and white chequered tiles amongst the grass, the remains of a lavatory floor (once situated off the entrance to the ball-room). The tiles are in good condition, the white ones even look clean. A few dead leaves have settled on them as if someone had left a door open.

After the fire the house was rebuilt with stone. Leverhulme, who had made his fortune from packaging soap, was one of the wealthiest industrialists on the planet and he poured money into his hilltop home. Photographs from its brief heyday are otherworldly: wooden pagodas beside a Japanese lake, a glass-roofed pergola, a minstrel's gallery above the ballroom, fluted pillars, Flemish tapestries, an 'orchestra' lawn. An entire hillside reclaimed from the moor and sculpted into ornate Italian gardens, boating lakes, waterfalls, terraces of rhododendrons. When Edith Rigby was reconnoitring the house for her arson attack she walked through the grounds passing grazing herds of llamas, kangaroos and ostriches. She noted how the animals seemed better housed and fed than many people on the land.

I stand up from the sundial stump where I ate my lunch and start to drop down off the hill, walking through the gardens. Everywhere the moor has crept back in. The croquet lawns are thick with rushes, the lakes silted up and grown over, the summer houses in brambles. Along the terrace steps, in the Italianate archways, you can see the detailed craftsmanship in the stonework. Then I am out of the terraced gardens onto a change in gradient. The ground begins to level and I think this is where the zebras and ostriches must have grazed, where Edith Rigby parked her car before the long slog up the hill with the paraffin kegs. The paths here are deeply grooved by runoff from the moor. Allotments, school playing fields, the woods giving way to the creased edge of the town.

* * *

A few years after Edith Rigby burnt down his home, Leverhulme bought the islands of Lewis and Harris in their entirety. The village where William MacGillivray went to school as a boy, Obbe, Leverhulme renamed after himself, changing its name to Leverburgh. A century on from the meeting between MacGillivray, his uncle and the laird over the tenancy of the farm at Northton, the same land disputes continued to flare through the islands. In 1919 a group of crofters from Northton challenged their new landlord, Leverhulme, with his lack of empathy for their need for land, with the same passion as MacGillivray had done when he confronted MacLeod and his duplicitous factor, Stewart. In a letter from 1919 petitioning the Board of Agriculture for the farm at Rodel, ten crofters from Northton wrote:

We shall never submit tamely like our forefathers. We shall not be compelled to leave our native land without struggle. If something is not done soon, I am afraid we shall be compelled to take possession in our own way. The following are those who wish to be given a small-holding on Rodel without delay ...

When MacGillivray opened up the kestrel to inspect its stomach he found, for the most part, the hair, bones and teeth of mice and shrews. But also, he wrote,

167

I have found the remains of young larks, thrushes, lapwings and several small birds both granivorous and slender-billed, together with the common dung-beetle, many other coleopteran, and the earthworm.

Add to this: the occasional lizard, rat, mole and slug (one kestrel was observed carefully skinning slugs, lifting them up to its bill, swallowing the slugs whole, a residue of slime glistening on the kestrel's foot). The kestrel is somewhere between a specialist and generalist, some-where between the short-eared owl, with its dependency on voles, and the more omnivorous buzzard. The kestrel can adapt its diet, diverge from voles when it needs to, but field voles are its mainstay; it cannot completely do without them. Population density, breeding success: both are impacted by the availability of voles. Starvation, the most common cause of mortality in kestrels (juvenile birds especially), is most prevalent in poor vole years, or when the voles are sealed by heavy snow.

They live short lives, these small falcons. There is none of the slow burn to adulthood you find in larger birds of prey. Kestrels can breed in their first year. The majority die before their second. They can be sedentary or migratory; much, again, depends on voles. There is an emptying out of kestrels from the uplands in winter; some birds migrate long distances, others remain in their breeding territories year round. Nest is a hole in a hollow tree, a disused crow's nest, a scrape on the side of a cliff (like all falcons, the kestrel does not build a nest). On treeless Orkney, where there are no foxes, kestrels nest in deep heather. Buildings serve as stand-in cliffs; in German the kestrel is the *Turmfalke* (the tower falcon). Window boxes, windmill ledges, church steeples, gutters ... as long as the site is sheltered, out of reach of ground predators, and will contain and hold their eggs.

There is a risk we take this common bird of prey for granted, that we view the kestrel as more adaptable than it is capable of being. The kestrel is not as common as it used to be. Since the mid-1970s its population has declined in England by more than a quarter. Scotland's population has also plummeted in the last two decades. If we destroy the habitats for field voles, the meadows and field margins, the tangled unkempt places, kestrels will find it hard to cope.

From the town I keep looking back towards the moor and the wooded slopes below Leverhulme's home. It is not so clear-cut, the switch from moor to town: the two can mingle and fuse with one another. Kestrels move easily between the two spheres, hunting over the moor, nesting on the town's buildings, on its disused factory chimneys. And sometimes the town slips out of itself to re-emerge up on the moor. In September 1896, 10,000 people walked up through the streets of Bolton, climbing up onto the hill in a mass trespass to stake their right to follow a path over the moor, the buildings emptying that morning and the noise of the exodus like a slow exhalation of the town's breath. Gamekeepers and policemen met the trespassers at the edge of the moor, noting ringleaders, the crowd churning past them through the disputed gate.

During the war a replica town was built up on the moor: a decoy, constructed of lights and long channels laid over the turf. The lights were used to resemble a poorly blacked-out town, leaking light from its doorways and factory furnaces. The purpose was to fool enemy aircraft into thinking they had reached their target. Fuel in the channels was ignited then flooded with oil and water so that it looked as if a town was already burning (and exploding) down there. The decoy was built on the moor to protect the crucial royal ordnance factory near Chorley. The fuel tanks, pipes and poles with lights on top of them stayed in place up there, on the hillside to the west of Belmont, for the duration of the war. Not so much a replica town, more the idea – the thought – of a town sketched onto the moor. A town stripped down to its circuit board.

I am walking through the suburbs of Horwich now, heading towards the M61 motorway. The hum of its traffic has been with me all morning. On one street, in a tiny front garden, there is a birch tree with all its leaves shaken out. A collared dove is perched in the tree like a bulb of grey light. MacGillivray paused near here on route to London, recharging his spirits in a public house in Chorley, sitting beside the fire, smoking a pipe, deciding then to not give up, to shun the stagecoach seat, and carry on with his walk to London, *although*, he wrote, *my stumps should be worn off to the knees ...*

I turn left off the street into a thin alleyway that runs along a row of back gardens. Old grass cuttings, tipped over the fence, are suspended in bramble bushes like frozen spray. The ground is slippery from the mulch made by the cuttings. In places logs have been laid across the path to serve as stepping stones. The other side of the path is flanked by the embankment of a disused railway, its slope rusty with discarded Christmas trees. Birch and hawthorn take over as the path becomes muddier and I drop down towards the edge of the town.

The rest of the day I spend walking beside the motorway through the wet fields on either side. This is where I hope to find the kestrel, in the tall grass along the motorway's sidings, between the slip roads and roundabouts. I use the footbridges over the motorway as lookout points, scanning the embankment with my binoculars, swaying above the traffic. A farm track leads to a tunnel under the motorway; it is a quiet echo chamber, lit with puddles, with a high ceiling to allow farm vehicles through. The tunnel is a good place to pause a while away from the wind and whoosh of the motorway. Its arched entrance frames the view of where I have walked today: the hill, now clear of mist, the wooded slopes of Leverhulme's old home, the town across the fields to the east.

If you transplant something ingrained in a landscape to somewhere new, can the object still retain the semblance of itself? Or, once it has been removed, does it start to die a little in its new surroundings? When I was on the Moray Firth I did not feel I could gather up the stones I found along the shore because it seemed that to remove them would somehow have diminished them.

There is an anecdote about Lord Leverhulme, that he took a liking to a wooden fireplace mantel in a public house on the Isle of Lewis. It was an ancient slab of oak and for generations families had carved their names in the wood. The owners of the inn would not part with it. So Leverhulme bought the entire building instead, extracted the mantel and shipped it down to his summer home at Rivington, where he had the mantel installed to support a fireplace alcove in the ballroom.

The stone used to build this motorway tunnel was transplanted from the moor above the town. Thirteen feet of stone were skimmed from the hillside to lay the foundations for the motorway. And it's almost as if I have not left the hill at all, that I'm still walking over the moor – or a memory of it – as I criss-cross the motorway. The stone removed from the moor was replaced with soil which washed off the hillside in the next heavy rain, pouring down the lanes and spilling over the main road in a thick black waterfall.

Nothing is static: even a hill can suddenly burst and wash half its face away; a bog is always breathing, changing its shape in its sleep; a kestrel appears to be still as she hangs in the air but really she is moving, pushing against the wind.

This is where I hope to find the kestrel and this instead is where I find the buzzard, flapping low over the scrubby no-man's-land between the railway and motorway. And then, because buzzards will often do this – will often draw your eye to something else – I spot the kestrel, hovering above the junction roundabout. I get as close as I can to the motorway and prop myself under an oak tree overlooking the slip road and roundabout.

The kestrel holds herself at a steep angle against the wind, tail spread to increase the lift, wings shivering. Her strikes come regularly: once, often twice, a minute. A staggered descent through the air, the angle almost vertical, checking her drop 5 feet above the ground, a slight adjustment to left or right, then a final plummet into a splash of grass. Those last seconds, when she pulls her wings up behind her before she hits the ground, I can see the pale white flash of her underwings and tail.

When the kestrel leaves the roundabout she heads south-east along the motorway. I scramble after her and the last few hours of daylight are a rush along hedge-rows, muddy underpasses, splashing across fields. There are snatched glimpses of the kestrel, often in the distance, hanging above the motorway. To catch up with her is just to push her out of reach again. Half a field away is as near as I get before she banks and arcs across to the adjacent field. In a farmyard I am slowed down by a herd of cattle, their breath smoking in the cool air. Curious and nervy, they bunch and heave around me, make sudden splatter-ing retreats through the mud, remuster and hunker back towards me in a swaying huddle, heads low to the ground, huffing, yellow tags hanging from their ears like bright fruit.

As the sun is going I am in a field above the motorway. Jackdaws and rooks are heading to roost in ragged flocks, the smaller jackdaws weaving amongst the rooks, the molecular structure of the flock. I am watching the kestrel perched in a hawthorn bush, her folded wings twitch and jerk above her long tail. The motorway is a streak of yellow light. The low sun has brought out the orangey reds of the kestrel's back. She is surrounded by the darker, deeper reds of hawthorn berries. I stand behind her and watch her shape turn black.

Montagu's Harrier

The Fens

One night, on route to London, MacGillivray dreams of flight:

> I dreamed the other night that I was winging through
> the air in a large area about three or four feet from
> the ground with great velocity, and I felt so very
> happy that I scarcely remember to have ever felt

happier ... the impression which this aerial tour
made upon my mind was so strong that for some time
after I could not prevail upon myself to believe that it
did not actually happen and I can scarcely believe
that it is not possible.

All flight, dreamed or otherwise, falls short of the bird I
am watching from this hedge. Montagu's harrier: a bird
given over to buoyancy and lightness of drift. Flying, like
MacGillivray dreamed he did, 4 feet from the ground. An
adult female, working her way down the purlieu of the
hedge, coming towards me in lilting flight. All wing:
there is nothing there but wing and nothing for the wings
to do but stretch and glide. I have never seen such buoyancy, never known something so undeterred by gravity.
That she does not stall, flying so low and slow above the
ground, is a miracle of design. And there is no wind
today, nothing to hold her up, just heat and a thick stillness clogging the day.

I am on the edge of The Fens. It is the middle of July
and the air is furrowed with heat. I have found a place
inside the hedge which allows me to swivel easily and
look out over the fields on either side. The hedge is tall
and frayed, more like a loose phalanx of trees. There are
deer gaps and fox gaps and some openings that are so
wide they could be sluice gates left open to let the wind
rush through unimpeded. The bulk is hawthorn and
hawthorn's companion, elder. There is also blackthorn
with its darker, glossier leaves. And a dead oak, cloaked
in ivy, standing up to its knees inside the hedge. The

fields on either side are wheat and barley, the wheat greener, paler-looking, the barley crackling and popping in the dry air.

When MacGillivray came down out of the north on his walk to London, he suffered a sort of vertigo – an inverse vertigo – or rather, a dry form of the bends, descending too quickly from the northern uplands. It left him homesick and irritable. His instinct, like a ptarmigan's, was to cling to the high ground for as long as possible.

In Keswick his Bank of England note is changed at last. He heads out of the town on the Borrowdale road and the rain comes on again. He stops to ask directions for the way to Ambleside but ignores the advice that he should return to Keswick to take the regular road as it goes against his determination to see the mountain. Because mountains will do that to him: pull him to them, not for the sake of climbing, but because he wants to see what is growing on their slopes, what alpine flora can survive up there. Sometimes it feels as if every plant – or the prospect of a plant he has not seen before – has this magnetic pull on him. And I cannot fathom, with every mile along the road an infinity of distractions, how he is able to walk to London as quickly as he does.

So MacGillivray follows this new diversion and heads up on the footpath over the fell. On the outskirts of a village a dog rushes at him with such fury he has to yell at it to get back. The noise of its barking – and the sound of his shouting – is such a shock after so many miles of silence. And the dog's sudden burst of fury is not unlike the London juggler, *driving like fury at his squeaking fiddle*, whom he sat beside in the Keswick inn, falling foul of his rum, trying to dry out in front of the fire after his shivering night in that hayloft outside Carlisle.

Still raining as he enters the valley and he can see the rain on the mountain *glistening on the face of the dark rocks*. He feels himself being ballasted with tiredness. Sometimes he feels so tired he does not recognise himself, as if a part of him has travelled on ahead and knowledge of who he is, or that absent part of him, grows blurred and strained. He struggles, for instance, to remember his age, as if he had mislaid it, or mislaid a year. It plagues him for mile after mile, this dizzy insecurity, and he is only rid of it – this giddiness – when he grasps that what is really happening is that all this time alone on the road has left him, despite what he says, unsure of his own company, of who it is that is walking in him. He finds it hard to recall the person who left his house in Aberdeen a month ago. He would like to ask him, his distant self, what on earth it is he is doing scrambling up this mountain in the near-dark in Cumberland. At such moments he wants to abandon the walk, return to Scotland, cloak himself in study, *become useful* ... But he has walked so many miles over the years, back and forth from Harris to Aberdeen and all the digressions in between. So he knows too well that walking will do that to a person, that something in the friction of momentum, in the pounding of the road, unsettles the soul so that it becomes frayed and loose till it drifts up and away from the body like a kite. And it's at that moment, when the soul hangs flapping above the body, that he loses sight of who he is and finds himself running through the check-list of himself, fumbling, struggling to reconcile himself and haul back in the errant soul.

He reaches the summit of the mountain at dusk. The plants here: savin-leaved club-moss, prickly club-moss, common club-moss, fir club-moss and the starry saxi-frage. He has, by now, lost the path completely. So he heads down the mountain through the closing dark, picking his way across the scree.

A whitethroat scolds me when I arrive at the hedge. It keeps leaving and returning and each time sounds a little less agitated. The Montagu's harrier's nest is in the deep barley field in front of me. For much of the day the female harrier has been circling above the nest. Occasionally the sun catches and brightens the dim white colours in her wings. There is no sign of the male. He has another nest – another mate with young – a mile away in a dried reed bed. I would love to see him, the ash-coloured male. MacGillivray wrote that the male Montagu's harrier was *remarkable for its slender form and the great length of its wings*. He is the lightest of all the harriers. He has the largest wings compared with body size of perhaps any bird of prey. Low body weight accentuated by long wing length: this is the ratio which gives the Montagu's harrier its extraordinary buoyancy, its ability to keep on sailing out low over the ground for mile after mile. The birds are all wing and can easily spend half the day on the wing. At a steady 20 mph gliding over the land, the distance covered in a day by the Montagu's harrier could be anywhere between 50 and 100 miles.

He is not a static hunter. He is nothing like the kestrel who waits up inside the wind, or the patient goshawk who sits in ambush on its forest perch. The Montagu's harrier hunts on the move, a low-level, long-distance forager, drifting out to scour the land. Like other harriers, Montagu's hunt by sight and hearing, using the cupped disc shape of their face as an owl does, funnelling any noise they detect onto their ears. The Montagu's harrier's face is a listening device and, flying as low as they do, they can pinpoint a locust by the sound the insect makes feeding on the branch of a cotton bush.

Lightness and lift: if he finds an updraught, the male Montagu's settles into it, gives his light frame over to the rising current of air, so that he is carried up and away like pollen. In this way he is able to reach hunting grounds miles from the nest site. For such a large bird, if you picked him up, his pumice lightness would startle you. I heard a story of a male Montagu's harrier found floating in The Wash one year after he collided with a wire. When the drowned bird was pulled out of the sea there was nothing to him: he was all feather.

I am willing the male Montagu's harrier into view. It is easy, when you are straining for a glimpse, to over-anticipate the bird, to try to make its outline fit onto a different bird. I have often tried to squeeze goshawks into buzzards, sparrowhawks, even, into fast-flying pigeons. Late in the morning a marsh harrier floated inland, a male, coming in across the barley field, and I missed a beat thinking it might be the male Montagu's harrier returning to the nest, till the marsh harrier's harlequin colours took hold, creams and blacks and reds. The marsh harrier flew close to the Montagu's nest and I skipped another beat because the female Montagu's was away from her nest and, in her absence, I wondered if the marsh harrier would swoop down and try to take her young. But the marsh harrier flapped on, following the line of a hedge, black wing tips against the yellow field.

After the marsh harrier had gone, the female Montagu's drifted back across the field. She stood in the air above the nest for a while, circling there. Then she turned, drifting quickly away. A glider, light as balsa, floating across the fields. The narrow line of her outstretched wings met and matched the line of the horizon, and as she moved further away from me her outline began to shimmer in the haze. There was a gold tint to the feathers on her underside. Then she disappeared in the heat and when I picked her up again she was beside a wood two fields away, her shape brought back into focus by the dark trees. She was climbing, and as she cleared the top of the wood a buzzard rose from under her, heavy and broad-winged and flapping to heave itself up. The harrier began to rise in a wide corkscrew pattern above the trees. The sky over the wood was very bright. As she circled there, the white bar of feathers joining her tail to her body seemed, against the backdrop of white sky, like a gap opening up across her middle. For a few seconds, her tail looked like it was chasing – trying to rejoin – her body.

* * *

Montagu's: after the English ornithologist, George Montagu (1753–1815), who was the first to accurately describe and identify the harrier as a different species from the hen harrier. His identification came after centuries of muddle and it can still be difficult to tell the two apart. The adult male Montagu's harrier is a slightly darker, slightly dirtier grey. A black bar runs across the middle of his upper wings, one bar on each wing like a reflection of itself. Two parallel grey-black bars run along the underwings. His chest and the underside of his upper wings are flecked with a rusty patterning; the female Montagu's also has this reddish-brown blotching on her feathers. The ruff (the wreath of feathers that circles the head) is less pronounced in both sexes of the Montagu's than it is in the hen harrier. The male Montagu's is a more intricately patterned bird, his underside daubed with reds and browns and blacks; the dots of red look like a street of distant lights. The male hen harrier, by comparison, has a clean white undercarriage, unpatterned, brightly lit.

All of these variants are mostly undetectable, even through binoculars. It is easier to look to the bird's shape and the feel of its flight. Look especially at the shape of the wings: the Montagu's has longer, narrower wings with three long-fingered primaries; the hen harrier's wings are broader, blunter at the ends. The difference in wing length is especially noticeable when the birds are perched: the Montagu's long wings extend as far as the tip of its tail. Gravity, as well, works differently on the two species. The hen harrier, with its longer legs, stands taller. The Montagu's harrier, at rest, has a lower centre of gravity, sits more squat to the ground; in flight, gravity seems to have no bearing at all on the Montagu's harrier.

In the early afternoon high cloud begins to collect, thin streaks finding then plaiting each other. There is a slight shift in the light as the day's glare dims under the cloud. When the female Montagu's harrier rises high above the field the backdrop of cloud articulates her outline beautifully. Her three long primaries are clearly visible, the first time I have been able to count them accurately. When she holds her wings out behind her, before she goes into a glide, the tips of the wings have a falcon's sharpness.

I spend the whole day not getting used to her. Each time she comes into view I am amazed by the length of her wings. She is so loose and willowy, so relaxed in her flight. And unlike any other raptor I have seen in the way she does not flex her speed and strength. She is more like a gull in this respect, languid, unhurried in her flight. She keeps her speed in check: an adverse wind specialist, flying into the wind to slow herself down so she can scan the ground. Until the moment she spots her prey and you see how in fact she is primed with speed, is capable of a sudden shock of speed and will often carry on past her prey then turn rapidly around, backtrack, and use the wind's momentum to make her strike.

Striking at: skylark, meadow pipit, lizard, partridge chick, reed bunting, common vole, field vole, grasshopper, cricket ... In their African and Asian wintering grounds, locusts are an especially important prey species for these harriers. The Montagu's harrier can switch between small passerines and small mammals and, though it is not as dependent on voles as some other birds of prey, there are locations where voles are a significant part of the Montagu's diet and the harrier's breeding success is strongly influenced by the vole population.

Lightness and lift, will-o'-the-wisp, the soul set adrift like a plume of smoke … The poet John Clare described the Montagu's harriers he saw from his home on the edge of The Fens as *swimming close to the green corn*. It is in her lightness and ease of buoyancy that the corn-swimmer is most distinct from the hen harrier, the heather-wanderer, a sense that you have met, in the Montagu's harrier, the epitome of lightness and drift, that you could not perceive any creature more buoyant than this.

If I were to mark a halfway point on my journey I think it would be here on the edge of The Fens. The place feels like a junction of sorts, a crossing point between the north and south. At least, I have the sense that I have crossed a border between birds, between the hen harrier who breeds on the northern uplands and the Montagu's harrier who, on the edge of its northern range in England, breeds in the fenlands and chalklands of the south country. It is a border which dissolves outside the breeding season when, at the end of summer, Montagu's harriers depart for the locust-rich habitats of sub-Saharan Africa, returning again in the spring. In the interim, a change of shift: hen harriers come down from the moors to over-winter in the lowlands, sometimes moving into the vacuum left by the departed Montagu's harriers.

There used to be more interaction between the harrier species in this country, more blurring of their breeding range. Historically the Montagu's harrier has never been a numerous summer migrant to the British Isles, but there are accounts of it breeding alongside hen harriers and marsh harriers in The Fens. There are records of the birds being snared and their eggs sold when the collect-ing rage was at its height in the nineteenth century (a male Montagu's harrier in good condition could fetch 20 shillings; eggs could go for a similar sum). So this border between birds – this north–south divide between harrier species – is not a natural one. The hen harrier's breeding range is only confined to the northern uplands because persecution forced it to retreat to the far north and west, and it has never recolonised the extent of its former range. In tandem, the Montagu's harrier's breeding range (which historically had been more widely, though still thinly, scattered) has contracted to the opposite corner of these islands and today the Montagu's harrier only breeds in tiny numbers in the south and east of England.

Dissolve the border: bring the different harrier species together, let their territories overlap (as they do across their global breeding range). It is then that you really see how the birds differ. Within a shared habitat each species of harrier is its own specialist. The marsh harrier, with its longer legs, hunts over the taller reed beds; the

Montagu's, with its shorter tarsi and claws, ranges inland across shallower vegetation, pursuing smaller, more agile prey and with a tendency to be more insectivorous than its larger neighbours, the hen and marsh harriers. Even their breeding seasons are staggered so that the different harrier species avoid competing with each other when the demand for prey to provide for their young is at its height. Marsh harrier, Montagu's harrier, hen harrier, pallid harrier (which overwinters with the Montagu's in India and Africa and has a shorter wing and faster flight), they have all evolved to coexist.

Dissolving borders, the interchange of land and water, the blurring of the two together: welcome to The Fens, where the land is lower than the sea and everywhere is peat and silt and water. And if it is not water then it is land reclaimed from water, and land taken from water is land that has a memory of water, or land that tries to dream the water back to life. A place where water loses its identity, where there is no gravity to instruct the rivers, where salt and fresh water meet and meld and sometimes meet so destructively, like two avalanches rushing at each other, that the land is drowned for weeks on end. A place where a plough working a black field miles inland can exhume the skeleton of a whale from out of the peat; where once, during a winter flood, a ship ran aground on a submerged house and, thinking they had struck a rock, the sailors committed themselves to God and saved themselves only by clinging to the roof.

* * *

She is still coming towards me down the side of the hedge. Through my binoculars I can see the cupped disc of her face and the dark bands across her tail. When she veers close to the hedge the white rump at the top of her tail looks like a splash of hawthorn blossom against the hedge. It is the most conspicuous part of her, this white strap across her middle, the most brightly lit part of her plumage, flashing, signalling across the fields. She is moving quickly and I wonder if the lack of wind means she is finding it hard to steady her pace. I try to stay hidden. I don't want to startle her with my presence and so I burrow a little deeper into the hedge, combing the long grass over my back and around my head. My worry is that she will notice the sun glinting off the glass lenses of my binoculars. I watch her as she keeps to the same course, the same linear route across the field.

Lines are an important feature of the way a Montagu's harrier hunts. The birds will often head out from the nest site in a straight line following a hedge or the side of a wood, foraging along its tangled margin, looking to come across prey by surprise. The birds rarely deviate from this flight path, continuing to head out on the same trajectory, sometimes for up to 12 kilometres from the nest site, a much greater distance than hen and marsh harriers forage from the nest. In this way the Montagu's harrier reads the landscape differently from the hen harrier. The latter is more inclined to hunt by hugging contours, dipping and rising with the swell of the land. The Montagu's harrier is a bird of grids and patchworks,

of roadside verges and ditches, utilising the linear struc-
tures we have drawn across the land.

And there is no landscape more linear than The Fens, no
place I have come across in these islands that has been
so straightened by drainage and agriculture. Here is an
uncovered landscape, the inverse of what happened at
Culbin, where the land was smothered by the sandstorm,
and the valley of the Upper Tyne, when it was flooded by
the building of the Kielder dam.

Before it was uncovered – before it was fully drained
– much of The Fens was known as 'half-land', ground
that was neither permanently flooded nor high enough
to escape the winter floods, a place where the border
between land and water was constantly breached and
blurred and the boundary between fresh and salt water
was often hazy. Sometimes spring tides would breach so
far inland that deposits of silt would be left like a smear
of grease across the peat. Beneath the peat of the southern fens and the silt zones to the north which border The
Wash, there is such an interchange of marine and freshwater deposits layering the soil, it is impossible to tell
where the sea began or the rivers ended.

How do you begin to bring such a disobedient landscape under control? It took centuries of incremental
progress, of drainage schemes that could be undone by a
single night of heavy rain, a drain left unmaintained, or
somebody's pigs rooting over a dyke. For every acre of
reclaimed land, the fen would revert to water at the
slightest opportunity. Often drainage works would be

sabotaged by locals fed up with the taxes levied on them to pay for the schemes and the disruptions that drainage caused to their livelihoods, to navigation, fishing and wildfowling.

But the land's potential to be made profitable drove the drainage schemes on. Rivers were straightened and diverted, cuttings and outlets excavated, outfalls dredged of silt. Sluices, locks, scoop wheels, pumping stations were implemented; windmills, then steam, then diesel, drove the pumps. The old scribbled, sluggish routes of the rivers that choked and spilled across The Fens were diverted, dried up, became ghost rivers, extinct waterways, void of all but their names – a *roddon*, a *slade*. Extinct, but still visible – made ghostlike – from their residues of silt and shell marl winding across the dark and shrinking peat. Shrinking because if you take the water out of peat it is quickly replaced with air, oxidation follows and then bacteria set to work, breaking down the peat so that the plant materials decompose. The impact of this is dramatic: the peat shrinks and the land drops away from under itself, leaving behind the strangest of landscapes, a place where rivers have to be carried like aqueducts above the constantly shrinking fields, where houses are left with their front doors suspended 12 feet above the ground, where trees sit on top of their exposed roots.

And linking the ghost rivers – the roddons and slades – are the outlines of eviscerated lakes or meres, the lakes' white freshwater chalk deposits and marls, like pale birthmarks, still visible against the black peat. Huge lakes were drained and disappeared: Trundle, Ugg, Brick, Ramsey, Benwick, Whittlesea ... all names of lakes that have vanished from The Fens. Whittlesea Mere: the second-largest lake in England, which in the space of two years between 1851 and 1853 went from a place of pleasure yachts and sudden storms to fields of yellow corn.

I watch the female Montagu's harrier circling for a long time with prey in her talons. She seems hesitant about returning to her nest and instead lands several times a good distance away. Then she is up again, circling, the prey still clutched beneath her. Something is unsettling her. I move back deeper into the hedge. Then I notice the farmer has parked his car at the edge of the field and he is slowly walking through the crop, waist-deep in barley. As he walks he picks the occasional barley ear, rubs it against his palm and inspects the grains. They are skittish birds, Montagu's harriers, they live the jittery, nervous life of a ground-nester, often unsettled by the presence of a large animal near the nest site, anything from a passing roe deer to a pheasant. Eventually the farmer leaves the field and the female is quickly down onto the nest.

It is a strange spot for a bird as rare as this (the rarest British breeding bird of prey): a busy habitat, a steady flow of traffic down the road that borders one side of the field. Walkers and horse riders pass along a bridleway which separates the wheat from the barley crop and I notice how the harrier uses this path and the adjacent hedge as one of her linear hunting routes. There is a village two fields away, a glimpse of brick and flint through the trees, though the buildings are barely visible in the shimmering heat. The nest is monitored by the RSPB, and before the field is harvested, the immediate vicinity around the nest is cordoned off and the young harriers fenced in so they do not disperse through the crop when it is being cut.

If a ghost is nothing more than the trace left behind, the scent or spoor of something vanished like a line of snowy shell marl from an extinct river, semi-luminous against the black peat, then the Montagu's harrier is like a ghost over the English fenlands. She is so rare and dwindling a species in these islands, she is barely here at all and exists on the verge of vanishing. She hunts over a landscape that has changed beyond all recognition. A place so drained and straightened that her long-distance linear flight paths could be a symptom of the landscape, a heading out indefinitely in search of a less sanitised – a more disobedient – version of the land.

Huge crowds gathered to witness the draining of Whittlesea Mere. People waded across the wet mud with boards attached to the soles of their shoes, scooping up the thousands of stranded fish into sacks and baskets. The mud was so thick, the boards on their shoes so cumbersome, the fish-gleaners moved like cattle across the lake bed, slow and heavy. Eels shivered and flickered through the remaining pools as if the water was boiling over. So many fish were gathered up that day that several carts were filled and the catch wheeled off to the markets in Birmingham and Manchester. Some months later, after roads and farms had been marked out across the reclaimed land, heavy November rains swelled the rivers causing the dykes to burst, and within hours the lake was a lake once more.

The breached dykes were repaired and reinforced. An Appold pump with a 25-horsepower engine was put to work and Whittlesea Mere was drained again within the space of three weeks. Then came the drying and the cracking of the mud into thousands of fissures and crevasses. Horses were out of the question: even if they were shod with wooden boards the mud was too thick to take their weight, and when it dried the cracks too wide and deep for horses to tread safely. To make the mud pliable the new ground had to be harrowed over and over again by hand. Coleseed and Italian ryegrass were planted first; the ryegrass did better in the wet conditions.

As the mud was worked over it dislodged things – treasures – of startling antiquity: items, lost from storm-havocked boats, that had lain at the bottom of the lake for centuries. Objects caked in mud that when picked up felt heavier than mud and possessed the hint of a bright undercoat, a tincture of light seen through cracks in the mantle. Two of these treasures, a fourteenth-century gilded silver censer and an incense boat, are on display in the Victoria and Albert Museum in London. I went and found them one afternoon in their glass case in a basement room of the museum. Both objects are assumed to have belonged to the Benedictine monastery at Ramsey Abbey situated a few miles from Whittlesea Mere. The censer and incense boat are the only surviving examples of their kind; all similar ecclesiastical treasures were confiscated and melted down during Henry VIII's Dissolution of the Monasteries.

Survivors, gilded rarities, they shimmer under the glass. The deck and hull of the incense boat is worn silver accentuated by a rim of gold leaf around the gunwale. A ram's head at either end, carved into the stern and prow, with curved horns like tiny mollusc shells. The fleece down the rams' necks is plaited drops of silver. The engraving along the gunwale is very delicate like a seam of stitchwork. Next to the boat, the censer is brighter, entirely covered in gold leaf. About the size of a child's face, the censer is designed as a medieval chapter house, complete with miniature lancet windows, battlements, parapets ... The lights in the museum are so bright they make a shadow of the lancet arches in the censer's charcoal-scuffed centre.

As the Montagu's harrier ages there is a gradual uncovering of the bird's eye colour. Both sexes are born with their eyes brown, though their underlying colour, like the mud-coated censer, is a bright jewel-like yellow. Whilst they are still in the nest the males' eyes quickly change to a greyish-brown (a useful indicator in sexing the birds at this age). By their first winter the males' irides have changed again from grey-brown to a clear bright yellow. The brown in the females' eyes fades more slowly, gradually revealing glimpses of the yellow beneath as the brown dissipates. For several years, whilst the brown slowly gives way to the underlying yellow, the female harrier's eyes appear orange. By her third or fourth year her eyes have cleared to the same bright yellow as the male.

For nearly an hour through the heat of the early afternoon I do not see the female. Then at 2.10 p.m. she startles me by flying straight past my hiding place in the hedge – long wings and a whoosh of air. By the time I pick her up again she has reached the end of the hedge. She turns around and begins to fly quickly back down the side of the hedge towards me, twisting, flickering low across the field. As she draws parallel she tilts her head in my direction. Her face seems very small, more like an eye than a face. I can see the dark shading on her cheeks and the white patch around her eyes.

She keeps to the same line, tracking along the side of the hedge. At the point where she passes the dead oak tree she is briefly surrounded by a flurry of white shapes. It looks as if a pillow has burst around her. I refocus my binoculars: the downdraught from her wings is disturbing a cluster of white butterflies. Everywhere butterflies are being shaken up towards her, dusting around the harrier as if she has entered a sudden snow shower.

IX

Peregrine Falcon

Coventry

When I reach the bench I find them as I had left them the week before. Both birds are perched above me, the male on a ledge high on the spire of Holy Trinity, the female on the flèche of the new cathedral, directly opposite her mate. The bench sits in the ruins of Coventry's old cathedral. It is a contained space away from the noise of the city, not unlike the corrie on the side of the mountain in Sutherland, a place of enclosed stillness, where the ruin's walls hold and amplify the sound of the falcons calling to each other.

Coventry is not far from where I live and I was able to visit the peregrines there on several occasions. My frustration with this journey, trying to find the different birds of prey, is that my time with the birds – in each place – was so transitory. I always left reluctantly. I felt acutely the need to spend more time among the birds. So with the peregrines in the centre of Coventry I was fortunate that I could keep returning to them. One June, whenever I had a spare morning, I hurried back to the cathedral ruins, arriving at the bench soon after dawn, the sun turning the cathedral's sandstone a deep chestnut red, flocks of gulls passing over the city in their silent morning height. The falcons were always there, at home, often perched in the same place I had left them.

June: the peregrine's month, when skies are pierced with the male's hunting tracers, when cliffs echo with the begging calls of young falcons who rush towards flight so rapidly they have different names for almost every passing week: an *eyass*, then a *ramage hawk*, then a *brancher*, all before the young have left the nest and learnt to soar.

I used to spend hours as a boy in a secretive glen near our home. Its steep, bracken-covered slopes cut if off from the world; a refuge for roe deer, a waterway for dippers. In the summer months I camped down there amid the reek of wild garlic, swam in the burn's slack elbows.

Bright, cold water: lovely to drink, so cold it burnt your teeth. Halfway up the glen, around a sharp kink in the burn, was the peregrine's cliff. At the foot of the cliff the rock was curtained by a deep bank of moss where dippers hid their nest. The water was so clear I sometimes watched the dippers treading the shallows after the caddis and mayfly nymphs. The current, where it met the dipper's breast, shaped the water like bracken fronds when their young necks are fiddleheads.

Dippers were my water scouts, leading the way up the burn. A sharp *zeet* call, then a short dash upstream to the next boulder where they waited for me, bobbing above the rushing water, their lit breasts, like white aprons, signalling. The dippers lived on the cusp of worlds, half in the water, half out. Jettisoning their buoyancy, they somehow, miraculously, walked along the river bed, foraging there, head first into the fierce currents.

Back then peregrines were scarcer, birds of the peripheries, of upland crags and seabird islands. Their population was still recovering from a dramatic crash in the middle of the twentieth century. From the early 1950s through to the mid-Sixties peregrines had been somewhere awful. Poison seeped into their world: agricultural pesticides trickling down the chain from seed to pigeon to falcon. Organochlorine compounds built up in the tissues of peregrines (also other raptors, notably golden eagles and sparrowhawks). The effect of these compounds was to reduce the supply of calcium carbonate (critical in the egg-formation process) to the egg shells. It caused the shells to thin and grow so fragile that the eggs would crack under the weight of the brooding adult birds. Thieves, looking for eggs patterned with the swirling reds and browns of Mars or Jupiter, found only broken shells. The birds' behaviour addled. Female peregrines brooded empty scrapes or sat for weeks on the wreckage of their eggs. Some peregrines took to ousting kestrels from their nests, hatching and then raising kestrel chicks instead. The population crashed. The birds died like a language, receding to the outer skerries of our world.

They were fiercely territorial, those falcons that came to nest each spring in the glen. Launching themselves from the cliff, tearing down towards me, screaming as they swooped low over my head. I would hurry on up the glen, criss-crossing the burn, then climb one of the steep banks, past the falcons' plucking post, a puff of pigeon feathers turning in the breeze, to where I could watch the birds through binoculars without disturbing them. My memory of the glen is of a world of terrific speeds, the falcons rushing high above me or tearing past my head, the young peregrines chasing after their parents along the cliffs, begging for food. Nothing was ever still in their world. For a few months in spring and early summer the glen was pierced with noise and speed.

The pesticides were banned, the bans enforced: it was not after all too late. Peregrines pulled back from the brink. The population slowly recovered. Old eyries on the cliffs of Devon and Cornwall were tenanted once more. Flocks of pigeons coming in off the Bristol Channel scattered like seed. Rock doves learnt to hug the cliffs rather than expose themselves to the falcon's swoop. As peregrine numbers swelled, the falcons, for so long a bird associated with the margins of these islands, began to colonise urban spaces. Peregrines found sanctuary in our towns and cities, habitats where they were left undisturbed to nest on the tall cliffs of buildings and hunt the large urban populations of feral pigeons. What occurred was an unexpected breaching of worlds, a shift from the depopulated corners of these islands into the centres of population. Peregrines came to live amongst us and their wildness pulsed through our cities.

Listen! Look up! When I hear the falcon I do not hear anything else. The city drops away from under me and there is just the sharp, piercing *kee-errk, kee-errk* cutting through the warm air. The surrounding buildings bounce the sound back so that it rushes at me, amplified, the call rising in pitch, the second note sounding more drawn out. I try to pick out the phonetics of the falcon's call, *ee-ack, ee-ack; kee-errk, kee-errk* ... but it's hard to transcribe and my notebook scrawls with imitations until the page looks like something from a codebook.

From the bench I watch the male – the tiercel – leave his perch and circle out in a wide arc back to the spire on Holy Trinity. A flexing flight, a pirouette: no intent to it. He lands on the spire's weather vane and his landing sets the vane rotating. Every few seconds, as he spins around the circumference of the spire, the tiercel's profile changes, black wings rotating through the mottled white plumage of his chest. The vane keeps on spinning like this, absorbing the force of the bird's landing; for several minutes the whole city lies under the tiercel's rotating gaze.

I get up off the bench and walk around the perimeter of the cathedral ruins along the adjoining streets. In drains and gutters lining the cathedral's walls I find the detritus of falcon meals: parcels of bone stringy with dried sinew, feathers matted with skin, a pigeon's claw with a turquoise ring around its ankle.

Too far inland to be bombed, at the beginning of the war Coventry and the Midlands were felt to be out of range of the Luftwaffe. When France was invaded in the spring of 1940 children who had been sent to stay with relatives on the English south coast were pulled back by their families to Coventry, to the distant safety of the Midlands. When the bombings began to reach the outskirts of the city in June 1940 they did so tentatively like the first wisps of an approaching shower. A ruined house was a novelty, buses did a good trade taking Sunday afternoon sightseers to see the damage. Bomb fragments were much sought after, treasured like pieces from a meteor.

June bends towards July. The light tilts. The air thickens with heat. The bombing raids become more familiar. The falcon young have flown and passed into another stage of their nomenclature: they are *soar hawks* now, learning what they are capable of. Very few of them will survive beyond the winter. On 1 July 1940 the Secretary of State for Air issues the Destruction of Peregrine

Falcons Order. Adults, eyasses, eggs are destroyed up and down the land. The peregrines pose too great a threat to carrier pigeons, lifelines for the military. The order lasts the duration of the war. Cliffs are overseen instead by ravens, the falcon's grudging neighbour.

To reach Coventry, to plot their way accurately, German pathfinders follow a system of radio navigation beams that lead the pilots to their target. A main approach beam is intersected by a series of cross-beams which mark off the decreasing distance to the drop zone. Fifty seconds after the planes pass the final cross-beam an electric circuit on the bomb-release clock closes and the first incendiaries fall over Coventry, lighting up the city for the subsequent waves of bombers.

Peregrines will return to the same nest sites year after year. Signs on the cliffs can help to guide the returning birds: green stains where nutrients in the droppings of last season's young have spilled down the rock and lit it up with algae blooms.

By early autumn 1940 Coventry is increasingly deserted at night. The doors of empty houses are marked *S.O.* in chalk – the wardens do not wish to risk their lives searching for people who are not there. *S.O.* stands for *Sleeps Out. Out* means the surrounding countryside, sleeping under hedges, bridges, in barns, burrowing under ricks of hay. Cars parked in pools of darkness. A shilling a head the going rate if you could find a bed at a farm or someone's house, baths were extra. Each evening at rush hour the nightly trek begins, thousands streaming out of the city, prams and wheelbarrows carrying bedding, a long procession of torches glittering in the cold air.

Almost half the city empties out like that each night. The wealthy have places to stay, cars to take them; the poor walk and sleep beneath tarpaulins in the woods. And the countryside at night so vivid and strange: bedding down with the noise of the roe in rut; finding piles of crab apples spilt from hedgerows like pools of green and yellow light; and once the noise of badgers rummaging through a wood, sounding like the wood was murmuring to itself. Hearing the raids coming in, the ground guttural, rumbling. An aftertaste of gasoline in the air. Fires breaking out across the distant city. Then back again come morning, stiff and dewy, the streets smelling of smoke. Dust on everything like a thin layer of snow. Searching for homes and finding just the staircase, the ribcage of the house, leading into thin air.

So that autumn of 1940 there was a constant flow, tidal in its regularity, between the city and the surrounding countryside, a crossing over from one zone to the next, from the dark of the blackout city to the deeper dark of the city's periphery. The city slept outside itself and every morning sleepwalked back into its own skin.

Between the Leisure Centre and the underpass I find him, banking above an empty car park in a tangle of crows. I hear the crows, look up, and there is the tiercel's sickle shape cutting away to the north. All morning I follow him through the city. The old cathedral looms like the great sandstone cliffs of Hoy. I see his reflection swipe the glass front of the museum. Sometimes I lose him behind a building until scolding crows give him away and he appears once more, quick and low over my head.

When he perches, often for long spells, I perch beneath him, keeping watch from a shopping centre, a bench outside an office block, through the window of a bar, open at 8 a.m., *the only place round here you can get Newkie Brown*; the tiercel outside, shifting.

A pub in Birmingham, 14 November 1940. The moon so bright it finds the glasses' sheen. A man in grey overalls bursts in, out of breath. The moonlight seems to clean his clothes. He stands there, gannet-bright. *Just come in the lorry from Coventry*, he says. *You want to go outside and take a look: they're getting it badly tonight.*

The first sign of the raid: dogs barking through the city, hearing the drone of the planes before anyone else. Then incendiaries making swishing sounds like heavy rain. People running into the streets with wet rags to put the fires out. A lady with white hair wears a colander on her head to stop the aircrews spotting her. Bombs coming down like hailstones. Shelters filling up. Candles are lit in upturned plant pots. Blown-off doors are used as stretchers. Hospitals spill over with the wounded. The fires and the moon feeding off each other make it light as day; one boy tells his mother he doesn't like this sort of sun. The air is hot and acrid. Then the electricity and gas are cut. The fire crews have no pressure in the water. Parachute mines look like German airmen bailing out;

people run to apprehend them with sticks, axes, anything to hand. The explosion stops their lungs.

He is hunting now and everything has changed. A falcon at rest creates a truce and the world beneath his perch is suspended for a while. So pigeons can pass casually by, a dipper can glance from rock to rock. But once the peregrine is up, the world that hangs beneath the hunting bird is suddenly charged. Everything is in flight from the falcon. Pigeons sharpen into speed, become almost falcons in themselves: compact shots of speed. Hunted birds have been known to be shocked into tameness, seeking out the safety of people, even allowing themselves to be picked up. Some birds grow so paralysed with fear there are accounts of people walking along a shoreline beneath a hunting peregrine gathering up the cowering snipe, placing them in the warmth of their pockets, each snipe a trembling, unexploded ordnance.

Even a falcon's absence can be felt. The presence of other birds of prey like the kestrel or merlin can sometimes indicate the absence of a peregrine, as if the smaller raptors have moved into a zone of refuge created by the absent falcon. Those peregrines, pesticide-addled, that reared the kestrel young were raising prey. Almost all birds are at risk from peregrines. There are records of geese, black-backed gulls, even buzzards being struck down. MacGillivray was told about the remains of a black grouse found at a peregrine's eyrie on the Bass Rock. The falcon would have had to carry this heavy prey a distance of 3 miles from the mainland. In falconry's heyday peregrines were trained to bring down birds as large as red kites and herons. But prey of this size is really an anomaly; peregrines are essentially a specialist predator in that their preference is for medium-sized avian prey. In these islands, pigeons (specifically rock doves, feral and homing pigeons) are by far the most common source of food for peregrine falcons. Depending on season and habitat, marine birds are also taken, especially black-headed gulls and fulmars. Additionally, corvids, red grouse and waders such as lapwings, golden plover and redshank can be locally important prey species for peregrines.

Some birds, conversely, are pulled towards a falcon's presence. The tiny wren will often nest close to peregrine eyries, gathering feathers from the falcon's plucking posts to line its own nest. Geese, too, have been known to cluster their nests close to peregrine cliffs, benefiting from the falcons' protection against ground predators such as foxes. Gauntlet-runners, the geese choose to walk to and from their nests, rather than risk drawing attention from their hosts. Once, in the glen near home, I took a dog with me and the presence of the dog seemed to ratchet up the falcon's fury. I had a glimpse of how unrelenting and aggressive the birds could be to foxes that strayed too close to their nests. The falcon rushed at the dog (and me), screaming, swooping low over our heads. All I wanted to do was get out of the way.

* * *

Towards eight o'clock the first incendiaries hit the cathedral, singeing the frost from its roof. Four men are on duty to defend it. The fires work through the building, moving from nave to vestry. A large incendiary lands amongst the pews and it takes two buckets of sand to extinguish it. The men rescue what they can: the altar cross and candlesticks, a silver wafer box and snuffer, a wooden crucifix ... They are soon exhausted, soaked in sweat. Steel girders twist in the heat. The organ (which Handel played) is a concentrated blaze. They can hear the drip of molten lead as the roof begins to melt. Throughout it all – throughout the night – the cathedral's tower clock keeps striking the hours. People across the city, when they hear the chimes, presume the cathedral has survived.

Suddenly he is alert, restless, clicking his gaze through every inch of sky. Three pigeons, flying just above the rooftops, seem to slow as they pass beneath him. The tiercel tilts towards them, slips from his perch, throws himself at the pigeons. The city rushes towards him. The pigeons blur then fracture. They drop down into the safety of the street, killing the falcon's space to swoop. The hunt is abandoned and the peregrine is back on his glaring perch.

One hundred and fifty, 180 mph a falcon reaches in its stoop. Waiting-up in the clouds or, when prey is spotted, climbing rapidly to position itself above the target. Then wings are folded back and the peregrine hurls itself at an angle of 30°–45° to the horizontal, sometimes almost vertical. Occasionally aiming wide and then striking from below as the falcon surges up out of the stoop. Often, the force of the impact is such that prey is knocked out of the sky and the peregrine then has ample time to glide down to the crash site. More often than not the falcon misses. If the hunt is not abandoned then the peregrine will beat back up to gain sufficient height to launch another attack, wings folded back, tearing down through the astonished air.

Later that morning he makes a kill. I miss the moment. It happens somewhere out on the edge of the city where I lose him in a fury of speed. When I find him again he is plucking at something on a ledge of the new cathedral. All I can see of the kill is a boil of red flesh. The female stands to one side calling to him, bobbing, agitated. When he has finished feeding he shifts his perch and begins to preen. Feathers drift away from him like thistledown.

Sounding the all clear, crawling out of shelters, mist over the city, a slow drizzle in the cold dawn. Everywhere the crunch of glass underfoot. A butcher's shop still burning, the smell of roasting meat. Houses quiet, missing the whirr of gas and electricity meters. Dust in the food. Kettles filled from rainwater butts. Fires lit. Tea made. Someone serves out treacle tart for breakfast. The outer walls of the cathedral enclose a great pile of smoking rubble. Incredibly, the tower is still intact, blackened down one side from all the smoke.

* * *

Then I am up in their realm. One wing flap and the falcons could reach me. I have climbed to the top of the old cathedral tower, miraculous blitz survivor, 295 feet high, the third-tallest spire in England. There are squirrels carved into the tower's stonework representing the medieval woods that surrounded the city. A slow coiling climb, past bell ropes, their sallies hanging in dusty stillness.

The night of Friday 15 November the Luftwaffe's main bombing force is dispatched to London. Only six or seven planes reach Coventry and drop 7 tonnes of high explosive. It is so trivial compared with the night before that the raid is barely noticed. The roads out of Coventry are streams of refugees wading through piles of glass. The roads have turned to quagmires from all the mud the bombs threw up. Aftershocks: delayed-action bombs, fires reigniting, shattered nerves, screaming when the sirens start again. The night following the raid the city is emptier than at any time for half a century.

From the top of the spire I can look directly across to the tiercel and the falcon still perched on the flèche of the new cathedral. The falcon – the female – is preening. The male has begun his ballet of agitation, flicking his gaze across the city. I am exhilarated by this new perspective, to be among the falcons, at the same height as the birds, looking down their avenues of sky. The female is taller than I had expected. In some artists' depictions of peregrines the birds often seem too tall, their necks elongated as if the perspective is not quite right, but I can see now that once the female stretches out of her hunched perch she unravels a long back. Her tail hangs behind her, tapering to a narrow end. The wrists of her folded wings protrude up to her neckline, making the wing-wrists look like shoulder pads.

Counting the dead. The first mass funeral of the war. Aid pours in to Coventry, donations from across the globe. Four lorryloads of shoes are dispatched from Leicester. In the ruins of the cathedral, on Christmas Day 1940, the Provost broadcasts to the world: *We are trying, hard as it may be, to banish all thoughts of revenge.*

The male flexes his wings, peers over his ledge and drops. From the tower I can keep track of him more easily. I watch him gaining height, circling over the city. He moves towards the north through a vast acreage of sky. I can see for 20 miles in every direction. I watch him hanging above the city and for long periods he is just a black speck against the cloud. I follow him as he starts to track to the east and suddenly I am aware he has dipped into a stoop, my binoculars trembling to keep up with his change of speed. The next ten minutes I spend trying to locate him over the city's outskirts. I trace my binoculars over every corner of sky and pause to unpick each speck and dot against the blue. But the heat blurs things and I have lost him again in the rising haze of the day.

I walk around the roof of the tower still trying to spot the male. My feet crunch the claws and bones of pigeons that have dropped from the falcons' plucking post above. I find a jackdaw's head lying on the roof. Dried, mummified in the heat, not yet a skull. I crouch down to take a closer look. *One for sorrow, two for joy ...* The rhyme starts before I realise my mistake: a magpie's head, a seam of metallic green running through the black feathers.

I cannot find the tiercel. He is shimmering somewhere above the city. I walk around the roof of the tower and pause opposite the falcon still on her perch on the new cathedral. I can see the yellow orbit of her eye, the black sunspot in the centre of it. Then she lifts, turns, and flies towards me.

Red Kite

Upper Tywi Valley, Wales

MacGillivray reaches Manchester on 13 October, the distance he has come starting to resemble a migration. Six hundred and fifty-six miles since he left Aberdeen thirty-seven days ago, a steady bearing southwards, picking up momentum, barely stopping now, as if London were all downhill from here. Weaving through the streets of Manchester, trying to find lodgings for the night, but everywhere refusing him. They only need to open the door a chink and take one look at his mud-splattered coat, his worn-out shoes, his grass-stained knapsack … It is not that they doubt he can pay, rather, that if they let him enter, they fear they would be letting in the weather.

Manchester is a low point. The miles are starting to tell. MacGillivray is exhausted and cannot shake off the feeling he is being followed through the streets. It is strange he should feel so haunted here amongst the cluttered city when the loneliness of the moor has never troubled him. He is trying to persuade a landlady to give him lodging for the night; she is wavering in the doorway and all MacGillivray wants to do is find a place to rest. He would like to curl up there and then and I wonder, if he could find a quiet spot away from the crowds, the coal wagons and beer wagons, could he not make a nest from all the plant cuttings he has in his knapsack and bed down instead in them for the night.

There is a species of goshawk, the beautifully named Dark Chanting Goshawk, that builds its nest by selecting twigs with social spiders living on them. The spiders quickly consume the hawk's nest with their silk so that the structure becomes hidden – concealed from predators – by a bulb of silk. If MacGillivray could build a nest like that, which hid him, protected him, he could forgo the lodging house and sleep instead amongst the noisy streets of Manchester, despite the sewer stench, the stink from all the tanneries, the butcher stalls and tallow chandleries.

There is no doubt now, there is definitely someone following him. He has had enough of this and so he whirls around to face his stalker:

– Sir (*the man says to MacGillivray, as if he had spoken to him*).

MacGillivray says nothing.

– Do you know me?
– No, I do not.
– Upon my word, I beg your pardon. I thought your name had been John Parkins.

I love these tetchy conversations MacGillivray has along the way, these brusque rebuttals. It seems that anyone who spoils his momentum is unwelcome. Pity the farmer, for instance, he met on the road outside Lancaster who was foolish enough to remark that MacGillivray seemed in a great hurry ...

– What? (*MacGillivray answers*).
– You are in a great hurry.
– No I am not.
– Aren't you?
– No.
– Where have you come from?
– From the North.
– Is there any quarrelling there? Any fighting?
– No.

- From what part of the North have you come from?
- From Scotland.
- Where are you going?
- To London.

MacGillivray becomes so irritable he almost punches him. Poor man, he starts to back away:

- Farewell, farewell, good morrow, good morrow ...

The only exception to these prickly exchanges I can find was the poor man, *turned off by his laird*, that MacGillivray passed on the road outside Elgin when he was walking home one time to Harris from Aberdeen. MacGillivray stopped and gave the man a shilling and apologised it was not in his power to give more, and the man blessed MacGillivray and said he had given too much.

MacGillivray leaves Manchester at ten o'clock next morning. When he reaches the outskirts he joins the London road and settles, more relaxed now, into his stride. Behind him the city's factory chimneys look like colonnades of rain. What did the farmer he barked at mean by *any quarrelling, any fighting?* MacGillivray is leaving Manchester just a few weeks after the Peterloo Massacre, and though he does not mention this in his journal, he must have been aware of what happened, that the region felt charged and changed and fragile. What with his experience of these forces at work in the

Hebrides, of the wholesale displacement of people, he must have recognised what happened at Peterloo – the charge of the cavalry troop into the crowd – as another, more brutal branch of this work, the clearance of people who are in the way.

He passes a milestone – *To London 182 miles* – and his spirits begin to lift. For the first time, London – the British Museum with its great collection of birds – starts to feel in reach. He walks through Stockport and on through Cheshire, approaching the green hills of Derbyshire. His pace picks up, he even (whisper it) starts to feel quite cheerful. A quick calculation: yesterday he covered 24 miles, London is now 158 miles off. Today is Friday. MacGillivray proposes to be in London by two o'clock on Thursday. That's 26 miles a day on a budget of one and twenty pence per day. He would like (of course he would!) to travel more cheaply, but why torment himself with bad meals and scratchy beds when there is no need for that. After all, he has nothing to prove: he is confident of his ability to walk for miles without food. He once travelled 240 miles on just twelve shillings, but there was also the occasion when he spent (he shudders to recall the lack of prudence) fifteen shillings in a day! These are his extremes.

Red Kite

The mouth is wide, measuring an inch and
two-twelfths across … the oesophagus six inches and
a half long, the crop two inches in width; the stomach
round, and two inches in diameter, its muscular coat

very thin. The intestine five feet long, from four to two and a half twelfths in width, until the commencement of the rectum, which is half an inch wide, and forms a large globular dilatation ... Wings extremely long, broad, narrow, but rounded at the end; the third quill longest, the fourth almost equal, the first short; the primary quills of moderate strength, broad, toward the end tapering, in-curved, with the tip rounded, the outer five having the inner web cut out ... Tail very long, broad, forked, or emarginated, of twelve broad feathers ... The flight of this bird is remarkably elegant, the lightness of its body, and the proportionally great extent of the wings and tail, producing a buoyancy which reminds one of the mode of flying of the Gulls and Jagers ...

I am sitting on a wall at the far end of a car park in Llandovery, strapping the tent to my rucksack. Late February, a granite light, the sky looks like it has been washed with silt. A pair of red kites come in low over the town from the north. They circle above the car park, one of the birds calling a high, echoing whistle. Not unlike a buzzard, but the kite's call sounds higher, quicker, less resonant.

I drive north out of the town following the river Tywi into the hills. Higher up the valley the land is under mist. Blocks of conifers are darker shapes inside the mist. There are glimpses of oak woods on the steep banks above the river; birch trees in amongst them lighten the oaks' colour. I have to slow the car to crawling pace, put the fog lights on and creep along the narrow road. Through a village smoking in the mist, then a bridge across the river and the road is suddenly even narrower. I park up, wedging the car out of the way under a tall bank. Tree roots, crimson ligaments, show through the turf where the bank has been cut back. Then the familiar ritual, feet up on the car's rear bumper, boots loosened and threaded, backpack tightened.

If the Montagu's harrier is all buoyancy, lightness and drift, then the red kite is pure agility, pure manoeuvrability. And if the Montagu's harrier is all wing, then the red kite is all tail. MacGillivray wrote, *It is his tail that seems to direct all his evolutions, and he moves it continually*. In the Upper Tywi valley the kite is known as *Boda wennol* (the swallow-tailed hawk). Further south in Wales, she is *Hebog cwt-fforchog* (the falcon with the forked tail).

Everything in the kite's design lends itself to agility: long-winged, light-framed, with a tail that is shaped to decrease drag and increase lift, a tail that can perform miracles inside the air. The 'swallow-tailed hawk' has swallow-like agility. A kite can hold itself inside the bumpiest of thermals, constantly adjusting its tail to keep itself in place to scrutinise the ground below. And a kite can suddenly turn on a sixpence, despite its great size, in order to twist around and take a closer look at something it might have missed. What is so mesmerising about the red kite is that a bird of its size – a bird with such long wings – can perform such aerial acrobatics.

You would think that it was too gangly for such aerial dexterity. The kite's size constantly belies its behaviour in the air.

The forked tail enhances manoeuvrability, it gives the bird stability through the tightest of turns. The span of the fork can be varied depending on how wide or tight the turn. The sharper the turn, the wider the fork, and vice versa. It is no good, such a forked tail, in a densely packed habitat like a wood, as the tail's outer primaries – the long exposed sides of the tail – are vulnerable to damage through snagging branches. So kites prefer to nest in roomy deciduous woods with ample space to reach their nests. The sparrowhawk, in comparison, has a long straight tail which is less vulnerable to damage as it hunts at speed through the clutter of a wood.

What the kite needs – like the swallow, like the harrier – is open space to range and forage over. Woodland is used by the kite only for nesting and roosting. The rest of its time is spent hunting over open landscapes. Of all the birds of prey the kite is the one that lives the most inside the air. She does not belong on the ground, does not make sense unless she is in the air.

I pass through a quiet farmyard. Nobody about, not a soul since I left the village. But I notice, as I brush close to it, the warmth coming off the bonnet of a tractor. I follow a quad-bike track out of the farm, spilled wisps of hay in the mud. A path filters off the track and starts to climb between gorse and hawthorn, across beds of flattened bracken. This is the kite's backyard, the *ffridd*, the tangled vole-rich lower slopes, equivalent to the margins between the moor and fields the hen harriers frequent over Orkney. Unkempt no-man's-land, so critical to foraging birds of prey.

The path takes me through a small wood, dripping and still. A kite turns out of the mist and flickers slowly over me. I have seen several kites already including the ones over Llandovery, but every kite is a gift because its flight is rarely hurried and you have time to follow it, watch what the bird's gymnastics do to the air. I think how different the experience is to following the merlins out on the flows of Sutherland, those tiny balls of energy fizzing out across all that distance. The kite is the least linear of raptors, it spends its time unravelling imaginary balls of string in the air.

I walk for several hours into the hills. The mist accentuates the quiet. I find fox prints in the mud, and at one point, the mist stirs enough for me to make out three chequered black and white wild ponies grazing on the hillside. An hour before dusk, I make camp in a small oak wood hanging above the river. I pitch my tent on a narrow clearing in the bracken. As I work a kite takes off from one of the trees in front of me and glides across the river. An hour before dark the mist lifts and I can see clear down the valley. It is clearer now, at dusk, than it has been at any time during the day. The kite is still in view and I watch the bird working her way down the valley, backlit by a thin layer of blue.

* * *

Each kite is a gift because more than any other bird of prey they are indulgent of you. They don't mind you being close to them and, outside the nesting period, are little troubled by human presence. One afternoon I followed a red kite foraging over the ground between a busy ring road and the outskirts of a town. The kite banked above houses, hunting over side streets and alleyways. At one point I watched it hovering just above me and saw it drop something, a vole I think. But before the vole could reach the ground the kite swooped down after it and retrieved it in mid-air. What I remember most from the incident was not the showy acrobatics, more the bird's dramatic turn of speed. All afternoon it had glanced over rooftops and hedgerows so slowly it was fairly easy for me to keep pace with it. But when the vole was dropped, the kite paused for a split second then burst after it in a sudden flex of speed.

They are more tolerant, red kites, of human beings and human spaces than other birds of prey. Kites are essentially scavengers, and like other scavenging raptors, such as vultures, they are often drawn in large numbers to the rubbish produced by humans. Some Asian cities have large resident populations of black kites, and English cities too were once home to substantial numbers of red kites, protected by royal statute because of the important role the birds performed in gleaning the filthy medieval streets. Medieval London was famous for its red kites and the birds so brazen in their interaction with people it was not unknown for a kite to snatch bread from a child in the street, or a cap from off a man's head to line its nest with.

Piratical; fanatical nest decorators: it is not improbable that London's medieval kites were as bold as this. Kites are well known for their piratical habits of harassing corvids and other raptors to drop their prey, utilising their aerial agility to harry the other bird into spilling its catch. Then it is the simplest thing for the kite to swoop down and pluck the tumbling item out of the air. Nests are adorned with anything that comes to hand: caps, handkerchiefs, plastic bags, discarded lottery tickets …

In Wales I found red kites over car parks, playing fields, allotments, as well as across the Cambrian mountain heights. There seems to be no other bird of prey that crosses over so fluidly, so constantly, into our world. The red kite is a bird that lives in the slipstream of human beings, gleaning, foraging around us. They will follow ploughs and harvesters and take scraps left out in people's gardens. They have even been known to tear net curtains from open windows to decorate their nests.

I sit outside the tent as it grows dark. Cold air has sunk into the valley and my breath is suddenly visible. Moths are out, flickering over my hands, whirring past my ear. There is a scuffling in one of the trees, something scratching at the bark, then a red squirrel scurries down the trunk and hops away over the crunchy leaf litter. If I had not seen it first I might have thought a larger animal, a deer or sheep perhaps, was moving through the spinney; in its frenetic scrabbling, a squirrel can make so much noise inside a wood.

All afternoon kites had come down out of the mist like sudden angels. As I walked up the valley I kept putting up a buzzard that flapped heavily away from me then waited round the next bend before I came into sight again. The buzzard seemed huge and slow in comparison with the flickering, twisting kites. Halfway into the hills a raven flew close and low, its glossy blackness lit up against the winter grass. There was frogspawn all over the hillside, stranded on clumps of reeds, as if it had drifted there like blown sea spume.

The light going now and at the last, before I turn in for the night, a buzzard rushes into the spinney, just a few feet from where I am sitting. It swerves between the trees and I think, because it is flying so fast, it must be hunting. But then it lifts out of its flight and lands on a wide branch. There is very little light now but I can just make out the dark shape of the buzzard, settling its weight on its perch, preparing to roost.

I am up before it is light. I did not sleep much. There was a small stream a few feet from the tent and all night, with my ear pressed against the ground, I kept waking to the sound of water, sounding as if it was running under me. As I sit outside the tent at dawn, making tea, there is a movement in the bracken. Stepping out into the clearing, right in front of me: a fox, white-chested, a brightness to her coat, made brighter – redder – by the rusty bracken behind her. Then she turns, coils away from me, and begins to climb the steep bank. After a minute she stops, glances back towards me. She repeats this several times, pausing, turning her head to look in my direction, finally disappearing into the bracken.

Take a hammer or an axe, whatever is to hand, swing it round and round you in a circle by its handle and, at the point of greatest energy, or before the dizziness over-whelms you, let go the handle and let the hammer fly. Retrieve it, and when you do so, mark the spot where it has landed. Then walk back to where you started and repeat the action. But this time send the hammer off in the opposite direction, until you have flung it out to every compass bearing. Then draw a line between all the spots where the hammer landed. In this way you can mark out the perimeter of your territory, your plot, your home.

This is how squatters in the first half of the nineteenth century would claim a patch of ground for their own on the marginal lands, the *ffridd*, of the Upper Tywi and elsewhere in rural Wales. The point where you swung the hammer had to be the front door of your house. But the house (and herein lay the catch) must be built in a single night in order for the squatter to validate their claim on the land.

Ty un nos: a one-night house. The key was to prepare the roof in advance and gather as many friends as possi-ble to help with the night's work. The walls and roof had to be up and, crucially, a fire lit in the hearth so that smoke could be seen drawing from the chimney at dawn. Surprise: a house!

I looked for traces of these houses while I walked through the hills of the Upper Tywi, drawn to poking about ruins marked on the map. In most cases I found very little, just the skeletal outlines of buildings, soothed over with mosses, riddled with bracken. These one-night houses in Wales coincided with the advance of Parliamentary Enclosures in the first half of the nineteenth century. Access to common lands and upland pastures was rescinded by landlords, forcing the poor to try and make a living from the scrappy wastelands around the margins.

A clearance is an ongoing process. It only succeeds in displacing a people to somewhere they will be in the way again. I found this with the story of the people shunted around the Morvern peninsula until they ended up dumped on the barren outcrop of Oronsay. But even there, of all the godforsaken places, they were not allowed to settle long before they were picked up and herded on. A common name for the Welsh one-night house was 'labour in vain'. More often than not the squatters' cottages were destroyed by farmers who felt their own grazings were being encroached. Fences, hedges, those hammer-marked perimeters, were dismantled and often just as quickly put back up again by the squatters. Disputes rumbled on like this for years. Sometimes squatters' houses were destroyed decades after they had been constructed when commissioners judged that the land they were on should be enclosed. You try to establish a toehold on the land, try to cling on to it, but that hold is just as soon pulled from under you.

* * *

In the first half of the twentieth century the hills and hanging woods of the Upper Tywi became the red kite's last refuge in these islands. A tiny, remnant population, dwindling, clinging on. At their lowest ebb, in the 1930s and early 1940s, there were perhaps no more than ten pairs. They entered a genetic bottleneck and for a long time afterwards all Welsh kites could trace their ancestry to a single female bird. That was how close the birds came to extinction in the British Isles.

Despite its remoteness, its largely un-keepered woods and hills, the Upper Tywi was never a safe refuge for kites. It was just where they ended up after they had been driven out from everywhere else. But the bird's status there was always precarious. Egg collectors, the limited gene pool, the climate of those rain-drenched, infertile hills: there were so many ways for the kites to fail in Wales. And for decades the few remaining birds lived a miserable banishment, their toehold on the land constantly pulled from under them. Even some of those responsible for safeguarding the few nests were corruptible and eggs were frequently stolen to order. When the Welsh kite population did finally begin to increase in the 1960s it was not because more birds were being born, rather that fewer adult kites were dying.

Britain's commonest bird of prey reduced in the blink of an eye to a rump, to just a handful of birds. The kite's undoing facilitated – accelerated – by that tolerance of human beings and human spaces. A large, slow bird swimming leisurely overhead made the easiest of targets; its propensity for carrion made it just as easy to trap or poison. We preferred (we still prefer in some cases) our birds of prey to be banished to the margins. We drove them to the furthest reaches, to the outliers of these islands, like the last lone sea eagle living out her days on Shetland. The Upper Tywi was the red kite's Shetland, its Oronsay.

But when we let them back in, as we have recently with the red kite through successful reintroduction schemes in England and in Scotland, their presence is transformative. The birds transform – they restore – the land. A landscape without raptors is an unnatural one.

People were found to be in the way once more in the Upper Tywi valley in the mid-twentieth century. The first the farmers of the area heard about it was a summons to a public meeting at Llandovery Town Hall on 18 November 1949. There they were told, abruptly, dismissively (in English), of the Forestry Commission's scheme to plant the largest forest in Wales, covering 20,000 acres, swamping forty-eight farms. The forest would take forty years to come to fruition. Farmers could volunteer to sell up or, failing that, the Commission would have no alternative but to issue compulsory purchase orders.

So the 'Battle of the Tywi' began and the farming community, angered by the manner and tone with which the Forestry Commission had proposed the scheme, organised itself to resist and petition against the purchase order. The 'battle' rumbled on for several years and ended with this statement in the House of Commons on 31 January 1952:

– Mr Baldwin asked the Minister of Agriculture whether he can yet make a statement about the proposals for the compulsory purchase for afforestation of a large area in the Towy Valley.

– Sir T. Dugdale: Yes. I should welcome an opportunity of explaining the position. A draft Order for the compulsory purchase of some 11,450 acres was published on 18th September, 1950, objections were lodged and a public local inquiry into them was held. The report of the inspector appointed to hold the inquiry was submitted to me on 20th November, 1951.

I have examined the proposals and considered the objections as reported by the inspector. After considering all the circumstances, including the country's financial and economic situation, my conclusion – with which the Forestry Commission concurs – is that it is not expedient to proceed with the project, which would involve heavy capital expenditure as a preliminary to a programme extending over 20 years. I have, therefore, after consulting my right hon. and learned Friend the Home Secretary and Minister for Welsh Affairs decided not to make an Order.

I sit down in a small field just above the river. For a while I watch a pair of ravens, vocal, busy about their nest site on a cliff high above the valley. Then a kite glances above the ridge. The rest of the morning I spend sitting at the edge of the field following the kite as it hunts slowly over the adjacent hillside. Behind me, great tits call and skitter through the hanging oak wood. Sessile oaks: hobbled and mossy, ferns growing along their thick shoulders. Sheep are inside the wood. Four skittish ewes with winter coughs, coughing at me when I disturb them coming down through the trees.

Sometimes the kite drifts towards me and hangs above the river. Its tail tips a fraction, pitching the bird into another angle of drift. The tail is almost fishlike in its flickering, waving movements. Other kites pass across the valley and I try, unsuccessfully, to distinguish the sexes. I read that the male is a fraction smaller, a fraction lighter, more agile, his tail working, flexing constantly. The female's tail is not as deeply forked, her wings are slightly longer, broader, more pointed at the tips. Later that day I watch a pair of kites flying close together, mirroring each other, one kite riding 8 feet above the other, a synchrony, a courtship in the air.

Throughout the morning buzzards and ravens interject into the kite's airspace. The kite amongst its neighbours is so much slower and less purposeful; even the buzzards are usually heading somewhere, crossing from left to right, or working to gain height. The kite, it seems, is not going anywhere. It is too intent on scrutinising the ground, rotating, adrift in its own gyre.

During the nesting season the relationship between the three species – kite, buzzard and raven – is fraught with squabbles. Red kite nests situated close to breeding ravens will often fail. If you hear the unmistakable quick-fire coughing of a raven's alarm call it is almost certainly aimed at a kite or buzzard passing through the raven's territory. Mid-air skirmishes, dive-bombings, are commonplace at this time of year and the cliffs ricochet with the ruckus.

Despite its size, the kite is not a powerful bird of prey. It relies on the stronger-beaked buzzard or raven to puncture a new sheep casualty. So the dynamic between the three birds can shift as the kite waits its turn behind buzzard and raven in the pecking order at a carcass, with the usual attendants – carrion crow and magpie – darting in between to snatch what they can. There is also a staggering of laying and hatching dates between the three species, as there is between the harrier species and between other raptors that share a habitat. Red kites breed seven to ten days earlier than buzzards, enabling the kites to feed their young on the potential glut of young black-headed gulls, corvids and woodpigeons; buzzards time their nests a little later to coincide with the abundance in young rabbits and voles.

Kites also take voles, immature rabbits, leverets, though rarely anything larger than a small rabbit. Live prey is usually dispatched with the bill, rather than the kite's relatively weak talons. Field voles, as with so many British raptors, can be a locally significant prey and fluctuations in the vole population can impact on the kite's breeding success. Red kites in Wales bred poorly in the years when myxomatosis in rabbits was at its peak. But no raptor is more of a generalist, more adaptable, more omnivorous, than the kite. It seems to have a characteristic taken from almost every other bird of prey I've met.

As much a scavenger of carrion as the sea eagle, it will also forage for worms alongside buzzards on moist fields in the early mornings, or hawk for dragonflies and crane-flies like a hobby. It will eat anything that is dead or nearly dead. Lambs' tails and lambs' scrota are a favour-ite titbit in Wales, even the rubber rings used to dock them are consumed. Fish, reptiles, amphibians are also taken across the kite's European range. A nineteenth-century egg collector in Wales used to warn people climbing up to kites' nests to *Beware of half-killed adders!*

Communal winter roosts can attract spectacular numbers of red kites. So many birds flocking together to spend the night you wonder how the trees can bear their weight. MacGillivray relates an incident at a kite roost of fog suddenly freezing one night and affixing the birds' feet to the boughs of a tree. In the morning some boys clambered up the tree and retrieved fifteen red kites, prising the birds from the branch as if they were dislodg-ing a row of icicles.

More gregarious, more relaxed about territorial spac-ing than most other raptors, kites can concentrate in very high densities. Their only territory is the immediate vicinity around the nest. Everything else is air! Adult birds are also prone to returning to their natal nesting areas to breed. So there are pockets of the country now where you can walk all day through a swirl of red kites. The birds function as a community: red kites are chiefly scavenger birds, foraging in loose groups, 'network foraging', relying on each other to pass the word along when a carcass has been spotted, much as vultures do. But this tendency to bunch together, to concentrate their numbers at high densities, also exposes the kite to harm. Still today, when carrion is laced with poison and deliberately planted in a red kite area, there follows a wholesale destruction of the birds. Other scavengers – buzzards, corvids, foxes – will be casualties too, but kites invariably pay a heavy price.

After the compulsory purchase order was dropped, the Forestry Commission employed softer tactics in the Upper Tywi. This time they approached farmers individually, using Welsh speakers as intermediaries. Many of the hill farms were still reeling from the losses to their flocks during the harsh winter of 1947, and once one had been persuaded to sell, many others followed suit. In the end more land in the Upper Tywi was afforested than had originally been proposed. Farms were cleared, even the oak woods were cleared to make way for the conifers. The stubs of one-night houses were covered over, the kites' foraging grounds covered over.

In the afternoon I return to the car park in Llandovery. I climb the small hill in the rain and stand amongst the castle ruins. Jackdaws spill, squabbling and chattering, from the town hall roof. Then two kites come into view, glancing over chimneys and television aerials. I watch as they drift across the town, unhurried, checking every yard and garden. One of the kites adjusts its path and starts to glide towards me. I can see its ash-grey face and nape, the white markings on its underwings, the flash of red between its tail and breast. Then the kite ducks out of sight behind one of the castle walls and I think I have lost it, but next moment it is suddenly above me, holding itself in the rain just 10 feet from my head. Face tipped downwards, beak angled towards the ground. Its eyes follow the line of the beak. Its beak opens, as if it is going to call.

That day the Isle of Sheppey felt abandoned to the birds, utterly given over to them. The marshes under ice, the ditches frozen, snow banked up on the windward side of dykes. I spent the day from dawn to dusk walking over the island's eastern marshes in an ice-shot wind beside a frantic sea. That wind never let up, never moved on; it had snagged itself on the island and spent the day trying to tear itself free. All day snow clouds waited off the coast, banked above the brown sea, waves of snow rolling in over the mudbanks and brittle reed beds. But when the snow hit the wind took it and flung it out across the marshes so that it was nothing like snow, had none of snow's quietness. It was snow corrupted into ice, snow consumed by wind. It made the day impossible, a madcap wind that yelled and spat at me relentlessly: *Keep your gloves on*; *face away from me*; *stop dilly-dallying* ... And I found that even taking my gloves off for a few seconds was so painful I gave up on trying to write notes or photograph. What was there to photograph? The land speeded up in a blur of snow and wind and snowflakes smudging the camera's lens.

But birds were there on Sheppey in their thousands, huge flocks of woodpigeon, lapwing, curlew and starling. And none of the flocks, it seemed, were deterred by the wind. At least, they had not been grounded by it and were buoyed and buffeted and flung everywhere inside the wind's madness. A small covey of red partridges split from under me and the lunatic wind grabbed the birds and hurled them across a ploughed field. The partridges whirled away so fast, I thought: they will not be able to stop, unless they can turn into the wind they will be flung across the marshes, over the mudbanks and out to sea. And if they reach the sea I knew I'd lose sight of the birds, not because of the distance (the sea was only two fields away) and not because the waves might grab the birds, but because the sea was so churned with mud and sand it had lost its usual grey and turned a muddy brown, so that the partridges, when they cleared the last field, would simply blend into the ferrous backdrop of the sea.

And in between the restless flocks – between the passerines, the waders and the ducks – were the flocks' magnets, the avian specialists: merlin, sparrowhawk and peregrine.

If I had to fold one of the places on my journey onto another, it would have to be Orkney folded onto – twinned with – Sheppey. Not so much for the wind or the sting of the sea's breath on everything, nor for the fact that if Sheppey broke its moorings and floated out of the Thames estuary, it would be blown north like the dregs of the Armada until it crashed into Orkney and wedged itself in one of the steep-sided geos on South Ronaldsay. Rather, for the sense that birds had overrun – had inherited – both island landscapes. Also, a sense that I had caught up with many of the birds again from Orkney here in their winter quarters on the north Kent marshes: curlew, lapwing, hen harrier and merlin.

I am crouching in the lee of a sea wall eating a freezing lunch (my water bottle has turned to mushy ice), trying to ignore the wind's harassment: *Go away wind*; *leave me alone*; *I'm trying to eat a sandwich*; *look what you have done to my fingers … they have turned a colour I do not recognise* … Then, above the pale reed bed, a sickle-shape echo from Orkney, from the Flow Country, from the mountains of Lewis and Harris. My first thought: a peregrine. But, no: too small, too low, skimming far too low across the saltmarsh. Not peregrine, but merlin.

Of all the raptors the merlin is the blink-and-you'll-miss-him bird. And in the seconds it takes me to gather my things, pack up my lunch, he is gone. This merlin was so charged with wind he could have been flung as far as Essex or Orkney for all I knew. But I find him again high above the marsh and it is as if he clears a space around him, as if the sky is purged of all other birds until there is just the merlin, an erratic black dot – an eye spot – backlit by the snow clouds. Kinetic, wind-invigorated, he rushes across the grey sky then drops suddenly down, flicking small birds out of the reeds, veering after them. I follow him across the marsh, thinking: is he hunting, what is he doing? He seemed to be testing the birds, looking for the stragglers, the slow-to-react. The reed birds spat out from under the merlin but he did not latch on to a pursuit, he just ploughed on, flushing out the tiny birds, broadcasting them like seed. The last time I see him he is perched on a bank of snow, catching his breath, glaring back at all the dislodged birds in his wake.

* * *

If a day can give up on itself long before it is over, even before, for goodness' sake, it has reached its midpoint, that winter's day on Sheppey was such a day. But then the day never really stood a chance faced with all that wind and snow. It was better that it closed itself down and let the onslaught continue through the dark. So it was strange to see figures coming towards me across the marsh just at the point, in the early afternoon, when the light was being raked out of the sky and the day was perishing. Wildfowlers: coming out of the grey and the snow with their dogs, faces buried under balaclavas, bulky camouflage jackets, shotguns sleeved over shoulders, nodding as they passed me. Strange apparitions, they were only briefly real. Though I knew they were not spectral because, at the moment we passed each other, I heard them cussing their dogs to keep back.

The first marsh harriers I met on Sheppey were a pair. Huge dark brown birds, untroubled by the wind, working a small field that bordered the marsh. I stood above the harriers, looking down on them from a slight hill. They shifted through the wind lifting over hedges and fences, peering into field margins, scanning the dead winter grasses. More than their size, their slow flight made them conspicuous. They were using the wind to hold themselves up, turning in to the wind to slow and steady their flight. The wind was so strong, at times it held the harriers static, pinned them in the air like giant kestrels. They were a female and male. Too distant to make out the patterns of their plumage but the male lighter, greyer; the female, when she came close to the male, noticeably larger, heavier.

I was so pleased to see them. There are some days when I spend all day searching and find nothing and that's as it should be. But it is such a relief when I do catch up with the birds. I was worried that the day's weather would have grounded any harriers who had stayed on Sheppey for the winter, but they were unmistakably harriers, could not have been anything else, gliding on V-shaped wings, sliding over the ground, foraging, occupying the harrier zone which is theirs and theirs alone, those first 2 to 6 metres above the ground, within earshot of the slightest squeak or rustle. Sound-gatherers, radars, listening in to the undergrowth as no other bird of prey, except for those great auditory hunters, the owls, can do.

I walked down the hill towards the harriers, hoping to get a closer look at the birds' colours. The male marsh harrier does not have the pearl-grey colouring of the male hen and Montagu's harriers. Instead the male marsh's plumage is a distinctive tricolour, black wing tips, light grey wings, a chestnut undercarriage. The contrast between these colour bands is like early morning fireplace ash before it is disturbed, the undercoat of grey, the black charcoal splints, the red fibrous imprint of the burnt-out logs.

I stalked the two harriers under the cover of a hedge which fell down towards the marsh like a slipway. But when I reached the field where they had been hunting the harriers had split apart and were a long way off, heading east, flapping slowly along the high-water mark.

Even within that harrier zone there are demarcations – holding patterns – for each of the harrier species. The marsh harrier tends to fly a little higher than its congeners, the hen and Montagu's harrier, relying more on its eyesight than the other species to peer down into the tall reed beds that make up so much of its hunting range. The hen harrier (the greater vole specialist) hunts perhaps the lowest of the three, scything the ground. The hen harrier also has the most pronounced facial ruff of the three resident British harriers. And as the ruff is the harrier's radar rim, of the three species, the hen harrier has evolved the most efficient sound detector to pick up the minute patter of a vole moving through its grassy tunnels.

But the marsh harrier is as much a sound detector, as much a listener-in as its harrier cousins. And the panicked splashing of a duck with her flotilla of ducklings through the reeds must flood the marsh harrier's hearing. At night, roosting on the ground, often in open spaces, harriers depend on that hearing to listen out for threat. Roosting sites are selected for their acoustic properties: reed beds, barley crops, dried mudbeds, all places that crackle and ripple when entered by a predator. A bird that can detect the sound a locust makes feeding along a branch must also hear the footsteps of a fox.

The harrier's face is a scoop, a shallow drinking cup, an Elizabethan face, rimmed by the silky, light-reflecting ruff. The ruff itself is like a thick plait, a ring of closely packed barbules layered around a rim of skin. The ruff can inflate, puff out, increasing the surface area of the face, increasing the harrier's ability to capture sound. The face is really a giant ear. It works like an ear, or, rather, serves the ears, scooping up sounds and channelling them into the large ear openings set behind the eyes. The harrier's facial disc is always working, drinking up sounds, weighing them, tasting them in the feathers' nerves, reflecting them back off the ruff, through the ear-coverts, into the large ears.

I walk north-east across the saltmarsh, following behind the two harriers. In the distance: a hamlet crouched low on the headland, hunkered in on itself. It is slow going against the headwind and I am amazed any bird could beat into such a wind. Then I reach the island's east coast and there is the sea again, brown and unrecognisable. I walk up over the dunes and peer down at the beach. Between the narrow road and the dunes is the most incongruous sign, as bizarre as my ostrich encounter in the fog above Bolton: *This Stretch of the Beach is Dedicated to Naturist Bathers*. The thought of being able to take your clothes off, let alone bathe in such a place … It is impossible to imagine the beach in light and warmth. There is no shelter, even among the dunes, and the beach is all crashing, roiling noise, spume-flecked, wind-wrecked, abandoned to the gulls and wading birds. Past the dunes: a bric-a-brac of summer beach huts and hauled-up, upturned boats, the colour gone out of them, everything shut down and weighted down by stones and ropes. A place in such deep hibernation you could kick and yell at it and it would not stir. In front of the huts the beach is demarcated with wooden groynes, the space between each of them filled with wind and shrieking gulls.

I turn at last inland. A brief dose of wind-relief as I shelter behind a caravan on its breezeblock stilts. I watch a flock of lapwings shivering over the fields. Then, glancing past the lapwings, closer to me, a marsh harrier: a male, working the seam of a ditch, gliding low over an abandoned saltworks, flying into the wind to slow himself down.

The harrier hunts through an interplay of sight and sound. The harrier's ears are not positioned asymmetrically (like an owl's), so it does not possess the owl's supreme ability to pinpoint prey in the dark. But, for the harrier, hearing and vision work off each other and a movement through the reeds can first be detected through the ears before it is homed in on with the eyes.

The marsh harrier is as much a generalist predator as the red kite and sea eagle. Almost anything is taken where available: insects, crustaceans, fish, snakes, birds, small mammals ... In the British Isles the largest prey is an adult duck. Unlike the other harriers, the marsh harrier will also occasionally feed on carrion, its larger size and larger bill enabling it to compete amongst the other carcass-squabblers, the corvids, kites and buzzards. The marsh harrier specialises only when there is something to specialise on, when there is a glut in a particular

241

prey species. But it is not reliant on a specific prey as other raptors – the vole specialists – are. Young moorhens, coots and rabbits are taken in the summer months. Also, partridges, skylarks, rats, small coypus, where available. In Kent, the marsh harrier is known as the *coot-teaser* (other local, archaic names include: *bald buzzard*, *white-headed harpy*, *duck hawk*, *moor buzzard*). It will repeatedly dive at coots and water-rail to exhaust and drown them, much as the sea eagle does. Marsh harriers have been known to barge the smaller Montagu's harrier off its prey. They have even been observed trying to knock an adult female pheasant off her feet to get at her chicks sheltering beneath.

They are more methodical too, marsh harriers, in their hunting than the hen and Montagu's harrier. Marsh harriers do not range as far when hunting (certainly nothing like as far as the long-distance foraging of the Montagu's harrier). The marsh harrier will work a patch of reed bed over and over, scrupulously checking it for the slightest movement, the slightest leaf shiver.

They rarely give chase. Marsh harriers rely on surprise and ambush, coming across prey unawares in the reed beds and ditches. But just as they hunt through the interplay of sight and sound, marsh harriers also hunt through a blend of search and flush, alternating their speed and height, leaning, like the other harriers, into a head wind to slow themselves, rising to take a closer look inside the reed bed, or, rushing low over a drainage dyke, hoping to surprise prey feeding on the marsh below the dyke. The male marsh harrier, his pale underside merging his outline with the sky, hunts more than the darker female over open spaces. The larger female is the reed-bed specialist. But both sexes prefer a broken landscape where they cannot be seen coming, where they can utilise landscape features – ditches, hedges, field edges – to surprise their prey. Often the harrier spots prey having already flown over it, performing a split-second somersault, tracking back to drop with wings held back and legs stretched out in front to make the strike.

Mostly it misses: most birds of prey miss most of the time. They are not the super-efficient predators we take them for. Five to 10 per cent is around the average success rate for raptors. Estimates for the marsh harrier are slightly higher, 5–17 per cent. One study in East Anglia gave a success rate of 27 per cent, though killing is hard to monitor because so much of it goes on out of sight in the deep reed beds. Young raptors chase everything and miss almost everything. They learn quickly what is suitable and what should be left alone. They learn to read the signals: coots flick their white tails at marsh harriers when they are still a long way off, saying, *We have seen you, we can see you coming, don't bother yourselves with us.* Skylarks, singing vociferously over the moor, are saying to the merlin, *Listen, I am loud and fit and can climb as far as the clouds if you try to pursue me. Save your energy, don't bother with me.* The myth is that killing is easy, that all the osprey has to do is turn up and fish will float to the surface, belly-up in submission. Most raptor prey is quick to adapt to predation. Raptors tend to hunt routinely, predictably. A marsh harrier will cover the same ground daily, often for years on end. Their prey know they are there: many small mammals seek out the cover of denser vegetation or make use of heavy rain (which grounds birds of prey) to do their foraging.

The marsh harrier kills with its talons, a seizure in the foot. The rear and front talons grip then squeeze, puncturing the prey from either side with the harrier's long sharp claws. If this does not result in death, prey can be stabbed with a talon or, more rarely, with the bill. Larger mammals are then skinned, the skin pulled down neatly like a sock from the head down over the rear legs. Avian prey is plucked then stripped of its flesh by the harrier's strong bill.

Enemies: heavy rain, bitterns, foxes, egg collectors, wild boar, mink ... Bitterns (who will eat anything, including marsh harrier chicks) are the marsh harrier's sworn enemy. As the raven is to the red kite, so is the bittern to the marsh harrier. Bittern-baiters, harriers will persistently mob any bittern that comes too close to their nest. The marsh harrier will swoop down at the bittern, veering up at the last moment as the bittern jabs its long spearlike beak at the harrier to ward off the attack.

I stand beside the caravan for a while, enjoying its shelter, hoping the marsh harrier will come back. But he has moved on, hunting the fields way over to the west, so I turn north and walk along a frozen farm track. I pass some outbuildings on the edge of a farm. I can see just an arm's depth into their open doorways, bridles on a nail hook, a lasso of blue bailer twine. Manure heaps beside the track are bulbous under the snow. I can still hear the sea. Between the track and the sea there is a narrow field with a thin windbreak of stunted birch trees.

I don't know why I stop there on the track, gazing through the swept-back trees at the muddy sea. I think I am just tired after walking into all that wind and I like the shape the dungheaps make under the snow, glandular, like giant puffballs. But then, out of the trees, racing towards me: a female sparrowhawk, the last bird I expect to see out here in the marshes. A burst of speed, then my binoculars find her and I can see the black and white patterning of her breast. It makes no difference to the hawk that I am here. What happens next carries on around me and close to me as if I'm not here at all. I stand on the track and watch the hawk fling itself at a black-bird, a glossy black male. The blackbird is on the ground, close to the fence that borders the track and the field. He is scolding hysterically, frantic with alarm. With its first stoop the sparrowhawk misses, lands on the ground beside the blackbird and proceeds to pounce at it, stabbing at the blackbird with its long yellow legs. The black-bird easily dodges the stabs. So the hawk tries again, lifts up, hovers a couple of feet from the ground, and flings itself once more at the blackbird. Again the blackbird easily steps out of reach and it seems to hold the advantage, the hawk has lost the element of surprise and it has too little space to use its speed. The blackbird, it seems, has no intention of taking flight. But the hawk will not give up, it keeps lunging at the blackbird until the blackbird has pressed itself right up beside the bottom of the wire-mesh fence, as if it is trying to squeeze itself under the fence. The hawk cannot risk flinging itself at the blackbird in case it misses and crashes against the fence. So it is finished: the hawk lifts off the grass and flies straight back into the trees. The blackbird, still scolding, shoots off low across the track and into the adjoining hedge.

I thought that was it and the sparrowhawk had gone. But she is suddenly flying back out of the trees and flinging herself at a large mistle thrush crossing the field between the track and the wood. The gap between the two attacks is barely a minute. The hawk seems exhausted, grabbing at the thrush, stabbing at it with its legs. Always missing, the thrush easily dodging the hawk's talons, feinting, checking, sidestepping away from the hawk. And once the thrush has twisted out of the momentum of the hawk's attack, it is over and the sparrowhawk turns away and flies back into the bare wood. For a few minutes afterwards I watch her burning in her hunger-rage through the trees, unsettled, skidding from branch to branch. Above the spinney, flocks of woodpigeon, like a weather system, stream over the trees on their way to roost.

Of all the British birds of prey the marsh harrier inhabits the most specialised habitat. It is a bird of the reed and the wet, the marshlands and fenlands, the border zone between land and water. The reed bed is the marsh harrier's backyard; in French it is *le busard des roseaux* (the harrier of the reeds). To hunt across such a landscape it needs to be able to listen deeply, see deeply and stretch deeply. So it has evolved the longest legs and largest feet of all the harriers and its greater size enables it to kill much larger prey than the hen and Montagu's harrier can.

Where it nests, in the deep reed beds, amongst bulrush, bur-reed, reed buntings and bitterns, is as remote and inaccessible as the peregrine or golden eagle's cliffside eyrie. A reed bed is the most difficult, unnavigable landscape to try and move through. I tried it once, late one summer (after the nesting season was over), walking through a huge reed bed on the Tay estuary. It was muggy and the river smelt of warm mud and rotting vegetation. On the path beside the river I almost stepped on a rabbit with foamy myxomatosis eyes. The rabbit sensed me and leapt awkwardly to the side, spraying dew from the long grass where it landed. I walked down a steep bank through thigh-deep thistles. Reed buntings were clicking all around me and through binoculars I could see the streaked patterns on their pale breasts and the distinctive black heads of the males. A female marsh harrier was cruising over the beds below me, her brown back the same colour as the reeds' seed heads. I could just make out her pale silver throat and nape. She circled briefly over a cornfield above the river, stirring up house martins that looped around her in agitation. Then she was out over the beds again, sweeping their expanse. In the distance, I watched her suddenly check her flight, turning right around. She swooped down towards the reeds, paused, then dropped into the reeds and out of sight.

I found a narrow path somebody had cut into the reeds and followed it. More like a tunnel than a path, the reeds completely dwarfed me and leant over to touch each other to form a roof. But then the path just stopped and I was confronted by a 10-foot-high wall of reeds in every direction. I tried to wade into them but it was impossible, I could not see where I was going and I needed a machete or stilts, or both. It was the most claustrophobic space I have been in, the reeds were so ungiving. So I gave up and waded back to the small clearing where the path ended. When I had stopped and caught my breath it was quiet inside the reeds. The place had its own acoustic reach, insects – the whirr of mosquitoes – were amplified inside the reeds. The floor of the bed was an oily black mud, I would have sunk into it if it wasn't for the broken reeds that lined the path and supported my weight.

Later I found a section of the path where the reeds were not quite so high and I could stand looking out across acres of reed bed. I enjoyed this new perspective, eye level with the tops of the reeds, at the same height as the marsh harrier cruising over them. I often seek out these sight-angles, try to get myself, if possible, at eye level with the birds. I had done this with the peregrines at the top of the cathedral tower in Coventry, the red kites on the hill above Llandovery and the golden eagles on the mountain tops of the Outer Hebrides. With harriers there is much less of a climb, you just need to find somewhere suitable to hide. Then wait, keep watch: the harrier's flight level is often as low as your eyes.

Perhaps more so than any other bird of prey the marsh harrier just needs to be left alone. They need the isolation – the strange quarantine isolation – of the reeds. They are the most fragile and flighty of raptors, easily spooked, easily disturbed. It does not take much for them to desert their nests: children splashing in a nearby pond, pleasure-boaters, a clumsy wildlife photographer ... The Danish ornithologist, Henning Weis, who studied both marsh and Montagu's harriers in West Jutland between 1913 and 1918, put it best when he described the marsh harrier as *a creature of infinite caution and wariness towards everything unknown*. One incident Weis records in his beautiful book *Life of the Harrier in Denmark* perfectly illustrates this caution in the bird. Weis was attempting to photograph a family of marsh harriers when the adult male bird spotted him crawling out of his hide in the reeds close to the harriers' nest. Weis at once destroyed his shelter but neither of the harrier pair landed in the nest again. Instead they dropped food down to the young as they flew over the nest. Eventually the adult birds persuaded the young harriers to abandon the nest site and move to a new location some distance away.

Henning Weis felt that this innate wariness was probably the only reason the marsh harrier still existed in Denmark, though he was pessimistic about its chances of surviving as a breeding species after the brief respite of the First World War. Once wildfowlers returned to the marshes again after the war was over Weis was sure the marsh harrier would be done for in Denmark. In Britain extermination of the species was more advanced. The last known breeding pair of marsh harriers were trapped in Norfolk in 1899. They had once been so common in that county they could have been named the *Norfolk Harrier*. And across the border in what is now Cambridgeshire, Whittlesea Mere, before it was drained, had been a mecca for the harriers, a place where oologists returned again and again to collect their eggs.

Gone by 1899; crept back in 1911; bred again in Norfolk in 1915. But the marsh harrier's status was so tenuous, so precarious, for many decades it was easily Britain's rarest bird of prey, rarer even (and you would not think this possible) than the red kite still clinging on in Wales. Numbers were boosted a little by wartime coastal flooding where land was deliberately flooded to deter invasion. Even more land was abandoned to the reeds along the Norfolk and Suffolk coasts after the devastating tidal surge of 1953, and by 1958 there were fifteen nests in Britain. Then came the pesticide years: eggshell thinning, convulsions, death by poisoning. By 1971 their numbers had plummeted to just one nest in the entire country, and the marsh harrier was the country's rarest breeding/not-breeding bird of prey again. Just as the red kite was exiled, banished to the remote Welsh hills for the first half of the twentieth century, so the marsh harrier, during the same period, was kept in check, contained within a small corner of the Norfolk Broads.

For decades the marsh harrier existed as a fragment of itself, a sprinkling of birds holed up – held up – in the marshes of Hickling and Horsey. The birds were held there in a quarantine of sorts, any attempt to colonise neighbouring areas being met with persecution, exclusion.

Marsh harriers were not resettled – not reintroduced – in the way that the red kite and sea eagle have been. They just came back of their own accord once the persecution abated. There are now over three hundred breeding pairs in Britain and they can be found in wetland habitats between the east coast of Scotland and the south coast of Dorset. Some of these, like the Montagu's harrier, are migratory, but recently, as winters have become milder, British marsh harriers have also begun to over-winter here.

In the end all landscapes tell the same stories, everywhere is layered with the same strata of clearances, displacements, resettlements. Around the Isle of Sheppey, in the mudbanks and creeks of the Medway, there is everywhere the legacy of enforced detentions, segregations and quarantines. Lazarets and prison ships: vessels on route to London from plague-infected ports were placed in quarantine in the creeks off Sheppey; hulks stuffed to the brim with French prisoners from the Napoleonic wars were also moored in the Medway. The prisoners died from smallpox, typhoid and cholera in their thousands and were buried in the surrounding marshes. Deadman's Island, lying just off Sheppey's west coast, became an island tomb. If you go to Deadman's Island today it is a place strewn with human bones, spilt from their graves by the sea's gnawing.

After the sparrowhawk encounter I head west across the fields towards a long, sinuous reed bed. The light is going and in the middle of one field I disturb a dozen swans, camouflaged against the snow. The swans rise heavily into the dusk. A merlin is here too, still charged with energy, still flickering intensely. He darts past me, skimming the ground, checking nothing is loose.

I wait beside the reed bed and watch as marsh harriers come in off the white fields making for their roost. Dark and slow, low-flying shapes folding into reeds. A large dark brown female with a reddish tint to her tail comes very close. At the last moment, when she sees me, she banks away, tipping herself over the edge of the reeds. Her pale cream face a faint light inside the dusk.

XII

Honey Buzzard

The New Forest

I reach the New Forest in the middle of August when the place is locked in its own microclimate of humidity. In deep bracken, beneath holly trees, I clear a space to pitch my tent. Bracken, cut and flattened, softens the floor to sleep on; in the Forest, for centuries, it was harvested as litter and bedding for animals. In the autumn, huge bracken stacks, tall as houses, grew up next to farm steadings as if the buildings had sprouted – bloomed – sudden strange appendages. Some of the stacks were so vast it looked as if an old rusty sun had been rolled into the farmyard and left there to burn itself out. And the smell! The great bracken-rich smell of the forest come out of the forest to linger in people's homes and hair and skin so that the smell pervaded everything.

There are holly trees all around my tent. Birch and oak are here too but holly dominates and I am glad of its shade and the way its thick screen hides my tent. Holly is hospitable like that, protective, nurturing: the humus it lays down helps oak and beech to get a footing in the degraded acidic soils of the Forest. A 'holm' in the New Forest is the name for a dense stand of holly. You see the holly holms rolling over the higher ground above the valleys like storm clouds snagged on the heath. I like that a holm can also, for a while, be a *home* to other species, to oak and beech and yew and rowan, nurturing them, protecting these trees from the voracious grazing of the Forest's deer and ponies. In places around my tent the ground is ankle-deep with brittle holly leaves, the floor crackles when I step on them. In among the leaves are dried whorls of pony dung, baked hard and white by the sun. When I flick the droppings with a stick to clear a space for my tent, underneath the baked exterior the dung is black and moist and pitted with tiny insect burrowing.

Holm is a common place-name in the Forest. As is 'hat', an older word for holm, and a lovely term which describes the prominent shape and stance of the holly stands sitting up on the high ground. Though such is the age of the New Forest, many of the 'holm' or 'hat' place-names no longer have hollies (or sometimes any trees) growing there, the original hollies having died and been replaced by open heath or other species of tree.

Often a place forgets its given name. Landscape is always changing and it can quickly become remote and unreconciled from the meaning of its name. So a holly holm becomes a home for something else, and 'hawk hill' or *Cnoc na h-Iolaire* (the eagle's hill) may not have seen a bird of prey for centuries. But the name remains to document the absence. And sometimes all you see of a place is what is missing.

The experience of absence was the most important experience of my journey. More often than not, that is the experience of searching for raptors: the birds are not where they might be, or not where you want them to be. Many birds of prey lead evanescent, hidden lives and many species are instinctively wary of man. Even buzzards, which are now quite common throughout much of the country, never let you get that close, always exiting their perch just ahead of your approach. Most of my time out looking for the birds was spent not seeing them, not finding them. Sometimes, as with goshawks in the Border forests or sea eagles in the Morvern penin-sula, I went for days without seeing the birds. So I was confronted all the time by their absence and I came, gradually, sometimes reluctantly, to appreciate the experience of that absence as being crucial to experiencing the birds, to appreciating their rarity and fragility, to respecting their space, to acknowledging the distance the birds needed to put between us.

Everywhere I went – from Morvern's empty glens to the abandoned one-night houses of Wales – I witnessed absence, or, more accurately, the legacies of absence. A journey through Britain's landscapes is a journey through narratives of absence. The land is so much emptier than I had imagined. Sometimes I found it difficult to separate the two strands of my journey: the stories of the birds, and the stories of the landscapes I went to search for the birds in, were always interacting, always working off each other; human and raptor fusing, each one inhabiting the other. You cannot separate the story of Britain's birds of prey from the birds' relationship with man. That relationship *is* the birds' story. So the narratives of absence I kept coming across in the wider landscape often, unavoidably, tangled themselves with the stories of persecution, removal and extinction that mark the narrative of so many of our birds of prey.

I went to the New Forest to try to get better at not seeing, not finding the birds. I wanted to be more patient, to not always be impatient to try to tick the birds off with a sighting. I wanted not to worry too much if I did or didn't find the birds. I wanted to appreciate more the experience of not seeing them. Historically, traditionally, honey buzzards have bred in the New Forest. Perhaps they were there when I visited, perhaps not; I was determined to not really mind, to let go of minding. Some birds live cryptozoic (hidden) lives and I wanted to respect that. My aim was simply to immerse myself in the honey buzzard's forest habitat and spend some time amid the possibility of the birds.

I am drawn to cryptozoology, the study of hidden animals, the searching for creatures that may not (and are unlikely to) exist. Most scientists think cryptozoology a nonsense and a waste of time, searching for Yetis, Loch Ness Monsters and the like. But I'm drawn to cryptozoology as a depository of metaphors, that searching for something that may not be there, the questing after absence. Cryptids (the creatures that cryptozoologists study) are things of absence or such elusiveness that they only exist beyond our reach or ken. Sometimes on my journey it felt that I was searching for birds that had slipped beyond my reach. Birds of prey can be so elusive, so unattainable, they can feel, at times, like cryptids themselves.

If I had to pick one bird of prey to represent – to epitomise – absence, it would be hard to choose from the roll-call of candidates. So many of our raptors are synonymous with absence. Several, still, are conspicuous by their absence. But if I had to choose, I would choose the one that lives the most cryptozoic life. The honey buzzard is a bird of such elusiveness and strangeness that it teeters on the brink of myth, a bird whose presence here is so short-lived and secretive it is barely here at all.

* * *

The first visitor to my new home – to my clearing in the bracken – was a robin. I heard its tiny feet on the leaf litter and noticed the bracken fronds shifting as the bird brushed against them. The robin hopped closer, paused, tilted his head towards me then skittered across the leaf fall, his feet over the dry leaves making a soft scratching sound.

After the robin had gone there was a long stint of quiet. I sat outside the tent until it was dark. Then the owls began. Right over my head the first tawny owl sent out a sharp, piercing *k-wick*, answered by a long-drawn-out *hal-loo*. For the next half an hour the owls took over and the noise of their calling was all around me. The tent caught and amplified every sound that touched it and I heard one owl leave its perch and zip over the top of the tent to land in the nearest holly tree. There must have been only an inch or two between my face and the owl as it skimmed over the canvas. Then it was quiet and I slept a little and woke again at 2 a.m., woken not by any noise but by the silence. It was so still, so strangely quiet, as if the forest was listening to itself.

At dawn, all new sounds: a blackbird scuffle, a jay's scratch, a woodpecker's yaffle. I get up and wash my face in a rusty brook, stirring up clouds of iron breath. After washing, I push, by mistake, through a cove of spiders' webs strung between pine branches, feel the threads prickling, sticking to my damp hair and skin. Beside the brook are several birch trees, their trunks so wrinkled with age they look like oaks.

The rest of the day I spend wandering through the Forest. For long periods I just sat, waited and listened. And wonderful things came to me that way: a nuthatch, a lesser spotted woodpecker, a squirrel-shower (beech leaves spluttering down on top of me from where a squirrel leapt). Tree stumps were dinner plates for pine-cone seeds left there by the squirrels. The air among the spacious rows of pine was cooler where the breeze had more room to flex. The pink skin of Scots pine showed through the cracks in its fissured bark. Ponies stood in swishing pools of shade amongst the trees.

The New Forest is such a vulnerable, fragile place, encircled – periodically threatened – by development. It is an environment which endures massive pressures on it, from recreation to livestock grazing; in places the forest is so sparse, grazed down to its bare knuckles by the ponies and deer. Only the unpalatable species remain: wood spurge, wood sorrel, butcher's broom ... The forest understory is such a depleted space, you can see a long way – unnaturally far – through the trees. What is abundant – what is luxuriant – in the Forest is the great diversity of bryophytes, the mosses which love to fur the moist south-western side of trees and the lichens which blotch and crust the rest. And everywhere too in the Forest there is an abundance of decaying wood. Old trees take so long to die and in their long death the Forest's ancient trees are home to many insects. All the dead-wood tenants are here: flies, beetles, bees and wasps. And they are here like nowhere else in the country, the diversity of invertebrate species is quite exceptional. Thirty species of bees and wasps alone in the New Forest and, of the wasps, the common wasp is found here, also the German wasp, the red wasp, the tree wasp and Norwegian wasp.

Wasps: they are the reason the honey buzzard is here. They are the reason the bird migrates in summer from sub-Saharan Africa into Europe and Russia. Wasps are the reason too why the honey buzzard lives such a cryptozoic, secretive life and why it is so unlike any other bird of prey. An old name for the honey buzzard was *bee-hawk* and that is a more true description of what the honey buzzard is, though *wasp-hawk* would be more accurate still. For, despite its beautiful name, the honey buzzard does not eat honey, nor is it a buzzard. What it does eat – what it loves to eat more than anything – is wasp larvae.

Unlike any other bird of prey is the way its claws are blunt and almost straight (not sharp and curved like other raptors). For the honey buzzard is a walker, a burrower, a digger-out of wasp nests from underground, a bird-badger. And it is a good walker, not awkward on its feet like other large birds of prey. MacGillivray noticed from his dissecting table that the bee-hawk's claws were *long, rather slender, arcuate, less curved than in any other British genus*. He noticed too in the specimen of a young male honey buzzard killed near Stirling in June 1838 which came into his hands on the 9th of that month, *when it was perfectly fresh* that its *soles were crusted with mud or earth; the claws very slightly blunted*.

Also unlike other birds of prey in the way its bill is more delicate. It needs to be, to enable the honey buzzard to carefully extract the wasp grubs from their cells. For the same reason, the bird's tongue is also highly distinctive, fat and tubular, designed for prising – perhaps sucking – the larvae from their chambers. The adult honey buzzard feeds its young like this, plucking out wasp grubs one at a time from the wasp comb then presenting the grubs to its chicks. It is a delicate, tidy procedure, the comb is handled carefully until every grub has been removed. Only then is the comb discarded, often trodden down into the detritus of the nest.

Even the honey buzzard's internal organs (MacGillivray would love this observation) are distinct from other birds of prey. Their gizzards are lighter and their small intestine much shorter than in most other raptors because the soft wasp larvae are more easily digested than the flesh and bones and fur that many other birds of prey consume. Also, wasps are the reason the honey buzzard rarely regurgitates pellets. It rarely needs to, because, again, the softness of the insect larvae is easy to digest, unlike the indigestible matter – the bones and feathers – which other birds of prey expel in their pellets.

Wasps are crucial, they are integral to what the honey buzzard is. But wasp larvae are not the only thing honey buzzards eat, the larva is not always available. In Britain, when the first honey buzzards arrive from their migration around the middle of May, wasps are largely inactive. So the birds top up their diet and, importantly, the females increase fat reserves before laying, by feeding on nestling birds (especially pigeon squabs), frogs, lizards and other insects. Dungheaps are favoured resources for excavating grubs and worms. Beetles, weevils, earwigs, ants ... have all been found in a honey buzzard's stomach. The stomach of the male specimen that MacGillivray dissected *was filled with fragments of bees and numerous larvae, among which no honey or wax was found*. Bee nests are frequently raided by honey buzzards. In the British uplands, where bumblebees are common on the heather moors, the bees are a significant prey species for the birds. Sometimes young honey buzzards become gluey with honey that leaks from the combs brought into the nest by the adult birds, leaves and twigs stick to the legs of the chicks as they wander about the nest. In poor wasp years, bees can provide an important supplement. Also frogs, which are usually skinned first by the adult birds before they are fed to the young.

But even when wasps are inactive, the honey buzzard is thinking about wasps. It has to think about them – to anticipate the wasps – in order to survive and rear its young. So after laying and during the long period of incubation the male honey buzzard becomes a map-maker, a cartographer of wasp nests. He does not raid the nests during this period as they are not sufficiently developed. Instead he makes a survey of his patch, recording – storing – the locations of all the wasp nests he can find. Later in the season, he will draw on this memory-map to return and plunder the nests when they are more advanced and stocked with fattening grubs.

But all birds of prey are map-makers. They rely on intimate knowledge of landscape to hunt, routinely returning to the places where they know prey can be found at certain times of day. Routine is everything. Landscape is memorised, landscape *is* memory. But the honey buzzard's map is more enhanced in scale. It deals in the minutiae of place, in the minuscule world of invertebrates. The woodland clearing, the forest ride and forest purlieu, these are the honey buzzard's theatres, its zones of interest. Dense forestry plantations are no good, they suffocate everything. The honey buzzard needs woodland that is light and roomy. It needs glades and tracks, woods that intersperse themselves with openings. The honey buzzard sits in a tree on the edge of these clearings, keeping watch, static hunting. And when it spots a worker wasp heading back to its colony, the honey buzzard slips from its lookout branch like a shadow unhooking itself and follows in the wasp's wake, tracking the wasp back to its nest.

But if the weather closes in, smudging everything, then wasps can be hard to track like this. And it's then that the honey buzzard's memory-map of wasp-nest locations becomes a lifeline. By storing the locations of wasp nests early in the season, the honey buzzard is laying down a cache of knowledge. And this enables the birds to be more climatically resilient than it's often assumed they are. It enables honey buzzards, for instance, to breed just as successfully in the British uplands (where it is generally cooler and wetter) as they do in the more benign lowlands. If wasp numbers are seriously depressed this can impact honey buzzard breeding success. But wasps are also more climatically resilient than we assume and the insects have been observed to forage even in heavy rain.

Perhaps more than climate – more than temperature and precipitation – soil consistency is what limits the distribution of honey buzzards. The earth needs to be diggable, friable. The honey buzzard is a miner of wasp nests, it needs to be able to extract the nests from the ground. So heavy clay is no good, hard, arid ground is no good for honey buzzards. Even where wasp numbers are high, as in Mediterranean countries, honey buzzards are scarce because of the difficulty of getting at the wasps in such a dry, baked landscape. Light sandy soils are good, ground covered in a thick mulch of pine needles is good. The bird's digging instinct is so strong that young honey buzzards are known to scrape holes in the bottom of their nest, occasionally to such an extent that their digging undermines the stability of its structure.

Nothing like a raptor, it digs like a dog, scratches away, deeper and deeper until the bird can sometimes disappear into its own hole. So absorbed in the task of excavating the wasps' nest, it is said that you can walk right up to a digging honey buzzard. Though this is not advisable: where a honey buzzard digs there are likely to be furious wasps, made more furious by the fact they cannot do anything about the honey buzzard and have been known instead to turn their fury on anything else to hand, ponies, dogs, passing ornithologists ...

The honey buzzard seems to work at its diggings with impunity. Wasps will swarm about the bird but appear not to harm or deter it greatly. It's possible the bird releases a chemical to calm the insects. The thick scale-like feathers on its face (which other raptors do not possess) may also offer protection from stings (like trying to sting through a pineapple's skin). Even so, sometimes a honey buzzard will be driven back by a ferocious onslaught from the wasps. But after a respite of head shaking, shrugging and intensive preening the honey buzzard usually resumes its pillage. Sometimes wasps and bees are snapped at by the bird, plucked from the air (often decapitated) and eaten. The whole process of digging out the wasps' nest can last for hours, with the nests often awkward to get at, lodged under layers of grass and tree roots. And once the nest is accessible the process of feeding from it can last for days, with the honey buzzard returning again and again to retrieve chunks of grub-rich comb.

Nothing like a raptor, but not exempt from the raptor's fate. You would think a chiefly insectivorous bird (a predator of wasps no less) might be immune from persecution, even welcomed. But when the war against birds of prey was at its height during the nineteenth and early twentieth centuries, there was little discrimination between raptor species. The *Birds of Hampshire* notes that twenty-four honey-buzzard nests were recorded in the New Forest between 1856 and 1872; at least twenty of these were robbed of eggs or young birds and the adult honey buzzards killed.

* * *

One evening in the New Forest, walking back to my tent through the trees, I heard a bird of prey calling. It was a loud, piercing call, agitated, persistent, a long whistling note, rising in pitch. It confused me, I couldn't identify the caller. It was roughly the same volume and pitch as a common buzzard but it sounded different, deeper, more plaintive. At least, it sounded different from the soundtrack of common buzzards I was so used to hearing at home. I walked towards the call, trying to get a bearing on where it was coming from. I searched for half an hour, pausing and listening, scanning the branches of tree after tree. Nothing. I found it impossible to pinpoint the sound in the deep foliage of the trees. Instead I tried to memorise the call (*ke-yeeeep ke-yeeeep* ...) and when I got home I spent a whole morning of confusion, listening to recordings of common buzzards and honey buzzards, trying to convince myself that what I had heard was a honey buzzard.

I went to the New Forest determined to be more patient about not finding the birds, but it would be dishonest to say that I didn't mind not seeing a honey buzzard. I longed to see one. And I explored as much of the Forest as I could in my search for the birds, even following wasps to see if they would lead me to their nest (they never did). I tried, but I could not shake that longing to find the birds. Not seeing them only made me dream of honey buzzards incessantly. Perhaps that is what a cryptozoologist is, somebody who dreams about the same creature over and over again; perhaps that is what a cryptid is, a creature that hides inside dreams.

After I got home from the Forest I read a fascinating paper hypothesising that the juvenile plumage of honey buzzards has evolved to resemble the plumage of common buzzards. Goshawks predate honey buzzards (especially when pigeons and rabbits are scarce), but goshawks are more reluctant to predate the sharper-clawed, more aggressive common buzzard and so juvenile honey buzzards, to deflect the risk of predation from goshawks, have, through a process of Batesian mimicry, adapted their plumage to more closely resemble their more robust cousins. The two species – common and honey buzzard – are difficult enough to tell apart; that the honey buzzard should try to absent itself even more by hiding in another bird seems somehow apt for this most cryptozoic bird of prey.

But how absent are they? Perhaps not as much as we tend to think given the honey buzzard is so good at being overlooked. MacGillivray wrote in his book *The Natural History of Deeside*:

Even on the border of the most frequented paths are many things travellers have passed by unheeded or unexamined.

The honey buzzard, despite its size, is an easy bird to pass by unnoticed. Still, it is only here in fairly small numbers, roughly sixty-plus pairs. But there is room – plenty of room – in these islands for many more. Anywhere that is diggable, friable and waspy is good for the wasp-hawk.

* * *

The sections I keep returning to in MacGillivray's journal of his walk to London are the lists of flora he recorded along the way, each night writing up the Latin names of all the plants he'd seen that day. Between the Bridge of Dee and Upper Banchory, alone, he notes down fifty-seven species of plant in flower and sixty-two out of flower (all of these committed to memory as he walked along).

There are moments in his journal when he seems to conjure beauty out of nothing, out of nowhere. For instance, a quarter of a mile on the road out of Buxton he pauses to listen in the clear morning air to larks singing and out of the corner of his eye he sees a plant he does not recognise, a musk thistle (*Carduus nutans*), *the most beautiful thistle*, he writes in his journal, *which I have yet seen*. Soon after this he finds the common carline thistle and, at that point, *everything*, he writes, *conspired to render me cheerful*.

Some of the plants MacGillivray collected on his walk to London have survived and are held at the University of Aberdeen's Herbarium. I spent a whole morning in the Herbarium going through the collection, looking at the sheets of plants exactly as MacGillivray had left and labelled them almost 200 years ago. Hundreds of specimens from a lifetime's botanical wanderings and all of them presented and organised with such clarity. I found plants he picked on his 1819 walk to London and many he collected from the high Cairngorms in the summer of 1850, just two years before his death. Several of the mountain ferns and grasses still had residues of peat tangled in their roots. Some of the flowering plants, remarkably, still retained the colour in their petals. The purple flowers of *Statice armeria* were paled and rusted but still had hints of pink in them. The note that MacGillivray wrote beneath each specimen (his hand-writing straight and neat across the page, no archaic floridness to it) was usually the plant's Latin name followed by the place and date he had collected it. I thought that if I spent enough time with his collection I could draw a map of all the places he went in search of plants. I could trace MacGillivray's movements across the land, across the years, that way. That would be how I would write a biography of William MacGillivray, his life told through his plant cuttings, his botanical wanderings ...

- Deschampsia Flexuosa: Gathered on Ben Nevis, Inverness-shire 16th September 1819, by Mr MacGillivray.
- Statice Armeria: Summit of Benvrotan near one of the Sources of the Dee, 10th September 1819.
- Statice Armeria: By the Dee, 8 miles from its mouth, May 1819.
- Asplenium Adiantum nigrum: Wall of the Marquis of Abercorn's orchard at Duddingston, near Edinburgh, 1st January 1820, 1 A.M. moonlight.
- Lycopodium Selago: Lochnagar, 8th August, 1850.
- Carex Saxatilis: Corry of Lochan uain, Cairntoul, 12th August, 1850.

Dear William, I am sorry for their desecration. After twenty minutes of searching the New Calton cemetery in Edinburgh I have found William MacGillivray's grave. For a while I was concerned I might not find it at all, several of the headstones in the churchyard have keeled over and I was worried his might be one of these. But I found it in the end, a great pink-flecked slab of granite with an Iona cross set in a Celtic scroll at its head. The long inscription a little faded inside the granite, though still legible:

> In memory of William MacGillivray, M.A., LL.D., born 1796, died 1852. Author of A History of British Birds and other standard works in Natural Science; Professor of Natural History and Lecturer on Botany in Marischal College and University from 1841 to 1852. Erected in 1900, together with a memorial brass in Marischal College, Aberdeen, by his relatives and surviving students, who affectionately cherish his memory, and by others desirous of doing honour to his character as a man and to his eminence as a naturalist.

It is a fine spot, his grave, with views out across to Arthur's Seat, a bird-busy place with gulls coming and going from off the Firth of Forth. But the shock is what has been done to his gravestone. Somebody has hacked away at the granite and stolen the brass plaque that had been fixed to the base of the stone. I have seen photographs of it before it was vandalised, the plaque had been beautifully cast with the image of a golden eagle modelled from one of MacGillivray's own paintings of the bird.

I kneel down and run my fingers along the jagged edge of the granite where it has been hacked and chipped. It is still possible, just, to see the eagle's outline imprinted on the stone. It's as if the shape of the metal cast has branded – seared – the stone beneath. *Sear*: flip the verb into a noun and a 'sear' is also the 'foot of a bird of prey', from the Old French *serrer* to grasp, lock, hold fast ... I can see in the stone the line of the eagle's back, the curve of its chest, its long tail. All that is left is the faintest trace of the bird, a ghost eagle scratched into the stone, a hieroglyph.

XIII

Hobby

Dorset

Anything to make him feel less absent. With the brass plaque on his gravestone stolen, presumably melted down, I went in search of MacGillivray's painting of the golden eagle which the plaque had been modelled on. There are over 200 of MacGillivray's paintings held in the library of the Natural History Museum in London. Most of them are watercolours of birds and there are also several paintings of different species of fish and mammals. MacGillivray's intention was that the bird paintings would be used to illustrate his five-volume *History of British Birds*, though, tragically – and it is tragic because the paintings are quite exceptional – in the end the watercolours were left out of his books because MacGillivray could not afford the printing costs of including them. MacGillivray's son, Paul, donated his father's paintings to the Natural History Museum in 1892, where they sit in storage and seldom see the light of day.

But that is MacGillivray for you, a man eclipsed, the legacy of his work eclipsed by his contemporaries, Darwin, Audubon and Yarrell (William Yarrell, whose own more accessible, more popular, *A History of British Birds* was published in 1845). So that MacGillivray himself could be said to have become a type of cryptid, virtually unknown, hidden from view, forgotten. When I started to research this book I had no idea who William MacGillivray was, but then a brief quotation led me to his work on birds of prey, *Descriptions of the Rapacious Birds of Great Britain*. And of course the book was out of print and impossible to find but, when I finally tracked it down and began to read it, I could not stop reading. And soon I was trying to find and read everything I could by MacGillivray. His descriptions of the natural world felt chiselled from hours of careful observation. His account of watching hen harriers in his book *Descriptions of the Rapacious Birds* led me to his great work, *A History of British Birds*, where I sought him out and found him

kneeling on the side of a hill, watching, this time, a
different pair of hen harriers:

Kneel down here, then, among the long broom and
let us watch the pair that have just made their
appearance on the shoulder of the hill ... How
beautifully they glide along, in their circling flight,
with gentle flaps of their expanded wings, floating, as
it were, in the air, their half-spread tails inclined
from side to side, as they balance themselves, or alter
their course! Now they are near enough to enable us
to distinguish the male from the female. They seem
to be hunting in concert, and their search is keen, for
they fly at times so low as almost to touch the bushes,
and never rise higher than thirty feet. The grey bird
hovers, fixing himself in the air like the Kestrel; now
he stoops, but recovers himself. A hare breaks from
the cover, but they follow her not, though doubtless
were they to spy her young one, it would not escape
so well. The female now hovers for a few seconds,
gradually sinks for a short space, ascends, turns a
little to one side, closes her wings, and comes to the
ground. She has secured her prey, for she remains
concealed among the furze, while the male shoots
away, flying at the height of three or four yards,
sweeps along the hawthorn hedge, bounds over it to
the other side, turns away to skim over the sedgy
pool, where he hovers a short while. He now enters
upon the grass field, when a Partridge springs off,
and he pursues it, with a rapid gliding flight like that

of the Sparrow Hawk; but they have turned to the right, and the wood conceals them from our view. In the meantime, the female has sprung up, and advances, keenly inspecting the ground, and so heedless of our presence that she passes within twenty yards of us. Away she speeds, and in passing the pool, again stoops, but recovers herself, and rising in a beautiful curve, bounds over the plantation, and is out of sight.

There is a warmth and intimacy to the writing, also a passionate energy; MacGillivray's voice, in this respect, feels different from many of his Victorian contemporaries'. He draws you in: *Kneel down here, then, among the long broom and let us watch …* He himself is so palpable, so present in his work; you cannot help but warm to him. MacGillivray's friend and correspondent the ornithologist James Harley wrote of MacGillivray's writing:

Having for several years past paid considerable attention to the Ornithology of the British Islands, I would venture to recommend the beautifully written and elaborate History of British Birds, Indigenous and Migratory, by Mr MacGillivray, as being the best work in that department of science yet published. There is a peculiar mountain freshness about Mr MacGillivray's writings, combined with fidelity and truths in delineation, rarely possessed by Naturalists, and hitherto not surpassed. To the Ornithological Student this charming History of British Birds ought

to become a hand-book – to the observer, a
companion – and to the rambler in woods and wilds,
a guide and pole-star.

MacGillivray wrote in the journal he kept of his walk to London a sort of manifesto of how he intended to write the journal. In these notes to himself, these memoranda, you glimpse a little of where that *peculiar mountain freshness* to his writing is drawn from:

- I shall write it with as much freedom as if I were
  convinced that no person should ever read it. At
  the same time it must be so written that others may
  readily understand it ...
- I must avoid obscurity ...
- I despise opinion unsupported by reason, detest
  bigotry, and rejoice in persecution, that is in being
  persecuted, but not in exercising any authority,
  much less persecution, over others ...
- But while I write with the intention of benefitting
  others, and of gratifying my own vanity, I also
  write from the conviction that my notes will be
  useful to myself on many future occasions, yea
  even unto the day of my death.
- Partly from the instigation of vanity, and partly
  from other motives, I refrain from laying down any
  general or particular plan either for my journey or
  journal. Only I shall drink a mouthful from the
  source of the Dee, and give three cheers to myself
  on the top of Ben Nevis; and till that time keep a

regular list of all the plants and birds which may
occur.

Hobby, from the Old French *hober*: to move, to stir, to
jump about. The hobby is the most kinetic bird of prey I
know. It is all zip and dash and rushing speed, like a frantic whirligig of the heath. Its scientific Latin name, *Falco
subbuteo*, simply means 'smaller than a buzzard'; its
Greek name, *Hypotriorches*, translates as 'somewhat
near a bird of prey' (the hobby's original scientific name
was *Hypotriorchis subbuteo*). Both definitions are so
wonderfully hazy in their description of the hobby,
strangely, paradoxically, they actually capture the difficulty of grasping this small falcon as it rushes past you in
its blur of speed.

A hop and a skip from the New Forest and I cross the
border from Hampshire into Dorset. I head east from
Wareham down a narrow road across the dusty heath to
the Arne peninsula, a fist and outstretched thumb of land
that juts out into Poole Harbour.

Walk due north from the tiny village of Arne, following the track across the heath, till you come to a scatter-
ing of birch and oak which lines the top lip of Arne Bay.
Enter the trees and wade through the undergrowth of
bracken, pausing when you reach the first lunar white
birch. You will know it because of the way its trunk
glows like a bar of light inside the wood. Turn left at the
birch and you will come to a great oak draped in honeysuckle and ivy. Try to go there when the honeysuckle is

in flower, when its flowers glow like small pale suns amongst the oak's dark leaves. You will know the oak for sure because one of its huge arms has broken off and is lying amongst the bracken beside the base of the trunk.

That is where, in a shallow hollow next to the huge oak, I slept that first rainy, windy night. A night of not much sleep, woken by rain and by deer sheltering from the rain; sika deer with their white mottled red-brown coats and their high-pitched alarm calls sounding like a bird's screech. I can't remember if I was asleep when the branch from the oak cracked then split and crashed to the ground, but it was a heart-thumping moment and I was up and out the tent within seconds peering into the gloom till I noticed that something was wrong with the tree, that it did not look right. Then I saw the branch sticking out of the bracken like a half-submerged wreck and the crashing noise suddenly made sense and, a little less spooked, I crept back inside the tent. Earlier, before the wind got up, I heard music coming from a bar across the harbour. Then, much closer, a churring noise as nightjars began to whirr across the heath.

MacGillivray's paintings have been arriving all afternoon in huge green boxes wheeled down on trolleys from the museum's storage. Wearing vinyl gloves, I lay the paintings out on a table one by one and write my notes in pencil.

- Here is his kestrel, a female, flaring red. He has the bird's bright chestnut colours, the detail of its down feathers, the cupped disc beneath the eye, the steep cliff-drop of its beak, the beak's black tip, the marble blue of the beak below the cere, the faint yellow of the cere itself, a black glint to the claws, a thread of ivy winding round the rock the bird is perched on; the kestrel poised, about to take off.
- Here is his ptarmigan with its feathered feet and semi-winter dress, painted 'from an individual purchased in the Edinburgh market October 1831'. What is beautiful about his ptarmigan is the way he captures those feathers dissipating as they ermine from gold and grey and black to northern white.
- Next, a storm petrel, 'from an individual caught off the Isle of May, 1832'.
- Then a pair of buoyant, bobbing wrens, 'shot in the Pentland Hills in the Summer of 1832'.
- His water ouzels, 'from individuals shot near St. Mary's Loch, September 1832', one in its first year of plumage and one young bird after moulting, the red-brown colours of its chest just starting to leak through.
- Sparrowhawks: an old orange-eyed female, long stretching talons, long legs, grey-black back.
- A tall, broad-chested, yellow-eyed female peregrine and a juvenile (I think) beside her with a reddish chest and heavy chainmail streaks across its breast.

- His merlins are precise: the blue of the male's back, the black wing and tail primaries, the orange blush of his chest; the female's lesser reds, her brown back, longer wings, longer tail; the juvenile's crenulated brown and chestnut patterning, mantling a ring ouzel which is almost the same size as the merlins.
- Ah, and here is his honey buzzard, that male 'taken near Stirling in the beginning of June 1838'. What a dark brown bird it is, so uniformly brown except for the grey above the cere and the light russet plumage above its legs.
- A red kite, another kestrel (the two red raptors next to one another).
- An osprey with the incomplete painting of the fish it's caught, just a pencil sketch of where the fish should be. One of the osprey's talons is also unfinished, lodged into the unfinished fish.
- And here is the painting of the golden eagle I was looking for. It is the last to emerge from storage. In fact, two paintings of eagles. One, like the osprey, is incomplete, only the cere and bill are painted. The other is of the eagle MacGillivray's gravestone plaque was modelled on, the eagle's thick talons embedded in a rabbit, the rabbit's right eye wide and bright. The painting feels a little artificial: the eagle is standing too tall, not mantling its prey, and the rabbit, despite the eagle's talon puncturing its neck, seems very much alive. A juvenile bird with white feathers showing on its tail and legs and

wing, every feather delineated, the base of its tail
all white except for the black trailing band.
Demerara hues in the feathers along the eagle's
crown and nape.

Hobby, *hober*: to move, to stir, to jump about ... I never
learn; better to stay put and wait for the birds to come to
me, don't wander aimlessly about the heath all day.
Which, of course, is what I do, and do not mind because
I see so much that way. I am looking for the flash of white
of a hobby's throat lit up against the pine greens of the
heath. And so everything that is white draws me in:
egrets, an albino sika deer, black-headed gulls, a pair of
spoonbills in the shallows, shelduck further out in the
bay. In the woods I disturb a herd of deer and walk
through the warmth of where they had been.

What am I looking for? A bolt of speed, a disturbance
amongst the swifts. Something 'smaller than a buzzard',
something 'almost like a bird of prey'. The hobby's jizz –
its feel – the gist of it: somewhere between a peregrine and
a swift. It has the peregrine's black moustachial stripe, the
falcon's sharp-angled wings; it has the swift's sickle,
boomerang shape in flight. Prey: anything from a flying
ant to a turtle dove. But especially dragonflies, moths,
beetles, small birds, willow-wrens, chiffchaffs, tits, pipits,
hirundines (swallows and martins), swifts, bats ... The
hobby is the only British bird of prey agile and fast enough
to catch a swift, a bat, or a swallow in mid-air.

Just as the honey buzzard times its arrival and nesting
to coincide with wasps, the hobby breeds in sync with

the glut of young hirundines and July's crop of dragon-flies. That the hobby (like the honey buzzard, osprey and Montagu's harrier) has to get out by autumn, migrating to sub-Saharan Africa, shows just how insectivorous a bird it is. Diet dictates migratory behaviour: the general rule of thumb is those raptors that feed on warm-blooded prey stay put, those that feed on cold-blooded species get out for winter as their prey dries up in the north. But why come back in spring? Why bother with such a long, hazardous migration twice a year? Why not stay in their wintering grounds, where it is generally warmer, where there is still food even for the insectivorous raptors in winter? Because the north in summer can be a land that is overbrimming, a place which offers much better opportunities for these birds to breed successfully. The pull of the north in spring is overwhelming. Hobbies have been recorded migrating northwards at an average speed of 71 kph (the return journey south in autumn is usually much slower than this). The journey – the awful journey – running the gauntlet of storms and Maltese gunmen who will shoot any migrating raptor within range, is not the point. It is getting back to the fickle north with its promise of all that light to work in.

Diet dictates migratory behaviour but also – for MacGillivray – diet dictates everything. To properly understand the bird, he felt, you needed to understand the mechanics of the bird:

> ... although I have selected the digestive organ as
> pre-eminently worthy of attention, I have not done so
> because I suppose them capable of affording a key to
> the natural system, but because the structure of the
> food determines not only the form and structure of
> the bird, but also the greater part of its daily
> occupations.

Wasps and other hymenoptera (bees especially) are integral to what the honey buzzard is; dragonflies and hirundines to what the hobby is. Especially dragonflies: in the British Isles, in recent decades, hobbies have been both increasing their numbers and spreading northwards out from their traditional heartland, the downlands and heathlands of southern England. Increase in dragonfly numbers has been an important factor in enabling hobbies to spread like this. There are roughly 2,800 hobby pairs now breeding here. Blink, and you will miss them.

The hobby in its winter quarters becomes a rain bird. It follows the rain, tracking thunderstorms and bands of rain that sweep south through southern Africa at this time of year. The hobby is much more insectivorous here than it is in its summer breeding territory. It can afford to be, can afford to hunt and eat less without the burden of young to raise. So the hobby tracks the rain, flies through the rain, flitting from rain cloud to rain cloud. Because the rain releases – induces – insects in their millions: locusts, flying ants, termites ... The hobby is just one among many species of raptor that follows these insect blooms. After the rains come grasshoppers, beetles, dragonflies, small birds such as queleas, pipits and cisticoles.

I spend a lot of time walking along the north shore of the Arne peninsula. A fringe of gorse and birch separates the shore from the heath beyond. I enjoy slipping through this curtain of trees and scrub, from heath to shore and back again. The heath feels as remote as anywhere I have been on this journey, yet I just need to step through a gap in the gorse, breach the border, and there are the office blocks, the flats and cranes of Poole, and a parting in the trees is suddenly filled by the vast bulk of a ferry coming into dock. The heath is like a pulse of wildness nudging the fringes of the town. A deer's alarm bark is followed by a lorry's warning alarm as it reverses along the quay-side. I go from the blue-green glint of dragonflies flickering over the heath to sunlight glinting off the windows of houses in Poole.

MacGillivray loved this zone, where the city gave way to the countryside. Faced with a disappointment or difficulty his instinct, usually, was to walk to the edge of the city and dip himself in the surrounding fields. It's not that he was fleeing the city, he simply walked out to its margins, took stock, reorientated himself, then walked back into town again. Often he would jot down some notes on the geological features he observed at the edge of a city (on an excursion to the south of London he was delighted to have the opportunity to study the chalk there, a geological district he had never seen before). On a visit to Glasgow in 1833 he finds the museum he wishes to visit closed and writes in his journal:

> I then proceeded to the College, whence I was, however, obliged to return, the Museum not being open. So I had recourse to Nature, as I often have under more grievous disappointments, and betook myself to the margin of the city ...

Recently some birds of prey have come to live amongst us in our towns and cities in ways that they have not done for many centuries. Peregrine and red kite, most notably, can now be seen across many of our urban centres. Some of the most memorable encounters I've had with birds on this journey have been in built-up areas. I once spent a morning standing behind a huge oak doorway that led out onto the flat roof of a church tower in the centre of a large town in South West England. Three spy holes had been drilled through the door. Before I put my eye to one of the holes I could smell the falcons: it was a warm day in June and the place reeked. So this is what a raptor's eyrie smells like ... It was as if I had climbed to the top of a cliff, poked my nose over the brim of a nest and inhaled the pungent carcass stench of the place.

I put my eye to one of the holes in the door. The roof was littered with feathers, small fragments of bone; I could just make out a pigeon's leg. And there, in the far corner, were three young peregrines, well feathered, the odd clump of down sticking to them like candyfloss. The birds were only 6 feet away from me behind the door. They were lying flat with their chins pressed to the floor, long necks stretched out behind their heads. One of the birds was panting in the heat.

The adult female was perched above the roof on a corner spire. Dark bars drawn across her breast. Heavy, muscular chest. Bright yellow talons: scaly, reptilian. The black moustachial stripe running down her cheek was like a long drip of wax. She kept twisting her head back, glancing up at the sky.

What happened to Arne was another form of clearance. Just as a slice of the moor above Bolton was commandeered during the war as a decoy to draw bombing raids away from the ordnance factory at Chorley, they also built a decoy on the Arne peninsula to draw the Luftwaffe away from the crucial Royal Naval cordite factory at Holton Heath to the west of Poole. Arne was a small rural community: if the decoy worked the majority of bombs would fall, it was hoped, on heathland, oak woods, saltmarsh and that rare, beautiful space where oak woods hem a saltmarsh.

On the night of 3 June 1942 the Luftwaffe come over to destroy the cordite factory. Searchlights go up from the garrison on Brownsea Island and the first decoy fires are lit on Brownsea and Arne. Old bathtubs packed with wood and coal are ignited. Lavatory cisterns flush paraffin and water down pipes into the burning tubs. With every flush the fires flare up violently in simulation of a bomb blast. Acres of scaffolding, constructed to resemble a giant warehouse, are set alight with tar barrels and paraffin. So it looks, from the air, as if one of the warehouses at Holton Heath has gone up in flames. Everywhere the stench of paraffin. People run to cellars, ditches, cram into cupboards under stairs. One man can't bear the shaking of his garden shelter and decides, though the others in the shelter beg him not to, to sit the raid out in the woods instead.

It is a terrible night on Arne. But the deception works. Five hundred tonnes of bombs are dropped on Arne that night. So many bombs explode on the woods and heaths that the topography of the place is changed. The land is pockmarked, pitted with craters. Two hundred and six bomb craters are counted across the peninsula. And Arne burned and burned. The oak and birch woods burned, the bracken and the heather burned. And the peat burned. Above all, the peat, the underlying structure of the heaths. Once the fire took hold of the peat it would not go out, would not be put out. For weeks Arne smouldered like that. At night planes could see patches of the heath glowing red. The fire brigade would come and put the fire out. Then hours later a rush of oxygen would flush through the peat and stoke another fire into life.

After the raid the people were evacuated. They were given a month's notice and everyone on Arne left the peninsula. A dairy herd on one of the farms was so traumatised by the raid that the cows took sick with milk fever (their milk congealed inside them) and they all had to be destroyed. Four weeks to sell up and get out.

Livestock sent for auction. Boats sold off on the cheap. It was such a hurried thing, the evacuation; they could not even stay for the harvest. Some families went to Blandford, some were given replacement farms elsewhere. Then the army moved in for the duration of the war and Arne was closed off, taken over by the military as a training centre.

After the war a few people came back to live on Arne, but very few of those who left in 1942 returned. The place was in ruins, the village derelict, its houses in an awful state, bullet-chipped, tiles ripped, smothered in ivy. Most of the buildings had to be pulled down. Meanwhile fields had grown rushy, scrub had invaded the ungrazed heath. And hundreds of bomb craters had become pools for dragonflies.

Dawn and dusk. Sometimes it feels like these are the best times to see raptors. You have to get up early for hawks! And so many diurnal birds of prey are surprisingly crepuscular. I have watched buzzards, in particular, hunting through the last dregs of light when it seemed there was barely enough light to fly in, let alone hunt. Hobbies, too, with their large eyes, can hunt for bats and insects deep into the twilight. So I go back out onto the heath in the evening and settle down to wait and watch for hobbies.

A kestrel is here and I watch it above me, quartering the heath. It has young in a pine-tree nest on a slope above a boggy sump. Every time the adult kestrel swoops close to the nest the young call loudly to it with their shrill begging *keeks*. The sound the young kestrels make carries right across the heath. Then, after ten minutes, a falcon's shadow flashes over me. I presume it is the kestrel back again, swooping through another arc of air. But the speed it is going is nothing like a kestrel.

Hobby! At last! Shooting low over the heath, long, sharp wings, a hundred times faster than a kestrel. Hobby: using up every ounce of sky, flinging himself at the air.

This heath is not big enough for him. He circles it in seconds, crosses from one end to the other in a blink. Can he even slow down? Could he go any faster? He is quicker, by far, than any bird I have watched. All the books say the peregrine is the speed master but this hobby feels so much faster than any falcon I have seen. Because he is flying so close to the ground the effect is that the ground is always rushing away from him. He needs to run and run. And then he needs to climb, to fling himself up, only to dive straight back down again to skim the ground. No bird I know flies like this. The closest thing he resembles is a swift, but a hobby is a swift enhanced. Even merlins, those compressed balls of energy, do not burst apart the air like this hobby.

He is hawking for dragonflies. I watch him seize one mid-air. Then, still on the wing, the hobby brings his foot up to his beak. He plucks at the dragonfly, peeling off the chitinous layer, the legs and wings, before he eats the insect. Fragments of dragonfly elytra drop beneath him as he feeds. Then he is on to the next (feeding like this can be frenetic, up to a dozen insects per minute).

A woman from the village has walked out across the heath and has sat down on a bench behind me. I want her to see what I am seeing too. Has she seen the hobby? Surely she cannot miss him, he is mad with speed. I stand up from the heather, grin and point at the hobby. God, what must I look like ... But the woman smiles, waves and her wave seems to say, yes, I am seeing him – witnessing this – too.

What is unique about this experience is that the hobby is not going anywhere. I am not going to lose him suddenly over a ridge or in the depths of a wood. I do not have to try and keep up with him or go looking for him. The heath this evening is his patch. He is not going anywhere else and appears to be feeding for himself, rather than taking prey back to the nest. I just need to sit here and watch as he whirls around me. The only effort in finding him is trying to keep up with his speed.

What is the hobby doing to the air? As he accelerates the air itself accelerates around him, down and back, lifting, thrusting the hobby forwards. In his wake he leaves behind air in mayhem, air like a whirlpool, several whirlpools swirling around each other. He makes a cauldron, a Corryvreckan of the air. He stokes, he concertinas it. The air cannot know what has hit it. If we could see what the hobby does to the air as he smashes through it we would see air in storm, vortexes, geysers, collisions.

* * *

A hobby in its northern breeding quarters is the inverse of its winter self. It is no longer a chaser of rain clouds. The damper western coasts of these islands are not ideal for hobbies; they prefer drier, warmer, insect-alluring habitats. Above all, they are a bird of open spaces, of heathlands, marshlands and farmlands where they have the space to fling themselves after their avian and insect prey. Woods and trees are only for nesting in, these cluttered spaces are the hawks' hunting territory. Hobbies only step into the woods to nest and, crucially, such a wood must provide its own abandoned nests. For hobbies, like all falcons, are squatters, not nest builders. In England, abandoned crows' nests are especially favoured, so much so that hobbies may well depend on a healthy crow population for their own breeding success. You would think that a falcon on its nest would be a no-go zone for other birds. In fact, sometimes the reverse is true. As with geese nesting close to peregrine eyries, so pigeons have been observed to nest in close proximity to hobbies. It is thought that, like the geese, pigeons do this to benefit from the hobbies' fierce protection of their nest sites against predators. Ravens and goshawks, in particular, are abominable to hobbies and the small falcons will harangue these larger predators at every opportunity.

Landscape can be lost, persecuted, reduced as much as any bird, as much as any species. In Dorset only a fraction of the heaths remain which were there in the early nineteenth century. Heathland – that difficult, acidic, nutrient-poor habitat, with its low-growing, woody, oily, inflammable plants (that burned for days on Arne) – has everywhere shrunk. Across southern England, heath-land has receded by more than 70 per cent over the last 200 years. Agriculture, afforestation, development have all chipped away at the heaths. What are left are isolated fragments, adrift from one another. What we do to land-scape is interrupt it. We plant blocks of conifers across the peat bogs of the Flow Country and cut the bog off from itself, squeezing out the moorland specialists, the golden plover, dunlin and merlin. We flood the Upper Tyne and Upper Tywi valleys with water and forestry until the land no longer recognises itself. Lives, land-scapes are interrupted.

If MacGillivray could have afforded to include his water-colours of birds in his *History of British Birds* would that have changed things for him? Would it have changed how his work was received? Would the paintings not have stilled the reviewers who so dismissed the books, their classification scheme, MacGillivray's 'affected' prose, almost everything about the work, even the 'spirit' of the 'Practical Ornithology' sections (his fieldwork notes), which, to my mind, soar with spirit and show how he – William MacGillivray – was one of the finest field naturalists this country has ever known? If MacGillivray had been able to include, for instance, his life-size painting of a grey heron or his watercolour of three linnets perched on a beech sapling, would that not have stopped the critics in their tracks? How might his paintings have rescued him?

The American ornithologist and great bird artist John James Audubon said this of MacGillivray's paintings:

In short, I think them decidedly the best
representations of birds I have ever seen, and have
no hesitation in saying, that, should they be engraved
in a manner worthy of their excellence, they will
form a work not only creditable to you, but
surpassing in splendour anything of the kind that
Great Britain, or even Europe, has ever produced.
Believe me always your sincere friend, John J.
Audubon.

Audubon, who leaned on MacGillivray, needed him, needed MacGillivray to help him write his *Ornithological Biography*, the accompanying text to his illustrated *The Birds of America*. Audubon, who came knocking on MacGillivray's door in Edinburgh one day in October 1830 looking for help. And MacGillivray agreed to assist Audubon with his work and correct his manuscripts, his wobbly English and hazy scientific descriptions of the birds for a modest fee of two guineas per sheet of sixteen pages.

The collaboration between Audubon and MacGillivray that ensued was the coming together of an ornithological dream team, the two great American and Scottish ornithologists of the age working together in a haze of bird skins, paper and ink. Audubon starting work early, MacGillivray joining him later in the morning but then working on late into the night. And they worked at such a pace, columns of manuscripts rising up around them. The pair were consumed – swamped – by birds; at night they dreamed of nothing else. They worked like this, on and off, for the next nine years until Audubon's five-volume *Ornithological Biography* had been completed. In the gaps between writing Audubon travelled back and forth between the United States (to procure more bird specimens) and Britain (to write and garner subscriptions for his book). After each field trip to America, Audubon would return to Edinburgh – the engine room – and seek out MacGillivray to resume the writing again.

They would bicker about technicalities, classification, the correct order to arrange the birds. But despite the occasional quarrel and the sheer intensity of the work, the pair became very close friends, working together, walking together, shooting birds together. MacGillivray named one of his sons after Audubon; Audubon named two species of American birds after MacGillivray, *MacGillivray's shore finch* and *MacGillivray's warbler*. Their sons, John MacGillivray and John Audubon, also became friends. John MacGillivray once crashed through the Audubons' Edinburgh home breaking a glass case that housed one of Audubon's birds. If Audubon disapproved of this clumsiness, he and MacGillivray must surely, on another occasion, have secretly approved when their sons were caught poaching together in Ravelston Woods outside Edinburgh and had their guns confiscated by the keeper.

If MacGillivray was not adequately acknowledged by Audubon for his part in the *Biography*'s completion, well, that is MacGillivray for you ... self-effacing, not especially concerned with accreditation. But subsequently others have acknowledged that MacGillivray's role was crucial, that without his contribution the *Ornithological Biography* could not have become the great founding work of American ornithology that it is. The American ornithologist Elliott Coues attempted to set the record straight when he wrote of Audubon's *Biography*:

> MacGillivray supplied what was necessary to make his [*Audubon's*] work a contribution to science as well as to art.

But Audubon was not ungrateful. In the entry for *MacGillivray's warbler* in the *Ornithological Biography*, Audubon wrote:

> I cannot do better than dedicate this pretty little bird to my excellent friend William MacGillivray Esq. I feel much pleasure in introducing it to the notice of the ornithological world, under a name which I trust will endure as long as the species itself.

Still, MacGillivray's name has not endured. He has slipped from view, his books and paintings have slipped from view. And *MacGillivray's shore finch* was later renamed the *seaside sparrow*. Audubon, by contrast, is renowned the world over and his paintings sell for vast sums today.

In his introduction to volume V of the *Ornithological Biography*, Audubon wrote:

> Allow me also to mention the names of a few friends to whom I shall ever feel most deeply indebted. The first on the list is William MacGillivray, and I wish you, Reader, and all the world besides, knew him as well as I do.

I envy Audubon greatly, that he knew William MacGillivray so well.

The hobby is still here, hunting over the heath. Fast and low, charging straight up, then down again to skim the heather. Sometimes he hangs a while in the air not unlike a kestrel. But never for long and he is always off again running into the wind. As the sun drops lower I see the hobby more sharply: white face, black hood, grey-black dorsal, a faint rusty orange high up on the underside of the tail and around his legs. Every time he turns into the low sun I can see the mottled white patterns of his breast and the reds below his chest.

When the hobby passes close to the young kestrels in their pine-tree nest, the kestrels call to him. They must confuse him for their parent, that sharp-winged falcon shape. They are roughly – kestrel and hobby – a similar size, though the hobby appears a little smaller when he perches briefly on a fence post. He seems to shrink into himself then, much as I've seen sparrowhawks do when they are also perched.

I clamber out of the heather and walk over to the woman still sitting on the bench behind me. *Fast as a peregrine!* is the first thing she says to me. She has lived in the village for fifteen years, she says, and has never seen anything as impressive as this hobby's display. We stand there together for a while in the middle of the heath. Then the woman is turning to head for home, *Goodbye, well that was very special, wasn't it ...*

I don't want to leave. I think the hobby is still out there, but the light is hopeless now. The last thing I see before I go is an egret flying slowly up from the shore, crossing the heath in front of me, heading for the wood to roost. A slow, heron-heavy flight, porcelain white. As the egret passes in front of the pine trees that skirt the heath, the bird suddenly brightens, becoming whiter against the dark backdrop of the pines.

XIV

Buzzard
River Teign, Devon

MacGillivray leaves Buxton on the Friday at twelve o'clock. It is one of those rare days when he is immune from melancholy. Crossing the high hills of Derbyshire he feels like he is soaring there and, for the first time on his marathon, he senses he is closing in on London.

Buxton to Derby: 34 miles
Derby to Leicester: 26 miles
Leicester to Northampton: 32 miles
Northampton to London: 66 miles

Up on the hills, that day, he sees: skylark, rook, starling, hedge sparrow, pied wagtail, wren, chaffinch, magpie, yellowhammer.

That night, in a scruffy, smoky lodging house outside Ashbourne, MacGillivray sits up late, smoking, comparing Scots Gaelic to Irish Gaelic with an Irish pedlar, then trying out his Latin on a young Italian salesman to see how the Italian and Latin words relate to one another. How these sister languages fit inside each other is not dissimilar to the ways that different species of birds coincide and resemble one another. Through his dissections, his close observations of anatomy, plumage, diet and behaviour, MacGillivray tries to see how the birds converge and form a passage into one another. In *Descriptions of the Rapacious Birds* he writes:

The genera Circaetus and Harpyia connect the eagles and osprey with the buzzards, while the Morphni would seem to unite them with the asturs. But of the birds that occur in our country, none are intermediate between the eagles and buzzards.

The next morning, two miles from Ashbourne, the musk mallow is in flower, and further on MacGillivray finds the ivy-leaved toadflax growing on a bridge. In Derby he buys bread and cheese and eats it in a field where water figwort is showing. He leaves Loughborough at three o'clock and the air is sharp with frost. There are vines growing up the sides of houses with tiny embryonic grapes. Field-mouse-ear chickweed, black horehound and common creeping cinquefoil all delay him. It is a day of sudden bursts of light: a glint of green beside a stream is a kingfisher and, in the dusk, as MacGillivray passes through Leicester, he sees, briefly, the Aurora borealis dancing, lighting the clouds to the north. Later it begins to rain and he finds a barn and buries himself in a heap of straw with his knapsack for a pillow. But it is far too cold to sleep and around two o'clock he gets up and continues walking. The dark propels him as if he had somehow grown much lighter. Figures loom towards him through the darkness and he flinches as they pass, but nobody tries to hassle him and he seems unaware how intimidating he must have seemed to others on the road, what with bits of straw still sticking to him and his knapsack swelling – doubling – his size in the dark. At first light the land is under frost and MacGillivray shoves his hands (he lost his gloves three weeks ago) deep into his pockets to muffle them. His feet ache and he is dizzy with weakness. The next milestone is the 80th from London.

Bread for breakfast and, cutting it with his knife, MacGillivray slices his thumb to the bone. Near Northampton he finds specimens of common nightshade, greater knapweed, dwarf mallow. And that evening, despite walking 51 miles without sleeping, he is able to write this wonderful sentence in his journal:

Flora still continued to smile upon me and in the
evening I found the Common Traveller's Joy which I
examined in the Inn.

The inn is at Grafton Regis between Northampton and
Stoney Stratford. That night MacGillivray sleeps under
warm blankets and wakes at nine. Fifty-eight miles to
London and he only has thirteen pence halfpenny left.
So onwards without eating and the hard road is gnawing
at his feet. His shoes and stockings have dismantled
themselves and he has become such a ragged, hobbling
thing. He buys some bread to chew and by midnight he
is passing through St Albans. He lies down under a tree
and tries to grab a few hours' rest, but then he is up again
and crawling on – cocks crowing – a herd of oxen swaying down the road – still 18 miles to London – heavy rain
– threepence halfpenny remains, he can hear the coppers
sloshing in his pocket – a bite of bread – an apple – god,
how his feet ache – how his thumb aches – his clothes
are soaking – it is still raining – his long blue coat is
heavy with rain – soon after midday MacGillivray is staggering through Highgate – 838 miles since he left
Aberdeen – his knapsack, his 'machine', so stuffed with
specimens of plants it looks like he has grown some
strange herbal appendage on his back … Jolting, grimacing, dreaming the final mile into London.

Buzzard

The upper and fore part of the cere is bare, but its
sides are covered with bristly feathers, which are
downy at the base; the space between the bill and eye
is pretty closely covered with radiating bristly
feathers, slightly downy at the base; the sharp
projecting eyebrow bare; the edges of the eyelids
furnished with ciliary bristles. The plumage in
general is full and soft, but rather compact and glossy
above, although the margins are loose. The feathers of
the head are small and narrow, those of the neck
larger and more rounded, of the other parts broad and
rounded; but the plumage has not, as some allege, any
decided resemblance to that of the owls, being, in
fact, as firm as that of the goshawk, and, in proportion
to the size of the birds, as that of the eagles.

Coming down the lane in the car through blue June
warmth. Just before we splash through the ford I see the
buzzard.

- Boys, look up!
- What is it, Dad?
- A buzzard, can you see it?

I stop the car.

A commotion in the high branches of an oak. The
leaves obscure what is happening but there is a screech
and flash of magpie. Then a glimpse of buzzard, 20 feet
away, trying to untangle something from the tree.

- What is it, Dad?
- Is it an eagle?
- There it is!

We see the buzzard detaching itself from the branches and the thing dangling from its talons gives the buzzard a different profile in the air: a limp, black shape only identifiable as a fledgling magpie because the two adult magpies are in the field beneath the tree, bobbing, yikkering with distress.

Buzzard
The bill is black, near the cere greyish-blue, its soft
edges yellow; the cere and bare space over the eye
greenish-yellow; the irides yellowish-brown; the feet
bright yellow, the claws like the bill.

From Dorset I turned west then south to Dartmoor. I wanted to walk along a stretch of the river Teign and follow the river from its source high up on the moor down through its wooded, buzzard-rich valley to the east.

I reached Chagford in the early afternoon and set off walking over Meldon Hill to the south of the village, weaving through banks of gorse, ponies parked in amongst the gorse, stubs of granite around the summit. Coming down off the hill into deep, high-banked lanes; sunken, subterranean pathways, you cannot see out of them until you pass a gateway cut into the side of the hedge. It's only then you catch a glimpse into one of the small fields that flank the lanes. Those fields seemed so remote, enclosed by their tall, thick hedgerows. In one of the fields I glimpsed, through its gateway, a flock of rooks and jackdaws, the jackdaws noisy in their squeaky chatter, bobbing around the larger rooks.

Then, climbing out of the lanes, approaching the moor, and up ahead a buzzard rises from the verge. It grows in flight! Huge, broad, long-fingered wings unfolding. It lands a little further up the road on a wooden telegraph pole and I sit down on the bank to watch. The dark creosoted pole accentuates the bird's greys and whites. Its grey face twitches and bobs, scanning the field in front. Then it is dropping from its perch in a low glide. Lands in a hunched pounce, talons first, stabbing at something in the grass. Misses: is quickly up again, this time landing on another pole further up the road.

Just as the kestrel hangs inside the air – hovers there – the buzzard, so often, hunts statically, scanning the ground from its perch in a tree, on a pole or fence post, waiting, listening for a vole to crinkle the grass below. And so often, as with so many British raptors, it is field voles (short-tailed voles) that a buzzard is hunting. Voles (particularly during the winter months) are a staple of the common buzzard's diet. If not voles, then: rabbits, insects, moles, frogs, earthworms, carrion, road-kill and, during the breeding season, fledgling birds. Insects (grubs and beetles especially) are also consumed in large quantities by buzzards. As are rabbits, notably in spring and early summer, when buzzards need to hunt through all the long daylight hours to provide for their young.

Rabbits and voles are to the common buzzard what wasps are to the honey buzzard. Without these crucial prey species the common buzzard would struggle to rear its young successfully.

The buzzard is both a static hunter, a hoverer and a low-level searcher. Sometimes I have seen buzzards poised in strong wind like a kestrel, their carpal joints pushed forward, their wings braced back so that the bird assumes a tight, streamlined shape, nothing like the broad, upcurved wings and fanned tail of a soaring buzzard. Other times I have watched buzzards hunting low and fast across the ground much like a golden eagle. And seen them too hunting like a hawk, swerving fast through woodland. The buzzard seems capable of taking on the hunting guise of many different birds of prey.

High-up soaring buzzards are not hunting. They are displaying, marking their territory, making the most of a rising thermal. The smaller, lighter male can rise more quickly than the female; often, when you see a pair of soaring buzzards, they are layered, one above the other, with the male invariably the higher bird. When the pair come together, as for example when the male swoops down at the female in his spectacular display flight, the difference in size between the sexes is clear. Soaring buzzards often call to one another and their calling will sometimes draw in other buzzards from adjoining areas to join their circling flight. On a still day their calls travel far. Cliffs ricochet a buzzard's call, making it sound sharper; woods soften and dampen the call; valleys carry it along their alleyways, extending it. A buzzard's call is among the most beautiful sounds I know.

A hunting buzzard is altogether different, capable, despite the buzzard's reputation for sluggishness, of astonishing bursts of speed. Many times I have been taken aback by a buzzard's turn of speed and on several occasions have wished-mistaken a buzzard into a hawk because it was flying so fast through the trees. Once, in a wood near my home, a bird rushed past me just 10 feet away and landed on the long thick branch of an oak. In the moment between it brushing past me and landing, before I could focus my binoculars, I was convinced, because of the speed with which it had shot into the wood, and because of the bird's size, it must have been a goshawk. But no, it was a buzzard, an adult, who, as soon as he touched down on the branch, was joined by a juvenile. The adult bird dropped some prey on the branch then quickly left. The young bird picked up the prey item in its beak, swallowing it whole.

Buzzards will also hunt on foot and, even when on the ground, can surprise you with their speed. They will graze through a field on damp early mornings for earthworms, or stand beside a mole run and wait for the earth to quiver, sprinting across to grab the mole where it surfaces.

I sit on the bank for half an hour watching the buzzard hunting from its perch on the telegraph poles. Head bobbing, judging the distance and angle of its swoop. Then: launch, glide, pounce, stabbing at something in the grass before returning to its lookout on one of the poles. On it goes like this. When the buzzard finally flies off, I get up and follow the small road west into a large conifer plantation. The wood is dripping, glittering from a recent heavy shower. The rocks and trunks are coated in moss; in places, where the light reaches the wood's understory, the moss emits a brightness, a green luminescence. Then I am out of the wood and dropping down a slope and I can see the headwaters of the North Teign in front of me, deep-pooled, fast and black. I walk down to the river, pick it up like a path, and follow it up onto the moor.

South-west, due west, north-west: erratic thing you are up here, river, trying to figure out a way off this vast granite plateau. I am looking for a place to camp the night near the river's source when I see another buzzard, querying the moor grass, hunting low like a harrier. And for a moment I mistake it for a harrier until I can see the bird is definitely a buzzard, a shape-shifter, flying much lower than I'm used to seeing, but the broadness of its wings – the sheer bulk of the bird – gives it away.

An hour later the moor is cooling fast and in the dusk light, sitting outside my tent, I have a wonderful, unexpected visitor. A merlin lands on the stone dyke just 12 feet away. If, that is, you can say a merlin ever really lands, ever settles properly. It is a bird that is always on the point of leaving, a quivering pause before it springs off again. Sharp-pointed wings, forked behind her like a swallow. Hello merlin, how good to see your shape again … Please don't go just yet … But when I shift my binoculars a fraction she is off, fast and low over the moor. Hello-goodbye-gone! Messenger from Orkney and The Flows and the winter marshes of Sheppey. Almost at the end of my journey and what a gift to have it linked up like this, a line drawn by a merlin from Orkney all the way to Devon.

In the morning: thick, cold mist. I can see only a few yards around my tent. The end of September and the high moor is already in another season. The moor has drifted so far ahead into autumn it has become inexplicable to the land – the *in-country* – below. A pony comes out of the mist like an apparition and wanders through the reeds in front of me. Its mane is beaded with dew, its coat is a tinny, bracken-red colour. I will not see any birds until this mist has burnt off, so I strike camp and walk on up the river to try to find its source.

London is: MacGillivray getting out of his drenched clothes; his feet exhaling; collapsing at the home of Mr Cowie, 31 Poultry (whose address MacGillivray had been given by his friend, Dr Barclay); washing his feet with warm water; opening a letter from his aunt, Mary MacAskill from the Isles; his feet are barely recognisable, they are so pale and crinkled they seem mummified; 838 miles since he left Aberdeen; *what a queer sort of dream this journey of mine has been*; then sleep and sleep and waking at nine into (oh bliss!) fresh clothes.

Before he heads out to explore the city he remembers he has forgotten to mention in his journal the plants he examined on the outskirts of London. And I am amazed in the blur and agony of those final miles he had the wherewithal to even notice these things:

> I forgot to mention in its proper place that I had examined on Tuesday the Blue Bramble Rubus caesius. It occurred in several places by the road, and I eat a great quantity of its berries which I find delicious and quite unlike those of the Common Bramble Rubus fruticosus which are most nauseous. Yesterday I found and examined another plant by the road near the fifteenth milestone, the Wild Succory. The Small Bindweed I found very common, but it is out of flower. I have now finished my journey and I am satisfied with my conduct.

London is: snowing heavily on the night of 22 October 1819; MacGillivray walking everywhere; climbing the Monument and peering out across the city through the smoky air; paying three shillings to visit the sad collection of animals at the Exeter Change menagerie; stopping to listen to a young girl singing in the street; dipping inside Westminster Abbey and MacGillivray coming out grumpy and angry at all the monuments to generals and admirals (what about the scientists and poets, he cries!).

Monday 25 October, 1819. MacGillivray is one of the first through the doors of the British Museum when it opens its rooms at eleven o'clock. He gravitates past the displays of minerals and shells towards the collection of British Birds, which has a room all to its own. What happens to MacGillivray in that room? He has walked all the way from Aberdeen to here, for this. It is an important moment. For ornithology, as significant, surely, as MacGillivray's meeting with Audubon. What is important about the time MacGillivray spends drifting through the collection is that it gives him confidence. He realises that his own self-taught theories of ornithology are accurate, that his intuition about these things is correct. That knowledge gladdens him, warms him inestimably. The ways the birds have been arranged according to their genera are much as he would have arranged them (though he also feels he could improve on the museum's system). What is most significant about his visit to the museum is that MacGillivray comes away from it knowing for certain that this is what he must do with his life. He *must* study the natural world but, above all, he knows that this approach – the sterility of the museum, all those specimens locked behind their glass cases – that approach is not for him. If he is to study the natural world, it must be out there – *he* needs to be out there – immersed, on the interface with nature:

> I felt my love of Natural History very much increased
> by the inspection of the museum. At the same time I
> felt convinced that to study nature I must have
> recourse to nature alone, pure and free from human
> interference.

What MacGillivray writes in the closing pages of his journal, he does not need to. Already – for some time now – he has achieved what he aspires to:

> Ornithology is my favourite study and it will go hard
> with me if I do not one day merit the name of
> ornithologist, aye, and of Botanist too – and moreover
> of something else of greater importance than either.

The mist is clearing above Whitehorse Leat. The first inkling, a thinning where the sun is a faint laser trying to burn through. Then, quite rapidly, the mist is being disassembled and I can see a tor's rubbled top, its clitter spill. Then I see the sharp spruce edge of Fernworthy running down the long back of White Ridge.

There is a kestrel over the ruins of Teignhead farm. Below the kestrel, downstream beyond the clapper bridge, a buzzard is rising. Though he may take on the hunting guise of so many different birds of prey, this morning, soaring above the river, the buzzard is himself, calling his high echoing call that is unlike any other raptor's. Sometimes I think I can detect a *w* or *p* sound in a buzzard's call: *wee-ooe* or *pee-ooe*. The first syllable usually short, followed quickly by a longer, wavering *ooe* sound. Other times, though I try to decipher it, I cannot hear any 'letters'. It is just two high notes with the second note sounding – feeling like – a reverberation of the first. It is always unmistakably a buzzard but the call (that second note especially) can vary in length and pitch. Sometimes that note is left to carry, other times it is brought up short and raised in pitch. Occasionally the first note is so short-lived the call feels like one long note, rather than two in quick succession. In late summer, while they are still in the vicinity of the nest and being fed by their parents, juvenile buzzards call a great deal and their call is distinctive, sounding longer, sharper, higher-pitched than the adult bird's. This morning, above the moor, the buzzard's call lingers on and on with an echo's resonance as if the bird is testing – using its voice like sonar – to gauge the depth of the valley.

Buzzards call in aggression, agitation, in courtship, to ward and warn off other buzzards. They are tenacious in their defence of territory and pursuits and squabbles with trespassing buzzards are vociferous affairs. Kestrels call often too with their high trilling whistle, but I don't think any other bird of prey is as conspicuous by its call as the common buzzard. Often you will hear a buzzard before you see it. How different, in this respect, the buzzard is to the largely silent golden eagle. I have watched buzzards flanked and jostled by a mobbing raven, the buzzards calling in what sounds like annoyance or frustration. The call always sounding shorter, more agitated, when the buzzard is being mobbed like this. Most of the time a buzzard's calling is prompted – is a part of – the bird's territorial display. A buzzard calling while it soars above its patch is like an acoustic 'beating of the bounds' of its parish; the long-drawn-out calls carry to the boundaries where they reverberate then settle.

Cattle are out along the side of Great Varracombe. I walk through them as I climb the bank up to Teignhead farm. Campfire pits in amongst the ruins, their ashes congealed to a black mulch, rain-prints dent the ash. A small shed with a rusty, sphagnum-coloured, corrugated-iron roof. The walls of the old farmhouse are huge, thick slabs of granite. How many ruins have I rummaged through on this journey? That abandoned house far out on the Caithness flows; the empty shell of Coventry cathedral; the chequered black and white floor tiles that were all that remained of Lord Leverhulme's home on the side of the hill above Rivington; the view from the open window of the abandoned croft on Oronsay across to the hills of Ardnamurchan ... It is strange how a ruin can pull you in, compel you towards it from miles away.

What happened here at Teignhead? The farm's build- ings were substantial: a large courtyard with its own walled-in dung-pit, a sheep-dip, paved paths leading out to the moor, clapper bridges laid across the brook and river ... A leat is cut to carry water from the hill to a well outside the front door. Gateposts are quarried from the rock on Magna Hill and left there until a fall of snow allowed them to be strapped to sleighs and sledded down to the farm. Seventeen eighty, the first tenant moves in. Sometimes the farm is cut off by snow for weeks. But even more than snow, it is the mists that cut the place off, stubborn, heavy mists that will not shift, that snag over the farm for days on end. It is as if the moorland bogs somehow engineer the mists, breathe them into being. By 1808, 1,551 acres of the farm have been enclosed and the long stone walls that have been built across the moor (one of these is where I had seen the merlin) are causing offence to the Gidleigh commoners who feel their rights and access to the common grazing lands are being encroached. Eighteen seventy-six, the incumbent tenant is evicted by the landowner, the Duchy of Cornwall, because the tenant's rent is in arrears. Nineteen forty-two, the land is requisitioned by the War Office and troops move in for training exercises. The following year, 1943, the last tenant leaves Teignhead farm (bundled out with some compensation from the War Office) and goes to live with a relative in Chagford. As happened at Arne during the war, the military take over the area completely. But unlike at Arne, after the war was over and the army had left, nobody moves back to Teignhead. By 1950 the place is in a bad state, the enclosure walls have begun to split, the buildings disfigured by the wind and vandals working off each other.

What happened at Teignhead is what happened to Leverhulme's summer home on the moor above Rivington. It is the same trajectory, the same story. Encroachment is followed by retraction, and before you know it the place is crumbling and the moor has crept back in again. What happened to Teignhead is also what happened to the hill farms of the Upper Tyne and Upper Tywi. There is an inevitability in the way it ends for these upland farms, as if these places endure a different level of gravity, as if something is constantly pushing down on them so that in the end it becomes impossible to cling on up there.

Dartmoor has always been drawn over, sculpted, its surface etched with standing stones and monoliths. Its granite outcrops are beautifully irregular and the wind like a potter continues to work at them. More recently, the peat (no longer accumulating on the high blanket bogs because of climatic shifts) has begun to shrink. The ensuing erosion looks as if someone has torn chunks out of the ground, pools and canyons weaving around islets of peat.

In the nineteenth century a great redrawing of the moor took place. Stone dykes were erected and charged off into the distance. Rapidly the moor was repatterned, made linear. On Dartmoor the term for this newly enclosed land was 'newtake' and by the end of that century the northern part of the moor had been completely severed from the southern by newtake walls. Inevitably, there were disputes: occasionally you still come across walls on Dartmoor that suddenly peter out, where the commoners had managed to assert their grazing rights and halt the enclosure. Besides these enclosures made by the larger tenant farmers (as at Teignhead), many small enclosures were made by the commoners themselves, appropriating, parcelling off tiny pockets around the edge of the moor. Often these small enclosures were thrown up in a single night, claimed and asserted in the same way that the 'one-night houses' in the marginal lands of rural Wales were.

Debatable, Batable, Disputed ground ... Every seven years on Dartmoor parishioners go out to beat the parish bounds. The boundaries themselves are often hazy, fluid, contentious things. It is not so clear-cut where the moor (the Forest) and Common divide. And boundaries can be porous, shifting lines. So every seven years people from the parish walk out along these boundaries, repairing, extending, adjusting the lines. Traditionally it is an exercise conducted in a spirit of subversion and the purpose, wherever possible, is to infringe anything imposed by the landowner. As they circumnavigate the parish, whenever the party arrive at a significant boundary marker, the custom is for the oldest man in the group to pick up the youngest boy, flip him upside down, and tap the youngster's head on the boundary marker to ensure that the younger generation stores, and does not forget, the position of the border.

MacGillivray wrote:

> A river is nothing but a continuous series of
> continually renewed drops of water following each
> other in a groove.

But when I drop down off the moor and pick the river up again in the shade of the woods, it is unrecognisable. All that moorland energy has dissipated, it has settled into itself. It has become a river of deep pools and sandy beds, a hoarder of leaves and branches, tucking them under its rocks to store there. And fish hang in its pools like shards of mica.

For the rest of the day I follow the river eastwards. Often it does not want to be seen, hidden under dark banks of rhododendron, contour-screened. And that is fine, I am just as happy to follow its sound-road, to veer away but to stay within earshot. The path deepens as it drops down from the moor, becomes a cutting, almost a tunnel. Holly and gorse line the high banks on either side. Badger runs criss-cross the path, I can see their claw marks in the soil where the bank is steepest. A buzzard drops from a tree and swoops low and fast through a narrow gap in the hedge. Its face is a light grey colour; wings and back a sandy brown. Again, I am struck by the huge bird's agility and turn of speed. A tussle through the hedge-gap with a crow: then gone.

The way frost peels and recedes across a field until there is just a small pocket, a corner of the field, which the low winter sun cannot touch and where the frost sleeps all day, that is what happened to buzzards in the nineteenth century. They were exterminated from lowland Britain, peeled back, like the red kite (and for the same reasons as the kite), to the corners, the fringes of these islands. Devon and Cornwall, the New Forest, parts of Wales, the West of Scotland and North West England held remnant populations of buzzards. That the buzzard has crept back across most of the rest of the country (becoming our most common bird of prey), spreading east, colonising old lowland haunts, is a remarkable turnaround, explained by a new era of tolerance and by the buzzard's adaptability, its versatility to both a variety of habitats and a variety of prey.

Bird of woodland, bird of farmland, bird of moorland, wherever these places meet and mix. The ideal buzzard habitat is one which contains a bit of each. Mixed, irregular farmland is ideal. A monochrome landscape is not so good, at least when it comes to breeding success. The buzzards I have watched closely hunt especially over the brambly, rabbity, vole-rich, unkempt no-man's-lands, the steep banks and field edges that are so important to so many birds of prey.

And buzzards, too, will often lead you to other birds, often other birds of prey. They are such a conspicuous, vocal bird. When you see a buzzard it frequently draws your eye to something else that has been drawn in by the large bird's wake. I have watched a sparrowhawk displaying in early spring beside a rising buzzard, seen kestrels and ravens and other corvids (especially ravens) sparring with buzzards. Throughout this journey buzzards have been a helpful guide, more often than not standing in for other raptors I have been searching for, but sometimes, too, helping me to find these other birds.

Downstream, in deep woods, the valley narrowed to a gorge. I'm trying to make out the mix of leaves gyrating slowly, a slack flotilla in the river's current: beech and birch, maple, alder, oak, some pheasant feathers in amongst the leaves. What is flushing the pheasant poults out of the trees and across the river? Something is panicking them. There is a Coke can floating in the shallows. I wade out to retrieve it and the water is lovely and cool on my moor-weary feet. An otter has left its tarry spraint, bitty with tiny bones, on a mossy boulder. A buzzard has started calling somewhere above the river.

To be stilled – stopped – that is what birds of prey do to me. There is a phrase particular to Dartmoor: *The Ammil*. It describes the phenomenon, occasionally witnessed on the moor in winter, when everything exposed to the air, every blade of grass, every rock, every twig, becomes encased in ice. The Ammil is the thaw put on hold, paused for a while. The temperature suddenly drops below freezing and the thawing, dripping, running world is held in check, suspended, so that everything, even the great rocky outcrops of the tors, is sheathed in ice. *Ammil*: from *ammel*, the Old English term for enamel, to encrust, to coat with a vitreous sheen. A rare event. The moor is decorated, it glistens. The land is stilled, and to witness it is also to be stilled.

XV

Sparrowhawk

Home

Home is: three doors down from the end of a street on the edge of a small village. The street ends at a kissing gate. The gate leads through to a grassy field, boggy around the gate, rising quickly to a steep bank. Hawthorn, elder, gorse and bramble grow along the bank, sporadic oak and ash trees too. Bracken dominates the western end. In May, before the bracken takes over, there are thousands of bluebells. I love the range of colours along the slope, there always seems to be a brightness there: the elder in flower, hawthorn blossom, the pink rosebay willowherb. Even in winter there is yellow on the gorse. Foxes have their den deep within the gorse. Ravens nest in a Scots pine windbreak above the slope. At the eastern end, where the trees thicken to a spinney, there is an ancient badger city, a lumpy quarried place. Roe and muntjac use the bank for cover. Fallow make channels through the bracken in summer. From the field – from the washing line in my back garden – the top of the bank forms the horizon. Sometimes a swollen moon seems to snag itself on the bank as its huge pale dome rolls along the horizon. The soil is heavy clay. The field is full of wounds, the slightest rain sets it weeping.

To the west of the field there is a large wood. A medieval bank marks its edge. Ancient ash stools, like eroded gargoyles, line the bank. Dog-rose and bramble form a hedge between the wood and field. The wood stretches west for nearly a mile and goes through different belts of trees: larch, spruce, sweet chestnut, the occasional colossal beech, its trunk black with rain seep. But here, in the corner closest to the field, it is mostly oak with hazel coppice. Ash grows around the wood's edge and there are some dark pools of holly in amongst the hazel understory.

For many months I walked all over the wood and further into the fields beyond looking for sparrowhawks. I walked miles searching for the birds. But my technique was all wrong. They are like ghosts, sparrowhawks, they cannot be tracked or followed; they appear from nowhere in a rush of speed and then they are gone. Sparrowhawks operate in a different dimension from other birds of prey. They live in the pocket of air that hugs the surface of the land. Quick and low, they cut the ground like a scythe.

Still, I pursued my wanderings through the wood and fields. Sometimes I came across a hawk's plucking post and occasionally – more rarely – there was a snatched glimpse of hawk disappearing through the trees. In deep summer, when the wood droned with the sound of hoverflies, I often heard the sharp begging calls of young sparrowhawks. All these things encouraged me into thinking I was getting closer to the birds. But that was never true: with every rare encounter the hawks would briefly shimmer then dissolve. Always, though, the encounters, when they happened, were breathtaking. Once when I was walking down the side of a field towards a brook there was a movement 10 feet away. Rising out behind a bramble thicket beside a gate was a female sparrowhawk, wings spread and tail opened in a fan as she rose. I could see the dark striped bars running across the underside of her tail. As she climbed above the thicket she dropped something, a grey shape. I waded through the brambles and there, next to the gate, was the body of a pigeon, head missing, a deep red gash down its breast.

Most encounters happened when I was not looking for the birds. Early one morning, putting a bag in the boot of the car, the quiet street suddenly interrupted by a clatter of pigeons and in their wake a sparrowhawk sheering over the kissing gate. I would sometimes see sparrow-hawks when I was driving slowly through the village. Once I pulled the car up beside a hawk I had seen land on a neighbour's wall, so close I could see the speckled patterning on her breast and the yellow flash of her eye. Another time – an astonishing encounter – a hawk flashed low in front of my car and slid over a garden gate. The hawk looked like it was going to collide with the front of the house, but at the last moment it shot straight up, glanced over the roof, and dropped down into the back garden. I had never seen any bird steer itself past objects at such speed. No bird I know flies this fast and low.

Sometimes garden birds would warn me of a hawk approaching, chaffinches and great tits at a garden feeder suddenly ratcheting up their anxious chatter. Sure enough, three seconds later, there was a male hawk swooping across the lawn and, as he rose to clear a hedge, I could see the rusty orange flecks that lit his breast.

In early spring the washing line is a good place to watch. On a fine day in March I sometimes see sparrow-hawks displaying above the bank. My elderly neighbour often pauses by the fence to chat while I hang the washing out. I like to linger there as much to talk to him as watch for birds. Sometimes he brings offerings from his garden: potatoes, small thick cucumbers, delicious red and yellow tomatoes. Grass snakes lay their eggs beneath the empty plastic compost bags in his greenhouse. He walks slowly and explains his hip is no good since a shire horse backed into him when he was young as he was leading the horse through a narrow gate. His anecdotes animate the field, the bank and the wood beyond. Tanks, he tells me, were parked at the bottom of the garden during the war and tested on the bank's steep gradient. The army camped in the wood and bartered sugar and tea for vegetables from his parents' garden. He remembers a Wellington crashing on the bank and he and his classmates rushing out of school and up the hill to find the plane on fire. I ask if he remembers the bombers coming over on their way to Coventry. He nods and tells me that there used to be a farmer who kept a few chickens up on the hill above the village. One night during the war a German bomber returning from a raid (and needing to jettison an unused bomb) must have seen the light from the farmer's torch glittering as he locked the chickens up. *Missed by a mile, thank God, but for a long time you could see the hole made by the bomb up there.*

Often, while we chat, buzzards run the gauntlet of the raven's airspace above the bank. A raven's loud, rapid croaking usually indicates a buzzard has appeared. Recently red kites have settled in the area and I see them almost daily now, their ash-grey heads conspicuous as the birds perch on top of a bare winter ash. I doubt these birds have been seen over the wood for two hundred years. Very occasionally I hear one calling, a high thin whistle, thinner than a buzzard's call. The kites appear taller than the buzzards when they perch, their long folded wings give them a longer back. Perched and silhouetted against the sky, the kites can seem huge; clear winter skies seem to magnify them.

William MacGillivray's home on Harris is a ruin now, the buildings from his uncle's farm commandeered for a sheep fank, a maze of gates, walkways and holding pens. The floor of the fank is littered with scraps of wool. The ruin sits on the lower slopes of Ceapabhal, looking east across the great expanse of Scarista Sands and north to the mountains of Harris. This was MacGillivray's childhood home and somewhere on Ceapabhal's rocky neck was the pit where he concealed himself to shoot the golden eagle. The low walls of the ruin are blotched with amber-coloured lichen, nettles grow in the cracks between the stones. The lush machair runs down from the ruin to the beach, its seed-heavy grasses pricked with yellow, white and purple flowers: eyebright, red clover, birdsfoot trefoil … A smaller ruin, 40 feet by 12, stands to the side of the old steadings. It is being used to store coils of fencing wire. Sections of its walls have been patched with mortar. Meadow pipits, with their streaked breasts, flicker along the top of the wall. The way the pipits blend into the backdrop of the stones, when the birds skitter about the ruin, it looks as if the wall itself is trembling.

From MacGillivray's Hebridean journal:

Monday 10th November, 1817
Today I rose early, drank warm milk at the gate as
yesterday – then walked along the shore of Tastir,

over Traigh-na-clibhadh, and along the rocks to the upper end of Moll-na-h-Uidhadh, then crossed Ui to the great sand, and returned along its margin. In this course the birds seen were the Starling, among the cattle and in the corn-yard, the Shag on the coast, the Common Gull in South town and on Ui, the Great Black-backed Gull on Moll-na-h'Ui, the Curlew on Ui in large flocks, the Wren on the marsh dyke of Ui, the Meadow Pipit on the shore, the Hooded Crow on Ui, the Raven on Fastir, and the Ringed Plover on the sands …

I have determined to describe all the birds found in Harris & shall fall to work immediately. In the evening I went to Moll to search the shores for shell-fish …

Wednesday 12th November, 1817
… The description of birds should be made in the following order. Name, (Linnaean, English, Gaelic) Description proper, very minute. Bill, feet, irides, general colour, dorsal, sternal, colours, habitation, migration, nuptials, nidification, ovation, incubation, education, food, use. Bill, dimensions, colour, shape, nostrils, tongue, shape, colour, mouth colour, eyes, appendages – feet, legs, shape, colour &c. toes number, nails.

Monday, 27th April, 1818
… I have not yet seen an account of the Birds of Britain with which I am entirely pleased; and I have

of late been thinking upon the subject. Perhaps it might not be a mad scheme to attempt the Ornithology of Scotland. I certainly would not engage for more. But whether this alone would be acceptable I cannot yet determine. However I shall begin to note every particular regarding it, which I can observe, or collect from creditable authority. The time I occupy in this will not be misspent, even at the worst. For I will thus perhaps acquire habits of attention, observation, and activity.

After his visit to the British Museum, MacGillivray left London on 28 October, returning to Aberdeen by sea. He did not have enough money for a cabin and took passage instead in the misery of the ship's forecastle. Perhaps someone took pity on him there or he pleaded a discount, for after two uncomfortable days he was upgraded to a cabin and arrived back in Aberdeen on Saturday 6 November, 1819. The return journey by sea was about 450 miles. In all, since he walked out of his front door in Aberdeen two months earlier, MacGillivray had covered 1,288 miles.

From Aberdeen to Gretna: 501 miles
From Gretna to London: 337 miles
838 miles
From London to Aberdeen by sea: about 450 miles
In all: 1,288 miles

The last entry he writes in his journal:

My journey is now finished. I arrived here early on Saturday the 6th after a disagreeable passage of ten days from London in the smack Expert. I am again plunged into the gulf of actual existence, and I can scarcely brandish a quill. Sapient remarks and practical conclusions, and resolutions sine fine should now be made, but all these fine things I must defer till I have another journey …

Vanity of vanities – all is vanity. What profit hath a man of all his labour which he taketh under the sun? For he that increaseth knowledge increaseth sorrow.

For the next few years, after the walk to London, it is hard to keep track of MacGillivray. There are hints here and there of his whereabouts. The plant specimens he collected, carefully labelled with a date and location, offer clues as to his wanderings. Scotland in the 1820s becomes triangular for him and he seems to have travelled regularly between the three points of that triangle: Harris, Aberdeen and Edinburgh. Harris is where he hones his fieldwork, where he *hammered at the gneiss rocks, gathered gulls' eggs, and shot plovers and pigeons* … and where, in September 1820, he marries his aunt's younger stepsister, Marion McCaskill.

Edinburgh in the 1820s is where he has not yet settled into himself. He attends the lectures of Professor Jameson, who held the Regius Chair of Natural History at Edinburgh University. And Jameson must have seen something in MacGillivray, something glinting there, because MacGillivray becomes Jameson's secretary and assistant in 1823 and he is also put in charge of Jameson's substantial Museum of Natural History. A dream job, a kid in a candy store: the museum held specimens of birds, rocks and minerals in their thousands. And for a few years MacGillivray is pin-down-able, working at the museum, testing his knowledge, starting to publish papers in journals on all aspects of natural history from geology to botany to ornithology. There are drawings from this period MacGillivray made of microscopic fossil sections which are beautiful in their precision. He becomes fluent in conchology, in mineralogy and lichenology (in a lovely phrase in his book *A Natural History of Deeside* he wrote that he was *especially addicted to Lichenology*). He meets Darwin (then a student at Edinburgh University); to Darwin, MacGillivray appears a bit uncouth, a bit ragged-looking: *He had not much the appearance and manners of the gentleman* ... But the two absorb themselves in natural history talk and Darwin, in his autobiography, remembers MacGillivray as being *very kind to me* and giving him some rare shells for his own collection.

In 1826 there is another lurch, another breakout from the city. Perhaps the museum and/or Jameson had become too stifling, perhaps the claustrophobia of the museum grated at him. Whatever the reason, MacGillivray quits working for Jameson, flits the city to continue his *observations in the fields* ... And for a few years he disappears, lost to the hills. Income, often precarious for MacGillivray, is perhaps most insecure during this period; by 1829 he has five children and he is trying to support both them and his fieldwork through what he calls *my labour in the closet*, editing, translating, piecemeal writing.

Eighteen thirty is an important year for MacGillivray. He is settled back in Edinburgh and books and papers start to come in a flurry. His writing begins to take on the pace of his walking. In 1830 he publishes a revised edition of Withering's *A Systematic Arrangement of British Plants*, which he abridges from four volumes into one. *Lives of the Eminent Zoologists, From Aristotle to Linnaeus* quickly follows this. Then a translation from the French of *Elements of Botany and Vegetable Physiology* in 1831. In September 1830 he is appointed to the role of Conservator of the Museum of the Edinburgh Royal College of Surgeons. The following month, October 1830, John James Audubon knocks on his door to ask for MacGillivray's help in writing his *Ornithological Biography*.

The 1830s are a giddy blur of work for MacGillivray: by the end of the decade he will have published thirteen books. How he manages to juggle everything seems extraordinary. His work for Audubon, and especially his work at the Museum of the Royal College of Surgeons, is hugely demanding. At the same time there is his teaching, editing, journal publications, fieldwork, his painting and draughtsmanship. And despite all of these commitments he somehow manages to pull together what he considers his proper work. *Descriptions of the Rapacious Birds of Great Britain* is published in 1836. It is the warm-up act for what follows, his monumental five-volume *A*

History of British Birds. Volumes I–III are published between 1837 and 1840. The final two volumes are published in 1852, the same year MacGillivray died.

The breakthrough in my search for sparrowhawks came in late summer when I found a feather. For several weeks I had been coming across the aftermath of hawk kills, the downy snow of pigeon feathers sprayed across a path or snagged in a hedge. On one occasion a goldfinch, tiny black and yellow feathers in a bright wet pile at the edge of a field. There was a pattern to these kills. The hawks were hunting in a radius which took in a corner of the wood, the field and the back gardens along my street. So I slowed my wanderings down to concentrate on this area. Then one evening, walking along a track, I found a scattered bloom of pigeon feathers; not that many, but enough to suggest hawk work. I wondered if the attack had been aborted, if the sparrowhawk had swiped but failed to grip the pigeon. The way the pigeon's feathers were smeared across the track suggested this.

Many sparrowhawk attacks are aborted, the majority fail. Juvenile hawks, especially, can misjudge prey and attempt to tackle birds that are too large. A woodpigeon is too heavy for a sparrowhawk to carry far and only female hawks are large enough to tackle such heavy prey. Female sparrowhawks are substantially larger than males, the size difference between the sexes greater than in any other British raptor (males weigh around 150 g, females around 290 g). Such is the difference in weight that female sparrowhawks are known to occasionally kill and eat males. Sometimes a female sparrowhawk can lump a pigeon a short distance, but she would not be able to fly more than a few feet above the ground with such a load. So usually pigeons are plucked and eaten close to where they are killed, the tell-tale sign a circle of feathers spread around where the hawk has worked. Sometimes a large prey item such as a pigeon will not be killed outright and the hawk will simply pin it down and begin to eat while the pigeon is still alive. There are several accounts of sparrowhawks being disturbed at their plucking and their prey then flying, stumbling away.

In amongst the pigeon feathers on the track was a sparrowhawk's feather, a primary, with a deep notch and narrow leading edge. Pale white at the base along the trailing edge, brown towards the top. The reverse side much paler than the front. Five brown bands running across – interrupting – the feather's white, the hint of a sixth at the top but too faint to make out against the darker brown. I wondered if the hawk had lost the feather in the maelstrom of the attack. I picked the feather up and took it home with me.

Finding the feather was the culmination of feeling that I was always a step behind the hawks, always arriving just after they had left. So I decided, as I had done with the sea eagles on Oronsay, to stop my wanderings and instead sit tight and wait for the sparrowhawks to come to me. Twice a week, just before first light, I would position myself at the end of the track where I had found the feather, tuck myself in to a tall hedge, and wait. From there I had a clear view of the eastern and southern edges of the wood and also a large swathe of the canopy where the wood stretched away from me to the north and west.

In 1841 MacGillivray is upgraded. It is about time. By the end of the 1830s he has written himself tired. His great friend Audubon has returned to America for the last time. Money is still a struggle and by 1841 there are nine children (two have died in infancy, William and Marion's tenth and last child is born in 1842). The first three volumes of *A History of British Birds*, pummelled by the critics, are a flop and his publishers are stalling on bringing out the final two volumes. There are hints of the impact of these pressures expressed in a letter MacGillivray wrote to Audubon in 1836:

> You desire to know how I am 'going on with the world.' The world and I are not exactly as good friends as you and I, and I am not particularly desirous of being on familiar terms with it. I have got rather into difficulties this year, but I do not exactly know the state of my affairs, and must take a few days among the hills by myself before I can understand how I am situated.

The godsend, in 1841, is that MacGillivray is appointed to the Regius Chair of Civil and Natural History at Marischal College in Aberdeen. The appointment is a hugely impressive coup for MacGillivray. Competition for the post is fierce but MacGillivray gets the nod and his family move from Edinburgh to Aberdeen, to the city of his birth.

Aberdeen is: MacGillivray walking everywhere, walking his students out of the lecture hall and into the fields and hills. Now in his late forties, he teaches on the move. Students who were taught by MacGillivray recall always struggling to keep pace with him on those outdoor lectures. His advice to one student on an excursion: *Keep your knees bent as you climb a mountain. You thus avoid having to raise your body at each step.* If you passed MacGillivray walking along the street in Aberdeen between his home and college, sometimes to St Machar's Cathedral, where he loved to sit and listen to the scriptures being read, you would notice a small, thin man walking quickly. Lately he has been walking so much and sleeping so little his clothes have become loose about him. Eyes fixed on the ground in front, he would not look up as you passed one another. Usually alone, to bump into him by mistake would be to nudge the greatest ornithologist in Europe into polite apologies and earnest concern for you. He was deeply (unusually so for the time) concerned for his students. One of them wrote of MacGillivray's teaching:

His interest in the habits of his students was remarkable. If he saw a good student careless he would remonstrate with him privately; while earnest attention gained his favour. With his rapid power of observation he could detect even a temporary lapse from diligence. His lectures were carefully written out, and he dictated an epitome of them once a week. Now and then he gave out a subject for an essay, say 'The Sparrow,' and he indicated a preference for a paper bearing on its habits and life on the street and on the wing. As an examiner he was patient, tender and gentle, unwilling to say an angry word. He would rather help out the hesitating student; but it was easy to see that carelessness was an abomination to him.

His lectures are so popular students and members of staff from different faculties enrol to hear them. His pupils come to him, as if he were some sort of oracle, with specimens of rock and mollusc for MacGillivray to identify for them.

In Aberdeen MacGillivray's writing is re-energised and books and papers start to flow again. *A Manual of British Ornithology* in 1842 (revised and published in a new edition in 1846); *A History of the Molluscous Animals of the Counties of Aberdeen, Kincardine and Banff* in 1843; a revised edition of Thomas Brown's *The Conchologist's Textbook* in 1845; *Portraits of Domestic Cattle of the Principal Breeds Reared in Great Britain and Ireland* in the same year. In the summer of 1850, aged fifty-four, MacGillivray makes a six-week field trip to the valley of the Dee and the Cairngorms to study the geology and botany of the region. His son Paul, and latterly one of his daughters, Isabella, accompany him and together they climb the mountains, collecting plants from the high corries.

A year after the trip to the Cairngorms MacGillivray's doctor orders him to spend the winter of 1851–2 in Torquay, rather than expose his fragile health to the blasts of an Aberdeen winter. From Torquay, he writes in the preface to volume IV of *A History of British Birds*, finally published in early spring 1852:

> As the wounded bird seeks some quiet retreat where,
> freed from the persecutions of the pitiless fowler, it
> may pass the time of its anguish in forgetfulness of
> the outer world, so have I, assailed by disease,
> betaken myself to a sheltered nook, where,
> unannoyed by the piercing blasts of the North Sea, I
> had been led to hope that my life might be protracted
> beyond the most dangerous season of the year. It is
> thus that I issue from Devonshire, the present
> volume which, however contains no observations of
> mine made there, the scenes of my labours being in
> distant parts of the country.

While he is still in Devon, MacGillivray's wife, Marion, dies suddenly in Aberdeen in February 1852, aged forty-seven. Audubon had died a year earlier in America. MacGillivray's health deteriorates further and he returns home to see out his final days in Aberdeen. Volume V of *A History of British Birds* is published in the summer of 1852; in its conclusion MacGillivray writes:

Commenced in hope, and carried on with zeal, though ended with sorrow and sickness, I can look upon my work without much regard to the opinions which contemporary writers may form of it, assured that what is useful within it will not be forgotten, and knowing that already it has had a beneficial effect on many of the present, and will more powerfully influence the next generation of our home ornithologists. I had been led to think that I had occasionally been somewhat rude, or at least blunt, in my criticisms; but I do not perceive wherein I have much erred in that respect, and I feel no inclination to apologise. I have been honest and sincere in my endeavours to promote the truth. With death, apparently not distant, before my eyes, I am pleased to think that I have not countenanced error, through fear of favour. Neither have I in any case modified my sentiments so as to endeavour thereby to conceal or palliate my faults. Though I might have accomplished more, I am thankful for having been permitted to add very considerably to the knowledge previously obtained of a very pleasant subject. If I have not very frequently indulged in reflections of the power, wisdom and goodness of God, as suggested by even my imperfect understanding of his wonderful works, it is not because I have not ever been sensible of the relationship between the Creator and his creatures, nor because my chief enjoyment when wandering among the hills and valleys, exploring the rugged shore of the ocean, or searching

the cultivated fields, has not been in a sense of His
presence. 'To Him who alone doeth great wonders,'
be all glory and praise. Reader, farewell.

William MacGillivray dies in Aberdeen on 8 September
1852; he is fifty-six.

MacGillivray's writing, for me, is a *way* of seeing. He
misses nothing. And he misses nothing out in his descriptions of the birds. His accuracy is so unflinching I use his
guides to the birds to check and identify what I see (or
think I've seen) in the field myself. He brings the birds
into view, his descriptions more acute than any illustration or photograph. Sometimes I just want to hand everything – how to find the birds, identify them, how to write
about them – over to him.

If, sometimes, he appears daunting and off-putting, to
an extent he brings this on himself. In the preface to
volume V he describes his ambition for *A History of
British Birds*:

Accordingly, each of our many ornithologists, real
and pretended, has a method of his own, one
confining himself to short technical descriptions as
most useful to students, another detailing more
especially the habits of the birds, as more amusing to
general readers, a third viewing them in relation to
human feeling and passions, a fourth converting
science into romance, and giving no key to the
discrimination of the species, bringing his little

knowledge of the phenomena under the dominion of imagination, and copiously intermingling his patchwork of truth and error with scraps of poetry. The plan of this work is very different from that of any of these and is not by any means calculated to amuse the reader who desires nothing more than pleasant anecdotes, or fanciful combinations, or him who merely wishes to know a species by name. It contains the only full and detailed technical descriptions hitherto given in this country. The habits of the species are treated of with equal extension in every case where I have been enabled to study them advantageously. The internal structure has been explained in so far as I have thought it expedient to endeavour to bring it into view, and, in particular, the alimentary organs, as determining and illustrating the habits, have been carefully attended to. If imagination has sometimes been permitted to interfere, it has only been in disposing ascertained facts so as to present an agreeable picture, or to render them easily intelligible by placing them in relation to each other.

Resolute, ambitious, impatient of others who did not share his approach (some just found him rude), he did not exactly court the favour of his fellow ornithologists. So it's not surprising that they, in turn, relished the opportunity to lay into MacGillivray when *A History of British Birds* was published. But his writing – his approach – is never as austerely technical as his preface to volume V implies. And although MacGillivray may not approve of *converting science into romance*, he himself turns science into poetry on every page. Describing a night-time walk returning from Loch Muick, *a moderate weight of granite specimens* rattling in his pockets, MacGillivray reached up towards the clear sky, and wrote:

> One beautiful cluster of stars I put into my vasculum among the plants.

At a ceremony held on Tuesday 20 November, 1900 in the Natural History classroom at Marischal College, Aberdeen, several people who had been taught by him and some who had latterly been inspired by his work assembled to pay tribute to William MacGillivray and to erect a tablet in his memory. Many subscribers, among them former students and relatives of MacGillivray, contributed to the cost of the memorial tablet, and at the same time they commissioned the granite tombstone which was erected above MacGillivray's grave in the New Calton cemetery in Edinburgh. For forty-eight years, before the monument was commissioned, MacGillivray's grave had simply been marked with the letters W. M. on the grave's lower cornerstone. So the ceremony at Aberdeen, and the commissioning of the gravestone in Edinburgh, was an attempt to secure William MacGillivray's legacy, to halt the slide into oblivion. One of those who spoke at the Aberdeen ceremony, Professor Trail, who had studied MacGillivray's work whilst a student at Aberdeen University, addressed the gathering:

> I did not know Professor MacGillivray personally, but I have learned to know him in a way that, I think, perhaps not very many know him, through his works; and through these I have learned to revere the man and to love his memory ...

The last to speak was Professor J. Arthur Thomson, then the Regius Professor of Natural History at Aberdeen University:

> Every one in Britain who cares much about birds does, in a real sense, know MacGillivray, for he left a lasting mark upon ornithology. May I explain in a minute why one says so. It is because, until 1837, no one in Britain had seriously tried to found a classification, or natural system of birds except upon external characters; while MacGillivray – a trained anatomist – got far beneath the surface and showed that a bird is not always, nor altogether, to be known by its feathers ...

Add to these tributes: Alfred Newton's comments in his book *The Dictionary of Birds*:

> I may perhaps be excused for repeating my opinion that, after Willughby, Macgillivray was the greatest and most original ornithological genius save one

(who did not live long enough to make his powers known) that this island has produced.

One night MacGillivray dreamt that four hooting owls dropped down his chimney, alighted on his dissecting table and began to rummage about in the midst of all his books and papers:

They [*the owls*] had probably been attracted by the odour emanating from a Buzzard's skull which I had recently dissected.

In his dream the owls proceed to bicker and complain about what they find on MacGillivray's desk. They criticise his work as being too preoccupied by technicalities, as not inhabiting – not sufficiently imagining – their lives:

'Nothing here but dry sapless stuff. MacGillivray's Raptors, etc' observed one of the owls; 'Gutts and gizzards' quoth another, 'fit only for Turkey vultures' tedious technicalities and objectless digressions,' shrieked the third. 'Besides' said the fourth, 'the fellow ought to imitate us, he has no respect to the majesty of nature …'

The dream ends abruptly when, as MacGillivray recalls,

Hardly knowing to laugh or cry, I awoke.

The owls are far too harsh on MacGillivray, he is anything but the tedious technician they dismiss him as. His genius, as Professor Thomson stated in his memorial address, was to get *far beneath the surface* of the birds. And it is not solely through his anatomical scalpel that he achieves this. Much more so, it is the way MacGillivray responds to the birds, the way he describes them in their natural setting, the ways he uses language to get *far beneath* the birds and lift them into being:

A flight of sandpipers is a beautiful sight; there they wheel around the distant point, and advance over the margin of the water; swiftly and silently they glide along; now, all inclining their bodies to one side, present to view their undersurface, glistening in the sunshine; again, bending to the other side, they have changed their colour to dusky grey; a shot is fired, and they plunge with an abrupt turn, curve aside, ascend with a gliding flight, and all, uttering shrill cries, fly over the stream to settle on the shore that settles out towards Barnbogle ruins.

The great loss is that some of MacGillivray's writing has not survived. There are three journals in existence: one that records the year he spent in the Outer Hebrides between 1817 and 1818; one that records his walk from Aberdeen to London in 1819; and another which records a journey he undertook while working for the Museum of the Royal College of Surgeons, who commissioned him to visit and report on other museums in Scotland, England and Ireland in 1833.

Though only three survive, everything points to MacGillivray having kept a journal throughout his life. He spent his whole life walking, exploring the natural world; it seems improbable that he did not keep a written record of these expeditions. In his book *The Natural History of Deeside* he describes an incident where he is suddenly enveloped in a thick mist on the summit of Ben Macdui. In order to describe the mountain in more detail, MacGillivray then quotes in the book from the notes he made in his *1830* journal in which he had sketched an outline of the geology and appearance of Ben Macdui:

> Now this Ben-na-muic-dhui on which we now stand
> 'consists,' as I find recorded in my journal of 1830, 'of
> a huge rounded mass of granite, which on the
> western side, towards the summit, presents a corry
> formed by a semicircular range of precipices, the
> rocks of which are marked by nearly perpendicular
> fissures, with transverse rents, covered toward the
> base by débris, and sloping into a small lake named
> Lochan-Uaine (green little lake), the waters of which
> are singularly clear, and have a bluish-green tint,
> which has a remarkable effect as contrasted with the
> ordinary tints of the Scottish lakes. On these
> precipices, as well as on other parts of the mountain,
> patches of snow remain unmelted during the
> summer and autumn. On the opposite side the
> mountain declines irregularly toward the head of

Loch Aain, terminating in a magnificent range of precipices.'

So there is proof that he kept a journal in 1830. But I'm sure there must have been shelves of his journals stretching right back to 1817 (the year he began his Hebridean journal), perhaps earlier. And I'm sure, too, that MacGillivray must have drawn on his backlist of journals as he might an encyclopaedia, to shake his memory, to check the name of a plant he had momentarily forgotten.

In the Hebridean journal of 1817–18 MacGillivray mentions a long walk he plans to make once he leaves Harris, walking through Skye, the Western Highlands and the far north of Scotland. If he did manage to complete that walk it is a great shame his journal of it does not survive. I would have loved the chance to read his account of these landscapes, their extraordinary geology, their birds and plants. To have MacGillivray as a guide to these unique, dramatic landscapes: what a thing that would have been.

The assumption is that after MacGillivray's death his son, Paul, took all of his father's journals and papers with him when he emigrated to Australia and that the journals were later destroyed in a fire there. If this is indeed what happened to MacGillivray's journals then it is a tremendous loss to the natural history writing of these islands. But read them – those journals that have survived – and, like Professor Trail in his memorial address, you cannot help but *to revere the man and to love his memory.*

Sparrowhawk
There it comes, silently and swiftly gliding, at the
height of a few feet, over the grass field, now shooting
along the hedge, now gliding over it to scan the other
side, and again advancing with easy strokes of its
half-expanded wings. A beautiful machine it is
certainly, and marvellously put together, to be
nothing but a fortuitous concourse of particles, as
some wise men, believing no such thing themselves,
would have us to believe. As if suspecting the
concealment of something among the grass, it now
hovers a while, balancing itself with rapid but gentle
beats of its wings, and a vibratory motion of its
expanded tail; but, unable to discover any desirable
object, away it speeds, bounds over the stone wall,
and curving upwards alights on that stunted and
solitary ash, where it stands in a nearly erect posture,
and surveys the neighbourhood.

From now on, this is my routine. I slip into the hedge at
the end of the track while it is still dark and watch the
light rinse the field. Who is here? First up, a roe deer and
her well-grown calf. They are wading back through the
high dewy grass towards the wood. The calf is skittish,
all sprints and feints around its mother. It is September
and their pelts are a deep red, turmeric and umber
colour. Next come the kestrels, a pair, flying low across
the field, chittering, yattering, chasing each other. Then
pigeon after pigeon, breaking from the wood at speed.
Each sudden burst of pigeon briefly holds the possibility

of a hawk hidden in its shape. But it never is, and when it comes the hawk is altogether something else. Different shape, different poise, different bent: hawk, it could not be anything else. The sparrowhawk lands on the dead branch of an ash tree on the edge of the wood, quivers there. Straight away, like a conjuror's hat trick, another hawk is pulled out of the wood and lands beneath the first. When it lands it tips the other hawk from its perch and then the pair of them are off, skittering, chasing after each other through the trees.

The next half-hour is a whirl of hawks, flickering, twisting, speeding through the trees around the edge of the wood, careering through the branches. Glimpses of them: racing, swerving through the foliage, dark long-winged shapes. Here they come again, one after the other, popping out of the wood to perch together in the ash tree. But too restless to stay there for long, they are off again skidding through the trees. They move so quickly it's hard to get the colours of their plumage right but the impression is of a mostly brown dorsal and a pale breast. I also find it hard to judge if they are a pair, a male and female. I presume they are and that I have just caught them emerging from their roost in the wood. But, again, the speed at which they chase after each other makes it hard to appreciate the size difference between the sexes. I notice, when the birds are perched, how they blend in amongst the brown clumps of dead ash key seeds, I keep mistaking the seeds for hawks.

A kestrel comes in. He is much stiffer in flight than the hawks, sharper, narrower-winged, nothing of the hawks' fluidity. The sharp angles of his wings make him seem a little larger than the sparrowhawks. The kestrel lands at the top of the ash tree and his tail bobs up behind when he lands, as if the action of the tail balances his landing. Immediately the hawks join him, shuffling around on the lower branches. For a while I watch a laddering of raptors: kestrel – then hawk – then hawk below.

The sparrowhawk is not a specialist. It does not rely on a particular prey species, as the honey buzzard does with wasps or the kestrel with field voles. It is, however, an avian specialist, as its diet is almost entirely made up of small to medium-sized birds. Some small mammals are taken, young rabbits early in the season, field voles especially in plague years, bank voles in the woods. But live birds predominate. It is also, like its larger accipiter relative, the goshawk, a woodland specialist, able to pursue prey at speed through the narrow airspace of a wood. A wide variety of bird species are predated: everything from wren (rarely) to woodpigeon (often). But locally, certain species will provide the bulk of the sparrow-hawk's diet. Fledgling songbirds in June and July are crucial. Sparrowhawks synchronise their nesting to coincide with the availability of songbird fledglings, and without this glut of vulnerable prey in the summer months the hawk's ability to breed successfully would be severely impaired.

Important prey species in the British Isles include starling, chaffinch, song thrush, blackbird and woodpigeon, especially in spring and summer; fieldfare and redwing in winter. Birds of deep cover like the wren and blue tit are far less vulnerable to sparrowhawk predation than more conspicuous species of open spaces like the robin and redwing. Vocal, displaying songbirds in springtime are especially vulnerable. Male hawks take a higher proportion of smaller prey species than the females. The males also tend to hunt in more concentrated woodland; female hawks tend to range further afield and hunt in more open landscapes.

The sparrowhawk is not the efficient predator of garden birds we tend to assume it is; its prey species are efficient at avoiding it. Alarm calls warn of a hawk's approach and give the chance for smaller birds to seek cover – about three seconds is all they need to make their escape. With the slightest head-start most birds will escape, as the hawk cannot follow them into dense foliage. A woodpigeon can outfly a sparrowhawk with relative ease. Once its prey has put sufficient distance between itself and the hawk, the sparrowhawk does not waste its energy and, unlike a merlin, usually gives up the pursuit. The hawk's agility does not always mean it can outmanoeuvre smaller, more agile prey. Starvation is a major cause of mortality for sparrowhawks, especially between March and April, the hungry gap, when winter migrants have left these islands and summer migrants have not yet arrived.

Sparrowhawks can be a major cause of mortality for certain birds during certain narrow windows in the year. These windows are defined by the stage of abundance and vulnerability of the prey. So fledglings, when they have just left the nest, are at their most vulnerable to predation. Despite this heavy predation, as Ian Newton explains in his great study of the raptor, there is no evidence that sparrowhawks have any long-term effect on the size of their prey's population. In other words, if the hawks were removed from the environment, there would be no noticeable increase in their prey species. In the absence of their major predator, other mortality or 'controlling' factors, starvation in particular, would come into play on these birds. The best evidence for this occurred when sparrowhawks *were* removed from large parts of the British countryside in the late 1950s and early 1960s through poisoning by organochlorine pesticides. During this period, despite the absence of their major predator, the songbird population remained the same. Neither, when sparrowhawks returned to the ecosystem, was there any noticeable decline in their prey species.

To catch its prey the sparrowhawk relies on stealth and surprise. It uses obstacles, hedges and walls for instance, to conceal itself, at the last minute rushing up over a hedge to attack prey on the other side. It flies as close to the ground as possible and conceals its approach by flying, when conditions allow, with the sun behind it. I have seen a sparrowhawk fly so low up a road in front of me there seemed to be no visible gap between bird and tarmac.

The reason you rarely see sparrowhawks is because to hunt – to survive – they rely on concealment. Sparrowhawks can (more rarely in Britain than on main-

land Europe) suffer predation themselves, so concealment also helps to negate this risk (goshawks, peregrines
and tawny owls have all been known to kill sparrowhawks). If a hawk perched on the top of a tree like a
kestrel does, every songbird in the neighbourhood would
yell: *Hawk!* The sparrowhawk must always be just out of
sight; that is where you will find them.

I am in the hedge before dawn. I'm glad of the track, the
way it allows me to avoid the wood, to slip into the hedge
without waking the wood. I'm just in time to catch the
change of shift: a muntjac crossing the field, heading
back to the wood; crows and jackdaws, coming the other
way, pour from the trees like black smoke.

The early morning soundscape (in this order): tawny
owl, the screech-echo of a pair; jackdaw chatter; a moorhen's alarm from the moat behind the track; a raven's
croak; pheasant (very loud inside the wood) sets off
another pheasant a whole field away; a buzzard calling
on the soar; a magpie's rattle ... Next comes the staggered departure from the roost: crows and jackdaws the
first to leave in their tatterdemalion flocks, magpies in
their slipstream, then the kestrel, keeking, wide awake.

The dawn itself is split between the buzzard-light,
which is a murky pre-dawn light, and the hawk-light,
which comes soon after dawn. The buzzard is always out
of the roost before the hawk, hunting when there seems
barely enough light to see in. It is only when the light has
really broken through, cleaned and sharpened the edges
of the wood, that the sparrowhawk comes out of the trees

from its roost, silent, quick, broad-winged. Sometimes a single hawk, sometimes a pair, chasing each other low across the field, turning knots through one another, playful, sinuous like otters. Usually just a fleeting glimpse: the hawk bursts out of the trees, shoots low across the field and is gone.

But that brief glimpse is enough. I long for it, and long to get back to the hedge. Some mornings I do not see the hawks, but because they use the wood to roost, I often catch the birds when they depart at dawn. And so, over the weeks and months, I build up a store of hawk sightings, a steady accumulation of wonder. One morning I return to the hedge to find it has been cut right back by a tractor's hedge cutter: it is almost unrecognisable, a shredded, splintered mess. I feel miserable and a little silly that I have become so possessive of a hedge. But I realise it will grow back and thicken up in the spring and there is still space for me to slot in and conceal my shape.

There are some mornings when the wind seems to get inside the birds. Jackdaws are bundled out of the wood in erratic, swirling columns. Pigeons pour out of the trees in their hundreds. A red kite comes over high and fast through the dawn with the wind behind it. A tiny goldcrest is made larger – rounder – by the breeze puffing out its feathers.

A hawk goes up from the wood, squabbles with a crow, then dives fast and steep back into the centre of the wood. Then she is climbing again, spinning up from the trees. She banks slowly around above the wood and out across the field. Another hawk joins her there and they reel together high above the village.

Because I am so absorbed in watching the hawks, I do not notice that a deer has walked right up to me. So when I look down, I am astonished to see her: a diminutive muntjac, just three feet away, her black eyes staring at me. I freeze, but the deer hasn't got a hold of me, hasn't seen me properly. The hedge, despite its crew cut, seems to still disguise me. The muntjac ambles past; stiff, stumpy gait, lumpy brown coat. Then my scent pricks her: she kicks her hind feet up, and bucks away across the field, white rump flashing as she goes. When she reaches the wood she slows to a trot, glances back, barks, then hurries on into the wood. For a while I can see her white tail signalling, like a light fading inside the trees.

I leave the hedge and walk back along the muddy track. Blackbirds are out along the path, scraping through the leaf litter. A moorhen makes a dash for cover. Through the gate, turn right, and up the street. Coat off, kettle on, binoculars back in their case.

Upstairs, on my desk, I keep a jar of feathers – kestrel, magpie, buzzard, pheasant – keepsakes from the fields and wood. My children also bring me feathers they have found, knowing that even a bedraggled pigeon feather fished from a drain will make me smile. The collection keeps growing; sometimes, when the light inside the room is thin and closing, it looks as if my desk has grown a wing.

Through the window three magpies have lit up the pale winter lawn. In the branches of the apple tree – the old, gnarled Russet – a clump of mistletoe is a ball of green light. There is a faint hum inside the room; the fan on my laptop, which I barely notice, has noticed one of the feathers – a buzzard's – and is breathing gently against it. The downy barbs around the feather's quill shiver and lift.

Bibliography

I Hen Harrier

Armstrong, Edward A. – *The Folklore of Birds* (Dover, 1970)

Balfour, Edward – 'Observations on the Breeding Biology of the Hen Harrier in Orkney' (*Bird Notes*, 27, no. 6, 177–183, no. 7, 216–224, 1957)

Barkham, Patrick – 'The mystery of the missing hen harriers' (*Guardian*, 13 January 2015)

Berry, R. J. – *Orkney Nature* (T. & A. D. Poyser, 2000)

Bevis, John – *Direct from Nature: The Photographic Work of Richard and Cherry Kearton* (Colin Sackett, 2007)

Cuthbert, Olaf – *Eddie: An Orkney Ornithologist Remembered* (Felix Books, 2005)

Eagle, Raymond – *Seton Gordon: The Life and Times of a Highland Gentleman* (Lochar, 1991)

Fenton, Alexander – *The Northern Isles: Orkney and Shetland* (John Donald, 1978)

Firth, John – *Reminiscences of an Orkney Parish* (W. R. Rendall, 1974)

Gordon, Seton – *Thirty Years of Nature Photography* (Cassell, 1936)

— 'Bird Photography 70 Years Ago' (*Country Life* Magazine, 8 April 1976)

Hamerstrom, Frances – *Harrier, Hawk of the Marshes: The Hawk that is Ruled by a Mouse* (Smithsonian Institution Press, 1986)

Hedges, John W. – *Isbister: A Chambered Tomb in Orkney* (B.A.R. 115, 1983)

— *Tomb of the Eagles: A Window on Stone Age Tribal Britain* (John Murray, 1987)

Kearton, Richard – *With Nature and a Camera* (Cassell, 1902)

Mackay Brown, George – *An Orkney Tapestry* (Quartet Books, 1978)

Meek, E. R., Rebecca, G. W., Ribbands, B. and Fairclough, K. – 'Orkney Hen Harriers: a major population decline in the absence of persecution' (*Scottish Birds*, 19, no. 5, 290–298, 1998)

357

Morrow, Phyllis and Volkman, Toby – 'The Loon with the Ivory Eyes: A Study in Symbolic Archaeology' (*Journal of American Folklore*, 88, no. 348, 143–150, 1975)

Pitts, M. – 'Flight of the Eagles' (*British Archaeology*, 86, 6, January–February 2006)

Rainey, Froelich – 'The Ipiutak Culture at Point Hope, Alaska' (*American Anthropologist*, 43, no. 3, 364–375, 1941)

Redpath, S. M. and Thirgood, S. J. – *Birds of Prey and Red Grouse* (Stationery Office, 1997)

Scott, Don – *The Hen Harrier: In the Shadow of Slemish* (Whittles, 2010)

Scottish Natural Heritage – *Substitute Feeding of Hen Harriers on Grouse Moors: A Practical Guide* (SNH, 1999)

Scrope, William – 'Days and Nights of Salmon-Fishing in the Tweed, with a short Account of the Natural History and Habits of the Salmon, Instructions to Sportsmen, Anecdotes, &c' (*Quarterly Review*, 77, December 1845)

Simmons, Robert E. – *Harriers of the World: Their Behaviour and Ecology* (Oxford University Press, 2000)

Taylor, Timothy – *The Buried Soul: How Humans Invented Death* (Fourth Estate, 2002)

Thomson, David – *The People of the Sea: A Journey in Search of the Seal Legend* (Barrie & Rockliff, 1965)

Watson, Donald – *The Hen Harrier* (T. & A. D. Poyser, 1977)

— *In Search of Harriers* (Langford, 2010)

Whyte, Craig – *The Wildlife of Rousay, Egilsay and Wyre* (Brinnoven, 2004)

Wilkinson, Benjamin Joel – *Carrion Dreams 2.0: A Chronicle of the Human–Vulture Relationship* (Abominationalist Productions, 2012)

Willis, Douglas P. – *Moorland and Shore: Their Place in the Human Geography of Old Orkney* (Department of Geography, University of Aberdeen, 1983)

II Merlin

Avery, Mark and Leslie, Roderick – *Birds and Forestry* (T. & A. D. Poyser, 1990)

Bibby, C. J. and Nattrass, M. – 'Breeding status of the Merlin in Britain' (*British Birds*, 79, no. 4, 170–185, 1986)

Crampton, C. B. – *The Vegetation of Caithness Considered in Relation to the Geology* (Committee for the Survey and Study of British Vegetation, 1911)

Land, Michael F. and Nilsson, Dan-Eric – *Animal Eyes* (Oxford University Press, 2002)

Lindsay, R. A., Charman, D. J., Everingham, F., O'Reilly, R. M., Palmer, M. A., Rowell, T. A., Stroud, D. A. (ed. Ratcliffe, D. A. and Oswald, P. H.) – *The Flow Country: The Peatlands of Caithness and Sutherland* (Nature Conservancy Council, 1988)

Mabey, Richard – *Home Country* (Century, 1990, pp. 119–131, 'Away Games')

BIBLIOGRAPHY

Munro, Henrietta – *They Lived by the Sea: Folklore and Ganseys of the Pentland Firth* (Henrietta Munro and Rae Compton, 1983)

Nethersole-Thompson, Desmond and Maimie – *Greenshanks* (Buteo Books, 1979)

Newton, I., Meek, E. R. and Little, B. – 'Breeding Ecology of the Merlin in Northumberland' (*British Birds*, 71, no. 9, 376–398, 1978)

Nicolaisen, W. F. H. – *Scottish Place-Names* (John Donald, 2001)

Orchel, Jack – *Forest Merlins in Scotland: Their Requirements and Management* (The Hawk and Owl Trust, 1992)

Orton, D. A. – *The Merlins of the Welsh Marches* (David & Charles, 1980)

Proctor, Noble S. and Lynch, Patrick J. – *Manual of Ornithology: Avian Structure and Function* (Yale University Press, 1993)

Ross, David – *Scottish Place-names* (Birlinn, 2001)

Rowan, W. – 'Observations on the Breeding-Habits of the Merlin' (*British Birds*, 15, no. 6, 122–129, no. 9, 194–202, no. 10, 222–231, no. 11, 246–253, 1921–22)

Sale, Richard – *The Merlin* (Snowfinch, 2015)

Stroud, David A., Reed, T. M., Pienkowski, M. W., Lindsay, R. A. (ed. Ratcliffe, D. A. and Oswald, P. H.) – *Birds, Bogs and Forestry: The Peatlands of Caithness and Sutherland* (Nature Conservancy Council, 1988)

Trobe, W. M. – *The Merlin* (Oriel Stringer, 1990)

Withers, Charles W. J. – *Gaelic in Scotland 1698–1981: The Geographical History of a Language* (John Donald, 1984)

Wright, Peter M. – 'Distribution, site occupancy and breeding success of the Merlin (*Falco columbarius*) on Barden Moor and Fell, North Yorkshire' (*Bird Study*, 44, no. 2, 182–193, 1997)

— *Merlins of the South-East Yorkshire Dales* (Tarnmoor Publications, 2005)

III Golden Eagle

Campbell, Laurie and Dennis, Roy – *Golden Eagles* (Colin Baxter Photography, 1996)

Gordon, Seton – *Days with the Golden Eagle* (Williams & Norgate, 1927)

— *The Golden Eagle: King of Birds* (Collins, 1955)

Harvie-Brown, J. A. and Buckley, T. E. – *A Vertebrate Fauna of the Outer Hebrides* (David Douglas, 1888)

Haworth, Paul F., Mcgrady, Michael J., Whitfield, D. Philip, Fielding, Alan H. and McLeod, David R. A. – 'Ranging distance of resident Golden Eagles (*Aquila chrysaetos*) in western Scotland according to season and breeding status' (*Bird Study*, 53, no. 3, 265–273, 2006)

Hunter, James – *The Making of the Crofting Community* (John Donald, 1982)

Lawson, Bill – *The Teampull at Northton and The Church at Scarista: Harris Churches in their Historical Setting* (Bill Lawson Publications, 1993)

Lockie, J. D. – 'The Breeding Density of the Golden Eagle and Fox in Relation to Food Supply in Wester Ross, Scotland' (*Scottish Naturalist*, 71, no. 2, 67–77, 1964)

— and Stephen, D. – 'Eagles, Lambs and Land Management on Lewis' (*Journal of Animal Ecology*, 28, no. 1, 43–50, 1959)

Love, John A. – *Eagles* (Whittet Books, 1989)

Lynch, Michael – *Scotland: A New History* (Pimlico, 1995)

MacGillivray, William – *A Hebridean Naturalist's Journal 1817–1818* (Acair, 1996)

Macpherson, H. B. – *The Home Life of a Golden Eagle* (Witherby & Co., 1909)

Moisley, H. A. – *Uig: A Hebridean Parish* (Geographical Field Group, 1961)

Newton, Ian – *Population Ecology of Raptors* (T. & A. D. Poyser, 1979)

Tomkies, Mike – *On Wing and Wild Water* (Jonathan Cape, 1987)

— *Golden Eagle Years* (Jonathan Cape, 1994)

Watson, Jeff – *The Golden Eagle* (Second Edition) (T. & A. D. Poyser, 2010)

Whitfield, D. P., Fielding, A. H., McLeod, D. R. A. and Haworth, P. F. – *A conservation framework for golden eagles: implications for their conservation and management in Scotland* (Scottish Natural Heritage Commissioned Report no. 193, 2008, [ROAME no. F05AC306])

Whitfield, P. – 'Golden eagle (*Aquila chrysaetos*) ecology and conservation issues' (*Scottish Natural Heritage Review*, no. 132, 2000)

IV Osprey

Abbott, C. G. – *The Home-Life of the Osprey* (Witherby & Co., 1911)

Bagnold, R. A. – *The Physics of Blown Sand and Desert Dunes* (Chapman & Hall, 1971)

Bain, George – *History of Nairnshire* (Nairnshire Telegraph, 1893)

Ball, Philip – *Flow: Nature's Patterns – A Tapestry in Three Parts* (Oxford University Press, 2009)

Brown, Philip – *The Scottish Ospreys: From Extinction to Survival* (William Heinemann, 1979)

— and Waterston, George – *The Return of the Osprey* (Collins, 1962)

Dennis, Roy – *A Life of Ospreys* (Whittles, 2008)

Fenech, Natalino – *Fatal Flight: The Maltese Obsession with Killing Birds* (Quiller Press, 1992)

Forestry Commission Scotland – *The History of Culbin* (Forestry Commission, 2012)

Gordon, Seton – *In Search of Northern Birds* (Eyre & Spottiswoode, 1941)

MacGregor, Alasdair Alpin – *The Buried Barony* (Robert Hale, 1949)

Macpherson, H. A. – *The Visitation of Pallas's Sand-Grouse to Scotland in 1888, together with an account of its nesting, habits, and migrations* (R. H. Porter, 1889)

— *A Vertebrate Fauna of Lakeland* (David Douglas, 1892)

Poole, Alan F. – *Ospreys: A Natural and Unnatural History* (Cambridge University Press, 1989)

Rubinstein, Julian – 'Operation Easter: The Hunt for Illegal Egg Collectors' (*New Yorker*, 22 July 2013)

St John, Charles – *The Wild Sports and Natural History of the Highlands* (John Murray, 1948, first published 1846)

— *A Tour in Sutherlandshire* (David Douglas, 1884)

Thomson, David – *Nairn in Darkness and Light* (Hutchinson, 1987)

V Sea Eagle

Cameron, A. D. – *Go Listen to the Crofters: The Napier Commission and Crofting a Century Ago* (Acair, 1986)

Craig, David – *On the Crofter's Trail* (Pimlico, 1997)

Crawford, Carol L. – *Bryophytes of Native Woods: A Field Guide to the Common Mosses and Liverworts of Scotland and Ireland's Native Woodlands* (Native Woodlands Discussion Group, 2002)

Drever, James – '"Taboo" Words Among Shetland Fishermen' (*Old-Lore Miscellany of Orkney, Shetland, Caithness and Sutherland*, 10, part 6, 235–240, 1946)

Edmondston, Thomas – *An Etymological Glossary of the Shetland & Orkney Dialect; with some derivations of names of places in Shetland* (Adam & Charles Black, 1866)

Fenton, Alexander – 'The Tabu Language of the Fishermen of Orkney and Shetland' (*Ethnologia Europaea*, 2–3, 118–122, 1968–69)

Fraser Darling, F. – *Natural History in the Highlands & Islands* (Collins, 1947)

Gaskell, Philip – *Morvern Transformed: A Highland Parish in the Nineteenth Century* (Cambridge University Press, 1968)

Gelling, Margaret – *Place-Names in the Landscape: The Geographical Roots of Britain's Place-Names* (Phoenix Press, 2000)

Gray, Robert – *The Birds of the West of Scotland, Including the Outer Hebrides* (Thomas Murray & Son, 1871)

Harvie-Brown, J. A. and Buckley, T. E. – *A Vertebrate Fauna of Argyll and the Inner Hebrides* (David Douglas, 1892)

Jakobsen, Jakob – *An Etymological Dictionary of the Norn Language in Shetland* (David Nutt, 1928)

Lodge, George E. – *Memoirs of an Artist Naturalist* (Gurney and Jackson, 1946)

Love, John A. – *The Return of the Sea Eagle* (Cambridge University Press, 1983)

— *A Saga of Sea Eagles* (Whittles, 2013)

McClure, J. Derrick – 'Distinctive semantic fields in the Orkney and Shetland dialects, and their use in the local literature', in Millar, Robert McColl (ed.) – *Northern Lights, Northern Words. Selected Papers from the FRLSU Conference, Kirkwall 2009* (Forum for Research on the Languages of Scotland and Ireland, 58–69, 2010)

Mackenzie, Osgood – *A Hundred Years in the Highlands* (The National Trust for Scotland, 1988)

Macleod, Norman – *Morvern: A Highland Parish* (Birlinn, 2002, first published 1863)

Marquiss, M., Madders, M., Irvine, J. and Carss, D. N. – *The Impact of White-tailed Eagles on Sheep Farming on Mull: Final Report* (Scottish Executive, 2004)

Martin, Martin – *A Description of the Western Islands of Scotland Circa 1695* (Birlinn, 1999)

Morton Boyd, John and Bowes, D. R. (eds) – *The Natural Environment of the Inner Hebrides* (The Royal Society of Edinburgh, 1983)

Murray, W. H. – *The Hebrides* (Heinemann, 1966)

Napier Commission – *Evidence Taken by Her Majesty's Commissioners of Inquiry into the Conditions of the Crofters and Cottars in the Highlands and Islands of Scotland* (Neill & Company, 1884)

— *Report of Her Majesty's Commissioners of Inquiry into the Condition of the Crofters and Cottars in the Highlands and Islands of Scotland. With Appendices* (Neill & Company, 1884)

Saxby, Henry L. – *The Birds of Shetland with Observations on their Habits, Migration, and Occasional Appearance* (Maclachlan & Stewart, 1874)

Scottish Natural Heritage – *Is lamb survival in the Scottish Uplands related to the presence of breeding white-tailed eagles (Haeliaeetus albicilla) as well as other livestock predators and environmental variables: A pilot study into sea eagle predation on lambs in the Gairloch area* (Commissioned Report no. 370, SNH, 2010)

Thornber, Iain – *The Gaelic Bards of Morvern* (Iain Thornber, 1985)

Willgohs, Johan Fr. – *The White-tailed Eagle Haliaëtus Albicilla Albicilla (Linné) in Norway* (Norwegian Universities Press, 1961)

VI Goshawk

Aitken, A. J. – 'Scots', in McArthur, Tom (ed.), *The Oxford Companion to the English Language* (Oxford University Press, 1992)

Diener, Alexander C. and Hagen, Joshua – *Borders: A Very Short Introduction* (Oxford University Press, 2012)

Forestry Commission – *Britain's Forests: Kielder* (HMSO, 1950)

Glauser, Beat – *The Scottish-English Linguistic Border* (Francke Verlag, Bern, 1974)

Jameson, Conor Mark – *Looking for the Goshawk* (Bloomsbury, 2013)

Kay, Billy – *Scots: The Mither Tongue* (Mainstream, 2006)

Kenward, Robert – *The Goshawk* (T. & A. D. Poyser, 2007)

Kenward, R. E. and Lindsay, I. M. (eds) – *Understanding the Goshawk* (The International Association for Falconry and Conservation of Birds of Prey, 1981)

Lamont, Claire and Rossington, Michael (eds) – *Romanticism's Debatable Lands* (Palgrave Macmillan, 2007)

Llamas, Carmen – 'Convergence and Divergence Across a National Border', in Llamas, Carmen and Watt, Dominic (eds), *Language and Identities* (Edinburgh University Press, 2010)

McCulloch, Christine – 'Dam Decisions and Pipe Dreams: The Political Ecology of Reservoir Schemes (Teesdale, Farndale and Kielder Water) in North East England' (D.Phil. Thesis, University of Oxford, 2005)

Macdonald, Helen – *H is for Hawk* (Jonathan Cape, 2014)

Mack, James Logan – *The Border Line: From the Solway Firth to the North Sea, along the Marches of Scotland and England* (Oliver & Boyd, 1926)

Mackay Mackenzie, W. – 'The Debateable Land' (*Scottish Historical Review*, 30, no. 110, 109–125, 1951)

Marquiss, M. and Newton, I. – 'The Goshawk in Britain' (*British Birds*, 75, no. 6, 243–260, 1982)

Neville, Cynthia J. – *Violence, Custom and Law: The Anglo-Scottish Border Lands in the Later Middle Ages* (Edinburgh University Press, 1998)

Northumbrian Water Authority – *Kielder Water Scheme: A Bibliography* (Library and Information Service, 1982)

Robson, Eric – *The Border Line* (Frances Lincoln, 2006)

White, T. H. – *The Goshawk* (Jonathan Cape, 1953)

Wilson, Keith and Leathart, Scott (eds) – *The Kielder Forests: A Forestry Commission Guide* (Forestry Commission, 1982)

VII Kestrel

Baillie, S. R., Marchant, J. H., Leech, D. I., Massimino, D., Eglington, S. M., Johnston, A., Noble, D. G., Barimore, C., Kew, A. J., Downie, I. S., Risely, K. and Robinson, R. A. – *Bird Trends 2012: Trends in numbers, breeding success and survival for UK breeding birds* (British Trust for Ornithology Research Report, 644, 2013)

Dobinson, Colin – *Fields of Deception: Britain's Bombing Decoys of World War II* (Methuen, 2000)

Evans, Darren M., Redpath, Stephen M., Elston, David A., Evans, Sharon A., Mitchell, Ruth J. and Dennis, Peter – 'To graze or not to graze? Sheep, voles, forestry and nature conservation in the British uplands' (*Journal of Applied Ecology*, 43, no. 3, 499–505, June 2006)

Hesketh, Phoebe – *My Aunt Edith* (Lancashire County Books, 1992)

Hutchinson, Roger – *The Soap Man: Lewis, Harris and Lord Leverhulme* (Birlinn, 2003)

Lane, Dave – *Winter Hill Scrapbook* (Dave Lane, 2009)

Nicolson, Nigel – *Lord of the Isles: Lord Leverhulme in the Hebrides* (Weidenfeld & Nicolson, 1960)

Rawlinson, John – *About Rivington* (Nelson Brothers, 1981)

Riddle, Gordon – *Seasons with the Kestrel* (Blandford, 1992)

Risely, K., Massimino, D., Newson, S. E., Eaton, M. A., Musgrove, A. J., Noble, D. G., Procter, D. and Baillie, S. R. – *The Breeding Bird Survey 2012* (BTO Research Report, 645, 2013)

Salveson, Paul – *Will Yo Come O Sunday Mornin? The 1896 Battle for Winter Hill* (Red Rose Publishing, 1982)

Shrubb, Michael – *The Kestrel* (Hamlyn, 1993)

Smith, M. D. – *Leverhulme's Rivington* (Nelson Brothers, 1984)
— *About Horwich* (Nelson Brothers, 1988)
Tattersall, F. H., Avundo, A. E, Manley, W. J., Hart. B. J. and Macdonald,
   D. W. – 'Managing set-aside for field voles (*Microtus agrestis*)'
   (*Biological Conservation*, 96, no. 1, 123–128, 2000)
Videler, J. J., Weihs, D. and Daan, S. – 'Intermittent gliding in the hunting
   flight of the kestrel (*Falco tinnunculus* L.)' (*Journal of Experimental
   Biology*, 102, 1–12, 1983)
Village, Andrew – *The Kestrel* (T. & A. D. Poyser, 1990)

VIII Montagu's Harrier

Arroyo, Beatriz – 'Breeding Ecology and Nest Dispersion of Montagu's
   Harrier (*Circus pygargus*) in Central Spain' (D.Phil. Thesis, University
   of Oxford, 1995)
Childers, J. W. (ed.) – *Lord Orford's Voyage round the Fens in 1774*
   (Cambridge Libraries Publications, 1988)
Clarke, Roger – *Harriers of the British Isles* (Shire Natural History, 1990)
— *Montagu's Harrier* (Arlequin Press, 1996)
Darby, H. C. – *The Changing Fenland* (Cambridge University Press,
   1983)
Dee, Tim – *Four Fields* (Jonathan Cape, 2013)
Delamain, Jacques – *Why Birds Sing* (Victor Gollancz, 1932)
Dormer, Sally – *Twenty Objects for Twenty Years: The Ramsey Abbey
   Censer and Incense Boat* (Victoria and Albert Museum website, July
   2013)
Fowler, Gordon – 'The Extinct Waterways of The Fens' (*Geographical
   Journal*, 83, no. 1, 30–39, 1934)
Garcia, J. T. and Arroyo, B. E. – 'Food-niche differentiation in sympatric
   Hen (*Circus cyaneus*) and Montagu's Harriers (*Circus pygargus*)' (*Ibis*,
   147, no. 1, 144–154, 2005)
Godwin, Harry – *Fenland: Its Ancient Past and Uncertain Future*
   (Cambridge University Press, 1978)
Image, Bob – 'Montagu's Harriers taking prey disturbed by farm
   machinery' (*British Birds*, 85, no. 10, 559, 1992)
Kingsley, Charles – *Prose Idylls* (Macmillan, 1873)
Miller, Samuel H. and Skertchly, Sydney B. J. – *The Fenland Past and
   Present* (Longmans, Green & Co., 1878)
Montagu, George – *Ornithological Dictionary* (J. White, 1802)
— 'Some interesting Additions to the Natural History of *Falco cyaneus*
   and *pygargus*, together with Remarks on some other British Birds'
   (*Ornithological Papers, Transactions of the Linnean Society*, vol. IX,
   1808)
Robinson, Eric and Fitter, Richard (eds) – *John Clare's Birds* (Oxford
   University Press, 1982)
Rosén, Mikael – *Birds in the Flow: Flight Mechanics, Wake Dynamics and
   Flight Performance* (Department of Ecology – Animal Ecology, Lund
   University, Sweden, 2003)

Simmons, Robert E. – *Harriers of the World: Their Behaviour and Ecology* (Oxford University Press, 2000)

Skertchly, Sydney – *The Geology of the Fenland* (HMSO, 1877)

Stevenson, Henry – *The Birds of Norfolk* (John Van Voorst, 1866)

Summers, Dorothy – *The Great Level: A History of Drainage and Land Reclamation in the Fens* (David & Charles, 1976)

Weis, Henning – *Life of the Harrier in Denmark* (Wheldon & Wesley, 1923)

Wells, W. – 'The Drainage of Whittlesea Mere' (*Journal of the Royal Agricultural Society of England*, 21, 134–153, 1860)

IX Peregrine Falcon

Baker, J. A. – *The Peregrine* (Collins, 1967)

Bird, David M., Varland, Daniel E., Negro, Juan Jose (eds) – *Raptors in Human Landscapes: Adaptations to Built and Cultivated Environments* (Academic Press, 1996)

Drewitt, Ed – *Urban Peregrines* (Pelagic, 2014)

Frank, Saul – *City Peregrines: A Ten-year Saga of New York City Falcons* (Hancock House, 1984)

Harkin, Trevor – *Coventry 14th/15th November 1940 Casualties, Awards and Accounts* (War Memorial Park Publications, 2010)

Howard, R. T. – *Ruined and Rebuilt: The Story of Coventry Cathedral 1939–1962* (The Council of Coventry Cathedral, 1962)

Longmate, Norman – *Air Raid: The Bombing of Coventry 1940* (Arrow Books, 1979)

Macdonald, Helen – *Falcon* (Reaktion Books, 2006)

The Provost of Coventry Cathedral – *The Story of the Destruction of Coventry Cathedral November 14th, 1940* (Edwards, 1941)

Ratcliffe, Derek – *The Peregrine Falcon* (Second Edition) (T. & A. D. Poyser, 1993)

Ratcliffe, D. A. – 'Changes Attributable to Pesticides in Egg Breakage Frequency and Eggshell Thickness in some British Birds' (*Journal of Applied Ecology*, 7, no. 1, 67–115, 1970)

Stirling-Aird, Patrick – *Peregrine Falcon* (Bloomsbury, 2015)

Treleaven, R. B. – *Peregrine: the private life of the Peregrine Falcon* (Headland, 1977)

— *In Pursuit of the Peregrine* (Tiercel Publishing, 1998)

X Red Kite

Carrell, Severin – 'Scottish bird of prey colony hit by mass poisonings' (*Guardian*, 3 April 2014)

Carter, Ian – *The Red Kite* (Arlequin Press, 2001)

Condry, William – *The Natural History of Wales* (Collins, 1981)

Cross, Tony and Davis, Peter – *The Red Kites of Wales* (Subbuteo Natural History Books, 2005)

Davis, Peter – 'The Red Kite in Wales: setting the record straight' (*British Birds*, 86, no. 7, 295–298, 1993)

Davis, P. E. and Davis, J. E. – 'The food of the Red Kite in Wales' (*Bird Study*, 28, no. 1, 33–40, 1981)

— and Newton, I. – 'Population and Breeding of Red Kites in Wales Over a 30-Year Period' (*Journal of Animal Ecology*, 50, 759–772, 1981)

Evans, A. H. (ed.) – *Turner on Birds: A Short and Succinct History of the Principal Birds Noticed by Pliny and Aristotle, First Published by Doctor William Turner, 1544* (Cambridge University Press, 1903)

Evans, John – *The Red Kite in Wales* (Christopher Davies, 1990)

Forestry Commission Wales – *Stories from the Forest: Newsletter of the Forests in the Rural Community Project* (Forest Enterprise, 1st Edition – August 2002 and 2nd Edition – November 2002)

Hansard – *Afforestation, Towy Valley (Government Decision)* (HC Deb 31 January 1952 vol. 495, cc50-1W)

Jones, David J. V. – *Before Rebecca: Popular Protests in Wales 1793–1835* (Allen Lane, 1973)

— *Rebecca's Children: A Study of Rural Society, Crime, and Protest* (Oxford University Press, 1989)

Lovegrove, Roger – *The Kite's Tale: The Story of the Red Kite in Wales* (RSPB, 1990)

May, Celia A., Wetton, Jon H., Davis, Peter E., Brookfield, John F. Y. and Parkin, David T. – 'Single-Locus Profiling Reveals Loss of Variation in Inbred Populations of the Red Kite (*Milvus milvus*)' (*Proceedings of the Royal Society of London B*, 251, no. 1332, 1993)

—, Wetton, Jon H. and Parkin, David T. – 'Polymorphic Sex-Specific Sequences in Birds of Prey' (*Proceedings of the Royal Society of London B*, 253, no. 1338, 1993)

Owens, Nerys Elisa – 'The Shifting Governance of State Forestry in Britain: A Critical Investigation of the Transition from Productivism to Post-Productivism' (Thesis, School of City and Regional Planning, Cardiff University, 2009)

Spence, Barbara – *The Forestry Commission in Wales 1919–2013* (Forestry Commission Wales, 2013)

Thomas, Adrian L. R. – 'On the Tails of Birds' (Dissertation, Department of Ecology, Lund University, 1995)

Walpole-Bond, J. A. – *Bird Life in Wild Wales* (T. Fisher Unwin, 1903)

Walters Davies, P. and Davis, P. E. – 'The ecology and conservation of the Red Kite in Wales' (*British Birds*, 66, no. 5, 183–224, no. 6, 241–270, 1973)

Ward, Colin – *Cottars and Squatters: Housing's Hidden History* (Five Leaves, 2002)

Wildman, L., O'Toole, L. and Summers, R. W. – 'The diet and foraging behaviour of the Red Kite in northern Scotland' (*Scottish Birds*, 19, no. 3, 134–140, 1998)

XI Marsh Harrier

Axell, H. E. – 'Rare birds: the marsh harrier' (*Bird Life*, 7, no. 4, 98–101, 1971)

BIBLIOGRAPHY

Burd, Fiona – *Erosion and vegetation change on the saltmarshes of Essex and north Kent between 1973 and 1988* (Nature Conservancy Council, 1992)

Buxton, Anthony – *Fisherman Naturalist* (Collins, 1946)

Chamberlain, Paul – *Hell Upon Water: Prisoners of War in Britain, 1793–1815* (The History Press, 2008)

Clarke, Roger – *The Marsh Harrier* (Hamlyn, 1995)

Daly, Augustus A. – *The History of the Isle of Sheppey* (Simpkin, Marshall, Hamilton, Kent & Co., 1894)

Gillham, E. H. and Homes, R. C. – *The Birds of the North Kent Marshes* (Collins, 1950)

Harrison, Jeffrey – *The Nesting Birds of Chetney Marsh* (Kent Ornithological Society, 1969)

— and Grant, Peter – *The Thames Transformed: London's River and its Waterfowl* (André Deutsch, 1976)

Hosking, Eric J. – 'Some Observations on the Marsh Harrier' (*British Birds*, 37, no. 1, 2–9, 1943)

Nature Conservancy Council – *Wildlife Conservation in the North Kent Marshes: A Report of a Working Party* (The Nature Conservancy, 1971)

Oliver, Peter – *Bird Watching on the North Kent Marshes* (Peter Oliver, 1991)

Riviere, B. B. – *A History of the Birds of Norfolk* (H. F. & G. Witherby, 1930)

Simmons, Robert E. – *Harriers of the World: Their Behaviour and Ecology* (Oxford University Press, 2000)

Underhill-Day, J. C. – 'Population and Breeding Biology of Marsh Harriers in Britain since 1900' (*Journal of Applied Ecology*, 21, no. 3, 773–787, 1984)

— 'The food of breeding Marsh Harriers (*Circus aeruginosus*) in East Anglia' (*Bird Study*, 32, no. 3, 199–206, 1985)

Weis, Henning – *Life of the Harrier in Denmark* (Wheldon & Wesley, 1923)

XII Honey Buzzard

Appleby, Ron – *European Honey-buzzards (Pernis apivorus) in North Yorkshire: A Breeding History on a Learning Curve: 1895–2010* (Hobby Publications, 2012)

Bijlsma, R. G. – 'Impact of severe food scarcity on breeding strategy and breeding success of Honey Buzzards (*Pernis apivorus*)' (*De Takkeling*, 6, no. 2, 107–118, 1998)

— 'Do Honey Buzzards (*Pernis apivorus*) produce pellets?' (*Limosa*, 72, no. 3, 99–103, 1999)

— 'Use and function of eyelids in European Honey-buzzards (*Pernis apivorus*)' (*De Takkeling*, 10, no. 2, 117–128, 2002)

— 'What is the predation risk for European Honey-buzzards (*Pernis apivorus*) in Dutch forests inhabited by food-stressed Northern Goshawks (*Accipiter gentilis*)?' (*De Takkeling*, 12, no. 3, 185–197, 2004)

— and Piersma, T. – 'Internal organs and gastrointestinal tract of European Honey-buzzards (*Pernis apivorus*) in comparison with non-insectivorous raptors' (*De Takkeling*, 10, no. 3, 214–224, 2002)

Buxton, Anthony – *Sporting Interludes at Geneva* (Country Life, 1932)

Clark, J. M. and Eyre, J. A. (eds) – *Birds of Hampshire* (Hampshire Ornithological Society, 1993)

Cobb, F. K. – 'Honey Buzzard at wasps' nest' (*British Birds*, 72, no. 2, 59–64, 1979)

Diermen, J. van, Manen, W. van and Baaij, E. – 'Habitat use, home range and behaviour of Honey Buzzards (*Pernis apivorus*) tracked on the Veluwe, central Netherlands, by GPS-loggers' (*De Takkeling*, 17, no. 2, 109–133, 2009)

Duff, Daniel G. – 'Has the plumage of juvenile Honey-buzzard evolved to mimic that of Common Buzzard?' (*British Birds*, 99, no. 3, 118–128, 2006)

Edlin, H. L. – *Trees, Woods and Man* (Collins, 1970)

Forestry Commission – *Tourism and Recreation Conflicts in the New Forest* (Forestry Commission Report, 2004)

Harrison, J. M. – 'Food of the Honey-Buzzard (*Pernis apivorus apivorus*)' (*Ibis*, 1, no. 4, 772–773, 1931)

Heuvelmans, Bernard – *On the Track of Unknown Animals* (Kegan Paul, 1995)

Holstein, Vagn – *Hvepsevaagen Pernis Apivorus Apivorus (L.)* (H. Hirschsprungs Forlag, 1944)

Irons, Anthony – *Breeding of the Honey Buzzard (Pernis apivorus) in Nottinghamshire* (Trent Valley Bird Watchers Nottinghamshire's Ornithological Society, 1980)

Koks, B., Straathof, A. and Bijlsma, R. G. – 'Common Wasps (*Vespula vulgaris*), insecticides and Honey Buzzards (*Pernis apivorus*)' (*De Takkeling*, 5, no. 3, 16–19, 1997)

Kostrzewa, Achim – *The Effect of Weather on Density and Reproduction Success in Honey Buzzards (Pernis apivorus)* (World Working Group on Birds of Prey and Owls, 1987)

Lascelles, Gerald – *Thirty-Five Years in the New Forest* (Edward Arnold, 1915)

Ogilvie, M. A. – 'European Honey-buzzards in the UK – correction to breeding totals' (*British Birds*, 96, no. 3, 145, 2003)

Pasmore, Anthony – *Verderers of the New Forest: A History of the New Forest 1877–1977* (Pioneer Publications, 1977)

Rackham, Oliver – *Woodlands* (Collins, 2010)

Roberts, S. J. and Lewis, J. M. S. – 'Observations of European Honey-buzzard breeding density in Britain' (*British Birds*, 96, no. 1, 37–39, 2003)

— and Coleman, M. – 'Some observations on the diet of European Honey-buzzards in Britain' (*British Birds*, 94, no. 9, 433–436, 2001)

—, Lewis, J. M. S. and Williams, I. T. – 'Breeding European Honey-Buzzards in Britain' (*British Birds*, 92, no. 7, 326–346, 1999)

BIBLIOGRAPHY

Spradbery, J. Philip – *Wasps: An Account of the Biology and Natural History of Solitary and Social Wasps with Particular Reference to those of the British Isles* (Sidgwick & Jackson, 1973)

Trap-Lind, Ib – 'Observations on a Honey Buzzard digging out a wasps' nest' (*British Birds*, 55, no. 1, 36, 1962)

Tubbs, Colin R. – *The New Forest* (Collins, 1986)

White, Gilbert – *The Natural History of Selborne* (Letter XLIII) (Dent, 1974)

Wiseman, E. J. – 'Honey Buzzards in Southern England' (*British Birds*, 105, no. 1, 23–28, 2012)

XIII Hobby

Ashley, M. – 'On the Breeding Habits of the Hobby' (*British Birds*, 11, no. 9, 194–196, 1918)

Atherton, Peter F. – 'Barn Swallow giving specific alarm call for Hobby' (*British Birds*, 90, no. 11, 526, 1997)

Baker, J. A. – *The Hill of Summer* (Harper & Row, 1969)

Blomfield, R. M. – *Poole: Harbour, Heath and Islands* (Regency Press, 1984)

Chalmers, John – *Audubon in Edinburgh and his Scottish Associates* (NMS, 2003)

Chapman, Anthony – *The Hobby* (Arlequin Press, 1999)

Clarke, A., Prince, P. A. and Clarke, R. – 'The energy content of dragonflies (*Odonata*) in relation to predation by falcons' (*Bird Study*, 43, no. 3, 300–304, 1996)

Davis, Terence – *Arne: A Purbeck Parish in Peace and War* (Dorset Publishing Company, 2000)

Dobinson, Colin – *Fields of Deception: Britain's Bombing Decoys of World War II* (Methuen, 2000)

Fenech, Natalino – *Fatal Flight: The Maltese Obsession with Killing Birds* (Quiller Press, 1992)

Forty, George – *Frontline Dorset: A County at War 1939–45* (Dorset Books, 1994)

Fuller, R. J., Baker, J. K., Morgan, R. A., Scroggs, R. and Wright, M. – 'Breeding populations of the Hobby (*Falco Subbuteo*) on farmland in the southern Midlands of England' (*Ibis*, 127, no. 4, 510–516, 1985)

Green, George – *The Birds of Dorset* (Christopher Helm, 2004)

Insley, Hugh and Holland, Maurice G. – 'Hobbies feeding on bats, and notes on other prey' (*British Birds*, 68, no. 6, 242, 1975)

Nethersole-Thompson, Desmond – 'The Field Habits and Nesting of the Hobby' (*British Birds*, 25, no. 6, 142–150, 1931)

Trodd, Paul – 'Hobbies nesting on pylon' (*British Birds*, 86, no. 12, 625, 1993)

Walpole-Bond, John – *Field-Studies of Some Rarer British Birds* (Witherby & Co., 1914)

Webb, Nigel – *Heathlands* (Collins, 1986)

XIV Buzzard

Baring-Gould, S. – *A Book of Dartmoor* (Methuen, 1900)

Burnard, Robert – *Plundered Dartmoor* (Dartmoor Preservation Association, 1896)

Christensen, Steen, Nielsen, Bent Pors, Porter, R. F. and Willis, Ian – 'Flight identification of European raptors' (*British Birds*, 64, no. 6, 247–266, 1971)

Crossing, William – *A Hundred Years on Dartmoor* (The Western Morning News, 1901)

— *The Teign: From Moor to Sea* (Quay Publications, 1986)

Dare, Peter – *The Life of Buzzards* (Whittles, 2015)

English Nature and Dartmoor National Park Authority – *The Nature of Dartmoor: A Biodiversity Profile* (English Nature, 2001)

Fryer, G. – 'Aggressive behaviour by buzzards at nest' (*British Birds*, 67, no. 6, 238–239, 1974)

— 'Buzzard and crows at Magpie nest' (*British Birds*, 79, no. 1, 40–41, 1986)

Fryer, Geoffrey – 'Notes on the breeding biology of the Buzzard' (*British Birds*, 79, no. 1, 18–28, 1986)

Harvey, L. A. and St Leger-Gordon, D. – *Dartmoor* (Fontana, 1974)

Hemery, Eric – *High Dartmoor: Land and People* (Robert Hale, 1983)

Martin, E. W. – *Dartmoor* (Robert Hale, 1958)

Moore, N. W. – 'The Past and Present Status of the Buzzard in the British Isles' (*British Birds*, 50, no. 5, 173–197, 1957)

Picozzi, N. and Weir, D. – 'Breeding biology of the Buzzard in Speyside' (*British Birds*, 67, no. 5, 199–210, 1974)

— 'Dispersion of Buzzards in Speyside' (*British Birds*, 76, no. 2, 66–78, 1983)

Prytherch, Robin – 'The breeding biology of the common buzzard' (*British Birds*, 106, no. 5, 264–279, 2013)

Ryves, B. H. – *Bird Life in Cornwall* (Collins, 1948)

Tubbs, Colin R. – *The Buzzard* (David & Charles, 1974)

Tubbs, C. R. – 'Population study of Buzzards in the New Forest during 1962–66' (*British Birds*, 60, no. 10, 381–395, 1967)

Wareing Ormerod, G. – 'Notes on the Geology of the Valleys of the Upper Parts of the River Teign and its Feeders' (*Proceedings of the Geological Society*, November 1867)

XV Sparrowhawk

Baker, J. A. – *The Hill of Summer* (Harper & Row, 1969)

Barlow, Nora (ed.) – *The Autobiography of Charles Darwin* (Collins, 1958)

Deane, Ruthven – 'Unpublished Letters of William MacGillivray to John James Audubon' (*The Auk*, 18, 239–249, 1901)

Newton, Alfred – *A Dictionary of Birds* (Adam & Charles Black, 1896)

Newton, Ian – *The Sparrowhawk* (T. & A. D. Poyser, 1986)

Newton, I., Bell, A. A. and Wyllie, I. – 'Mortality of Sparrowhawks and Kestrels' (*British Birds*, 75, no. 5, 195–204, 1982)

Newton, I., Dale, L. and Rothery, P. – 'Apparent lack of impact of Sparrowhawks on the breeding densities of some woodland songbirds' (*Bird Study*, 44, no. 2, 129–135, 1997)

Nicholas, W. W. – *A Sparrow-hawk's Eyrie* (A. Brown & Sons, 1937)

Owen, J. H. – 'Some Breeding-Habits of the Sparrow-Hawk' (*British Birds*, 15, no. 4, 74–77, no. 11, 256–263, 1921–22)

— 'The Feeding-Habits of the Sparrow-Hawk' (*British Birds*, 25, no. 6, 151–155, 1931)

— 'The Hunting of the Sparrow-Hawk' (*British Birds*, 25, no. 9, 238–243, 1932)

— 'The Food of the Sparrow-Hawk' (*British Birds*, 26, no. 2, 34–40, 1932)

Perrins, C. M. and Geer, T. A. – 'The Effect of Sparrowhawks on Tit Populations' (*Ardea*, 68, 133–142, 1980)

Pounds, Hubert E. – 'Notes on the Flight of the Sparrow-Hawk' (*British Birds*, 30, no. 6, 183–189, 1936)

Tinbergen, Lukas – 'De Sperwer als Roofvijand van Zangvogels/The Sparrowhawk as a Predator of Passerine Birds' (*Ardea*, 34, 1–213, 1946)

Yapp, W. B. – *Birds and Woods* (Oxford University Press, 1962)

General

Aberdeen Free Press – 'In Memoriam. William MacGillivray, M.A., LL.D., Professor of Natural History and Lecturer on Botany, in Marischal College and University, Aberdeen; 1841–1852' (*Aberdeen Free Press*, 21 November 1900)

Audubon, John James – *Ornithological Biography*, volumes I–V (Adam & Charles Black, 1831–39)

Balmer, D. E, Gillings, S., Caffrey, B. J., Swann, R. L., Downie, I. S. and Fuller, R. J. – *Bird Atlas 2007–11: The breeding and wintering birds of Britain and Ireland* (BTO Books, 2013)

Bannerman, David A. – *The Birds of the British Isles*, volume V (Oliver & Boyd, 1956)

Baxter, Evelyn V. and Rintoul, Leonora J. – *The Birds of Scotland: Their History, Distribution, and Migration* (Oliver and Boyd, 1953)

Bijleveld, Maarten – *Birds of Prey in Europe* (Macmillan, 1974)

Bircham, Peter – *A History of Ornithology* (Collins, 2007)

Birkhead, Tim – *Bird Sense: What It's Like to Be a Bird* (Bloomsbury, 2012)

Broun, Maurice – *Hawks Aloft: The Story of Hawk Mountain* (Dodd, Mead, 1949)

Brown, Leslie – *British Birds of Prey* (Collins, 1976)

— *Birds of Prey: Their Biology and Ecology* (Hamlyn, 1976)

Cade, Tom J. – *Falcons of the World* (Collins, 1982)

Campbell, Bruce and Ferguson-Lees, James – *A Field Guide to Birds' Nests* (Constable, 1972)

Chalmers, John – *Audubon in Edinburgh and his Scottish Associates* (NMS, 2003)

Cobham, David and Pearson, Bruce – *A Sparrowhawk's Lament: How British Breeding Birds of Prey are Faring* (Princeton University Press, 2014)

Cocker, Mark and Mabey, Richard – *Birds Britannica* (Chatto & Windus, 2005)

Corning, Howard (ed.) – *Letters of John James Audubon 1826–1840* (The Club of Odd Volumes, 1930)

Craighead, John J. and Craighead, Frank C. – *Hawks, Owls and Wildlife* (Dover, 1969)

Deane, Ruthven – 'Unpublished Letters of William MacGillivray to John James Audubon' (*The Auk*, 18, 239–249, 1901)

Fairbrother, Nan – *New Lives, New Landscapes* (Penguin, 1972)

Ferguson-Lees, James and Christie, David A. – *Raptors of the World* (Christopher Helm, 2001)

Frederick II, Emperor – *The Art of Falconry being the De Arte Venandi Cum Avibus* (Oxford University Press, 1955)

Gordon, Seton – *Hill Birds of Scotland* (Edward Arnold, 1915)

— *Wild Birds in Britain* (Batsford, 1938)

— *In Search of Northern Birds* (Eyre & Spottiswoode, 1941)

Greenoak, Francesca – *British Birds: Their Folklore, Names and Literature* (Christopher Helm, 1997)

Hardey, Jon, Crick, Humphrey Q. P., Wernham, Chris V., Riley, Helen T., Etheridge, Brian and Thompson, Des B. A. – *Raptors: A Field Guide to Survey and Monitoring* (Stationery Office, 2006)

Harkness, Roger and Murdoch, Colin – *Birds of Prey in the Field: A Guide to the British and European Species* (Witherby, 1971)

Harrison, J. C. – *Bird Portraits* (Country Life, 1949)

Hart-Davis, Duff – *Audubon's Elephant: The Story of John James Audubon's Epic Struggle to Publish The Birds of America* (Phoenix, 2004)

Holloway, Simon – *The Historical Atlas of Breeding Birds in Britain and Ireland: 1875–1900* (T. & A. D. Poyser, 1996)

Jonsson, Lars – *Birds of Europe with North Africa and the Middle East* (Christopher Helm, 1992)

Lensink, Rob – 'Range expansion of raptors in Britain and the Netherlands since the 1960s: testing an individual-based diffusion model' (*Journal of Animal Ecology*, 66, no. 6, 811–826, 1997)

MacGillivray, William – 'Journal of a year's residence and travels in the Hebrides by William MacGillivray from 3rd August 1817 to 13th August 1818 Vol. I' (Manuscript, University of Aberdeen Special Collections, 1817–1818)

— 'Notes taken in the course of a journey from Aberdeen to London by Braemar, Fortwilliam, Inveraray, Glasgow, Ayr, Dumfries, Carlisle, Keswick, Kendal, Manchester, Derby and Northampton in 1819' (Manuscript, University of Aberdeen Special Collections, 1819)

BIBLIOGRAPHY

— (trans.) – *Elements of Botany and Vegetable Physiology by A. Richard* (William Blackwood, 1831)

— 'Report on Visit to Museums' (Manuscript, University of Aberdeen Special Collections, 1833)

— *Lives of the Eminent Zoologists, From Aristotle to Linnaeus* (Oliver & Boyd, 1834)

— (ed.) – *The Edinburgh Journal of Natural History, and of the Physical Sciences* (The Edinburgh Printing Company, 1835)

— *Descriptions of the Rapacious Birds of Great Britain* (Maclachlan & Stewart, 1836)

— 'Autographic Notes Chiefly on British Birds' (Manuscript, University of Aberdeen Special Collections, 1836–1840)

— *A History of British Birds, Indigenous and Migratory*, volumes I–V (Scott, Webster, and Geary, 1837–52)

— *A History of British Quadrupeds* (W. H. Lizars, 1838)

— *The Travels and Researches of Alexander Von Humboldt* (Harper & Brothers, 1839)

— *A Manual of British Ornithology: Being a Short Description of the Birds of Great Britain and Ireland, Including the Essential Characters of the Species, Genera, Families, and Orders* (Scott, Webster, and Geary, 1840)

— *A Manual of Botany: Comprising Vegetable Anatomy and Physiology, or the Structure and Functions of Plants* (Scott, Webster, and Geary, 1840)

— *A Manual of Geology* (Scott, Webster, and Geary, 1840)

— 'Testimonials in favour of William MacGillivray, A.M.' (University of Aberdeen Special Collections, 1841)

— *A History of the Molluscous Animals of the Counties of Aberdeen, Kincardine, and Banff* (Cunningham & Mortimer, 1843)

— (ed.) – *A Systematic Arrangement of British Plants by W. Withering* (Adam Scott, 1845)

— (ed.) – *The Conchologist's Text-Book by T. Brown* (A. Fullerton, 1845)

— *Manual of British Birds: Including the Essential Characters of the Orders, Families, Genera, and Species* (Adam Scott, 1846)

— *The Natural History of Dee Side and Braemar* (Private publication, 1855)

— *A Hebridean Naturalist's Journal 1817–1818* (Acair, 1996)

— *A Walk to London* (Acair, 1998)

MacGillivray, William and Thomson, J. Arthur – *Life of William MacGillivray* (John Murray, 1910)

MacGillivray, William – *A Memorial Tribute to William MacGillivray* (Edinburgh, 1901)

Mead, Chris – *The State of the Nations' Birds* (Whittet Books, 2000)

Meinertzhagen, R. – *Pirates and Predators: The Piratical and Predatory Habits of Birds* (Oliver & Boyd, 1959)

Meyburg, Bernd-Ulrich and Chancellor, R. D. (eds) – *Raptors in the Modern World* (World Working Group on Birds of Prey and Owls, 1987)

Mullarney, Killian, Svensson, Lars, Zetterström, Dan, Grant, Peter J. – *Collins Bird Guide* (HarperCollins, 1999)

Mynott, Jeremy – *Birdscapes: Birds in Our Imagination and Experience* (Princeton University Press, 2009)

Newton, Alfred – *Ootheca Wolleyana: An Illustrated Catalogue of the Collection of Birds' Eggs Formed by the Late John Wolley, Part I. Accipiters* (John Van Voorst, 1864)

Newton, Ian – *Population Ecology of Raptors* (T. & A. D. Poyser, 1979)

— 'Raptors in Britain – A review of the last 150 years' (*BTO News*, 131, 6–7, 1984)

Nicholson, E. M. – *Birds in England: An Account of the State of our Bird-Life and A Criticism of Bird Protection* (Chapman & Hall, 1926)

Porter, R. F., Willis, Ian, Christensen, Steen, Nielsen, Bent Pors – *Flight Identification of European Raptors* (T. & A. D. Poyser, 1981)

Proctor, Noble S. and Lynch, Patrick J. – *Manual of Ornithology: Avian Structure & Function* (Yale University Press, 1993)

Ralph, Robert – *William MacGillivray* (HMSO, 1993)

— *William MacGillivray: Creatures of Air, Land and Sea* (Merrell Holberton, 1999)

Richmond, Kenneth W. – *British Birds of Prey* (Lutterworth, 1959)

Ritchie, James – *The Influence of Man on Animal Life in Scotland* (Cambridge University Press, 1920)

RSPB – *Birds of Prey in the UK: Back from the Brink* (RSPB, 1997)

— *Birds of Prey in the UK: On a Wing and a Prayer* (RSPB, 2007)

— *Birdcrime: Offences Against Wild Bird Legislation in 2012* (RSPB, 2012)

Self, Andrew – *The Birds of London* (Bloomsbury, 2014)

Snow, D. W. and Perrins, C. M. – *The Birds of the Western Palearctic*, Volume 1, *Non-Passerines* (Oxford University Press, 1998)

Thompson, D. B. A., Redpath, S. M., Fielding, A. H., Marquiss, M., Galbraith, C. A. (eds) – *Birds of Prey in a Changing Environment* (Scottish Natural Heritage, 2003)

Thompson, Des, Riley, Helen and Etheridge, Brian – *Scotland's Birds of Prey* (Lomond, 2010)

Videler, John J. – *Avian Flight* (Oxford University Press, 2005)

Walpole-Bond, John – *Field-Studies of Some Rarer British Birds* (Witherby & Co., 1914)

Watson, Donald – *Birds of Moor and Mountain* (Scottish Academic Press, 1972)

Whitlock, Ralph – *Rare and Extinct Birds of Britain* (Phoenix House, 1953)

Yarrell, William – *A History of British Birds*, volumes I–III (John Van Voorst, 1845)

Yosef, R., Miller, M. L. and Pepler, D. (eds) – *Raptors in the New Millennium* (International Birding and Research Center, 2002)

Zuberogoitia, Iñigo and Martínez, José Enrique (eds) – *Ecology and Conservation of European Forest-Dwelling Raptors* (Diputación Foral de Bizkaia, 2011)

Acknowledgements

I am grateful to The Royal Society of Literature and The
Jerwood Charitable Foundation for an RSL Jerwood
Award for Non-Fiction in 2011, and to The Society of
Authors for an Authors' Foundation Roger Deakin Award
in 2011.

Thank you to my agent Jessica Woollard;
Nicholas Pearson, my editor at Fourth Estate, and Kate
Tolley at Fourth Estate; Andrew McNeillie for his
support and encouragement and for publishing
work in progress from this book in *Archipelago*
magazine; Robert Macfarlane and Robin Harvie for
their encouragement; Antony Harwood for his patient
support.

Thank you also to Sophie Wilcox at the Alexander
Library of Ornithology in Oxford; Jim McGregor at the
University of Aberdeen Herbarium; the staff at the
Special Collections Library, University of Aberdeen; the
staff at the Natural History Museum Library, London;
Alyson Tyler at CyMAL Museums Archives and Libraries
Wales; George Deane in Bolton; Bob Image and Jim Scott

in East Anglia; Eric Meek on Orkney; David Pearce in Gloucestershire; Norrie Russell in Sutherland.

Above all, my thanks to Nicki.